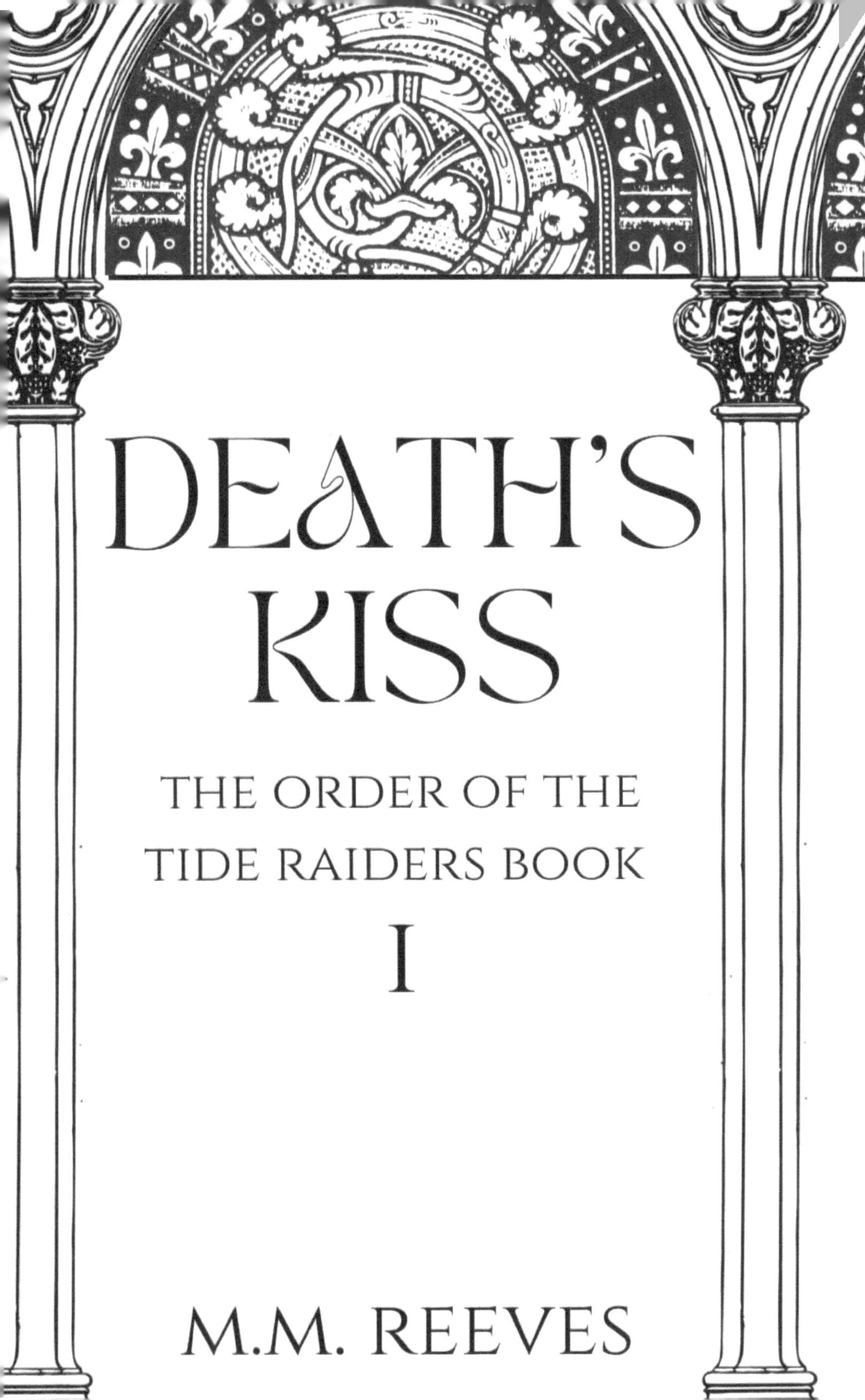
DEATH'S
KISS
THE ORDER OF THE
TIDE RAIDERS BOOK
I
M.M. REEVES

The Cardinal North Order
THE BONEYARD
DOCKS FOR THE SOUTH,
EAST & WEST CARDINAL SHIPS
OUTDOOR TRAINING LYCEUMS
THE BAY
GIANT'S CROOK
NORTHERN FORTRESS
N
W
E
S

CONTENTS

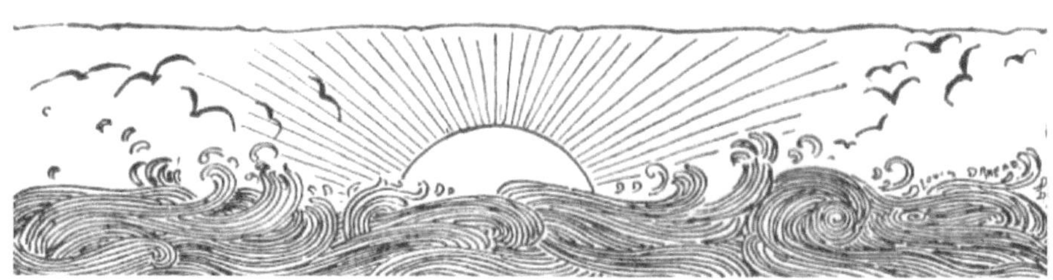

SOUTHERN DIALECT TRANSLATIONS

Chapter 6.

— *Fortasse pater meus dabit te mihi* = **Perhaps my father will give you to me**

Chapter 7.

— *Vos omnes sunt futu idiotae* = **You are all fucking idiots.**

Chapter 9.

— *Subtus mihi* = **Beneath me.**

Chapter 13.

—*Abeamus* = **Let's go**.

Chapter 14.

—*Vide nonnihil vos lubido?* = **See something you like?**

—*Quare non vos futuere her iam?* = **Why don't you fuck her already?**

—*Noli vi ego posuit a rostrum in te.* = **Don't force me to put a muzzle on you.**

—*Scis quid acciderit cum ignis et glacies miscentur... res admodum humidae fiunt.* = **You know what happens when fire and ice mix... things get very wet.**

—*Illa facit vultus bonum on sua genua, annon?* = **She does look good on her knees, doesn't she?**

Chapter 18.

—*Quoniam nullus of hic est real, ego opinor id nolo materia.* = **Since none of this is real, I guess it doesn't matter.**

Chapter 19.

—*Deos sub superficie* = **Gods beneath the surface**

Chapter 24.

—*Futuere mihi. Vos vultus sicut peccatum.* = **Fuck me. You look like sin.**

—*Donec deinde tempore, mea divinus cruciatus.* = **Until next time, my divine torment.**

Chapter 26.

—*Quod suus 'fraudando* = **That's cheating**

Chapter 33.

—*Vos habet nullus notio omnes vias ego vellem efficio vos imploro* = **You have no idea all the ways I would make you beg.**

Chapter 35.

—*Tu minoris aestimo quam iucundus esset experientia.* = **You underestimate how enjoyable the experience would be.**

Chapter 43.

—*Volo facere inenarrabilia sunt ad vos* = **I want to do unspeakable things to you.**

—*Committens hoc to memoria* = **Committing this to memory.**

—*Quomodo sunt vos melius etiam quam mea phantasiae?* = **How are you even better than my imagination?**

Chapter 44.

—*Paenitet, sumusne interpellatione aliquid?* = **Sorry, are we interrupting something?**

—*Iustus paulum negotium* = **Just a little business.**

—*Quid negoti? Genus ubi illa terminus sursum nudus in lecto tuo?* = **What business? The kind where she ends up naked in your bed?**

—*Nonne iam dixi tibi non loqui de puella?* = **Didn't I already tell you not to talk about the girl?**

—*Technice vos dixit nobis non loqui puellae directe.* = **Technically you told us not to talk to the girl directly.**

—*Ea satis peritissimus gestatio equitatio lunalevius, ego bet illa posset accipere te ad somnum per noctem enim semel et det manum tuam quietem* = **She's quite skilled at riding a moonlighter, I bet she could get you to sleep through the night for once. And give your hand a rest.**

—*Depone arma nunc!* = **Lay down your arms now!**

Chapter 47.

—*Deos meos* = **My gods**

—*Non possum credere stupri hoc nunc fieri.* = **I can't believe this is fucking happening right now.**

Chapter 48.

—*Tu es dulce. Fortasse pater meus dabit te mihi.* = **You're sweet. Perhaps my father will give you to me.**

Chapter 49.

—*Deos supra et infra* = **Gods above and below**

—*Hoc tam durius futurum esse quam putabam.* = **This is going to be so much harder than I thought.**

Chapter 50.

—*Bene. Ophios fuit amissa causa aliquamdiu nunc quae excusatio tua—Uthra?* = **Fine. Ophios has been a lost cause for some time now, what is your excuse—Uthra?**

—*Vide eam!* = **Look at her!**

—*Quum femina sicut gloriosus sicut illud, ostendit tibi etiam exigua de studium vos have ut pounce! Mea Deos—non est mea culpa quod illa est unus opus artis!* = **When a woman as glorious as that, shows you even a little bit of interest you have to pounce! My gods—it is not my fault she's a masterpiece!**

—*Quid ego docui tibi de continentia?* = **What have I taught you about self-control?**

—Non potes permittere puellam valde splendidam a pari calliditate et calliditate monstri, quod sub superficie iacebat, te avocare. = **You cannot allow for a very gorgeous girl to distract you from the equally cunning and calculating monster that is lying just beneath the surface.**

—Videstine quam deos-damnatum ieiunium erat enim ea in venire sursum cum quod? = **Did you see how godsdamned fast it was for her to come up with that?**

Epilogue

—Vos habes nulla idea quid genus sordidus res ego volo audire vos dicunt vel modus ego volofacere te gemere. = **You have no idea what sort of filthy things I want to hear you say, or the countless ways I want to make you moan.**

—Et sicut ego cogito vos vult mox recordo ego semper id quod volo. = **And as I think you'll soon remember, I *always* get what I want.**

ABOUT THE BOOK

This book contains some explicit content and dark elements that might be triggering for some but is in tune with the harsh world of the Tide Raiders.

For a full list of warnings, please turn to the last page.

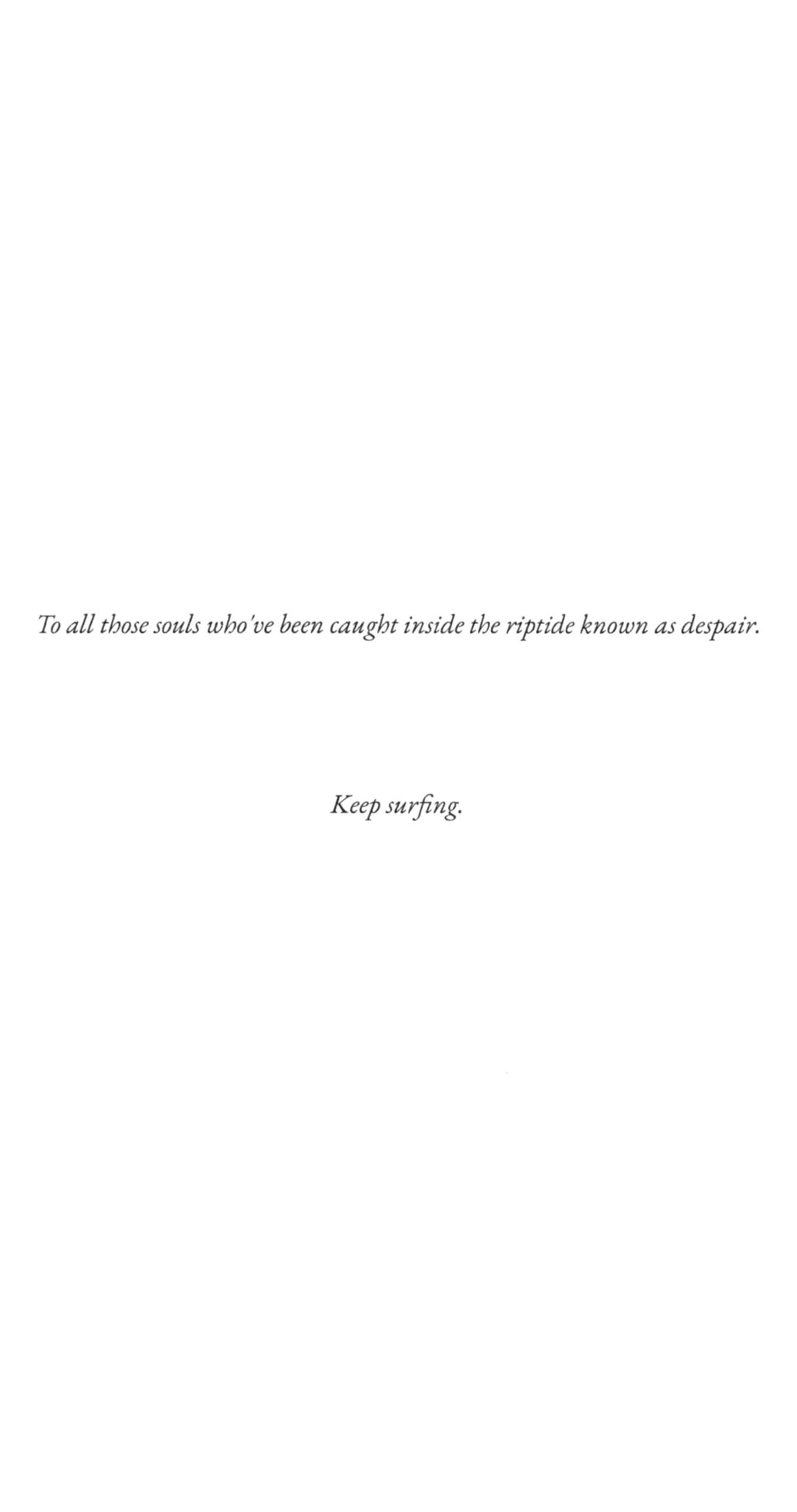

To all those souls who've been caught inside the riptide known as despair.

Keep surfing.

1. OVER MY BURNING CORPSE

In order to contain the drowned souls of the sea, it is highly important for one to bring a sturdy enough glass.

"Not so loud, Greer!" Kleio chides the fiery redhead, who's been whooping with delight since making it past the last bend in their path. They're now out of view entirely from that black-spired fortress each of them knows unfortunately well.

A hand comes to twist the end of Kleio's long, dusky braid, while her heart-shaped face pinches in admonishment. Greer flashes her a straight, white grin, full of the promise of mischief in return.

"She's going to murder you for this. You know that, right?" Herse snarks from the other side of Kleio, her chin-length onyx hair shining under the star-studded sky.

Kleio presses her cupid's bow against her lower lip in a frown, no doubt mulling over the tongue-lashing that'll be had after tonight. Her quiet deliberation is quickly replaced with a shrug. "She'll come around."

Herse shakes her head with a faint, disbelieving snort yet doesn't counter. She knows better than to argue with the crew's second-in-command.

There is only one person on all of Pontus whom Kleio both loves and fears enough to listen to. And it seems as though that one person in particular has been very *conveniently* left out of tonight's events.

The twins, Prisca and Nephthys, run past Kleio in a blur of copper skin and dark, coiled braids. They burst out into identical peals of laughter when finally reaching the highest hillcrest of the dark coastline. The tides rolling out in their loud pattern of oceanic noise are enough to muffle most of the group's subsequent howls and cheers at the beguiling sight laid out before them.

Tonight, those waves tumbling along the dark shores belonging to the Cardinal North are no ordinary tides. Tonight, the waters are ablaze with tiny pinpricks of brilliant purples, blues, and greens as thousands of star-like dots fill the heaving seas and shatter against the black sands.

Kleio gasps outwardly, her hand clutching a crystal vial hanging from the neck of her navy-colored northern raider uniform. In the warm midnight breeze, stray chocolate curls have slipped out of her normally rigid braids and flutter against the sides of her suntanned face.

It really is such a beautiful sight.

The crew's second-in-command is likely wondering why on Pontus they should be denied this. Why, on their one single day of autonomy, they can't experience true freedom. But that's the way of things. None of them will ever be let off the leash, not entirely. The Order of the Tide Raiders owns every single one of them. The brand wrapping around each of their left wrists is proof enough of that.

That leash agitates Kleio more than the others. It chafes her to a point where she takes idiotic risks like the one being taken tonight, just to get a taste of life before. Perhaps it's because she's had a taste of true freedom in her past. Maybe it's because she actually has something out there left to remind her of it.

The group of six hellions stand close to the sparkling water's edge and begin stripping off their uniforms down to their water-suits with a nervous sort of excited energy. Greer, the crew's fourth-in-command, leaves her spot gazing at the ethereal waters and comes to stand beside Kleio. The impish light in her olive eyes has died down to something like worry.

There's an air of seriousness to what they're about to do, a hint of treachery.

"You don't think—" Greer starts and then pauses, looking back at the swelling ocean before swallowing nervously. "You don't think she'll be too upset, will she?" Her olive eyes flicker to the black hillcrest behind them and the ominous black fortress of the North Order beyond.

Herse snorts a derisive laugh from Kleio's other side. "Oh, she's gonna lose it."

Kleio shoots a dark glare at the crew's third, to which Herse shrugs, before answering Greer. "If she does lose it, then it will be on me and me alone. None of you will be in any trouble, I swear it. I'll accept the punishment in full and anything else that comes with it."

That appears to do little to ease Greer's newfound nerves. The others have also stopped their idle banter and absent laughter. Each one of them appears somewhat stricken now that the topic has turned to *her*. How *she* might react. How *she* might perceive this.

Nimra, the youngest of them both in appearance and in years, moves her weight from heel to toe anxiously while asking Kleio, "Should we have asked her to come with us?"

"No!" Kleio, Herse, and Greer all respond emphatically at once.

"Gods, no," Kleio adds firmly, looking paler by the second. "Let's just get what we came here for, alright? We'll be back before she's even awake, and none will be the wiser."

She looks each one of the other five present crew members in the eye, waiting for a challenge. When none comes, Kleio peels off her northern raider uniform down to the water-suit beneath with that crystal container now secure in her hand.

A moment later reveals Kleio slowly entering the sparkling waterline with bated breath. It's been seven years to the day since any of them have come into contact with the drowned souls. The others waiting anxiously on the dark sandy shores quickly follow her lead.

Peals of delight ripple into the night as their movements in the tides make the divine ocean stars glow brighter before beginning to change shades of color. Green turns to blue to purple, and so on. Even Herse eventually shrugs off her uniform to join the others in the celestial waters.

But time passes by all too quickly.

It can't possibly have been long enough before the winds begin to shift. Kleio appears to sense the slight change in their surroundings before any of the others.

No.

"Get to the shore!" Kleio orders, and they all follow her command without hesitation. The six of them begin staggering out of the rumbling waves toward their discarded uniforms, just as the sound of kicked sand emanates from the black dunes towering above.

Kleio's face dons a well crafted mask, one that's been forged from years within the North Order, before turning to discover the reason for the shifting winds. Standing atop the hillcrest, his shoulder-length black hair looking all the more inky under the moonlight, watches Preceptor Bealu. He gives them an oily smile by way of acknowledgment.

They're screwed.

Completely, utterly, entirely, *fucked*.

Kleio could scarcely imagine the punishment Preceptor Bealu would inflict for their infraction tonight. She often tried to hide it, but Kleio had never fully recovered from his rather disturbing teachings during levels six and seven.

Bealu's dark, soulless eyes land right on the crew's second-in-command, sending a suffocating wave of dread rolling out and over the six below.

This was such a horribly asinine idea. What possible reason could there have been to take this sort of moronic risk?

Bealu's grin is serpentine in response to Kleio's clear terror. It's a smile that promises hours upon hours of misery-fueled torment.

"Raider Hiraeth, why am I somehow not surprised?" he hisses, addressing Kleio directly while slowly shaking his head of inky hair in mock disappointment at them all. In the wake of her stunned silence, the oily preceptor adds, "And just where is your captain tonight?"

Bealu feigns looking around the dark beach, but his eyes never actually leave Kleio's face. He's enjoying the taste of her fear, no doubt.

Kleio appears at a loss for words. Her chocolate curls drip with star-flecked water, and heavenly droplets slide down damningly onto the black sands beneath their feet. She struggles to keep her calm, to keep from trembling with panic.

Preceptor Bealu's voice lashes out into the night like the whip he so prefers. "Well then, Raider Hiraeth, it appears you are the highest ranking here. How do you see fit for punishment?"

Kleio grapples with herself, and that mask of false calm begins to slip. She opens her mouth, undoubtedly in order to tell him she would be taking on the punishment herself in full. Because no matter how utterly terrified of Preceptor Bealu Kleio is, she won't allow for anyone else to take on his form of discipline. Even if that means another day of horror for her.

And Bealu knows it.

There's anticipation brimming in those soulless eyes of his, eager as ever to feast upon any remaining joy that might possibly exist within her after these last seven years of hell.

Over my burning corpse will I allow for that to happen. No matter how absolutely livid I am with her. With *all* of them.

"Actually, Preceptor, *I* would be the highest ranked here," I drawl casually, deciding now's the time to finally leave my concealed viewing post behind the nearest blackened sand dune.

I've been waiting down here ever since the six soaking-wet idiots standing down along the shore snuck out of our cabin, thinking I wouldn't have heard them. That was almost an hour or so ago now. They really and truly should have known better than to presume I'd be asleep.

Standing from my vantage point with a lazy stretch, I nonchalantly brush off the onyx sands clinging to my captain's jacket before strolling their way. I'm immensely thankful not to have worn my full garb tonight. The air is far too balmy.

Preceptor Bealu whips around to watch my approaching figure with a look of complete surprise. That look quickly turns to something like annoyance and then swiftly into disappointment.

I smirk at him in turn.

You see, I'm not much fun for someone like Bealu to play with. His affinity, the individual power gifted to a raider from the drowned gods' blessing, feeds upon the pain of others. The pinguid man delights in watching the joy seep right out of those unfortunate enough to earn his punishments, stealing whatever happiness from prior memories they might contain in tow.

I make that charming little pastime of his damn near impossible.

Kleio lets out a choking sort of sound at my sudden appearance, while Greer and Herse both look like they might vomit. The rest are deadly silent, and I don't so much as glance in their direction. My anger is a terribly behaved beast that I struggle daily to leash.

"Ah, Captain Boreas." Preceptor Bealu recovers himself quickly with a false smile, emphasizing the use of my bastard name. Boreas being the name given to those bastards of the north. He's disliked me since the day I washed up here. I'm one of the few castaways the North Order has ever accepted, and likely only because of my highly unusual affinity.

I don't let it bother me. Not really. Not anymore.

Instead, I give him a cold nod of deference in return, as I've been trained to do.

"You will be accepting the punishment for your crew, I assume?" Bealu inquires, his voice dripping with barely concealed disappointment.

"I will," I agree with another nod, still refusing to look at my six on the shores below.

Kleio finally finds her voice. "N-*No*. You can't, Merena." Her face has turned ashen while her curls continue to drip with that incriminating oceanic starlight.

Preceptor Bealu raises his eyebrows in response to Kleio's apparent defiance towards me, towards her captain. My second's next words are directed at the dark preceptor, but her eyes are locked on mine. "This was my idea, all mine. I dragged them all out here without Captain Boreas's—"

I shoot my second a warning glare before cutting her off sharply. "Stop. Talking. Now."

Idiots, the lot of them.

My attention returns to Bealu, whose expression can only be described now as put out.

"I'm Captain. This is my crew. I will be accepting the punishment in full." My tone offers no argument; the cold in it is biting.

His depthless eyes study me for a moment, looking for something to correct, anything to pick apart and swallow whole. He frowns at the lack of ammo I have for him to prey on before sighing in obvious disappointment. "Fine. Captain Boreas, you will follow me to the Grand Preceptor's quarters. He will be the one to determine a fitting punishment for you."

I hesitate for no more than a blink, but it's enough. Preceptor Bealu's serpentine smile makes a reappearance. His infernal affinity can sense even the fleeting flicker of agitation that the mere mention of our Grand Preceptor causes.

"Oh yes," he affirms, excitement returning to his eyes. "I'm afraid with your new promotion to captaincy, all discipline will have to go through Grand Preceptor Skelm. Although after tonight, who knows how long you have left with that title?"

I can both see and feel the pure panic rippling off Kleio and the others. I throw them all a dark look that promises consequences if they attempt to intervene any further.

After a brief glance towards the dawning horizon, Bealu says gleefully, "Well, let's not dally. I'm sure Hymir will want to deal with this swiftly." Then he pivots on a heel and begins stalking back down the dark sand dune path without another word.

I take a quick study of my crew, all of whom are standing like statues. Each of them stares up at me with varying shades of shock and nausea playing about their features. My gaze cuts over to Kleio last, who looks like she wants to scream.

"Raider Hiraeth, get them all back to the cabin. I expect a full debrief when I return." My cutting voice is devoid of all warmth.

Kleio swallows down her tears before they have a chance to shine on the surface of her sepia-shaded eyes. She then clenches her fist to her heart in salute before dipping her chin in understanding.

With one last frigid glance at my crew and the tempting waters beyond, I too pivot and begin stalking down towards my impending discipline.

11. PUNISHMENTS & LEECHES

The Grand Preceptor's quarters are situated at the top of the largest spire of the dark, imposing stronghold that houses the Cardinal North Order of the Tide Raiders.

His office's veranda opens out to the harsh arctic waters beyond while also providing a clear view of the stone courtyard directly below. The room he claims for himself is brimming with excessively lavish furniture crafted in foreign lands I've never seen. Every available surface is dotted with priceless trinkets from his glory days sailing under the previous Tide Raider King.

A fact he never lets us forget.

I stand paused in the open entranceway to his quarters, my feet unwilling to enter of their own accord. The Grand Preceptor's well-muscled back faces me from the opposite end of the room, where a large marble mantle yawns open wide. The flames inside grow hotter and wilder under his careful prodding. I shove down the incessant hammering inside my chest and will the proof of fear sliding into my palms to freeze over.

A mask, crafted of carefully carved ice, slides perfectly into place along my features just as our Grand Preceptor turns around. He gives me a thin-lipped grimace before returning the hot poker to its metal stand. The golden patch that covers the sunken hole where his left eye should be gleams in the firelight, directly at odds with the neat crop of his silver-streaked hair.

Even in his waning age, Grand Preceptor Hymir Skelm is nothing less than formidable.

When he speaks, finally addressing me, his voice is rough and admonishing. "I must say, it's rather unfortunate to find you back here again, Raider Boreas."

His head gives a slight shake of disapproval before he walks over to the impressive oaken desk that sits just before a wall of wrought iron windows. I grind my teeth together to stop myself from correcting him and calling myself captain like some whiny little level-three.

"Yes, Grand Preceptor," I reply, giving a dutiful bow of my head and avoiding looking directly at him.

"Well, don't just stand there. Come in," he snaps, glancing up from where he's begun rummaging around in his desk. "And shut the doors, would you?"

I can tell from the shadow passing through his single eye that he enjoys just how uncomfortable this makes me. He wants to see me squirm and delights greatly in finding all the ways to break me.

Pity for him, I've nearly perfected my own guise over the years.

I sweep coolly into the room and turn to close the doors without a moment's hesitation. I'm no longer the washed-up level-one who cried herself to sleep every night, praying to all the gods who might listen that she would choke to death on her own tears.

Skelm's sun-weathered face reveals nothing of what's to come, but he gestures with a leather gloved hand to a familiar crystal bowl sitting atop the shelf nearest to me. It's filled almost to the brim with hundreds of small copper-colored seeds.

Kratosbane.

It takes every shred of my self-discipline to clamp down on the immediate refusal that radiates from every fiber of my being and instead pluck one of the copper kernels from the container before tossing it into my mouth casually.

Even more horrible than what's undoubtedly about to occur here is the immediate feeling of being cut away from my affinity. I can only think to compare the sensation to a keen blade slicing through the connections between my mind, body, and soul.

Skelm waits until I swallow before continuing.

Coward.

"Now, Boreas, you've been promoted to captain for all of what? One week, is it? And your crew has already begun to run rampant." His frown tightens around the gold-covered socket of his missing eye.

Rumor had it that a seajay plucked that eye straight from his skull in the middle of a raid near the Foggy Isles only a few years into his own captaincy career. By all accounts, it's only served to make our Grand Preceptor more terrifying. Not to mention the chip it left on his shoulder.

For me to speak now would be a mistake. One that I have made before and then swiftly learned from. I have to stop myself from rubbing the phantom ache in my forearm at the memory. Skelm absolutely hates fidgeting. He calls it the "calling card of liars."

I bite my tongue while watching his bejeweled hands come to rest atop the oaken desk. A deep frown appears permanently etched onto the planes of his aged face. The largest ring he wears, a golden sea serpent wrapped around the length of his index finger, taps idly against the wood.

"Explain this to me," he says, and I can feel his one good eye practically boring a hole into the spot between my brows. "Why is it that we do not permit raiders to visit the shores on a night such as this one, Raider Boreas?"

I swallow once before answering. "Because of the Sál Moon, sir."

Skelm nods, his frown deepening. I know I'm meant to continue.

"Because of the incoming sacrifices. Going into the waters on this night could disrupt their path to us." He nods again before removing his hands from their resting place atop the desk.

This night is indeed a sacred one. Not just to the Order, but to the whole of Pontus. Every landmass, encompassing sea, drifter, and minuscule island knows the significance of the Sál Moon night.

It's the night when the veil between our realm and the below realm of the netherdepths we call Nawai is thinnest. On this night, the drowned gods may choose the sacrificed children from the landmasses, or those youths carelessly tossed to the sea, for a second life.

They're then guided by the Nix's will to the religious cult of the drowned gods, known as the Sons and Daughters of the Deep. Which, by extension, leads them to the Order of the Tide Raiders.

This divine tradition dates back to the first sacrifice, known as *The Soteria Daughter*. It was her sacrifice, made nearly a thousand years ago, that saved our world of Pontus from a disastrous event known today as *The Great Deluge*.

"So you do understand the severity of what your crew has risked tonight. Good. Explain, then: why should you be allowed to retain your captaincy following this incident? All signs point to future mutiny." Skelm spits the last word out with a mouthful of disgust.

His insinuation has me biting the inside of my cheek until I taste blood on my tongue in order to keep from saying something that will surely end with a week in the hole, strung up in iron. The terrors of that particularly dark period from level-four still manage to drive me from sleep some nights.

Our Grand Preceptor looks me in the eye again, signaling that he expects a response. He wants me to answer for the sins of my cabin. As always, I oblige.

"I take full responsibility for their... *transgressions*, sir. This sort of behavior will not happen again. I can assure you of it." My tone doesn't allude to even an undertow of fear.

Skelm gives me the severe look of scrutiny I've come to expect from him. It's no different than the one he gave me on that first night, filled with quiet calculations. I wait in practiced silence for him to pretend to weigh out his options.

After a moment, he furrows his graying brows in mock contemplation. "I suppose, as it was during your all's day of liberty and they could not be directly commanded by you—fine. I will preserve your title. This time."

I dip my chin. "Thank you, sir. That is very generous."

Although we both know he couldn't have taken my title. Not for an excursion that occurred on this day in particular. It would be a direct violation of the Tide Raider Code. By the way his thin lips curve into a cat-like smirk, I know he's daring me to point that out. But I hold my tongue.

"There will still need to be consequences, of course. The single rule we set for you all on this day of freedom was broken. That cannot be allowed to go undisciplined."

Nodding in silent agreement, I hear him sigh, like he's exasperated with an unruly child.

My vision drifts away from the Grand Preceptor and instead settles on the iron-crossed windows facing the newly dawning sky. The waters that lie far beneath are sadly no longer aglow with the strange spirit magic.

Standing, Skelm removes his cloak and gloves before rolling back the cuffs of his navy uniform.

I watch the sea birds darting low enough to skim the volatile waves and admire their daring as they pull up on the winds at breakneck speeds. Meanwhile, Skelm meanders back over to the roaring fire. He grabs something from the golden stand and prods around in the flames once more.

I've always hated fire.

Even as a child. Even before I was given a real reason to. I've always disliked its wild, unpredictable temper. Always loathed the way it consumes anything and everything in its path without thought. No one ever comes away from its touch unscathed.

Intrinsically, I'm repelled by it.

I abhor it.

My attention remains fixed on the newly agitated sea beyond Skelm's windows. If I focus hard enough, I can feel the salty breeze on my face. Sometimes I focus so hard that I swear I can hear the water's pulsing heartbeat. It's a practiced method that takes me away from reality, if only for a few precious seconds at a time.

"I must admit, I find it quite fascinating after all these years," our Grand Preceptor remarks after a few moments more spent digging around in his inferno before turning back to face me. "Your aversion towards fire is every bit as potent as that first night."

The birds must have found something, I think. More and more of them are flocking to some invisible speck in the water. They begin dive-bombing in groups of twos and threes. Soon their jewel-feathered bodies are swarming whatever unfortunate sea creature has risen to the surface.

Skelm's steely voice slices through my reverie. "I think eight is appropriate today. One for each of those little *transgressions* under your charge, and an additional one for the clear lack of proper control being held over your own godsdamned crew, *Captain.*" He hurls my title like a curse.

I don't talk back as I might once have done. Rather, I begin silently removing the jacket of my uniform and untucking the thin summer shirt beneath before tugging it over my head without complaint. My startlingly white hair is twisted neatly around a golden pin and back into a low knot—a gift from my chosen second for my promotion to captaincy.

Skelm motions for me to turn around, and it's a struggle to tear my eyes away from the distraction of the windows. Of course he would take even that small relief away.

Our Grand Preceptor's affinity gives him the advantage of sensing a person's greatest fears in the form of pain. And, by default, anything that might lessen that pain. He holds out the item he'd been searching his desk for earlier: a roll of leather.

I take the offer without a word. No need to break a tooth just to prove a point. Well, not again.

I slide the roll between my lips and focus my thoughts on the future. It's so close now I can just about taste it. The day we finish the eighth level. Before, it seemed so unlikely. But now, it's only a mere year away.

Skelm doesn't bother warning me before pressing that searing hot poker of his into the sprawling affinity mark along my backside. I bite down on the leather strap hard.

No matter how many times, I never become immune to the pain of this. It never seems to lessen. Which is also precisely why this is the chosen method of discipline for me. I work to ignore the fiery agony and think about the day we might be chosen to sail under a TideLord's fleet instead.

I focus on the beautiful possibility of leaving the Cardinal North at long last. The next brand sears into me even hotter than the first.

I think about what it would be like to have the wind at my back and open water before me as far as the eye can see. I remember the untethered excitement in Kerau's electric-blue eyes just before he left. I can almost feel that yearning ache from watching him stride onto TideLord Raimbaut's ship.

He never looked back.

Skelm's third burning stamp makes me cry out in extreme pain through the leather. The sound of my torment is followed by his chuckle.

I think, if I try hard enough, I can hear the ocean thrashing about somewhere far below. My imaginings turn to how it might feel to captain under a TideLord myself. To take on assignments and earn our own spoils.

The fourth and fifth strikes blind me with fresh pain. My legs give out, and I'm forced down into a kneeling position. Sweat slides down my temples, and my shoulders begin to shake.

I focus on my crew. The sacred eight. I imagine how it would be to live a life with them, out on the open tides. All of us safely far away from this hellish place.

Skelm makes sure to press the last three brands deep into the planes of my already ruined back.

My screams come out clear through the leather. The shrill pitch of them pierces the air and travels all the way out to the newly scattering seabirds flying up and away from the tides beyond my sight.

Black spots pulse and grow along the edges of my vision until the world fades out of view entirely. All the while, I hold onto the thought of never, *ever* being forced to separate from my affinity again.

Scents of lavender and chamomile swirl through the air and tickle my nose, reeling my unconscious self back to the surface.

My vision is blurry when I first try fluttering my eyelids open. It feels as though a haze of algae has been wrapped around my corneas.

"Wha—" I begin to say, or rather moan, pushing up with arms that are now apparently beneath me. Pain laces up my back, so fresh it's blinding. I think I let out a shout. Maybe it's another scream.

"Hey—whoa, now don't get up. Come on—lay back down," coos a familiar voice.

From the sound of the quickly approaching footfalls, the owner of said familiar voice is heading toward me. Wherever that is. I continue struggling upwards and curse viciously at the pure agony now known as my back.

"I'm serious, Merena!" snaps the voice, now right beside me.

So much for soothing.

I drop my arms and huff out a breath as my chest thuds back onto the cushioned cot beneath me. My hands raise slowly to rub the blurriness from my eyes before finally peering up at the golden-maned girl currently frowning down at me. The bronze dusting of freckles splattered across her nose is all the more prominent under the sickbay's orb lights.

"Hi, Vi," I mumble.

Davina's frown deepens, and her eyebrows knit together in concern. "So they went through with it, then?" Her question is blunt, her mouth pursed into a line of barely concealed outrage.

I do my best to nod in my current position. "It would seem so." I let out a sigh. "You're the only one to miss out on all the fun."

Davina is the only member of my crew who wasn't down there on the shore, actively disobeying the Order's rule. She shakes her head, her hazel eyes a kaleidoscope of hidden thoughts, constantly changing and morphing from one to the other. Blue to green to brown to gold.

"I was with the other leeches at the ceremony," she explains, before turning and heading for one of the many sun-stained tables that frame the back part of the sickbay. I observe her as she begins pulling down various bottles and herbs from the cabinets above her workstation.

"I know. I figured they would've pulled you for it. Is that why Leech Vitasan isn't here?"

Davina turns around from where she's now begun steeping a silver ball into a pot of steaming hot water. "Yeah, she's still down there. Big catch this year. Over forty of them in total. The Sons and Daughters seem to think it's auspicious."

"They always think it's auspicious," I snort.

My mind begins wandering to the unsettling image of the ocean-worshipping cult members and their hollow eye sockets. A disturbing chill spiders down my spine at the memory, and I force my train of thought to pick a different track.

"Were any of them—" I start.

The inquiry is one Davina knows is coming.

"No," she cuts me off with the answer to my unfinished question. "None of them were anything like you. I inspected each one myself, promise."

I sense that her normally sharp tongue is trying to be gentle.

I hate that.

Turning my head away from where she works, I instead face the wall of glass that looks out into the bay belonging to our northern isle. I watch the many fish who pass by the glass in curious silence. Their colorful scales, glimmering under the orb lights, are somewhat soothing.

I've spent more time in the sickbay than probably just about any raider here. Particularly during levels one through four.

I knew this Sál Moon wouldn't be any different. I knew the likelihood of any of those poor kids who washed up last night looking anything like me was a long shot. Yet still, every year without fail, I somehow get my hopes up.

I can't help it. I look for any trace of who I am in every single stranger I meet. The slope of their nose, the shade of their irises, even the pout in their lips. Suffice to say, I've yet to come across anyone that might be a familial relation.

"Here," Vi offers, returning to my cot at last with a low black ceramic dish in her hands. It's filled with half an inch of hot, scented water, and I prop myself on my elbows to take it from her.

The liquid tastes like peppermint and burns nearly as hot as Skelm's poker while sliding down my throat. I close my eyes and shudder in response to the sensation before slumping with the intense relief of reconnecting to my affinity. An icy breeze flits about the room from a small burst of power, and Vi tightens the jacket of her leech's uniform.

"Thank you," I manage to croak out, relishing the comforting chill blooming into every inch of me. Apart from the devastation on my back, that is.

It's silent for a beat before Vi whispers, "I'm so sorry, Merena."

My eyes reopen, and I look up through thick lashes to find guilt coloring her face.

Davina swallows thickly and walks away again before I can say anything in return. She begins crushing something or another with a jade mortar and pestle. The constant sound of her angry mixing is the only thing to break the room's silence.

"I'm sure Kleio has her reasons," I comment after a few minutes of the stifling quiet.

Vi doesn't reply, and I close my eyes. Lingering, searing pain is the only reason I'm not drifting off to sleep right now. A few more minutes, and a cooling paste is dolloped along my back.

My eyes snap open in a moment of agony, and I inhale a steady breath through my nose to a count of four, as we've been taught. The ointment is then generously spread over my wounds, and I hold my breath for another four before exhaling on the same count.

Preceptor Darood would be proud.

I do this repeatedly until the paste is no longer painful and is instead a blissfully cold antidote to the heated wounds. I count the fish who swim past and stop to watch me as the miracle salve, blessed with Davina's affinity, sinks into the brands.

In an hour or so, there will only be thin white scars left. In a day or less, they will have vanished entirely to the outside eye. Only I alone will remember the pain of them.

I am marked with countless invisible scars.

Once finished, Vi quietly watches me pull back on the top half of my uniform, re-strap the buttons, and adjust my hair so it's tightly coiled around the golden pin once more.

"I'll see you at the cabin?" I ask.

Unlike the other members of my crew, Davina's schedule revolves around the leeches, not the raiders.

She nods, her kaleidoscope eyes churning with the track of her thoughts. I give her a suppressed smile, which she doesn't return, before passing through the familiar archway and leaving the sickbay at last.

III. RUMORS

Returning to mine and my crew's cabin, positioned on the far back side of the sprawling fortress, I'm unsurprised to find Kleio pacing in the main room.

I'm also unsurprised to find the green-veined marble fireplace that sits against the front wall of the main area has noticeably been extinguished. Upon my entry, my second pauses her anxious walking and turns to me with an anguished face drained of all color.

"Merena, I—" she starts with a step in my direction.

I hold up my hand, halting her mid-sentence. Fortunately for Kleio, the ache in my back is slowly but surely easing with every passing moment. Thank all the fucking drowned gods for leeches.

"I do not want to hear an apology," I snap, and it's an effort to keep from shouting. "I know you, Kleio. You're only sorry because you all were caught."

She looks at me like I've just slapped her. I have to restrain myself from grabbing hold of my second by the shoulders and shaking until some sense finally rattles round in that stubborn fucking head. Kleio folds her arms over her chest as if she can read my thoughts.

"If this was last year, you would have been the one leading us out there! You wouldn't have had an issue with it, you—"

"I wasn't a captain then, Kleio!" I exclaim, effectively cutting her off again. "Last year and all the years prior, I was nothing. I had nothing to lose. There was nothing they could take from me."

I watch as the typical warmth in her brown eyes cools. "Nothing? You had *nothing*?" she argues, her voice rising an octave.

I gaze up to the thick wooden beams lining the cabin's ceiling and back at my second in exasperation. Then I bite down on the side of my fist to stop myself from saying something I shouldn't and stride into the main room.

Shaking my head silently, I ease into one of the two armchairs facing the dead hearth. One of my hands goes to gingerly hold my back while proof of the lingering pain slides through my teeth. Kleio's eyes soften again as she watches me carefully position myself so my still-healing wounds don't touch the chair.

My voice is a bit more controlled when I finally reply. "Obviously I had you. I had all of you. But as my allies, not as my crew. I wasn't in a position to affect your futures, to give you all a shot at freedom—or as close to it as we can ever really get."

I try selecting my next words carefully. "I'm one of only two captains, Kleio."

"I know that!" she practically explodes.

The chocolate curls framing her heart-shaped face shake with the force of her voice. "Do you really think that I don't already know all of this? You don't think that there must have been a great godsdamned reason I was down there?" Tears begin to betray her eyes. "You cannot seriously believe your newly minted second-in-command would risk my own captain's neck for a night of rebellion, can you?"

"Alright, then let's hear it!" I hurl back at her, thankful the others have obviously been sent out to observe morning colors. "What was so incredibly important for you to take my crew, under my nose, and gallivant down to the one fucking place you weren't allowed to be last night?"

It feels good to yell.

It feels good to rage against something.

Anything.

Frost begins covering the arms of my chair, and I spot Kleio trying to hide her shivering.

Huffing in irritation, I reel back my affinity before looking to my second in expectation for her response. She hesitates, tucking a loose curl behind her ear and looking anywhere but my eyes.

I groan, a hand coming to pinch the bridge of my nose as my eyes squeeze shut. "I swear, if this has to do with Vash fucking Larceon, I will—" I begin to warn, and her eyes flash at the implication of my words.

"It isn't about Vash! It's about something he said," Kleio snaps defensively.

As if that somehow makes it better.

Kleio's current entanglement and I have a long history of mutual dislike, but that isn't what sparks my aggravation. That's more or less due to the amount of times I've heard his name from her lips in the last seven years. On and on and *on*. Ever since we were thirteen.

I curse beneath my breath but motion with my free hand for her to explain.

She's hesitant with her next words. "There is a rumor. A rumor going around the levels that the Vault has risen up this year."

Now that has my attention. I lean forward too fast, and merciless agony flares up my still-healing back. "Shit," I curse between my teeth, and Kleio's eyes widen with worry.

"The Vault?" I echo, my mind narrowing in on the improbable possibility at hand. "Vash actually told you that *the* Vault has risen?"

Kleio eyes me for a moment, and I know she's thinking about my wounds. She also knows much better than to try and coddle me in this state.

Fun fact: I bite when smothered.

My second gives a stiff nod of assent. “He did.”

The hand still pinching the bridge of my nose drops to grip my chin in thought. If it had been a rumor heard by any other ears, I’d dismiss it entirely. But coming from Vash, the only other captain in our cardinal, there must be some weight to i t.

Also, there’s the fact that his affinity tells truths from lies, among other talents. It further indicates this is very likely real.

My mind begins racing at nauseating speeds. Possibilities jump out at me with every passing thought. The doors this could open—the opportunities. Not only for myself but for all eight of us.

The Vault in question is not your typical guarded chest containing some trivial bout of treasured possessions. This Vault was crafted by the drowned gods themselves. Or so legend claims. It rises from the netherdepths only when sensing there is a Tide Raider among us worthy enough to enter its gilded doors.

Of course it’s not as easy as being chosen, the Order would never allow for that. So there are challenges, or rather *Pillar Trials,* put in place for those who might gain entry. Only level-eight captains from one of the four Cardinal Orders are eligible.

“You know,” Kleio says, her tone noticeably lighter, “almost every single captain who's ever been chosen by the Vault became a TideLord later on in their career.”

“It’ll be a bloodbath,” I reply, still lost in thought,

“Why do you think we went down to the water?” she responds slyly.

My gaze slides right back over to lock with hers. I watch as a mischievous smirk—one I’m guilty of encouraging over the years—tugs onto her rosy lips. And I have to fight my own grin threatening to make its appearance before finally shaking my head in defeat.

Only Kleio could get away with the bullshit she pulled last night.

Capturing a soul in a bottle was a very tricky thing indeed. But if you were able to manage it, which from the look on my second's face tells me that she *did*, you could tell it a wish before releasing it back into the sea.

The tradition being that the soul will then tell the drowned gods of your prayer when it returns to the spirit world of Nawai. If you're lucky, the gods might just choose to answer it.

It's the closest thing we have to an actual shot of hope around here.

Our first official week of level-eight passes by without another hiccup.

My cabin, having been thoroughly reprimanded by myself and given the task of walking the courtyard for two nights straight, is on its very best behavior. I still haven't entirely forgiven Kleio, although now having the facts, I do understand her reasoning.

After her public discipline, a requirement of any crew member who disobeys or shames their captain, I find it much easier to meet her newly blackened eye. To Kleio's credit, she wears the shiner like a crown and actually laughed when I asked if it hurt.

"You should really work on that left hook, but I appreciate you using your off hand."

No more words are heard or spoken regarding the Vault until our weapons class the week directly following the Sál Moon. The class in question is headed by Preceptor Oplon, a now middle-aged raider who'd previously made his career as one of the most sought-after gunners in all of the Order.

His training is held within one of the largest chambers carved deep beneath the dark fortress of the Cardinal North. Today, we work in pairs with weapons called dancing discs. The twin circular blades are one of my favorites. They're incredibly fast and have the ability to match their wielder's fighting patterns after only a few moves.

We're currently tasked with using the two discs with another person. Working as a team is proving to be much harder than working alone.

"Merena—catch!" Javin shouts before streaking across the training grounds ahead of me in a blur of cropped dark hair and bronzed skin.

Javin Supad is my assigned partner for today's lesson. His affinity for speed makes him a worthy opponent and an even more challenging partner. Preceptor Oplon is always sure to pair me with whoever he deems most difficult based on the weapons we're training with.

I follow the line of the disc's flight and dive for the spinning blade. My hand catches the slim leather-bound grip just before it makes to cut through my thigh. The disc in my left hand hums with excitement at the presence of its twin in my right.

I scan the training chamber and find Preceptor Oplon watching our exchange. He gives me a shallow nod of praise, and I bite back a smile. There are very few instructors here who don't outright try to increase my chances of failure. Oplon has always been tough on me. He's always pushed me harder than the others and expected more. But with him, I know it has nothing to do with my origins.

"Good catch there, Captain," Oplon calls across the set of mats that make up our training sectors. His salt-and-pepper hair is tied back in a low bun that continues down into a matching beard. He motions for me to come over to him, and his mouth twitches with the threat of a smile.

I give him a nod in understanding before setting the discs carefully in their holder along the wall covered floor-to-ceiling in weapons, then head his way. Javin is gulping down water when I come near.

"Good session, Supad," I say in passing.

He gives me a wink and replies suggestively over his flask, "Let me know anytime you need a good workout, Boreas. I'd be more than happy to oblige, Cap."

I roll my eyes and throw him a one-finger salute before jogging over to where Preceptor Oplon stands with Captain Larceon at his side. Javin has probably slept with half our level at this point. Although his flirtatious attempts have never landed with myself, I can't say the same for all of my crew members.

Upon my approach, Vash gives me no indication he knows why we've been called over. Instead, he pushes back his sweat-laden bronze hair before flashing a roguish grin—the kind that drives almost all the girls in our level and many below crazy. As always, it only serves to amplify my own annoyance, and my attention turns toward our instructor.

"Captains," Preceptor Oplon says by way of greeting, his gray eyes shifting between us. "You two have been called to the Regent's quarters and are expected to report there immediately."

"Did she say why?" Vash asks before I can.

Oplon's painted smile reveals nothing. "I would guess she's expecting you any minute now, and I wouldn't keep her waiting if I were you," he warns, leaning on the silver stingray cane that betrays his irreparable shoulder injury. It's for that reason he no longer sails under the current Tide Raider King and is instead stuck here training us.

He gives us a grimace before turning around in dismissal and heading for the training mats directly diagonal. Oplon's voice takes on a thunderous edge when growling out, "Eiran! What did I say about spatial jumping during the lesson today? You're going to end up in front of a disc, and I am not in the mood to clean your guts off the stone!"

We leave before hearing Eiran's typical smartass retort.

Vash doesn't even look worried that his third is currently tempting fate, both with the dancing discs and Preceptor Oplon. On the contrary, his angular face is uncharacteristically reserved on our walk through the tunnels leading back up to the main levels.

For a while, only the sound of our footsteps fills the halls until eventually rock becomes wood.

"I know that you know, Merena," Vash states, breaking our silence and abruptly derailing me from my current train of thought.

"What?" I ask, looking over at him, having to tilt my head up to fully meet his green-speckled gaze.

It doesn't seem like so long ago that he was shorter than me. Then, in levels three and four, he grew so we were exactly the same height. It drove him mad until level five, when he hit a growth spurt, dropped his voice several octaves, and became more popular with the girls.

By level seven, he'd won just about everyone else over, as his later promotion to captaincy proved. But Kleio has been infatuated with him since that first night.

His mouth tugs into a half-smirk, and green eyes glitter with amusement. I just might detest his affinity most of all. His ability to tell the truth from lies—and, in turn, to pass on lies as easily as truth—has always left me feeling off-footed.

And I hate feeling anything less than certain.

"The Vault," he comments casually. Like he's mentioning something about the weather and not the biggest opportunity in the last decade.

I give him a small frown. "I might have heard a rumor about it. Why do you bring it up?"

Vash laughs, and the sound of it is so at odds with the dark-stained wooden halls we walk that I can't help but smirk a bit. But anytime I've thought about the Vault this last week and what it could mean, I feel a dangerous amount of hope flutter inside. So naturally, I do everything in my power to smash it.

Clamping down on my smirk, I force my face into an expression of cool indifference.

"Why else would the old bat be calling us to her office?" he adds, giving me a sidelong glance.

Taking the end of my long white braid from where it hangs over a shoulder, I begin twisting the thick strands around a finger before answering in mock innocence, "Maybe she wants to have tea and give us sweets as a congratulation for our promotions."

Vash snorts a laugh, and I suppress my own.

The thought of Regent Beldham doing anything of the sort is about as ridiculous as the Sol Emperor himself showing up to the Order with a hand-stitched white flag. Which is to say, completely absurd.

"Okay, smartass," Vash rolls his eyes. "Have it your way."

His steps slow, and I realize that we've made it to the tall black doors marking the entryway to our Regent's quarters. I'm about to retort when the sound of Beldham's voice stops me.

"Larceon, Boreas, do not make me wait any longer than I already have," she clips briskly from the other side of the doors.

I bite my tongue and slip inside after Vash.

IV. REMEMBER THE CODE

Preceptor Beldham's quarters are vastly different from Skelm's, although nearly as big.

With her being our Regent, Beldham has, of course, been afforded the next best quarters. The office itself is circular in shape, with three arching windows revealing just how close we are to the lethal cliffside serving as our isle's borders. Those windows are the only speck of wall not covered in bookshelves or swathed in maps.

Standing at attention before the unique ring-shaped desk Beldham sits behind, I scan the stacks of papers and books crammed into every curve and ledge of her worktable. I always feel a bit overwhelmed when inside her quarters. My eyes tend to wander, hungry for any scrap of information about the outside world.

Vash stands at attention beside me. I force myself to focus on our Regent and not the large, detailed map of Pontus that hangs on the wall just to my left.

For several moments, Beldham doesn't so much as glance up from the scroll unbound before her. Her rich umbra skin stands out against the shock of aging white hair that's been pulled back into a severe bun. We wait as her cornflower eyes rove back and forth over the report in her hands, one that I itch to see.

After another minute, she sighs and re-rolls the report before setting it on a pile of nearly identical others stacked precariously close to the edge of her desk. Her startling blue gaze assesses Captain Larceon and then myself. "Go on now. Let's not waste any more time," she clips, gesturing with a hand toward the wooden spindle chairs across her desk.

I take my seat carefully, and Vash does the same.

I never know exactly where I stand with our Regent. On principle, she doesn't actually favor anyone, but she's also one of the few instructors here who hasn't given me a reason to hate her. Beldham is tough as fucking nails, but she's also fair.

"I've called you here on behalf of some rather... *unexpected* news. News that will directly affect the both of you," she states calmly, steepling her hands on the table.

I can't help but admire the many different rings that adorn her long, slender fingers. Each one of them signifying a promotion or achievement during her career. The largest of which being the Polaris signet, marking her as Regent to the Cardinal North Order.

Ignoring Vash's glance in my direction, I cross my arms in question. "Oh?"

Her lips form a tight line when nodding. "It seems our Raider King has been given scouting reports of the Vault ascending. They claim it's broken the surface."

So we're cutting right to the chase today.

"You're joking," Vash remarks with unnerving conviction, his arms coming to cross themselves.

"I never joke, Captain Larceon." Beldham's tone is crisp. "The report has been confirmed, and the other three cardinals have already made their preparations and begun sailing this way."

"This way?" I ask, my voice higher now with genuine surprise.

The Pillar Trials are normally held on neutral soil or sometimes neutral waters. The different cardinal captains are always kept separate.

Beldham's eyes appear to flash with irritation, but I get the sense it's not directed at either of us sitting before her. "Yes, this way," she affirms with a sigh. "It has been decided that the Cardinal North will be hosting the Pillars this time around. With uprisings springing up on every other landmass, not to mention the coups on the drifters—well, anyway, the Grand Preceptors thought it best to hold them in one place."

This was quite an unexpected change of plans, one I had not in my wildest dreams anticipated. From the way Vash sits in equally stunned silence next to me, I know he's just as surprised.

"I assume you two have put the pieces together by now, but in case Preceptor Oplon's training today knocked something loose, I will lay it out plainly. You will both be participating in the Pillar Trials," Beldham states, her expression unreadable.

That's the other thing about the Vault: it's not a choice. As a captain of my cardinal, I'll be made to participate in each deadly task until getting a shot at the Vault itself. There's no debate, no escape, not even if I wanted to. The risks are high, but the reward...

"Thank you, Grand Regent, it is a great honor," I acknowledge, giving her a respectful tilt of my head.

Vash echoes me in words and movement, his voice much quieter than normal. This new tidbit of information must have thrown him off even more than myself.

"Yes, well," Beldham begins, standing from her chair with catlike fluidity. We follow suit while she continues. "I do expect you both to prove exactly why you were chosen as captains. I look forward to seeing another northern raider as Vault champion once more."

Her words are clipped, but there's a shine of anticipation in her eyes. The sight of it brings the shadow of a grin to my lips. "We'll flatten them," I promise.

The hint of a rare smile crosses our regent's face. "See that you do."

We trek back down the creaking wooden hallways in silence.

I make to turn left toward the dining chamber when Vash reaches out and grabs me by the neck of my uniform. Before I can tear myself from his surprisingly firm grip, he's pulled me through one of the many alcove balconies lining the dark fortress's upper corridors.

"May I *help* you?" I hiss through my teeth once he releases his grip before beginning to straighten my uniform back out in visible annoyance.

Vash laughs at my irritation.

I have to ball my hands in order to keep from grabbing one of the blades strapped to my thigh and stabbing him as I wish to. Maiming another captain a week after my crew's incident would not bode well for me. And I'm determined not to mess up the impossible opportunity that's just been laid before us.

Raising both hands in mock surrender Vash says, "Sorry, honest. I just wanted to talk to you about what Preceptor Beldham said. You know, captain-to-captain." He emphasizes this by turning around and latching the alcove's windowed doors.

"For future reference," I all but snarl, "I prefer to be *asked* to chit-chat, not dragged by the nape like a fucking grimalkin whelp."

Vash looks on the verge of laughing again, but he sees the intensity of my glare—feels the temperature steadily drop in the air around us—and thinks better of it. "Noted," he confirms.

I cross my arms with a huff of annoyance. "Well? I'm here."

My fellow co-captain runs a telltale hand through his bronze waves while gazing out at the glacial waters crashing violently against obsidian rocks. After a moment he pivots in order to lean against the stone balcony wall and face me. "What do you think about the other cardinals coming here?" Vash asks, crossing both arms before a broadened chest.

I glance at the sky, shaking my head in exasperation. "I think that the Order doesn't give a single shit about how either you or I feel regarding the subject."

He studies me, those green eyes growing uncharacteristically serious. "But you heard what Beldham said," he pushes. "About the landmasses and the drifters."

"Yes, I heard her." I suck in a breath. "Why do you care?"

"Why don't you?" Vash counters, his voice low. "Don't you see? The Order doesn't just change its traditions on a whim. It's calculated. Something is—this whole thing—it just feels off." His brows knit together in concern.

My head tilts as I study him. "Are you saying Beldham lied in there?"

Vash's gaze cuts to mine sharply, and he presses his lips together for a moment before stating, "I'm saying she *withheld* something. Or skirted around a bigger truth—I'm not sure. But I am sure that putting the four cardinals together is a big fucking gamble. Skelm is an asshole, but he isn't an idiot."

My eyes, nearly the same exact shade as those crystal waters below, flit around the alcove and the doors tightly sealed behind us. Skelm might also be missing an eye, but his ears are literally everywhere. And I keep my voice low when responding while taking a step closer to where Vash leans against the stone.

"Captain-to-captain here," I whisper, and he nods before inclining his head closer. His irises have a strange golden flicker to them when I come near. "I'd advise you to keep those thoughts to yourself. I suggest you get your eyes on the fucking prize and let the Order sort out its own shit. Whatever is or isn't going on out there is not our concern. Our concern is gaining entry to the Vault."

Vash's eyes narrow, a scowl pulling on his mouth.

"If not for yourself, then for your crew."

Uncertainty briefly crosses his face and I take that as my out. Turning back around, I move to unlatch the alcove doors before throwing icily over a shoulder, "Remember the code, Vash. A captain's duty is to the crew, no matter the cost. Personal or not."

"And so, due to the sudden and immediate collapse of the Northern Empire, a period of chaos ensued. Can anyone tell me what that period was called?"

A sharp and unexpected kick to my ankle has me lurching forward in my chair.

"Yes, Captain Boreas?" Preceptor Chie calls, mistaking my reaction as an attempt to get his attention.

I look over to Kleio, who winces before mouthing "sorry." But there's amusement dancing around the edges of her warm sepia eyes, and it doesn't slip my notice.

"The, uh—Era of Discordia, Preceptor," I call back.

It's a guess, a shot in the dark. Whatever the old man has been droning on about for the last hour is beyond me. But I've found that nearly seven out of ten times he's rambling over this particular portion of history.

Truth be had, I'd been slowly drifting off to sleep in my seat before now. Preceptor Chie's voice is so dull it's actually rather relaxing. And after staying up half the last few nights since meeting with Beldham, reading anything I could get my hands on regarding former pillar tasks, I was just tempting fate.

"Correct. Very good, Captain Boreas," Preceptor Chie praises, twisting the end of his long silver goatee between two gnarled fingers. From the narrow of his ancient eyes, it's clear he isn't entirely fooled, but he resumes the lecture without further question.

I relax back into my chair and try incredibly hard to focus on the board before us. It's filled with periods of time and the events that mark them. By all accounts, this class should be fascinating to me—being the only frame of reference I have to the world outside these dark walls. But the excitement of learning the history of Pontus has only seemed to dampen with each passing level. All I've gained in these classes is the depressing knowledge that the world has and always will revolve around power.

Those who have it and those who want it.

The rest of it is just a repetition of the same wars parading about under different names. It's mainly bullshit, in my opinion. There is never any 'right' or 'wrong' side because, at the end of the day, the winners half will be the only part of the story you're told.

Not that anyone asked me.

Chie's lecture ends just a few minutes later, and I'm saved from his dangerously tranquil voice before I can fall into another slump. I leave the dim bell-shaped room with Kleio on my heels and Greer and Herse only a few steps behind. The twins and Nimra have been selected to help train the new level-ones. Davina is most likely either being used by the leeches or sleeping during whatever brief respite of time she has.

We make our way to the outdoor lyceums situated across a long stone bridge connecting our cliff-bound fortress to the rest of the minuscule island. Being that it's the end of summer, we won't be able to utilize the outdoor spaces much longer. The rainy season won't be far off now, and Preceptor Ersatz is determined to use every last day possible outside.

We're about halfway over the open-air trestle before Kleio speaks. "So how much longer are you planning to pull these all-nighters? I mean, normally I'm happy to kick you awake, but this last time I thought you might actually freeze my ass to the seat. You had that scary little look in your eye."

My third and fourth snort their laughter from behind, and I throw them a glance over my shoulder. The kind that has them both pressing their lips into hard lines of silence.

"Yep, that's the one," Kleio sing-songs, pointing a finger towards my ice-cold glare.

I try and fail to keep a straight face, my lips pulling upward in eventual defeat. "It's not like I haven't tried sleeping—I just can't," I begin to explain. "Anytime my head hits the pillow, my mind starts running—no—sprinting in a million different directions. There's so much I don't know about the trials and the other cardinals. It's overwhelming."

Kleio sucks on a tooth, her eyes skimming over our approaching exit in thought.

Then Greer chimes in from where she keeps pace with Herse just a few steps behind. "Let us help you, Merena."

I pause my strides and turn to find my third nodding in agreement. "Yeah, 'Cap. Give us each a tome or two and we'll knock it out. No problem."

"Oh—yeah. That would be great, actually." My voice is suddenly, stupidly thick.

I'm still getting used to this—to having *actual* friends. Having people that I care about and who seem to care about me in turn. Most days I don't truly let myself believe it's real.

For a while there at the beginning, the Order pits each of us raiders against the others. The idea being that it will ensure only the strongest of us emerge. Those casualties in the first few levels—either by our cardinal or sometimes even by our own hands—well, they were weaklings and would have sullied the reputation of a raider. At least, that's what we're told.

Each and every one of us has had to fight and scrape our way through, just to make it to the eighth level alive. It wasn't even until around level four that those making up my crew started becoming allies. I would not have considered us friends at that point. Not by a long shot.

Except for Kleio. We became a duo years before accepting the others. She drove me nearly half mad those first few levels. I couldn't stand her constant talk of home. I also wanted to smash my head into a wall every time I heard her swooning over Vash Larceon.

Back then, I kept mostly to myself. Partially because I didn't care to make any friends, but mostly due to the fact that I'm a castaway with a bastard's name. Not to mention the fact that I was singled out regularly for disciplinary measures. They all left me to my own isolation on purpose. Honestly, though, it was in everyone's best interest to keep their distance.

Except for Kleio. She could never leave well the fuck alone. She just *had* to go and risk her neck in level three for me.

Idiot.

The point being that even now—even when working with my own crew—sharing the load does not come naturally.

"Well, that's settled," Kleio quips, her fading black eye squinting in the sun-light. "Now we can go and enjoy Preceptor Ersatz's famously inspiring and always uplifting class."

"You will all die. Every last one of you."

Preceptor Ersatz's lectures before affinity training are exceptionally harsh and unforgiving. Her black boots shine in a rare appearance of the sun peeking out from behind its usual refuge of clouds as she paces up and down the grassy floor of the lyceum before us. But then she halts her stalking for a moment to turn and face the line of us level-eights. We're currently spread out in a crescent shape against the pine-strewn borders of the outdoor training grounds.

The preceptor who trains our affinities is middle-aged with piercing gold eyes and deep wine-stained lips that stand out starkly against the porcelain skin of her face. Her long, burgundy hair has been tied back into a mass of various braids and I think she would have been beautiful if it wasn't for the crazed light that often shone in her eyes. It's particularly bright when she's describing to us the various horrific ways in which we will no doubt each reach our end.

"I would kill for a good coma right about now," I mutter beneath my breath, to which Kleio tries and fails to hold back a laugh.

Ersatz notices the exchange, and I curse.

Nothing gets by that psychopath.

She turns her razor sharp focus onto me, her yellow eyes alight with the possibility of carnage. "Something to report, raiders?" Ersatz purrs, a small smile playing on her merlot mouth.

"No, Preceptor," I reply, and Kleio echoes.

Ersatz tilts her head of maroon braids and takes a step toward where I stand at one end of the crescent-shaped lineup. There was a time when that one step alone from this preceptor in particular would have sent me running for the hills. But now I don't even flinch. In fact, I don't move a single muscle.

Her smile widens incrementally when pressing, "Was there something funny, then? Something humorous about you all dying?"

Running my tongue against the inside of my bottom lip, I contemplate just how much the list of sarcastic comments I'm itching to respond with would cost me. But then, from the corner of my eye, I catch Greer shifting her weight at the opposite end of the line and I'm promptly reminded that this is not a normal year. It's no longer just my own skin I risk when talking out of turn.

Damnit.

The words I chose slip out from between my teeth. "Not particularly, no."

Preceptor Ersatz's hawkish gaze narrows ever so slightly. I've held a very special place on her shit list these last few years. Ever since she realized I possessed one of the only affinities she couldn't steal. One of the only gods-given blessings she couldn't imitate with her own freakish power. Elemental affinities are apparently too wild and unpredictable for her own to wield.

I think she's about to push again—to force me into saying something that will absolutely end with a flogging—and I find I'm too exhausted to care. I wasn't kidding about the coma; I can feel myself falling asleep standing up.

But instead, she turns away in a flash of brilliant speed. I hear Javin Supad gasp and then swear sharply from somewhere nearby at the feeling of her snatching his affinity for speed.

"Enough distractions, raiders," she lashes out, brandishing her words like a blade. "We will be going over fatal blows today. I want each of you to work on at least five ways in which your blessing could kill. No weapons involved or partners allowed."

I'm onto my seventh technique for a fatal blow—this one being a bit of a stretch. Technically, the ice daggers I've crafted *are* weapons, but since they've been crafted by my own affinity, I say it counts.

"That would be cheating."

The unexpected sound of Captain Larceon's chiding makes me loosen my hold on the daggers, and they splinter midair.

"Damn it!" I snap, glaring at Vash whose appears on my left.

Damn him and his stupid stealth abilities.

"You've already come up with five. Don't tell me you're playing at being Preceptor Ersatz's pet now," he snarks admonishingly.

"No. I just so happen to have a plethora of ideas on how best to maim and murder." I give him a false smile before adding sweetly, "What can I say? It's a gift."

He laughs, and I find the sound of it unnerving. My eyes quickly find Kleio standing across the outdoor lyceum. She grins at us, and we both wave back at her in turn. My second is quite annoyingly determined to force Vash and myself into a camaraderie of some sort. A very difficult task indeed, considering the rather grim history between us.

"Any reason you've chosen to disrupt my concentration today?" I ask airily, more irritated than usual. Which is undoubtedly due to my lack of sleep. At this rate, I'll have to skip water combat training and slink off to our bunks just to avoid tearing someone's head off before dinner.

"They're coming tomorrow night," Vash reveals, no trace of humor left in his voice.

I look back up at him, my brows lifting in uncertainty. "You're sure?"

He gives a sharp nod, the angles of his face drawn and slightly pale. "I'm positive. Raider Oneiros had a dream last night."

Glancing away from Vash, I look over the scattered level-eights, all sharpening their affinity to kill. Searching further, I find Riggs Oneiros sitting in a patch of honeysuckles several yards away from the bordering pine trees. Preceptor Ersatz mostly ignores him and anyone else with an affinity the Order has deemed *Vek*. That is to say—not lethal, and therefore unworthy.

Raider Oneiros is a big kid, always has been. He's the tallest in our level by at least a foot, with pasty arms and legs the size of tree trunks. He could probably palm my head with his hand if he wanted to. I'm sure our Grand Preceptor—and the rest of the Cardinal North, if we're being honest—were positively devastated to find out he didn't possess a mean bone in his body.

Choosing him as fourth in command for their crew was a strategic move on Vash's part. I'll give him that. Even if Raider Oneiros can't fight worth shit, the value of his so-called 'Vek' affinity to dream in visions has been unforgivably underestimated in my opinion.

"Well fuck," I mutter before turning my gaze back on Vash. "Thanks for the heads-up," I say, and mean it.

He gives me a smile in return that doesn't quite reach his eyes. And I watch as his golden-flecked gaze flickers to something behind me. "No problem. They're supposed to hit Giant's Crook at sundown. Riggs thinks we'll be expected to receive them at the docks."

"I'll be sure to bring my most welcoming attitude," I promise, my grimace falling right down into place.

V. BREK & VEK

The next afternoon I speak with Preceptor Darood before water combat training, and he agrees to allow me to cut out of class early.

This was of course under the premise that I do, in fact, need to look presentable for the arrival of the other cardinals. We were all officially informed this morning that they'll be joining us in time for tonight's grand welcome dinner. Just as Raider Oneiros predicted.

I head to our cabin and strip off the sweat-soaked training uniform that's been clinging to my skin since our afternoon shoreline run. It's then that I find a letter has been left for me upon the small table between the two armchairs facing our green marble hearth. One look at the wax seal portraying a star constellation in the form of a small bear, tells me it's from Regent Beldham.

I know what it contains before even ripping open the message; all three cardinals will dock today at sundown in the wharf of Giant's Crook. The letter details the expectation that the northern captains and their crews will be part of the receiving party. Formal wear is expected. And a meeting concerning the trials will directly follow this evening's feast.

Next I bathe and change into the midnight-blue dress regalia reserved for special occasions such as this. My white hair is then carefully braided into a long, uniform plait that ends at my waist. The golden hairpin I've begun to treasure above all other possessions cuts through the braid menacingly, just at the nape of my neck.

I'm adjusting my dark navy captain's cape and securing the ornate bronze clasp across my collarbone when the others finally arrive, dripping with salt water.

"Dress regalia tonight, ladies," I announce, my smile grim, to which they all moan loudly in complaint.

The cool breeze slipping past my cheek promises autumn is right around the corner, and with it, the rainy season. I wait before a stone balcony perched just outside our bunk room while the others rush to get ready. The sun has begun to droop lower and lower, and it won't be long now before we need to start heading for Giant's Crook.

My elbows move to rest atop the stone-carved terrace as I lean into the nippy air, letting its chilly caress soothe the ragged edges of my nerves. The water far down below—a beautiful arctic shade this evening—clashes nervously into the giant, black, teeth-like rocks.

Three black spots mar the fading horizon.

My insides twist with the knowledge of what and who they carry.

"Oof, looks like you're screwed."

Turning back sharply to face the intruder, I find Greer, my fourth in command, behind me. Her wild red hair has been wrangled into a sleek twist, and her midnight-blue uniform is in perfect adjustment. The bronze chains across her jacket gleam gold in the approaching light of dusk.

"I'm what?" I ask, my voice a touch cold.

Greer inclines her head to the edge of my captain's cape, and I look down to discover it's twisted around a stray nail that juts out from a crease in the stone. "You're screwed," she repeats with a small chuckle. "Here, let me help."

I'm motionless while my fourth carefully untwists the edge of the fabric from around the bit of metal and successfully liberates it without a single thread snaring. "Thanks," I murmur, my tone turning unusually soft.

Greer gives me a rare smile. Not a grin or a smirk, or any number of false expressions she paints across her freckled face daily. A rare and true smile, one that lights up the olive color of her eyes.

"No problem, Captain," Greer responds before moving to stand beside me against the terrace edge. She too begins studying the three ominous spots, becoming more real with every passing minute.

It's silent between us for a few beats before she asks, "Do you remember back in level four, that day that Preceptor Bealu was instructing us on the difference between Vek and Brek affinities?"

My eyes linger on the anxious waves. "I do."

"And do you remember the demonstrations he had us perform? The ones meant to show us all just what made a power Vek or Brek?" Greer prods, still watching the approaching ships.

I glance sideways at her, now beginning to wonder where this line of questioning is heading. I very much do remember that day. It's one that's extremely difficult to forget.

Preceptor Bealu instructed us in a course that is now mercifully complete. His methods were... *dark*, to put it lightly. We never knew exactly what he would show us or expect from us in turn. The day Greer is referring to specifically in level-four was just an introduction to what we would deal with later on in levels five and six.

"Yes," I answer, swallowing tightly.

Greer laughs, but the sound of it doesn't hold an ounce of humor. "I'll never forget that day," she tells me, her olive-colored gaze appearing somewhere far away. "When he ordered you to freeze off my fingers and nose to demonstrate the uselessness of my ability to transfer energy elsewhere. To show everyone in our level that it was Vek. That *I* was Vek."

I too will never forget it. I can practically feel that jolt of shock that ran through me in response to his unprecedented order. Shock that quickly transformed into untethered rage. I'd never forget the panic in Greer Abaft's painfully young face as she realized just exactly what Bealu was demanding of me.

What he intended to *demonstrate* to the class.

My fourth laughs again, but this time it's real. She laughs so hard that her shoulders begin to shake with her rippling amusement. The sudden change in tone nearly gives me whiplash.

"And then—" Greer struggles to get out the words in between breaths. "Bealu's face—" she manages before another round of laughter, "—when you told him he could go fuck himself into next year—right after you *spat* on him." She dissolves into a fit of fresh mirth, leaning against the terrace to keep herself upright.

Her laughter is infectious, and possibly it's the tight ball of nerves inside of me or the recent lack of sleep, but I begin laughing too, until we're both in near hysterics. It was one of the best and worst days in my years within the Cardinal North.

"I got him pretty good," I admit through a winded gulp of air.

"You hit him in the *eye* with a glob of ice-spit. Lessons for the upper levels had to be held off for an entire week while he was down with the leeches," Greer wheezes, one hand holding onto her abdomen.

It's an effort to rein in my deviant grin. Preceptor Bealu's look of sheer disbelief, that swiftly evolved into pure loathing as the ice wad began to spread—quite painfully, I might add—is honestly one of my fondest memories.

"Then you spent a week down in the hole because of it," my fourth remembers, her voice softer.

The wave of amusement between us has begun to fizzle, and there's a pause of sound. We both take a moment to catch our breath and look again toward the approaching ships.

"We weren't even allies," my fourth all but whispers, breaking our brief respite. "I don't think I'd spoken more than ten words to you in all four of the years we'd been here together at that point." Her fiery head drops low, feigning observation of the ocean beneath us.

My throat becomes uncomfortably tight, but I lift a shoulder casually. "To be fair, most everyone had spoken less than five words to me at that point. So ten words is actually pretty good."

Greer doesn't laugh at my attempt for levity. She shakes her head slowly, not looking my way.

"You don't realize just how terrifying you are sometimes, Merena. I've never seen anything like it. Not here, and certainly not during my life in the sunken isles. How very strong you are. How Brek. Not just your affinity—*you*." Her voice rises with each word. "You do not bend. You do not break. No matter what they've thrown at you year after year, you always manage to endure it."

My fourth takes a breath and straightens, now turning to face me head-on. Light shines on the edges of her olive irises and illuminates the smattering of copper freckles across the bridge of her nose.

"I did learn that day the difference between Vek and Brek, but not because of Bealu. Because of you. It's one of the many reasons why I was so proud to be chosen as one of your crew members. It's why I know that you will be unbending in these trials, no matter what they throw at you."

I swallow again, not trusting myself to speak.

Greer's hand comes to rest lightly on my shoulder. "No matter what other assholes are on those ships, just remember that we know—your crew knows—you are unbreakable. You are *Brek*."

Captain Larceon and I stand side by side in identical stances, hands clasped behind our backs.

We watch in practiced reserve as the first of the three cardinal ships is docked. The air teems with the sounds of Giant's Crook longshoremen—mostly low-level criminals from the various landmasses whose debts were sold to the raiders for labor hands—as they rush to secure the massive vessel.

This first ship stands several stories high, making the mountain-covered wharf of Giant's Crook look small. Its hull is crafted of iron-bound, beautifully carved, dark-stained wood that feeds out to matching grand polished decks. The vessel itself is large and sturdy, made to take on any number of natural disasters or monstrous creatures lurking beneath the waves.

Its staggering masts reveal flags of deep emerald, and the emblem of a great hound in the form of a constellation can be found rippling in the stale saltwater breeze. There's more clamoring as the ship's gangway is pulled out and down to the dockside, where Grand Preceptor Skelm awaits. Regent Beldham and the remaining preceptors are all lined up along the dock behind him.

Meanwhile Vash and I, along with our crews, flank the opposite side of the berth. *To be seen and not heard*, as Skelm so lovingly put it. The rest of our level, and those below, are back at the dark-spired fortress, awaiting our arrival and the feast to follow.

A minute passes before the shape of a willowy woman appears at the top of the gangplank. She's bathed in gold from the shade of her hair down the flowing fabric of her robes. The beautiful age lines gracing her sun-kissed face only serve to make the golden willowy woman more striking. Her descent is masked with an air of authority and poise.

"Ah, Krasinu," Skelm says in welcome, lifting a gloved hand to assist her in making the last step onto the wooden pier.

She brushes him off and clears the gap in one graceful leap. Which is highly impressive, considering the length of her robes. "I s'ink you mean Grand Preceptor Vedet," the woman replies loftily, her accent a rolling wave of soft vowels and harsh consonants.

A man I hadn't noticed before appears at the eastern grand preceptor's side. He's thin, both in face and body, but his hair is thick and dark, accompanied by a matching mustache. He measures about half a foot shorter than Grand Preceptor Vedet.

Skelm turns his one good eye on the male with a barely restrained sneer, completely ignoring Vedet's earlier correction. "And you brought the mutt, I see."

It's only due to years of training that I'm able to refrain from choking on my own surprise at Skelm's scathing words. Vash appears to have the same struggle. His eyes widen while glancing toward me.

What the fuck is that about? he seems to say.

My own eyes widen back in turn. It's the only signal we pass. *To be seen and not heard.*

The slim mustachioed man beside the eastern grand preceptor laughs, his dark eyes giving Skelm a once-over. "I'm surprised you even recognized me, Grand Preceptor. V'hat v'ith only half your vision still intact," he ripostes with a cruel smile.

Beldham intervenes in the next moment. Probably because of the way Skelm is looking at the man—like he wants to wear his skin for a cape. "Grand Preceptor Vedet and Regent Nagual, please follow me. I'll show you to the North Order. We have a feast prepared and awaiting your arrival."

Beldham's crisp voice offers no argument, and she's already begun leading the way out of the wharf before either can so much as comment. Vedet lifts her chin and delicately sniffs the air with disdain before following. But Nagual turns to face the deck of the behemoth ship. "Captains, fall in!" he orders.

I discover two new forms have already appeared at the top of their gangplank. Nagual then turns with the sweep of his auric cloak and follows after Vedet and Beldham's retreating forms.

The eastern captains march down the steps in a dutiful procession, one male and one female, each no older than twenty. They look as though they could quite possibly be siblings, twins even. Both have tied back their long, dark hair into plaits, not unlike my own. They possess rich olive skin with very similar almond-shaped eyes that glitter like cut garnet in the shadowy wharf.

The two of them match completely in their deep emerald uniforms trimmed with a tan-colored lining. I watch the captains descend the short gangplank down to the pier in eerie unison before pausing in sync to wait for their crews to join them.

Vash and I begin studying our competition from across the dock, and they scrutinize us in turn. I can see their narrowed eyes on us. They're more than likely trying to calculate exactly why we were made captains and what power we must hold. It's precisely what we're trying to discern about them.

When the last of the eastern crews make it to the pier, they file behind their captains, who begin marching after their superiors. Skelm and the other Preceptors ignore them entirely. Their attention has already turned to the next ship in line.

I observe the Cardinal East's dutiful procession until they make it out of the mountain-covered port entirely. Only then do I turn my attention to the current vessel being unloaded. The smell of newly mixed salt water fills the air while the sounds of workers continue to clang about.

I know from the silver flags hanging from the masts, with a sea-goat constellation upon them, that this craft belongs to the Cardinal West. It's sleek and narrow, designed to cut through storms. If I had to guess, it's likely also fast as all hell. I'm suddenly itching to step aboard it. There's a need inside me to see just how many knots it could do in open water if pushed.

My initial assessment is proven correct only a few minutes later when their footbridge is pulled out and down to the pier. Their ship is lower in stature than the first, so there isn't the same awkward gap as the eastern order's had.

A stern-looking woman—as old, if not older than Beldham—draped in a flowing cloak of charcoal, sweeps easily down the steps. She's followed by a tall, somewhat portly man. His rounded head is barren of all hair and his uniform is one shade lighter than the severe eldery woman's. But what stands out most is the thick black markings traced around his eyes and angling downward with what I assume to be kohl.

"Grand Preceptor Ator," Skelm boasts, addressing the older woman as she makes it off the gangway.

Her time-weathered hand goes to pat the silver hair that's been carefully coiffed into the sterling coronet-style headpiece adorning her head. "Yes, yes," she chirps, giving an idle wave of her hand. "Would it be possible to skip the formalities this evening, Hymir? I need to sit soon or I shall begin to wilt."

Skelm nods curtly. "Of course. Preceptor Ersatz will show you all the way." He extends a hand to where Ersatz stands nearest to the exit.

Ersatz flashes a wild sort of grin at the recognition before turning to lead them to the North Order. And I swear I catch the old woman rolling her eyes before following.

Skelm flat out ignores the portly, kohl-marked man, who I can only guess is their Regent. I'm surprised to catch Preceptor Bealu giving him an oily sneer as he walks past. So far, Bealu has remained silent at Skelm's side—no doubt plotting in his own sinister ways. And from the way the western regent chuckles at Bealu's expression, there must be a history.

No one commands the rest of the western raider's to follow, but their captains promptly begin leading their crews down from the ship in dutiful rows of uniformed twos.

Vash and I study the next male and female pair as they step onto the pier. Unlike the East Order, the western captains don't even bother to look our way. The girl is rather pretty, her head full of long, beautiful black braids with silver charms coil around them here and there. Her upturned eyes look almost predatorial, and I can feel myself narrowing in on her as a major threat.

She'll be someone to look out for.

I can feel it.

The boy is handsome, of medium build and taller than average height, with his inky hair tied back into a bun atop his head. They both wear light gray dress regalia with dark capes similar in style to our own. I have to wonder what Vash's thoughts are.

The western captains move at a calm and unhurried pace after their grand preceptor and regent. Some of their crew members whisper to each other while throwing curious glances in our direction. I stare forward icily, and when any of those gazes do land upon me, I find they look away almost immediately.

The west trails out just as the final craft moves up to dock. My stomach is starting to bark at me impatiently, and I can only pray this last arrival is quick so we can join the dinner unfolding.

The remaining preceptors seem more on edge than they did a moment ago. Except for Skelm who remains as unruffled as always. His one eye steadily tracks the ship being brought forward. This last vessel appears to be made entirely of iron or some other dark metal. There are curious markings along its hull that look almost like burn marks and create an odd pattern on its edges. The shape of it is both hulking and sleek—like the best parts of the other vessels have been stolen in order to create this one.

Flags the color of spilt blood wave in the idle cavern breeze and reveal four golden stars arranged into the infamous southern crux of the South Cardinal Order. It is perhaps the most terrifying ship I've ever seen. The dark cruiser glides in near-perfect silence and makes me want to test it out all the more.

I watch the dockhands trying to secure the vessel and almost flinch when a loud, booming voice shouts, "Oh, do get out! The last thing I need is your filthy hands touching my ship. My raiders will drop the brow. Scurry off like the disgusting rats you are!"

Risking a glance across the way, I find Grand Preceptor Skelm smiling—*actually* smiling—in the direction of the gruff shouting.

The ironclad walkway is then lowered from the ship's side with one easy, fluid movement. The mark of well-practiced raider hands. And from the dark beast of a ship emerges the outline of an equally morose man.

His hair is onyx and wild as it falls to his shoulders in unruly curls. The long black goatee he sports has the beginnings of silver streaks running up from the ends, and his deep-set eyes flash about the pier below him in a menacing sort of search.

It's a pity Preceptor Ersatz has already left. I have a feeling the two might just have had a love-at-first-batshit-crazy-sight moment.

Those sunken eyes of his find Grand Preceptor Skelm, and his face breaks into an awful sort of expression that I think is supposed to be a grin. "Hymir!" he growls in exclamation, throwing up his hands and striding down the metal gangway.

I notice that one of his hands is entirely made of metal, starting halfway down his forearm. The metallicity of it shimmers in the orb lights as they clasp hands, and the southern Grand Preceptor pulls Skelm into a hug of sorts. I clench my jaw to make sure it's not hanging open.

"Saubarag, you old sea devil!" Skelm growls affectionately after releasing him from the embrace.

"It's been too long!" his southern counterpart barks back in agreement.

Their regent ascends the walkway next, more silent than a shadow. He's a tall slip of a man, thin yet tan from time in the sun and cloaked in a uniform of deepest onyx. The male's hair is devoid of almost all coloring but it's not the same damning white of my own. Rather a pale yellow, like the shade of old milk. He stands beside Saubarag before giving a pointed nod to Preceptor Bealu and then Preceptor Oplon a little further down the line.

Bealu inclines his head back with more respect than I've seen him bestow on just about anyone other than Skelm.

Incredible.

Now there's two of them.

Preceptor Oplon merely looks away blankly.

Interesting.

"These are your captains this year, Skelm?" Saubarag questions. His deep, rumbling voice rises while turning to where Vash and I stand at attention, with our crews lined in perfect formation behind us.

Skelm's single eye narrows directly in on me, and I can read his darkening expression with perfect clarity. *Do not make a fool of me, or I'll have your hide for a rug before my hearth.*

Amusement flickers in the corner of my mouth.

Were it any other year, I just might have.

But sadly not today.

Saubarag's sunken eyes study Vash at my side, and after a minute he grunts—or maybe it's a laugh. He and Skelm then have some wordless exchange before his attention turns itself on me.

Saubarag's eyes rove over every inch of my person in a way that makes my affinity coil tightly. He studies me for a noticeably longer time than Vash. And it takes every ounce of restraint I possess not to send the temperature around us plummeting. Instead I lift my chin to his piercing stare with my own freezing gaze, refusing to look away.

A dark grin creeps across his battle-worn face, before he turns back to Skelm with a laugh. "You've certainly got your hands full here, I should think. Well, you showed me yours, Hymir—I'll show you mine. Agni! Leporem!" He barks out the names as a command.

A quick glance upward reveals his demands are met in record time. Another pair of captains have already emerged at the top of their iron bridge. One male and the other female. Albeit I don't actually even glance at the girl to be sure.

My attention is now wholly, absolutely, locked elsewhere.

VI. SOUTHERN TONGUE

I don't know what exactly is wrong with me.

My last disciplinary meeting must have knocked something loose inside. Or maybe it's a delayed reaction to one of the leeches' various antidotes. Although I know neither is likely, seeing as over a week has passed since either event occurred.

Yet there's no other way I can make sense of it.

Why can't I stop staring?

I can only think it must be because he's so utterly different from all the others that it feels like some kind of a physical shock to my system. Because I watch with an unreasonable amount of curiosity as the male South Order captain strides down the steps slightly ahead of his counterpart. He moves with such an easy, swaggering arrogance it looks like a birthright.

The captain is broad with chiseled muscles and *tall*. Even from this distance, I can tell he'd probably measure up to Riggs in height, which is truly saying something. His arresting features are bronzed from the sun, and his midnight hair appears roughly tousled. Then there's his eyes. They're a curious shade of amber, made all the more striking by the scarlet coloring of his uniform.

But it isn't the southern captain's compelling looks that have taken my interest captive. Rather, it's the way in which he moves, the boldness about him. How his gaze scans the mountainous chamber, completely unimpressed and damn near insolent.

Something about him is so... *familiar* to me.

Yet entirely foreign.

The sound of a strangled cough comes from nearby, and I shift to find Vash giving me a warning look. My attention darts to the dockside across from ours, discovering Skelm watches me closely. The shadows playing about his weathered face provide me a clear warning signal. *One toe out of line and I'll have it cut off.*

Eyeing the cavern ceiling, I swallow tightly before allowing my attention to drift back to the southern entourage. My expression now reflects complete and total disinterest. This is, of course, the same moment that I discover a pair of scorching amber eyes have fixed themselves on *me*.

The instant my gaze locks with his, something visibly *flashes* across the southern captain's face. An array of tightly concealed emotions I'll never be able to place. He's staring at me so intensely, I have this uncanny feeling like someone is bottling my soul. My blood turns colder the longer those eyes hold me prisoner. Setting my jaw, I lift my chin and refuse to be the one to look away.

One second. Then two. Three. Four. Five.

He doesn't break eye contact, and neither do I.

It isn't until the southern captain's crew members begin descending the gangway, and a raider directly behind nudges his shoulder, that I realize he's stopped walking entirely. The male shakes his head of messy waves with a sneer before ripping his gaze from mine and turning to who I assume is his second.

The possible second is nearly as tall as his captain, corded with muscle, and sports shoulder-length sandy hair. Which is currently half-tied back. I watch as he raises a pair of thick black brows in regards to his captain's outward annoyance. I get the imression he finds this irrational behavior somewhat humorous.

Meanwhile amber eyes over there cuts me a vicious glare, as if blaming me for his own hesitation, before turning away and continuing toward their grand preceptor. All remaining crew members file in afterward, and Skelm announces their imminent departure. Vash and I, along with our crews, are to bring up the rear of our welcoming party.

We've left the confines of the mountain-covered wharf and begun trekking up the winding cliffside path. The uneven terrain is only made more treacherous by the swelling darkness of the impending night.

Herse starts her report from my side, while Kleio walks in step on my left, listening intently. The other five are in close formation, just a few paces behind. From their unusual silence, I know they're all concentrating on her debrief. "The eastern captains," she begins in a low, breathy tone.

Vash and his crew are only a few meters ahead of us, and we're not about to give him any leg up. North Order allegiance or not.

"Those weird little twins?" Kleio interjects, to which Herse nods in confirmation, and I let out the quiet murmur of a laugh.

"The girl's name is Dhara Ghosh, and her affinity is some sort of internal radar," my third quietly informs me.

I utter a sharp-tongued curse.

"So what? Is she part delphis?" inquires Nephthys, her laughter floating up from behind. Turning around, I find those caramel-streaked black coils of hers have been braided and bound prettily into two tight buns atop her head.

I shake my head tersely at the eldest twin. "She can see incoming threats—probably already knows the tunnels beneath the North Order as well as you or I—and she'd be a killer threat out on open waters."

Nephthys and the others are silent at that.

Herse carries on as we continue struggling up the cliffside. "The male captain is Reed Namak and is apparently her boyfriend. They do look oddly alike, but there's no familial connection."

I think I hear Greer gag from behind me, and I make an effort to smother my amusement.

"He can manipulate minerals and crystals. I'm not really sure what that entails, but I know we've never had that affinity here in the north," Herse discloses quickly.

I run my tongue over the back of my teeth, thinking over the strange ability. It must be powerful enough to warrant a captaincy, but I honestly don't have a clue how it could make him a threat. After a moment, I nod at my third to keep going.

"The western girl with the charms in her braids." Herse starts again, and my focus sharpens in response to any information regarding the predatory girl. "Name is Brisa Bedivere. She has a gravitational affinity and can turn on and off gravity for herself or manipulate stuff near her."

I don't say a word in reaction. Instead, I work on beating back the rising anxiety in order to mull over the information as we get closer to the dark fortress.

I knew she would be a threat.

"Ansil Tetsuo is the boy," Herse whispers in continuation.

"And a pretty boy at that," Prisca chimes in, not bothering to lower her voice. The others snicker their agreement while irritation flashes darkly across the face of my third.

Herse huffs in annoyance before stating flatly, “He can manipulate magnetic fields.”

I note it and force myself to worry about both of those staggering amounts of power later. “And the male captain from the South?” I can’t help but ask. My curiosity regarding him has become as sharp and gnawing as a hunger pain.

Kleio glances over a shoulder, and I catch her passing unspoken words with Greer. Herse remains uncharacteristically quiet for a moment. My eyes squint through the dark, trying to read their faces.

“What?” I finally snap, my tone cold.

“He is supposed to be very powerful..." Herse answers slowly. "More so than the others."

I know there’s more to it.

“And? He’s a captain—of course he’s powerful. What’s his affinity? Don’t tell me he’s some sort of shadow wielder or death charmer or something else boringly predictable,” I drawl, remembering the obsidian color of his hair and the darkness in his gaze.

“He’s an elemental,” my third admits, her eyes no longer meeting my own.

“Oh? Of what sort?” I push.

Raiders with elemental affinities like myself are incredibly rare. I’ve only ever known of one other to exist besides myself in all my time within The Order.

“It’s fire, Merena,” Kleio divulges, her voice echoing into the darkening night.

The resounding silence from my crew is heavy. I chew on my lip while something in my gut twists uncomfortably. Then I quickly switch my attention onto the rocks beneath my boots while we climb higher up the trail.

Fire.

Of course it is.

I snort derisively and feel seven pairs of eyes instantly upon me so I continue prodding “What else?” I need to steer the report along but still feel that insistent curiosity regarding the southern male.

Herse doesn't respond immediately, clearly not having expected me to move on from the shocking knowledge so quickly. "His name is Olsson Agni. He's supposedly from some ancient line of highborn royalty who now lord over a grouping of isles under the Sol Republic."

"And the girl?" I ask next, not particularly caring but needing the intel all the same.

"Corvina Leporem. She isn't supposed to be much of a threat when it comes to weapon play, but do not underestimate her," Herse warns.

I turn to my third in question at the new venom in her tone. We're close enough now to the front entrance that the distant orb lights reveal the set in her jaw.

"She can sirenspeak," Herse states, before adding swiftly, "Also, she and Captain Agni are a thing—or at least they were."

"What is it with these captains all dating each other?" I ask, my mouth turned down in distaste. I'm suddenly brimming with disgust at the cavalier way the other Cardinal captains appear to treat their positions.

Greer laughs from somewhere behind Kleio on my left. "Not everyone can be as single-minded as you are, Merena," the redhead points out teasingly.

"What are you implying? It's not like I'm some novice—I've *been* with a male before," I snap, immediately defensive.

"Yeah, and when was that again?" Greer chides. "It's been almost two years since Captain Tharos left for TideLord Raimbaut's fleet. And I don't believe you've had anyone warming your bunk since."

"I can attest to that," Kleio adds unhelpfully, with a taunting grin thrown my way.

Seeing as we've co-bunked the last few years—mine on top and hers on bottom—she'd be the one to know. My scowl is dark in response but I have no actual argument to make.

Yet the mention of Kerau sends a rush of unwarranted memories running through my mind. I never pinned for him. There was no teary, heartfelt goodbye when he was chosen to captain under TideLord Raimbaut at the end of his final year. Yet from time to time, I do miss the nights we shared. The things he taught me. The way his fingertips sent volts of lightning skittering over my bare skin—literally *and* figuratively.

The others pick up their chatter and teasing as we make our way through the skull-like entrance and into the dark fortress. By the time we arrive inside the large vaulted dining chamber hosting the evening feast, my mood has steadily darkened into a budding storm.

I hardly notice the idiotic looks of intrigue from the visiting cardinal raiders as they take in our dining hall. It's framed by walls made from stained glass, each one depicting a different story from *The Days of Many Waters.* Those same curious raiders begin craning their necks to view the massive skeletons of mythic creatures haunting the arched ceiling high above.

My gaze scans the wooden tables crammed full with the addition of the other cardinals. It snags on arrogantly ruffled hair the color of oblivion and eyes that flicker with malice.

The southern captain, Olsson Agni, has his attention focused on the sandy-haired raider next to him. The same one who nudged him out of our staring contest earlier. They're angled toward each other with voices lowered, while the six other males around his table watch and listen intensely. I'm positive he's being given a report similar to my own.

I don't linger, and instead stride for our table at the front of the dining hall, parallel to Captain Larceon's. Kleio and the others are already there. I glimpse the quick squeeze Vash gives my second's hand. They share a brief smile, filled with flirtatious promises, before parting. And I claim my chair at the head seat wordlessly.

I don't taste the dinner I eat tonight. I honestly couldn't even tell you what we were served. My eyes wander up the gilded staircase where the preceptors sit at their tables on the large platform balcony before us. I halt my careful scan when finding a new arrival.

Next to Preceptor Oplon sits a surly-looking man I'm sure I've not seen before. His hair is a faint reddish blonde, his nose crooked, and eyes a boyish blue. The middle-aged raider is elbowing Oplon while they share a laugh. Studying the stranger closer, I note he wears a plain uniform of lackluster sage. But nothing about it tells me to whom he belongs.

I move my assessing gaze over to the three other corners of the room where the captains and their crews have been intentionally placed so that we're as far away from each other as possible. That's when I spot the female southern captain at last—Corvina Leporem—sitting head of the table parallel to Captain Agni's. I can't tell her height from here, but she appears petite. I can tell she's slender and toned, as most raiders are. Her face is as pretty as a painting, with large doe eyes of emerald green and sharp cheekbones to match an equally sharp chin. All of which is framed by a canopy of raven hair cleverly twisted back into a low knot.

The remainder of the evening I spend eating and drinking on autopilot. I don't join in on my table's conversations. And when Grand Preceptor Skelm announces the end of dinner with the captains' meeting to follow, Kleio has to elbow me in the ribs to get my attention. To which I bristle and adjust myself before leaving my crew to follow the other captains.

The meeting is held in a small reception hall located just off the dining chamber. Without the stained-glass windows and odd fantastical creature skeletons dotting the ceiling, it's rather shabby in comparison. The room is mainly stone, with colorless patterned rugs here and there, and a floor-to-ceiling fireplace made of black marble taking up the far wall.

Vash and I stand near each other toward the front of the room, as far from the newly raging fire as possible. The eastern captains, Dhara Ghosh and Reed Namak, have their heads inclined toward each other as they speak in hushed words under the single window in the room. Brisa Bedivere and Ansil Tetsuo are both chatting with the western grand preceptor and regent near the oblong table filling one side of the room. I spot Corvina Leporem and Olsson Agni lounging lazily on the patterned chairs before the hearth.

Skelm and Saubarag, their regents, plus the surly man I spotted eating next to Preceptor Oplon, enter the room in a wave of low arguing voices. They abruptly stop when stepping inside. Grand Preceptor Vedet and her mustachioed regent move up from where they've been scheming in the back shadowed corner at their arrival.

The rowdy buzz of raiders leaving the large chamber next to us and heading toward their various cabins overtakes the room. Until Beldham shuts the large oaken door with a tight *click.*

Once it's silent, Skelm announces, "Now that we're gathered, I would like to introduce to you all our officiant for the upcoming Pillar Trials. Raider Horas Dornon. He's come here to us on behalf of our Raider King and his Driftwood Court."

Raider Dornon smiles, and the crookedness of his nose becomes even more noticeable. "It's a pleasure," he says, a hand on his chest, his voice low and gruff. "I am aware, as you all are, that it has been an age since the Vault last opened. Before some of us had even taken up the title of grand preceptor." Dornon addresses the room but waves a freckled hand idly in Grand Preceptor Vedet's direction.

She stiffens but doesn't argue, and I wonder just how recent her promotion in rank is. The last trials having been a decade ago, she can't have been in charge of the Cardinal East for very long.

A pair of bright blue eyes find each of us eight captains. "I have been sent on behalf of King Nereus to preside over these auspicious trials and feel it's best if we review the rules and expectations of the events to come. As you well know, the TideLords will be joining us for the challenges to act as impartial judges. They will rank you individually based on scores given after every event."

I swallow down the nerves triggered by the mere mention of the TideLords. Of course I knew they would attend. Historically, they've always acted as the judges. Yet the idea of having them see what I can do firsthand—even if I don't win The Vault—could still be a way to secure a ship in one of their fleets. A way to get myself and my crew out of the north.

Permanently.

Raider Dornon's rumbling voice carries over to me again. "Each of the four tasks will test a pillar of your training under the TideRaiders. The first, of course, being endurance and survival. In one month from today, the first Pillar Trial will be held. It will be observed by your peers and judged by the TideLords. You can expect a test over that very first lesson taught by each of your cardinals."

I watch his blue eyes dim, and he meets the gaze of each grand preceptor and their coordinating regent. "There will be no hints and no help allowed. You can bring with you a single weapon of choice and your affinity."

Raider Dornon finishes with a curt bow to the room. "I wish you each the best of luck. To Nawai and back."

Half an hour or so later, I stroll down one of the last stretches of alcove-laden hallways that make up the path to mine and my crew's cabin.

But something more instinctual than rational has me frowning and reassessing my familiar surroundings before coming to a halt. Scanning the corridor, I quickly discover the reason for my impulsive pause: A tall shadow lingers just outside one of the many nearby stone recesses.

I note that the windowed doors, normally latched against the outside world, are currently ajar. From the faint light provided by tonight's slender claw moon, I can just barely make out the sight of black windswept hair. It's Captain Agni, and he's—I turn my head to check up and down the hall—*alone*.

Is he waiting for someone?

That idea seems unlikely, but why else, and how else, would he have managed to make it down here?

I decide the strange movements of the southern captain are not worth my time or attention. And I continue strolling back down the hall toward our cabin. I make it about five steps before the smell of a spice-burdened smoke laces its way through both the air and my resolve.

Stopping short again, I turn back around to discover that shadow no longer lingers on the opposite side of the alcove's doors. Captain Agni leans casually against the stone corridor wall. A set of burning ember-like eyes stare back at me from beneath the shadowed hood of a crimson captain's cloak.

"May I *help* you?" I ask, my tone sharper and colder than a winter gale.

It would normally be enough to make any other raider turn tail. But this one only chuckles. The sound is a deep rolling timbre that sends a wave of gathering energy rumbling somewhere deep below my affinity.

"*Fortasse pater meus dabit te mihi,*" he replies, his voice so low and dark it emulates smoke sliding over gravel. Meanwhile his eyes rove up and down my person appraisingly.

I blink in surprise at the strange language from his foreign tongue. "What?"

The southern captain brings a hand to his mouth, revealing a line of rolled paper attached to one of the many golden rings that adorn his calloused fingers. The source of that spice-scented smoke. He brings his other hand to the end of the aroma-laden stick, and a small blue flame appears at the tip of his index finger. It takes every ounce of self-discipline I possess not to flinch at the sight of that flame. To push down all the horrors associated with it and package them away into a box of trauma I can deal with another day.

I watch Captain Agni as he breathes in the burning spices and exhales out a narrow stream of smoke, sending it through the open alcove door and out into the night beyond. All the while, his eyes never leave mine.

The living embers in his irises appear to be shifting between interest and amusement while searching for something in my face. I don't have the faintest idea what language he's spoken, but it must be common to the south. His arresting features form an expression that appears even more bemused by the fact that I clearly haven't understood him.

I wonder for a moment if perhaps he and the others can't speak our dialect. But then he pushes off from the stone wall with predatory fluidity, before saying in perfect northern tongue, "Good luck with the trials."

The captain's gaze remains on me while flicking the end of his rolled spices out the alcove opening. The shadow of a smirk pulls up onto his lips before he turns around and begins sauntering down the corridor from the direction I've just come.

I lay awake that night for a long time, replaying the troubling interaction over and over. It's not until an unreasonably late hour that exhaustion finally drags me under.

VII. THEORY OF WAR

After all the events of yesterday, I'm up early today. I've decided to work off my increasing stress levels in the pool chambers.

Located in the maze of tunnels that make up the belly of the North Order, the pool chambers are one of my only places for solace. And if I'm there early enough, solitude. In level-one, we spent most of our time training down here, learning to swim and dive and control our breathing.

It's also where Preceptor Darood holds water combat training when the harsh, wintry ocean tides become too much for even his thick skin to push through.

The familiar scents of saltwater and minerals never fail to ease the tightness in my shoulders. Lap after lap, my agitation slowly begins to recede as my body rhythmically pulls its way through water. I relish the feeling of my muscles tiring and the way it allows my brain to quiet. I can sort through my array of thoughts better in motion and surrounded by water than anywhere else.

What's more, I can allow myself *not* to think.

By the time I've completed my workout and slipped back to our cabin to change, I'm in a much more agreeable mood. Breakfast passes easily and I find I can once again taste the food.

I walk with my crew to today's first lesson and my favorite course taught by our Grand Regent: Theory of War. My mood lifts while joining in on the conversation as I slowly begin feeling normal once more.

However, once we're through the arched entrance and into the dim, windowless room, I stop in my tracks. Prisca nearly runs right into me from behind at my abrupt halt. I hear her grumble something unintelligible but the others remain silent as they too study the scene before us.

The reason for my pause.

There was no announcement. No one even *mentioned* the combining of our lessons with the other cardinals. I suppose I assumed they would be taught on their ships or something.

It seems slightly more obvious when I really think about it. Yet I'm still blind sighted, finding Captain Agni's towering form holding court at the front right table belonging to me and my crew.

Shifting fractionally, I observe Kleio, Greer, and Herse exchanging equal looks of displeasure, mirroring my own. But it's Nephthys who finally utters what we're all thinking.

"Those little southern *pricks*."

Captain Agni sits lazily in the chair that belongs to me and tests my restraint. The same chair that I've sat in every day for the last seven years of this course. I watch as he tips it backward while laughing at whatever the dark-haired boy on his right has just said. Something about that careless, arrogant motion breaks me from my indifferent demeanor.

I might as well be back in level-four.

"You're in my seat," I hear myself state before striding over to the southern captain, cold irritation coating my every word. The eyes of Kleio and the others are on me. I can feel their presence like a silent force from behind.

Captain Agni looks upwards, a thick, dark brow lifting in surprise. "*Oh*?"

I give him a false smile, nodding in confirmation.

He proceeds to rake his amber gaze over me like he's never seen me before in his life. Like all of yesterday and last night was just some dream on my part. One corner of his haughty mouth lifts and I wait for him to retort, already poised to hurl back my own retaliation. But then he does something infinitely more infuriating.

Agni turns back around to the males seated around him as if I haven't spoken at all.

The insult of his blatant disregard sends a searing kind of cold into my veins. It's a familiar feeling I have no problem leaning into. Before I know it, I've closed the gap between myself and him, and I'm leaning down to the male with maddeningly messy hair.

My demand is uttered in a soft, venomous voice, dangerously close to his ear. "Get *out* of my seat." The air around us drops an easy twenty degrees and multiple curses are thrown about the room at the sudden crispness.

Captain Agni tilts his head back to glare at me without the typical mixture of fear and surprise I'm anticipating. On the contrary, he looks at me like I'm no more than the dirt beneath his nails. His mouth twisting into a sneer.

The south order captain snorts before standing from my chair. His towering stature forces me to tilt my head back in order to meet his scorching stare. He's somehow even taller than it appeared last night. His shoulders seem broader in the light of day. And his muscles strain against the thin red shirt of his uniform when crossing his arms before the width of his ridiculously solid chest.

What *are* they feeding these southern boys? Even Kerau wasn't quite as monumental nor so ridiculously brawn.

"You want me to give you back your seat?" Agni inquires, voice low, amber eyes flickering with unchecked malice.

My jaw ticks but I nod sharply, ignoring the growing snickers from his friends avidly watching our standoff.

Agni takes a page from my book and leans down to rest his lips beside my ear. His voice is a mockery of my own bitter tone when whispering in reply. "Make me, *squid*."

The southern captain may have whispered the words, but those assembled have grown so silent that the comment ripples outward for everyone to hear. The six of my crew members behind me freeze, struck dumb with the shock of hearing those words spoken aloud.

To a captain.

To *their* captain.

I stiffen and blanch while the jackass drops down into the seat that belongs to me. Agni leans back again in the chair, throwing a lazy smirk my way.

There's a roar in my ears that I haven't heard for some time now. A rush of emotions unlike any I've allowed myself to feel in years comes crashing through me. Invading my senses. I wouldn't be surprised to find I'm vibrating with the freezing rage now licking up my insides.

I can't recall exactly when the last time was that I heard that slur directed towards me. The ugly term for unwanted children. Castaways. Those deemed no more useful than fish food.

Squids.

It's almost embarrassing how utterly incensed I am after only a few words from this southern boy. But the way his expression flashes with anticipation while watching my face tells me he'd love nothing more than to watch me come undone before him.

Kleio is the first to break out of mine and my crew's momentary stupor. I hear the unmistakable sound of her abalone hilted blade as she pulls it from her side. "You little *son of a—*"

I turn, stopping Kleio with the light press of my palm against her rising shoulder. Agni watches the death threat of my second with barely a hint of interest in his eyes. The two males seated opposite him, however, have both placed their hands on the hilts of their own carrying weapons.

"We'll deal with this in the trials," I grit out.

The words are aimed at my crew, but my attention doesn't waver from Agni. His smirk deepens in turn, and I fight to keep my temper tethered.

Turning away from the cruel delight playing along the razor-sharp edges of his aristocratic features, I aim for the empty table closest to the entrance. Kleio slides into the seat beside me and Herse drops into the one opposite. The remaining four take their usual spots. But Davina is, of course, with the leeches.

The seven of us are silent while eying the males who've stolen our table, now loud with laughter and chatter in that odd southern tongue. But then a prickling on my neck has my gaze shifting to the table just behind Agni's, I hadn't even noticed it was occupied until now. The girl with emerald eyes and a lovely doll-like face is glaring daggers at me. I hold the female southern captain's stare with my own.

When I don't look away, Corvina's green eyes harden. The south has apparently made it their personal mission to test my practiced restraint. And I've just about fucking had it.

I blow her a kiss with my captain ring finger, earning me a round of snickers from my crew. Captain Leporem's lip curls up high in disgust, and the girl next to her with tawny skin, topaz eyes, and tightly coiled ebony ringlets bares her teeth at me.

I smirk in return, this must be Corvina's second.

Preceptor Beldham breaks the building storm as she sweeps into the windowless room in a flurry of navy. Captain Larceon and his crew, along with several other stray level-eights, file in after her.

Vash passes by our new seating arrangement and catches my eye. He raises a bronze brow in question, to which I answer by shooting a black look in Agni's direction. His questioning gaze seeks out Kleio next, but for once, she doesn't notice his attention. All her concentration and palpable anger seems to be reserved for the eight southern pricks.

"Seats seats!" Beldham calls, weaving through the tables. Our preceptor takes her place behind the wooden podium at the front of the chamber, pulling out several scrolls, epistle bottles, and carefully laying down a carto-sphere before finally addressing us. "We will be beginning where we left off last. I expect those joining today to pay close attention and speak *only* when prompted." Her piercing cornflower eyes scrutinize the room before pointedly landing on the group of south order males.

Captain Agni nods to her curtly in confirmation.

Seemingly satisfied, Preceptor Beldham sets the carto-sphere atop the silver disc on her platform. The round glass ball lights up immediately to refract a 3D image in the air above us. We're told it's top of the line technology, courtesy of raids made in the Sunken Province.

The image projected is that of a ship. It's ugly, bulky, and robust, with mismatched wood and a deep-set hull of solid iron.

"Who can tell me what kind of vessel we're looking at today?" Beldham questions, her hands coming to rest along the edges of the wooden podium.

"A merchant," I answer easily.

"How can you tell?" Beldham counters, expectation clear in her eyes.

I angle my head towards the image slowly rotating above us. "That boom there on the mast. It's used specifically for lifting cargo."

The barest hint of a smile pulls on Beldham's mouth. "Correct, Captain Boreas." With a twist of the sphere from our Grand Regent's hands, the image enlarges. "And just where is this particular merchant vessel from?"

I study the ship, having to lean forward to do so, and mentally curse out the jackass in my seat for the terrible position we're now forced to observe from.

Captain Agni's deep, gravelly voice answers from my stolen chair, "The Nation of Jetsam."

"How can you be sure?" our preceptor prods, her stoic face giving away nothing.

The jackass sighs before crossing his arms and tipping back the chair legs in a way that sets my teeth on edge. "You mean apart from the ragbag mix of materials they've put that ship together with? Or the depth of the hull on it due to the heavy-duty ballast tanks needed in order to survive their nightmare of a sea?"

Beldham blinks once in silent confirmation to continue.

"The ID is right there, MV-4687-NJ." Olsson motions with a ring-adorned hand to the starboard side of the ship's transom and I notice the engraved markings upon it for the first time. "MV stands for merchant vessel, the four-digit number is the ship's naval code and NJ is the Nation of Jetsam." His explaining drawl is insolent at best.

I see a rare look of surprised approval color Preceptor Beldham's expression and I'm forced to bite down on my lip to keep from scoffing. "Very good," she praises. "We haven't gotten to hull identification numbers yet in this course. I applaud your previous instruction, Captain Agni."

Olsson glances over his shoulder at me with a smile so smug it nearly sends me into orbit.

Get a godsdamn grip, Boreas.

Preceptor Beldham moves right along with the lesson. "Alright raiders, now let's say in this scenario you've been given the task of targeting this particular vessel. Why is it important not only to know the type of craft you're dealing with but also where it originates?"

"You can use the information against them. Learn their weak points, cultural vulnerabilities, fears, needs, etc." Vash answers from the table in front of ours.

"Yes, *precisely*. Know thy enemy," Beldham agrees, rapping a knuckle hard against the edge of her dais. "Thank you, Captain Larceon."

I notice the way Captain Agni's entire table subtly shifts to glance at Vash. Their stares aren't exactly threatening, more calculating. But Vash is too busy throwing Kleio a wink to notice. My eyes study the ceiling in exasperation at their constant flirting.

"That leads us to our main topic of discussion for this year: psychological warfare," Beldham announces. "There are several tactics you can deploy based on the target at hand. But for the sake of time, we're going to stick with the merchant vessel from the Nation of Jetsam today. Let's begin with their vulnerabilities, what are they?" she inquires, opening the discussion once more.

"Their visibility systems," calls out Aoi Nakai, fifth in command of Vash's crew. When Beldham looks at her pointedly, she explains, "Like Captain Agni mentioned, their ships are a collection of various remnants and scrap pieces. Which means so is their technology. I'm betting that causes most of it to go haywire pretty often."

"Yes. Good. What else?" our preceptor inquires.

People begin shouting out possible weaknesses, such as weather, isolation, and resources. I take note of each answer with their reasoning. However, none of them seem to be exactly what Beldham is looking for.

Herse's husky voice is the one to answer correctly at long last. "Their governance," she says, not need prompting to continue. "The Nation of Jetsam is ruled by five clans; they're almost always in the middle of some sort of conflict. If you wanted to take one of their merchants, just stage a false attack. Draw up flags with one of the clan's insignias, then send out a distress signal. Let them come to you."

I can't help but smirk at the brilliance of my third.

Preceptor Beldham all but beams. "I couldn't have said it any better myself, Raider LeRoi."

Captain Agni's second—the male with tied-back sandy blonde hair and chiseled square jawline—looks at Herse in interest. She responds by studying her nails with cool indifference, and I catch a flicker of annoyance alighting his navy irises.

My smirk deepens.

The lesson moves into a lecture regarding the importance of knowing the background to each and every landmass. Class concludes with the promise of more physiological tactics to come and a debate in our next meeting.

We share history with the East and water combat with the West. But the Grand Preceptors have all decided to keep our affinity training courses separated to ensure fairness in the trials. However, weapons training the following week consists of all four Cardinal Orders.

The practice chamber Preceptor Oplon favors is by far the largest and can more than hold all level-eights assembled. The former renowned gunner has strategically separated us eight captains as far from one another as physically possible. He's also made sure to assign everyone partners within their own cardinals. At least while we settle into this new arrangement.

I'm positioned in the far left corner. My designated partner this time around is Herse. Which is useful as we're practicing the use of her preferred weapon of choice: the evening stars.

It's a difficult weapon, favored by those with superb balance and control. It consists of two metal rods joined together by a bit of chain and adorned on each end with evening stars, of course. The spiked midnight spheres themselves are coated with a paralyzing poison. Even the *faintest* of scratches and its lights out until you're given the antidote.

Hence the name.

I study Herse intently, noting the way her feet move about in a series of dance-like steps. She lurches forward without warning in a swift diagonal strike. Acting on instinct, I stretch out the two iron rods of my weapon and block her attempted maneuver in the space above our heads.

We grunt in unison from the impact of our collision. Sweat slides down the sides of my temple and my shirt sticks uncomfortably to the skin beneath. We've been going at it for nearly an hour.

"So, in Beldham's class last week," I start up casually, ignoring my own labored breaths.

Herse grabs one end of her dark metal rod and whips out the other half in a horizontal swipe. In turn, I maneuver mine from one side of my body to the other in a quick double-sided block.

"Yeah?" she asks, stepping back to regain her balance.

"You mentioned the five clans in the Nation of Jetsam—" It's my turn to go on the offensive and I swing a single chained rod above my head before bringing it down with blinding speed. "I'm guessing you had family in one?"

Herse is already there, both rods folded together as one, rebuking my attack. "My brothers," she grunts out in reply.

I step back, flipping one stick over my arm in readjustment. We begin to circle each other while breathing a bit raggedly. I'm trying to decide how much I dare pry. Herse is tight-lipped about most of her past life. She was sacrificed, of course, having originated from noble blood of some sort in the Nation of Jetsam. The youngest of three with two older brothers. This much is all I know for sure.

It's not uncommon for raiders to avoid their previous lives, to push themselves away from the past knowing it won't ever be their future. Most, if not all, prefer to keep their former life buried deep down inside. Except for Kleio, she's the only raider I've ever met who talks about home like it's a place she might one day get to return.

"Do you think you could feign a distress signal?" I ask, moving in for a quick side swipe.

"What?" she barks back in confusion while deflecting my weapon. The venomous black spikes of an evening star swipe less than an inch from the thin fabric of her shirt.

"I mean—" I grunt, twisting away before knocking down her next incoming strike. "Knowing you have family there—people that could be on a vessel we target. Could you go through with it? The plan you laid out in Theory of War?"

Herse feeds the evening stars behind her back and comes at me with one stick spinning like a motor blade. "Are you asking me if I would *betray* you?" Her words are sharp and I barely have time to meet her blow when she lashes the still-spinning rod out like a whip.

"No—*gods* no. I'm just asking—" I duck under the swing of her rod. "I don't even know what I'm asking." I swing my own weapon upward and Herse drops back just in time. "I guess—I just wanted to see if you were alright. If talking about targeting your home like that—" I'm stumbling over my words when she swipes for my legs and I'm forced to jump back out of range.

"You're one of my crew," I try again, willing her to understand my reason for the query.

Herse's violet eyes are filled with determined light as she gracefully whips the evening stars around in a fluid butterfly formation. I don't catch onto her strategy before she's folded them in two and aims a well-placed jab to my ribs with the blunt end of the rods. *"Fuck,"* I hiss as pain blooms along my side.

That's going to leave a right nasty bruise.

"They sacrificed me, Merena. My own mother slit my throat and tossed me into the sea," Herse says, stepping back to regain balance. "As far as I'm concerned, that place means nothing to me. It can burn for all I care." The set of her jaw beneath the blunt cut of her onyx hair tells me not to push.

But it's harder for me, not knowing or remembering my own origins, to understand the others on this level. The landmasses are few and far between. The drifters are basically floating specks. Every inch of known territory is under extraordinarily strict population control. Most families are only allotted one child, those of noble blood may be afforded two. Any *extras* are to be disposed of.

That's where the Tide Raiders come in.

Those with highborn blood may be raised for sacrifice on the Sál Moon instead of merely being put down. There's no guarantee the drowned gods will choose them. No promise or assurance that the will of the Nixes will bring them back from Nawai and lead them to the Order.

Even if they do, even if the stars align and your child is sent to one of the four cardinals, the question becomes, what sort of life are you subjecting them to? I suppose the way I see it, it's a second chance for your child. A shot in the dark maybe but a shot nonetheless.

Herse lunges forward to resume our spar as a voice unlike anything I've heard reaches my ear. It's as lovely and bright as the stars on a winter's night.

"Don't move," the voice commands.

I instantly obey the order, desperate to hear more of its beautiful tenor. I don't understand the mixed look of confusion and fear in Herse's eyes until her evening-star spikes rake straight across the front of my chest.

"*Merena*!" Herse shouts as I stumble and fall backwards onto our training mat.

The pain bursting inside of me is sharp and biting.

"Merena, why didn't you *move*?" my third demands, rushing to my side.

I shake my head in confusion. There's an odd sort of pounding that's starting to sound in my ears. The pain located in my chest grows keener and I try sitting up so I don't choke on my own saliva. That's when I spot the swish of long raven hair retreating to the far side of the chamber.

Raising my hand slowly, I point it towards Corvina's backside while black spots begin dancing along the edges of my vision. "Sirenspeak," I manage to spit out over the hammering inside my head.

Herse's violet gaze follows my line of sight and before I can stop her, she's up and running for Captain Leporem. The world next takes on a very strange greenish hue. I watch in ultra-slow motion as Herse tackles Corvina down to the ground.

"Herse what the *hell* are you—" Kleio yells from somewhere further off. There's muffled shouting and then my second's voice is closer by. "Oh my fucking gods—*Merena*!"

I hear other people's voices too. I think they come from nearby but I can't be sure.

"Someone start explaining, now!"

"—then she just freezes out of nowhere and–"

"*Three* fucking gashes—"

"Where is Raider Supad?"

"—left with Captain Larceon almost an hour ago."

Nameless voices carry in and out like the tide of my subconscious but I can barely string the conversation along. The painful hammering inside my head has turned into a dull and heavy beat. My fingers and toes feel significantly lighter, my breathing slower. And the searing agony from earlier mercifully begins to fade. I start to think this might not be so bad.

"*Vos omnes sunt futu idiotae,*" mutters an angry voice like smoke. The stranger's deep tenor slices through my newfound peace and stirs up something that had just begun to slumber.

Then suddenly, I'm airborne.

I think I might groan out in protest but it's hard to be certain of anything external. Internally, I struggle and fight with all my waning strength to kick up to the surface of my own consciousness.

"Whhhat's *'appening*?" I demand, breathless.

It takes nearly all my energy to get those two words out and they sound deranged even to my own ears. I'm held captive inside a steady rocking motion, like relentless waves beating against solid rock. The comforting rhythm does little to keep me cognizant.

A dark huff of annoyance, a curse, and the bitter-sounding words "déjà vu" are all that accompany me while tumbling down into that sweet soporific abyss.

VIII. Affinity Measuring

I wake up gasping for breath.

There's a ringing in my ears and a blurriness to my vision that only intensifies my immediate need for air. I take it in great big gulps, my body shuddering with the effort. The gasping leads to a fit of spluttering coughs that have me pushing myself up into a forced seated position.

"That's *twice* now in the first three weeks! I thought you'd changed your ways since being sworn in, Captain Boreas," someone scolds from nearby.

I don't need to rub the blurriness from my eyes to know the voice. It's one I've gotten accustomed to hearing over the years. Specifically while confused and in the thralls of fading agony. "Leech Vitasan," I croak, my voice raw and ragged.

She 'tsks' from somewhere on my right. There's a nauseating dizziness in my head that has me placing my skull between the safety of my thighs and squeezing my eyes shut tight.

"Lucky to be alive," Leech Vitasan continues on in her exaggerated reprimanding.

My voice is somewhat muffled from the current position I'm in while grumbling back defensively, "Two weeks, actually."

There's a too-long pause followed by a scuffling of feet that makes me think the other leeches have left the sick bay. A hand comes to squeeze my shoulder lightly, hesitantly. "Three weeks," Leech Vitasan repeats softly.

My head snaps up from between my thighs and I look at her in bewilderment. The older woman's sun-spot speckled face is clouded with concern while meeting my puzzled stare. "What are you *talking* about?" I snap, suddenly angry.

The hard-won age lines around her rheumy teal-colored eyes deepen in worry. "You've been out for a week, I'm afraid, Captain Boreas," she explains. The unexpected information startles me into another fit of coughs that leave me lightheaded and breathless.

"Now don't go undoing all the work I did here—" Vitasan's wizened hands press lightly against my shoulders, easing me down to the soft cushions below. "There we go. I'll let Davina know you're awake. You need another night's rest, a bit of food, and perhaps you'll be ready to rejoin classes in a day or two."

My gaze trails Leech Vitasan's movements for the next few hours as she moves from one task to the next. Eventually, she slides from the room altogether on the premise of grabbing a plate from dinner. I keep my eyes closed and my breathing rhythmic as she passes by on her way out.

I wait one minute, then two, before cracking open my eyelids and silently shifting upwards. Sliding my legs over the side of the cot in one swift movement, I quickly gather my belongings from the end of the cot and slip out the unwatched door.

My hands slide familiar blades into place along my hips and thighs and I pick up the pace walking down the winding passageways. It would be just my luck for the seasoned leech to forget something and catch me.

A quick peek down the fresh cotton tank I wear reveals thick bandages bound around my chest, they smell of mint and eucalyptus. I wince at the pain that lingers beneath them and keep going.

I finally make it back to our cabin after what feels like hours. The journey has left me winded and a bit nauseous. My sigh is long and low when opening the door to find the others have not yet returned from dinner. And I half-drag myself to the cushioned chairs before the absent fire, stifling a groan while easing into the plush seat. It's so comfortable and I'm so relieved that I haven't a clue when my eyelids began to close.

"*Captain?*"

My eyes snap open at the sound of a soft, inquiring voice. I find a pair of honey-ringed pupils peering down at me in surprise. Shaking my head, I resituate myself, having slid down low in the chair, so that I'm properly seated one more.

"Nimra," I breathe, rubbing a hand down the side of my face. I can only imagine what I must look like right now.

"The leeches let you *go*? We didn't even know you'd woken up!" she exclaims.

I twist with a grimace at the sting beneath the bandaging around my chest that follows. "Not exactly," I admit to my seventh through gritted teeth. "More like... I let myself out."

"Leech Vitasan is going to kill you," Nimra states, her soft voice unusually stiff.

Glancing upwards, I discover her petite form studying me closely, her doe-like face cautious. "Where is everyone else?" I grunt out, beginning to stand while ignoring her truthful statement.

Nimra takes a step forward to help me but I stop her with a pointed look. "They're down at the shore, keeping Herse company while she completes her punishment," she explains.

My eyebrows lift in question and Nimra tilts her head. "How much do you remember?"

Clearing my throat, I begin sorting through the blurry memories. "I was sparring with Herse and then—then she got me. I was cut by an evening star but—hey *wait*—they're not—they can't be punishing her for that!"

I straighten too fast and abruptly hiss in pain. *How fast can I make it to Grand Preceptor Skelm's quarters in this state?*

"No." Nimra gives a slow shake of her chestnut braids. "She isn't being punished for hitting you during Oplon's class."

The vise around my chest eases.

"She's being punished for attacking a captain," my seventh explains. "Captain Leporem, the girl from the south order. She used her affinity on you while you and Herse were sparring."

My fingers come to massage either side of my temples while working to remember. Brief flashes dance in my recollection and they all hold that same strange green-hue. There *is* an image of retreating raven hair that stands out.

"And then what?" I croak in question.

Nimra exhales slowly, deciding best how to answer. "Well," she begins, her hands coming to hold one another behind her back while switching her balance from heel to toe. "You know Herse—she, uh—went a little *psycho* after realizing what the southern captain had done."

I narrow my eyes in signal to continue.

"She tackled Captain Leporem and started swinging on her, pretty hard. Kleio tried pulling her off until she figured out what had happened." Nimra grimaces tightly. "Then Leporem's second came to break it up, her and Kleio started getting into it. By the time everyone realized how badly you'd been struck... it wasn't good."

Nimra's constant movement gives away her nerves and intensifies my current nausea.

"Vash and his crew had already left and Oplon was furious. I thought he was going to strangle the southern girls." Her words begin to tumble more freely. "I don't think anyone knew. Oplon said it only caused paralysis but—" Nimra stops, cutting herself off abruptly, looking like she's said something she shouldn't have.

"But what?" I push.

One of her hands begins twirling a braid absently. "But the *other* southern captain said something was wrong. He said that you shouldn't be fading the way you were. Except no one was paying much attention with all the fighting going on. So Captain Agni took you to the sick bay himself." Nimra's voice drops to a whisper. "I'm pretty sure he sprinted the whole way there. Davina told us later that night that it wasn't evening star poison in your system. It was ekhinos."

Ekhinos.

The name echoes around in my head searching for the information I'm certain I have. It's on the tip of my tongue but for the life of me, I can't find it. Looking to my seventh, I shake my head in a defeated sort of confusion.

"We call it the serpent's egg where I come from," she tells me, her face clouding over. "It's extracted from the spine of a leviathan's clutch. They say even breathing in the poison is a death sentence. We thought for a minute there that you were a *goner*." Nimra's voice breaks on the last word. She clears her throat before blinking rapidly and looking to the hearth behind her.

There's an awkward silence between us. It's not in my nature to comfort and it's not in hers to care. Luckily, we're both spared the uncomfortable moment.

The door to our cabin bursts open, and the room fills with a cacophony of dark grumblings, swearing, and many chiding words. The cacophony of noise abruptly halts one second later.

I turn to face the rest of my crew with a smirk.

"Miss me?"

We stay up much too late and I'm heavily regretting it by the time morning comes. My limbs feel worn out and sluggish while hauling my body through its morning swim. I'm determined to return to my usual routine, but my brain is still foggy from recovery.

Kleio was stunned, then overjoyed, and finally furious by my unexpected return. She threatened to drag me back to the leeches if I didn't let her swipe me a plate of dinner from the kitchens. Herse was relieved, and exhausted, *and* soaking wet. Apparently her punishment for the last week has been to swim across the bay and back at night.

Every night.

The rest of my crew filled me in on the gaps where Nimra left off. And unfortunately, it appears I do indeed owe a life debt to Captain Agni. The idea is equally repulsive and confusing and I'm determined to avoid that little reality at all costs. Though some deeply buried, noble part of me nags from the back of my mind that a 'thank you' is in order.

Returning to classes is a relief, even though they add to my stress after being out for an entire week. The first trial is now only seven days away, I've wasted so much time. I've barely done any research into the many, *many* possibilities of what our first challenge could entail.

In Preceptor Chie's class, we start a new lecture series about the early rise of the Sol Republic and their ever-growing crusade bleeding into our world today. We next practice carrying tender's along the beach and into the tides during water combat training. Preceptor Darood makes us drag them until we're all vomiting lunch onto the black sands.

Preceptor Ersatz has us working on adaptability with our affinities and has created her own demonic version of an obstacle course. We're to complete each section by using our affinity alone. No outside help, weapons, or partners allowed.

In Theory of War, we've moved onto the next form of psychological warfare: propaganda. Which simultaneously ties in with Preceptor Chie's current lecture series.

I'm surprised to find the South Order Regent now sits-in on Beldham's class. The pale slip of a man perches just behind my crew's new table and sets my teeth on edge with his presence. It appears to annoy our own regent just as much as it does the rest of the northern raiders.

When I return at long last to weapons training, I'm immediately pulled by Oplon. My mouth opens in affront. I'm ready to argue, both angered and surprised he wouldn't allow me to return to train, but he silences me with the raise of his hand.

"You're needed elsewhere at the moment I'm afraid, Captain Boreas. It seems the other Grand Preceptors already let their captains know when and where to meet. However, Raider Dornon here will escort you and Captain Larceon," he explains.

"For what?" I ask, glancing at Vash standing at the chamber's entrance, chatting with our strawberry-blonde officiant.

"The affinity measuring. It's standard procedure. Shouldn't take but an hour or so." At the look of worry that crosses my features, Oplon leans over his stingray cane, saying quietly, "I'll keep the training chambers open late. Should you care to practice afterwards."

I give him a small smile in thanks and he motions for me to get going.

Affinity measuring is held in the same hall as our first meeting regarding the Pillar Trials. Vash and Raider Dornon chat the whole way there, apparently they originate from islands not far from each other. I let them prattle on about things familiar to them and focus on my breathing. My fingers tap together rhythmically in order to ease the incessant anxiety.

Upon entering, I discover a new face among the other raider captains gathered. Or perhaps an old face is the proper term, as the stranger's skin is weathered and his hair little more than tufts of white. The uniform he wears is a deep ocean green ombre beginning at the ends of his robes that lightens all the way to a cream color along his shoulders. A sash of conjoined shells, crab claws, and various sea creature bones surrounds his waist. Threaded seaweed ties in a band around his head, covering the holes where his eyes should be.

As a member of the 'The Sons and Daughters,' he forfeited those orbs long ago in exchange for what they call 'true sight'.

I try my best not to stare at the chain of razor-sharp teeth encircling his neck. They appear to belong mainly to various breeds of sharks but a few of them are so large they must have come from a more fantastical creature of The Deep.

Since my own Sál Moon ceremony, I haven't seen another member of the Sons and Daughters. The Hiereus's unexpected presence does little to quail the nerves prickling their way up and down my limbs, demanding I run as far from this room as possible. Vash has become quiet and the other captains eye the ocean-worshiping cult leader uneasily.

The ancient hiereus chortles beneath his seaweed veil and I give us all a little credit for not flinching at the unearthly sound. Raider Dornon clears his throat, announcing Hiereus Philistos will perform the assessments one by one. We are then instructed to remove the clothing needed in order to expose the markings of our affinities.

"I'd prefer he bought me dinner first," mutters Brisa Bedivere, one of the western captains, from my right.

I actually snort a laugh at the unexpected comment and we share a brief glance of amusement while the others begin shimmying out of their uniforms. Her steel-colored eyes, the same shade as the charms in the dark braids of her hair, assess me with less edge. United in fear, it seems, if only for a few moments.

I unbutton my uniform jacket and quickly remove both it and the thin navy shirt beneath. A moment later, I catch amber eyes staring at the bandages wrapped tightly around my breasts. The scent of menthol and eucalyptus on them is fresh, Davina having replaced them for me this morning in an effort to steer clear of the sick bay and Leech Vitasan's wrath.

I give Agni a cold glare, to which he answers with a sneer, before beginning to undress himself. Averting my gaze, I try ignoring the constant feeling that I should thank him somehow. Regardless of his name-calling and constant vexing, he did rather unfortunately save my life. Whatever honor I do in fact have demands that it can't go unnoticed.

Hiereus Philistos begins his assessment with the Cardinal East. And Reed Namak, the male captain who Herse reported has some ability with minerals, goes first. He's now shirtless like myself and several others while turning to expose the seven intricate, circular markings equally space along his spine.

The unsettling old man places his gnarled hands atop the marks, proceeding to rub his palms up and down Captain Namak's back. He hums to himself almost the entire time, sometimes stopping to mutter "*good*" or "*yes, yes, just as I thought*" before resuming his assessment. Once finished, he clicks his tongue and motions for Reed to step back so the next captain may take his place.

Dhara Ghosh, the female eastern captain, steps before Hiereus Philistos and extends both arms to him. She's lucky enough to have the thick black bands marking her affinity wind up from her wrists to the edges of her toned biceps in even one-inch spacing. They're simple yet exact.

The room is quiet as he taps his fingers along each black band and I watch Captain Ghosh's unreadable face as he does so. "Sharp, sharp," Hiereus Philistos mutters to no one in particular. "Mmhmm." He tuts to himself, barking out, "Go on, swim along now!"

Dhara flinches out of his grasp and moves back to stand in the shadow of her boyfriend.

Ansil Tetsuo of the west goes next, revealing the palms of his hands and soles of his feet. The affinity markings he's been gifted portray deep charcoal rings encircling each other, growing larger and larger as they extend outward.

I hear Vash stifle a laugh from beside me as the old man has Captain Tetsuo sit on the floor so he can cup the soles of his feet. The western captain throws Vash a dark look that has me wrangling my own lips together in a tight line.

"Push and pull, push and pull, so do the tides go," Hiereus Philistos sings to himself while Vash and I exchange mixed looks of amusement and unease.

When he's finished with Captain Tetsuo, Philistos moves onto Brisa and actually cackles when first touching the dark blue radiating lines along her shoulders. "On the shoulders, oh, of *course.*" He laughs again and this time it verges on insanity.

Brisa looks pointedly over at Ansil, who gives her a wide-eyed shrug in response. Her judgment ends with Philistos lightly patting her markings before stating, "I get the joke," in dismissal.

Corvina looks a bit worse for wear when stepping before the old man. From the circles beneath her eyes, it doesn't appear that she's had much sleep. I watch her through a frigid glare. It's up to the southern Grand Preceptor how she's punished but I'd like to know exactly what's been asked of her. It had better be worse than Herse swimming across the bay every night. A punishment that has thankfully ended since my awakening.

The midnight blue symbols of her affinity begin just at the hollow of her throat and are undeniably some of the most beautiful markings I've ever seen. They swirl in thin curving lines that sprawl down to bloom like saltwater flowers along the breadth of her chest.

The hiereus uses two wrinkled fingers to jab along the floral design, as if taking her pulse. "What a pity," Philistos laments after a moment, and Corvina's emerald eyes flash in warning. "Only one half." He heaves a disappointed sigh. "Well, dear, just give it more time."

I can't help but smirk at the utter indignation coloring Captain Leporem's face. She wastes no time in storming away from the elderly cult-leader and yanking on the scarlet jacket of her uniform.

Next comes Olsson Agni and it would be a lie to say I wasn't more than a little interested in his affinity mark. Other than Kerau, he's the only elemental I've ever come into contact with.

Being that the southern captain is so tall, Agni opts to sit backwards in one of the chairs lining the center table so Hiereus Philistos can reach him. I work on controlling my curiosity as he reveals the sprawling affinity mark covering the entirety of his backside. In the center of his spine lies a perfect circle of obsidian and an intricate diamond pattern forming what appears to be rays of the sun spreads outward. From there, a design portraying wisps of smoke swirl and curl all the way over his shoulders to twist around his biceps.

His markings are unlike anything I've ever seen before. The longer I study them, the more nuanced shapes I find. From the looks being thrown around the room, I know I'm not alone in my newfound dismay—or jealousy.

Hiereus Philistos places both palms on either side of Captain Agni's back. "Oh, I *see,*" he mutters, swiftly dropping his hands to pick up the end of his weird shell-and-skeleton sash. I watch in disgust as he lifts one end of the belt to his mouth and begins sucking on a crab claw.

The southerner throws a dark scowl over his shoulder, aimed for the hiereus.

One aged hand belonging to Philistos tentatively begins touching the muscles along Agni's shoulders, like the markings might burn him. "How... *unusual,*" he murmurs around the claw hanging from the corner of his mouth, running a crooked finger up Agni's spine. The old man begins rubbing something invisible between his thumb and middle finger, mumbling, "As above, so beneath. *Hm.*"

Captain Larceon volunteers to go next and stands almost awkwardly motionless while he holds either side of his rib cage. As I've known Vash now for almost eight years, I'm already aware what his affinity mark emerges as. A labyrinth of lines and symbols scales either side of his ribs but never quite connects one to the other.

"Such murky depths," the hiereus muses, shaking his seaweed-veiled head. "Which path, which path indeed," he remarks, ending Captain Larceon's evaluation quicker than the others.

I take a quick breath before trading Vash places.

The others have begun dressing and now talk quietly with one another so I don't feel quite as anxious coming to stand before the hiereus. He motions for me to turn around and I do so. Although I am a bit puzzled by how he already knows where my affinity mark lies without eyes to actually see it.

"Does she even *have* one?" Corvina whispers snidely to Olsson. He snorts faintly in response before resuming to watch my assessment in a state of passive calculation.

I keep my mouth shut from the smart-ass remark I'm tempted to make as my gaze finds Corvina's. I give her a freezing stare, one that I hope she feels inside her bones. Her jaded eyes glimmer while giving me a saccharine smile in turn. Yet I note the way her jaw sets, and I track the thick swallow she aims to hide. She knows this dance is unfinished and I have plenty of time to retaliate.

My smile is faint when releasing her gaze and returning my attention to the old man. He's current observing the unusual white marking gracing the expanse of my back. His gnarled fingers lightly trace the wild and unruly patterns bursting across my shoulder blades and streaming down to the base of my spine. It's silent for a moment.

"This won't do," he tuts.

The sound of something snapping echoes from behind. I look back in time to see he's yanked one of the large, razor-sharp teeth from around his neck. I'm too surprised to even think about stopping him before Philistos has swiped the edge of that massive tooth across the skin of my exposed flesh.

I bark out a curse and hear Vash suck in a sharp breath as the room grows several degrees warmer. A thin line of crimson appears beneath the cut. And quicker than should be possible, the hiereus runs his finger over my fresh wound before touching it to the tip of his tongue.

I freeze.

I'm so stunned by the bizarre sight that I can't form a coherent sentence in my own mind beyond the words *what the fuck.* Which I replay over and over and over again. I'm positive this image will star in many nightmares to come.

Hiereus Philistos clicks his tongue against the roof of his mouth. Twice. And a deep frown etches into his ancient face when shouting shrilly, "*Fine*. Keep your secrets then!"

IX. ABHORRENCE

We're only one day away from the first challenge, and I'm spending every free moment either studying or training.

Preceptor Oplon has graciously agreed to leave his chambers open far later than usual this past week, allowing me to make up the time lost after Corvina's little stunt.

I still don't know how to face the fact that Captain Agni saved my life. It hasn't appeared to change his attitude toward me in the slightest. On the contrary, he's been even nastier than usual. Always quick to embarrass me in class, always talking and laughing loudly in that southern language he knows I can't understand. If anything, he's gone out of his way to make it well known he views me as little more than a sea slug he'd delight in crushing beneath his heel.

The memory of his foul words and equally irksome actions steels my resolve to win these trials. The look of shock and disgust on his face when I'm the one to enter the Vault will be all the sweeter. I head back down to the training chambers after dinner every night to practice, sometimes with one or two of my crewmembers in order to spar.

Tonight is no exception.

Tomorrow we are expected to meet near the docks that curve along the North Order's bay. We can each bring one weapon and our affinity; no other hints have been gifted since Raider Dornon's official introduction. My crew and I have scoured the very few scrolls and tomes available recounting previous pillar tasks, but no solid answers have ever revealed themselves. The tests change each time around, and Kleio informs me the same lack of intel is true for Vash as well. We'll be going in blind.

A grunt escapes me with the effort it takes to hurl the heavy tactical ax across the self-made training area and lodge it onto the target board. It is admittedly my very worst weapon. But I figure if the trials are meant to test you, then surely I should work on my weakest points.

Hence the ax.

I begin walking over to the board with the aim of dislodging the ugly thing when a dark, rumbling chuckle halts my steps. Stopping mid-stride, I turn toward the open doors of the chamber to find a towering form watching me through near-glowing ember eyes.

I haven't technically spoken a single word to Captain Agni since he saved my life. We've exchanged plenty of sneers and murderous glares, but any time there's an opportunity to speak, I feel this terrible urge to thank him. It's disgusting.

"The training chamber is closed," I announce icily, resuming my path to the weapon-laden board.

Removing the ax takes little effort, and I turn around in time to find Captain Agni staring at me. The expression he studies me with is like that of a predator deciding whether to bother devouring such minuscule prey. My eyes narrow down to slits, and the sneer he gives me in return is well practiced.

Agni steps into the training room, ignoring my comment altogether. I notice that he's brought his own weapons. A pair of tenebrous broadswords intersect across his back, peeking over the tops of his shoulders menacingly. Holding my ground, he swaggers closer, his chin lifting incrementally when surveying the room. "Practicing alone, I take it?" he asks, his deep voice a heavy drawl.

"Someone's astute today," I quip, my tone as biting as a cold snap, throwing a scowl in the direction of his approaching figure.

His lips form a brief smirk, and a shadow passes over the sharp planes of his face. "My, what a temper you have. It's incredible no one's beaten that out of you yet." He tuts in mockery.

I give him the sliver of a grin and say with false sweetness, "Trust me, they've tried."

Captain Agni throws me an unimpressed look. "You do know that it won't make any difference, don't you?" he questions airily, continuing his casual stroll across the empty chamber.

"What?" I twirl the wooden ax once in my palm. Frost patterns begin skittering up the handle from my sweat-soaked grip.

"This," he answers simply, gesturing to the training room around us before stopping a few meters from my mat. "It won't do you any good. No matter how hard you train or the time you put in, none of that will erase the fact that you *do not belong* here."

His words are harsh yet familiar. They're no different from what I've been told repeatedly since the day I washed up here and the Cardinal North Order was forced to accept me.

"And you think you're the first one to tell me that?" I huff a mirthless laugh. "Hate to break it to you, Agni, but you aren't special." I enjoy the slight way in which his nostrils flare at my disrespectful use of his name without his captaincy title. "Now, like you so kindly pointed out, I'm practicing alone and I'd prefer to keep it that way. So *leave*."

His expression appears unruffled, but I note the way those flickering flames in his eyes darken until they're nothing but searing black coals.

"When will you learn, *squid*? I will not ever take orders from the likes of you." He's sure to put as much repulsion into the slur as possible.

I hold my weapon tighter, wishing it was one of the ones I favor instead of my worst. Captain Agni's head cocks to the side, and my jaw clenches at the way his menacing gaze scrutinizes me.

"What is your *problem* with me?" I hiss through gritted teeth. It's a slip on my part. A question I've longed to hear the answer to. Not just from this foreign captain, but from all the others who have come along years before him. The ones who judged, looked down on, underestimated, and discarded me.

"I don't think we have time for that. The first trial begins in only twelve hours," he taunts.

"Funny," I spit back.

Agni chuckles, the sound dark and hollow. "What can I say, *squid*? I find your mere existence more than reason enough. But if you really care to know, I can name a few others."

My shoulders tighten as he takes another step across the training chamber.

"For starters, you're a mistake, a blip, an *error*. You weren't sacrificed—you were unloved," Agni states, his voice so matter-of-fact it makes me irate.

"You don't even know me," I growl, my feet shifting to properly balance my weight.

"Oh, but see, that's where you're wrong," Agni chides, a hint of his southern accent trilling over the last word. "Captain Boreas, isn't it?" he inquires, as if we haven't just spent the last few weeks in class together. I don't bother answering, but he carries on anyway. "So, not only are you a castaway but a bastard to boot." He lets out a bitter laugh. "I'm told you didn't have the faintest idea of your past life, weren't even positive in your own name. You washed up here with the markings of an undesirable and nothing else. Have I got it right so far?"

Agni takes my silence as confirmation. He nods to himself with an unsavory chuckle. "Thought so. The fact is, you're here in place of another child. One whose parents had no choice. Someone who was actually wanted. Someone born with the power you *stole*." He spits out the last word, and it's an effort not to wince at the disgust in his tone.

The room feels warmer.

He keeps talking.

"As if that weren't enough, you're hellbent on taking more. You've risen to captain—a title, I might add, that has been made comical with the use of your bastard name. Now you think you're good enough to compete with us? You're truly arrogant enough to believe you're actually worthy of entering the Vault?" He gives me a look of deepest disdain.

"The drowned gods chose me!" I snarl, finding my voice at last. "I didn't ask for this. I didn't ask for their blessing or their gifts. As for my title—I was voted in as a captain by the raiders of my cardinal order. I was chosen by my peers. The same as *all* of you."

"Interesting." Agni's lips twitch and the beginnings of a cruel smile pull at the corners of his mouth. He takes another measured step in my direction. "Did you know there hasn't been a single squid to compete in the trials for the last thousand years?" His head cocks to the side before musing, "I wonder... why do you think that is?"

My voice takes on a tone so sweet it's sickening. "Probably because of insecure assholes like you—too scared to allow a castaway to be voted into captaincy. Likely due to your very apparent paranoia that maybe it's not only your highborn mommy and daddy who don't love you." I smirk. "At least, *not enough*."

His eyes again turn coal black before he lets out a low chuckle. The sound is so unexpectedly sharp and bitter that I almost flinch. I watch as a new, terrible thought crosses the planes of Captain Agni's exquisitely carved face, and I take an involuntary step backward. "You know, now that I think about it," he draws out his words slowly, tracking the movement of my unease, "you remind me of one of those wild creatures that roam the open seas near here." His eyes dip to where my braid is tossed over my shoulder, and he reaches out a hand as if to grab it.

I flip the ax once around my wrist in warning, and Captain Agni chuckles again. "So vicious," he taunts, making a *tsk-tsk* sound, as if I'm only proving his point. "I have to wonder if that affinity of yours comes from one of them."

At my look of confusion, his lips curve into a wicked sort of grin.

"With as wild and unrefined as your power is, it would only make sense. I mean, any common gutter whore can be rutted by a monster, can't they?" Agni's eyes glimmer with meaning. "I hear kelpies can sometimes take the shape of men."

His words have the intended effect.

My self-control evaporates, and the room drops rapidly in temperature. Ice instantly spiders out along the dark stone floor surrounding where I hold my ground. A rush of fury swallows up my restraint, and like a moronic level-two, I swing on him with emotions running exponentially high.

Agni catches my arm with surprising agility for someone so big. In one swift movement, he dislodges the weapon in my hands while simultaneously drawing one of his own. The ax skitters noisily across the cold stone floor.

I feel like a novice. There's a deep flush creeping into my face. I can't even remember the last time I've been disarmed and never so quickly. It honestly doesn't seem like he's really even trying.

Agni's free hand catches me by my braid. He tugs it sharply backward while placing one of his twin blades beneath my throat, forcing me to glare up into his burning eyes. I bare my teeth, and his breathing comes out in clouds, like puffs of smoke between us.

"You know what else I've heard about kelpies?" he asks, his hand now winding my braid like a rope. "All you need is a *bridle* in order to control them."

There's a mean glint in the amber of his eyes as he tugs down on my hair for emphasis. The scents of citrus and saffron begin wrapping around my senses. Hatred like I've never known rushes through my veins. "Why did you save me—why not just let me die?" I hiss through clenched teeth. It's the unsolvable mystery that's been preying on my mind for nearly a week straight.

The edge of his blade presses perilously tight against the skin of my throat as I meet his dark glare. For a brief moment, I think I glimpse uncertainty flicker in the shadows of his eyes, but in a blink, it's gone. I'm sure I imagined it to begin with .

Agni wets his lips before swallowing tightly, his throat bobbing with the movement. "I took you to your healers that day *only* so that I wouldn't miss out on the joy of watching you realize your place." His words are blazing. His mouth is now only inches from mine.

"And what place is that?" I'm seething.

His face moves even closer to mine, and I catch a wicked gleam in his gaze before he whispers just beside my ear, *"Subtus mihi."*

I'm about to lash out in vexation at the use of his foreign tongue—blade beneath my throat be damned—when, with abrupt force, he lets me go. I stagger back from his unexpected release. White strands of hair flutter in the air between us and down onto the black stone floor.

Swiftly snatching the discarded ax from the ground, I pivot back to face Agni. My heart is thundering painfully against my chest in outrage. I wonder if he can hear it. I now know with absolute certainty that I have never hated a person this much in my life. The only thing I want more than to watch that highborn head fall from his shoulders is to be the one swinging the sword.

I find my thoughts reflected in Agni's face. Unfathomable rage kindles those living embers in his eyes. The sight is almost enough to send a shiver of terror down my spine. It's clear that whatever loathing I feel for him, he feels for me in turn. I don't understand it. Perhaps I'll never understand it. How those sacrificed can feel such sheer hatred for a castaway. As if I had any say in the matter.

Lesser still can I understand how someone I scarcely know is able to detest me with such vibrant animosity. Including this interaction, I can count the number of times we've spoken on one hand. Yet every single thing I do repulses him.

Enrages him.

Offends him.

Captain Agni slides the tenebrous blade across the length of his broad back and deftly turns away from me. I can damn near hear his smirk as he swaggers out of the training chamber, leaving me standing there fuming. It's not until the last of his infuriatingly messy hair is almost out of sight that I remember the weapon in my hands.

I fling the heavy ax with all that pent-up rage writhing uselessly inside my veins. It rotates through the air with startling speed before making a satisfying *thunk* as the blade sinks itself into the entranceway. The sunken edge struck just barely above where his disappearing highborn head would have been.

What a pity.

Small white petals of frozen moisture begin falling in the air around me as I continue standing there shaking, staring at the hilt. My chest rises and falls in tune with the beat of my fury.

I make a vow to myself.

I promise to earn his abhorrence any way I can.

X. THE FIRST PILLAR

Vash and I are pulled from the dining chamber just as breakfast is ending.

I barely feel the squeeze of reassurance Kleio gives my hand before standing from the table and leaving for our impending task. Northern raiders shout words of encouragement as I pass by but I'm so distracted that their voices all sound muffled, like they're coming to me from under water.

Beldham marches us both swiftly across the open-air bridge, past the outdoor lyceums, and down to the rocky pathway leading to the bay. The three of us are quiet and Vash looks uncharacteristically pale. I'm fervently glad to have stuck with a bit of toast this morning.

We make our way down the cliffside, rounding the hilly pathways until we're welcomed by the sight of a wrought-iron stadium that has seemingly been erected overnight. The towering metal structure lines the circular edge of the bay and faces out towards the incoming waters, where dark storm clouds can be found forming along the horizon.

Our regent freezes and turns on a heel to face us. She studies Vash and myself for one brief moment before stating, "The two of you are remarkable raiders. Among the finest we've brought into the fold. I trust you'll bring honor to our cardinal today."

My tongue suddenly feels like sandpaper against the roof of my mouth. That's the closest thing to kind words I've ever heard spoken by our Grand Regent. Vash and I manage to nod at her by way of a response.

The unease that's been sitting in my chest since morning tightens its grip, coiling like a vice around my ribs.

"We'll flatten them," I assure her with false bravado.

Beldham inclines her chin with a tight-lipped smile in acknowledgement of my earlier promise.

A violent clap of thunder rumbles across the sky and I wince beneath its otherworldly edge.

Our regent indicates to the bottom level of the newly erected stadium where a line of coverage has been crafted from sage-colored tarping. "Those are the captain's quarters," Beldham explains. "Go in through there and wait until you're given further directions. Once inside, you'll stay put until it's your turn. The TideLords, the other preceptors, and I will oversee everything from the stands with the rest of your peers."

"Thank you, Regent Beldham," Vash and I say in unison.

Beldham purses her lips and nods tightly for us to move along.

I begin to follow Vash when Beldham's voice stops me. "Captain Boreas, a word?"

Pausing, I glance over my shoulder and then again towards Vash, who is now already too far down the path to hear. With the wind that's begun to rip through the air and the constant ominous thunder, I don't think he'd notice even if I shouted at him.

"Yes?" I ask, turning back hesitantly.

Surely my crew hasn't gotten into more trouble already. *Have I done something?*

Beldham looks at me almost uncomfortably, her weight shifting with uncharacteristic unease. The unusual sight of her discomfort makes my stomach plummet in trepidation.

"I just wanted to say—" Her piercing blue eyes, so startling against the umbra tone of her skin, find a spot above my head to focus on instead of my face. "The hardest trials often disguise themselves as the simplest. From what I've seen, wit and tactics hold more weight than sheer ability, but you seem to possess all three."

I remain frozen as those startling eyes meet mine.

"I do suspect that your unusual origins will only prove to make your success all the more spectacular," she concludes with an air of finality.

My stumbled words of gratitude are swallowed up by another clap of thunder. The hair on my neck stands on end as the sound reverberates out across the darkening clouds. Then the rolling boom morphs into a higher and higher pitch until a primal chilling wail echoes around us. I look back at our regent in alarm, but she appears distracted.

Beldham clears her throat, advising, "Best to get going."

I don't argue before jogging down the rest of the path and rejoining Vash just as he's entering the tarped-off captain's quarters. "About time," he snaps, green eyes wide. "I heard that siren go off, and when I turned around, you were gone. Thought you must have stopped to re-lace a boot or something."

Ducking under the lifted canvas opening, I enter behind Vash. "Is that what that was? A siren or some sort of alarm signal?"

He looks over a muscled shoulder to glance down at me in confusion. "What else?"

"I don't know—nothing. I'm just a little on edge," I surmise, shaking my head.

We walk further into the tarped enclosure to find the captain's quarters have been sectioned off by the colors of our cardinal. We pass by a sector of tan-trimmed emerald, then one made from shades of charcoal, next a division of pure crimson, before finally one of deepest navy.

Entering our private section reveals a table and two chairs have been provided. The table is chock full of plates with food and cups of steaming liquids. My attention travels from the seating arrangement facing away from the bay and over to the opaque panel lining the back of our sector. Moving to the edge of the small space, I lay my hand flat along the solid vinyl fabric. Even though I can't see it, I can *feel* the storm brewing on the bay's horizon as it journeys ever closer. A traitorously craven part of me wonders if they'll have to call off the first trial.

The sound of ruffling canvas has me spinning back around to find Raider Dornon's strawberry blonde head sticking in through the makeshift opening of our northern captain's sector. "Larceon, Boreas, let's go!" he barks in that gruff voice, motioning his head backwards.

The excited light in his blue eyes does little to calm my nerves as we follow his command and leave the sanctuary of our designated area. We aren't the only ones to have been ordered out. The other six captains have left their sections as well, and we gather in the long, sage-colored passageway connecting them.

A rumbling of boisterous noise sounds from overhead. It contains the movements of hundreds of feet along with nervous laughter and excited chatter that rains down upon us. It's an unnecessary reminder that our peers, in addition to the preceptors and the TideLords, are all here to watch us. The weight on my chest grows impossibly heavier.

Scanning the faces of the other captains, I'm secretly grateful to find they look nearly as nervous as I feel. All except for Captain Agni, whose expression of unease comes across much more flustered than anxious. I can't help but wonder if his demeanor has anything to do with the small groups of girls I've seen starting to follow him and his crew about.

I've caught a few of them lingering after our lessons and even some dawdling down near the wharf where their ships are kept. The groups vary in levels and even cardinal orders. It seems as though the customarily divided raiders have apparently all come to a consensus in finding a new heartthrob, vile and callous though the prick may be.

Poor Corvina.

I suppose with the way the raiders cherish cruelty, it should come as no surprise to me that others would find him desirable. But all I'm able to see when looking at Olsson Agni is pure, incomprehensible loathing. Even so, it's hard to picture him truly concerned about a few admirers when the weight of our looming judgment rumbles overhead.

There's a twisting in my gut that worsens each time the shrill, otherworldly thunder breaks through the noise of the assembling crowd. I have a sickening feeling that it isn't any sort of siren or alarm bell.

Agni's gaze catches mine before our instruction begins, and I find those amber eyes of his brimming with amusement. My own eyes narrow on him in confusion. His lips twitch upwards in response, like he might actually laugh out loud.

What in the depths?

"Alright captains!" Raider Dornon calls to our group, stealing my attention with an excited clap of his hands. "As previously mentioned, this first task is meant to test the first pillar of knowledge instilled in you by the Order: endurance and survival." The crookedness of his nose makes our officiant's eager grin appear more sinister than enthusiastic.

"In order to test this knowledge, we've come up with a trial that I think you'll find to be quite *unique*. But first, how do we decide the order in which you'll participate?" he questions us before answering himself. "We've made it simple. You will go in order of arrival of the cardinals, beginning with our hosts. So we'll start with the north, then east, west, and lastly south."

My insides take a nosedive with the news.

This means Vash and I will be the first captains tested. Best-case scenario: I'll get a few extra moments to panic within the confines of our sector. The *worst* case...

"You will all flip a coin to determine who goes first within your cardinal. Here—" he rummages in the breast pocket of his sage-colored uniform, pulling out four golden coins and gifting one to each of our captain pairs. "North, you go ahead."

Vash turns to face me. "You call it." He nods to the coin in his open palm.

"Heads," I call not daring to watch as the golden piece flips in the air and lands back on Vash's hand. He covers the coin before turning it over into the opposite palm.

Raider Dornon leans over to inspect. "Tails!" he announces, and I feel the bit of dry toast begin making its escape. "Captain Boreas, you have the high honor of opening up the Pillar Trials."

Wonderful.

I'm made to wait for the next ten minutes before the midpoint opening of the tarped off level. Raider Dornon explained what announcements to expect before the official start of the Pillar Trial, but most of what he told me was lost to the increasingly loud pounding of my heart. It's a real struggle getting my feet to pull from the ground when finally hearing the signal I've been waiting for.

The eruption of cheers emitted from the gathered crowd at my entrance is deafening. I glance up and around, hoping to spot familiar brown curls, a slash of black hair, or flaming red locks, but there's too many raiders gathered to locate my crew. The stadium is a blur of faces and roars of excitement. So I swallow my agitation and continue steadily along the path.

As Dornon explained before leaving our group, there's a line of neon flags that mark the walkway to the groyne extending out into the bay. The darkened sky makes it appear to be evening rather than morning, and the flags I pass flap wildly in the brutal winds.

Tapping my fingers rhythmically against each other, I begin counting to quell my nerves until making it to the edge. My feet stop themselves at the end of the wooden track stretching across the familiar waters, precisely where I've been instructed to. With the wind and the constant shrill of sirens and thunder, it's almost impossible for me to hear the announcer's distant voice. Yet it's imperative that I do.

When I said we were going in blind, I meant it.

I still have no idea what I'm about to face.

My hand travels down to the borrowed hilt of the blade Preceptor Oplon leant to me for today. Gripping it somehow fractionally eases the pounding lodged somewhere inside my throat. Enough, at least for me to hear the announcer's next words.

"Here we go, Raiders! To set us off on what will no doubt be an unforgettable year of trials we have before us, Captain Boreas. Our first captain here represents one of two from the Cardinal North. Not only is she the first castaway *ever* selected to compete for the Vault, but as her name gives away, she's bastard-born to top it off. Truly history in the making here with this one!"

My teeth stack themselves tightly in response to the booming voice.

Just get to it already.

I begin eyeing the sea wall directly across the bay. The new structure extends from one end of the curved waters to the other, effectively closing out the ocean beyond. Growing ever anxious, I start bouncing between one foot and the other to keep my muscles loose while striving to hear what's being said to the crowd at my back.

"You all may have noticed the weather has taken a bit of a turn—"

I'm trying to make sense of his words when another high-pitched shrill pierces the sky. It's so close now that the sound reverberates through the groyne under my still-bouncing feet.

"—generously donated by TideLord Nero specifically for this first pillar!"

A clamor of rowdy cheering erupts from behind, and I look backwards in bewilderment at the new commotion. I didn't hear what he said. Panic flares up inside of me, bright and pungent.

What? What did he say? What's the task?

My head is swinging around in all directions as if the answer might just be written somewhere when a large groaning noise emanates out from across the bay. My eyes snap back to the waters, and my hand tightens its grip around the hand-me-down hilt. The seawall separating the bay from the outside ocean has begun to *move.*

"—selected based on the findings of Hiereus Philistos."

What is he talking about?

I'm only catching snippets of information due to the level of noise surrounding me from every possible angle. The words that I do manage to catch don't make any sense. They're too jumbled and sporadic for me to piece together the intel properly. The seawall continues stretching outwards with a grating sort of sound. There's a sliver of an opening forming in the center, directly opposite from where I currently stand. My pulse hammers faster and louder.

I can just barely make out what appears to be some sort of a massive cage on the other side of that narrow opening. The clouds above gather tightly while the winds rise up and whip greedily through my long braid. Small pinpricks of water start to fall from the sky.

Shuffling as close as I dare to the edge of my designated starting position, my eyes strain to see what lies beyond that enclosure. I cover my brow from the rain just as the alarm-like sound from before, that otherworldly piercing shriek, shatters the sky and damn near splits my eardrums. This time it comes from the cage, now fully wedged into the seawall opening. Understanding dawns on me at last, and my knees begin to shake.

The next proclamation from the booming announcer echoes out to the gathered crowd before being carried to my ears on savage winds. "We welcome our captains to their first challenge: The taming of the kelpie!"

The front of that iron enclosure slams open at the sound of the announcer's signal. And all I can think is that I should have gone with the broadsword.

XI. THE TAMING OF THE KELPIE

What comes out of that cage across the bay is no mere water spirit of legend.

It's a hurricane incarnate.

A natural disaster given shape.

A nightmare presiding as a maelstrom.

A kelpie.

My insides feel like they just might fall out while watching in mute horror as a swirling vortex of terror rips out and into the waters. I can't even get my feet to move. I'm just standing there stock-still with my weapon arm raised like a *fucking* moron.

The miniature typhoon bolts out across the other side of the bay, tearing up great swells of water in its wake. While watching it, I finally registered the reasoning behind Grand Regent Beldham's unexpectedly kind words. I'm going to die today. That was my eulogy.

Swallowing tightly, I squint through the misting rain to better study the shifting storm. The unruly winds and spray of saltwater give way to glimpses of a colt-shaped spirit within.

What am I supposed to do again? Kill it?

No—the announcer said taming. I remember now.

They want us to break the kelpie's in, which means I need to get this thing to heel. How in the *fuck* am I supposed to do that when it doesn't seem to note let alone care about my presence?

The more I observe it, the more I notice that the kelpie avoids just about anything that isn't water. It doesn't come close to the shore and steers clear of the extended pier on which I stand.

I quickly deduce that it must not be able to survive too long outside a water source.

There's an idiotic plan forming in my mind, and it's almost certain to get me killed. Running my tongue back and forth against the inside of my lower lip, I consider just exactly what I'm about to do. Unfortunately, I don't see another option.

After a few more motionless moments, I heave a sigh and step over the groyne's safety out onto the danger-filled bay. The water beneath my approaching footfall solidifies into a step of ice.

It sounds as though there's a collective gasp from the crowd behind me in response to the use of my elemental affinity, although I don't dare turn to confirm. Willing the ice to form into a patch big enough for me to comfortably stand on, I pause and reevaluate.

The kelpie is running up and down the sea-wall's edge, begging to be let loose. The waters surrounding my small haven shake from the efforts of the creature, but not enough to destroy my rapidly firming ice. He still doesn't appear to notice me, so I think I'm safe for the moment.

I wade out a little further out into the bay, solid ice meeting my every step. Once I make it to the halfway point where a red buoy bobs in the center of the choppy waters, I push out my power gently. A ten foot-wide frozen circle forms around me.

I've no more than placed my palm along the frost-covered red buoy when the winds shift.

My eyes dart over to the kelpie to find it's finally stopped its pacing. The vortex of violent air and brutal sea turns my way. Squinting through the drizzle, I glimpse what looks like a lifted stallion's head sniffing the breeze. The world is somewhat calm for one single merciful second.

Then the winds shift again.

I observe, with no small amount of fear, as the wild tempest rears up. It allows me another peek at the savage spirit beneath as it swings its ferocious head angrily. Eyes like a living maelstrom lock onto me from afar, and my blood turns cold.

One heartbeat later, and the monsoon comes barreling my way at top speed.

From this rapidly reducing distance, I can fully appreciate the way its thunderous near-corporal hooves pound against the water with breathtaking power. A breath catches in my throat at the sight of it. I've never seen anything like it in all my life.

It's terrifying.

It's *beautiful.*

If this creature is what kills me, then I think it might be a worthwhile death.

Forcing myself to remember the plan, I dig my heels further into the ice at my feet. I steady my weight on bent knees as the living hurricane aims itself for me. One hand grips my borrowed weapon while the other comes out to improve my odds of balancing. White strands of hair sever from my braid and slice through my vision.

Adrenaline sharpens my focus. The blood rushing in my ears is the only sound I register.

"Come *on,*" I mutter impatiently.

As if the chaotic spirit can hear my whispered urging, it increases in speed and charges straight for my icy respite. I'm bracing myself, preparing my body while mentally trying to time the jump, but the kelpie kicks it up one more knot at the very last possible second.

I've miscalculated, is my one and only thought before being hit with a wall of solid wind.

No—not *hit*—sucker punched.

My entire body is sucker punched by a wall of solid fucking wind.

The attack is almost too swift for me to make sense of. One moment I'm waiting for the right instant to jump in the hopes of landing on something resembling its back, and the next I'm spluttering up saltwater, fighting to keep myself conscious. At least I'm cognizant enough to send a silent prayer to the drowned gods that I haven't just been paralyzed.

I can only imagine the reactions from those watching. The panic from Kleio and the rest of my crew is likely staggering, but I don't have time to dwell. Not with the kelpie now circling me.

The literal eyes of a storm have narrowed onto my struggling form.

Treading water I use the breathing techniques we're taught in order to ignore the type of pain currently flaring through every inch of my body. My focus never leaves the wild creature bounding around my position with its slitted gaze pinned on me. I keep my head above the bay and study its movements. To my surprise, the kelpie begins to morph.

The lawless storm begins taking shape. Storm clouds and saltwater combine into an almost completely corporal form, and I'm left gaping over the heaving tides at the massive silver colt.

"Of fucking course," I mutter as a memory drags itself before me.

I recall quite clearly the amusement brimming in Agni's amber eyes in the tarped off captain's quarters. The way his mouth twitched like he just might laugh whenever he looked at me.

He knew.

I don't know how it's even possible that he knew, but I'm suddenly certain of it.

The savage otherworldly creature continues parading around where I fight to tread water, a much harder task with a veritable whirlpool nearby. When it shoved me off my icy ledge, it made sure to do so far enough away that I'd have to make it past him in order to get back to safety.

There's an unmistakable shine of intelligence glinting in those eyes as it passes by.

"So you're a clever one, are you?" I call out over the swelling waves, barely avoiding a mouthful of bay water in the process.

The silver kelpie swings the length of its sparkling head back and forth while making a strange noise that I can only describe as a whinny of derision. I have an uncanny feeling that the creature can somehow understand me. Albeit, I honestly have no idea how intelligent kelpie's actually are. They're so rare we only went over them for a week at most in level-two.

I've begun measuring the distance each time the kelpie makes a loop around me. The racing pulse of my heartbeat acts as a timer. In order for this to work, I have to clock it just right.

Now.

My hand shoots up and out of the water, aiming for the beast, and a sheet of ice instantly crystallizes right in front of his watery hoofs. The kelpie stumbles and slides onto the now rapidly generating ice with an angry shriek that cracks the sky. I don't waste a single second.

I swim for my patch of safety like my life depends on it because I'm certain it does.

For once in my entire godsdamned, or rather gods-blessed, existence with the North Order, I am beyond grateful for Preceptor Darood and his insane water combat training class. I swim as fast as I can, my arms and legs moving against the weight of my waterlogged clothes while barely giving myself time to breathe. Ignoring the protest of my muscles and the pain that still stings sharply along my body is an ability earned only from his courses.

My hand smacks onto the icy ledge, and I hurl myself up before barrel rolling onto the tiny glacier just as the kelpie comes back for more. The sterling colt tries his earlier move, running straight at me at top speed in an effort to knock me off the patch of frozen water again. But I'm a quick learner. I wait until he's only meters away and drop down flat on my stomach.

The kelpie storms over the air above my head, missing me entirely.

He makes an angry sound somewhere between a snarl and neigh before whipping off to the sea wall in a rage-fueled burst of speed. I pop back up on my feet, water pouring from my soaking person while clocking his movements. For a minute, I think the creature's trying to barter for its freedom along the blockade, keeping him locked in with me, but then I grasp his true intention.

Looking around at the choppy waters, I try formulating some sort of strategy as the kelpie uses the sea wall like a springboard and rebounds this way at heart-stopping speeds.

Miraculously, I find I've managed to keep hold of my weapon thus far. Not that it's done me any good, but still. The hilt in my hand makes me feel just a tiny bit better about the newest suicidal scheme I'm now banking on.

I have to break it, which means I have to get *on* it first.

Shaking out the nerves from my legs and arms, I take what just might be my last breath before beginning to sprint across the water straight for the kelpie, advancing me head-on. A narrow tread of ice appears under my swiftly moving feet. The storm spirit is so bewildered by my rapidly approaching form it actually slows its strides. It's exactly what I'm hoping for.

I take advantage of the momentary lapse and use my building momentum to leap off the icy landing and onto the back of the freshly startled tempest. The kelpie rears its magnificent head in outrage. For a moment, I start to think maybe I can do this. Maybe I stand a real chance.

Then the beast dives headfirst into the upset waters, dragging me down along with him.

Thankfully, I have the good sense to gulp down a precious bit of air before I'm unceremoniously plunged into the bay's depths. It takes all my concentration to hold onto the ever-changing storm spirit as it twists and turns, trying to wriggle free inside the murky depths.

Then the kelpie leaps back up through the air in an effort to buck me off, but that only allows me another breath before it drags me back under. My thoughts are frantic, and I'm trying not to panic, but honestly, I didn't think I'd get this far.

I hold on for dear life as he spins us into an underwater tornado before shooting forward at vomit-inducing speeds up and out over the waves.

Now what? How the hell am I supposed to tame it?

I'm wracking my brain and finally beginning to crack when terribly crude words—words that make me want to punch a wall—echo from the back of my mind. A deep, dark, smoke-wrapped voice laughs mockingly in the back of my memory.

All you need is a bridle to control them.

Shoving down the sickening feelings and enraged thoughts erected by that memory, I force myself to focus on the task at hand. A bridle. I need a bridle. In order to manage that, I need—

"Oh, you have got to be fucking kidding me," I grunt in complaint.

Imagining a certain southern captain's face, I kick the side of the kelpie's underbelly *hard*.

The creature roars in outrage before plummeting back under the water in fresh fury. He drags me with vengeance now, rolling and bucking in a whirlpool of angry movements. Too angry to even notice what I'm doing on his back.

My hands work as best they can, while my thighs feel like they might set themselves on fire from overuse. Then I take the blade from where I'd shoved it beneath a strap along my leg and kick the kelpie once more. The spirit surges up out of the water in one enormous leap.

It opens its mouth to bellow its rage right as I shove the frozen blade into its mouth. One swift movement and the reigns of ice I've crafted latch onto the side of its mouthpiece in my last trick. The effect is mercifully immediate. His bucking and thrashing finally stops, and the uncontrollable storm at long last breaks.

The kelpie ends its tantrum, and I sigh in relief as it comes to an effortless trot along the waters.

Shaking my head, I work hard to dislodge the water from my ears. When I stop, I hear the sound of thunder rumbling violently from behind and my gut squeezes in alarm. The kelpie beneath me turns us both, and I discover the thunder is actually riotous cheers from the crowded stadium before us. Their shouting is so loud I actually think I've lost a bit of my hearing.

The water spirit whinnies up at me, and I see that gleam in his eyes from before.

It's as if he's saying, *Let's give them a show.*

Taking the ice reigns in my hands, I give them the slightest flick. The kelpie bolts forward and begins galloping across the waters with wondrously powerful strides. It doesn't feel like I'm holding onto a storm for dear life anymore. It's like I'm running with the winds.

The thrill is exhilarating—a complete and total rush.

The sterling beast heads for one edge of the shoreline without encouragement, and we race past the stands. Raiders are on their feet, clapping and cheering like mad. Voices begin shouting out my name, but I'm too distracted by the upcoming groyne to take much note.

I brace myself for impact, certain I'm about to lose any points or interest I might have gained from the Tide Lords, when the silver kelpie clears the entire pier in one jump. The crowd goes absolutely wild for it, and now I look a thousand times more skilled than I actually am.

I crow out loudly when we land. The adrenaline high from riding the creature pulses through me gloriously. It's an even better rush than the ice-surfing competitions we have here in the darkest months. This is freedom. Pure, unrestricted freedom. Something I've never had before.

I could get addicted to this.

The kelpie chortles like he's heard my most recent thoughts, and I can't seem to wipe the grin from my face. He makes one final victory lap before finally trotting over to the end of the groyne.

Then the kelpie bows his magnificent shimmering head low enough for me to dismount. The incredible beast stays for a moment and allows me to stroke his mane before *nuzzling* my palm for a few impossible heartbeats. I feel an unexpected pang of sadness knowing our time is up.

Now that he isn't trying to actively murder me, the kelpie is actually kind of adorable.

In a string of deft movements, I reach down and pull a ball of ice from the bay waters. My nimble fingers work fast to mold the sphere into a makeshift apple. The kelpie promptly bites it right out of my outstretched hand with alarming speed.

My laugh is real and deep and long before giving him one last stroke of affection.

Then I stride down the neon-flagged path like the agony rippling through my body isn't real.

I'm escorted back into the captain's quarters by Raider Dornon immediately following my exit.

A towel is given to me along with a fresh uniform, but I'm told to wait for a leech to come and inspect my wounds before changing. I didn't even realize there was blood running from my arms and legs. I guess rolling through patches of underwater plants and rocks will do that to you.

The pain I register is focused on the lower half of my body still recovering from being body-slammed by a kelpie.

Only moments after I'm finally left in peace, the navy-colored entrance flap to our quarters zips open. I then find myself fighting for air around the person currently squeezing me to death.

"Good to see you too," I murmur, my voice muffled by the rich brown curls pressed tightly against my face.

I can feel Kleio's body shaking beneath mine, and I pull her from our embrace as gently but firmly as possible. My hands push her shoulders back to find her face pale with a tinge of green. There are marks from where her nails have dug anxious holes peppering both her cheeks.

"I thought you were going to *die* out there, Merena," Kleio states, looking so tightly wound that she's actually turning more green by the minute.

"Hey—I'm okay—you see." Removing one hand from her shoulder, I motion down to myself. My bloody, soaking wet, towel-wrapped self.

I grimace at the fresh alarm in her gaze. "Okay, maybe this isn't my shining moment, but I'm fine, Kleio, I swear." Meeting Kleio's painfully worried stare, I will her to believe my claim.

"You were incredible. I—I still can't believe it," my second confesses breathlessly, some color coming back into her face at last.

"Yeah?" I ask, still in disbelief to have completed the pillar at all.

"I mean I *also* thought you were even more of a brash fucking idiot than I already know you to be. Especially when you started running straight *at* that demon waterhorse." Kleio laughs, and I join her. My amusement is shaky and filled with leftover nerves.

"Yeah, that was a spur-of-the-moment idea," I admit through more relieved laughter.

A familiar voice interrupts our reunion saying, "Alright, Kleio, you've had your turn. Now let me get our captain treated." I look over Kleio's shoulder to find Davina standing in the dark blue tarp entrance. Her expression is cool and collected, but those kaleidoscope eyes studying me shine with scarcely concealed worry.

"Go watch Vash. He's up next," I insist, giving Kleio one last squeeze. "He'll be alright," I whisper in added reassurance before letting her go.

She nods, more to herself than to me, before flashing a quick grin. I watch her slip past Vi and hurry back to watch Vash with the rest of our crew.

Davina surprises me by closing the short distance between us and swiftly pulling me into another rib-cracking hug. Her mane of golden hair evades my senses for a brief moment. Then she lets me go just as quickly before barking at me to sit down so she can inspect my injuries.

Once my wounds are cleaned and sufficiently mended, Davina leaves to rejoin our crew in the stands. Raider Dornon pops back in after I've changed to inform me I'm allowed to either wait in my cardinal section or move to the common area at the other end of the tarped off quarters.

As I'm the only one so far to complete the trial, I watch Vash's round in the common area alone. His turn goes by surprisingly fast, or maybe it just feels that way since I'm no longer the one having to accomplish it. Regardless, his affinity for stealth is a powerful ally in this challenge.

Vash's kelpie, nearly invisible with its watery mane, is *quick*. There was a moment where I truly feared for his life. His beast did *not* take well to Vash's attempts at getting on its back. The kelpie reared up to its full might and kicked Vash square in his chest, sending him crashing into the bay waters with the creature diving in after him.

I watched with bated breath as the formidable creature led him through a series of maneuvers that would have made me lose my seat in an instant. Yet Vash hung on, eventually resurfacing with a fistful of seaweed from the waters beneath.

He worked strategically, and it finally paid off when the heavily knotted seaweed bridle slid into place and reigned in the spirit at last.

I'm selfishly grateful he survived intact. I need my second at her best.

Vash Larceon's untimely death would devastate Kleio, to say the least.

As previously foretold, the East Order made its debut next. Dhara lost her coin toss and went first, although I couldn't find it in myself to pity her. Her sonar abilities were borderline unfair.

Vash and I watched in silence as she outmaneuvered her beast time and again. To a point where the creature became reckless. Dhara used that in combination with her chosen weapon, a long leather whip. It was over as soon as she figured out how to get it over the kelpie's head. The only reason I can find her losing points is her time. She wasted most of it riling the beast up.

I was keen to observe Reed and his strange power, but it became too difficult with the pouring rain and ceaseless winds brought in by each new kelpie. From the commentary of the obnoxious announcer, I learned he crafted reigns of solidified salt straight from the bay after trapping the creature in a cage of it. I believe that was also *after* his kelpie dislocated the captain's shoulder.

The west provided an interesting watch.

Captain Tetsuo went first and came out swinging with his control over the magnetic fields around him. At first, his affinity actually appeared to only cause more of an issue. Each time he would try utilizing it, it would cause his kelpie to ripple with menacing lightning so that his efforts only intensified the creature's power.

He quickly learned from his mistakes and managed to reign in the spirit at last by manipulating the metal of his weapon. He *almost* got away without a scratch. Right before being broken, the kelpie twisted beneath his rider so viciously that I could hear the nauseating 'snap' of Ansil's leg all the way from inside the viewing area. That is a sound that will be difficult to forget.

Brisa is just as lethal an opponent as I suspected.

All five of us studied her in contemplative quiet as she increased and decreased the pull of gravity for her kelpie and was able to mount it on the first try. It looked effortless as she went lap after lap with him. I took mental notes of her power and watched with mixed feelings of jealousy and awe.

The south comes last, and I'm dismayed by Corvina's ultimately successful trial.

I'm not exactly sure what it was she did. The announcer even had trouble explaining her methods. Captain Leporem stood out there at the very edge of the groyne and just *waited.*

It took much more time than I'd have risked wasting, but eventually the kelpie came to her. After making a few passes back and forth, it stopped, as if it were incredibly exhausted, and went to heel before Corvina sleepily. I'd never audibly admit it, but I have to wonder if she just might have us all beat.

Finally, the moment I've been waiting for arrives at long last. Captain Agni's turn.

I prayed to all the drowned gods of Nawai and the Celestial realm for his death during these trials after last night's interaction. Here's hoping I get to witness it firsthand.

Seven of us captains now, many of them heavily bandaged and one on crutches, line up along the clear vinyl screen serving as our window. Corvina, having just made it back, watches from the furthest end with a towel draped around her dry shoulders. The other cardinal captains begin talking in hushed voices, but I keep my silence.

I fully intend to enjoy every moment of this.

Captain Agni's towering frame stalks down the neon-flagged path in a leisurely gait. He exudes his typical arrogance with every swaggering step. I notice that he's stripped down to the thinnest layers of clothing beneath his uniform. The scarlet stitching on his otherwise midnight wetsuit stands out threateningly beneath the dark skies.

The clouds rolling overhead are the most ominous by far. Flashes of gold light up the near pitch-black horizon over the sea wall's edge like live artillery.

Just like each of us before him, Captain Agni stops at the edge of the pier, extending a third of the way into the bay. His obsidian hair runs wild with the raging winds surging past. A black fabric mask has been pulled up to just over the bridge of his nose.

The sound from the crowd above is horrendously loud. The whole common area vibrates with the force of their excitement. I find myself holding my breath as that siren-like sound erupts with a glass-shattering screech from the other side of the slowly opening gate.

I can tell, even from this distance, that the cage being revealed bit by bit in the middle of the sea wall is larger than any of the others. My own sterling beasts included.

The signal is given, and the ironbound prison door falls open wide.

XII. THE TIDELORDS

I am admittedly overly eager to watch Captain Agni's trial, but not just because I hope to watch him meet the end he so deserves firsthand. It seems a shame to have met one of the only other elementals in the entire world and never to have even seen them wield.

Olsson has brought with him only one of his twin tenebrous broadswords, which is intriguing considering I'm positive they would consider the pair as a single weapon. He doesn't even draw it. Instead, he faces the oncoming storm with only those unique blue flames at his fingertips.

Corvina gasps from down the line of captains as the monstrous spirit prowls out of its enclosure. The creature is crafted of black tumultuous clouds that writhe and curl in wisps of gray smoke while flashes of golden light spark menacingly from within. Agni doesn't wait for the creature to notice him. He raises his hand and shoots up a flaming ball of azure fire like a flare gun.

His spirit isn't nearly as sporadic as the others. It's rather strategic in its movements.

The savage clouds around it condense into the size of a small ship, and its rippling hide emulates the color of hell itself. Eyes like the inside of a wrathful volcano narrow on the harrowing male waiting at the end of the groyne. The beast flicks its smoky whip of a tail and blasts a shot of aureate lightning straight for Captain Agni.

This kelpie has been waiting.

Screams erupt from the crowd above as Olsson drops flat against the ground, narrowly avoiding the lightning strike. After its power has ceased, the kelpie bellows while rearing its terrible head with a chuff before beginning to sprint across the bay like its brethren. Agni rolls to the side of the groyne, remaining flat against the wooden planks as the spirit hurtles across the waters.

The kelpie isn't using its power, like it's saving the lightning just for him.

The tempest pulses with pent-up energy while making circles around the restless bay. Then the demonic storm makes another pass, closer this time. Agni blasts a condensed ball of flames at the beast before rolling off the groyne entirely and down into the bay.

I'm shocked by his move. To willingly go into the water near a kelpie is idiotic at best.

The tempest roars out in outrage at the fire, having just barely missed its hide.

My brow furrows while studying Agni's movements as I try to decipher what on Pontus his strategy is. He surfaces at different points around the bay, striking the kelpie with his power before vanishing beneath the waves again. There's no attempt at subtlety. If anything, he goes out of his way to announce his location with a loud splash or a shout in the tempest's direction.

"What is he *doing*?" Vash mutters from beside me.

"I think he's trying to lure it," I answer in a hushed voice. "But I'm not sure why."

The Southern captain's actions seem to be riling up his kelpie. Shadows coil off its shifting form, momentarily parting to expose the fierce golden light surging within. Across the bay, Agni emerges once more, unleashing another wave of fire. The flames streak past the kelpie, barely clipping the edge of its flickering tail.

A guttural, otherworldly cry rips from the creature as it rears up, its body trembling with fury.

The sound is unbearable. It's so sharp and unnatural it feels like it's splitting my head open from the inside out. All seven of us captains bark out curses with hands firmly planted on either side of our heads. The terrible shriek eventually relents, and the tempest begins mutilating the bay waters, sprinting in the direction of Agni.

In no time the massive creature makes it over to where the southern captain was last spotted, only for him to re-emerge at the opposite end of the bay, now well past the red buoy. There are shouts of confusion and concern from the crowd overhead as Agni continues like this back and forth across the bay.

The kelpie is all but consumed with wrath as the charade ensues. When he finally emerges again at the now fully closed sea wall edge, I start putting together the pieces of his plan. He blasts an additional ball of fire, and this time it's angled straight above his head like another flare signal. The kelpie hears it and streaks off across the waves in a fit of rage. Auric-hued lightning writhes inside of it, just begging for release.

"*Move*! What are you doing?" Corvina shouts as Olsson continues treading water.

The kelpie is only meters from him at best.

He's still there when the hellish spirit rises up on his hind legs again and the golden energy inside explodes from it with another mind-numbing shriek. Corvina sucks in a sharp breath of terror, and she's far from alone. I'm likely the only one in the entire stadium who remains utterly silent as a thousand bolts of resplendent energy race for Captain Agni's heart.

Unfortunately, my dreams are dashed in the next moment.

Too fast for my eyes to break down the movements, Olsson snatches both hands out of the water and *grabs* onto the lightning aimed directly at his chest. I have to grip the sides of my jaw to keep it from hanging open as he steals the bolt of power from the beast and throws it back like a lasso around the kelpie's head. The tempest bucks and rears, yanking him from the waters.

Agni uses it as leverage and swings himself skillfully onto its back.

What.

The.

Fuck.

The second he takes his seat, the storm spirit goes mad. It shoots out across the bay like a black comet, thrashing and rolling in a raging cyclone of movement. Impossibly, Agni holds onto the lasso of charged energy the entire time. It looks as if he'd been born to ride kelpie's. The tempest only attempts diving below the surface once and almost immediately roars up to the dark sky with a thunderous cry before resurfacing.

"What was that?" Vash demands, his arms crossed before his chest and his brow furrowed in deep concentration regarding our competition.

"He heated up the bay," I reply, almost spitting the words in regards to Agni's cruel genius.

Vash turns slightly to where I still grip my jaw in one hand, my mouth an angry line. I meet his questioning eyes with a huff. "Each time Captain Agni resurfaced, he taunted the beast before diving back down again. He was using the distraction and time under the waters to heat up the bay. Now the kelpie can't drag him below."

Vash nods as understanding glitters in the gold flecks of his irises.

We continue judging silently as the violent kelpie rips around the waters faster than any of the others. The crackling golden light tells us Agni is somehow managing to hold on. My adrenaline spikes as they race past. If he were to fall off at these speeds, they'll be picking him up in pieces.

The rippling light begins to stretch and elongate from somewhere inside the raging storm, and I know Agni's next move. He's forming a bridle of its own power in order to tame the beast. From the looks of it, he's almost there. The kelpie is slowing in speed, and I can *just* about glimpse the staggering male on its back. All he's missing is the mouthpiece.

There's a hush in the captain's common area as we watch Agni lean down close to the tempest's head. Lightning is taut between his hands as he makes to secure the last piece of the bridle. He's up on his knees with his arms extending carefully as the beast makes a completely unforeseen move.

The demonic cyclone corkscrews at the very last second.

The unpredictable maneuver sends Captain Agni crashing right into the wooden pier. Its pent-up lightning sputters throughout his person as he goes. A heartbeat later reveals Olsson's body lying limp among broken boards and razor-sharp rocks.

Gasps and cries ring out from the stands overhead. Crimson spills down his face and chest, swirling through the water in dark, winding tendrils. Corvina rushes out of the common area with a hand over her mouth and a hysterical sob in her throat. I assume she's going to get their grand preceptor, but for what reason I'm not sure. Even Saubarag can't interfere in the trials, not once they've begun.

The storm spirit has become corporal again while creeping closer to where the southern captain's broken body lies. Power pulses within the beast as it bows its terrifying head down to graze the captain's obsidian hair. At first, I mistake its movements for simple curiosity. But then that potent spark coils up bright inside, and realization steals the air from my lungs. I now know, without a doubt, the kelpie is about to kill Captain Agni.

My mouth hooks up in one corner.

I cannot believe my luck.

The wild creature makes for a death blow, but Agni reacts in the final heartbeat. His hand emerges from the crimson waters in a lash of scorching blue fire. It carves across the kelpie's form in brutal efficiency just before he rolls away. A split second later, a jagged bolt of lightning channels into the exact spot where the captain had been lying.

The kelpie's bellow warps into a piercing cry of anguish.

Agni doesn't waste a moment.

He's back up on the creatures in a matter of seconds. Despite the blood soaking him, Agni's work is swift. Fire surges between his fingers, weaving around the spirit like a net before he drives the final burst straight into its open jaws, cutting off its tormented cries. The moment the fire-bridle locks into place, the kelpie goes eerily still.

A very odd, hair-raising noise begins forming in its chest.

Agni slides off the newly broken kelpie's back and down to the half-destroyed groyne. He turns back towards the stadium as the beast begins swinging its head from one side to the other in agitation.

With an unevenness about his steps, Agni makes his way down the flag-lined path. I spot several members of his crew racing from the stands to help him. He waves them all off and I note that one of his arms looks like the bone might have been snapped in half. That thin black fabric mask of his is now down around his neck, exposing the right half of his face is drenched in crimson.

I don't give anymore attention to his wounded form. My eyes find the dark kelpie still moving anxiously to and fro. The noise emerging from it almost sounds like a sob. Others are noticing the creature's strange behavior as well. I have the strangest impulse to go to it.

The world around me becomes wholly silent as the terrifying wild spirit sinks down onto its darkly beautiful haunches and lets out a long, mournful wail. It causes a perilous chill to envelope my person, all the way down to the bone. I find myself shuddering in physical response, it feels like something is tearing inside my soul. And I think the pure, unspeakable sorrow in that sound might just haunt me forever.

I watch on in agony as the kelpie's midnight head turns at last to reveal a massive brand has been sliced right across both of its once fiery eyes. Agni stole the creature's sight, but what's worse, he mutilated it with a brand.

My stomach twists, bile stinging the back of my throat.

It's true we learned little of the water spirits during our earlier levels. But from what I remember for certain, a branded kelpie cannot ever find its one true mate. There's nothing more devastating that could have befallen the creature.

We've lined along the narrow dock directly in front of the newly crafted stadium while a light drizzle drips down on us. I have yet to glimpse any of the six TideLords who will be judging this first task, but I'm already anxious to see the seventh. Raider Dornon informed us they would be deliberating privately on scores before announcing them.

Only one of us is still missing.

Captain Agni hasn't been seen since his exit.

I'm wondering if perhaps he'll be too injured to join us for scoring when a thunderous wave of applause rips me from my hopeful reverie. At first I think the TideLords must have come back, but then I spot the approaching figure heading for his place at the opposite end of our line-up.

Agni's arm is locked against his side, wrapped so tightly in cloth that it barely moves. One half of his face is obscured, hidden beneath layers of fabric stained a disturbing red. It doesn't appear he's even changed clothes yet. The southern captain takes his spot next to Corvina before raising his good arm to the crowd in thanks for their praise.

I resist the bitter urge to swear.

Raider Dornon announces then that the TideLords will enter shortly to give their scores. He's noticeably less jovial than he was at the start of the trials. The twinkle in his blue eyes has dimmed, and the scars on his face are made more prominent on his noticeably paler face.

Unlike when Agni made his recent entrance, the crowd becomes deathly silent, and everyone stands at attention for the TideLords stalking back into the open air box located in the center of the stadium. Only the wind and rain dare to make a sound in their presence.

My breath is stuck somewhere between my chest and my throat while watching them enter one by one. The first TideLord is tall and predictably well built with hard-earned muscle. Black corded dreads fall to his shoulders, and a neatly trimmed onyx beard takes up the lower half of his face. His uniform is the exact orange hue of a sun on the brink of death.

I know without looking at the unmistakable gold earring on his left lobe or the ring adorning his right index finger, who stands above me. TideLord Hiwaye Kufko, or as the land masses better know him, 'The Clawmaster'. He peers down through tangerine-tinted spectacles at us with cool amusement in his russet eyes.

I barely have enough time to absorb the sight of the first TideLord when the next one waltzes into the judges platform. He's shorter than Kufko and noticeably leaner but his teal-dyed crocodile kurta adds on plenty of bulk. From one ear hangs a long, vicious-looking polyphyodonty tooth. It's the same length as the Lord's dark silky hair.

His uniform is only one of the many reasons they call him 'Crocsbane'. Tide-Lord Jaladhi Bombay gives a nod to Lord Kufko before standing beside him and looking down to us in observation.

At the appearance of the following Tide Lord, I find myself scanning the stands for a familiar pair of electric blue eyes. I don't find any trace of Kerau. I knew I likely wouldn't, especially when it's only the first trial, but I suppose a teeny tiny part of me had hoped. A *bit*.

TideLord Regis Raimbaut sweeps in with the flourish of his long ruffled cape; its remarkable pigment fades from ashen pink to soft cerulean into a coral hue. The uniform beneath is a crisp white, appearing almost neon against his sun-tanned skin. The Lord is middle-aged and quite handsome. His expertly trimmed black hair has a few grays, as does his shadow of a beard.

It's true that TideLord Raimbaut is one of the more *colorful* lords to emerge from The Order, but don't be deceived. In the seas of Pontus, the more vivid a creature's exterior, the more dangerous. He wasn't given the title 'The Bright Terror' without earning it.

The only current female TideLord swaggers in next. She's even smaller than the rumors, although you'd never know with the way she throws her weight about. The dark brown of her uniform is dripping with black pearls; they twist thickly around her slender neck, and strings of them droop from the epaulets at her shoulders.

Her midnight hair is shorn tight against the hollows of her delicate cheekbones, revealing a row of tightly studded gems along both ears. I work to keep my face neutral while watching TideLord Mei Li Tiamat join the others. Her reputation for leaving every skirmish with her enemies not even able to recall her face is legendary.

There's no wonder why the landmasses know her as 'The Faceless Devil'.

She's my hero.

Lord Tiamat is followed by an extremely intriguing TideLord Kazuo Kurage. His otherwise standard uniform of dull gray is made utterly transfixing by the outer cape adorning it. The storms have brought in a dark enough sky to reveal the bioluminescent lining of said cape that extends along up and over the edging of his hood.

Even with the rain continuing down between us, I can clearly make out his famous gloves lighting up the darkness. Those gloves are the only thing shielding anyone near from the fatal touch of Lord Kurage or more fittingly, 'The Reaper's Hand.'

The last TideLord to arrive is one whose name needs no introduction.

He's as cutthroat and vicious as they come. His finely tailored uniform is a deep tartarean and fashioned with golden armor around both his midsection and shoulders. A cape of matching obsidian falls from the auric plates atop his shoulder. That sharply lined, square-shaped face of his is handsome and expertly groomed.

TideLord Orcus Nero, also known as 'The Kraken King'.

I wonder how our Tide Raider King feels about one of his lords holding a title to rival his own.

Lord Nero's dark eyes scan over each of us; his attention lingers on Captain Agni and his bandaged body the longest. Jealousy twists my insides in response to the TideLord's blatant interest. I *have* to stand out to one of them. This is our best shot at the closest thing to freedom that exists within The Order.

The crowd cheers wildly once all of the TideLords have taken their places. The announcer then informs the stadium that the scoring will begin with the first captain to complete the task, *me*.

I steady myself as TideLord Kufko lifts his board to reveal my score.

He turns it over and I blink to find a nine. A fucking *nine*.

I'm floored. Looking upwards, I give what I hope comes across as an appreciative grin. Kufko returns it with a cool nod in acknowledgment, and I clamp down on my budding excitement.

TideLord Bombay gives me an eight, and I'm once again stunned by the score I don't quite feel deserving of. I then receive a seven from Lord Tiamat and another eight from Lord Raimbaut. I keep myself firmly grounded when Lord Kurage gives my next seven.

This is followed by TideLord Nero, who hands me my lowest score, a three.

A portion of the crowd actually boos at Lord Nero's score. A portion that is most definitely *not* under his command. It doesn't make me feel any better. One of the most revered TideLords in the history of The Order views me as a *three*. It stomps on something previously budding inside.

I end up with a total score of forty-two. But I don't know yet whether or not that's going to be competitive. Droplets of water begin clinging to the white hairs marring the edges of my vision as I wait and watch while the others receive their results.

Vash is given a final score of thirty-nine, his highest points coming from Lord Tiamat. Dhara comes out hot on my heels at forty-one. Reed is in the mix at thirty-eight. Ansil isn't far behind at forty, while Brisa earns herself the very first perfect ten from TideLord Bombay.

I'd be lying if I said I wasn't green with envy at her forty-six.

I'm actually surprised Corvina only earns a total of thirty-five but clearly time was more of a factor than I'd already anticipated. I wonder if she was also penalized for her lack of actually *riding* the creature. It's quite obvious that The Order wants these trials to be a show.

Captain Agni goes last, and I'm impatient.

The mournful wailing of his kelpie has mercifully stopped, but I know that I won't be able to get the memory of the creature's heartbreaking scream out of my head for a very long time.

I smirk when Lord Kufko gives him a six to kick it off. Bombay holds up a seven, followed by Tiamat's score of another six. Raimbaut gives him a six as well, and Kurage adds another seven to his total. There's true joy fluttering inside of me when tallying him up at thirty-two with only TideLord Nero and his repeatedly low scoring to go.

Not to mention the fact that the kelpies were donated by him to begin with.

Beating Olsson is almost the same as winning as far as I'm concerned. Lord Nero turns his score over at long last, and both my stomach and jaw drop at the perfect *ten* he's given Captain Agni.

Leaving him with an outcome of forty-two.

He's now tied with me for second place.

XIII. THE NETS

The stars seem particularly bright tonight.

Holding up my hands, I form an open circle between my thumbs and index fingers. I challenge myself to find and name each of the different constellations. They're all scattered like hidden worlds across the wide midnight plain above me.

Sounds of laughter and shouting and even whistling reverberate from both above and below where I currently lie in mine and Kleio's secret spot. My back rests flat against the knotted cords of black netting holding my horizontal body aloft. The nets themselves are strung around each of the thorn-like spires and border every edge of our northern fortress, but I have no idea why.

Not even Skelm could claim they're for safety measures and keep a straight face.

My personal purpose for them is for nights exactly like this one. When the outside world has become too much to process and my numerous facades much too heavy to wear.

The TideLords left directly after the close of the first pillar trial. We were assured that the seventh Lord, the only one missing from today's events, would be there to judge the next. A part of me can't help circling back to Vash's earlier suspicions and wondering if there's any weight to them. *Should* I be concerned about what's going on with the landmasses? The drifters?

Anytime I begin mulling over his worries, I myself just can't seem to find the point. Why bother caring when they're just as likely to be our allies one day as they are our targets the next?

Besides, I'm a castaway, I don't see what good the landmasses are to me anyhow.

I stop searching the celestial seas in order to turn over my left arm for inspection.

My thumb brushes absently over the brand around my wrist. The one that claims me as gods-blessed and supposedly determines me worthy enough to come back from Nawai. Worthy enough to be sent to the The Sons and Daughters and, by extension, the Tide Raiders.

Yet not worthy enough to retain my memory, apparently.

The brand is bright against the fading summer tan of my skin and it encircles my wrist like a bracelet. It depicts a skeleton belonging to some great sea serpent eating its own tail.

We are told by the Sons and Daughters after washing up on the Sál Moon that the unique mark symbolizes our descent to the netherdepths and subsequent return from it. It symbolizes the great cycle between us and the spirit realm of Nawai, just beneath the veil. Although personally, the longer we're here, the more I find it appears eerily similar to a shackle.

While others have varying different shades coloring their Tide Raider brand, like hues of greens, blues, purples, black, or even gold, mine is indisputably *white*. As is my affinity mark and even my hair.

White is a blatant sign given from the drowned gods to signal a castaway.

Without family, without home, without *color*.

In my case, also without memory.

“Pouting?” A familiar taunting voice shouts down at me from above.

Tilting my head backwards towards the spire window now fully open, I spot Kleio grinning in my direction. She lifts up a bottle of liquid recklessness and I can’t help but chuckle with the shake of my head. My amusement only grows while watching her climb through the awkward opening and roll down onto the nets, managing to stick the landing without spilling a drop.

“Why would I be pouting?” I ask easily as Kleio carefully makes her way over to where I lay before the very edge of the nets.

"Oh, I know how you hate to lose. Though I myself wouldn’t consider the second highest score in the first pillar trial losing by any means, I’m well aware of your aversion to anything less than first,” she teases, finally reaching my spot and sliding down to sit beside where I lie.

"I'm not technically second," I remind her with a roll of my eyes. “I’m tied for second, which practically makes me third. Even worse, I’m tied with that fucking jackass so yeah—it kind of does feel like a loss.” Each word grows more heated until I’ve completely proved her point.

Kleio snorts a laugh over the glass bottles' rim before tipping it backwards and taking a lengthy drink. She pushes the liquid recklessness into my hands next. “Well then, drink up, loser.”

My second always knows precisely what to say to turn my moods and I find it impossible to restrain my own snort of amusement. I swipe the bottle from her hands before promptly tipping it back myself. The green liquor slides down my throat with an electrifying sort of sensation.

“Where on Pontus did you manage to get a bottle of anquil liquor from?” I demand.

Kleio answers simply, "Vash," before stealing back the bottle.

I huff in acknowledgement before lying back down, both arms coming to rest behind my head. “I do appreciate the pep talk, Hiraeth but I’m really alright. You should head back inside and rejoin the others.”

Kleio swallows, sliding closer to where I'm strung out along the netting. I accept the bottle she hands me, choke down two rather ambitious mouthfuls, and send it her way once more.

"Liar," she mutters beneath her breath.

Her tone is too uncharacteristically snappish for me to disregard. My gaze flickers over to find her eyes locked onto the stars.

"I *know* you, Merena," Kleio states, after a moment, exasperated. "And you've been off since the start of this level. Even before the trials and the other cardinals arriving. You're just so—" she motions with a hand for emphasis while taking another sizzling gulp, "*restrained*."

My lips form a line while twisting the golden band around the middle finger of my right hand. It's one of my very few, and therefore highly treasured, possessions. A four-star compass is engraved on top with a burning blue gemstone in place of the north symbol. My captaincy ring.

"Comes with the territory, I suppose." My voice is barely more than a distracted murmur.

Kleio eyes me for a moment. "Just because you're a captain doesn't mean you're no longer entitled to having feelings or reactions of any kind. We chose you because you're a leader, one that *doesn't* follow every single order rule. I actually seem to remember you spent most of your first five years here, breaking as many as possible."

I listen to her speech while sipping on the bootleg bottle.

The pleasant heady buzz filling me, courtesy of said bottle, allows my next words to slip past my tongue easier than usual. "I did, and as *I* remember it, that rule-breaking and back talking didn't get me anywhere except into more trouble. Trouble that led to rather unpleasant punishments."

Kleio winces, and the brown curls of her high knot start pulling loose in the midnight breeze.

"If I seem restrained, it's because I know I'm not the only one who can be subjected to the disciplinary procedures that *will* follow." I pause in order to swallow. "I'm not just risking my own neck anymore when telling a Preceptor to fuck off. If I'm caught sneaking out or breaking curfew or even throwing a punch the next time someone calls me a name—do you seriously think it's only me who'll be suffering those consequences?"

My voice has started to rise, and I gruffly hand the anquil to my second. Her face studies the sky while mulling over my rant. After a moment, Kleio says, "We can handle it."

I snort, moving up to my forearms and giving her a look with brows raised. "Oh? Is that so? Let's say they toss you to Bealu the next time I decide to get a little mouthy. You're telling me that you'll be just fine with that?"

Kleio's face pales before turning a bright pink as she pulls again from the bottle. I mentally replay the look of absolute terror on my second's face that night they were caught on the shore by him. I recall quite clearly just how suffocating the threat of his vile affinity was to them all.

"I can handle Bealu, Merena," Kleio states evenly, and my brows raise further. "Okay, no, I don't happen to love his method of ripping out my few happy memories, but it isn't like he hasn't done it before." The following sigh she emits is long and low.

Kleio shifts to meet my gaze, and I discover the usual warmth in her eyes has dimmed, it makes something painful constrict in my chest. "I think you forget that we made it through all seven years of hell too. We *all* made it to the eighth level. Each one of us has earned our place here. We are not innocent, we are not soft, we are not in need of your protection at every twist and turn."

My teeth bite the inside of my lip while my second's assessment washes over me.

After a considering pause, I nod quietly to her in acknowledgment.

Kleio's voice comes out softer now. "I think you also sometimes forget who it was throwing punches right beside you whenever anyone called you a name or made crude jokes about your memory loss or any number of other terrible shit they threw your way."

The anquil makes my head a bit lighter, and it's easier to relax deeper into the netting while letting out a breathy chuckle. "How could I *ever* forget you slamming that poor level-six into one of your energy shields until his nose shattered?"

Kleio lets out a guffaw at the memory. "Poor level-*six*? We were only in level-four! It was his fault for picking a fight he couldn't win."

My grin isn't forced one bit as I gaze up towards the velvet sky.

"Today, or I guess by now it was yesterday, *whatever*. When you were facing that kelpie—I damn near lost it. I mean, I think Herse and Greer were holding me back by their fingernails at one point." Kleio snorts faintly to herself. "So I do understand your instinct to protect us."

We each take another drink.

"And it's not that I don't love watching people shit their pants whenever you give them one of your I-will-end-your-next-breath glares. I really and truly enjoy seeing the fear in their eyes as the temperature *plummets,*" Kleio adds. Her hands come whooshing down to the nets in emphasis.

"You are such a sadistic little shit," I tease while laughing up to the wide open night.

Kleio laughs long and hard, the sound of it is as close to a home as I've ever known.

"Coming from the stone-cold-bitch herself, I'll take that as a compliment," she quips, pushing the significantly lighter bottle into my hands.

We sit in comfortable silence for a few beats, my eyes traversing the celestial realm above.

"So that Olsson kid," Kleio comments, breaking our peaceful quiet and I take a rather long drink. "I cannot believe the stunt he pulled. That poor kelpie's cry nearly broke my heart."

"Mine too" I agree, the sound of its devastation is still fresh in my memory. "But it honestly doesn't surprise me. He's a fucking psychopath." I have trouble holding back my sneer.

Kleio watches me grapple with contempt. "He really gets under your skin, doesn't he?"

"And he doesn't get under yours? You were ready to fucking stab him on our first day sharing class together," I point out.

She smiles with a shrug. "He called you a squid. I'll stab anyone who makes that mistake."

The memory of that day makes my teeth grind together in annoyance.

I sincerely hope his injuries are too fucked for him to return.

The noise from inside drifts downwards, becoming impossible to ignore with its rising volume. I shift my gaze back to Kleio, the slight movement making my head dizzy. "You can head back, you know. Go enjoy celebrating with Vash and everyone else. I'm much better now." I flash her a grin for proof.

She snorts in return. "I'd rather be here with you. I mean, after seeing you out there today, I'm not wasting any of our very likely short time left together." She gives me a teasing grin, and I give her a playful shove in response.

"Vash was out there too," I remind her. "Don't you want to spend your time with him?"

Kleio laughs, and I swear it carries all the way up to the scattered stars above. "Vash is just a boy," she states airily.

I eye her incredulously, and my second sticks out her tongue, making me chuckle.

"Okay, he is a boy that I've been more than a little obsessed with for a few years, but he's still just a boy. You're my best friend. You're my sister." Her eyes shine with so much warmth it makes my throat feel too tight.

Her choice of words also reminds me of something. "You know," I say casually, gauging her reaction. "If by some miracle I happen *not* to die in the rest of these trials, we could be sailing under a TideLord. We might even get some assignments near the Pearl Sea."

"Asha," Kleio breathes, the name full of meaning.

I nod before adding, "We could start looking for her, get intel from any islands or drifters nearby. If I won, I bet I could even put in a request with the TideLord to help us gather news of her."

Kleio swallows thickly, her eyes brimming with unspoken hope. "I would never ask that of you—"

"You would never have to," I cut her off firmly. "Like you said, we're sisters. Which would make Asha kind of like a little sister too, of sorts."

Kleio looks to the stars, letting a few rare tears fall. "You would love her. I mean, she would also definitely annoy you to death with her babbling. You have no idea, she can just go on and *on*."

I give Kleio a pointed look.

"Hm, I have *no* idea what that must be like."

My fervent wish from the night upon the nets appears to have been granted.

We resume courses as normal just a few days after the first pillar task. Entering Preceptor Beldham's class finds Captain Agni's pack of males holding our usual table hostage. However, the head seat is noticeably *empty*.

A delightfully sinister smile curves my lips, and I beeline for the empty chair. I don't have to check to know the others have followed my line of thought.

I've spent a lot of time marinating over Kleio's words and decided she made some solid points. I've been restraining myself to the point of chafing at nearly every point of conflict in order to shield my crew. I'm not about to revert all the way back to the little bastard-born menace of years prior, but perhaps somewhere in between.

Balance.

Captain Agni's second, Vagar Ophios, glances up in obvious dislike at my sudden presence.

"Hi boys," I purr, my eyes scanning each of the southern males occupying our seats. "You'll be giving us our table back today, seeing as how your king appears to be missing and therefore unable to claim his throne."

Something unreadable passes in the navy irises of Captain Agni's second.

"Fuck off, northern bitch," barks out one of his other crew.

My attention slides over to the boy sitting directly across from Vagar. His upturned features are haughty, and his dark hair is shorn tight on the sides. Jade-colored eyes watch me with clear disgust.

Adiram Uthra, Captain Agni's third in command.

I 'tut', my hands curling on the back of my chair. "I guess I shouldn't be too surprised they haven't taught you all manners down south, but since you're here residing in the *civilized* north, it's customary to return things to whom they belong. Like my seat."

In one swift movement, I pull out the wooden chair and plop myself down before anyone has a chance to object. My smirk meets each of their murderous faces. All seven pairs of eyes around the table now reflect Adiram's disgust.

I promised to earn Agni's abhorrence, and I intend to do just that.

Placing both my legs up on the table like a personal footstool, I lean back with a bemused expression. "Now, why don't you all pretend to be gentlemen for a minute and give my girls their seats back. Bonus points if you pull the chair out for them."

Vagar's eyes burn with anger, and his mouth turns downwards in a sneer, *perfect*.

He moves to grab me, but quicker than a ligetung eel, Herse's hand slams down, and a butterfly blade nails the sleeve of his crimson uniform into the wooden table. Vagar's gaze flashes to my third with a look of real surprise. She gives him a cool smirk in return.

"Careful," I croon. "Herse has plenty more of those, and I would hate to see you lose something *infinitely* more valuable than a shirt next time." My eyes flicker below his belt with meaning.

"Get out of our captain's seat, you *squid*," growls another of Agni's crew members, his hands slamming down flat on the table before him.

My brows raise when finding the culprit, this one appears a bit more fiery than the others. There's a thick white scar across his tanned face, stretching from just under his left eye over the bridge of his nose and ending at the top of his right cheekbone. The male's inky hair is pulled back in a similar style to Raider Ophios, his lip curls under my study.

Giving him a sickly sweet smile, I purr in return, "Make me."

A cold snap abruptly whips down on his exposed hands as hard as any switch. He yelps out loudly in pain before spitting what I'd guess is a string of profanities in their southern tongue.

Vagar is fuming, and he stands up from his spot so violently that his chair clatters back to the ground. He plucks the butterfly blade from his pinned shirt and keeps his gaze locked on Herse while sliding it into the front pocket of his jacket. Her violet eyes narrow dangerously in turn.

"*Abeamus*," he grunts towards the rest of Captain Agni's crew, still watching the exchange. The males leave their spots begrudgingly and follow Vagar with looks of deep hatred thrown my way.

Kleio slides into her usual seat on my left with an approving grin that matches the rest of my crew's expressions. I smirk and enjoy allowing myself a bit of leeway on my own personal leash.

"Better watch out you southern shits!" Prisca calls across the room.

"Prisca darling, I believe the official title they prefer is South Cardinal Order shitheads," Nephthys chides her sister while imitating their haughty southern accents.

"Oh yes, quite right, Nephthys dear. My deepest apologies, how very uncouth of me. Wouldn't want to offend their more *delicate* sensibilities," Prisca agrees, giving the one with a scar a wink.

If looks could kill, I'd be out two crew members.

Sliding deeper into my seat, I relish the feeling of reclaiming my spot.

I spend the rest of Preceptor Beldham's lecture imagining the look on Agni's face whenever he deigns to rejoin us again.

XIV. SCARRED

The rest of our first week after the initial pillar task passes in blissful ease.

Without Agni there to vex me at every turn, the other southern raiders are much more manageable. And by manageable, I mean easier to ignore.

Even Corvina is suspiciously quiet, though I still find her gaze on me often. I'm aware when she leans in to whisper something snidely to one of her crew, exactly *who* it's regarding. But she hasn't made another move against me. I wonder if she isn't waiting for me to make mine first.

When Corvina isn't whispering nasty pointed insults, she's cooing over Olsson's supposed heroism in the trial. I've overheard her chatting loudly with several other southern raiders about his horrific injuries. They lamented weepily for days about how very unfair it was for him to be given a beast so much more dangerous than any of the others. Including her own.

My blood thrashes in memory of just what exactly the prick did to his kelpie, but I keep my mouth shut.

Agni isn't the only one absent after the first pillar.

One of the western captains, Ansil Tetsuo, is said to have spiral broken his leg and hasn't been seen since. Reed Namak, the eastern captain, only returned just yesterday. Vash was lucky enough to get away with some tonics from the leeches and claims his cracked rib is a scratch.

We're down to three weeks until the next pillar trial, and Preceptor Oplon has begun assigning us opponents outside of our cardinal. So far, the experiment hasn't gone too poorly. Only a handful of prohibited affinity fights have broken out. Nearly all of them started by the south.

I've been paired up against almost every other captain's second in command.

The toughest to win by far was unsurprisingly Corvina's. Aella Bellum, I've now learned, is her name. Raider Bellum is just as skilled as I suspected, maybe even more so. Her strikes with the bo-staff we practiced on were damn near lethal. I managed to outmaneuver her in the end with quick footwork that Herse has helped to drill me on, but my shins are still barking in protest.

Today Preceptor Oplon is having us return to the basics in an effort to determine next week's pairings. We'll be partnered with someone outside our cardinal and expected to use three blades of choice as our allotted weapons. The first one to submit, of course, loses.

I'm sent to the far left corner per usual and begin stretching while awaiting my opponent.

A shadow falls across one side of the mat I occupy.

"Ah, so it's the squid for me today," someone says from above, the deep male voice like smoke sliding over gravel.

I turn around, and my eyes dart upwards. There's a scowl already plastered across my expression and a smart-ass retort just waiting on my tongue, but I stop short at the sight of Agni's face.

He's come back marked.

My swallow is tight.

The scar is wild and jagged as it slices through his left onyx brow, just narrowly missing his eye, before scattering down to the edge of his sharp jawline in the unmistakable pattern of branched lightning. The marking is made even more shocking by its odd coloring. Its strange hue reflects that of molten gold, the exact same auric shade of his kelpie's lighting.

It seems as though he was branded in turn—*interesting.*

"*Vide nonnihil vos lubido?*" Agni asks, his tone mocking.

His foreign words snatch me from my thoughts, and I realize I've been staring. Standing up from my sitting position on the mats I glower at him in an effort to hide the flush creeping up my neck in embarrassment. His smirk lets me know that whatever he said was somehow insulting.

"So the asshole survives," I muse while tightening the gold pin in my hair and checking the security of my blades. "What a pity. I already had my pyre-burning outfit all picked out."

Those amber eyes flicker, his mouth twisting into a familiar sneer. "Sorry to disappoint."

I'm silent while watching the southern prick move into position at the other end of our mat. He pulls out three daggers from his person, they look so different from any I've seen before that it's a struggle to conceal my curiosity. The blade on them is violently jagged, and the metal is a dark obsidian shade that shines with a curious ruby hue under the nearby orb lights.

Agni tosses two of them onto the side of the mat, and I look at him in question.

He scoffs in return. "I can handle *you* without needing any weapons. But I say we make today's challenge a bit more interesting." The jackass is sure to put enough emphasis on the word 'you' to convey the many layers of loathing and disgust that he associates with who and what I am.

"Oh? Do tell," I drawl, my tone bored. Though, annoyingly, I'm rather intrigued by the dare.

Agni's eyes darken before me. "I say one blade each, otherwise hand to hand. Unless you're too scared, of course," he taunts with another smirk. "Last time you did go down *pathetically* easy."

My face sours at the memory of him disarming me. I can't resist the temptation of a challenge, however, and begin discarding my weapons one by one over to the pile where his own lies.

"Fine by me. One blade is all I need to give that pretty little scar of yours a twin," I mock, resuming my position at the opposite end of the mat. His eyes on me smolder with contempt.

"Ready?" Agni asks with the sharp tilt of his chin.

I nod in silent confirmation, and our dance begins.

I strike first, relying on the one edge I have against an opponent as massive and powerful as the Southern captain—speed. Moving fast, I go for a deceptive maneuver, a swift feint followed by a sharp kick, a tactic that has never failed me before.

Agni dodges my blade with infuriating ease before catching my leg in the next moment.

"Predictable." He 'tsks' and the room moves in a blur of motion as I'm promptly slammed onto my back. The impact is sudden enough that I'm left without air. Suffocating fury rises up inside.

I've kept my grip on my dagger, so I focus first on getting a breath inside my lungs, then I lunge for his thigh second. He knocks away my attack with a lightning swift block from his forearm, but I still manage to graze him with the passing edge of my blade. Using the impact of his block, I roll out from under him with a grunt, and in a flash, I'm back up on my feet.

"Effective," I counter, nodding to his torn sleeve, now budding a line of cherry.

He gives a cold, unfeeling laugh before pouncing, his jagged blade slicing through the air with deadly precision. I sidestep him, feeling a rush of air pass dangerously close as the ruby weapon narrowly misses my shoulder. I move in next for a quick counterattack, aiming a punch at Agni's torso. He blocks it effortlessly, and I swear as the impact of his deflection vibrates up my arm.

"Anyone ever tell you before that you fight like a drunkard?" Agni inquires snidely while deftly moving around my person. "Must be a sign of bad breeding."

My teeth clench together, and my jaw sets in annoyance. I'm determined to catch him off guard. I need to find his weak spot—any vulnerabilities in his fighting-style that I can exploit.

"Anyone ever tell you to shut the fuck up?" I snap before launching a series of quick strikes, aiming for any gap in the southern captain's defense.

He parries each blow with preternatural skill. His movements are so impossibly fluid and controlled that it's throwing me off my game. I've never seen someone move like him, and that includes the entirety of the Cardinal South Order raiders.

Agni catches my next blow with his free hand. He gives me a flash of his capricious smirk before yanking my captured arms, so I'm forced to spin until my back hits the solid wall of his chest.

"*Fuck.*" I'm practically seething.

My chest heaves with renewed fury. He's so obnoxiously tall that slamming my head backwards won't make any kind of impact. His weapon arm is now across my upper ribs, and it feels like solid steel. I'm effectively held prisoner against the unyielding planes of his stupidly firm body.

Agni hisses in my ear with the slash of a wicked smile, "Just as *wild* as ever I see."

"Fuck you," I spit before stomping down on his foot as hard as I possibly can.

"Godsdamned—*brat*" he barks out in pain, loosening his hold.

I tear free from his clutches with a laugh before whirling back around to face him, the dagger still in my grasp. Others have stopped their practice to watch our spar. I can practically feel the eyes of his crew as well as my own burning onto our backs. I don't allow for the distraction.

Agni comes at me next with a self-assured blow that's poised for my neck when I spin around and kick. My mouth hooks upwards as I finally feel the satisfying 'thunk' of my blow landing.

Even better, I managed to kick his weapon arm.

The ruby-hued blade in his grip goes flying to the end of the mat. I laugh again, and the sound of it, mixed with the loss of his blade, sends a wave of rage rippling across his striking features.

I take advantage of his lack of a weapon and move with a well-placed jab to the throat. He dips at the last second, and my blade kisses the air above his head. The southern prick grabs my arm next, and something in my gut twists as I realize the obvious move he's about to pull on me.

I'm such a fucking moron.

Agni yanks me forward before flipping me around his body so that I smack down hard onto the ground once more. Vital air is once again stolen from my person, and I gasp.

"As I said, *predictable,*" he sneers.

It's almost not possible to believe his arm appeared snapped clean in half only a week ago. If I hadn't witnessed it with my own eyes, I'd have said they lied about the extent of his injuries.

There isn't any breath left in my lungs to respond to his insults. Not letting my affinity escape is my main focus. The use of our powers is strictly prohibited during Oplon's class, not to mention the embarrassment of not having it under control as a level-eight.

Quick as a sail catches wind, he maneuvers my hand into an unbreaking hold before driving his knee into my ribcage. My breathy cursing is guttural, and I feel the room temperature both rising and falling around me while a flush blooms inside my chest. A mixture of wrath and humiliation begins simmering in my blood as Agni forces the weapon from my grip.

He takes my borrowed blade and lightly grazes the lethal edge of the gleaming dagger down my cheek in mockery of my recent taunt regarding his scar. His quicksilver grin above me is smug.

Then he angles the dagger beneath my neck, and I go still.

"And you wonder why I know I'm better than you?" Agni murmurs, almost to himself.

The pure arrogance in his eyes is kindling to my ire. I rear up and spit in his freshly scared face, nicking myself in the process. His smugness turns to unchecked outrage in a blink, exactly as I had hoped.

Agni's arm instinctively moves to wipe his face, and I take that as my cue to push upwards with all my strength. The southern captain makes a dark sound of annoyance as I roll out from beneath him and jump back up to my feet.

I laugh without amusement. "Come again? Last I checked, our scores were tied, asshole."

He shakes his head at me like my very existence is a troubling question to him. Before he can make another move, I go for his feet with brazen speed and swipe them out from under him. The staggering male goes down satisfyingly hard.

I'm on him in an instant.

Without a blade, I'm left to my own devices, and my arm squeezes around his neck in a vise. Unfortunately for me, instead of grabbing for release from my hold as I'd expect, he gets his hands on the back of my thighs and twists. I lose my leverage as Agni rolls us until he's on top.

My gods.

His forearm presses down against my throat while his muscular body lays firmly between my thighs. There's no chance of repeating my last escape. All I can see are the fiery embers of self-assured satisfaction in his eyes. All I can feel is the pressing weight of him against me.

I'm acting out of instinct now, and a free hand goes for a punch to his vulnerable throat.

He catches my fist with blinding speed just before I make contact in a grip of solid iron and pins it down against the mat above my head. Removing his forearm from my throat, he grabs my other tightly balled fist and pins that one up above as well with an aggravating smirk.

"I *am* better than you, there's no doubt about that fact," he mutters before lowering himself closer to my person. "As for the scores, you got lucky the Tide-Lords took pity on a squid."

My vision reddens around the edges.

Piece. Of. Shit.

Agni's face moves slowly down to mine as if I'm some sort of strange creature he'd like to inspect. He comes so near that his lips almost brush against my own. I discover his new scar is even more menacing up close, and a craven breath catches in my throat.

I hate him.

I hate him so much it's suffocating.

Agni moves back a touch while his eyes flicker down my person with dark brows furrowed in disdain. "How are you this little?" he mutters in question, sounding somehow both irked and surprised by the obvious difference in our statures.

My blood damn near freezes beneath his study. Locking my legs behind his back, I give all my effort to buck him off and pray to the drowned gods that he's unbalanced enough for it to work. Unfortunately, the gods do not care about my wishes.

My bucking only serves to spark up something wicked in his eyes. They glitter maliciously before he pins me down harder. Every plane of his body is now driving me into the mat, and I think I catch something like starvation flitting briefly through his gaze before his teeth clench.

My breathing hitches from the impact of his added weight.

A muscle in his jaw flickers.

"*Quare non vos futuere illa iam?*" someone asks, disrupting our brawl with a barking laugh.

Glancing up, I find it's his second in command, Raider Ophios. I *hate* not knowing what they're saying, especially when it's so obviously about me. From the mean glint in Vagar's navy eyes, I can tell Captain Agni's second is far from over our little table debacle.

His gaze never leaves mine even while snapping back at Vagar, "*Noli vi ego posuit a rostrum in te.*"

Raider Ophios lets out a dark chuckle in return to whatever terrible comment his captain has no doubt just made about me. Then, with sudden abruptness, Agni lets go of his hold on my wrists before getting off of my person entirely. I begin inhaling greedy gulps of air while he stands.

The south captain tosses my blade back onto the mat beside me before turning to collect the one I disarmed from him along with the rest of his discarded pile at the end of our makeshift area.

He nears his second, and I hear Vagar whisper to his captain's passing figure, as if I can even understand them. "*Scis quid acciderit cum ignis et glacies miscentur... res admodum humidae fiunt.*"

Agni glances back at me, and I notice his obsidian hair is indecently messy from our brawl. I've moved up to a kneeling position, currently focusing on the free expanse of my ribs as I can finally breathe again. His full lips pull upward in the corners, and cruel amusement is plain in his gaze while amber eyes access me once more.

"*Illa facit vultus bonum on sua genua, annon?*" he asks Vagar with a wink.

His second almost chokes on his resounding howl of a laugh.

Fucking mongrels.

I'm left rising from the mat, shaking in a freezing rage. I don't bother waiting for my crew to finish their rounds before storming out of the training chambers in the wake of my growing abandon. I'm crammed full of emotions that I'm decidedly not equipped to handle.

Uncomfortable heat and embarrassment and loathing and something else I can't quite place consumes me. Whatever it is, it writhes inside of my veins like a living being and stirs my affinity into a foreign frenzy of unrest. My power is straining at the leash, begging to be untethered.

Regardless of the conversation I had with Kleio and regardless of my resolve to give myself a bit more leeway, the same *cannot* be said for my affinity. To let it loose is far more dangerous than allowing myself some backtalk.

I tear down the rocky tunnel passage, my thunderous thoughts surrounding Agni and his cretinous southern tongue. Laughter from ahead drifts out to bait my straining temper, laughter I recognize from its musical quality. I know it's Captain Leporem before rounding the corner.

Corvina and two of her crew members chat in an alcove of the hallway before me in barely hushed voices. One of the two is her second, Raider Bellum, the other is a tall, slender-built boy. His brown hair is cut short, and his nose is strikingly sharp. I don't know the male's name, but the vicious glimmer in his eyes tells me what they've been laughing about.

Or rather, *who*.

Corvina's smile is feline while taking in the state of me. I can only imagine what sort of dishevelment I'm in, but I don't care. There is ice, bitter and cruel, thrashing inside of me, demanding to be heard. It's taking the better part of my focus not to allow for that. She steps into my path, as do her two crew members, and I bite back a growl of annoyance.

"Move," I bark out.

It's both a warning and a demand.

Her emerald eyes glitter like venom against the sheen of her silky raven braid. "Why would I do that? You didn't even ask politely." Corvina fakes a pout with the cross of her arms.

"Fucking *move,*" I demand, my voice low and vitriolic. The power is building into a pounding headache, and my temples are beginning to throb. I need to get out of here as quickly as possible.

Her smile widens to a grin while looking me up and down. "Maybe I should *show* you how asking politely is done," she purrs darkly. Raider Bellum and the unnamed male on her right snicker, clearly in on the joke.

Corvina's voice takes on an ethereal tone, like snow falling on calm midnight waters, as she orders, "Get on your knees and beg me, *squid.*"

"Oh Olsson is going to fucking *love* you for this," the male raider jeers, his eyes alight and greedy to watch me grovel.

My body moves without permission. I find my knees slamming into the stone floor of the tunnel. Rock bites into my skin and I think I hear something splinter. The voice that slides past my lips is not my own when I plead, “Please move.”

They all roar with laughter.

"Ugh, you’re every bit as pathetic as Olsson said. I’m not even sure you really have an affinity. You certainly are *weak* for an elemental.” Corvina’s smile turns saccharine. “Beg me again.”

“P—please move, Captain Leporem," I beg, my body and voice no longer under my command. I’m struggling to keep a hold of my affinity in its increasingly feral unruliness.

There is both keen amusement and and an edge of hunger in Corvina’s gaze. She doesn’t even have a clue as to what kind of danger she’s in. Perhaps that’s my own fault. I probably should have retaliated sooner, should have given them a taste of who I really am. So they would understand that there is in fact a monster lurking just beneath my skin.

Clearly, what she’s asked of me is not enough.

Corvina tilts her head and speaks again with that bewitching voice, "Oh, you can do better than that *surely* after all the trouble you’ve caused. You’re nothing but an offensive little mistake, you know that? Your entire crew should have their sanity checked.” Her own crew members' laughter encourages the silver-tongued captain further.

“So why don’t you tell us how you’re just a pathetically worthless squid first, apologize for being so rude to Olsson second—” the thrashing power in my veins revolts with a vengeance at the mention of his name. Corvina’s eyes flash before she finishes her listed demands with, “And then... then I think I’d like you to kiss my ring.”

She extends her hand out to me.

Raider Bellum sucks in a breath of shock.

What she’s demanding from me is the utmost insult a captain can ever bestow. To fall into her affinity’s trap and kiss her captaincy ring would be akin to removing my own title. I cannot begin to fathom the hatred and monstrous thrill in Corvina's expectant gaze. Clearly there's an issue here going a hell of a lot deeper than The Vault.

She's fucking insane.

Corvina pushes her hand out closer to me with a widening smirk.

The cold inside of me is nothing now compared to the wild pounding that's begun from the other side of my affinity. It's an impudent feeling, one I've been trying desperately to avoid triggering. It hammers brutally inside of me, the beat is deep and heavy and *savage*.

"Aw, she's trying to fight it," Corvina coos, like my resolve is adorable. The nameless boy lets out a mocking laugh, but Raider Bellum is silent as she watches me through suspicious eyes.

"Well, I'll make this easy." Their captain's gaze narrows into slits. "Kiss. My. Rings." Her enchanting words are full to the brim with absolution.

If it wasn't for the roaring in my head, I would have heard her. I would have grabbed her hand and kissed her rings and disgraced myself and my crew. I would have thrown away our future in one moment of weakness.

Unluckily for Corvina, I don't.

The palpable fury that's been licking me up from the inside, courtesy of my recent time spent with the *other* southern captain, explodes in a wave of violent, unchecked power. Her crew members are flung backwards with the impact of a freezing cold blast. Their bodies smack *hard* into the dark stone walls and crumple with a sickening thud.

Corvina looks around in startled surprise, the only one not having been thrown.

Standing from the frigid floor, I very much enjoy the trepidation that begins creeping into her eyes. As if she's just now realizing what exactly she's provoked. I take a measured step in her direction, my affinity urging me on, whispering to me its hungry plea for violence.

"I never got to repay you for that incident with the evening stars," I say, taking another step closer. Captain Leporem's eyes are calculating. Her mouth opens, and I'm sure she's poised to spout those entrancing words once more, but the thudding of something beneath my affinity is deafening.

I reach out with a hand and find it next around Corvina's delicate throat before it's slamming her against the dim tunnel wall. She splutters with the impact, and I slam her again, delighting in the cracking sound of her skull against stone—a little *too* much.

My hand quickly becomes a vise around her most potent weapon. "I was going to just forget you tried to *kill* me and move on, you know," I whisper, enjoying the way her eyes widen in alarm as I cut off her air source.

Corvina struggles to speak through my freezing grip. "I didn't know–know about the–the ehkinos," she chokes out.

The look I give her is full of disbelief. Frost has begun coating the tunnel, and my breaths start coming out in little clouds. There's a blue tinge to Corvina's lips now that has nothing to do with her current lack of oxygen. Releasing my grip from her throat, she gasps out loudly for air.

Her eyes darken on me, and I know her next move will be a mistake.

"You fucking bitch!" She seethes through bared teeth. "You should be *dead*. You and your entire crew are worthless, pathetic, cunt—"

I stop her mid-sentence with a cold snap, shoving her harshly against the wall. The pounding inside of me isn't finished, it guides me in pulling the moisture from the air and freezing her to the spot. Finally, I seal Corvina's lips together. Her wide eyes stare at me with true horror.

Good. Let her see what I am.

What I battle with every single day.

I lean in close to whisper in a deadly sort of calm, "*Never* insult my crew."

Glancing up to where ice shackles currently pin her arms up above, I notice that her ring-laden hands are slender, elegant, and exposed. A truly sinister smile dances along my lips as I pluck one of those hands free to inspect it. Corvina sounds like she might be trying to shout something, but her lips are still frozen tight.

"You wanted me to kiss your ring, right?" I ask sweetly, turning her struggling hand over to expose the golden bands. Captain Leporem makes a throaty sort of growl in return, and I bring her hand closer with a smirk. "I think I can do you one better."

Her emerald gaze is wide, but I'm too heady with the thumping rhythm of something far more barbaric than my affinity to stop. If there's one thing I learned shortly into my time with the Tide Raiders, you have to cut off threats before they become promises kept.

I take the finger adorned with her southern captain's signet and press my lips upon it. Her eyes widen even further before a scream attempts to escape her locked lips. I watch in satisfaction as her finger blooms purple at the tip and begins to blacken as my kiss of deadly frostbite spreads.

With a snap of my fingers, she's released from the wall just as her friends are beginning to stir and gather their bearings. Her second in command looks around in startled confusion at the alarming sounds of Corvina's tight-lipped screaming.

"You'll want to get to the sick bay quickly," I advise their captain with a smirk. Her eyes on me are full of rage, and I add with a false smile, "If you wait too long, it'll be the whole hand they have to cut off. Somehow, I just don't think that'll be the sort of thing your *adoring* Olsson will be able to overlook."

Corvina gives me one last glare of utter repulsion before storming off down the tunnel in a panicked jog. Her two crew members look like they're still trying to piece together what's just happened, but at the sight of their captain fleeing, they quickly follow after with matching death glares thrown in my direction.

The incessant beating inside of me has at last eased, satiated by my ugly display.

The icy power belonging to my affinity dulls into its more easily managed state and coils back down inside of me like a slumbering hound. I'm left alone to ruminate over whether there's any truth in Corvina's confession before beginning to dread what that slip of power might cost me.

XV. THE OD

"Who can tell me the name of the first landmass to fall under the Sol Empire?" Preceptor Chie's leathery voice inquiries of our class.

I'm unable to so much as raise my hand without searing pain blooming along my sides, so I keep quiet, and one of the western raiders answers, "The Isle of Andesite."

Preceptor Chie nods while stroking the length of his powder white goatee. "Why is it that Andesite Isle fell first?" The same raider answers him without missing a beat, "Because of Mt. Zyphos. The rulers of Andesite agreed to an alliance in order to stop the impending eruption from wiping them out."

Our ancient preceptor nods again, his face grave. "Correct, the people of Andesite believed the eruption of Mt. Zyphos to be unavoidable, but Emperor Anatolius provided them with an alternative that could not be refused," he explains, hobbling to the back salt-stained shelves lining the walls of his lyceum. Each shelf is full of dozens of rows; every row contains countless objects and knickknacks.

Preceptor Chie pulls out something from one of the lower shelves beneath my eye level and stands, turning back to face us. He holds up what appears to be a mangled bit of rectangular fabric. I can tell the color of it is supposed to be white, but at this point it's so tattered it looks more gray than anything. From this angle, it's hard to be sure, but I *think* fish are beaded into the fabric to give the illusion that they're swimming up the swatch.

I lean forward to get a closer look and wince at the agony flaring along my ribs. Kleio's hand brushes mine, and I glance over to find her eyes brimming with worry. Shaking my head incrementally, I silently warn her *now is not the time.* She bites her bottom lip like she's debating arguing with me but then turns her attention back to the lesson.

After being unceremoniously ripped from my bed by an angry pounding at our cabin's door in the middle of the night, I was led up to our Grand Preceptor's quarters and made to wait before his freshly lit hearth until the others arrived. The 'others' being the accusing party of the South Order. I knew this would likely be the end result. I'm just grateful none of my crew were dragged down into it with me.

I lost control of my affinity. It would have been idiotic to think I might have gotten away with it.

Saubarag had come barreling in, holding her blackened finger aloft and waving it angrily in his metal hand. He claimed it would sabotage his captain's chances for winning The Vault.

Then hell froze over, and Skelm began questioning my defense. "Is it not true, Captain Leporem, that you used your own affinity against Captain Boreas here and asked her to kiss your ring?" Corvina was then forced to admit her own hand in the matter leading up to the incident. "And I am also correct in recounting that *you* were the one who intervened during Captain Boreas's and Raider LeRoi's training round? Leaving a northern captain *unconscious* for multiple days before the first pillar trial?"

By the end of his line of questions, Corvina looked ill, and Saubarag was almost white with rage at the information his captain had failed to inform him of before storming up here.

Skelm had growled angrily at the southern Grand Preceptor. "I looked the other way with that previous incident, *Deverell*. I allowed you to punish your charge however you deemed fit—which was *clearly* not effective. Do not mistake our history for a sign of deficiency." The skin around his golden-covered eye socket tightened with the warning. "This is my cardinal, and you are here as a guest. Do *not* abuse your welcome."

Corvina and I remained motionless as the two Grand Preceptors stood glowering at each other. Finally, Saubarag gave Skelm a relenting nod before dragging Captain Leporem back with him to their ships. I wasn't stupid enough to think my actions would go unpunished. Although I *was* surprised at Skelm's praise that followed the eight lashings I received, four on each side.

"Impressive bit of affinity work there. Something I believe that both Bealu and Ersatz have worked tirelessly to pull from you these last few years, to no avail." His one good eye studied me, dripping with blood on the rug before his blazing hearth as I struggled to see straight through the pain. "Perhaps they simply did not know the right *motivations* for you."

A shiver ran through me from the meaning in his words.

When I finally gathered myself to leave, Skelm added sharply, "Don't go to the sick bay or that leech on your crew for healing until after tomorrow's lessons."

Dispelling the memories of last night's events, I refocus on the lesson in progress and the tattered piece of material that Preceptor Chie continues to hold aloft for our observation.

"Can anyone tell me what this is?" he asks, his rheumy eyes scanning the rows of western and northern raiders.

I turn in my seat and catch sight of the western Grand Regent, who's started to sit in on this course as he shifts his weight beside the entrance. The dark khol around his eyes makes it almost impossible to tell what he's thinking, but his body angles slightly, seemingly in interest. No one speaks or raises a hand in answer to the preceptor's question. I personally have no idea where that swatch of embellished material might have come from.

Chie frowns, and his eyes dim with a nod. "This is the original flag of Andesite Isle. A flag that is no longer in use as its culture was swallowed up by the Sol Empire. The white of the flag once represented their independence, while the gold-beaded fish depict the auricfins that used to repopulate in great swells near their island."

He continues his lecture by listing the names of the subsequent islands that fell shortly after. Within decades of Andesite, we learn that the isles of Rhyolatia, Basulto, Pomice, and Dioriten all melted into the arms of the Sol Empire. Preceptor Chie tells us, "These first five land masses later went on to become the province we now know today as the 'Iron Fist' of the Sol Empire."

"That sounds like a sexual request, doesn't it?" I hear Nephthys whisper to Prisca, who tries to smother her laughter with an unconvincing coughing fit.

Kleio gives the twins a look of reprimand, but I catch how her mouth is fighting not to pull upwards. My own lips twitch in respite of amusement.

We leave Chie's class to make way for the outdoor lyceums, where Ersatz is still making us train even with the rainy season more than well underway. I think she enjoys the way the mud makes our obstacle courses that much more difficult.

My gait is stiff-backed while walking across the trestle, and I fight against the fresh pain along my ribs when turning a bit too sharply at the questioning call of my name, "Captain Boreas?"

Gritting my teeth through the agony, I discover Brisa standing beside the entrance to the open-air bridge. I glance at Kleio and nod, signaling for her to head on with the others to Ersatz class.

"Captain Bedivere," I return in greeting before striding her way.

Her charm-coiled braids, tied back in a high plait atop her head, give her upturned features a more regal than predatorial appearance today. Those steel-colored eyes flicker to the air above my head before glancing back at my approaching form.

"Your crew is very... protective," she comments with a small twitch of her lips.

I glance over a shoulder to find Kleio, Herse, and Greer all waiting on the other side of the open-air bridge with gazes narrowed in our direction. Rolling my eyes, I motion for them to move on with a huff of annoyance. The three of them look poised to argue but I give them a glare that has them thinking otherwise, and they finally depart for the rainy afternoon with Ersatz.

"They can be," I admit, meeting Brisa's gaze.

I don't mention that the events of yesterday have set my crew atop a razor's edge of suspicion towards every other captain here. I'm not positive I've talked Herse and Greer completely out of their brewing plot to somehow shave Corvina's head. The twins are incorrigible; they think my use of frostbite was a stroke of comedic genius, and they even asked Captain Leporem this morning at breakfast if they might get to sneak a peek at her new 'accessory'.

"I wondered if we might chat, briefly?" Captain Bedivere asks, her head angling to one of the open alcoves lining the hallway.

Raiders of all levels scurry around us in the brief period between lessons and training.

I eye Brisa with uncertainty. "Regarding?"

She laughs. "I'm not going to use my affinity to throw you over the side of the building if that's what you're worried about. I'm actually quite fond of my fingers," Brisa adds with a knowing smirk before heading towards the open alcove.

Against my better judgement, I follow.

My body is still yelping in protest with nearly every step, but I manage to join her on the ledge overlooking the crashing sea. I shut the glass doors behind me, knowing this might just be my last moronic move. Yet there's *something* about the western captain that I feel inclined to trust.

I'm not daft enough to be blind to the obvious threat she poses, but I can't help feeling her motives are not dissimilar from my own.

"Alright, let's chat."

I wait until the end of dinner before cornering Vash.

Well, I don't so much as corner him, as I do take a page from his book and snag Larceon by the neck of his uniform as he aims to leave the dining chamber. Ignoring his gasping sounds of choking, I drag him roughly into the nearest empty hallway before letting him lose again.

Vash whirls to face me with bewildered eyes. "You *yanked*?"

"I did," I agree, glancing around the empty corridor and realizing that it's not isolated enough, with various raiders spilling out from the nearby chamber. "We need to go somewhere more private," I mutter, trying to think of somewhere that might be quiet enough and away from unwanted ears to discuss.

Finally, it dawns on me. I know the perfect spot.

"Come on!" I call out, beginning to trek down the empty hall.

Vash watches me with uncertain eyes but eventually follows after. I take the winding staircase steps two at a time until we've made it to the top of one of the black thistle-like spires.

"Alright, lets go," I order, opening a large window that reveals black netting below.

Vash looks from me to the open window, then to the ten-foot drop onto dangerously wide knotted cording, his expression filled with alarm. "Are you insane? You don't know these nets are even stable! Wait—Boreas—is Captain Leporem making you do this?"

Giving him a side eye full of annoyance, I wordlessly crawl through the window and drop down to the netting, landing neatly on my feet. Looking up, I find Vash sticking his head of bronze waves out the open window with a frown full of unease.

"Come on, Larceon, your girlfriend makes this jump all the time," I taunt from below.

I don't deem it necessary to mention that technically we've never been on these *particular* nets before. Mine and Kleio's usual spot is around the second highest spire, or sometimes we walk the nets lining the edge of the, but I'd never show Vash either. These ropes feel sturdy as any others beneath my feet, so what he doesn't know won't hurt him.

Vash tumbles more than jumps from the open window, coughs on air, and rolls over the cording before finally making it to a sitting position with a dark scowl. I glance down at him with one brow raised. "That was *very* graceful. Truly. Your stealth affinity is one for the ages."

"Ha ha," Vash retorts, standing at last and brushing himself off. "Now will you tell me what the hell is going on? You're acting strange."

He's right, my weight keeps shifting from my toes to my heels with nerves, and I'm suddenly reminded of Nimra. I glance around once more to be sure there's no way for anyone to overhear.

Satisfied, the next words practically fall out of my mouth. "What if I told you I *know* what the next pillar trial is—or at least I know some of the major pieces?"

The golden flecks in Vash's green eyes brighten with intrigue before clouding over with doubt. "I'd ask how you could possibly know what it is and then follow up with—are you *insane*?"

I bristle at his words, explaining snappishly, "I know what it is because I was given a tip-off by a source that I'm very inclined to trust."

Vash eyes me like I really might've gone mad before swiping a hand down his face in exasperation. "You are *inclined* to trust? Sea hags tits, Boreas," he curses, shaking his head in disbelief before snorting. "Fine—just tell me what it is that you *think* you know."

My eyes narrow with a frown before answering him. "We won't be doing the next pillar task individually. We'll be working in pairs with our cardinal captains. It actually makes sense when you think about it. In levels one and two, we're taught endurance and survival but then in levels three and four, the training shifts into Vek and Brek and we focus on—"

"Alliances," Vash says, taking the word from my mouth. I nod, and he rubs the scruff along his jaw in contemplation. "Okay, that tracks, but there's always two ends to every pillar. If alliances are one end, then what's the other?"

"Weaknesses," I answer. "I don't know exactly how it will play into the trial, but I'd bet my captain's ring it has something to do with our affinities."

Vash nods again, looking over the netting and towards the darkened sea beyond, appearing lost in thought for a moment.

"And who is your source, exactly?" he suddenly asks, as if just remembering that tidbit.

My hands move to twist the end of my white braid around an idle finger. "I can only tell you if you swear an od not to reveal their identity to anyone."

Vash blinks at me in response. "You sure are wearing that dramatic flair today. Why is an od necessary?" He questions, crossing his arms before the width of his chest. "I am your co-captain after all. We've been through seven years—almost eight here together. I'm also currently dating your best friend. Do you seriously still not trust me?"

I tilt my head to the side and study him with a frown. "Od or no dice."

Vash sighs a long stream of annoyance. "Alright," he concedes, pulling out a piece of metal from the band around his arm and flicking out a menacingly sharp blade. I watch in silence as he swipes the edge across his palm, and crimson blooms beneath. Vash then tugs off his captain's ring from its spot on his right hand and grips it in his bloody palm.

The corners of his mouth pull down in irritation as he grumbles, "I swear on my captaincy title not to reveal the identity of your source, or may the drowned gods take back my affinity and pull me back down to their deep, dark netherdepths."

I give him a smile in satisfaction. "See, that wasn't so hard."

He gives me a look filled with ire. "Okay, now tell me."

"Captain Bedivere, from the West Order."

Vash's mouth hangs open. "You made me swear an *od* for that? Are you joking? Why on Pontus would you think that she would ever give *you* or *me* any sort of advantage? I swear, Merena, you've taken one too many hits to the head or—"

"She isn't trying to give us an advantage—she's trying to level the playing field!" I snap, sharply cutting him off.

Vash's expression turns curious, so I explain with a huff, "Brisa told me their Grand Preceptor already informed them it would be a partner trial and hinted about memorizing lunar patterns. She also said that Captain Tetsuo overheard the eastern captains discussing strategy for the second pillar and caught them studying a tomb about moon phases. They all *already* know."

"That makes no sense." Vash shakes his head. "Why would their Grand Preceptors risk telling them? That's absurd. Why would—"

"Because the trials are here in the north, Vash," I say through my teeth, effectively cutting him off again. "You said it yourself—they've never held trials at one of the cardinals before." The other Grand Preceptors view this location as more than enough of an advantage for us—Brisa told me she and Ansil *knew* about the kelpies."

At that admission, Vash looks somewhat stunned.

"They had time to prepare and form a strategy, just as the East did. Brisa wasn't certain about whether the South had, but I am. All of them already knew." My words have turned bitter, and Vash clearly notices, although he's clever enough not to comment on it.

"Alright, let's say that's true. I still don't understand why she would tell you any of this. Captain Bedivere is ranked first right now, and you're tied for second. Why would she risk that?" The suspicion in Vash's voice and crease between his brows tells me how truly unfathomable he finds it.

"Because she doesn't want to win that way!" I'm surprised by the rising of my own voice. I swallow and make an effort to keep my tone even. "It may come as a shock to you, Larceon, but some raiders do indeed hope to keep some shred of their integrity intact."

His angular jaw sets, and there's a cold gleam in his eyes. "What is that supposed to mean?"

My glare is dark. "You know exactly what that's supposed to mean."

Something flickers in his gaze—something calculating, a side to Vash Larceon that I've never forgotten. A piece of him that his stealthy affinity hints at.

"If you're referring to the incident in level four, then I'm surprised by your ability to hold a grudge. Really, I thought we were past all of that," he says, lifting his chin in disbelief.

I shake my head incredulously. "Level *four,* Larceon? How about the night I spent sleeping in the snow after that nasty trick in five? Or the stunt you pulled in six? Tell me, *who* was the first person in the north to ever call me a squid?"

Vash pales, looking at a loss for words for once in his life.

I save him the trouble of finding any.

"Just because you decided to play nice this past year does not mean I forgot the previous six. Kleio might have forgotten who you used to be, but she never saw how truly dark that side of you is to begin with, and I've never disclosed it to her. But I can promise you that I *will* if I see even a shadow of it returning."

"I apologized—I apologized for all of—" Vash starts up in his own defense.

"I am aware," I hiss back at him. "*That* is the only reason I'm standing here able to have a somewhat civil conversation with you. The only reason I haven't deterred Kleio and although I accepted your apology—it does not erase what happened."

Vash's jaw clenches, and he swallows with a nod, trying to ascertain how to go on from here.

I sigh deeply before adding, "Look, for right now we're partners. We should start researching together, our crews included, and find out anything we can on lunar phases or past trials that mention them. If I had to bet, Saubarag is giving the southern raiders more than just hints."

Vash agrees a tad briskly, "Aye-aye, Captain Boreas," before turning back to scale the side of the spire and slipping in through the window opening without another word.

I wander to the edge of the nets and sit to watch the last few rays of the sun melting into the chilly waves. My left palm opens and I trace the jagged line of my own od made earlier today to Brisa. I'm relieved Vash didn't ask exactly why it is that I trust her, relieved I wasn't forced to lie.

He would have picked it up immediately, given his affinity.

The truth isn't mine to tell.

XVI. UNDERGROUND DINNER PARTY

My crew, along with Vash's, spends the next few weeks reading over anything and everything containing lunar phases. Not knowing exactly *why* we need to memorize them makes things difficult, but having the hint at all helps to quell the anxious thoughts pestering me at all hours.

The morning before the second pillar trial, we received an unexpected request to dine separately from the northern raiders later that evening. We're to instead join the other captains and their superiors in one of the smaller chambers located beneath our stronghold.

The dress code is standard uniform attire, so I think little before changing into a fresh navy set, readjusting my hair around the golden pin, and strapping on my usual array of concealed blades.

I begin separating from the rest of my crew as they head for their own dinner, and I aim for the tunnels below. Kleio grabs my hand before I leave, telling me earnestly, "I'll wait up for you. I think I might have found something in that last tome you brought in. I can show you when you get back, and we can see if it's anything."

I give her a rare soft smile in thanks.

Kleio has been practically killing herself these last few weeks.

She stays up late almost every night, pouring over books and scrolls with me. She has quizzed Vash and me on every single moon cycle and its tiny significance, both to the Tide Raiders and the landmasses. I honestly think she's more prepared than either of us at this point.

I leave them at last and set off to wander the underground channels.

Tonight's dinner is hosted further down underground than I think I've ever been. I journey deeper and deeper beneath the North Order until I'm finally greeted by the twinkle of candlelight and the soft hum of idle chatter. I didn't recognize any of the last ten or so chambers I've passed, and I certainly don't recognize the one I enter now.

A grand mosaic covers every wall and even spans across the ceiling of the domed dining room. The tiles merge together to create an unmistakable image of a wave wrapping around the entirety of the large cavern. In inspection, I tilt my head up and discover little blue-tiled droplets falling from a collection of gray, shapeless clouds in the makeshift sky.

I come to recognize the scene at last.

'The Great Deluge' is what we raiders call it, but I've heard the landmasses have other titles, such as 'The Days of Many Waters'. It's the event that changed our world a thousand years ago, almost to the day. It's the reason behind the first sacrifice, 'The Soteria Daughter,' whom The Sons and Daughters still continue to worship fanatically.

Her sacrifice is said to be what stopped the great flood from wiping out the realm of Pontus.

Speaking of which, my attention flits to the long table filling most of the room; each one is bathed in blue silk cloth and dotted with candles. I glimpse the Hiereus who tasted my blood seated at the opposite end, and my stomach turns uneasily at the sight of his seaweed veil.

I'm made only more anxious upon finding our spots are assigned.

The four cardinal Grand Preceptors are already seated at the far end, chatting and drinking loudly. They don't pay any mind to us captains beginning to file in. I drift along the table's edge, hoping dearly that I've been placed as far from Hiereus Philistos as physically possible. I'm relieved when finding my name written on a plate near the middle of the table, far from him and his necklace of sharp teeth.

That relief is short-lived.

"You've *got* to be kidding me," mutters a deep voice from above.

I look up to find Captain Agni frowning down in obvious irritation at his nameplace on the seat next to mine. His scar is made more vivid in the light of the flickering candles. It shines like real gold, giving his otherwise perfectly sculpted face an overt warning sign. The sight of it up close is still so startling and brutal that I find myself blinking away in an effort not to stare.

Then, with an air of hostility not lost on me, the prick pulls out the chair on my left and slumps down into it. I shift away, determined to ignore his presence as best I can for the remainder of the night. I'm also determined to ignore the deeply buried sting that his outright revulsion towards me still impossibly inflicts. It's really quite pathetic.

"I thought I was due for a spot of luck."

Glancing up again, I find the owner of the pleasant, rolling timbre, as he slides easily into the chair on my right. Ansil, or rather Captain Tetsuo, gives me a half smile as I doubtfully meet his pale ashen eyes. His smile widens at my expression before he sweeps his gaze over me appreciatively.

Captain Tetsuo lowers his voice to ask, "There's no rule against admiring the competition, is there?"

My eyes roll upward at his shameless attempt at flattery, but I can't stop the small tugging from the corners of my lips when responding, "Not that I'm aware of, no."

"Well, thank the drowned gods for that. Otherwise, sitting me beside you would be grounds for sabotage," Captain Tetsuo responds with a roguish wink.

I take a sip of my water in an effort to tame the blush that's beginning to warm my neck. I refuse to notice the way Captain Agni stiffens from my other side in outward disdain.

Risking another glance at my new dinner companion, I realize with no small amount of surprise that my crew was correct about their initial assessment of Ansil. He *is* a pretty boy.

I've only ever observed him from across a room or training field, but up close it's more than obvious. His length of dark hair has been swept back into its usual top knot, and a tight braid has been carefully woven against the right side of his head. The potent angles of his face combine with the soft features of his nose and mouth, making him just as beautiful as he is handsome.

The rest of the captains find their seats, and I discover Vash has been placed on the opposite side of the table from me. He appears less than thrilled to be sitting between Corvina and Dhara.

Captain Tetsuo and I start up a surprisingly enjoyable conversation about how he's finding the North Order. We chat away effortlessly about the first pillar trial and how impressed he was by our leeches' handiwork in repairing his leg.

Once everyone has been accounted for, Raider Dornon stands between Grand Regent Beldham and the western Grand Preceptor Ator. His face is flushed from drinking, and he taps on his glass a bit too hard when calling our attention. "Captain's, I'd like to thank you all for joining us on the eve before your second pillar trial."

As if we had a choice.

"I think you'll all find this next challenge particularly unusual. It has been carefully crafted with the intent of testing you on the second portion of your education received within The Order, alliances and weaknesses."

I meet Vash's stare across the table, and we share a subtle look of understanding.

Our officiant sweeps his bright-eyed gaze over each of us in eager anticipation before raising his glass in toast. "As before, I wish you each the best of luck. To Nawai and back."

Our echoing voices fill the mosaic cavern.

I find the sound of it almost eerie.

After the first course is laid out and everyone has eased back into their conversations, Captain Tetsuo leans closer to me and asks with a conspiratorial whisper, "So, did you stab him with your fork or something?"

My eyes widen in confusion, and he nods over to Captain Agni, who's shifted so far away from me that he's practically on Brisa's lap. I barely refrain from grinding my teeth in annoyance and instead give my best attempt at a casual laugh. "Him? No, I think my presence alone is more than enough torment for poor little Agni."

A muscle in the southern captain's jaw feathers, and I swear the grip on his knife tightens, but Olsson gives no further indication that he's heard me. He continues to talk to Corvina, who is sitting across from him, as if I haven't spoken at all.

Captain Tetsuo's dark brows rise, and his gray eyes glimmer with amusement. "Well, *I* certainly don't find your presence tormenting. I actually have a question for you. Is it true that you northern raiders like to use glaciers in the colder months to balance on in the ocean?"

The interest in his face is so sincere, while his eyes twinkle with excitement, that I can't help but laugh a bit at his description as our empty plates are cleared and the next course is served. I'm surprised to discover we're being treated to an especially sweet wine.

“You mean ice surfing?” I ask, and he nods eagerly.

I laugh again before clarifying, "Well, they aren't glaciers, not really. We are *in* the north, but not far enough north for all that. In the deep winter months, tiny chips of real glaciers will sail down past our isle, and we'll use them to ride the curves of the waves all the way up to the shoreline. It's—fun.” I catch myself smiling and take an ambitious gulp of wine in an effort to stop.

“I'd wager that *you* are particularly good at that activity,” Captain Tetsuo says, his eyes flashing from over his wine glass before taking a drink himself.

I suppress my grin when admitting, “Current reigning champion.”

The western captain rests a hand against his chest in mock surprise. “I had no idea I was dining with such a renowned master! I should have brought something for you to sign.”

Rolling my eyes, I can't help but laugh again at his ridiculous display. On my left, Captain Agni downs the entirety of his wine in one swift drink before laughing in response to a comment from Corvina that I didn't catch.

"Oh, she's a cheat,” Vash chimes in from across the table, having obviously overheard our conversation.

“You're just upset to be runner up for three years and counting,” I toss right back.

He chuckles with a shrug of admission, and I flash a small smile in return. Vash and I have both made an effort to be more cordial since that evening on the nets. Our history isn't settled by any means, but if we're going to rely on one another in this next trial, then we can't afford to be at each other's throats.

“I'd like to see it sometime, this ice-surfing,” Captain Tetsuo comments, drawing my attention back to him and his charming smile. The candles glow brighter and taller as I shift an inch closer to the western captain while the next course is brought in and laid out.

“I'll show you one night, if you'd like,” I offer tentatively, taking another sip of the wine.

His charming smile broadens, and I'm surprised once more by his obvious beauty. "I'd really like that, Captain Boreas. Maybe I could teach you how to play rogue's gambit in return."

"What's that?" I inquire, immediately intrigued by the idea.

"It's a dice game and loads of fun. We play it whenever we're battened down until the storm makes its way through. I think you'd really enjoy it." His voice is low, and his eyes are playful.

"I do love a game. I'll hold you to it," I promise, and the room feels a bit warmer.

"Please do," he encourages with a look that makes a forgotten feeling in my core begin to stir.

I'm about to ask him more about the West Order, very aware of how we've begun to inch incrementally closer to one another in interest, when I hear the sound of glass shattering and feel the spray of liquid hitting the side of my face. Blinking in shock, I slide my gaze over to find Captain Agni's chalice shattered into fragments on the table before him. The wine managed to miss him entirely, spraying me and my plate instead.

"My *gods,*" I snap angrily, grabbing the newly soaked napkin that saved my uniform beneath.

"Don't be so dramatic," Agni snaps back peevishly with a wave of his bloody hand.

They're the first words he's actually spoken to me this entire evening.

"*Dramatic*?" I hiss, using the edge of the now purple cloth to try and blot the wine from my hair. Something in my gut turns unpleasantly as I counter furiously, "You just smashed a cup full of wine all over me!"

The southern prick rolls his amber eyes at the mosaic tiles above, as if he finds my argument tiresome. "It was an accident," he replies dryly. "Besides, you were barely even hit."

I twist fully in my seat to give him a glare while trying to get the red liquid out of my white locks. "You got it in my hair and ruined my food!" My voice rises an octave, and I ignore the other captains watching our interaction. The Grand Preceptors and Regents, along with Hiereus Philistos, are too locked in their own spirited conversations at the far end of the table to even notice.

"Oh, *please*," Agni drawls, glancing pointedly at my barely touched plate. "As if you were actually eating. That mouth of yours was far too busy yapping to bother picking up a fork." He scoffs.

My head feels fuzzy with the rise of my temper.

I curl a lip up high in anger. "Well I didn't realize you were paying such close attention. I didn't think someone such as yourself would ever deign to eavesdrop on a *squid*."

His gaze flashes with irritation, and his voice drops to a low, ominous rumble. "I'd hardly call it eavesdropping. Your pitiful attempt at flirting was loud enough for anyone with ears to note."

Blood heats my cheeks, and the fogginess in my head worsens. "I'm sorry that having a civil conversation with anyone outside of your own cardinal is so unfathomable to you, but not all of us have such a hard time comprehending what it is to be *pleasant*."

Agni's face pales with displeasure. From the way his mouth begins to twist, I know his next words will further prove my point. But before he gets the chance, something *strange* happens.

The pressure that's been building up and up inside my skull starts expanding into my vision.

Terribly familiar black spots begin dancing along the edges of my vision.

I suck in a breath of confusion as pain creeps into the base of my neck.

My mind works with aggravating slowness to put together the pieces. Too slow for me to turn to Vash to warn him. Too slow for me to even shift back properly in my chair. I'm barely able to breathe out two words before the world tilts on its side.

"*The wine.*"

With a merciless yank, the drugged liquor drags me under its dark velvet blanket.

The last thing I see is a wide pair of bewildered amber eyes before I fall utterly unconscious into Captain Agni's unsuspecting lap.

XVII. THE SECOND PILLAR

Drip.

Drip.

Drip.

My eyelids snap open as a stray droplet of water nails me in the spot right between my brows.

I groan and go to wipe it off with the sleeve of my uniform when a soft hiss of pain escapes my lips. There's a dull ache in my head and dryness in my throat, reminiscent of mornings after revels. Rubbing my eyes, I struggle to get them to focus on the dark room around me.

The memories of dinner start crashing into my still-adjusting brain. It feels like I'm taking bare knuckle punches to the head while the fragments of recollection each fall back into place. The last of which is the flash of shock in Captain Agni's gaze before everything is swallowed up into a world of darkness.

My pulse spikes in embarrassment regarding that last memory, and I shoot up into a sitting position. Arms come to hug my knees in comfort while taking in my unfamiliar surroundings.

It's rocks and shadows as far as the eye can see.

I chance a look upwards to where the rhythmic water droplets are stemming from and discover dangerously sharp stalactites distending downward. The floor appears riddled with protruding spikes of limestone, and the two come together to form an image of gnashing teeth.

My head is starting to throb from trying to bridge the gap between where I am now and the moment I realized the wine was drugged, when something shifts in the darkness. I'm on the balls of my feet in an instant. I send a prayer out to any watery deity who gives a damn that my array of knives is still securely strapped to my middle, and a moment later I sigh in relief.

The shifting form lets out a groaning sort of sound. I creep closer, one hand on a gods-blessed knife handle, and squint in the darkness. I'm able to dimly make out what looks like bronze hair.

"Vash?" I hiss, my voice low.

"*Whaaauh*?" Is the response I'm given.

Releasing my grip on the knife, I hurry over to Vash's body, now curled onto its side. His eyelids are blinking rapidly, and his breaths come in and out in swift succession while focusing on me.

"Merena?" Vash mumbles, his voice raspy, as he moves into a sitting position. "What—where are we?" His question echoes softly in the chamber as he scans the gnashing ceiling and ground.

I shake my head, still aching from the tampered wine's aftereffects.

The wine.

Understanding hits me like a sharp slap to the face.

My mouth parts a bit while reassessing our foreign surroundings before answering him in a shaky voice, "I think we're in the second Pillar Trial."

Vash's eyes go wide, and he stands on wobbly legs in order to pat himself down for his own weapons. There's a flutter of relief that crosses his face, telling me he has what he's looking for.

His throat bobs with a dry swallow before asking, "Boreas, do you feel *weird*?"

I've begun creeping towards the tunnel opening at the other end of the chamber. There's a soft, whooshing sound of passing air that tells me it leads somewhere. Looking backwards at Vash, I feel the ache in my neck keenly as it streams unpleasantly down my backside.

"Weird how?"

"Weird like... I don't know." Vash chews his lip, looking around the rocks and shadows before finally returning his attention to me with an idea in his eyes. "How do you feel about Captain Tetsuo? Do you find him handsome?"

"*What*?" I splutter, my expression one of alarmed disbelief.

"Just answer me. How do you find him after flirting all night?" He lets slip an irritatingly knowing sort of grin. "Do you think he's beautiful?"

"This is not the time—not to mention that it's none of your fucking business." My tone is a rising hiss of irritation. "I spoke to him for an hour at most, and it was *not* flirting. I don't *find* Captain Tetsuo any particular sort of way."

Vash's irritating grin fades into a frown, and he shakes his head. "Damn. I couldn't feel that you were lying, even though I *knew* you were. Our affinities are cut off."

If it wasn't for the fresh panic settling into my bones as I try and fail to use my power again and again to no avail, I would have struck Vash Larceon for his moronic insinuation.

I let out a groan of frustration. "*Fuck*. They must have laced the wine with kratosbane as well."

Kratosbane is the name of an otherworldly sea flower that blooms only in the dead of night, and its copper seeds can take a full week to wear off without the proper remedy. The kernels are both tasteless and odorless. I imagine they were ground up and mixed into the wine or sprinkled on the food.

Just when I thought we had a leg up, I'm blindsided once more.

Luckily, I happen to have a talent for faking nonchalance in the face of impending danger, so I hone in on that skill and will myself into a state of logic-based concentration.

"Those fuckers," Vash mutters to himself before looking back at me with a frown.

Vash also, fortunately, has a knack for indifference towards likely doomed situations and strolls easily to where I stand at the cavern's opening. He whistles into the dark tunnel before us, and it rings back in an ominous echo. "You think we just go for it?" My co-captain muses, squinting into the void. It does him no good; the tunnel is as dark as it can be.

I suck on a tooth in thought. "Might as well. I don't want to waste any more time."

Vash makes a grand, sweeping gesture towards the opening. "Ladies first."

Rolling my eyes, I stride into the mountainous mouth with Vash right behind me. After a few paces, I turn back around to study the chamber in order to note anything that might help me remember its location, but I find that where once was an arched opening is now solid stone.

"*Shit*," I breathe.

"No going back now," Vash announces grimly.

My hands find the rock-laden walls, and I'm about to suggest following the side of the tunnel with our hands when stars begin illuminating a pathway from above. No—*not* stars. Tiny pinpricks of green and blue light—thousands of them—dot the rocky ceiling and walls.

They're similar to those that fill the ocean tides on the Sál Moon. The tiny pinpricks appear to curve around the tunnel bend. They don't remove the chafing inside, but at least it's a start.

"Let's go," I urge, beginning to follow the twinkling trail.

Vash quietly joins me. His usual irksome joking manner is effectively suppressed under the unknown. We stroll in silence down the long stretch of cavern tunnel, my ears straining for any noise. I'm not sure if our paths will even cross with the other cardinals, but if they do, I have a blade perfect for Agni. He won't hesitate to use the cover the trials provide to his own advantage, and neither will I.

It's maybe ten minutes later when we come upon the first fork in the tunnel.

There are two identical archways in front of us, and as the brightening stars illuminate them, I can discern the carvings above. With a nudge of my elbow, I order Vash, "Look."

The one on the left has a crescent moon carved above it, while the one on the right has a first-quarter moon. A small knot in my gut untwists. Brisa was actually telling me the truth, both regarding the partners *and* the lunar signs.

"Okay, so crescent moons are signs of life and death and sometimes fertility. At least according to the tomes from the Selene Citadel," I state, recalling our previous studies.

Vash lets out a shaky laugh, still coming to terms with the fact that Captain Bedivere was actually telling me the truth. "Well, I don't love the sound of that," he admits before pausing in recollection. "Quarter moons are supposed to be related to strength and decision-making."

I give him a shrug. "That seems like the better choice, right?"

"I suppose we'll find out," he replies darkly, leading the way through the quarter-moon archway.

Following him, I pause to give another backward glance, and I feel a small jolt of horror as the opening is again sealed with solid stone. No way out.

"I really wish that would stop happening," I mutter, my insides are uncomfortably raw without connection to my power, and my shoulders slump beneath the pressing weight of the cavern.

The stars that are not stars take us further down until we hit a massive, impassable chasm.

“Well shit,” I grumble, assessing the dead end. There's nothing leading across the never-ending gulf, and there's no possible way around it. I begin scowling at the tiny green and blue dots with distrust.

“We should go back and see if we took a wrong turn somewhere,” I advise before pivoting backwards and Vash catches my arm.

"No, Merena—look," he says, pointing toward the chasm.

I’m straining to see what he could possibly be referring to when I realize that the blue and green dots have appeared beneath my boots. Taking another look into the chasm, I find our path has twisted, and the bioluminescent pinpricks now lead down the side of the large open expanse.

My head whips to Vash, who’s already grimacing. “You don’t think...” I begin warily.

He nods without a hint of his typical trickster self. “Unfortunately, I do.”

Letting out a heavy sigh, I start pacing while Vash examines the pit further to make sure there isn’t another route. “Normally, I would just craft some ice anchors to climb with, but without my affinity, that’s out of the question,” I begin stating my thoughts aloud. "That first little ledge is too far down and way too thin to chance jumping onto. There’s obviously no way across.”

"Well, we’ve got to get down there somehow.” Vash groans, running a hand through his hair, getting more frustrated by the lack of possibilities.

I stop my pacing, lean over the side, and squint down into the void before turning back to face my co-captain. “I think I have an idea.” I bite down on my lip in worry over the plan forming.

Vash looks clearly disturbed by my tone. “Why do I get the feeling this idea of yours might just end up getting us killed?”

"Oh, yee of little faith,” I chide, my expression grim.

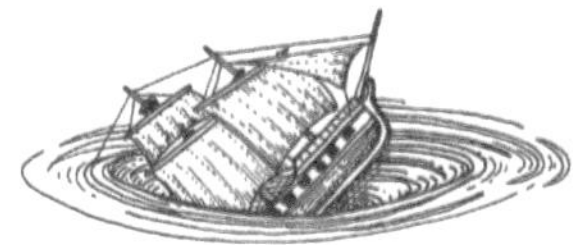

A few minutes later finds Vash dangling me over the side of the chasm.

"A little lower," I order, my feet fluttering for purchase. Vash makes a grunting sound in exertion while continuing to lean me down further until—*there.*

"I have it!" I announce, and my feet successfully hit the thin ledge. It juts out just far enough for someone to stand on.

From here, I can see the small pinpricks of light running down the side of the chasm into the dark unknown. My hands brace the rocky wall in front of me to test how damp it is. If I *only* had access to my affinity, I could easily scale down the side of this pit. Unfortunately, I have a feeling nothing about this pillar trial will be easy.

Vash asks, "What now?" as I remove two of the knives from around my waist.

Slamming the first blade into the wall, I grin in relief, as I'd hoped it sinks up to the hilt but doesn't budge further. "Now—" I call back in response, grunting as I sink another blade, this time lower. There's a newly illuminated ledge just a few paces away. "We stab and swing."

I demonstrate this by moving from one dagger to the next, then carefully removing the first while hanging onto the second. Vash leans out over the void, and his jaw drops at my idiocy.

One more stab and swing, and I've made it to the next ledge. Wiping the sweat from my palms on my pants, I shout up at his very alarmed face, "You coming or what?"

Vash grumbles something that sounds like, "Always in a godsdamned rush to find trouble," before turning around and carefully lowering himself to the first ledge. He clings to the stone wall, pulls out one of his own blades, and slams it in with a wince. It holds true, and Vash quickly copies my movements while I make my way onto the next ledge even further down.

After almost half an hour of this, my muscles are screaming in protest, and my insides are increasingly sore from the unnatural block to my affinity. I can literally *feel* my strength dissipating as I reach the final ledge and jump to the bottom of the chasm, now flooded with light. The glowing specks seem to sense our presence and only light up when we're near.

Vash follows behind me and jumps to the bottom with a small grunt before rubbing the soreness in his arms in protest. I'm not the only one unused to this change of circumstance. Being weak does not come naturally to a raider, and I have a feeling this first test took more than our wits.

"Let's get out of here," he growls in irritation before striding towards the new twinkling trail.

Another tunnel passage, and several quiet minutes later we hit a second fork almost identical to the first. Two archways again stand before us, but the carvings atop them this time are different. The engraving above the left shows a completely full moon, while the right reveals a new moon.

I'm once again the first to recount our gathered knowledge. "Full moon means something like completion, and it almost always has a positive connotation. Although I doubt we'll find anything even remotely positive in a single one of these tunnels."

Vash studies the two options for a moment before chiming in. "The new moon is about new beginnings and starting over." Glancing over at Vash, I find he's studying me. His green eyes reveal an unsettling calculation.

"If the last one meant strength and it literally *took* our strength to complete it, then the new moon might *literally* start us over from the beginning. Like circle us back around," I point out.

Vash's mouth forms a hard line, and his brows furrow. "Full moon it is then."

I nod in agreement before stepping through the archway with Vash close behind.

His familiar earthy scent is not one of comfort. I meant what I said that evening on the nets. Vash Larceon made my life a living hell for years and he did it so discreetly that barely anyone even knows the extent. Herse was the only one to suspect, and that's likely more to do with her own stealthy affinity than any slip on Larceon's part.

Though I'll admit, he has done a damn good job this last year of making me question his true intentions. It's forced me to wonder if maybe that darker side to him—maybe it's due to his unruly youth and landmass upbringing—maybe it's not *exactly* indicative of his true self.

As soon as we step through the archway, the opening again closes, sealing us in like a tomb.

I try very hard to ignore the anxiety that flares inside each time it happens. Without my icy affinity to soothe me, it's harder to concentrate. Vash lays a hand on my shoulder, and I barely contain my flinch before turning to glance at him. I'm startled to see the flecks of gold in his otherwise green eyes shimmer with understanding.

"We'll get out of here, Merena, don't worry. I know you hate closed spaces."

"It's just a stupid, irrational fear. I don't even know where it comes from," I lie, and Vash tilts his head to the side. I wonder if he's going to call my bluff. I wonder if he's able to without the aid of his power. When he doesn't, I break eye contact and turn back towards the path ahead.

Moving onward, we soon discover that there's more illumination in this cavern than just the green and blue speckles trailing the stalagmites above. A much more vibrant, silver-stained light comes from somewhere further away, towards the opposite end of the tunnel.

"You don't think this is it, do you? The way out?" I ask doubtfully.

"You mean, because we picked the full moon, symbolizing endings, that it would end the trial?" Vash sounds equally disbelieving.

I nod even though I don't actually think for a minute that The Order would ever make it this easy. Even if we came prepared, it feels suspicious at best. We make it to the hollow mouth of yet another large echoing cavity, and that distant pearly luminance begins bobbing closer.

With its eerie approach, the cavern before us brightens, revealing a labyrinth of tide pools.

We suck in sharp, identical breaths before stepping back to the safety of the path behind us. My eyes widen while studying the newly exposed room. The floor is a pattern of thin limestone walkways that criss-cross over depthless pools, each narrow gully no wider than my foot. Stone columns rise here and there to meet the high ceiling and cast ominous half-shadows.

"Well, there it is," Vash grumbles cynically.

"What?" I ask, my eyes still scouring the mystifying scene.

"The other shoe," he answers with a faint snort of disbelief.

I bite the inside of my cheek in thought before finally tilting my head towards the labyrinth of tide pools before us. "I think there's only one way, and that's through."

Before Vash can argue, I take a cautious step out onto one of the narrow walkways and tread slowly until reaching the first pool on my left. The waterline is several meters below our sliver of footpath, so I lean over in curious inspection. My heart stops dead in response to my findings.

Tightly curled, in a ball of unmistakable virescent, slumbers a *real* ligetung eel.

I clamp a hand over my mouth to keep from yelling in panic and motion at the pool for Vash to see. He edges onto the pathway behind me and leans over, before his eyes widen in equal horror.

The little silver radiance takes that as its cue to come closer. I watch as the light wiggles in between the stone columns, revealing itself as a small bobbing orb. It's beautiful really, like a miniature moon. I'm so distracted by the peculiar sight that I forget about the giant slumbering monster beneath us. The baby moon makes it past the last columns and meanders our way.

Its presence is like a physical shock to the tide pools nearby.

"Uh, Merena," Vash warns, his voice ripe with fear.

Turning backwards, I find him staring at the dozing eel, except its eyes have opened.

"*Oh gods*," I curse.

The orb, now floating above us, spins itself on a phantom wind, and the tide pools directly beneath it begin swelling with its rotation. The water rises higher the longer we stand there.

"We have to run for it," I tell Vash, straining to keep the panic from my voice.

"It's not safe, Merena. What am I supposed to do if you slip? Kleio will actually murder me in my sleep," he counters, shaking his head and looking back at the now unfurled ligetung beast in terror. The thing is a behemoth. The tide pool must sink down a hundred meters or more.

"We don't have a choice," I snap, even as my thoughts drift to Kleio. She was waiting up for me last night and has no doubt been worried sick since figuring out we weren't coming back.

"There's no telling what other things are in these pools, and we can't afford to wait and find out. Besides, I'm light on my feet. I'll be fine," I add more to reassure myself than Vash. "But we have to hurry."

His lips press together while glancing about the expanse once more, before swallowing and dipping his chin in silent agreement. We return to the cavern opening, and I select the path that seems widest before beginning to run as fast as I dare down the ledge with Vash right behind.

I try to keep my gaze averted from the stirring pools nearby, but it's damn near impossible.

The baby moon follows, and the water rises in turn. My attention quickly shifts to a rapidly swelling area on my right. The water is so high, it floods over the limestone edge and into the nearest pools. I pick up the pace, but the orb remains on top of us, its pearly glow throwing more horrors into stark relief. I keep running, determined to ignore the reservoirs brimming with undiscovered terrors, until a splash from behind turns my blood cold.

"*Vash!*" I scream, whirling back around.

His name reverberates throughout the newly empty chamber.

He's not behind me anymore, and the dark water of a rather large pool appears to be rippling with the evidence of Larceon's fall. I dash back as fast as I dare to the edge of that tide pool.

But I find *not* Vash bobbing just beneath the surface.

I let out a bloodcurdling scream at the sight of Kleio's long chocolate hair fanning out in curly tendrils several meters below me. The hand gripping my throat trembles uncontrollably as I stare at the impossible.

XVIII. DARKEST DESIRES

A deep violet hue now tinges Kleio's once lovely pink lips. Her skin reflects an unmistakably fatal blue-gray tone. Mercifully, her eyes are presently closed.

I think I'm going to vomit.

How could she possibly have gotten down here? Did they place her here as an added challenge?

What the fuck? What the fuck? What the fuck?

My thoughts are frantic and quickly running away from me. I don't have time for this. I don't have time to panic. All that matters now is saving Kleio. There *has* to be something left to save.

I won't even consider the alternative.

Stripping off my captain's jacket first, I tear off the arrangement of weapons from my person second, so as not to weigh me down. The mini moon has stopped spinning, allowing the other pools to settle as I plunge down into the blackness for the person dearest to my stone-cold heart.

Hitting the water, I let out a sharp bark of pain. It fills me with an agony I've never before experienced. I never had a reason to dislike the cold, and thanks to my affinity, I've never been more than slightly uncomfortable in frosty terrain, yet the frigid tidepool rapidly becomes unbearable. I search the black waters quickly for my second, whose body is somehow *missing*.

"Kleio!" I cry out in terror.

Her body was just *here*. It was just *right* here.

I call her name again, but it comes out strangled from the freezing pain beginning to cut into my bones. I have no choice. The water is quickly becoming deadly. I take a large gulp of air and dive fully beneath the surface before beginning to frantically search in a determined sort of frenzy.

A low guttural sound of grief emanates from my chest when resurfacing without her.

I can't understand it; she can't have sunk.

It's not possible.

I've begun splashing around in a torturously blind fit. The feeling in my hands and feet is lessening to a point of complete numbness, but I can't stop. I can't leave her *here*. My cries are little more than agonized pleas while screaming her name. I think I might even call for Vash.

The peculiar water is filled with so much pain that I almost don't register the voice yelling back at me. "*Boreas*!" Someone shouts again from above, his tone low and jarring.

Recognition of that voice calling my name rips me out of the suffocating nightmare for a single moment. Gazing upwards in shock, I discover Captain Agni scowling down at me from the ledge of the tide pool. His amber eyes flicker with annoyance when meeting mine.

Warmth blooms inside of me at long last. A warmth radiating from my own personal vibrant loathing towards the male above me. I hold onto it tightly—a single match in a maelstrom.

What Agni does next, however, shocks me more than anything thus far.

He holds out his hand.

The black water gripping me with its deadly clutches is growing more unbearable with each passing moment, but I shake my head at him in vigorous refusal. "N—no, Kleio is he—here. I saw her bo-body" I stumble on the last word, my voice breaking against the unnatural chill.

Agni heaves a frustrated sigh. He starts, "Your Kleio isn't here, Boreas—"

"No, she is! *She is*! I saw her—she was in *here*. She must have gone looking for us when we didn't come back from dinner and found an entrance to the tunnels and—" I cut him off, barely even able to finish the thought without hyperventilating.

The southern captain groans loudly into the echoing cavern, like he'd rather be anywhere else in the world but here. Yet he's quick, faster now even than he was on the mat. In one fluid motion, Agni leans down and grabs for my arms before forcefully wrenching me out of the black-cut waters, completely ignoring my shouts and struggles.

I'm about to swing at him, my body vibrating with outrage, when he captures my chin in his grip. His hand then forces my head towards the pool glimmering beneath the false moonlight.

"*See.*" He gestures towards the empty basin. My mouth parts in surprise, and my head begins throbbing painfully while my face turns back to his with an expression of complete confusion.

Agni shakes his head of messy obsidian waves. "All of these are just illusions. The pools are reflections of yourself. Your deepest fears, darkest secrets, other things..." His voice drifts off.

My teeth begin chattering from the black waters lingering chill. I'm no longer vibrating with outrage; I'm shaking from shock and cold. Agni looks down at my trembling form and rolls his eyes. "You really are pathetic," he scoffs with another shake of his head.

I can't even open my mouth to argue. I'm shivering so intensely it's starting to hurt. To my surprise, he snaps his ring-adorned fingers, and a wave of soft warmth instantly rolls over and through me. Delicious heat dries my clothes and dripping hair until I'm perfectly warm again.

I manage to grit out a bitter, "Thanks."

Agni laughs, but it doesn't sound real. It's not his typical scathing chuckle. This one is instead filled with all the heat of a beach bonfire. The sound skitters down my spine and does repulsive things to my insides.

Glancing back up, I find Agni staring down at me with a new sort of intensity.

It's different from the dark glares I normally catch him throwing my way. The look he's studying me with begins to toe the line between his usual simmering loathing and something... *else*.

I can't quite place it. I'm not even sure I want to.

Agni's ring-adorned hand reaches out and slides itself through my hair. I flinch at the unexpected movement. The white strands in his palm glow with a beautiful opalescent hue under the pulsing orb light. His eyes, still intently studying my face, shine voraciously.

"*Quoniam nullus of hic est real, ego opinor id nolo materia,*" Agni murmurs to himself.

I'm too stunned to fully grasp what happens in the next second. One moment we're standing there, and the next his hand is cupping my jaw while his mouth crushes itself to mine.

It's complete madness. Pure unexplainable mania. I might actually be going insane.

My brain feels like it's splintering.

His demanding, sultry lips taste like spices from lands I'm desperate to see, while his roving touch feels like playing with living fire. *Dangerous.* Another heartbeat passes with his mouth devouring mine and I discover, to my own shock and horror, that I'm suddenly ravenous.

I begin returning his hungry kisses with my own startlingly intense and passionate need.

I've never wanted somebody to touch me more in my entire life. Never felt like I might actually implode if they don't kiss me harder, faster. There's a concerning pounding beginning to beat louder and louder against my eardrums as I continue damning myself with the sin of his touch.

Gods I hate him.

I hate him so much that I think it just might fucking consume me. Sometimes I lie awake in my bunk at night, fueled by the obsession to take him down and watch him meet the end he so deserves. The echo of his mutilated kelpie's heartbreaking wailing still haunts my dreams.

I hate how he talks to me. I hate the names he calls me. I hate who he is, inside and out.

I'm burning with that hatred. I'm *freezing* with it.

I break away from Agni with a harsh shove from the very last remaining sliver of my sanity, and he looks down at me in stunned surprise. His lips are temptingly swollen, and his dark hair is indecently ruffled. Something awful grows warm inside of me at the sight of him so disheveled.

"Come on, *Boreas*," Agni all but purrs. "Don't you want to see what fire and ice can create?" To emphasize his point, a ball of living flame appears in his hand before vanishing just as quickly.

Shaking my head, I think back to his earlier show of power. "How is that possible?" I demand, my voice hoarse. "The wine had kratosbane in it. It cut off our affinities and—" I scan the otherwise vacant cavern. "Where is Corvina?"

Agni's smirk slips, but only for a moment before he takes a step closer to me; his movements are as predatorial and skillful as a panther. The branch of lightning that forms his scar appears hauntingly glorious under the pulsating light. It's like facing an extremely beautiful nightmare.

"Merena," he whispers darkly before taking another step.

"*Merena?*" I bark back in question, now entirely freaked out. "You have never, not once, called me by my name. I have only ever been *squid* to you."

Why are there tears in my voice?

Captain Agni frowns and tilts his head downward to study me. "Don't you want me to? Don't you like the sound of your name on my lips?" He then lowers his head beside my ear, and I go still. "*Merena,*" he whispers my name like a prayer. A shiver ripples through my person in response.

Then he says it much, much louder. "MERENA!"

I flinch away from him, but Agni grabs onto my shoulders and begins to shake me, *hard*.

"MERENA!" he shouts again. "*MERENA!*"

The southern captain sounds so completely petrified that I vomit.

Water, dark and salty, sputters out of me. I'm struggling to breathe now, gasping for air. When he continues shaking me, my hands fly to my neck. I cough again, and more water comes out.

"What the *fuck* is wrong with you, Agni?" I snarl, jolting upward and immediately hurling again.

"Agni? *By Nawai*—Merena, are you okay?"

I stiffen, my eyes squeezing shut and opening a beat later to find Vash leaning over me, concern and alarm coloring his face. His bronze hair shines from the distant glow of the mini moon, and I clamp my hands on either side of my head with a deep groan.

"No, no, no, *no*," I nearly sob, rocking back until my shoulders hit a wall. There's a pounding pressure born from madness compressing my skull, and I feel as though it really might crack.

"Are you real?" I choke out, looking at Vash with wild eyes, my voice verging on hysteria.

Vash gives himself a sweeping once over before staring back at me incredulously, and I realize he's soaking wet. I glance down at myself and see that I'm fully clothed, weapons and all, dripping with black water.

I let out a low whine full of confusion and fear, and Vash kneels down next to me.

He reaches an arm around my shoulders and squeezes me awkwardly in comfort as I shake with tightly restrained tears that I won't allow to fall. "I'm real, Boreas. I'm real." He repeats the words over and over until I've come to a calm, yet utterly mortified state.

The second I stop shaking and begin to take stock of our new surroundings, Vash releases his hesitant arm. We're at the other end of the cavern. The small moon's light is only a distant sliver.

"What happened?" I demand, my voice hoarse.

Vash's eyes tighten on my face. "I was actually hoping you could tell *me*. You were running ahead and I couldn't catch up. The ledges were too thin for me to run on and the light was chasing you so I couldn't see until—" His eyebrows knit together in doubt and he pauses.

"I think—I think you screamed my name maybe, and then—" his gaze becomes a bit lost.

"What?" I push.

Vash shakes his head like he's trying to rid himself of the memories. "I saw—*things*. Things that aren't actually possible and couldn't have been real. Let's just say that."

I swallow with a tight nod of understanding. "After that?"

His mouth twists, a hand coming to rub the back of his neck guiltily. "I was too distracted to notice the splash. It took me too long to get to you—you were floating at the surface, dead. I was certain of it. I'm really, so *sorry*." His voice cracks a bit on the last word.

"It's alright, Larceon—really. Those pools—they messed with my mind too," I admit with a trembling breath.

He lifts a brow, and I chew on a lip while trying to decide how much to reveal. “I heard a splash as well, and when I turned around, you were gone. It looked like you’d slipped. I called for you and there wasn't a response so I went back to the tidepool but when I got there, it—” My breathing hitches, and I work hard to shove the overwhelming emotions tied to the image flashing in my mind down and away. “I found Kleio floating there instead.”

Vash’s eyes flicker with a strange light as he begins standing. I grab his arm and state firmly, “Not real. Kleio isn’t here.” The look in his eyes takes more than a minute to fade.

“I thought I was jumping in after her, but it turned out to be a nasty trick, an illusion.” My voice becomes quiet at the memory of that very real illusion. The false image of Kleio’s dead body is too much to bear, so I take a deep breath and stand on wobbly knees. Vash joins me.

“I’m guessing it’s that way from here,” I say dully after a beat, motioning with a hand to the trail of stars winding outside the tidal labyrinth room. Vash agrees, and we head that way. The stone solidifying behind our backs to seal off the moonlit maze of terrors is, for once, a comfort.

We journey down the narrow tunnel leading away from that last horrible test. The sound of water dripping from our clothes and the squeaking of our boots echo around us. After a few twists in the path, Vash breaks our silence. “What happened after all that? I was trying to get the water from your lungs, and when you finally came, you were shouting Captain Agni’s name.”

My mouth forms a deep frown of displeasure at his inconvenient memory. “I was having a nightmare,” I answer stoically, daring him to counter.

His expression doesn’t change, but there’s a glint of something in his eyes. In this moment, I’m extraordinarily grateful they took our affinities.

Two more archways, two more dumbass lunar phases. One waxing, one waning. I clench my jaw in sopping wet irritation; none of the *weeks* worth of research we’ve done has even helped.

"Honestly, at this point, I say we just rock paper scissors this shit," I offer, looking between the two options with equal distaste.

Vash shrugs. "Fuck it."

Scissors beat paper, so we begin trekking down the waxing gibbous path. My mind has started cramming the memory of the mania-induced events within the tide pool into a small box that I intend to light on fire. Then I force myself to focus on the trial. We're close now. I can feel it.

I've begun imagining dry clothes, warm food, and soft sheets waiting in my bunk. The longer we walk, the more real those wishful thoughts become. My daydreams are so tempting they start clouding my actual vision, and I smack right into Vash's back upon his very abrupt halt.

"Ah—Vash, what the hell?" I snap, tasting blood on my tongue after biting the absolute living shit out of my lip. A quick scan reveals the path we've been journeying down has ended in a large circular room, one that is *already* occupied.

Corvina turns her lovely head of braided raven locks to glare at us in clear disgust. Yet I also notice something curiously like uncertainty hiding in her emerald gaze. I bristle immediately in response to the sight of her, and my hand goes to the knives around my middle on instinct.

If she's going to make another move against me, now would be the time.

Captain Leporem's lip curls at the movement, and her own hand goes to remove the dagger on her thigh. I notice the new silver metal finger-cap adorning the one I kissed with frostbite. A wickedly sharp nail gleams at the tip of her new accessory while I take a step closer.

Before either of us can make another move, a voice from the shadows drawls, "Don't go riling up the squid, Corvina. You know how terribly feral they are."

I turn to find Agni and his burning ember-eyes emerging from the dark bend. He sneers at the look I give him, and it feels like the mutual loathing between us has managed to intensify into something darker, something so potent it's almost tangible. My hand grips the knife handle tighter as he swaggers towards our group.

"Watch your mouth, Agni," Vash warns from my side.

How ironic.

Those amber irises barely flit in Vash's direction before the corner of his mouth lifts and his eyes return to mine. "Someone has to remind her of what she is, of her *place*." Agni's tone is mocking, a pointed reminder of that night in the training chambers before the first pillar task.

Water continues to drip from my soaking wet uniform, and I watch as cruel delight sparks inside Captain Agni's gaze. "Oh *no*, did the little bastard go for a swim? I thought it smelled like wet dog in here." He takes a pointed sniff in my direction.

Heat floods my face as hatred pumps through my veins. The tide pools sick fucking joke of an illusion was meant to crack my sanity. I'm certain of it. Seeing Agni's staggering form before me now—the one I know to be true—is enough to just about tip me over the edge.

To my surprise, Corvina actually holds a hand up in caution. "Olsson, we don't know whether they're actually—" But I don't hear the end of her warning.

I'm too busy chucking the knife in my hand for Agni's stupid fucking head.

In typical fashion, he's faster than I anticipated. Agni snatches the blade right from mid-air, and those amber eyes glitter with cool amusement before he chuckles. "Oh, it's her alright."

My face sours as he begins twirling the blade—*my* blade—in his hand and weaving it through his fingers with expert precision. He watches me watching him, and a smug smirk pulls on his lips.

I don't so much as glance at Vash, who's staring at me like I've lost my gods-damned mind. My attention is narrowed onto the male I want to strangle with my bare hands—and he *knows* it.

Cutting off my affinity has also clearly taken away my self-restraint.

"What did you mean you don't know whether it's actually us?" Vash demands, turning to Corvina in question.

Her gemstone eyes are glued onto Agni, who's currently doing everything in his power to rile me up further. She tears them away to snap at Vash, "I don't see how that's any of *your* concern."

He blinks in my direction as if to say, *Is she for real?*

I don't react to either one. There's a concoction of humiliation and unease churning inside, mixing with my usual hatred. A deep, dark part of me is panicking at the idea that Captain Agni might somehow know what I saw in that pool. His face is unreadable, but every time something flickers in his gaze, I'm thrust back into the false memory that I'm desperately trying to forget.

Vash moves towards me in an effort to get my attention, while Captain Agni also takes a step in my direction. The floor beneath us instantly flares to life with green and blue light.

My attention snaps downward to find a circle has been crafted from those glowing pin pricks, and they extend around the four of us now standing in the center of the round chamber.

Then the world begins to spin.

XIX. RIDDLES

The shrill sound of rock scraping against stone consumes everything else.

I clamp my hands over my ears with a grimace, and Vash follows suit. His eyes are wide with alarm as the tunnel exit seals itself before the walls begin rotating around us. Corvina stumbles backwards from the sudden change in motion, and Agni swiftly catches her in his arms before setting her back up gently.

A sharp, unexplainable tension manifests between my neck and shoulders at the sight of it.

Watching the cavernous walls spin, I palm another knife, then promptly lose my balance and jolt forward a step as the floor beneath us pushes *upward.* We're both rising and spinning now, like some sort of giant corkscrew. I look at Vash and see that he's also working to balance himself. The ground keeps rising for another minute before coming to a violent, screeching halt.

I begin inspecting our new surroundings, as do the others. We're still encircled by stone, but the walls framing us now contain two large colored gems on opposite sides, one blue and one green.

"Brilliant—what in the *fuck* is it now?" Captain Agni grumbles darkly after observing our new predicament with clear annoyance. I'd be inclined to share his sentiment if it wasn't repulsive for me to find myself agreeing with him about anything.

"Are we supposed to press them, or something?" Corvina questions her boyfriend, whose eyes are still scanning the walls.

As if in response to her question, the floor begins to tremble once more. I brace myself, but we remain mercifully motionless. Instead, an inscription on the floor reveals itself in a swirling script of radiant flecks.

In spirals of three, I hold the worlds
Each of them captured within a curl
The first of which you've been before
Yet to others is little more than lore
The second one is here and now
Once together but split by a vow
The third realm is bright and true
Only in the dark can you truly view

"It's a riddle," Vash states, taking in the newest addition.

"No shit," Agni deadpans, and Corvina laughs. "Good to know you weren't promoted into captaincy for your quick wits."

"Just shut the fuck up for one second, would you?" I snap, throwing a murderous glare in Agni's direction. "As Vash said—it is in fact a riddle. Ergo, we need an answer. Anyone have any bright ideas? Like it or not, we are currently trapped inside this hellhole together."

Agni scowls at me in return but shockingly doesn't argue. He folds his muscular arms across the width of his tightly corded chest, and I glimpse the cuts lining his hand from smashing his wine glass. My jaw locks angrily at the unsolicited reminder.

Corvina obviously takes her cues from him and begins studying the floor instead of hurling back the insult I'm expecting. Or maybe she's just fond of her fingers.

It's silent as we read and re-read the riddle below.

"Time," Corvina answers at last. "The first world is the past, the second is the present, and the third is the future," she explains, and for a moment I'm stunned by her cleverness.

The giant green stone on the wall lights up, and I think we've got it. But then the floor *drops*. We all stumble backwards and work to keep a shred of balance until the plummeting floor comes to halt a few seconds later.

"Ugh, okay, so not that," I mutter while re-steadying myself, and Corvina shoots me a nasty look. Rolling my eyes, I squint at the words still glowing beneath our feet, rethinking them while biting on a lip. It just seems like something I should *know*.

Another minute passes in silence before Vash and Olsson suddenly answer in the exact same breath. "The triskelion."

The word rattles around in my head until it finds purchase in understanding. The triskelion is the three-wave symbol that adorns the Raider King's Crown of Bone and Salt, and is the emblem stitched upon his flags. Each wave represents one world. The first being the spirit world of Nawai, the second being our world of Pontus, and the third being the Celestial realm.

The blue gem blazes brightly, and the stone around us rumbles once more as the walls begin to twist while we rise upwards. We move higher and higher, finally stopping with an eardrum-bursting stone shriek. We're closer than before, but our surroundings look exactly the same—rock walls with opposing blue and green stones as their only marking sign.

I instinctively look down, and a short breath later a new riddle flairs to life.

I am home to those who guide the way
I'll be here still long after your decay

My limbs do connect between the veils
For I am mother to the mighty trail
Innocents and miscreants come to me
A place to plead for dreams or mercy
You may find solace beneath my cover
But don't blame me for what you discover

We're all quiet in heavy contemplation until Vash breaks the silence. "A compass," he answers.

The green gemstone lights up the shadows, and I barely have time to brace myself before the floor buckles beneath us, and we plummet for far too many seconds before slamming to a halt. My hands hit the ground in front of me at the violent impact, and all four of us struggled to right ourselves. Looking upwards reveals we're almost all the way back down where we started.

My throat tightens in worry.

"*Deos subsuperficie*—don't just blurt out any errant thought that crosses through your fucking idiotic mind!" Captain Agni seethes while brushing himself off.

Vash glares back with palpable anger. It takes a lot to get under Captain Larceon's skin, and Agni has managed to wedge himself there in a notably brief amount of time.

Blowing out a breath, I study the words again and again until something finally clicks. A memory of the legends we're taught by the Sons and Daughters lends me the answer.

"The Sálix" Corvina and I answer in unison.

The Sálix is the name of the sunken sallow trees whose roots are fabled to grow between this world and Nawai. It's from this underwater shelter that the watery souls made into guiding Nix stars leave and return to on the night of the Sál Moon. They are like temples, sort of.

My narrowed eyes meet Corvina's across the room.

Blue light flares into the small circular chamber, and the floor rumbles upwards in success. I'm tempted to just sit down at this point. We stop once more at what I'm hoping is one of the last identical areas and wait for yet another cryptic question to appear.

It doesn't take long.

From darkest depths and skies aligned,
We remain forever intertwined.
Together we weave a timeless tale,
Of promises kept and lies unveiled.
A millennia may pass and the truth forgone,
But when reunited, we herald a new dawn.
Two spirits given form to play,
We'll rule the world with our might and rays.

Agni snorts with a disbelieving shake of his head. "This is fucking asinine."

I give him a look of annoyance, even though I myself can't find a correlation between any of the riddles. They're seemingly random, pointless even. My brows knit together in frustration.

"It's not the sun and moon; that first bit wouldn't make sense," I speak the thought aloud to make sure we don't go crashing all the way down with another impulsive answer.

The tension in our small space is increasing with every tight-lipped comment. My hand drifts back to the edge of a weapon handle, just in case. I begin pacing near Vash to think through the inscription. I'm worried that if we get it wrong, we just might drop all the way to the bottom level, and there may be no way back up. I chew over the words. They're disarmingly familiar.

Almost like fragments of a lullaby I used to know.

Then it hits me. It's so obvious I almost laugh.

"*The sun and the sea.*"

But my voice is not alone.

I scowl before pivoting on a heel to face Captain Agni, who's answered in the same breath as myself. My mouth curves downward in irritation and his expression perfectly mirrors my own.

Successful blue light illuminates our room, and the ground shakes once more. The walls no longer twist, but the stone beneath us continues its ascension. We pick up speed, and it's an effort to keep myself upright, I give Vash a look of dread when my ears pop from the incline.

The never-ending ceiling above us suddenly has an end, and it's a very solid one at that. We continue rising and rising while the teeth-like stones above us race closer at daunting speeds.

Incredible.

We're going to be fucking impaled in here.

Corvina screams as the sharp rocks come only meters from us. I grab a blade for comfort and close my eyes tight. But before I can meet a truly terrible end, there is suddenly bright white light flooding the chamber, nearly blinding me even through my closed lids.

The blinding light is followed by an eardrum-splitting roar.

XX. LEADER OF THE LEVIATHANS

The platform of limestone beneath our feet comes to a shuddering halt in the middle of an entirely enclosed arena. The roaring sound emanating from every direction is shouting and cheering, pouring out of a seriously packed stadium. One I don't recognize in the slightest.

I whirl around to scan the amphitheater of tide raiders packed in around us like sardines. There's noticeably more of them today than at the last Pillar Trial. The TideLords must have brought several captains and their crews to watch, but—how *would* they watch?

The announcer, whom I've yet to meet and whose voice grates even harder on my nerves each time I hear it, starts up his overly excited banter. "And there you have it! The first team to emerge from the second pillar trial, 'Lunar Partners'. Let's check in with our remaining group."

The crowd erupts in cheers and whistles as a projected image soars high overhead. It reminds me of the carto-sphere Preceptor Beldham uses in our Theory of

War class, except much larger. I squint and tilt my head back, finding it difficult to discern the exact image projected beneath it, but then I *hear* it.

"Alright, what do you think it is then, east?" Brisa's unmistakable steely voice snaps, reverberating around the large arena.

I cupped a hand over my mouth while watching Dhara glower in the space above us.

The four captains of the east and west continue bickering over a riddle engrained at their feet in a chamber identical to the one we just escaped from. Heat flares up my backside and spreads across my neck as I realize, with no small amount of horror, that this crowd of raiders, the TideLords, even our own cardinals, have been watching the *entire* thing.

While thinking through our last few hours and every miniscule moment of embarrassment, anxiety begins swelling up inside. Blood pounds harder inside my pulse until my angst-fueled rumination makes it to the labyrinth of tide pools, at which point I freeze. My eyes dart to where Captain Agni stands next to Corvina, as far away from us northern captains as physically possible.

His gaze locks with mine, and for one single absolutely ludicrous moment, I think I catch panic flashing through his eyes. A panic that seems to mirror my own disturbed line of thought.

His face is certainly paler than before; even his nostrils flare once as if in alarm. But no more than a heartbeat later, and the embers of his gaze have burned away all traces of emotion I might have mistook for anything other than hostility. I'm sure it was just in my head to begin with.

It was an illusion. Get it together, Boreas.

I school my features into a perfected mask of icy indifference and force myself to watch the second group projected above as they complete their final riddle.

The other four captains, like us, rise from below the floor. I note how the limestone floor breaks away, allowing their circular dais to push through. They look just as dumbstruck as I'd felt when blinking away the shocking light after spending so long, so far beneath the ground.

"—technology recovered from the sunken province. This riveting trial was truly spectacular to behold thanks to the incredible microscopic recording devices. With those lights being motion activated, we can be assured our judges did not miss a single moment in this challenge."

I blanch, keeping my eyes as far away from Agni as possible.

The blue and green pinpricks illuminating our path weren't stars or some natural cavern fluorescence. They were planted there to observe us in the trial. How could I be such an *idiot* as to assume otherwise? I resist the urge to swear.

Agitation floods me, not knowing what was seen or how much was heard. A feeling of shame and confusion, tinged with a hint of horror, churns my stomach at the thought of anyone ever discovering what I did in that illusion.

The foreign feeling is so distracting that I almost miss the arrival of the seventh TideLord as their group re-enters the raiders' stadium, their presence demanding a respectful silence. His golden hair's sheen catches my eye against the dark violet color of his uniform. He wears a cape similar to TideLord Nero's, but it appears to be made of some sort of soft chain metal. It follows his deep amethyst uniform in a resplendent silver cloak.

When the seventh TideLord turns to stand on the other side of Nero, I'm surprised by his youth. As the newest Lord, it shouldn't faze me; he's only ten years older than myself. He's also the most recent raider among us to have gained entry to The Vault.

I bite my lip in anticipation as his sea-green eyes sweep across us captains for the first time.

Impossibly, they linger noticeably longest on my own.

The hilt of his broadsword peaks out from his side, and I feel a flutter in my chest when studying the sea serpent wrapped wickedly around its handle. Vash coughs pointedly from beside me, and I tear my eyes at last from TideLord Blaine Dolion, leader of the leviathans.

I refrain from sticking out my tongue at Captain Larceon's knowing smirk. Crossing my arms in annoyance, I turn uncomfortably in my still-wet clothing and wait for the scoring to begin. I don't have to wait for long before Raider Dornon bustles down from the ladder leading up to the surrounding stadium with an air of excitement.

"Captains," he calls, walking the wooden path between our platforms.

Squinting at the familiar salt-stained wood, I don't hear our officiants' next words. I'm too focused on inspecting the crowd standing on iron rows bolted into the side of a mountainous rock until I finally realize where we are. It's just been so modified that I didn't recognize it until noticing the walkway beneath Dornon's feet.

The walkway that is actually a dock.

"Giant's Crook" I breathe, turning to Vash, whose attention is on the officiant. He turns questioning eyes on me and I hiss, "We're in giant's crook—the *wharf*." His eyebrows knit together while scanning the area with new interest and then recognition alights his eyes.

"Our TideLords will start with the first team to finish the pillar task, our captains from the Cardinal North and South Orders."

I'm promptly anchored back to the TideLords before us.

If I had paid attention to Raider Dornon, then I would've already heard that they were scoring us as a team this time around. The tallies begin with Olsson and Corvina. I watch with a set jaw as Lord Kufko, 'The Clawmaster', gives the southern captains an eight to kick off the results. Lord Bombay pulls another eight. His alligator-tooth earring shines under the orb lights, and I have to suppress a shudder at the memory it invokes from our affinity measuring.

TideLord Raimbaut sports a cloak of blinding azure and barely glances down before showing his score of nine. Lord Tiamet smirks as she reveals her score of seven. Lord Kurage's clothing doesn't glow quite as spectacularly with the lights around him today but I glimpse a sheen of blue-ish purple upon his gloves when lifting up another eight.

I'm starting to wonder which route the southern captains took when TideLord Nero draws the first ten of today's scores. The raiders around us begin cheering in deafening succession while anger burns bright inside my chest. TideLord Dolion ends their results with the lowest score yet, a *four*.

I don't bother biting back my grin.

Vash and I stand side by side, hands clasped behind our backs, waiting for the TideLords to tip the scales of our fate. Astoundingly, Lord Kufko starts us off with another nine, and my shoulders release a bit of tension as I give him a grateful smile. I nod in thanks at the seven that Lord Bombay offers and swallow the painful feeling of hope when Lord Raimbaut grants an eight. Lord Tiamat's face is amused when revealing another eight, while Lord Kurage's face remains hidden behind the black mask covering it from the nose down as he extends a seven.

I have no idea why I'm surprised by the three TideLord Nero gives. Yet it takes everything in me not to physically slump with the awful realization that Captain Agni will now be ahead of me.

Even if, by some miracle, TideLord Dolion were to—

A ten?

My blinks are rapid when gawking at the last TideLord's score raised high above us all. I don't quite believe what I'm seeing. A quick glance over reveals the same look of disbelief on Vash.

I meet TideLord Dolion's sea-green eyes again, and he *winks* at me with a small, handsome grin. I'm not positive whether or not Vash actually pulled me from that pool because this is too good to be true. I'm so stunned that all I can do is smile back and hope that the heat in my cheeks isn't visible from this distance.

Someone scoffs loudly after a moment, and I remove my gaze from the Lord only to find Captain Agni blatantly sneering in my direction. Corvina leans forward to whisper something to him, but I don't catch it. He snorts a laugh, and I turn away. For the duration of these pillars, I'm determined to ignore him as completely as possible.

The eastern captains manage to score a forty-eight while the west receives a total of fifty. Brisa now has the jackass known as Olsson Agni to deal with as they tie in ranking at ninety-six. My new, official, third-place title and personal score of ninety-four leave me with an unsavory taste in my mouth.

XXI. Nightmares & Sinkers

I toss and turn in my bunk the night following our second trial.

The sheets I've thrown aside twist up around my sweat-soaked body like a vise. My night terrors flash with images from the tide pools. Kleio's face, her blue lips, and her limp body make me cry out in horror. Yet that awful memory isn't what drives me from sleep.

Sometimes, on nights such as this one, I have these dreams that are too murky to remember in the light of day. They're a depthless dark around the edges, and the words sound like they're spoken from underwater. Faceless figures lurk in the shadows of my vision while a sense of imminent doom is all-consuming.

In the dream, I know that I'm quite young, but not much else.

There is a bright, shining light of pure halcyon that I follow through a hidden passage. Then I run with it as it leads—no, *pulls* me—while an uncontrollable wind tugs at my hair.

The sounds of distant screams, blood splattering, flesh tearing, and great, terrible crashes make me sob out in terror. Yet I don't stop running. I don't stop following that halcyon light, guiding me towards what I inexplicably know is safety.

The dream always ends the same way, with a hand outstretched. One that my dream self knows well, well enough to trust as I take their hand in mine. Right before I take a dagger to the heart.

But this time, when that wicked blade plunges itself into my chest, I look *up*.

Eyes that smolder and flicker with living flames stare back down at me. His golden scar flashes with a blinding light, and a dark kelpie's terrifying scream rips through the air.

I jolt awake, panting heavily as a frantically thundering otherworldly beat pulses in my ears.

That blinding light flashes again before thunder rolls from above while vicious winds whip around our room. I quickly realized that the light wasn't a scar from my dreams, but actual lightning. It wasn't the kelpie's scream but the wind's scream. The windows to our veranda have blown open, and it looks like a particularly nasty storm is making its way through.

The room around me is freezing cold, and I hear some of my crew groan out uncomfortably in their sleep. My palms and neck are slicking with sweat, and my throat is hoarse from shouting, but thankfully no one seems to have awoken.

I jump down from my bunk and scramble towards the veranda. Rain is thick and heavy outside. Thunder shakes the North Order's bones as another bolt of power streaks across the sky. I securely latch the doors before pausing to watch the ocean below as it thrashes with vengeance. The waves almost seem to heave in time to the pounding beat trapped inside my ears.

"Merena?"

I turn sharply to discover Herse standing in the doorway to our room; her bunk is in the room across the shared living area of our cabin. Lifting my hand, I wordlessly signal to her before swiping the blanket hanging off my bed and wrapping it around myself. I stifle my laugh at the sight of Kleio, who bunks under me, and her halfway-on-halfway-off diagonal sleeping position.

Herse has already disappeared, so I meet her out in the living area and take the furthest of the white armchairs for myself while she lights the green marble hearth. Noticing how her breath comes out in frigid clouds, I instantly feel the twist of guilt.

My first year here or so, I had this nightmare all the time. It pissed off just about every raider who ever had poor enough luck to room with me, as they'd oftentimes wake to find themselves and their sheets covered in a layer of frost. The reoccurrences eased a bit after that first year.

For awhile, it would only occasionally intrude on my other nighttime terrors. Then, after I became friendly with Kleio, maybe once a year. I haven't had that nightmare since level five.

Herse takes the chair beside mine and begins warming herself before the flames.

"Sorry," I apologize with a grimace. Herse turns to me with a manicured brow raised. "About the cold. I had the nightmare again," I clarify.

Understanding lightens her violet eyes, and she shakes her head of angular black hair. "Don't ever apologize to me for something outside of your control, Captain."

I incline my chin before leaning back into the comfort of the plush armchair. I know when Herse's words are final, and she knows that if I want to talk about it, I will. When I don't say anything more, she skillfully changes the topic. "So the dinner... was a rouse?"

"Sort of. There *was* an actual dinner, but the wine was drugged," I explain.

Herse snorts faintly in response, her eyes studying the heavy rain lashing against the windows high above the marble mantle.

"How much did you all actually *see* during the task?" I ask hesitantly. The question is one that I was too cowardly to voice after the trial's completion. But clearly it's eating me from the inside out if the new addition to my nightmare is any indication.

Herse glances away from the rain to give me a queer look. "From the moment you all wandered out of whatever underground chamber it was that they dumped you in. Why?"

"What about the labyrinth room, the one with the tide pools?" I hedge.

Her face pales against the sharp cut of her midnight bob. "You mean when you jumped into the water? Screaming for Kleio?"

I nod in response.

Herse no longer meets my eyes, and her voice is uncharacteristically thick when admitting, "I thought you might have died. You went under that black surface and the next time we saw you—" she shudders and her face turns unnaturally pale while something strange shimmers along her waterline. "Vash was dragging your limp body towards the end of the chamber."

My shoulders drop incrementally in relief as something unfurls completely in the pit of my stomach. I think I might even sigh out. It really had been in my head. That moment with Agni was just an illusion. A nasty trick. Very likely crafted with the intention of cracking my sanity.

Herse must notice my relief because her expression turns curious. "Was there something we missed?"

I blow out a long breath as thunder rumbles loudly overhead. If there was someone, anyone, that I could talk to about this, it would probably be Herse. "I saw Kleio's body, but when I went in after her, she was gone. Then I saw some other things in the water. Horrible things. Cruel illusions."

My third chews on a lip while her violet eyes study my face. The calculation behind those cunning irises tells me she knows there's more that I'm not saying, but Herse, true to form, doesn't push me further. "How long until the next trial?" She asks, changing the topic again.

"Three whole months this time," I answer, feeling lighter by the minute. "Our officiant told us after scoring that we'll be hosting the TideLords in a month or so for Luminalia. The third Pillar Trial isn't for another month and a half after that."

"The TideLords *here*? For Luminalia?" She echoes in wonder, and I tilt my head in answer.

Her expression becomes thoughtful and a bit distant. We sit and watch the storm in comfortable, companionable silence as it howls long into the deep, dark night.

Fuck.

There's a gods-awful soreness in my neck from craning it at such an odd angle in order to study the projected image Preceptor Beldham has displayed for us at the front of the room. What appears to be a large whale swims in place through the space above our heads.

Its movements are somewhat strange though, almost as if— "It's mechanical." I find myself blurting the thought aloud before meeting Preceptor Beldham's striking blue eyes.

Her gaze brightens, and she nods. "Correct, Captain Boreas. Excellent observation. This is one of the latest advances we've seen come out of the Sunken Province."

The image enlarges so we can view it in clearer detail, and I glimpse a HIN inscription along the backside of its massive tail.

"What are they calling them?"

I try not to flinch at the closeness of Captain Agni's deep questioning timbre.

Unbelievably, I've somehow made things worse for myself by reclaiming our seats in Preceptor Beldham's class. Agni and his crew finagled their way into convincing Corvina and her crew to switch tables with them, so now they sit directly behind us. His chair rests just a meter away from mine.

"Good question, Captain Agni. We have reports that they're calling them sinkers," Beldham answers with a curt nod of approval.

Greer snorts faintly from the other side of Kleio. "How clever," she mutters beneath her breath. The comment piques my interest, especially considering that my fourth originated from the Sunken Isles before being sacrificed.

"What other questions should you be asking?" Our Grand Regent inquires of the class, her gaze remaining on the enlarged image.

"How fast are they? How far can they travel?" I throw out without bothering to raise my hand.

"From what we know for certain, up to twenty knots, fully submerged, and as far as five hundred miles before needing to refuel." Her career rings tap against the wooden podium as she waits for more questions. I swallowed that daunting new knowledge thickly.

"How deep?" Agni asks from far too near my ear. My jaw clenches tight in irked response to the weight of his legs as he proceeds to prop them on the bottom ledge of my chair.

Beldham responds briskly, "This one in particular can delve roughly six hundred meters. However, there are reports of other sinkers similar to this that can go much, much further."

More raiders start spewing their questions, and I turn back to give Agni a glare full of ire in response to his incessant need to provoke me. It's been two weeks now since the second trial, and he's practically made it his personal mission to vex me at every single possible turn.

I don't know what's gotten into him.

It's gone past his previous desire to put me down, to make sure I'm aware of *what* I am.

Now it's like he can't resist even the slightest opportunity to thwart me, while I'm determined to ignore him as much as possible. After the events in the tide-pools, I can't find another way to get him out of my head. Agni, however, is determined to make that new resolution practically impossible.

He smirks at my outward annoyance and slides down further, so that his legs weigh even more on my seat. I throw him a withering glare before forcing myself to turn around and try my hardest to resist his goading. I'm resolved not to see those amber eyes every time I close mine.

I listen as best I can to Beldham's lecture over the new challenges these sinkers are creating, taking notes on how widespread they've become and what sort of weaponry we can expect them to contain. When the lesson finally concludes, I'm on pins and needles from restraining myself so forcefully in order to not give any sort of reaction to the male behind me.

At this point, I'm no better than a hound chafing at its leash.

So when I feel a sharp tug on my braid, I snap completely with a snarl of outrage.

Turning swiftly to find the culprit with my affinity poised to maim, I spot Captain Agni's retreating figure. My eyes narrow in on his broad shoulders, shaking with laughter.

My building rage is a palpable, dangerous thing.

XXII. THE BONEYARD

"Brek!"

"Brek!"

"Brek!"

Dancing back and forth on my bare feet, I find the gritty, sand-dusted wood beneath my soles is almost a comforting feeling. I move left to right in time with the familiar chanting tune of the northern raiders gathered around. Fresh blood paints my white cloth-wrapped hands crimson.

I hold them up before me in the proper stance we've been drilled on since level-one. Narrowing in on my opponent, I watch the rise and fall of his chest as he struggles to catch his breath.

"Brek!"

"Brek!"

The rowdy crowd of levels one-through-eight continues their chorus in the background. I work quickly to zone them all out completely and hone my focus on the rival opposite me.

There's a spot around the far bend of our tiny wintery island that we northern raiders call 'The BoneYard'. It's comprised of ancient ships broken beyond repair, whose current usage is for nights such as this one. When northern raiders of all levels slip out and away from our dark fortress quarters in order to gather and either watch or join in on affinity fighting.

I'm pretty positive all the preceptors know about it, but I'm not positive whether they're exactly allowed to acknowledge it. They turn a blind eye and deaf ear to our unsanctioned activities.

"Come on, Rivo!" A faceless voice shouts from somewhere in the tightly knit crowd beneath our wooden pedestal.

Kleio calls up to me with a sharp laugh, "Quit playing with the kid—end it, Boreas!"

My opponent, a level-seven named Roan Rivo, wipes the sweat from his bloody face and looks at me with renewed determination. I let my mind go absolutely blank as he lunges forward with a fist raised in distraction before switching into a kick for my ribs. My reaction is solely based on instinct; I shift my front leg to the back and block his attacking foot with my fist.

He loses his balance, and I take advantage of his off-kilter sway with a perfectly arched high-kick to the head. My foot makes violent, concussion-worthy contact, and Raider Rivo goes down with a powerful wooden *'thunk'* to an uproar of riotous cheers and feet stomping.

The level-seven lies there stunned for a moment. His eyes roll upwards before blinking hard, and I lean down with a hand out to pull him back up. It takes his gaze a troublingly long minute to focus on me, but once it does, he reluctantly accepts my help.

"Don't go to sleep until you've seen the leeches," I shout near his ear before thumping him on the back. He glances down at me and nods in agreement.

His expression remains dazed as he exits the wooden makeshift arena. Raider Rivo is set to be one of next year's captains. It's no wonder why, with his affinity for anticipating an opponent's next movements, he's an undeniable threat and therefore an asset.

It's taken me a while to find the trick in defeating someone with his particular skill set. Forcing myself into a zone of complete instinct seems to be the solution. The downside is that I *also* have to shut out my affinity in order to block his.

I scan the crowd while catching my breath.

My hair is piled high atop my head in a tight knot, and the loose strands framing my face are plastered to the sides of my temples and cheekbones with sweat. A droplet of perspiration slides down the bridge of my nose from laughing while watching the twins weave through the crowd, cashing in on bets made against me.

"Alright dipshits—pay up! Let's go!" They shout before aggressively shaking down a group of level-fives and sixes.

Raiders grumble as coins, small jewels, and other minor oblations are tossed into their pail. Being that I'm a bastard-born castaway, I did not arrive here with the usual pouch of small treasures that others do. There was no offering made to the gods on my behalf. No oblation from my parents with which to declare my reputable bloodline and potential inheritance of power.

It's safe to say I spent a lot of time down here in The Boneyard trying to amass my own.

But winning silvers isn't why I'm here tonight, nor is it why I've been coming here several nights a week for the last month. *That* would be due to the recurring nightmares driving me from my bunk just about every eve since the last trial. Flashes of amber eyes and mutterings of whispered foreign words right before a blade is plunged into my heart haunt me from dusk till dawn.

I've found that if I go to bed utterly exhausted, they don't seem to be able to find me.

So I'm down here to avoid those shadowy terrors, and it's also become a necessary release on my restraint due to my resolution to ignore Captain Agni entirely. And if I'm feeling honest, perhaps a small part of me is also down here to regain a bit of the self-assurance that Agni has managed to steal by beating me. *Twice.*

The admittance, even to myself, is so enraging that I have to physically shake my sweat-drenched head in order to remove it. That's when I spot them.

Across the blown-out ship hold we utilize to host these little fights come the other six cardinal captains. They slink in through the makeshift door, the one crafted from a massive discarded porthole long before I arrived here.

Several members of their crews aren't far behind, and soon I'm not the only one aware of their presence. The crowded ship hold goes silent as all raiders turn to view the intruders. I catch Kleio's eye from where she waits below on my left. My second nods once in understanding before quickly passing up the sling of weapons I'd discarded earlier.

"What do you fuckers want?" Vash shouts, now having climbed the steps of the wooden arena.

Both the east and west captains have the good sense to look slightly uncomfortable. Corvina appears annoyed to be here at best, downright pissed at worst. Captain Agni meets my quiet study from across the crowd, having to look slightly upwards to do so. I can tell he hates it from the clench of his jaw, so I flash him a smirk that's sure to spike his annoyance.

Captain Tetsuo's charming voice speaks up for the group. "We all heard the shouting and thought it best we come check to make sure you weren't under attack." There's a sincerity in his pale eyes as they meet mine that makes me glad for the blood already hot in my cheeks from my latest fight.

Brisa nods her agreement from beside him, two of her own crew members near the porthole door. I watch Reed and Dhara dip their chins in wordless agreement to Captain Tetsuo's explanation.

Do those two ever talk?

“Speak for yourself west.” Captain Agni’s voice rumbles from his menacing form as he sends a dark look towards Captain Tetsuo. His amber eyes flash back to mine before adding, “We thought it would be some sort of *freakish* northern ritual we might get to sneak a peek at.”

Corvina’s previously annoyed frown becomes a feline smile, and her eyes dart to mine.

Vash and the other northern raiders appear to size Agni up. Some of the lower levels nearer to him actually back away from the tenebrous blades hovering menacingly above his shoulders.

If he’s intimidated by a room full of raiders who clearly dislike him, he doesn’t show it. On the contrary, Captain Agni’s scathing eyes never so much as flicker from mine.

"Well, it *is* a northern ritual of sorts.” I join the conversation at last, coming to lean over a railing along the edge of the platform. "But it's not one that we'd ever allow little southern pricks like yourself to gawk at," I croon before flashing a sickeningly sweet smile at the southern captains and their arriving crews.

Laughter from my crew and others below ripples throughout the room; it serves to darken Agni’s countenance further and uplift my own mood. Before either of them gets a chance to retort, I explain, “You all have a choice.” My eyes scan the lineup of captains. “If you do wish to stay and observe our little *games,* then you’ll have to partake in them as well.”

Their dubious expressions have me glancing down at Kleio, her smirk the twin to my own.

“Who wants a shot at challenging a cardinal captain?” I shout in question to the mob of raiders.

Chaos breaks out at once. Raiders of all levels raise their hands eagerly while scrambling closer to the raised platform in order to be chosen. Level sevens and eights start roughly shoving the lower levels out of their way left and right, impatient to test themselves.

I jump down to the ancient shipwrecks' sticky paneled flooring, and Vash takes over choosing raiders for matches. The twins, along with Captain Larceon's second and third, have already begun taking down names, affinities, and odds. The wall of bodies around me now is too high to even glimpse the cardinal captains as they weave through the madness.

"So what—you too good to challenge me?"

Turning around, I find pale gray eyes shimmering with humor and fight back a smile at Captain Tetsuo's jest before answering, "No, I would just much rather watch you parade about up there than have to get my hands any bloodier." I wriggle my knuckles, stained scarlet, for emphasis.

Captain Tetsuo flashes me a pretty grin. "Ah, of course, I knew you only liked me for my body."

Tilting my head to one side, I ask, "And when did I ever say I liked you at all?"

He places a hand over his nicely sculpted chest before proclaiming much too loudly, "Captain Boreas, you *wound* me! Truly."

My eyes roll up so far that I think they might get stuck there. "Is that all you came to find me for? To heal your fragile ego?"

Captain Tetsuo laughs for real before admitting, "No. That's not the *only* reason." His voice is slightly more serious than before. I note the way he keeps shifting his weight from one foot to another before studying his face again.

"Oh?" I probe, intrigued.

There's an uptake in my pulse at the grin he reveals. If I didn't know better, I'd say there was a blush inching up the back of his neck, where his hand is currently resting. Ansil's next words lack their usual bantering tone. "I was wondering if you might want to—"

"Tetsuo! You're up!" Vash hollers and multiple people in the crowd begin pushing Ansil towards the raised fighting arena. I frown as he looks back at me with an apologetic grimace before turning towards the arena to see just who is so impatient to challenge Captain Tetsuo.

But of course. Of *fucking* course I'm greeted by the sight of Agni's smirk.

My expression grows cold, and my lips flatten into hard lines. The south captain stands where I stood only minutes before, already having taken off his broadswords, jacket, and undershirt to expose a rather obnoxious amount of perfectly sculpted golden muscles. His crew rallies beneath the corner he's clearly claimed for himself, and their jeering fills up the shipwrecked hold.

I feel Kleio's presence before hearing her voice. "You sure you know what you're doing here?"

Folding my arms, I turn to where she stands on my right and give her a look that says I won't tell her my plans anymore if she continues to question them. Kleio fights back a grin and wrangles her lips into a somewhat straight line. "You're the boss," she agrees, holding down a laugh.

There is actually a *third* reason I've been coming to The Boneyard nearly every night. Not just to get away from those nightmares or remember my own affinity's prowess. I also come down here with the long-shot intention of rousing the other captains in order to study their affinities.

Which, as of tonight, has finally proven to be successful

Our attention is drawn to the arena as the two captains begin to circle each other, sizing one another up. The raiders around us are shouting excitedly, and bets are exchanged from every corner. This evening is an unprecedented turn of events and fortunes for some.

As far as I'm aware, neither of these two captains in particular have fought each other in Preceptor Oplon's class with weapons or hand to hand. I know for certain that none of us have been allowed to fight with our affinities at all due to the trials. Strictly speaking, this little gathering tonight has the potential to earn me another week in the hole, if Skelm so decides.

I don't allow that troubling fact to deter my attention from the brawl at hand. I'm eager for any opportunity to watch another elemental use their affinity. Even if I am desperately hoping and betting a handful of coins, that said elemental gets his teeth kicked in.

The ground beneath Captain Agni trembles as Captain Tetsuo disrupts the magnetic fields nearest to him in a strategic effort to get the southern captain off his expert balance. Unfortunately, it does little to disrupt him. Olsson punches out with a blast of pure power, creating a searing barrier of colorful dancing flames that effectively repels Ansil's efforts.

I have to resist the urge to flinch when Olsson then goes on the attack. He steps forward with a whip of energy, which Ansil narrowly manages to dodge beneath. Another two movements are made with punches of equally brilliant flame, and Captain Tetsuo begins hurtling discs of his own condensed magnetic power back in an effort to both block and attack.

Agni burns each one away with maddening ease, chuckling darkly as he does. I find that watching him fight gives me the same tense feeling deep in my gut as watching the fire in Skelm's hearth.

His affinity is so fluid, moving from one movement into the next in a seemingly endless display of power. It looks as easy as breathing for him to control it. He effortlessly incorporates his power into his already extremely deadly hand-to-hand combat style. Meanwhile, it takes just about every ounce of strength I possess to keep a check on my own element and not allow it to run wild and violent as it desperately wishes.

It's difficult to stifle my irritation while watching Agni toy with Captain Tetsuo. It's clear now that there was no real chance for the western captain in the first place. For all his incredible power, Ansil is absolutely no match for Olsson. A horrible part of me enjoys that—is *relieved* by that, if only so I feel better about not being the only captain he's bested.

Their brawl comes to an end when Ansil, growing frustrated by Olsson's outright arrogance, condenses one of his fields so tightly that familiar energy glimmers in the air. I suck in a sharp breath as a thin line of electricity, different from Kerau's but deadly all the same, flickers into existence. Just as with the kelpie taming, I'm motionless as Captain Agni *snatches it* from the air between them.

A hand absently comes to rest around my throat as I'm struck dumb all over again by what I'm witnessing. The way he grips another element with ownership and, in turn, the way the lightning eagerly writhes up and around his wrist like some sort of weaponized accessory—I've never seen anything like it.

Impossible.

Agni's eyes are alight with cruel amusement as he raises his arm and aims a killing blow directly for Captain Tetsuo's chest. I manage not to gasp with the rest of the crowded room of gambling raiders as the mood shifts into a darker realm of our nature, but my knees do become a bit unsteady. Agni cocks his head toward Captain Tetsuo with an unspoken question.

Messy midnight hair falls across Agni's brow in menacing waves. There's barely even a drop of sweat anywhere on him. Captain Tetsuo's handsome face blanches, and after a beat he nods, putting up both hands in undeniable surrender.

Yet Agni still doesn't lower his hand, writhing with that malignant power. Instead, his gaze slides out across the throng of packed bodies until it finds its intended target.

Me.

A knot of nausea forms in the pit of my stomach as his lips curl into a taunting sneer. The deadly power around his wrist flashes against the scar marrying his exquisite face in a threatening pulsing light. It's a sharp reminder of what he is and what cruelty he's capable of bestowing.

I hold his gaze with my jaw set and try to tamp down on the newly pounding rhythm working its way into my blood. His eyes flicker at my willfulness, while Captain Tetsuo remains frozen, his face losing color by the second.

From the look Agni shoots down to his second, I realize that he thinks this is funny. It's a game to him, showing me the strength and depth of his affinity's cruel brutality. Aiming a sure-fire death blow at a boy whose only crime is being nice to me. Kind to a lowly, worthless, *squid.*

When he twitches his lips as if to laugh before lowering his weaponized hand, I know he does this just because he can. *Asshole.*

"What a sadistic little prince," Herse mutters, having crept up to join us without my notice. I silently nod in agreement, struggling to control my restless element.

Agni gives a finely practiced sneer to Captain Tetsuo before jumping from the platform and rejoining his pack of wild mongrels below. They all begin chanting his name, like some long-lost god.

The sadistic prince and his vicious pack of mongrels.

XXIII. EPISTLES

When dawn finally comes after a long night watching the other cardinal captains down at the boneyard, I slip away from our still slumbering cabin alone.

I make quick work of the wooden hallways and spiral staircases that eventually land me before a familiar, daunting archway. For a moment I stand there in frozen deliberation, trying to decide whether to turn back around and forget this ridiculous idea altogether.

The choice is made for me when a brisk voice calls from the other side of the archway, "Captain Boreas, are you a person or a statue? If it is the former, come on inside. If it is the latter, please go make yourself useful by deterring the seajays out on one of the alcoves."

Grimacing at her uncanny awareness, I hastily push open the large oaken door, revealing the Grant Regent's chambers. They are as intriguing with their organized chaos as I've ever seen. Beldham doesn't even bother glancing up from the scroll she's studying upon my arrival.

I take out the tightly rolled bit of paper that's been burning a hole in my pocket for the last hour or so and twist it between my thumb and forefinger while waiting silently. A few minutes later, her cornflower eyes at last stop their exploration of the scroll and turn my way.

“I was wondering if—” I begin a bit too loudly, pause to clear my throat, and then continue in a noticeably lower voice. "I was wondering if I might be able to use one of your epistles?" The words sort of cram up in my mouth , then fall out all at once under her piercing gaze.

In all my years in the north, I have never visited a preceptor's quarters without receiving a summons or a punishment. I have certainly never asked for anything from one of them. My insides squeeze uncomfortably as her lips purse tightly and I wonder idly for the hundredth time exactly how old she actually is.

Kleio and I have had a running bet since level four, but I'll never admit my wager.

Beldham looks away from me for a moment, and I'm about to call this stupid idea a wash and sprint down to the pool chambers to work off my impending mortification with a swim. Before I get the chance, our Grand Regent unexpectedly turns around in her irregular circular desk.

I watch hesitantly as she pulls open a low-level drawer, and the sound of glass clinking around fills the room. Curiosity gets the better of me, and I find myself leaning in just a bit to study her collections. Bottles of all sizes and shapes rattle around in the deep drawer. She carefully selects one that perfectly fits my purpose. Again, her uncanny perception is unnerving.

Having found the one deemed correct, Beldham swiftly slides back in the drawer before turning to face me. "This, I trust, should do the trick,” she states quite matter-of-factly, setting the epistle down on the tiny bit of spare space available on her desk with a firm ‘clink’.

I'm a tad stunned at how easy that was. Outside communication from your cardinal is not strictly allowed. I rationalize this unexpected outcome with the knowledge that she likely is granting me this kindness because I have no one else out there in the entirety of Pontus to communicate with. No family, no home, not even a memory of my past life.

Therefore, there is really only one candidate for whom I may be contacting.

"I assume you remember how to use them from my course?" Beldham inquires, her voice as crisp as the winter winds stirring outside her arched windows.

I dutifully repeat our instructions from her lesson over them in level-six. "Slip the message in, seal it with your signet, and drop it in a body of water."

Our Grand Regent's stern face reveals nothing as she nods her head, currently steepled upon slender fingers. "Don't forget to call out your intended receiver's name in full. Otherwise it could end up in only *the depths* know where."

"Thank you, Grand Regent." I acknowledge her unexpected kindness with sincerity before taking the epistle from her desk and turning to leave.

My hand grips the ornate handle of the exit, and I'm almost halfway through when her sharp voice calls back to me. "Captain Boreas, be sure to return the epistle to me when you're finished with it."

I've read and re-read the tightly rolled note in my hand more times than I will probably ever admit.

After the events of last night, I have questions that demand answers. Even though the thought of sending this message makes my stomach feel like it might just tear itself apart,

Winter is coming on strong, with its freezing rain and frigid winds that smatter and tear at bits of my hair while I slip the message into the glass epistle bottle. The black sands beneath my boots have a thin layer of morning frost upon them that sings to my affinity. I ignore the power inside of me that wishes to be allowed time to play and remain focused on the task at hand.

Once my note has settled securely inside the epistle, I push back the corked stopper. On the outer end of the cork is a black re-impressionable wax made for near infinite uses of the device. I press my northern captain's ring into it firmly as my sealing signet.

The seas today are calm despite the deepening cold; the swelling waves form a pattern of sea foam and cool azure tides. Inhaling the scent of salt and brine eases a bit of the tension that's been building in my neck and shoulders. As much as the wintry winds and frost-covered sands taunt my affinity, the pull and seduction of the seas calls to something far deeper inside of me.

Next, I locate a spacious black rock to stand on, free from the waves' current assault. Then I hold the epistle up high, the sea and sky bearing witness as I shout, "Kerau Tharos, Captain of 'The Challenger'," before flinging the bottle into the churning ocean before me.

As soon as it hits the water, the epistle disappears.

All I can do now is wait and hope that he'll answer.

If there's one tradition living within the raider ranks that I enjoy above all others, it's revels.

The order relinquishes their terribly strict hold on us a touch when it comes to celebrating our most treasured holidays. In the Cardinal North, Luminalia is the most cherished of them all.

Luminalia is a revel dedicated to showing deference to 'The Soteria Daughter' and the sacrifice she made to save the world of Pontus from The Great Deluge. The day chosen to celebrate this mythical seraph was said to have been her birth day. That having been a thousand years ago, I doubt the accuracy of it, but I enjoy the celebrations as much as the north enjoys throwing them.

This fact is further proven when it is announced that a market will be set up inside the wharf of Giant's Crook. My crew and I are thrilled by the prospect. Normally we wear our dress regalia for the revels, so it's a rare thing indeed to be offered the chance of an extravagant gown or finely tailored suit. I suspect Skelm is hoping to impress not only the other cardinals but also the attending TideLords with this spectacle. He's never been satisfied with his lot here, always itching to get back and rise into the newest Raider King's ranks.

Perhaps he sees this as a chance.

Regardless of the motives, I'm a bundle of cautious excitement as the eight of us journey down to the wharf during our allotted free day to pick out our attire for Luminalia. My crew's fur-lined cloaks are wrapped tightly against the icy winds and white flurries dancing about in the salty air.

"I want something pink—no orange—or maybe chartreuse. Gods, it's been *so long* since I've worn a color outside of boring old blue," Prisca laments as we descend the rocky cliffside.

Nephthys argues immediately, "Well, I'm wearing orange, so you'll have to pick a different color."

"I'm thinking of something with a pattern." Nimra's soft voice from the back of the group adds to the twins' conversation.

"Oh, you'd look incredible in a floral," Greer says thoughtfully.

Davina sighs. No doubt she's relieved to be given a break from the leeches, but I sometimes wonder if our company actually provides her much sanctuary or just adds to her stress. "I'm picturing green, but I'm not sure what shade," she muses aloud.

"You'll look good in any of them," Nimra remarks breezily with a wave of her hand.

"What are *you* going to get, Captain?" Kleio asks with a playful nudge of her shoulder.

"That is a great question," I answer vaguely.

I honestly have no idea what I'm searching for today. I've never worn a dress before, and I've also never gotten so much as a choice of the shirt on my own back. I'm not positive whether or not I actually even have a preference in colors.

"Something purple for me," Kleio announces with a grin.

"Ooooh, *shocking*," Herse teases from my other side.

Kleio has made it well known to us all of her favorite color time and *again* over these last several years. I huff out a laugh at the prickly pout she hurls immediately towards Herse.

I'm pensive the rest of our trek while the others continue on in their lighthearted chatter. It's been an entire week since I sent the epistle off to Kerau, and I've received absolutely nothing in return. Not even the godsdamned epistle bottle back so that I can at least make good on my promise to Beldham. I feel stupid for even reaching out.

Kerau has undoubtedly forgotten all about me by now.

As a captain under a TideLord, his horizons are far wider, brighter, and no doubt busier than I could ever imagine. I just wish he would send me *something*. Even if it's just a note telling me not to reach out anymore. Then at least I would know for sure he was the one to actually get my message in the first place. Gods forbid anyone else received the epistle.

The mortification of the alternative would surely kill me, but if not, then I'm positive Skelm would finish the job.

I've been too distracted by my own muddle of thoughts to realize we've made it to Giant's Crook already. Kleio's excited squeeze on my arm is the only thing that brings me back to the present. Regaining my attention and therefore my sight, I gaze up and around the wharf in poorly concealed amazement.

The stadium that was built inside the mountain cover has been completely torn down. The docks have been restored and expanded, with merchant stalls lining them up and down the sides. There's no sign of the northern ships that normally reside here, and I wonder idly where they've relocated them.

Not that I would ever go looking for them.

Well, not now that I'm a captain.

The sounds of filthy swearing and loud scuffling I've come to associate with Giant's Crook are even rowdier today. It seems that our typical wharf hands have been turned into shopkeepers.

The eight of us decide to split up and make a lap around the stalls first before choosing anything. We've all been given strict instructions of no more than two fabrics each. Any baubles or trinkets will not be provided for by The Order and must come from your own oblation stash.

Luckily, I've been building mine up this last month down at the boneyard.

Ten minutes or so later finds Kleio running her hand back and forth over a line of rolled silk in an orchid shade, her attention appearing to be somewhere far from the wharf. "Silver for your thoughts?" I tease lightly while coming to sort through the silken fabrics on the rack across from her.

She glances up, and the distance in her eyes is keen. There's a sad smile laid upon her lips when responding, "This just reminds me of a market back home." Kleio swallows back emotions foreign to myself before adding, "The locals called it the Cloth and Gem Quarter."

I nod in understanding, even though I do not understand, not really. I don't know what it's like to miss a place or to have memories that take me back to a different time. But for Kleio's sake, I joke, "Did it smell as awful as this?"

The corners of her mouth lift, and she shakes her head with a small laugh, " *Gods* no."

One of the dockhands playing merchant today makes a noise of indignation from where he stands behind a makeshift stall. I swivel my head backwards and give him a dark look of annoyance at his eavesdropping. "Busy body," I tut. I'm not wrong; it *does* smell. The mixture of stale saltwater and sweaty dock workers leaves a less than desirable scent in the air.

We proceed to the next stall, which displays rows upon rows of velvet swatches in every shade imaginable. The fabric is soft and warm beneath my passing touch. Kleio delves back into her own world as we continue on in our search.

"Did you visit it often? This market—or erm—*quarter*?" I feel compelled to ask.

There's an intrinsic need inside of me to do anything in my power to keep those shadows at bay. The ones that sometimes take away the wonderful warmth to Kleio's eyes whenever lingering too long on thoughts of her past life. I pretend not to watch her as intently as I am and hold up a swatch of putrid yellow, gazing at it as if it's something I'd truly choose.

"Every time there was an event or we had company to entertain, which was fairly often, yes. Asha's mother always insisted that I watch her while she shopped," Kleio answers while inspecting a lilac-colored roll.

Kleio and Asha are sisters, but only by half. Kleio came from a previous marriage. Her mother passed when she was too young to really recount how. Then her father, a highborn in the Oyster Court, remarried another highborn, and Asha was born soon after.

The next open-air boutique hosts a large plethora of wool and fleeces. Likely many of the outfits will be lined with one of the two. Luminalia is always held outdoors, deep into the winter months. I wonder idly what the other cardinals will make of it, if it will be anything like their own holiday celebrations.

"I'd like to see this quarter one day," I muse aloud.

Kleio nods with a reserved smile, as if she doesn't dare allow herself to truly hope. There was once a time when she did, and it kills some piece of me that The Order has taken that away, even if her fervent beliefs *did* used to drive me up a wall. Perhaps being so close to the possibility makes it harder to hold on, knowing the pain if it slips through your fingers.

I'm saved from trying to find the right words to comfort her by Greer calling us to come check out the stand next door. We join my fourth in command and find the rest of my crew has begun swarming the medium-sized booth as well. It takes only a moment to understand why the bolts of fabric before us are jaw-droppingly beautiful.

The textiles all vary in types of cloth and hues of color, but what's unique is that each of them is expertly embellished with unique designs or wonderous patterns. Some are made from lace, others feathers, a few with gemstones, and some even shimmer with flecks of gold and silver.

I join Herse, where she skillfully sorts through a rack of various darker-colored bolts.

Half an hour later, and my hands feel like they've been flitting along the spools for *hours*. It's almost too overwhelming to have so many options. I'm at a complete loss for what to choose. Each piece I see is lovelier than the last, but none of them truly feel like me.

The others have already made their selections and are in the process of choosing their gown design styles. We're meant to turn them into our Grand Regent upon our return in order to have them tailored. All this searching has me exhausted and verging on hangry. I'm about to just say fuck it and wear my dress regalia to the revel when Kleio whistles at me to come over.

My breath catches at the sight of the swaths of fabrics that Kleio and Herse have expertly layered atop each other and hold out in presentation.

"It's—it's..." I begin, unsure how to find the right words.

Beautiful, stunning, fetching.

"Brilliant," Herse finishes for me.

My second and third share equal grins of satisfaction as I take the bolts in my arms and carry them to the merchant stall as if they're incredibly fragile.

I'm quiet as he begins cutting the proper amounts according to Kleio's instructions. She and Herse then delve into the dress designs and begin plotting out my attire for the event.

Fiddling with my captain's ring, I study the trinkets set up at the front of the market stand. My eyes scour the jewelry situated behind a glass display before roaming over the basket of gem-studded hair clips and charms. All of them are undoubtedly worth double my entire stash of oblation scraps.

A shine catches my eye next, and I walk over to the far wall without giving my feet permission to do so. There are small wooden pegs lining the entirety of the ramshackle stand, each of them laden with what appears to be strands of precious metals. My fingers reach out and brush them.

A bundle of thin golden threads is braided together like real hair, and it feels just as fine as my own. I'm utterly perplexed by their possible usage. Maybe it's the detailing on the fabrics, if you want to embellish them yourself? That might be possible, I suppose.

My eyes hungrily searched the countless pegs. Bundles of copper, platinum, palladium, more gold, and silver all shine under the orb lights. On the higher pegs, some are strung with beads, gemstones, and even pearls. I can't even begin to imagine how difficult those would be to embroider onto a fabric.

"They're hair threads."

My head snaps over in question towards Kleio, who's appeared at my side. She stares almost wistfully at the various bundles. "They're *what*? Hair dipped in metal?" My revulsion for that idea and exactly how it would occur must be prominent in my expression because Kleio snorts loudly in amusement.

"No, nothing like that!" she exclaims before laughing again at my complete lack of knowledge about the outside world. I know with Kleio, there is no malice in it, and I bite back a victorious smile at the return of her laughter.

She then goes on to explain, "They're very finely shaved bits of precious metals that spin into hair-like fibers. It used to be a style a while ago, at least in the Oyster Court. People would tie them into their hair or weave them through their braids."

"Ah, I see," I muse, pretending to understand at last. My eyes travel up to the pricing at the top of the pegging board. The strands themselves are ridiculously expensive—nearly fifty silvers. Each.

I turn away at last and take my bag of fabrics from the dockhand without another glance.

XXIV. LUMINALIA

My swallow is tight while admiring myself in the floor-length mirror.

The dress design turned out even better than I'd hoped. The tips of my fingers, which Kleio insisted on painting black, trail over the multilayered fabrics at my sides as I twist to see my reflection from every angle.

Each way I turn it looks even better than the last, and I'm once again blown away by Kleio and Herse's invention.

The base fabric is a crushing black that hugs my every curve. It perfectly outlines the swell of my ample breasts down my waist before gliding over feminine hips to finally pool at my feet. It looks as though I'm bathed head to toe in midnight.

As if that wasn't incredible enough, the second layer is nearly invisible, save for the embedded crystals that begin in tightly knit clusters at the bust and expand wider near the hem. It also serves as the thin sleeves that are snug over my arms all the way down to my wrists, giving the illusion of being dusted with gemstones.

I turn around to admire my back once more, where the dress scoops just low enough to glimpse the dimples located at the base of my spine and show off the entirety of my affinity mark. Damning white coloring and all. I suppose it might look to be a bit of a statement on my part, exposing myself so intentionally.

But more than that I want to see the cape again, made entirely from that second fabric. It falls from the peaks of my shoulders down to just past the black silken trim at my feet.

My hair cascades to the base of my ribcage in its simple, natural state of loose waves.

Kleio insisted on a few touches of makeup, so there's a soft blush on my cheeks and a sharp black line of kohl jutting upward at the edges of my eyes that magnifies the cold sapphire shade of my iris. My lips only have balm applied as I have trouble keeping anything more colorful than that out of my teeth, so they're left to their natural pale pink hue.

I smile in admiration at mine and my crew's handiwork before stepping down for the twins, impatiently waiting to appraise themselves next. As promised, they're both dripping in color. Prisca is swathed in a sparkling periwinkle, while Nephthys chose a cool-toned peach. The dresses almost glow, illuminating the beauty of their coppery skin.

I grin while they spin before the mirror with hoots of identical laughter.

Nimra emerges next, dressed in a soft pink gown. Like mine, her second layer is a thin fabric with embellished designs. However, unlike mine, hers is crafted from an intricate lace that holds the illusion of falling petals. Davina did end up going with a green in the shade of seafoam. It brings out the gold in her hair and the colors in her hazel eyes. Greer also went with green, but her chosen shade is a deep forest hue, and layers of shimmering tulle make up her dress.

Herse appears after some time looking like she's been dipped in liquid silver. The cut of her dress is impeccable; from the body hugging silk falling off her shoulders to the flowing sleeves and narrow hem, she could be mistaken for a queen. A pair of pearl drop earrings makes the effect complete.

Per usual, Kleio takes the longest to get ready, although it's mostly due to her helping the rest of us along the way. True to her word, she ended up selecting dual fabrics of purple. The first layer is composed of a rich violet that plunges between her breasts artfully and flows slightly outward from her hips. The second is a light lavender tulle studded with gemstones that serves as her sleeves, which billow out from her shoulders before tightening around her wrists.

Her hair is styled atop her head in an intricate way only Kleio could manage. A long necklace of real diamonds wraps around her neck, and matching baguettes adorn her ears. Likely from the large stash of oblation items from her father. I grin at the excitement in her eyes meeting mine.

Tonight, Kleio looks every bit the Oyster Court highborn that she is.

I'm sure to strap a blade around my thigh before we leave and the slit running up my right leg gives me the perfect access.

The others shove their own weapons down their sleeves, around their waists, and into hidden folds. I even catch Nimra shoving what looks to be a dagger between her breasts. I'm deeply impressed as I watch it simply *disappear* from sight.

The outdoor lyceums are to be the grounds for tonight's Luminalia revel so we head for the open-air bridge normally crossed in warmer months to Ersatz class.

Due to my affinity, I'm the only one who isn't bundled inside a cloak matching the color of my dress. The winter chill does nothing more than ruffle my hair as we reach the bridge.

An archway of lights has been crafted to encompass the open-air trestle so we enter inside what appears to be a tunnel of brilliant, blazing stars. Kleio slings her arm affectionately through mine while we trail behind our crew, with Herse and Greer just a few steps ahead.

The sound of wild, pulsating music greets us at the halfway point while inside the dazzling overpass. Reeds and bone flutes combine with the strumming of a lyre and the beating of rawhide drums to concoct a tempting melody that urges us to come join the chaos unfolding.

Stepping out of the shimmering exit, I stop dead in my tracks.

"Skelm has lost his godsdamned *mind."* My voice is little more than a whisper while my eyes widen at the grandiose scene before us.

In the past, we've been treated to some string lights here and there, a bit of warm food and some traditional music. Wine and other such drinks are of course also a major part of the revelry but this—*this* is another thing entirely.

The outdoor lyceums, surrounded by a tall forest of newly decorated pine trees, are absolutely unrecognizable. A massive enclosure constructed from lavish garlands and fine white tenting spreads out wide along the training grounds. Towers of candles glow from within, swaying to the wild beat of the music drifting towards us from inside.

"Well, his loss of sanity is our gain in debauchery," Keio whispers back excitedly with a wink before tugging me along. I follow her and the others, walking through the entrance as if in a dream. My mouth is parted the entire time, I'm sure of it.

The inside is more unbelievable than the outside.

Level-twos stand on either side of the entrance and hand out the traditional Luminalia halos. I swipe one from their outstretched baskets without really seeing the lower-level raider before me. I'm too enraptured in our current ostentatious setting to pay much attention to the twisted winter wreath adorned with tiny glowing orb lights before placing the crown atop my head.

While the outside looked to be tented in white, the inside reveals the ceiling is actually made up of a clear translucent film. It opens up wide to the night sky above, undoubtedly in order to watch tonight's main event. Likely also to provide shelter against any freezing rain or snow should it cloud over.

The floor is made from glass and lights are beaded alongside the edges so we appear to walk atop radiant ice. Long tables are strewn about, each overflowing with candles, food, and drink. Raiders of various levels laze upon plush lounges and expensive-looking chairs. Under the open sky lies a massive dance floor, with plenty of room for the musicians and their instruments.

This is *only* the main area.

Swiveling my head, I discover there's various openings leading from the main space out into hallways and other smaller rooms beyond. I catch glimpses of darkened corners with scattered chaises and fertility-potent mistle bundles hung tauntingly near.

Kleio turns to me after handing her cloak over to the waiting level-two and the others begin shrugging theirs off in succession. "Drinks?" she asks hopefully.

I'm only able to nod in response, my eyes wide from gawking. I make an effort to close them while following her to a buffet crowded with cups of liquor. On the way there, we pass by a grand table crafted of sterling perched atop a glass platform on the other side of the dance floor.

I bite my cheek to control my own surge of excitement. TideLords Bombay and Kufko sit chatting and drinking with Lord Tiamat. The two males wear impossibly rich suits in their traditional colors. Tiamat dons a silken gown of dark russet. Pearls flow from her neck and arms in an astonishing show of casual wealth.

I glance around but don't spot any of the others though I'm certain they're here somewhere. We've been forewarned not to speak to any of the TideLords unless spoken to or contacted directly. The likelihood of which is low but I still find myself buzzing with newfound nerves at the opportunity of them being so close.

"Bottoms up, 'Cap!"

Tearing my gaze away from the trio of TideLords, I blink at the unexpected sight of an odd blue liquid before me. It glows faintly from inside what appears to be a shot glass. I take the offering from Kleio's extended hand and find that the rest of my crew have matching ones already.

Kleio grins fiendishly before raising her tiny glass, "To Captain Boreas and her incredibly ravishing crew!" The twins whistle loudly in agreement and I chuckle at my second's shamelessness before tossing back the luminous liquor.

"I'll drink to that," Vash announces, joining our group and throwing a suggestive grin Kleio's way. His own crew is currently selecting drinks from the opposite side of the table. Larceon has found himself a dark green suit that looks almost black in the dim lights and a matching Luminalia halo sits perfectly straight atop his bronze curls.

He looks like some sort of king out of a children's fable, someone aiming to be worthy of Kleio's obvious grandeur. After several minutes of chatting and heckling over Skelm's gaudy display, I take another shot of the blue liquid and wave Kleio off as Vash pulls her towards the growing dance floor.

The twins have already disappeared into the throng of spinning raiders with Javin and Eiran from Vash's crew. As expected, I have no idea where Davina has run off to, but I spot Nimra chatting to a level seven near some hors d'oeuvres.

My eyes flicker back to the glass platform, where the three TideLords still sit.

"Wine?"

Greer pushes a silver goblet into Herse's hand before extending an identical one to me. I take the drink, deciding that if by some small chance one of them does actually happen to speak to me tonight, it wouldn't hurt to loosen up a little.

I clink glasses with my third and fourth before taking a rather ambitious gulp.

"*Ugh*, am I about to watch Bealu and that skeezy little Regent from the South make out right now?" Greer asks with disgust.

Her comment is so unexpected that I choke on my wine. Glancing up through my coughing fit, I burst into laughter upon seeing her meaning. Bealu and the southern Regent are standing in a shadowy corner to the side of the heathen dancers. The way they're chatting closely with heads tilted, it really does look as if they might begin to kiss.

The thought of Bealu with absolutely *anyone* in that regard is vomit-inducing.

"Personally, I'm more interested in how Ersatz managed to fit her cloven hooves into those heels," Herse drawls, making me laugh again while searching the opposite end of the crowded floor. Ersatz, the she-demon herself, is cloaked in a seductive gown of darkest coal. Its plunging neckline appears to be doing very little in enticing Preceptor Oplon but the five-inch heels she wears *are* impressive.

I continue downing my liquid courage and chatting with Herse and Greer for the next half hour, all the while keeping my eyes peeled for the presence of other TideLords in the room. I've had two full goblets along with another shot, for good measure. I'm *just* about to slip away to strategically meander near the sterling TideLord table when someone grabs my arm.

I turn to discover Raider Dornon's unexpected boyish blue eyes and blush-filled face, likely the result of too much wine, as the culprit. "Captain Boreas, there you are! We're almost ready to begin. Come on now—quickly!" He drops his grip and ushers me to follow him through the now entirely packed tent.

I trail along, squeezing through tightly clustered bodies as ethereal-sounding music emulates from hidden musicians. "What—exactly—is starting?" I shout up at Dornon as he moves effectively through groups of people towards the front of the massive glowing floor.

He looks over his shoulder to bark back, "The opening dance."

I blink in surprise. No one said anything about a dance. I don't even have a partner.

"But the revel has already opened!" I counter dubiously.

My eyes automatically scan those raiders currently out dancing on the large floor to the musician's strumming tune. The halos adoring everyone's heads makes it look like we're a bunch of spirits here for a night of trickery from Nawai.

He gives me a look and says between a group of level-sixes, "It's ceremonial in name. *Obviously.*"

I frown before continuing on in his wake and we eventually make it to the general area that I was aiming to end up by in the first place. Vash stands alongside the dance floor edge with an open spot next to him so I beeline for it. He might not be my *favorite* person in the North Order, but he sure as hell is better than ending up with someone like Olsson Agni for a dance partner.

"Hey," I shout, nodding up to Vash.

"Hey," he shouts back in acknowledgment, seemingly unfazed by this last-minute tradition.

The noise level from music and rowdy laughter is at its peak right where we stand so it's hard to get more than a few words across to him. "Where's Kleio?" I holler in question, and he points over the crowd to the table I've just left, where my crew is now gathering, drinking, and laughing.

I'm immediately envious of their fun and wish to skip this stupid ceremonial event entirely.

As this song comes to a close, everyone is shooed off the dance floor. Those present are made to grab refreshments and watch as us cardinal captains are ushered onto the now barren space. I follow after Vash and take the hand he offers me, my pulse fluttering nervously.

Dancing is not what makes me anxious. We've been schooled heavily in dancing since level-three and I'm quite apt. As many of us hope to end up as hired eyes or swords for our TideLords, it is imperative that we have all the weapons needed in our arsenals.

That includes dancing, apparently.

What makes me nervous are the *seven* TideLords who are now seated at the grand sterling table. They peer down at us with varying expressions of amusement and mild interest. It also doesn't help that the bawdy tune selected for this dance is one I know to be a partner exchange.

The music hits its starting key, and we're off.

I try my best not to search the glass platform for sea-green eyes or the shine of a leviathan hilt.

My focus is solidly on following in Vash's swift lead yet I can't ignore how oddly silent he is while spinning me around the floor. He doesn't say one single word to me. We go through the motions of the dance but his steely reserve has me feeling off-footed and only adds to my growing nerves.

I'm actually a bit relieved at the first partner exchange when Captain Namak intervenes.

Reed has dressed himself in a fine suit the color of sand. Like me, he has also chosen to wear a cape this evening. However, his is fur-lined and of *much* thicker material than mine. I chance a glance up at his face while we turn to find his topaz eyes are far above my head. Reed is just as silent as Vash. The eastern captain's hand doesn't even place itself upon my back nor fully in my palm.

Impossibly, I begin feeling even more off-footed than when dancing with Captain Larceon.

Mercifully, Captain Tetsuo's turn follows suit. There's already a faint flush on my cheeks and an excited flutter in my stomach as he spins me away from Reed and into his charcoal-clad arms.

That excitement is quickly stomped on.

Even though Captain Tetsuo does give me a slight smile with a brief teasing, " *You clean up nice,*" he too is noticeably mute and quite physically distant as we twirl and dip. Those pale gray eyes, typically full of flirtatious humor, now reflect an invisible yet firm wall.

After another spin, I study the other mixed cardinal captain pairs and discover that none of them are as silent as my partners are with me. They all appear to hold their partners in the typical fashion, too. There's a sharp stinging sensation beginning to form along my face. Like I've been slapped.

The way Captain Tetsuo gazes pointedly above my head as we move around each other, as well as the fact that he does not fully touch any part of me when we come back together, further confirms what is happening here. A traitorously tight lump builds in my throat as I come to fully understand my dancing partner's peculiar behavior.

With the TideLords watching us intently from their dais above, and my boldness in the way I've chosen to expose the white branding of my affinity mark, their strange behavior checks out.

None of them, not even Captain Tetsuo, would dare to be seen enjoying the company of a bastard-born castaway, a *squid*. Not tonight. Certainly not in front of the TideLords. Lest they risk their future chances of earning a captaincy under the royal raider colors. I should laugh. It's painfully obvious now.

But I'm not in the laughing mood anymore.

As we continue our dance, I ignore Captain Tetsuo's shifting glances and instead choose a spot beyond him to focus on. I bite the inside of my cheek until tasting copper—a technique to keep the pricking behind my eyes at bay. Ansil's portion drags on for far too long. It's an agonizingly slow torture. Skelm should really be taking notes.

Finally, a voice like scorched gravel commands, "My turn."

I'm shaken from my grim resolve only to discover it's the worst person I could possibly be forced to deal with right now. Olsson *fucking* Agni.

Captain Tetsuo obliges without so much as a parting word. Even though I'm prepared for it, it still manages to feel like a physical blow. The cups of liquor have started catching up to me, making my usually reserved emotions concerningly potent.

I feel like an idiot, a complete and utter fool. To have worn this gown—to have actually believed I looked beautiful—it's all a joke. No matter how high I climb, I am and will always be less-than in their eyes. The disheartening awareness is so distracting that I almost don't hear Agni mutter something foreign beneath his breath.

"*Futuere mihi. Vos vultus sicut peccatum.*" His words come out oddly strained, like a swear. Given his very clear hatred towards me, it more than likely was.

My wintry gaze snaps up to his face. Anger is a familiar emotion and right now a very welcome distraction. Agni's eyes burn with those lifelike embers as he glances down at me, and his jaw tightens before we turn.

"Whatever insults you have for me tonight, you can say them to my face you fucking coward," I hiss, feeling the flush of liquor-laced ire rise up inside. Ignoring him this past month and a half has proven to be nearly impossible. He's made damn well sure of it.

Agni's hand presses itself so fixedly against my exposed backside that I can feel each and every one of his many hard-earned calluses through the thin second fabric. I look away from his gaze in an effort to shake any lingering traitorous images of the tide pools illusion out of my head.

That damn box just can't seem to keep itself closed.

"Where did you get this dress?" Agni asks abruptly, disregarding my seething words entirely.

My eyes leave the point on his chest I'd been staring at instead of his face to raise a dark brow in disbelief. "Why? You want one?" I return snappily. My hand is nearly swallowed whole inside Agni's and his grip is surprisingly quite firm. Possessive, almost.

If I didn't know better.

The southern captain scoffs out a laugh with an errant flicker of his gaze down the slight of his nose. It causes me to take in his chosen attire for the evening at last. He wears a classic suit, not so different from the captain's regalia, fashioned of midnight velvet and set with a hooded cape of embroidered gold.

Aurelian chains gilt across his chest and dangle opulently from his broad shoulders. They manage to bring out the shine of his scar even more than usual. He's topped off the lavish trappings by wearing his Luminalia halo at a ridiculously insouciant angle in his always carelessly tousled hair.

I understand his question now. Our outfits this evening are perfectly opposing and yet direct parallels. We look like some sort of sacrilegious union between the depths and stars.

I scowl down in annoyance, and a wave of warmth rolls over me from his continued closeness. He holds me so solidly in his arms that I realize he could probably burn the living shit out of my person if he so wished. But that fact does not hold my tongue and I'm now even more irked than before.

"What? All out of nasty remarks for me tonight?" I goad, meeting his blazing eyes once more.

Agni arches a brow at my ire, his mouth curving wickedly. "When will you learn, *little bastard*? I'll not ever take commands from the likes of you."

I feel our tether of mutual loathing go taut and in this one singular moment, I'm extremely grateful for it. I'm beyond relieved to feel anything other than like I've been playing as the night's grand fool.

"Is that really the best you can come up with?" I croon. "You're not losing your edge now, are you? I'm honestly disappointed, I expected more."

His mere presence stirs my inner need for conflict. The urge for a fight pulses through me, craving the chaos of a real challenge. The haze in my mind lifts, clearing any remaining stinging sensation from both my eyes and thoughts. Wonderful hatred burns everything else away.

Agni smirks before his hand, currently pressed unyieldingly against my back, slips beneath the thin layer of my cape and slides down *low*. His fingers halt in between the two dimples located at the base of my affinity mark. I swallow the spike in my pulse as said fingers begin lightly grazing back and forth over my exposed skin from one dimple to the other.

My eyes narrow down into slits and I shoot him a venomous warning glare.

"I'd suggest you remove that wandering paw of yours before I freeze it off." The words escape me through newly bared teeth. "Unless, maybe you would prefer a blackened hand? You know, to match with your girlfriend?"

Agni blinks down at me with a frown. "Who?"

I roll my eyes at his never-ending supply of arrogance and equally never-ending supply of females falling at his feet. "*Corvina*, you moron."

Dark brows rise in surprise before he lets slip a dark chuckle. "You really are quite a merciless little thing, aren't you?" Something in his tone makes it sound as though he's deeply pleased by the realization.

I'm poised to retaliate but Agni's eyes flit away from my face to a point behind me and his amusement fades away entirely. He lets go of his hold on me before inclining his head low in the mockery of a gentleman, stating, "*Donec deinde tempore, mea divinus cruciatus.*"

Only then do I realize that the song has ended.

The other captains have already left the floor. Raiders are now pouring in and the musicians start back up with a new tune. I find myself unable to stop watching Captain Agni's formidable form as the crowd appears to cut open a path just for him to rejoin his crew.

I'm at a complete loss for how to interpret this most recent interaction. But before I can begin ruminating over it for too long, there's a tap on my shoulder.

I spin backwards and a pair of electric blue eyes meet mine.

XXV. ELEMENTALS

"Kerau!" I exclaim in shock before promptly throwing my arms around the male.

He smells the exact same as when he left, like rain-soaked pine. Kerau squeezes me tightly in return while chuckling into the top of my head. "Hey kid," he mutters by way of greeting.

It's harder than I care to admit to break away from him but I force myself to before peering upwards. Selfishly, I'm relieved to find that he's more or less the same as when I last saw him. Same burnished gold hair, still resting just above his shoulders. Same chiseled face and easy smile. Maybe a few more scratches than before, and a bit more muscle. Like he *needed* any more.

"Is that a new scar?" I ask, squinting, to inspect the white line slicing through his upper lip.

He laughs before rubbing a sun-tanned hand against the mark. The familiar rumbling sound triggers an ache somewhere deep inside. "New to *you*, maybe. I earned this thing almost a year ago now," Kerau answers teasingly.

His vivid eyes study my face briefly before glancing down to my dress and back with a glimmer of something too intimate to acknowledge. Something that makes an old version of me raise its head once more. I work hard to ignore that former, very reckless, Merena.

"What are you doing here?" I have to shout the question over the music growing ever louder.

There's a flash of incredulity that crosses his features. "I got your epistle."

I stare at him, taken aback. Kerau looks at me in turn, as if it should have been obvious.

Raiders, now careless with liquor and heady with the unruly vibe of the revel, begin bumping into us left and right. Those dancing have gotten into the heathenly sway of our night's traditions and the floor around us quickly becomes a lust-filled battlefield.

"Let's talk somewhere more private," I advise.

Kerau nods, allowing me to lead the way back through the pit of hellions. Raiders part for us easily now and at first I don't understand why but then I look back and take in Captain Tharos again. *Really* take him in, beyond the male I used to know more intimately than any other.

Kerau wears the unmistakable white dress uniform of TideLord Regis Raimbaut. His captain's cape reflects a striking cobalt and a jewel-studded sword I'm sure he's never had before is strapped boldly to his side. On his right hand, he has an impressive ring that declares him a TideLord's captain, and I catch the shine of a new sapphire earring dropping from his left earlobe.

Due to his good looks and elemental affinity, Kerau has always been intimidating. He's always been seen as quite a dangerous force among us northerners. Honestly, that's what most attracted me to him in the first place, all the way back in level four. But now—*now* he looks like someone to give deference to. Someone that any TideLord with half a brain would be worried about.

Should be worried about.

I mull this over while swiping two silver goblets from the tables we pass, teeming with wine and liquor of every shade. My crew is completely scattered. Some are on the dance floor, while most of them are no doubt exploring what other pleasures this revel has to offer.

Spotting another passageway at the opposite end of the main tented area, I take Kerau's hand in mine and tug him in the direction of my thoughts. His expression hints at a nostalgic sort of amusement when allowing me to drag him through the opening, extending out to a stretch of many smaller rooms.

We pass by a few alcoves with more drinks and refreshments. Others contain groups of raiders loudly chatting and laughing. Even more are filled with shadowed couples. The sounds emanating from those rooms, in particular, are seedy enough to make my neck burn.

I hear the deep rumble of Kerau's easy chuckle behind me, intensifying that burn.

My gaze snags on the last room we pass in our search for privacy at the unexpected sight of maddeningly messy obsidian hair. I spot Captain Agni lying lazily along a plush settee with a roll of burning spices sitting between his lips. His head, adorned with the still-skewed halo, rests in Corvina's green velvet-clad lap and she softly strokes the edges of his face.

Voices belonging to raiders from both of the two southern captain's crews carry out from inside the room. It sounds like they're playing some sort of card or dice game, if I had to guess. Agni tips his head back further into Corvina's lap to laugh freely at something said by someone I can't see. Her hands run idly through his maddening waves as she too laughs in response.

There isn't a way to explain the feeling that runs through me at the sight of it.

Captain Agni's gaze then slides over to the open entrance, where I've evidently frozen without realizing. There's a gleam in his amber eyes that tells me something a bit more potent than usual is in that smoldering bit of paper. His mouth curves up sinfully when spotting me, just before Captain Tharos takes a backward step towards my halted form.

Olsson's attention moves over to Kerau, who now also resides in the small doorway exposure. In less than a blink, an unreadable mask swallows his aristocratic features whole.

I forcefully yank myself from whatever unexplainable trance I've fallen into and turn to Kerau, who gives me a playful tug towards the room next door. He flashes one of his handsome grins, the kind that never fails to ensnare me and I laugh when he teasingly crooks a finger in silent motion for me to join him inside the private alcove.

I don't miss the way in which the last of Agni's embers wink out as I follow.

The room we enter is the smallest I've seen by far.

It's much more private and intimate than any of the others and filled to near bursting with a single, high-backed, circular couch. Two small tables reside within the center and I set my cup atop one as Kerau places his on the other. He then motions with a grand wave of his hand for me to slide into the tiny seating arrangement first and I laugh again before obliging him.

The previously consumed liquor makes my mirth come easier.

Once I'm situated, Kerau closes the tiny room's makeshift door. It's really just two heavy bundles of decorated garlands that he unties, allowing it to shield us from any prying eyes or listening ears. It almost appears as if we could be inside one of the Luminalia halos. Except for the translucent ceiling opening up wide to the sparkling winter night above.

"So, *Captain* Boreas," Kerau teases, emphasizing my new title while sliding into the circular cushioned arrangement. His tall and well-built frame is comically large in the tiny space.

"So, *Captain Tharos,*" I mimic, hoping he can't hear the spike in my heart rate as we're forced into such close proximity. His gaze travels over my dress again with something bordering on hunger and a buzzing kind of energy fills the small space between us. The sort that has the power to lead us into dangerous territory if not carefully monitored.

"You got my note," I say, reminding us both as to why we're in this close-quartered situation.

Kerau swallows thickly with a nod. It seems like it takes a bit of effort for him to pull away and plaster on a casually friendly smile. He leans back into the cushioned seat before saying, in agreement, "I did, and I thought it wise we talk in person. Hence my presence tonight."

"Why?" I prod. It comes out a bit rudely so I'm quick to add, "I didn't mean to bother you or draw you from your captaincy duties. I just—I had a few questions and I didn't—I couldn't think of anyone else who might be able to answer them."

I take a sip of my wine, despising the pitiful truth in the words I was about to utter.

Didn't have anyone else to ask.

Kerau's gaze finds me again after having been studying a spot along the wall. His mouth twists, like he's having a difficult time selecting exactly the right words. After a moment, he begins with, "You asked about being an elemental," and I nod. "You wanted to know what all that entails. First, tell me why."

His calming scent of cloudy skies fills the space between us, encouraging me to ease into our old pattern of trust. "There's another competitor in the trials, another captain." My voice is low as I think of said captain's presence in the room next door. "He's an elemental."

For some reason, it comes out sounding like a confession.

Kerau has leaned in closer and he dips his head low before divulging quietly, “The one from the South Order, we’ve heard.” I glance at him in surprise and his eyes harden a touch before continuing. “They say he bends fire to his bidding.”

I nod, watching his thoughts churning inside those shocking irises. My eyes dart around our small enclosure uneasily before deciding to let Kerau in on the driving reason behind my epistle.

“But that’s not all he can do. I’ve seen him in the trials and he—” With Kerau's' attention so focused on me, I pause to find the right wording. “We had to tame kelpies as our first task and his was a bit more chaotic than the others. It spewed this lighting and he—I watched him *grab onto it*. He was able to manipulate lightning the same way you can—he can use it as a weapon.”

Kerau’s brows raise up to his hairline.

“I don't understand it but I’ve seen it twice now. I’m sure of it,” I affirm with the shake of my head.

His head is angled down towards the Luminalia halo that he’s removed and now spins around between his hands idly. I watch as his expression morphs from surprise into contemplative thought that borders on worry. My fingers trail through the top layer of my dress fabric, playing with the embellished crystals while he gathers his thoughts.

“There honestly isn’t much known out there about elementals. That kind of power is just as rare within the landmasses as it is among the raiders, even more so,” Kerau admits after a moment.

“Most of what *is* known is based on ancient myths and stories from before The Great Deluge.” I rub my left temple, beginning to ache, while he continues quietly. “In the landmasses, many people believe elemental powers are really just fragments of a greater whole.”

My head tilts to one side at his words, my eyes crowded with uncertainty.

"I mean to say that some elementals have a stronger foothold in their 'element,' so to speak." Kerau explains. “The more powerful they are, then naturally, the more control and access they possess. If the legends of Pontus are to be believed, fire and lightning are actually slivers to a much larger sum of energy."

He laughs at my expression, growing more skeptical with every claim. "Think of it like there's a wide array of potential abilities within a single element and all of them are little pieces creating a great big puzzle. Very few elementals, if any at all, have been powerful enough to access more than just one."

I ponder this idea while twisting a long, wavy strand of white hair around my index finger.

"So, what you're saying is that your affinity is really just a *fragment* of an element? Not an actual element?" I ask, my voice hoarse with disbelief.

Kerau's head tilts from one side to the other. "More or less, yes. The same way that *your* affinity for ice is really just a sliver or rather a subsection of its pure element. It's powerful, of course but it isn't access to or mastery over the complete domain itself or its source."

"So then Agni must have a greater hold over his element—he really *can* use more than one," I muse, not entirely sure whether I'm speaking to Kerau or myself at this point.

My insides feel as though they're starting to disintegrate. If what he's saying is true, then I don't know where this will leave me or my chances for The Vault. Panic twists my insides and the soothing chill of my affinity works to ease its grip. Kerau angles his head of burnished gold locks in an unspoken question and I realize my tiny misstep.

"Captain Agni. He's the elemental from the south that I mentioned," I clarify.

Something moves in the set of Kerau's jawline while his arms come to fold across the width of his chest. "You seem... *informal* with this captain," he comments, but my mind is still a bit too dazed to grasp how his eyes are studying me. After a moment of silence on my part, he asks bluntly, "So is he warming your bunk then?"

My eyes go about as wide as they can without falling right out of my skull. "*Gods no.* That's obscene—our relationship is about as far from that as you can possibly imagine," I sputter in surprised disgust.

Kerau narrows his eyes fractionally. "Well he could, you know."

I return him a look of complete disbelief, my mouth popping open slightly to gape in affront at his insinuation.

Kerau then scrambles to clarify. "I meant—only if you *wanted* him to I—I mean that you are free to take *whoever* it is you want to your bed," he rambles, waving a hand over me in emphasis. "I'm certainly not here anymore and I'm not an idiot—or some love sick level-five. I would expect you to have moved on to a new—well—*partner*."

By the end of his uncharacteristic babbling, Kerau's typically aggravatingly calm demeanor is nothing short of frazzled. One hand shields most of his face while the other tips his wine chalice back for a long drink. My lips press tightly against the laughter working its way up my throat.

Kerau glances at me through an opening in his fingers and groans outwardly in response to my clear amusement. "*My gods*—why am I so bad at this now?" He pulls at the collar of his pristine uniform. "I don't really know exactly how to act around you anymore, Merena."

"Why? Too intimidated by my captaincy?" I tease, flashing my brows with a playful shove to his knee resting solidly against mine.

Kerau shakes his head, a hint of a smile playing on his lips. "That and—" he falters with a thick swallow, his eyes roving over my person once more. The area inside our little alcove feels like it might be vibrating. "And you are *not* the same kid I left here." He shoves out the words with the shake of his head, like he has to physically force his eyes to remove themselves from me.

"I'd hardly say I was a kid," I remind him with the roll of my eyes. We're only two levels apart but Kerau has this terrible habit of making it seem like that might as well be decades.

His lips threaten to curve upwards. "Okay, then you were a very reckless *young adult* last time we were together." I'm primed to argue that point but he barrels onward. "I do believe you were the level-four I caught stealing a speeder to take out for a midnight joy ride, correct?"

A line of reluctance forms between my lips and I choose to sip my wine rather than answer.

Kerau laughs deeply. "That's what I thought! This was also the night after you'd *just* spent a week in the hole from freezing Preceptor Bealu's eye shut, wasn't it?"

I take another drink from my chalice, and my cheeks suddenly feel quite warm from the reminder of my prior escapades. Eyeing him over the burgundy liquid, I admit, "It was. But as *I* recall, a *certain* level-six showed me that very same night exactly how to put the speeder back so Skelm would never know it'd been taken out in the first place."

Kerau has the good sense to look a bit guilty before waving the facts off in nonchalance. We catch each other's eye again and promptly break into a round of breathy laughter in remembrance of that night. The first night we ever spoke.

"But what I can't quite remember," I add, leaning towards his electric eyes shimmering upon my approach, "is whether that was before or *after* that same level-six joined me in said joyride."

Kerau inches closer with a heart-rate-spiking grin just on the horizon.

My hand comes to brush along the side of my throat absently and his vivid gaze follows the movement before traveling slowly lower until my breath catches. I'm not sure at what point we stopped laughing and when we began closing that sliver of a gap between us.

In a flash of movement, his hands are on me.

One hand gently cups the back of my neck, and the other carefully holds the side of my face while softly pressing my lips against his own. Kerau even tastes just the same as I remember, like wildflower nectar. His mouth moves in sync with mine and electricity tickles the air between our tongues.

I'm thankful to have kept my hair down as Kerau begins lightly running his fingers through it. His hand on my face drops away to sneak beneath my gemstone-layered cape and gain entry to the open exposure of my back. His fingertips hold tiny pinpricks of real lighting while trailing up and down my affinity mark.

I arch into his touch and am unable to conceal the moan escaping my lips in response to that voltaic power along my skin. It's been so long since anyone has taken me to bed. Maybe *too* long.

Kerau makes a low sound in his throat before deepening the kiss. Frost spreads over the garlands decorating our little alcove as he then proceeds to pull me into a straddling position atop his lap.

My body begins reacting to the familiarity of his touch immediately and I can feel the very *prominent* way in which Kerau's is responding to mine. The firmness of him pressing into my thigh is nearly enough to make me forget about the rest of the evening and drag Kerau back to our empty cabin.

His tauntingly light caresses send bolts of buried desire skittering up and over my skin. My hands press down on his strong shoulders in order to gain some leverage as more breathy noises slide past my lips. I'm practically melting into his kisses and quickly growing impatient with my suddenly very real needs.

I've begun mentally calculating how long it would take to get to the cabin from here when someone clears their throat.

My eyes dart above Kerau's head to find a shadow standing in the garland entryway to the tiny room. A shadow whose eyes have darkened considerably from their usual glowing embers.

Scorching black coals glare at me.

XXVI. FIVE MEASLY QUESTIONS

I break away from Kerau's lips with a murderous scowl aimed at Captain Agni's bemused and intruding form.

He looks as smug as if he'd just walked into the damn Vault while watching us peel apart from each other. There's a wicked shine to the southern captain's eyes that tells me more than enough about what he's witnessed. I'm not entirely sure why but something curdles in my stomach at his expression.

"What do you *want*?" I snap as Kerau quickly slides me off his lap.

Agni's gaze finds mine and a shit-eating grin tugs on the side of his mouth. "I was given a message from TideLord Raimbaut for his—ah—*captain*." He says the title as if it means something more like servant.

Those darkened eyes brim with cruel amusement while watching Captain Tharos stand to straighten himself and my face reddens involuntarily. His hair is a touch tousled and his lips are more than a bit swollen but his expression doesn't come off ruffled in the slightest.

Kerau frowns incrementally as he takes in the dark form lingering in the garland doorway.

Captain Agni's head cocks to one side and I glimpse that abnormal gleam again in his gaze from beneath the light of his skewed halo. The one that makes it plain he's indulged in a little more than just wine tonight. There's an unforgiving cut to his sharpened features, a cruelness hidden in plain sight as he stares down Kerau.

"Well, go on then. What's the message?" Kerau asks, his voice a deep challenge.

The corners of Agni's upper lips twitch, like he might actually dare to laugh in the face of TideLord's captain. I feel the way in which Kerau's mood shifts. Tension begins building in the small space like a storm rolling in from the coastline. That jewel-encrusted hilt of his weapon glitters menacingly from his side while stepping closer to the exit.

If Agni feels the charged warning in the air, he doesn't let on. The southern captain merely shrugs in nonchalance. "How would I know? I'm not your messenger boy, *Tharos*."

I blink once in surprise that he already knows Kerau's name. Although I suppose I really shouldn't be, any captain worth their salt would gain immediate intel on any and all new threats. Especially one so incredibly rare and obvious as another elemental.

"*Captain* Tharos," Kerau corrects Agni pointedly.

"Yes, well, *Captain* Tharos. I've completed my task. Now you can stay and play with your little pet here or you can go fetch your master like the good dog I'm sure you are," Agni drones airily, ignoring the violent energy thickening around us entirely.

Kerau glances back to where I remain seated after having been removed from his lap. There's a hesitant deliberation in his eyes, so I motion with my head for him to go on. His presence here tonight was more than enough. I never intended to distract or draw him away from his duties.

Kerau rocks back on his heels before reaching into his uniform's inside breast pocket. "In case I don't get to see you again before leaving," he explains before tossing me the epistle bottle.

I catch it with a small grimace and nod in understanding. Kerau gives me one last pained look. "I'll write to you, I promise. Good luck, Merena—and I'm—I'm sorry," is all he manages to leave me with before quickly exiting the small room to find his TideLord.

I feel like a sail that's suddenly lost all its wind.

To go from such a grand high to a swift dropping low—it has the effect of raising my temper and darkening my mood. I'm trembling with barely contained aggravation while doing my best to brush out my hair with my fingers. Then I gather myself and head for the exit.

Captain Agni takes a step in front of me, effectively blocking me from my path out.

That's all it takes to send me over the edge.

"Are you directionally challenged now, Agni? Get *out* of my way," I demand. The frigid edge to my voice is damn near fatal.

This evening is too volatile for me to be interested in staying much longer. My highly irritated thoughts are mixing terribly with the liquor that's decided now is the time to make itself more prominent. The tortuous phantom feeling of Kerau's lips on mine also does nothing to help.

Agni sneers while looking down his perfectly straight nose at me before actually having the audacity to snap, "That's the thanks I get?"

"*Thanks*?" I echo him in disbelief.

"You're welcome," he quips, a capricious grin now eclipsing his features. My nails begin digging themselves into a palm in order to stop myself from grabbing the blade strapped to my thigh.

"Just what exactly do you imagine I would ever have to thank you for?" I manage to grit out.

His attention skips lazily to the halo still miraculously atop my head and his hand stretches out as if to touch it. I smack his attempt away angrily. He chuckles darkly in response to my obvious hatred while still acting as a solid wall between me and my escape route.

"I would have assumed your honorable little captain already made you well aware of the risks in associating with him tonight. Did he *not*?" Agni inquires, feigning shock.

The stark contrast between my previous interaction with the southern prick and the one currently developing leaves me feeling dizzy. I can't keep track of his mood swings nor do I have the patience left to decipher his senseless taunts.

My chin lifts. "Just get out of my way."

Agni does no such thing. On the contrary, he proceeds to take a step closer.

It's a small step but the room is tiny enough that it has my hand finding the comforting feel of a hilt at last. In a blur of movement, the end of my blade, once strapped to my thigh, now angles itself perilously close to his neck's primary artery. He glances down at that razor-sharp edge before returning to me.

Agni's responding smile is slow, like the last dying rays of the sun just before it slips beneath the cover of night. "You're going to regret doing that," he hums, eyes flashing.

I press the blade until it lies tightly enough against his skin to cut with any sudden movement. "I don't think I am," I counter. My head feels lighter with both wine and power wreaking havoc on my blood.

I am sick of him. Sick of his constant thwarting and ceaseless riling that has only increased exponentially these last few weeks. I'm sick of how he speaks to me. Sick of how he bests me. Most of all, I am sick of seeing his face every time I close my eyes.

"Then you *do* know the bylaws?" Agni challenges with a lifted brow.

I'm silent for a beat and he 'tsks'. The motion causes his neck to slice on the blade but he doesn't so much as blink. "Should any of the TideLords happen to have stumbled upon your little *mingling* in here—" Agni smirks so darkly at his choice of words that I start seeing red. "Well, that would have cost you your trip to The Vault."

"What are you talking about?" I snap. There's a prickling along my scalp, and a rioting sensation is developing near my gut. A droplet of crimson rolls from his cut down onto my weapon still intent at his throat.

"Did *wonder boy* back there seriously not even mention the rules you'd be breaking before swallowing your tongue?" Agni shakes his head distastefully while satisfaction gleams in his eyes. "No fraternizing with any raider belonging to a TideLord until after the completion of all pillar trials. Can't have them giving you any unfair advantages in the tasks."

Sadistic pleasure practically radiates off of him in the face of my silence, further confirming that he's telling the truth. My hands suddenly become numb. I drop the blade between us and take a dazed step backwards.

No.

No.

The thought of being disqualified for a law I haven't ever heard of sounds just as cruel as it is likely. That's life in The Order—nothing is fair. *Get over it.*

My breathing starts coming in and out too rapidly but I just can't seem to stop it. All I can think about is how I've just cost my crew their futures. They all chose me—they all relied on me. They believed in a worthless, unwanted child—a castaway. And I've *failed* them.

No.

"Oh, don't get so riled, *little bastard*. I don't have intentions of ratting you out."

I stop hyperventilating just long enough to lift my head and eye him dubiously.

Captain Agni's laugh is devoid of all mirth as he inches another step closer. "After all, where would be the fun in that?"

I subconsciously move backwards in response to his approaching form and my shoulder blades hit the furniture wall. "Then what do you want, *Agni*?" I hurl his name like the obscenity it is.

The sound of rushing blood pounds heavy in my ears. He looks every bit like the insolent southern highborn that he is. I hate that.

I hate *him*.

"A trade," Agni answers before snorting snidely at my look of wild confusion that follows. "Nothing of any tangible value, of course. I doubt anything you own is worth more than ten silvers. I'd like a trade in the form of truths, much more exciting."

My cheeks reddened at his apt insult. "What in the depths are you talking about?"

The scents of citrus and saffron overpower what little is left of the space between us. A perfidious part of my brain begins recalling the hallucination from the tidepools, how my insides felt like they might combust with his touch, and how his lips tasted of spice.

I quickly strangle that part of my brain into submission.

"Five questions of *my* choosing, whenever I decide to ask them and in which *you* will answer truthfully," he explains, holding up an open hand and waving all five fingers in emphasis. "And I'll know if you're lying."

"Why would you want that? Five measly questions—when you could just have me thrown from the trials altogether?" I don't understand whatever game it is he's playing.

The space between us is so small now that I can't breathe without brushing against him. Agni's hands then unexpectedly plant themselves against the furniture-based wall on either side of my head, effectively caging me in. I despise the rare feeling of true fear that begins pounding in my chest, and I hate how my breath hitches traitorously with it.

He tilts his beautifully carved face down at me in silent study.

"Because I'm bored," Agni answers after a beat, his scar appearing even more ominous up close.

My eyes narrow in disbelief.

His smile is thin while explaining, "You see, your little northern isle is rather dull and dreary. There's really not much here to garner my attention. I could use a source of—*entertainment*. This seems like the perfect opportunity."

"I don't see how me answering some questions would provide you any sort of entertainment," I retort flatly, my eyes tight with suspicion.

His responding grin is like quicksilver as it flashes before me in the shadowy room. "You haven't heard what I'm going to ask."

Ignoring the tightening in my stomach, I snap, "*Fine*. We'll make an od then. You promise not to rat and I promise to answer five stupid questions."

Agni sighs as if I'm being tiresome by forcing him into an official contract, but ultimately he inclines his head in agreement. "On the added condition that we use my blade. The gods only know where *yours* has been."

"Then go get it," I hiss back in annoyance.

His lips twitch before motioning with his chin down towards the waistband of his suit, while both his hands still rest against the wall on either side of my head. "You'll find precisely what you were just ever so *desperate* for right down there. Go on—grab it."

I pale, my affinity coiling tightly before throwing him a look of utter revulsion. "I will not you fucking *prick*."

Agni lets out a sharp barking laugh at my outraged expression. He drops an arm away from the furniture backing to lift up his suit jacket, revealing the ruby hilt of his dagger peeking out from a sheath strategically sewn into his waistband.

His shoulders shake in amusement as I come to understand his words.

"Oh," I say quietly, and try to ignore the flush of embarrassment at my assumption by removing the dagger from its sheath. I take my time inspecting the uniquely jagged blade as it shines that odd ruby hue under the lights of our halo's. It's really quite an exquisite weapon.

Agni's smoke-over-gravel timbre pauses my survey. "Not that I owe you any sort of explanation as to how I operate Boreas, but for your own reference—I enjoy only willing participants during my nighttime endeavors. And I can assure you, I'm never lacking in them."

Looking away from his intent gaze, my attention returns to the dagger in my hands. I make quick work of cutting open my palm. The blade stings like none I've ever encountered and I hiss from the unexpected pain. After completing my own half of the od, I pass Agni back his weapon.

"What type of blade is that?" I ask with a wince, holding my hand gingerly.

Agni smirks while slicing easily across his own palm and watching a long crimson line spring to life. "An old one," he answers simply after saying his own part in the od.

When he next holds out his hand to me, I blink in confusion.

"The od is done."

Agni chuckles as his messy hair shifts in the faint light. "The cuts can't seal until we shake on them." I look at him like this might be some sort of trick and he sighs in annoyance before explaining, "It's the blade. If we don't shake, then we'll both eventually bleed to death. But if you're willing to take that chance, then far be it from me to—"

"*Alright*, alright," I huff, holding out my wounded hand.

Agni takes mine in his and there's a strange, sizzling sort of sensation between the two od lines when they meet. Something unexplainable begins to hum behind that icy wall enveloping the back regions of my mind. Almost like the distant buzzing of energy.

He drops my hand as if I've just given him frostbite, which I *did* technically threaten to do an hour or so ago. I pull my palm to my chest, keeping it in a tight fist as the strange feeling fades into a dull ache. Agni looks down and studies my face with a peculiar frown.

I'm growing sick of his games. "Well, go on then. Ask me your questions before someone notices we're gone," I demand in irritation.

To my shock, he actually doesn't argue and instead asks, "When is your birthday?"

The question is so sudden and unexpected that I laugh in disbelief, to which Agni blinks in clear annoyance. "My birthday? You're serious? You're wasting a question on that?" I laugh again, holding onto my still-aching palm in surprise.

"Just answer it," he orders, obviously displeased by my mocking.

"It's today," I blurt, followed by, "why in the *depths* would you want to know that?"

"Because no one else does," Agni answers smoothly, dangerous amusement returning to his eyes. I bite my cheek to stop my runaway mouth.

He is correct, technically.

The Sons and Daughters were able to tell me a few trivial things that their 'true sight' lent them the night of my own Sál Moon. Two of those things being my birthday and physical age. They couldn't see anything I would consider actually useful, however, such as my name.

Days of birth are meaningless within The Order. There is no celebration or acknowledgment like the stories I hear told of the landmasses. I'd honestly expect a beating for even mentioning it to our ever-cheerful Grand Preceptor. The only person whose day of birth I actually know is Kleio's and that is something only my second would feel the need to make known.

She has, of course, asked for mine, and I simply told her I didn't remember. But I'm not about to reveal any of that to the male before me. Clearly, he already knows more than I'd thought, and I wonder, not for the first time, which of his crew members is his prime informant.

"Well, I have to admit I *was* expecting better inquiries than that," I goad, unable to hold my tongue or temper when it comes to Agni. "All of this just for you to question my day of birth—what would you like me to tell you next? My height? Favorite color? How about my hopes and dreams?" My lashes flutter mockingly.

Agni tilts his head to the translucent ceiling above and the sky beyond for a beat before exhaling deeply and looking back down at me. I watch his expression turn fiendish as a new idea alights his amber eyes. It makes that golden scar look all the more wicked.

I'm promptly made to regret my taunting when Agni re-plants both hands on either side of my head, once again imprisoning me between him and the furniture-based wall. He leans in closer than before and dips his head dangerously lower.

I freeze at the unexpected movement.

The room grows warm with his nearness and the savage drum beat inside of me picks up speed as I stifle the urge to squirm. He brushes my throat lightly with his nose and I jerk away as best I can while in my current position. "What exactly—is your game here—Agni?" I demand, hoping my sudden breathlessness doesn't hint at the mortifying fluttering feelings being erected traitorously near my core.

I can do little more than stand there as he continues on, completely ignoring my breathless inquiry. His nose comes to *barely* graze the outside edge of my ear before trailing softly over my jaw and down the side of my throat. My heart beats louder and faster with every descending inch.

I am acutely aware of the energy rippling off of him and the power he possesses. The element that has my own personal form of torment all these years. Just because the burns and brands along my body are invisible doesn't mean I don't still feel each and every one.

He chuckles darkly, his lips hovering over a noticeable pulsing spot located at the hollow of my neck. It looks as though my heart is attempting to hammer its way outside of my person.

"Are you afraid of me, Boreas?" Agni asks, with a smug half-smile.

His second question, accompanied by the rough smokiness of his voice, skitters across my skin, leaving goosebumps in its wake. My mouth instinctively forms the defiant word 'no,' but his amber eyes are before mine in a flash. They glitter with challenge, daring me to lie to him and see the consequences.

"Yes," I admit, swallowing quickly before wetting my lips.

While tracking the absent motion, a sort of frenzied light enters his eyes. The thrumming inside of me is becoming uncomfortable as the scent of spice invades my senses. A feeling reminding me of hunger pains grows keen and I take a deep breath in an effort to calm myself. My chest presses against him when inhaling and his gaze darkens in response to the contact before frowning.

"*Quod suus 'fraudando*," Agni mutters, shaking his head before giving me a quick once-over.

He sets his jaw and pushes off from the wall of furniture behind me, removing himself from my personal space entirely. My next breath is shaky while he turns around, aiming for the exit and I'm instantly flooded with fresh panic.

"But—that was only two!" I call out, horrified by the thought of him turning me in anyway. I mean, who are the Grand Preceptors going to believe? My money isn't on the bastard-born castaway.

Agni glances over a broad shoulder with an arrogant smirk. "You didn't really think I'd use them all up at *once*, did you?"

The idea sends my stomach plummeting; of course I had. I'd assumed he'd get out whatever humiliating answers he wanted from whatever terrible questions he had for me and I could just chalk it up to a shit night. Having to wait, knowing he could spring it on me at any moment, is infinitely worse. From the way his lips curve, the prick knows it too.

Agni meets the garland veil and turns back to face me as I'm collecting myself against the sofa frame. He holds up three fingers by his head as an obnoxious reminder. "Whenever *I* decide."

I cross my arms, glaring at his gloating when people begin cheering from the rooms outside. My gaze darts to the room's translucent ceiling. I know the reason for the commotion lies in the sky.

Sure enough, brilliant blazing lights colored in shades of amethyst, cyan, and jade all weave back and forth across the midnight plain in a divine sort of dance. Even with the current situation at hand, a smile splits my face from watching the wondrous display. Every year without fail, I get this inexplicable rush of happiness when watching them.

The Sons and Daughters claim them to be a symbol sent from the spirit world to remind us raiders of the important bridge we hold between the three realms. But for some reason I just can't explain; they always feel like some sort of inside joke I used to know. As if they'd been specially crafted for my eyes alone.

Like a secret gift from someone I've never met.

After a moment, I glance back at Agni, the display above having made me forget his unpleasant presence altogether. I find him staring at me and the smile still on my lips with an ambivalent sort of expression. One that's almost *painful*. It toes the line between bitterness and surprise.

Another blink and it's gone. A mask forged of iron has slipped securely down into place and I'm sure I must have imagined the ambivalent look to begin with.

Agni's voice comes out oddly strained when saying in parting, "Happy birthday, Boreas."

I watch with deeply furrowed brows as his tall figure disappears through the garland veil and returns to the revelry beyond.

Only a minute later does the screaming begin.

XXVII. FALLING STARS

Preceptor Chie's age-speckled hand makes loops and lines on the board in front of his room.

I read and re-read what he's just written but my mind is in such a deep haze I can't focus enough to register any meaning behind his scrawl. I can't concentrate on anything; I haven't been able to, not since the end of Luminalia.

That was almost two weeks ago.

I thought I'd been somewhat spiraling since the second task, like my mind really *did* crack in those tidepools and never really healed. But ever since the revel, I've been in an all-out free fall with no real end in sight. My nightmares have worsened to the point that even spending time at The Boneyard does little to put me to sleep. And if those dreams don't keep me up, then it's the feral pounding coming from the other side of my affinity.

It's constantly keeping me on edge.

Normally that rhythm is a warning signal that my power is growing unruly but lately it feels like it's some sort of harbinger. Like my affinity is trying to tell me that *something* is close.

But what?

I gaze down at my palm and the thick silver scar marring it. The one from my od with Agni, the one that *won't* go away. I've had Davina look at it, claiming to be an injury from Oplon's class and even her powers can't seem to make it disappear. What sort of a blade leaves a permanent mark on such a shallow cut? Od lines never take more than a day to disappear.

Kleio's eyes keep anxiously flickering over to me every few minutes. I've nearly bitten her head off for the constant worrying on three separate occasions. I know she can't help it but to have a member of my crew worry like that about their captain—well then I'm failing at my duties.

All of which to say I'm more tightly wound yet inexcusably drawn than I can ever recall.

I didn't even hear Preceptor Chie's question towards the class. I'm only able to catch on when the answer is given by Briggs, Vash's fourth in command. Due to the fact that their table is right next to ours, it would be impossible for me not to hear him.

"The night of the bloody betrothal," Briggs says in that unusually soft voice of his.

My head snaps up to the front of the room, gaining my attention at last. In any class, let alone Preceptor Chie's, it's not often that we discuss things believed to be complete myths or little more than Pontus legends. The man who prides himself on historical events and their accuracy.

The bloody betrothal is something like a children's fable. A bedtime story.

Yet his ancient eyes look out at us all with a very solemn seriousness. "Do you each understand the importance and significance of what has happened this last fortnight during the Luminalia revel? What monumental event we all bore witness to?"

The mere mention of that night makes me feel as though I might vomit. My face pales and I twist uncomfortably in my seat. Kleio looks at me again and I refuse to meet her gaze.

"The falling stars," Greer answers from the other side of our table.

I can still hear the shouts and screams rattling in my head from that night. I remember the way I'd practically dove for my blade on the ground in that tiny private alcove. Then I was sprinting out of there, hurtling towards the main area only a split second later.

The continued cries and panicked yelling that rose while I ran down that hall towards my crew made my heart feel like it might just stop beating entirely. Confused relief hit me square in the chest at the sight of my seven, all completely safe and well, staring up at the night sky in horror.

The mood felt unexplainably heavy, mournful even.

It was one of those times that I'm made keenly aware of my memory loss. Afterwards, when we'd been dismissed to our cabins, Kleio and the others had explained to me what the big deal was.

"Correct," Preceptor Chie agrees, looking away from us with a heavy sigh. He makes his way to the front of the room, one hand at the base of his rounded back. "Let us pretend that not all of you grew up with the tales sung by your mothers and the stories told by your fathers. What then is the meaning behind falling stars on Luminalia?"

"It's the signal that 'The Great Fall' is near." The sound of Brisa's voice has me chancing a glance her way. The western captain's face is as rigid as mine but I don't think I'm mistaking the shine of real fear in her eyes. The same fear I find is reflected in every raider in this room.

It hangs in the very air we breathe.

"Yes, 'The Great Fall,' also sometimes called 'The Second Wave'. The later title stems from the notion that some believe this to herald a second coming of 'The Great Deluge'." Preceptor Chie purses his mouth, wrinkles forming at the corners as he strokes the end of his beard.

From the grave looks between raiders, I now know many of those believers to be in the room.

Chie pulls himself from his ponderings to ask, "And this all ties into the bloody betrothal, of course; how? Your originating landmass version of the ancient tale is quite welcome."

I'm surprised to see Kleio's hand rise in response, and even more surprised to find that it looks like it might be trembling. Preceptor Chie nods for her to answer.

"In the Oyster Court, it's said that 'The Great Fall' signals the return of the Northern Empire. It's the heralding of their revenge for The Bloody Betrothal and the subsequent fall of *all* our worlds. It means that at some point, sometime somewhat soon, all three realms will be at war."

I understand the darkness pressing into every corner of the room a bit better.

Looking around, I have the startling realization that each of these raiders fully buys into this legend. Even my own crew members. I have to wonder if my face shows just how incredulous I feel in response to their dread over a *myth*.

Preceptor Chie nods in somber acceptance to my second's answer and motions for the next raider to tell their landmasses interpretation of the legend. It turns out there is quite a wide variety of different ways in which this particular story is told around Pontus.

All of which are brutal and bloody and end in total and complete annihilation.

Lovely.

"*Please* don't do this," I plead.

"I'm afraid you've given us no choice, Captain," Greer states with a sad shake of her head.

"Come on—let's just go back. I'm serious." I turn my beseeching eyes to Herse, who stands with her arms crossed and a stony gaze facing out toward the dark night.

She glances over a shoulder at me. "Oh no, don't you look at me to stop this. You brought this all on yourself."

"How?" I ask in pure disbelief.

Herse is poised to answer but the sound of sand being kicked over the hill at my backside hushes her unspoken words. I shift to watch Kleio jump down from the black dune behind us with fierce determination in those brown eyes.

"*How?*" she angrily echoes, striding for us with nothing but her wetsuit on. "You've been silent for the last *five* fucking weeks, Merena. Things were a bit weird after that last pillar task I'll admit, but you disappeared the night of Luminalia and came back *off*. You won't tell any of us what's going on with you, even though it's clear as godsdamned day that something is."

My second looks more furious than I've ever seen.

"You're being a bit dramatic," I breathe with the roll of my eyes.

"I am *not,*" Kleio says through her teeth, coming to face me head on and her affinity flickers in the air nearby. "You barely pay attention in class. The only time you're focused is during weapon training or mealtime, and you can't sleep through a single night without getting your ass kicked or exhausting yourself by kicking other people's asses."

I bite my thumbnail with cool indifference. "Is that all?"

Kleio shakes her head of dark curls currently braided into two uniform plaits. "How many times do I have to get this through your ice block of a skull, Merena? We. Can. Handle. Ourselves. Stop trying to protect us, you overbearing little deviant!"

"I'm not trying to protect you!" I snap, louder than intended.

Some of the others flinch from the slight burst of cold that expels from me unintentionally. Kleio, however, holds steady as a rock and raises an eyebrow skeptically. The only raider who's never been afraid of me or my power. No matter what terrible things she's seen me forced to do.

I take a deep breath to calm myself.

Kleio is right; things *have* only gotten worse since Luminalia. After the second pillar and my nightmare returning, I was at least able to right myself by spending time at The Boneyard.

Then I had to go and contact Kerau, whom I'm no longer sure if I can trust. I toss and turn with the idea that he knew the bylaws and was trying to get me thrown from the trials but that makes absolutely no sense. Yet the alternative is that he didn't know the bylaws that were given by his own damned TideLord which would make him an idiot.

Which he isn't.

I've recounted his apology when leaving the private alcove many times over. At the time, I thought it was just because he had to leave me to go to his TideLord but now I'm not sure.

Then there was the slap in the face I'd encountered just prior by the captains who did not wish to show any sort of friendliness with me in the face of the TideLords. Captain Tetsuo has tried to gain my attention several times since but he's been met with my very frosty stare at each attempt. I won't allow myself to be made a fool like that ever again.

It had stung worse than I'd ever let on.

Then there is the charming little fact that I'm currently indebted to Captain Agni, the very worst person possible to hold my secret. His goading has stopped being so outrageous and become more subtle, which is worse. He knows exactly how awful it is to keep this from my crew, and he makes a point of giving me knowing looks or passing comments that serve to confuse and rile them.

Just yesterday, after Beldham's class, in which I had kept my mouth shut to avoid Agni starting an argument on purpose, he waited for us in the hall. Waited for *me*, specifically.

I'd brushed past the prick without so much as a passing glance to him or his pack of jackals.

"*I have a question,*" Agni had called out, making my pulse come to a thudding halt.

The southern jackass flashed a smirk at the lack of color on my face before tilting his head in the direction of my crew, who all waited with mixed looks of perplexity. His eyes then landed on Kleio at my side. "Could you tell me, what is five minus two?" He asked her with a look my way.

Freezing cold anger nearly burned me from the inside out. Taunting me was one thing, but taunting my crew was entirely different. It took all my willpower to keep my tone casual as I swiftly intervened. "Why don't you have one of your little mongrels do your counting for you, eh? Might be good exercise for their stunted little brains. I'm sure they could all use it."

His crew abruptly stopped whatever it was they were laughing over in that odd southern tongue and Agni's mouth twisted with loathing. "Oh but I think I find yours more *entertaining*."

A flush graced my face at his pointed choice of words. Yet from the way his own crew was looking with uncertainty behind him, I got the strange feeling they didn't know about our deal either. That fact both confused and emboldened me.

So I gave him a false smile before grabbing Kleio's arm. "I beg to differ."

Those words sparked something menacing in his eyes; it made my legs feel too heavy and light at once. All it would take from him is one little visit with his Grand Preceptor and we'd be out of the chance of a lifetime. The idea made me feel like I might just pass out right then and there.

The crook of Agni's mouth twitched. "Alright, so long as I'm the one making you beg."

Then he'd turned around without another word, as if having lost all interest in his own game. He rejoined his crew, as if the exchange had never happened. To avoid further interaction, I kept my mouth shut and marched my crew onto water combat training without saying a word.

That had evidently been the last straw for Kleio.

"Okay—okay, maybe I am a *bit*. But it's only because I messed up in the first place—I made a mistake—a few of them, actually. It is my responsibility to correct them, and mine alone. I won't allow any of you to have your futures jeopardized because you chose to believe in some *worthless* bastard-born castaway who should have just been left down in the depths."

My crew members all inhale sharply at my words. I think I hear Herse swear low.

Kleio grabs me by the front of my shirt so harshly and unexpectedly that I don't even think to draw a blade. She bares her teeth at me when growling furiously, "Do not ever speak about *my* captain like that again!" All warmth is drained from her eyes, now brimming with outrage.

In response to my silence, she shakes me. *Hard*.

"You don't want to tell us what happened—*fine*. You want to take on full responsibility and once again refuse to share the load—*fine*. But what you do not get to do is question the choice we each made. Not for a single second do you get to tell us what it is we should see in you. I will *not* allow for you to succumb to the idiotic political bullshit that The Order loves to spew in order to promote animosity," she seethes no more than an inch from my face.

I swallow. This is perhaps the most terrifying I have ever seen Kleio look—my perfect second. Her affinity shields of violet energy buzz to life angrily in the air along the midnight shore.

"I will *not* allow for you to question your worthiness to be alive." She barrels on. "I swear to all the drowned gods that if I ever hear you question that fact again or even catch so much as a glimmer of the doubt that's been shadowing your eyes these last few weeks—captain or not—I will *personally* kick your ass. Got it?"

My lips flicker upwards in response to her threat. "Got it."

The relief in her expression at such a small gesture on my part makes me suddenly guilty. I never intended for her to worry so much. But that's Kleio; she can't help it. As much as these last few weeks have been eating me alive, it's probably taken something out of Kleio to watch.

"Good." She releases her grip from my shirt. "Now—shall we?"

"But I'm not in the mood," I whine for the hundredth time since being dragged from my bed in the middle of the night.

Kleio gives me a look that could peel paint so I hastily start stripping off my uniform down to my wetsuit beneath.

A few minutes later, and we're out amongst the freezing waves.

Luckily, my second's affinity is able to keep her and the others from truly feeling the bitter cold.

"Merena—this one!" Kleio shouts from across the choppy waters.

I lie flat on my stomach along the ice board I've wrangled and a quick glance backwards reveals there's a monster of a wave coming towards us. I turn around and give Kleio a thumbs up in agreement. Her grin is deviant with eager anticipation and I shake my head, laughing.

It feels nice to laugh.

Admittedly, I have a bit of a sixth sense when it comes to ice surfing. I'm able to anticipate just when the exact right moment is to catch a wave. It's like I can feel the way the current's rolling, almost like seeing the motion of it beneath the surface. I'll allow the tide to sweep me up inside until I find that perfect sweet spot.

Some, like Vash Larceon, call it cheating.

"Now!" I shout towards the line of my crew members before popping up on my board. They follow suit quickly, as the behemoth wave builds even higher upon itself.

I'm immovable from my tiny glacier board while beginning to descend the monstrous current at thrilling speeds. My balance is never better than when I'm out on the chaotic tides.

I hear the others high shrieks of enjoyment through the winds rushing past my ears and I smile.

It feels nice to smile.

As the lip of the wave spills over to my left, I aim for the hollow barrel forming and hear Kleio's loud whoops of enjoyment not far from behind. The ocean's power beneath the ice at my feet never fails to both excite and ground me in the moment. It forces my brain to forget about any other problems plaguing it and immerse itself in the now.

Navigating the water's constantly changing surface, I make my way for the slim lip and use it to three-sixty myself down into the widening barrel. My face splits into a wide grin when landing and sliding skillfully inside the pocket.

Nimra and Greer have already wiped out and Davina stayed back on the shore, claiming there would be no one to heal us if she snapped her neck on a rock. The twins are still hollering their enjoyment from somewhere farther off. Herse is the only one nowhere to be seen but she's like a ghost on the waters; you never know where she'll just suddenly *appear*.

Kleio has followed me, racing just meters away inside the rapidly forming curl. Reaching out my hand, I run a finger along the passing wall of saltwater. My pulse beats in sync with the ocean's steady undertow and my power arches into the temptation of the wave like a needy grimalkin.

Glancing at my second and her excitement-flushed face, I decide to allow my affinity to play.

The sea spray rapidly transforms into soft white petals, while the watery pathway beneath our glacial boards turns into a powdery tread. Kleio squeals out in delighted surprise as we go from surfing to snowboarding our way down the remaining wave and onto the black sandy shore.

After a few more rounds, I feel lighter than I have since the second pillar trial.

Regardless of this stupid fucking deal with Captain Agni, as long as I have my crew and the occasional escapade, things will be okay.

To further prove that point, tonight I sleep soundly without a single nightmare.

Leave it to Kleio to catch me in my free fall.

XXVIII. THE VEIL KEEPER

My expression is one of complete shock while reading the contents of the previously sealed scroll that has made its way into my hands this morning by two very timid level-ones.

I scan the neat handwriting, studying the unlikely words.

Though I know Preceptor Beldham would never lie about such things, I just can't quite believe it. It's the *morning* of our third pillar trial, after all. This is the one that's supposed to test our ability to surrender and evolve, which has to be the most ominous sounding yet.

"Merena, is everything okay?" Kleio takes a break from inhaling her breakfast long enough to ask. "Your face is doing that thing where it sort of looks like it might fold in half," she explains, bending the piece of toast up between her hands in demonstration.

I wordlessly pass my second over the scroll for her to read. It's then that I notice the wide-eyes belonging to said pair of timid level-ones *still* standing there, gaping at me.

I blink once at them in question.

"G–Good morn—morning, Captain B-Boreas," stumbles the pale, ginger-haired boy on the left before looking pointedly over at his partner.

"Hi," is all the umbra-toned boy on the right manages to squeak out. His brilliant green eyes, framed by cropped onyx hair, are the size of dinner plates.

It's unbelievable how young they look. They can't possibly be the same age as we were when first arriving here. Their awfully big uniforms hang off at odd angles and a bit of baby fat still rounds out their cheeks. Even their hair is youthfully mussy. They look like a pair of grimalkin whelps.

"Hello," I reply, but it comes out as a question. As in, *why are you two still here?*

Both boys glance down the table I occupy as head.

I follow their fear-stricken gazes to find the twins. Nephthys and Prisca seem to be in some sort of sibling spat and obviously haven't been paying attention to the exchange.

Propping my elbows up on the wooden dining table, I rest my chin on interlaced fingers and wait. It takes only a handful of seconds for them to have the good sense to cease their bickering and turn their attention my way.

The twins look over at the pair of level-ones and back at me with identical expressions that make a mockery of the word innocent. Knowing full well that the two of them, along with Nimra, have been tasked with helping the newest raiders this year only increases my darkening suspicions. My lips press together in silent analysis.

Not a shot in hell will I buy whatever it is they're about to try selling me on.

"What are you two little *sea devils* doing here, bothering our captain?" Nephthys aims for a casual chiding tone even while alarm flashes through her usual mischievous gaze.

Prisca nods a touch too emphatically in agreement. "Shouldn't you both be practicing your drowning down in the pool chambers right about now?"

Herse snorts a laugh and the level-ones instantly blanch.

The red-haired one starts up again, his tone now frustrated. "But *you said* that we could—"

"Whoa–baah-buh-bup-bup," Prisca interjects with a look that promises violence if he continues any further. The level-one throws a deep scowl back in her direction and it almost makes me laugh.

"What did you two tell them?" I demand, looking between my fifth and sixth through a narrowed gaze. They both quickly plaster on demure smiles that don't quite manage to hide the guilt from their eyes.

"Oh *nothing*," Nephthys assures me, giving an errant wave of her hand. "You know how much kids like to prattle."

Prisca is quick to agree. "No idea what they're blabbering about half the time."

"You said that if we did all of your tasks until the end of the year, Captain Boreas would give us each a kiss!" The green-eyed boy shouts in a surge of frustration.

Loud enough for just about any table near ours all the way down to the exit to hear.

My mouth pops open and Greer promptly snorts ice-water straight out through her nose. Herse begins banging the table with her fist while choking on her own unexpected laughter. The silverware and plates upon our table rattle around in an obnoxiously loud display.

If all eyes in the dining hall weren't on us already, they sure as shit are now.

Kleio drops the scroll from between her hands and it flutters down to land before her plate. With incredulous eyes, she slowly turns to fully gape at the twins. Nimra's soft honey irises are just as wide and anxious as the poor level-one's while looking between me and the two imps at the other end of the table.

"You—*what*?" I splutter in outrage.

Nephthys winces and slides down in her seat while biting a nail.

"It's not the end of the year now, *is it*?" Prisca hisses at the boys with a look that's intent on murder. They each turn a bit green beneath her gaze and shake their heads 'no'.

Sighing angrily through my nose, I turn swiftly around in my seat to face them.

I quickly study their faces to find them both fearful and yet idiotically hopeful. My eyes roll all the way to the skeleton-clad ceiling with a small shake of my head in utter aggravation.

"Just how old are you two anyway?" I ask, my voice hinting at the underlying disbelief I'm mentally grappling with in regards to the pure menaces that are my fifth and sixth.

"Thirteen," boasts the green-eyed boy, standing up a bit straighter.

"And a *half*," corrects the other before scrambling to push back the locks of red hair that have fallen before his eyes.

"Why don't you all try earning a kiss from one of the girls in your own level? I'm sure such strapping lads as yourself must have plenty of admirers," I say, trying for a smile.

Murderous thoughts regarding the twins make it difficult to pull off.

The boys exchange looks of total deflation and my brow creases in confusion.

"No—" starts the one on my left, beginning to push up his sleeve.

"We don't," finishes the other on my right, folding back the cuff of his uniform.

They hold up their exposed arms for me to view their raider brands. I study the identical skeleton of a great sea-serpent wrapped around their wrists to find both of their markings reflect a startlingly colorless shade of white.

Castaways.

A tingling sensation comes from the same blindingly white brand wrapped around my own wrist in acknowledgement. My heart stumbles a beat in response to the haunted look in their eyes, one I remember far too well. It used to greet me every day in my own grim reflection.

I sigh deeply before shaking my head at my own resolve.

Looking back at the level-ones standing before me, I motion with the crook of my finger for them to come closer. Then I gift them each with the very thing I wish someone would have done for me all those nights I spent drowning in my own tears. What I needed every time I'd prayed I wouldn't wake to see the morning.

A kiss on both cheeks.

The boys step backwards, dazed.

"Now hurry on along. Go tell all your little rivals that Captain Boreas always pays her debts. Even those made on *my behalf,*" I slide the last part through my teeth with a glare at the twins, who currently look as though they're trying to find a way to meld into the woodwork.

They nod, slack-jawed, before scampering clumsily away from our table.

I watch as they hold their hands firmly over each cheek as if to trap my kisses in while returning to their now gaping table of level-ones located at the other end of the dining chamber.

Pinching the bridge of my nose between my thumb and forefinger, I turn back to my crew.

"You two are both dead," I state, motioning with my free hand to Nephthys and Prisca, now sliding down ridiculously low in their chairs. "But I'm going to have to reschedule your execution because I'm currently booked for today. Kleio—walk with me."

Rising from the table and aiming for the nearest exit, my second quickly swipes the scroll from its spot before her plate and follows in my wake. Once we've made it out of the dining chamber, she blurts, "So the TideLords really won't be there?"

"It seems not," I reply, before beginning to rub small circles on the sides of my temples. A headache won't be far off. "Even our officiant won't be there today. I'm not sure how or if we'll be watched or scored, or what. Only what's written in that letter."

"When will you leave?" Kleio asks, just as worried about this unexpected turn of events as I am.

I shake my head. "I don't know. We were told to go about our day as normal and we'll be summoned when needed."

Kleio's brow furrows in concern but I shrug. "I'm sure it's fine. Honestly, it's better. At least now I can get in a swim and relax a bit beforehand. Go keep an eye on idiot one and idiot two for me. Have Herse and Greer start thinking up punishments. Tell them to get creative with it. Also make *certain* they haven't promised my kisses to any other level-ones. Please."

Kleio snorts a small, disbelieving laugh at the absolute absurdity of the twins' stunt. Then she gives me a brief but tight squeeze of my hand, along with a few words of encouragement for the impending trial, before leaving me to rejoin the rest of our crew.

I aim for the pool chambers, intending to make good on my previous statement and get in a nice long swim. It would be nice to work out my stress and also probably help stop this newly forming ache holding my neck hostage.

Unfortunately for me, however, a swim is not in the cards today.

Before I even make it to the entrance of the underground tunnels, a black bag is shoved down over my head while multiple strong hands contain my furiously struggling form.

If it wasn't for the familiar sound of Beldham's brisk voice right before wax is forced into my ear canals, I would have been slightly worried.

For the last hour or two, a steady rocking beneath my feet, alluding to the ocean's presence, has been my only companion. I pick at the stray skin around my fingernails, not needing my sight to do so, while playing a mental game where I try estimating how many knots we're doing.

My best guess is 19.5, and I'm almost certain it's correct.

It isn't until whatever carrier I'm journeying on comes to a halting, squealing stop that I begin feeling the first real jolts of nerves.

I'm yanked from my sitting position a moment later without any sort of gentleness.

My blindfold is then removed but not my ear plugs, and my hands remain tied behind my back.

So I stare blankly at Preceptor Oplon's moving mouth for almost a full minute, not hearing a single word he's saying. After a moment, I shake my head at him in complete confusion.

"So sorry about that, Captain Boreas. You can hear me now, yes?" He asks after taking out the earplugs and untying my hands. Preceptor Oplon appears to be almost as nervous as I am.

"Yes," I answer, repressing my own grimace while rubbing my newly freed wrists.

"Good—great. Now this is going to be a bit of an unorthodox task set before you today." I nod and he continues, "Obviously, with Raider Dornon and the TideLords absence, the cardinals are having to put on this trial on our own. So it has been decided that you are each going to complete your challenge entirely separate from the other captains."

I dip my chin in understanding and Oplon smiles briefly before finishing. "We're doing this in order of rankings. Both the west and south have each had a captain go already this morning."

Incredible.

I'm next brought up to the deck of the small ship to see where exactly I'll be performing this 'unorthodox' trial. It's then that my breakfast decides it just might make a grand appearance.

I gawk at the sight before me, my stomach rolling over in succession.

A massive skull, perhaps larger than the North Order's fortress itself, rests just about a mile out in the ocean before us. The colossal thing is angled slightly backwards with its monstrous jaw parted. It looks like a sunken giant's skeleton screaming at the sky.

Looking back over a shoulder in disbelief, I spot our Grand Regent as she makes her way towards the ship's starboard railing to join me. I turn forward again and silently stare at the otherworldly sight, barely even noticing Beldham's quiet presence.

My mouth feels more like sand the longer I continue to gawk.

"And the trial is what, exactly?" I finally manage to ask, hoping terror isn't obvious in my voice.

Beldham answers in her typical matter-of-fact tone. "Enter the grotto of the Veil Keeper and retrieve a single athanasia bloom."

My head whips 'round to face the old bat. "A flower? You're sending us in *there* for a godsdamn flower?" My voice is high with incredulity but I'm too shocked to apologize for swearing.

Our Grand Regents face remains stern but something softer resides in those cornflower eyes. Not that I would ever dare comment on it.

"Yes, Captain Boreas. You are going in there for a flower. One of priceless value and incredible importance to The Order, especially now." She sniffs the sea breeze and I squeeze my hands into tight fists in order to stop myself from retorting another snappish comment.

After a moment, I dare to inquire, "And how will I know it's this, athanasia bloom?"

Her lips look like they might have moved in amusement before answering, "They have petals of amethyst with stems of blue and they smell like death itself."

Of course they do. I huff a long sigh and return my gaze to the giant skull we're quickly approaching.

"I would expect you are aware of the other things you may face in there?" Beldham asks lightly.

Clenching my jaw tight, I nod.

"Good."

It's been a few years since we studied the Veil Keepers and their various ocean grottos but what we learned of them is terrifying enough that there's no chance of me ever forgetting.

The three realms of Nawai, Pontus, and Celestial used to coincide together with the drowned gods watching over them all. But when the Great Deluge occurred, something else happened. A veil fell between the realms and separated them from each other entirely, or so legend claims.

The Veil Keepers are said to be guarding posts, maintaining the veil. They uphold the necessary walls between our worlds and help to keep those terrifying creatures from Nawai and the Celestial realm out of Pontus. The kinds of creatures that only gods could hope to defeat.

Our boat approaches the open skeletal mouth until we're almost perfectly level with the beast's mandible. The Veil Keeper's closeness jolts me out of my grim thoughts, and my hands move automatically to inspect myself. I pat down one leg and the next with growing panic-fueled horror until Beldham holds up my sling of various small blades.

I'm then informed that the cardinal ship will be waiting for me at a safe distance from the extremely dangerous grotto. After that, I'm given a small flare gun and instructed to fire it once I've made it out with the bloom in hand. I'm able to read in between the lines.

Don't bother coming back without it.

Taking a leap off from the small boat's edge, I land with a rather annoying splash in the waters before the massive skull topper.

The behemoth head must have belonged to some sort of ancient god or other malevolent creature that roamed Pontus long before the massive flood. Preceptor Chie's musings over myths suddenly don't seem so insane, as I literally stare one right in the face.

The vessel behind me makes quick work of turning around and speeding back out to a safe distance from the Veil Keeper. I snort in renewed disbelief before removing one of the many blades now slung snugly around my middle. The hilt in my palm is as comforting as a child's blanket and I grip it tightly before angrily stomping through the ominous mouth.

The bad mood I'm in, stemming from the twins and their stunt this morning, is only further heightened when I stumble and trip within the first two seconds of entering the Veil Keeper.

My hands and knees promptly slam down onto what feels like stone and I swear so loudly that I'm sure even the gods in their watery depths can hear my fowl mouth before forcing myself up.

Furiously scanning my surroundings, I find the reason for my spectacular fall. The direction I chose inside the Veil Keeper is framed by a large lip of limestone and its presence hidden under the shallow waters. Just my fucking luck.

I next discover a single pathway extends out before me into the chamber beyond and my throat tightens at the sight it leads to. *This can't be right.*

This massive skull's interior is basically empty.

The singular pathway leads out to a ring of extremely tall stones set upon a strange circular platform in the middle of the watery cavern. There is no oceanic garden and certainly no flowers to be seen. My pulse quickens with concern—*is this the wrong place?*

Is that possible? There is quite literally nothing here except those monoliths.

Unless I'm meant to search the water?

A chill runs down my spine as I recount the various monsters and terrifying netherdepth creatures said to haunt the Veil Keepers like they're some sort of Nawai graveyard.

I decide to at least inspect the stones. Maybe there's an inscription on them with directions or perhaps this is just some big misunderstanding. Maybe we went to the *wrong* Veil Keeper?

The scuff of my boots against stone fills the enormous skull's hollow inside as I make my way over to the solemn rocks. I begin flicking the blade in my grip around my hand and through my fingers anxiously while reaching the monoliths rising all the way up to the gray cranium ceiling.

To my surprise, they *do* in fact have inscriptions etched into them but nothing I can make any semblance of sense out of. The swirling script embedded in the rocks is one I've never seen before, which is intriguing but ultimately doesn't mean much.

A few of them appear to have intriguing wave-like symbols further up along the stones.

Curiosity gets the better of me and I step into the center of the ring to get a closer look.

That's when the fog rolls in.

It's thick and heavy and absolutely wasn't there a moment before but suddenly the grotto is absolutely teeming with it. The white haze hovers over the ground, covering the waters below and completely hiding the one and only walkway available for exit.

I squint at the mist for a moment before turning around to face the towering boulders again, only to find that the strange script and symbols are now gone. That can't be possible.

My hand stretches out instinctively to graze over the stone and it is met with an invisible wall.

I watch as my fingers simply *bounce* right off of it. The sensation of the unseen barrier reminds me of Kleio's affinity and the violet-colored energy shields she's able to create.

"Weird," I mutter softly.

The word rings out and around the grotto, echoing loudly as if I had shouted it rather than whispered. I quickly rescan the eerie mist that's begun creeping up the sides of the monoliths and find it somehow has not entered the small circle inside them where I currently stand.

Deciding I'd better hurry up and get back out to let Beldham and the others know they were wrong about the bloom's location, or possibly even the Veil Keeper itself, I aim for the lip of the pathway. But when I try stepping over it, I am *again* met with that invisible wall.

"What the fuck?" I grumble, not bothering to keep my voice low. As before, my words repeat outwards in an irritating echo that seems to only grow louder with every repetition.

I try again and again. Each time I hit that same barrier.

Growling out in frustration, I grip my blade tighter. Fine. I'll just slip out one of the other narrow openings between the monoliths and scale back around the edge to the mist-shrouded walkway. I won't dare touch the water beneath that fog unless I have to. Only the gods know what lurks down there—likely creatures capable of breaking through ice with minimal effort.

Choosing the space between the closest set of rocks nearest me, I try again to exit and run smack into the concealed barrier. Spewing out a lengthy string of choice words that would make any raider proud, I have a brief moment of terribly irritated stupidity.

Without thinking, I hurl the knife in my hand straight at the invisible barrier in a fit of rage. I immediately recognize my own idiocy as the weapon rebounds off the barrier and comes racing back for its owner.

Ducking with the reflexes attained only through years of The Order's training, the blade whistles harmlessly in the air over my head.

I'm expecting the clattering noise it makes upon landing but I'm not expecting it to sound as distant as it does. Spinning backwards, I discover the knife has flown *through* the stone opening directly opposite me and landed on a previously unseen path beyond.

My eyebrows knit together and a lip slides between my teeth in confusion.

I'm positive that pathway wasn't there before. There was only one exit and entrance.

I'm sure of it.

XXIX. THE THIRD PILLAR

My steps are cautious while heading towards the discarded weapon.

No invisible wall springs into place, and at long last, my foot mercifully meets the other side of the ring. The strange new pathway appears to be real and solid so I take another step and leave that bizarre stone circle completely.

One more hesitant step and I make to scoop up the blade from the ground.

The ground that is now made of sand.

I just barely manage to grip the weapon's hilt before my pulse spikes in surprise at the sudden change in terrain. My eyes study the ground in front of me, which should be stone. I don't entirely believe the white sediment I see beneath my feet.

Slowly, my gaze parts from the sand floor and rises upwards to take in the space before me.

I clutch the knife to my chest in shock at my findings.

A yawning chasm, like one of the enormous trenches found in The Deep, stretches out as far as the eye can see. But it's not the sight of this outlandish ocean trench I'm evidently standing at the bottom of, nor is it the fact that I'm somehow breathing and moving inside the watery expanse as if it were air that steals all thought from my mind and grips my heart like a vise.

That would be due to the waterway's current occupants.

The otherworldly trench is teeming with countless bobbing medusae.

Each one of them glows with an ethereal light in a shade of silver-kissed-blue. I don't need any closer inspection to know exactly what they are.

Heimartai.

The name and its meaning evoke a memory from a few years ago. In level-five we're taught about some of the more nuanced beings that exist in the pockets of space between this realm and the others. I suppose the Veil Keeper would qualify as one of these 'pockets'.

The Heimartai are nightmarish creatures said to reside in the lands between life and death itself. Or rather the realms of Pontus, Nawai, and Celestial. If memory serves me correctly, then each one of them contains a single soul's prophecy. Each one holds a person's past and destiny—their entire life glows inside that silvery-blue medusa.

I also recall my horror upon learning their trick.

The Heimartai will tell you all you wish to know about your past and future, as long as you touch the *right* one. However, if you were to touch one that did not belong to *you* in particular, even the barest trace against them or one of their many long arms would spell certain death.

I flick the knife around my hand absently while analyzing the scene.

There are *hundreds* of them, thousands even, lining the waterway.

Chancing a glance behind me towards the ring of monoliths I just stepped out of, I find there is nothing but a solid wall of basalt. It appears I'm backed into the trench's corner with no way out but through. An ache begins forming near my temples before again facing the deadly trench.

Upon my second study, I spot something I must have missed in my initial assessment.

At the other end of the lengthy passage, an ocean grove sparkles into existence. Through the shadow-strewn water, I catch a glimpse of unmistakably vibrant amethyst petals.

My outward groan is long while rubbing my face with both hands in agitation.

Can't one of these trials be like semi-easy? Do they all have to be life or death? I'm starting to think that exceptionally high odds of maiming are a prerequisite when deciding upon the task.

My hands slide down either side of my face. This is impossible.

The medusae float menacingly above and along the trench's sides in tightly knit groups, illuminating a very fine path for me to tread. I'm forced to remind myself there isn't a choice.

Holding tight to my comfort weapon, I shove down all gnawing fears, precisely as The Order has beaten into me from day one and step out into the trench of horrors.

To my surprise, the first few meters into my suicide mission pass by without much problem. The few low-hanging Heimartai drift out of the way upon my hesitant approach. Only a few linger in my path and they're easy enough to skirt around even with their dangerously long arms.

I can't find the right words to explain the peculiar ocean-way. My movements and breathing are exactly like I'm above surface. Even my hair and belongings don't float in the water around me.

I suppose it's akin to moving within a dream, where logic and the laws of nature cannot intervene. Maybe that's what this is—the place in between life and death, a dream realm teeming with nightmares.

That sounds about right.

I maintain a slow enough pace so as not to disturb any of the deadly creatures but quickly enough that I don't waste any unnecessary time. My mind wanders to the TideLords and their absence. The tension in everyone since the falling stars on Luminalia is obvious yet I still haven't really grasped the consequences of such an event.

About a fourth of the way into my careful trek, things become significantly more difficult.

A voice unexpectedly calls out to me from above. It sounds like it might have come from another world, another realm. Perhaps it did.

The tenor is both cruel and sweet, familiar yet utterly alien, emanating from one of the many glowing Heimartai. "*The blade of one you love shall end your days,*" it whispers eerily down into the open waters; the prophetic words are carried on an invisible current to reach my ears.

I stiffen as the Heimartai's statement sends a chill racing down my spine. My mind flashes to the recurring nightmare where a blade is pushed into my heart by a hand I trust. The obvious correlation is enough to stop me in my tracks and peer upwards at the creature above my head.

The horrible being drifts down perilously close. That silvery-blue light inside of it grows brighter as if sensing it holds my attention. When it's only a single meter away, I hear its voice once more: "*You will fail to find what you seek and another shall take your place.*"

Before I know what I'm doing, my hand is outstretched and reaching eagerly towards eternal sleep. I almost graze its bulbous head when my voice of reason—Kleio's voice—shouts loudly at me from inside in my own mind. *Keep it moving, Boreas!*

I snatch away my extended fingers in a blur of motion with a gasp at my own stupidity.

The Heimartai must know it's lost its chance at ensnaring me, because I watch with trembling fists as it fades to a pale opal shade before floating off. That prophecy didn't belong to me after all. An odd shuddering sensation runs through me, like someone is bottling my soul.

Continuing requires forcing my legs to move one by one.

It quickly becomes evident that the Heimartai opened some sort of floodgate by speaking to me. The other medusae no longer remain silent or pliant, but instead begin calling out to me as I pass.

Some even fall directly into my path. Their ethereal voices reach out, more potent than their tendrils, trying to ensnare me with possible futures that may or may not belong to me.

The louder ones, the ones that block me from my path—those are the ones I feel some sort of unexplainable connection to. I don't know enough about Heimartai to know if that truly means anything. Only the voices of my crew members shouting inside my head have the power to stop me from touching the tempting ocean oracles and their sweet promise of death.

A part of me wonders if the Heimartai can somehow hear my crew's mental warnings. They're quick to realize the moment they've lost their hold on me and easy to get around once I know for certain that it's not my fate they're whispering about.

Each time one is dismissed, another will swiftly fall into place. I find that the things they say and the sound of their wonderfully horrible voices is a test in and of itself every single time.

One croons, "The heavens shall spill to you their greatest secrets; you alone can chart the path."

My skin rises with the chills I feel at the absolution in each of their soul's destinies.

I make it a few more paces before another promises, "*In the darkest hour, your burden will be to find the key. It's the only path to salvation.*"

The one to halt my progress next instructs, "*Follow the heart through the darkest night and into the sun's prison. It will guide you to your purpose.*" I'm halfway down the sandy trail and having to sidestep the onslaught of prophecies meant for other people's ears.

A shiver runs through me after another almost gains my full attention. "*Guided by the flame of old, uncover the realm of knowledge. The truth that was hidden must again be known.*" My hands twitch towards the Heimartai; a part of me desperately wishes to know the rest of its prophecy.

Even as my very bones shout that it is not meant for me.

"*When all seems lost and the tethers have snapped, you become the bridge.*" The enticingly silky words strum out upon a phantom current, but again, those voices in my head steer me away.

I'm close now; the shimmering ocean grove beckons near, and excitement pulses in my ears.

Thank the fucking depths, because my self-restraint is wearing thinner with every passing destiny. It's becoming harder to stop my curiosity-fueled impulsive reactions to them.

"*Always underestimated. Always the odd one out. How ironic that your decision will be the one to tilt the scales.*" The spiel of information from the wicked creature floating just above my head makes my skin crawl.

The sight of the athanasia's startling amethyst petals grabs my attention, and I force myself onward. Just a few more meters. I can do this. I can slip into the grove, steal one of the blooms, and be done in mere moments. Of course then that leaves the little question of how exactly I get back *out* from here but that's for future Merena to worry about.

I deftly duck and weave through the remaining few creatures of destiny until one last Heimartai drops down into my path. It's unlike any of the others. I watch stunned as it pulses silently before me, changing in colors from greens to blues to purples to silver and back again.

The rhythm of it matches the pounding beat within, that odd thrumming that comes from the other side of my affinity. I resist the knee-jerk urge to unleash my power. I've got a feeling in my gut that freezing one of these creatures would not bode well for my own survival.

The color-morphing Heimartai floats in my pathway, effectively nailing me to the spot. When the being speaks at last, it doesn't have the same odd mixture of tone as the others. Instead, its unusual voice is one I cannot place and yet somehow I *know* inside my very soul.

A male's voice, deep and rich and *familiar,* proclaims, "So, the daughter of tides approaches at long last. I've wondered when you'd finally find your way to me."

I can't make myself move. I can't tear myself away. Only one single thought keeps looping around and around inside my mind while I stand there as if frozen solid.

I know that voice.

I know that voice.

I know that voice.

Something inside of me hammers with an insistent beat. The wild thrumming feels like it is begging me to understand, begging to be remembered. As hard as I try, I'm met with the same solid wall of ice as always. I'm at a loss for words; my hands struggle to keep hold of their blades.

I know with absolute certainty that whatever this thing is about to spew, it is at last for me.

"And yet you are *not* you. Not quite."

If Heimartai could tilt their heads, I swear this one would.

"W–what do you mean?" I rasp out in befuddlement.

My affinity is coiled tight inside my chest, just waiting for the moment to pounce.

The medusa actually appears to muse for a moment.

Then, without warning, the colorful creature begins circling around me as if inspecting my person. I spin in place with blades held aloft, prepared to stab it if I must. Curiously, though, I get the feeling that harming this creature might just break something vital inside of me.

"You have the potential to become *you,*" it states slowly. "But you are not yet the you that's intended for this fate."

My mouth opens and closes like a fish out of water, which I suppose that inversely I am. A hot flush of confusion and irritation towards this peculiar spirit begins coloring my cheeks.

"Then tell me who I am. If you know my fate, then surely you know my past." I growl the words low and threatening to avoid them sounding like the plea that they very much are.

The Heimartai drifts back, cutting off my path forward once more. Its pulsing, color-changing beat only seems to amp up the one that's currently hammering me from the inside out.

"I could tell you about your past, but you wouldn't believe it, and it would do nothing to bring about the *you* that this destiny calls for. I'm afraid there's only one set of greater events already at work that can trigger your metamorphosis," the creature laments, sounding terribly sad.

I flounder around for the right words, but I'm too shocked and angry to think properly.

The Heimartai's light begins to dim, and I'm filled with a surge of panic that starts clawing inside my chest, demanding that I do something. I have to learn something—anything—before it fades away like the others. This may be my only chance to salvage a piece of my past.

"What events?" I plead, my hand stretching out as if to grab it.

The creature's color shifts into a deep indigo as it swiftly dodges my closely approaching fingers. "Do not make that mistake again, daughter of the tides!" It snarls angrily at me. "You are not yet the right *you* intended for this fate, and so my touch may very well bring about your death."

A feeling of crushing hopelessness at being so near my past and still being denied access all but consumes me. The Heimartai's light dims once more, and my opportunity slips away with it.

"*Please*," I beg the mythic being. "What events? What must happen for me to regain my memories? To become the one your fate is meant for? *Please,* I just—I'm so sick of not knowing."

The creature pauses briefly. "I cannot say. I only know for certain that you will rage against them, and in turn they will *shatter* you. We will meet again, daughter of the tides."

With that final piece of dreadful information, the medusae fades away entirely, and I'm left with an open path to the beckoning grove.

There's a heavy weight pressing on my chest when I ascend the ocean garden steps. I can't believe I was *so close* to my memories, and yet again I'm found unworthy. It's becoming a painful pattern in my life, one that I'm keenly aware of. I tread perhaps more angrily than I should through the coral, aiming directly for the athanasia bloom.

The flower is just as described, with petals of vibrant amethyst and, upon closer inspection, a stem of blue. I lean down to sniff, not positive I will even be able to do so in the dream-like realm, but sure enough, the potent smell of the flower hits me like a slap across the face.

The sickly sweet fragrance of carrion invades my senses and invokes images of rotting flesh and maggot-covered bones. I jerk away from the innocent-looking bloom and promptly double over.

Clutching my stomach tightly, I hold back the gags, wracking my body with everything I have.

I don't even want to know what it would be like to vomit in this pocket realm. My affinity works quickly to cool and soothe, taking away that gruesome scent along a frosty current.

"What in the *fuck* do they want with you?" I question, eyeing the flower testily after having regained some control over my bodily functions.

The flower, of course, remains silent.

Blowing out a short breath through my nose, I remove one of the more recently sharpened blades from the sling around my middle. It's easy enough to sever the bloom from its home. Re-sheathing my blade, I hold the deceiving flower outwards like it might explode at any minute.

Thankfully, I'm saved from a trip back through the trench of horrors. As I step down the ocean garden's steps, my foot lands on the pathway leading back out of the Veil Keepers mouth.

A quick scan reveals I'm back inside the monolith circle but now it seems I'm allowed to leave.

The fog has cleared entirely from the grotto, and I hurry towards the exit as swiftly as I can.

The amethyst petalled flower still held out carefully before me, like it might set itself on fire at any moment. I refuse to risk accidentally catching another whiff of its scent.

The last thing I need to add to this hellish day is to hurl my guts up before our Grand Regent.

XXX. BURNING PYRES

The completion of our third trial is unsettlingly different from that of the previous two.

There is no fanfare, no TideLords, no screaming raiders, no loud announcers, and certainly no afterparties.

Tonight is instead a soberingly somber affair.

My boots dig themselves into the moist black sands filling the bay's shoreline, while I stand with an otherwise statue-like stillness. There is a chill flitting about the midnight breeze, which has nothing to do with winter's lingering presence.

My breathing is a practiced steady thing whose current purpose is in tracking the morose movement of time. I count twelve inhales and thirteen exhales before the traditional sound of bone drums begins cresting up and over the towering cliffs at my backside.

The approaching beat is a dark and heavy dirge, so despondent in melody it might as well be dragging me down to the bottom of the ocean floor. My fifteenth inhale is greeted with the sweet aroma of ritual cleansing smoke. The heady white haze prowls throughout the space around us like an air-propelled leviathan, paving the way forward with its grievous scent.

Beyond the fragrant fog and haunting bone-drum lament, emerges the outline of a wooden longboat. I turn in time with the others gathered. My eyes automatically begin tracing the sturdy vessel making its debut against the backdrop of midnight's velvet curtain.

The body won't be far behind.

During the return journey to the north following the third task, I was able to glean just a touch more information from Preceptor Oplon regarding the current state of affairs within The Order.

From what little I was able to pry from our weapons master, it seems that the TideLords have all been called for an emergency meeting of the Driftwood Court. Our Raider King himself is said to have arranged it. Oplon theorized that the unprecedented timing was likely due to the events of this last Luminalia. The Sons and Daughters are, of course, in attendance as well.

While assembling the full Driftwood Court is in and of itself a phenomenon, it's not the only concerning tidbit I obtained. All four cardinal Grand Preceptors were *also* summoned to the Driftwood Court's assembly late last night. Skelm and the others left at dawn, the reason for their mysterious absence from today's pillar trial.

The morose rhythmic thrumming increases in volume with its persistent approach, and I'm careful to keep hold of my dependable glacial reserve while we stand at attention as one.

With perfect precision, each raider presents a clenched fist to the heart and moves it up to the brow in synchronized welcome of the cortege. Small torches have been afforded to those who lead and close the desolate parade with their cleansing driftwood smoke. They shed both lawless light and potent fog upon the marching crew of raiders, who carry their captain's corpse high atop a wooden pyre.

Holding my fist steady against my brow, I scan the raiders presently bearing their captain on their shoulders in his place of high honor. Their expressions all resemble identical grim veils, and I find their eyes brim with unshed pain. An unexpected tightness forms inside my throat.

It's been some time since we last set a pyre ablaze, at least for those of us in level-eight.

In the first few years, deaths are a pretty common occurrence. In most cases, you barely even know the name of the lost raider. When you *did* know of them, chances are you were hoping for their death in the first place, if not the reason behind it.

Animosity ran rampant back then.

The Order wants only those who are strongest, who represent 'Brek', to emerge from the ranks. They will ensure that the weak, those deemed 'Vek', are eventually sifted out. Pitting us against one another is just one of the many ways in which that can happen, and it *does* happen.

Later on, after around level-three, the deaths start to slow and become less and less routine. Once The Order has deemed us all sufficiently broken, they build us back up, promoting teamwork and unity in place of bitter rivalry. A change that takes several years to accomplish.

Afterwards, it is unusual to have more than the rare pyre burning amongst your own level.

To have a captain who has not yet graduated from their cardinal be the one upon that mortal heap is as close to a tragedy as The Order will ever acknowledge. Under ordinary circumstances, this would be completely unprecedented. The Pillar Trials provide the obvious exception.

I suppose to have managed three tasks with only one fallen among us is quite a feat. Although the majority of the bloodshed doesn't ordinarily take place until the fourth and final pillar when The Vault is up for grabs. A craven part of my insides turns over in response to that fact.

On instinct, I glance at Kleio standing to my right. Her sepia-shaded eyes slide to me in turn as the passing torches fling light onto our silent forms. A pressing weight sets itself upon my chest at the look she gives me. Her unspoken terrors are clear; it very well could have been *me* atop that pyre tonight.

The body finally makes it to the longboat set carefully along the dark shore's edge, and I find that dropping Kleio's heavy gaze brings physical relief. We pivot back as one unit to face the bay.

The bone drums cut off sharply, leaving us in an abrupt silence.

Facing us now with their backs to the waters are the four Cardinal Regents. Each one of them studies the procession currently handling the body with carefully obscured expressions.

True to tradition, Captain Reed Namak's corpse has been shrouded by both his emerald-colored captain's cape and the flag of his cardinal sewn together as one. The sight of that shroud as his body is laid inside its longboat tomb evokes a hollow echoing deep down inside.

I've never witnessed a captain's pyre burning before.

My attention sweeps over to Dhara, who stands at the very front of the gathered raiders now facing the Grand Regents. Her spine is unnaturally stiff, and her face appears unnervingly vacant. I don't think I've even seen her blink since we were called to gather.

Giving a once-over of her crew spanning the front row in their own emerald uniforms, I quickly discover similar grim veils draped over each of their own countenances. It strikes me then that her crew's grievances are worn for Dhara's sake just as much as the fallen eastern captain's.

Grand Regent Nagual steps away from the line to address those of us before him. His eyes, framed between dark hair and an equally dark mustache, look as though they might be gleaming in the torchlight. But when he speaks in that lilting eastern accent, his voice is strong and swift.

"We convene 'zis Eve to commit Captain Reed Namak back to 'ze eternal vaters, to 'ze spirit realm of 'ze drowned gods. For his second and final time."

Nagual's deep-set eyes flicker towards Reed's shrouded body tucked into the longboat.

"As you all are 'avare, it is no small 'ting to become a captain 'vithin a cardinal. Even greater to be chosen during a time 'ven ze Vault has opened. Captain Namak died valiantly and honorably in accordance 'vith ze raider code." The eastern Regent pauses to wet his lips. "Salt coursed through his veins as zick and true as any good Raider Captain. Ve 'vish his soul an easy journey back to Nawai and pray zat he finds his place 'vithin ze Netherdepths."

Our heads bow in ceremonial salute as the Grand Regent of the East steps back into the fold lining the shore. Water lapping continuously over the sandy shore provides the only sound.

Captain Namak's second in command, Raider Bedi, parts away from the group of those laying out their captain's shrouded form. His face is startlingly barren when stepping forward.

Bedi's shadowed eyes appear just as deeply crushed as the concern in Kleio's own foretold.

I remain motionless while he unfolds a roll of parchment from between his fingers before clearing his throat. This next part is a tradition among pyre burnings that I have not ever witnessed. None of us have.

It's called the death poem, written for lost captains by their surviving crew.

Raider Bedi calls out their short composition clear and true.

"Here is the day I've come to hate,
The one that stole your soul and sealed our fate,
Your laughter echoes 'round our heads,
I cannot stomach being in your stead.
Here is the day I've come to hate,
The one that forces on me an impossible weight,
Rest assured, your legacy won't end with me.
I shall shout your name from sea to sea.

Here is the day I've come to hate,
The one that made us seven instead of eight,
I'll count the days until joining you,
Not only my captain but my brother too."

Hair rises on my neck and arms with the rueful verses, and I spy Kleio swallowing thickly from the corner of my eye. When shifting slightly to better view the rest of my crew, I discover six pairs of tight, red-rimmed gazes locked on Raider Bedi. That hollow echoing inside grows.

I'd always thought of my captaincy as something like a tool for my crew to leverage. A way to further their careers and get something worthwhile out of this second life. I've honestly never before considered how my death might affect them merely beyond the inconvenience of it.

The reading of the death poem is promptly followed by the send-off ceremony.

Grand Regent Negual sends the longboat containing Reed's body out into the ominous waters as the four cardinals watch in hushed respect. The bone drums pick back up in their dark tolling knell, and the shuffling sound of arrows tells me Captain Namak's crew is preparing themselves.

I can't stop myself from glancing again at Dhara. Her empty eyes appear to be gazing at something far beyond the retreating longboat. She stares unseeingly all the way out to the midnight horizon, and perhaps even beyond that.

Seven blazing arrows fill the night sky like shooting stars.

One is fired from each of Reed's crew members. They arch gracefully through the night, with one chasing after the next before plunging down into their wooden target.

Captain Namak's boat burns brilliantly in varying shades of green while it drifts deeper into the bay. Waves sweep out in rapid succession, lulling the burning pyre into their eternal embrace.

The sea is eager, like a greedy miser, to call in on its returned soul.

Half an hour later, and I'm hiking back up the last few meters of the rocky cliffside far above that still-burning longboat.

My feet might as well be lead weights. I've been working hard not to allow myself to linger on that fiery vessel below. I find that each time my thoughts move in that direction, I'm filled with an overwhelming and completely irrational guilt.

Maybe it's due to the fact that I never spoke more than a handful of words to the eastern captain. Maybe it's some sort of survivor's guilt, having passed the last trial. Maybe it stems from watching the grief pass over Reed's crew, which I then found mirrored in the faces of my own.

Or maybe I feel terrible for *not* feeling that terrible over his death.

I honestly don't have the energy to unravel my own tedious complexity tonight. So I focus on shoving my iniquity down and away to be inspected at a later time until a piercing cry from below shatters my glacial composure.

Grabbing one of the small knives burdening my hips, my instincts pull me quickly towards the pathway's edge. I crane my neck out over the grassy bluffs and begin scanning the black beach for any signs of danger, only to discover Dhara's crumpled form down along the shoreline.

Blowing out a short curse, my shoulders immediately loosened in relief. I re-sling my weapon before shaking my head in annoyance at the eastern captain's ongoing display.

Girl's lost her damn mind.

Dhara has very evidently broken out of her prior stupor. With narrowed eyes, I watch the eastern captain claw at the dark sand below while screaming every last remaining breath out of her lungs. She then begins cursing both the sea and sky like a woman possessed.

The abnormal performance is, admittedly, morbidly transfixing.

Tide Raiders are expected to keep their emotions at bay no matter what. Captain's are required to anchor them so far down inside that not even a glimmer of sentiment should be hinted at upon the surface.

A strange coldness blooms inside of me upon witnessing her keening. One that does not belong to my affinity. I find myself hesitating, my thumbs squeezed inside the vices of my hands.

The rest of my crew were made to leave before the captains gave their final respects, so there's no one to urge me onward. I'm not entirely sure what it is that holds me down to the spot now. Perhaps it's just the sheer misery in Dhara's cry. Or possibly the fact that she's completely alone in a state of such despair, her own crew having been made to leave with the others.

Regardless, I'm now frozen in queer contemplation while the captain of the east spews her misery to the stars and tides. I feel trapped between minding my own business and overstepping The Order's firm boundaries.

I'm stuck inside this internal state of deliberation as a faint outline materializes along the bay's waterline, and observe as it crouches down next to Dhara's trembling body.

I blink once in disbelief, my mouth opening slightly.

It's been too long of a day for this to be anything more than my imagination. Yet the longer I stare, the more solid the form becomes. The outline radiates an almost imperceptible hue of emerald green. When it finally stands next to Dhara's crumpled body, I'm sure I'm dreaming.

It's *Reed*.

Or rather, a shadow of Reed. A glowing sort of shadow.

A *shade*.

The foreign word is plucked from someplace locked behind a wall of ice. As absolutely bizarre and impossible as it seems, I'm instantly certain that is precisely what I'm viewing.

With a shaky exhale, I study the apparition of Captain Namak moving in the ocean wind, turning his semi-corporeal head. His ghostly gaze reaches the summit of the cliffs before scanning up the rockside. My pulse thunders wildly in my ears as his spectral eyes fix themselves on *me*.

Reed's silhouette slowly extends his chin upwards before lifting a hand in a silent gesture of acknowledgment. Air catches inside my throat, and I fervently attempt to rub away the fabrication with the heel of my hands. Reopening my eyes proves my efforts to be futile, and I'm left to gape, completely confounded.

A bitter gale blows white tendrils through my eyeline while I watch Reed sign an old sort of gesture to me. It's one I'm sure I've never seen before, and yet somehow I *know* it. His arms bring themselves to cross at the wrists before his chest while his palms open in my direction, and he then makes a very low and deliberate bow.

It's an unquestionable sign of deeply pious regard. An extremely old and highly unusual one at that. Even the wintry winds pause their ancient howling to watch in astonishment.

Captain Namak's spirit then bends down to press a firm kiss upon his girlfriend's forehead. His apparitional fingers appear to stroke back the unraveled curls framing Dhara's hunched-over form until, at last, her shuddering sobs slowly subside. As she trembles, Reed's hand gently rests on her back in comfort.

Finally, Dhara gathers herself from the sands, her cries replaced by quiet suffering.

Standing once more beside his beloved girlfriend, Reed gives her one last kiss, which he gently presses against her lips. Dhara makes no sign of sensing his presence other than brushing a finger idly over her mouth while staring blankly towards the flame-dwindling longboat.

Captain Namak pivots before striding out to his watery grave with a sense of immense purpose. It appears as if he's simply reporting for his next duties. I can't help but think that maybe he is.

The scene leaves my perception of reality muddled.

Without thinking about what I'm doing, I take a careless, blind step forward. I'm too engrossed in the vision that my undoubtedly damaged brain has conjured up to realize my idiotic mistake.

I've taken a step *too* far.

Almost instantaneously, my heel slides on the cliff's craggy edge, throwing my balance to the wind. A rendering of my soon-to-be-broken body flashes through my head so vividly that screaming isn't even an option.

But in the next instant, I'm caught on something.

No—not caught—I'm *yanked*. Yanked backward by the neck of my uniform. The fisted hand at my nape grips me with an iron hold, dragging me to the safety of the weather-beaten trail.

A strangled sort of sound escapes my lips, but I'm otherwise breathless upon release, struggling to even swallow. I was certain I was dead. I should currently be dead. *Why am I not dead?*

The image of my broken, blood-splattered body shrouds all other thoughts.

I *should* be dead, but I'm not because—looking up to view my very forceful rescuer, I tense.

A pair of murderous ashen eyes glare back down at me. They hold such an overwhelming intensity that it's difficult for me to do anything other than stare like some petrified level-one.

"You think you could at least *try* not to get yourself killed for five *fucking* seconds?" Agni seethes down at me, the ridiculous muscles in his crossed arms bulging threateningly. His gaze travels over my person with a searching quality, like he's taking stock of something. "Honestly, it's a godsdamned wonder you've made it this long—you're practically suicidal."

Agni's visceral anger is like having a bucket of water thrown on me in bed.

It both wakes me up and turns my already dark mood pitch black.

"Oh well, *pardon me,* your highness." My lip curls in aggravation. "But I don't recall actually ever asking for your help."

"Spare me." He scoffs. "You'd be accompanying Captain Namak in his retreat down to the Netherdepths right now if I hadn't grabbed you." Agni's reddened hand rolls his jaw, while amber eyes move up and down over my person again.

I scowl, my fisted fingers itching for the comfort of a blade. "You can save yourself the trouble of your whole 'hostile hero' act for your fan club, Agni. I believe I saw several of them pretending to be lost down near the wharf if you find yourself in the mood to start handing out autographs."

It was aimed as a taunt, but it's also the truth.

His admirers have somehow managed to grow in numbers over the months.

There are now an obscene number of female and even a few male raiders whose sole purpose appears to be to monitor Captain Agni and his crew's movements. They wait for him between classes or even after meal times, throwing themselves into 'chance' encounters with the swaggering little sadist and his equally arrogant hounds.

Letters are left on his table before dinner, and countless notes are passed over to their group during lectures. Kleio, Herse, and I even caught a handful of level-seven's blatantly camped out near the boneyard a week or so ago. Agni and his crew have taken to using a few of the old outdoor rings near the ancient ship wreckage as their own personal training space.

Shirtless.

Absolutely shameless. Do try not to choke on your own drool, ladies. Herse had called over to those level-seven's rather loudly when we'd passed them and their very obvious fixation.

A sneer lies on his lips. "Oh now that is rich, coming from *you.*"

My arms cross themselves as my brows quirk in his direction. "In what way?"

"You tell me," Agni retorts arrogantly and his tongue presses out his cheek while amusement simmers in his gaze. "Kiss any good level-ones lately, yeah?"

My mouth opens and closes before a deep flush encircles my neck. His lips pull up into a sardonic grin at my surprise, then he lowers his head and waits mockingly for my contradiction.

The one he knows I cannot make.

Herse and Greer had better be making the twins' lives a living *fucking* hell right now.

My back molars scrape against the flesh of my tongue in bitter aggravation. The longer I'm silent, the broader his grin grows. I decide offense is better than no defense at all. "If I didn't know any better, Agni, I'd say you pay an unusual amount of attention to my daily life."

It's an off-handed remark without too much bite, yet it has an unanticipated effect on the southern captain. A faint redness begins to bloom beneath the perpetual tan of his face. Any and all hint of his prior amusement is suddenly gone.

"What were you even doing that close to the cliffside?" He asks snidely, changing the topic of our debate entirely. "Trying to see if you might sprout wings?" A strange edge sharpens his voice.

"I was—I heard a scream. I went to see what it was and lost my footing," I explain, my tone odd.

While it's all technically true, the look Agni gives me says he isn't buying it. His eyes narrow skeptically while scrutinizing my face. Countless arguments cloud the south captain's expression, but to my eternal surprise, he actually doesn't start a single one of them.

After a minute of silence, he makes a comment designed specifically to make my head spin.

"Your eyes have green in them."

I blink up at Agni. "*What*?"

I'm quite certain I've misheard him.

His dark, windswept head of hair weighs heavily to one side. I find those amber-ensconced pupils dilating incrementally while inspecting something about my face further.

"Right there in the center," he notes to himself. "*Hm.*"

Agni's ability to throw me off balance is quite honestly uncanny. My mouth parts itself slightly, but no sound escapes. The bizarre shift has left me at a complete and utter loss for words. My brain feels like it's been run through a bath, and I'm suddenly overly conscious of the growing silence between us.

He looks away from me and up to the nocturnal sky above us for one fleeting moment. The motion strikes me as odd—*boyish* even.

I try to formulate some sort of stinging comment, but to my horror, my usual arsenal is found entirely empty. He looks back down, scanning my face briefly before setting his jaw and abruptly turning around. I stare in stupefied silence as he stalks ahead, taking the second path and forging away from my own trail.

Shaking my head in complete confoundment, I drag myself up to the bleak, spired fortress.

When returning, I don't immediately slip back to my cabin as I'd previously intended.

Instead, I find myself gazing at one of the many rusted mirror wall-hangings lining the main level's backside corridor. I stand there for several minutes, peering intensely at a reflection I've never cared much to study before.

Agni was correct.

There, in the heart of my bitterly cold sapphire iris, ripples out a small halo of seafoam green.

XXXI. RAIDER HIRAETH

Level Three

My arms wrap themselves across my chest in practiced indifference.

I stand slanted against the wall opposite the dim entrance leading to our Grand Preceptor's quarters. The sound of Preceptor Raith's raised words is met with the chilling calm of Skelm's. Both voices tumble through the closed doors like ships in a storm, reaching where I batten down in a show of nonchalance.

Truthfully, my entire body is still sore from the last disciplinary meeting held on my behalf. My muscles are currently spasming quite painfully. Clenching my jaw tightly against the aches, I fist my hands beneath my arms to stop their visible tremors.

I refuse to let that one-eyed bastard see me cry again.

"That girl is a godsdamned menace! This is the fifth fight she's started this year already. Clearly, whatever discipline she's been given isn't nearly enough. I've said it before, Hymir—we need to seriously look at putting her down!"

I can't contain my flinch. My teeth lock together in poorly concealed outrage. They're actually discussing killing me in there. *Putting me down* like I'm some sort of ill-behaved beast.

The overheard discussion shouldn't be so unnerving. I should be used to this way of life, accustomed to just how little I mean to The Order. My attention shifts to the white Raider brand peeking out from around my wrist. The one that assures them I'm every bit as worthless as they believe me to be.

As I now frequently find, an untethered rage begins filling me from deep inside. It sometimes keeps me up at night with its gluttonous wrath and desperate need for violence. That rage drives me to lash out at anyone and everyone who dares to come near.

Someone swears low in response to Preceptor Raith's words, snatching my attention back.

I discover intolerable brown eyes gazing at me. My nostrils flare while my mouth turns into an unsavory frown. "What do you want?" I practically spit at the girl who has exasperated and frayed every last nerve of mine in the span of little more than two years.

Raider Hiraeth.

Even the thought of her name leaves a sour taste in my mouth. She looks slightly startled by my venom, but there's something in the twitch of her cupid's bow that leads me to believe she finds my acidic attitude amusing. I hold in a groan.

That is perhaps what annoys me most about this girl in particular.

My eyes narrow on her, where she stands just a few meters down from me, in irritation. There is a bruise along her cheekbone and a bloody gash that's begun crusting the side of her chin that matches up exactly with the torn skin along my damningly crimson knuckles.

"I'm here to speak with the Grand Preceptor," Raider Hiraeth replies with aggravating calm.

As if we weren't just in a full-out brawl within the last hour.

I don't allow my voice to allude to even an ounce of the fear that's been eating me alive since Preceptor Raith dragged me up here. "Why? You going to go in there and second Raith's request to have me executed? Go ahead. I'm sure our level—the whole North Order, actually—would praise you for it. Maybe one day they'll make you *captain*."

To her credit, Hiraeth doesn't so much as blink at my hate-filled words.

A small trail of still flowing blood on her chin, left over from my fist, drops down to the dark wood-stained floors. Shame kicks me so sharp and low that I'm forced to turn my face away from hers and instead look over towards the other end of the hall.

It hadn't been her fault today. Not really. Today just happened to be an awful morning, spilling over from a previously terrible day, overflowing from a particularly miserable fucking week.

The crime she committed was, admittedly, innocent enough.

All the girl did was ask about my affinity mark, but it had been in the presence of Vash Larceon and his overly eager lackeys. The former of which, by the way, she is agonizingly enamored with.

My second personal strike against Hiraeth.

Even after surviving the first two levels, Larceon, along with most of our peers, still looks at me like something they're all longing to watch get torn apart. Therefore, I have to make sure they all know the consequences of fucking with me. I have to remind them of exactly what prowls beneath my skin every single day of my continued existence in this hellhole.

Maybe I *should* be put down like the feral beast I'm turning out to be.

I catch Raider Hiraeth watching me again, and I glare until she looks away. The voices in Skelm's office have lowered, so neither of us can hear what's being said.

A few moments later, the wooden doors are flung open, with Preceptor Raith storming out in an angry flurry of navy.

My gaze ekes back over to the open entrance and the hearth that has begun flickering to life beyond it. I wince internally at the sight of those flames, knowing full well exactly what I'm about to endure. Exhaling the last of my nerves, I push off from my stance along the wall.

To my surprise, Raider Hiraeth slips into the daunting quarters just before myself. My brows crease while following her. Once inside, my attention flits almost immediately to the windows. *Ah*. My stomach anchors down deep upon finding them tightly shut.

Skelm sits behind his vast oaken desk; the shine of his golden patch is brighter with the awful dancing light from his inferno so near. My entire body tenses up as his dark eye narrows in on me, then slides down to my torn knuckles and across the damning blood-splattered shirt.

Only the talent for pure willfulness keeps my shoulders from sagging and my chin from wavering.

Focusing on my steps, I come to stand beside Raider Hiraeth, and we both dutifully wait for the Grand Preceptor to address us. I have a difficult time not fidgeting around him. A habit that, as I have recently learned from the healing fracture along my humerus, is absolutely not tolerated.

"Raider Boreas," Grand Preceptor Skelm says before leaning forward in his chair with a deep frown. "After your very recent punishment with Preceptor Ersatz, I thought you were grasping The Order and your place in it."

I fight the instinct to snap at Skelm's words. His calm intonation is so much worse than outright yelling, and it sends a flood of terror down my spine. All of my affinity's strength is barely enough to keep me from sprinting out of the room.

But then again, where would I go?

"Not only have you disrupted your peers' instruction, yet *again,* I might add. Now you've cost me a weapons master as well." His voice remains steady, but his words come out with a keen edge.

Lightheadedness crashes over me when coming to understand Raith's departure. For a moment, I struggle to track down any coherent thoughts beyond my trepidation and pressing panic.

Preceptor Raith has just—

He's—

I made him quit.

Soothing ice begins to cool over the slick sweat lining my palms and face in an effort to calm me down like some sort of mothering hen. It doesn't stop the dread from pooling down inside. I couldn't form words even if it was my turn to speak. Which, from the look in Skelm's eye, it is *not*.

"Preceptor Raith did, however, make a good point before informing me of his acceptance into the ranks of TideLord Nero. You may not be worth the trouble you've caused here, Raider Boreas. Elemental or not," Skelm says in that unnatural calm.

My chin dips incrementally.

I study the top of the report-strewn desk, the gold leviathan wrapping around Skelm's finger, anything other than his piercing gaze. There's a hollowness blooming in my chest that swiftly travels out to my limbs while comprehending where this conversation is inevitably going to end.

Retreating to a place deep inside myself, I barely even hear the Grand Preceptor. "Honestly, I'm inclined to believe Preceptor Raith. If this last incident is any indication, I'd say we should return you to the Netherdepths this very evening."

Cold internal walls slam down and lock tight to protect me in my reserve. Soon, I've zoned so far out from his morbid lecture that I almost miss Raider Hiraeth's unexpected outburst entirely.

"It wasn't her fault!" She snaps loudly, her face turning a deep scarlet. I damn near jump out of my own skin with how alarmingly adamant her voice is. At Skelm's disgruntled look, she adds a quiet, "Sir."

His single, beady eye roves quietly between the two of us before inquiring, "Explain then, Raider Hiraeth. What exactly occurred between the two of you today?"

Sucking on a tooth is the only way to avoid grimacing. I'm still too far removed to even consider intervening.

"It was my fault."

My mouth drops open slightly at that and I swiftly close it again. I glance over in time to watch Hiraeth's face harden before lifting her chin at the Grand Preceptor. If I didn't know any better, I'd say the look on her face was that of a challenge.

How badly did I hit her?

Is it possible my fist disconnected something critical in her brain? Skelm scrutinizes the girl with equal disbelief, both at Hiraeth's unyielding expression and the firmness of her words.

"It's true, I provoked her," she falsely states. "I claimed her affinity was Vek to the rest of our level. Raider Boreas is elemental; she had no choice but to defend that. She challenged me, but I don't think Preceptor Raith was paying any attention to us until after we'd already begun."

I work hard not to let my jaw hang open as she outright lies to the Grand Preceptor of the Cardinal North. Raider Hiraeth had claimed no such thing. No one in our level was *that* stupid, and I certainly was not honorable enough to challenge her.

Why is she lying for me? What could she possibly hope to gain out of this?

Skelm shifts back in his seat, his hands coming to lace themselves together as he weighs out his options. "Raider Boreas, do you confirm that this is the truth?"

Blinking away my shock, I give him a tight nod. I don't dare speak should my voice betray me.

"Alright—then you will remain here. But one more strike this year, *Boreas*, and I will not feel even an ounce of guilt watching you be fed back to the sea," Skelm warns me fiercely.

I do not doubt his claim one bit.

It's not until reaching the main level of the dining chambers that I realize Raider Hiraeth has become my shadow. Turning sharply back to face her, I again find that surprising hint of humor hanging about her expression in response to my frigid temperament.

I hate that.

"Are you following me, Hiraeth?" I snap.

The corner of her mouth hooks up before answering simply, "Yes."

Blowing out a stream of annoyance, I grumble, "And why is that? I can't compensate you for the lies you told." The next words have a bitter taste as they slip past my tongue. "I don't have any oblations to trade with, and I—I got banned from the boneyard."

"You're banned from the boneyard? *Why*?" Hiraeth's dark brows knit themselves together. "I don't think they mind you starting fights in there. I think that's sort of the point." She lets out a timid sort of laugh.

My face begins to burn without warning. I quickly look away from her and over to the mouth-like opening of the northern fortress. An idle palm comes to rub the base of my neck uncomfortably, and I feel the still terribly too-short edges of my tightly shorn hair against the back of my hand. In the last six months, it's only managed to grow a few pitiful inches.

"The new level-eight captains aren't allowing castaways to compete in affinity fights anymore, so..." The words drift off into the vacant corridor while I fight another flush of embarrassment beginning to engulf my neck.

Raider Hiraeth rocks back on her heels, and I'm immediately on the defense. "Look, I didn't ask for your help. You should have known I wouldn't be able to pay you back for it. I'm a fucking castaway *and* a bastard. That's your own damn fault for thinking otherwise." My tongue is just as impossible to control as my temper.

"You think I want you to *pay* me for not standing by and letting them *murder* you?" Her voice is high with incredulousness.

I pause for a moment to wrangle my own emotions before turning back to stare blankly at Hiraeth. I hate every single bit of the warmth in her sepia-shaded eyes. The warmth indicative of someone who's been loved before.

"I don't want payment, Merena." She utters the words quietly around a newly formed frown.

I can't stand to be here anymore. I can't stand to look at the blood and bruises on her otherwise lovely face. I can't stand to hear her call me by my name, as if she knows me. No one knows me. *I* don't even know me.

So I turn on my heel and head for the exit leading to the path towards Giant's Crook.

I only make it down the first rocky slope before her needling presence has me spinning back around. "What?" I growl out. "What do you want from me? I already told you I can't give you anything—there is nothing I can do for you. Go on to the sickbay." I wave my hands, gesturing towards her injuries. "Go get your cuts and bruises cleaned up. Just—just leave me *alone*."

Her reply to my exasperated and slightly broken bellowing is so quiet and rushed that I just about don't hear Raider Hiraeth's next statement. "I-would-like-to-be-your-friend."

"You want—*what*?" I falter back a step, positive I've misheard her.

She gives me a nervous bob of her chin in response, as if surprised by her own request.

I'm fairly acclimated to being on my own. I wouldn't go so far as to say I particularly enjoy it, but it's pretty much all I know. There are no other castaways or even bastards in my level. I've had to come to terms with isolation early on. Choosing to view my aloneness more as a way of life rather than something that's been thrust on me has been the only way to push forward.

The *incident* from six months ago has also not helped. In fact, it's managed to push me even further towards the outside recesses of The Order. A feat I hadn't before thought possible.

This must be some sort of joke, then. A prank that Raider Larceon or one of the others has coerced her into executing. Well, I won't be made a fool. My mouth twists into an ugly sneer.

"*No,*" I spit up at Hiraeth before turning around and storming down the next rocky hill.

The wind today is just unruly enough for my next intended venture but not so loud as to hide the sounds of the girl's continued stalking. Hiraeth is about to make me come fucking unglued, and that would be very bad news for the both of us. Waiting until I reach the bottom of the cliffside, I pause and then hurl my affinity back at her in a whip of merciless cold.

I expect to hear a yelp or even a shout of pain. When no such reaction reaches my ears, I peek back over a shoulder. In the space between us, the shield of her own affinity's power glimmers a pale violet shade. A scowl etches itself deeply into my expression at her unabating smile.

"Look—I'm not going to be your sad little replacement for Voss," I grit out.

Raider Hiraeth winces slightly at the mention of her friend's name. Her *dead* friend's name.

Raiders Voss and Hiraeth were pretty close throughout our first two levels. I think they both derive from the same landmass, but I've never felt inclined to ask.

Voss's pyre burning was a few months ago. Just another raider in our level lost to the unforgiving expectations of The Order.

Hiraeth had sobbed in her bunk for weeks.

It made me sick.

"Allies then—*maybe,*" she offers hesitantly.

Pushing out an aggravating breath, I look back at her in question. "Why? Did Larceon put you up to this? Because if I find out that he did—" My lip curls upwards. "I will freeze him from the inside out."

Her eyes widened slightly in response to my very real threat. Hiraeth is well aware of what I did to Raider Byron and the others. The whole damned north is aware, thanks to Raider Nell.

Good.

She should see me for the monster that I am.

Hiraeth recovers quickly to dispel my suggestion. "*No*, Raider Larceon did not. No one even knows I went to the Grand Preceptor's office. I just wanted to find you and—and apologize, and then I heard what Preceptor Raith was saying, and I—and I had to make it right."

"Apologize for what?" I question sharply, my eyes tightening with suspicion. We both know I started that fight without any real grounds to do so.

She shakes her head of braided curls. "I shouldn't have asked you about your affinity mark in there like that in front of the others. It was stupid—I should have realized what sort of position that put you in. I cannot imagine how hard it must be for you after what they—" A menacing growl escapes my lips at her implication, and she scrambles to change tact. "I think that we could make a good team."

One of my brows lifts, and she continues hurriedly, sensing my attention is fleeting. "I think maybe we could do well together, you and me. I—I think we'd be able to survive here together. If we each had someone to rely on. To—to talk to or *not* talk to."

My arms begin to fold themselves evenly across my chest. The winds whipping off the darkening waters run over the shorn sides of my scalp, a constant reminder of that nightmarish night.

"I've been doing just fine here on my own, Hiraeth."

She fidgets, her weight moving from heel to toe and back again. Raider Hiraeth's eyes study me. They trace over the uneven chunks left of my hair and then slide over the glacial plains of my features before admitting softly, "Well, I'm not, Merena."

I snort. "You don't say."

Her eyes flash, and I realize there's *anger* in them. It's a spark I'm not sure I've ever really seen in her. Hiraeth is usually far too kind and agonizingly positive for someone such as myself to stomach. Even as her arms cross and her gaze turns flinty, she remains silent.

That's *interesting*. My lips fight to stay in a straight line.

"Okay," I concede slowly. Partly because she's intrigued me and partly because I want to see just exactly how long she's willing to keep this up. Being alone *has* become rather dull as of late.

"Prove it. Prove to me you're being honest with this request. Prove to me your allegiance, and I'll consider becoming *allies,*" I challenge her.

Hiraeth's expression brightens immediately, and her voice carries varying levels of worry and excitement when asking, "How?"

My mouth curves upward into a very deviant grin before resuming the hike down to the wharf.

I call back over a shoulder to her, "Come along and find out, *Kleio.*"

XXXII. ICE SKATING

After yet another brush with death and Captain Agni, it has become glaringly obvious that it's time to come clean to Kleio and my crew about everything.

Mostly.

The week following Captain Namak's death, my second and I decide to reveal our special place among the nets to the other six. With a few bottles of liquor for courage, thanks to Vash and his improbable ability to get just about any illegal substance smuggled into the north, I set about unburdening my crushing load of guilt.

One damning story at a time.

Starting at the top, I fill them in on the night terrors, trials, and hallucinations still eating me from the inside out. I don't go into specifics on the tidepool's trick, but enough to get the gist of my mental undoing. I then divulge the details of my message to Kerau, as well as my embarrassing lack of knowledge about my own affinity. After that lengthy spiel, I give a rushed description of his brief appearance at Luminalia, quickly followed by his deceit.

I knew they hadn't been aware of Kerau's presence, but none of his crew members had been spotted either, apparently. In fact, I wasn't sure whether or not they had joined their captain in his return to the north at all. A fact I only now regard as strange.

The guilt of putting myself and my crew in such a precarious position feels like it might just swallow me whole. My heart hangs in my throat. My head hangs in my hands.

Saving the very worst for last, I finally explain to them my current od with Captain Agni and begrudgingly recount his latest *assistance.*

What I don't feel the need to mention is the very disturbing illusion that led me so near that treacherous edge in the first place. That little vision of insanity is something I myself am still attempting to detangle, and I'd prefer to deal with one psychosis at a time.

"Fuck—*Merena*." Kleio swears angrily. Not at me, but *for* me. A reaction I hadn't been expecting nor was I prepared for. "Gods, I didn't even think—Vash said Skelm already went over the bylaws with you guys. He said they were explained before the first trial!"

"Maybe he told Vash, but he sure as shit didn't think to fill me in."

When I mull that idea over, I come to find it is admittedly right on target for our Grand Preceptor in all things regarding me. This was just classic. I should have known.

"Did he happen to mention what all they were?" I ask through the spaces between my fingers.

Kleio's face is turning redder by the minute.

"There's just three." My second huffs before listing them. "No fraternizing with any raider belonging to a TideLord, any communication between participants and TideLords may only be initiated by the Lord, and no maiming or killing of another captain outside of the Pillar Trials. The penalty for each being forfeiture of The Vault."

"That little fucking asshole," Herse mutters to no one in particular while using one of her butterfly blades to pick dirt out from under her nails. She's still missing the one Vagar Ophios swiped from her. From the angry furrow in her brow, I wonder if she's remembering that fact.

"Which one?" Greer asks in a tone reeking of sarcasm while passing the bootlegged liquor bottle over to Herse.

"Both. They're both such fucking pricks," Kleio grumbles, her voice uncharacteristically dark as her hand squeezes my arm reassuringly. "I swear, if I see Captain Tharos again, those precious cheekbones of his will get well-acquainted with my bare knuckles."

Herse snorts a laugh, and it's accompanied by the twin's snickering from where they currently lay spread-eagled in the center of the netting. They both appear absolutely exhausted.

Good.

Since the stunt they pulled last week, Herse and Greer have overseen their punishment as I had requested. Prisca and Nephthys have been made to complete the chores of our *entire* cabin, along with treading water for two hours every evening down in the pool chambers. All done in an effort to remind them what it was like to be level-ones. With *one* other condition.

I also requested that they be creative with it.

Even with the overbearing guilt crushing down on me, the corner of my mouth has a hard time not pulling upwards when looking over at them. Or more specifically, when catching sight of the very blatant signs my third and fourth made and then stitched to the front of their uniforms.

In large lettering, their makeshift tags read, 'IDIOT. CANNOT BE TRUSTED.' I was informed that it's just until their month of hell is up. Only three weeks left to go.

I'm forced to duck my head to keep from snorting in amusement at the addition the pair made to their uniform requirement. With bandanas made of spare cloth tied around their foreheads, they've titled themselves 'IDIOT #1' and 'IDIOT #2.' In birth order, of course.

They made me crown them the evening following the unnerving pyre burning.

It was an official, completely made-up, and wholly ridiculous ceremony. It was also their heathenly form of an apology, one that was extremely difficult to keep a straight face while accepting. To be honest, after the heaviness of the night prior, I was more than glad for the distraction. They wear them every day, entirely of their own volition.

"Captain Agni truly saved your life, again?" Nimra's questions hesitantly from where she sits across the netting with her legs bent at the knees while the soles of her feet line up together.

"Technically—*yes,*" I slide the admission through clenched teeth, hating the way it sounds aloud.

"That would be the reason both his kneecaps aren't currently being shattered," Greer points out while attempting to re-wrangle her vibrant hair.

"I'm still debating it," Herse growls softly with the menacing flick of her blade.

Kleio huffs in agreement before her distant expression turns contemplative. "So you have now what—*three* questions left, is it?" She inquires, lifting her gaze to mine without an ounce of anger or blame. It makes me feel worse than I'd thought possible for not having confided in her sooner.

"Correct." I sigh, picking habitually at the skin around my nails. "They could be about anything. Strategy for the final pillar, your all's affinities, vulnerabilities—" All those months of anxiety and panic start welling up once more, making my voice come out tight and thick and *weak*.

I hate it. I hate Captain Agni all the more for it.

"Anything Agni can exploit for leverage, he will." My claim is gruff with finality.

"What if you got him to ask you something else, then? Something relatively harmless—like the first two?" Nimra asks, her fawn-like eyes imploring in the wake of my visible agitation.

Herse and I snorted our derision at the same time.

"And just how do you suppose she does that?" Prisca asks, stealing the sardonic question from its place along my tongue while her ridiculous bandana droops at a blasé angle atop her head.

A small grin I don't believe I've seen before tugs at Nimra's mouth. It reminds me far too much of the twins. Maybe having her help them in instructing the level-ones this year *was* a mistake.

"Well, the south captain does keep a pretty close eye on you," Nimra says slowly while measuring my reaction. "It seems to me like he has a bit of an odd fascination, maybe that could work to your advantage."

"In what way?" I snap, turning to get a better look at my seventh.

Nimra strokes back her dual chestnut braids absently, revealing the tips of her ears turning pink. "You *know*... get him alone. Be *interesting*, I suppose. Make him want to ask you things that aren't related to us or the trials or whatever else you want to keep secret."

A blush creeps over her cheeks under my look of dubiety.

"Nimra, you sly little minx," Nephthys teases, rising up from her deathbed to playfully shove my seventh's knee.

I think I would have been less dumbfounded had the girl risen up and slapped me across the face. "So you're suggesting I should, what? Get him to ask me my favorite color or something?"

Herse guffaws at the thought, while Kleio inches closer with a queer look on her face.

"No. Not exactly," Nimra hedges, twisting a braid around her index finger. "More like—

"What color *undergarments* you're wearing," Prisca supplies, throwing a suggestive wink towards my expression of complete bafflement. It sets Nephthys howling.

Davina, who has just taken a sip from the bootlegged bottle, begins promptly choking on the indigo-colored liquor.

"Have you two not been punished *enough*?" Herse hisses at the twins. The overt irritation in her voice doesn't hide the flicker of humor pulling along her mouth. Greer meanwhile runs a hand down her face in disbelief at their incorrigible cheek.

"Hang on I—I think maybe she's right, Merena," Kleio interjects, making my jaw hang open wider. I give my second a look of bewilderment before closing my mouth and shaking my head incredulously at them all.

"Hear me out," Kleio requests, her palms open in defense. "Nimra isn't wrong. Captain Agni *has* taken a particular interest in you since arriving here. I'm not suggesting you go to the extent of idiot number two's advice over here, but a little sweet talk might do more than you think."

My eyes narrow with a scowl. "Agni has made it crystal clear that he regards my existence as some sort of personal offense. His 'interest' in me is the same as every other asshole who is disgusted by the fact that I'm a castaway and yet alive. As if I had a choice in the matter," I scoff.

Kleio bites down on a lip before sharing a look with Herse that I don't catch the meaning of.

My scowl deepens.

"Right," My second agrees, drawing out the word slowly. "I'm not saying that his curiosity surrounding you isn't malignant in nature—I'm pointing out that for good or bad he *is* drawn to you. He's curious about *you* specifically, and that's something to leverage."

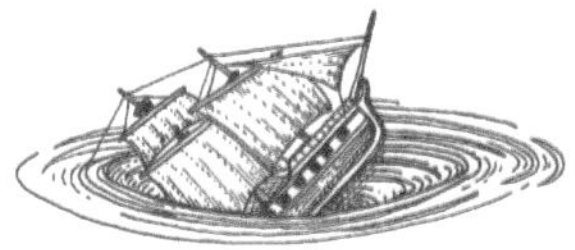

The weeks that succeed our night along the nets unfold at the pace of brine seeping through arctic ice. Which is to say, *painfully* slow, maddening even. However, these weeks also provide me with all the proof I need to determine both Kleio and Nimra were mistaken in their theories.

Captain Agni has apparently decided that I no longer exist.

There are no more taunts, no more pointed insults, no braid tugging, dark chuckles, or foreign words. Anytime we're forced together in a room, he keeps about as far away from me as physically possible. The whiplash in his behavior might just put me in a damn neck brace.

Our day-to-day life in the north has also taken an unanticipated turn.

Things have changed since the return of our Grand Preceptors.

The cardinals are now all kept mostly separated. We've even been given different eating schedules to decrease interaction. The few classes we have been allowed to continue sharing with the others are heavily watched. Affinity training is separated into Vek or Brek classes, and The Boneyard is now one hundred percent off limits.

For *everyone*.

Following the sobering death of another captain, a dense fog of grim reality appears to have slithered its way into every corner of our fortress. It finds me at all hours, even my morning swims aren't spared from its somber disruption. With the final pillar looming, I recognize its heavy presence in the faces of my crew members more and more each day.

The Vault is my top priority.

With the current lack of fighting pits at my disposal, I find myself returning to habits of younger years. Ice slides beneath my feet as I glide back and forth across the newly frozen bay.

The spring months are supposedly underway in the rest of Pontus, but our small island has just endured a winter storm. Originating from further up north, the frigid tempest barreled straight through the night. The ocean surrounding our cardinal has been spitting up glacial drifts onto the rocks and sand all day. The bay was already solidified in chunks, so I made it whole.

Sailing across the white expanse, I shift my weight from one leg to the other with easy precision. My arms move of their own accord up and out to keep my balance secured in their fluttering rhythm. The majority of my crew was out here earlier, when the sun was still up. I tried coaxing almost all of them into letting me at least slide them once across the bay.

Kleio, of course, allowed it, and Herse is never one to miss out on a thrill. Greer feigned a twisted ankle from Oplon's class, forgetting we've been practicing aim the whole week. The twins are both stuck fulfilling their daily chores, part of their enduring punishment.

Davina claimed she couldn't in case someone was injured, her typical response to anything deemed risky—fun included. Nimra made it to the center point of the newly frozen bay before asking me in a very urgent but small voice if I would take her back.

They cleared off not long afterward. Except for Kleio, who stayed to keep me company well past the sun's absence, and I put on a show in return for the company. Spinning and jumping and gliding—any sort of trick I could think of, I'd attempt. In turn, she'd reward each stunt by holding up a score with her hands and giving an awful impression of one of the TideLords.

Once, after gracefully landing an easy double twist, Kleio held up eight fingers before miming, putting on glasses, and crossing her arms. She gave me a cool upward nod and drawled in a deep baritone imitation, "That was sick. I'm going to chill out now. Pet my crabs. Or whatever the fuck it is, I do in my free time."

My ass still hurts from where I fell on the ice while choking on my own laughter. "Thank you, TideLord Kufko." I barely managed to get out between alternating cackles and groans of pain. There's going to be a bruise the size of the Sol Empire mottling my backside tomorrow.

Another time, I pranced about doing as many jump-and-spin combinations as I could before one finally took me down and out. Kleio revealed a score of two, held up by each of her middle fingers before crowing between cupped hands, "Boooooo! I find your beauty offensive, you little northern wench! Don't you know I only have eyes for big, strong, fire-breathing captains?"

She then made a mocking gesture of dismissal, to which I bowed low from my seat on the ice.

"My apologies, Lord Nero. I am well aware of your *preferences*."

If anyone heard us out here, we'd be murdered in our bunks before dawn.

Eventually Kleio left as well, off to spend time with Vash, as she should. If we won The Vault, there's no telling how often she'd get to see him. I try not to let my guilt over that add any more weight to my already crumbling stack. The bulk of which wavers precariously on the fact that I've not gotten even one single question out of Captain Agni.

The glass-like waters beneath my gliding feet snag, and I stumble for a moment before hitting my stride again. It's an unnerving development, his strange silence. It's worse even than his earlier methods of torture because it's become nearly impossible for me to end our od.

I cannot believe Agni and his absolutely worthless, highborn attention span. He's finally grown bored of targeting me and has completely forgotten about our little deal altogether. Now I'm stuck with the shit end of having to fulfill the od in order to get out of it.

Selfish fucking prick.

Anger and annoyance are all but consuming as I gain speed before shifting my weight onto my left leg. Cool air brushes soothingly against my face while extending my right leg behind me, and I relish the burning stretch through my back and hamstring. I bend slightly at the waist, and my arms reach out for balance, one forward, the other backward, to form a graceful line.

My left foot digs into the ice to create a steady pivot point, then I lean forward into a tight spin. The world around me blurs into nothing but velvety darkness and glittering celestial light. The moon bears witness to my secret pleasure, and my right leg lifts up higher, coming parallel to the ice before I extend it fully with toes pointed.

The sensation of pure exhilaration ignites my system.

It's the perfect blend of freedom and control.

Like surfing, the precision required to remain upright demands my full attention. My core engages as I spin faster and faster, and a laugh of delight escapes me. My spinning reaches its peak, and a rush of adrenaline crashes into me, sending shivers all the way down my spine.

Laughter slides past my lips in enjoyment.

Once I finally begin slowing, my eyes instinctually scan the swiftly passing shoreline.

I'm most definitely not expecting them to land on a dark figure watching me from halfway up the cliffside. I tense at the unexpected sight and instantly lose my balance, busting my ass for the second time tonight.

"*Damnit!*" I snarl in pain.

My hand reaches for one of the only pathetic blades I've brought with me onto the ice. The tall figure shifts, his chin lifting beneath a crimson hood to reveal scorching amber eyes, and I freeze completely. The pain in my tailbone is smothered for a moment by my stark surprise.

How long has he been here?

For the next minute, I don't move even a single inch until Captain Agni turns around and starts hiking up the cliffside without any sort of acknowledgement. The silver scar still prominently displayed across my left palm tingles as a reminder, spurning me to follow the southern prick.

I *have* to end this, the last pillar is only weeks away.

Gritting my teeth, I get back on my feet and sprint across the bay to grab my discarded weapons before jogging to the base of the rocky climb. Painful groans and curses spew from my lips the whole way there.

"Wait!" I call towards Agni's swiftly moving form once reaching the pathway's edge.

He doesn't turn or make any sign that he's heard me. Climbing as efficiently as I can, my thighs begin screaming out in protest, but I ignore them.

His stupidly long legs reach the top far sooner than myself, and I can do nothing as he deftly switches trails. But I know the route Agni's headed towards. It traverses over to the other end of the small island, where the cardinal's boats are all moored.

"Hey!" I shout upward, trying to get his attention again.

Agni still pretends not to hear me, and I'm forced to briskly pursue his staggering form up the last of the rock-strewn path. I'm swearing up a storm when finally reaching the top, only to watch as he vanishes into the bordering pines just beyond the outdoor lyceums.

Silence falls, and a growl sits restlessly in my throat. I owe him three questions, and I'll be damned to go into The Vault with an od tethering me to Olsson *fucking* Agni.

Using my intimacy with the island, I quickly find a shortcut to exploit.

Stepping into Captain Agni's path a few minutes later, I repress my own enjoyment as his amber irises flicker with barely contained irritation at my sudden appearance. He frowns around the roll of newly lit spices perched between his lips.

"Not tonight, bastard. I'm not in the mood."

They're the first words he's spoken to me in *weeks*.

My face tightens at his audacity while still working to slow my labored breathing. As if *he* didn't start this. As if *he* hasn't spent the last several months provoking me at every turn. As if *he* isn't the one who forced me into this ridiculous deal in the first place.

"*No*," I snap before shoving my scarred palm in front of his face. "Ask me the rest of your moronic questions so we can be done with this!"

Agni takes a leisurely drag from the smoldering herbs, glances indifferently at my silver wound, then blows a cloud of smoke directly above my head.

Prick.

"As I believe I've said numerous times by now, I do not take orders from the likes of *you*." His cutting timbre is barren of all levity. "I also believe that the od was made with the condition that *I* would decide when and what to ask, and I am telling you I am not in the mood. Now leave."

In the same warning breath, the kindled end of his ensconced spices illuminates that savage scar. It's frightening yet also a bit transfixing. A quick study of his expression reveals the southern captain does indeed appear more pissed off tonight than usual.

I should hold my tongue.

I should set back off for my cabin and let the sadistic prince brood on his own, as he wishes. But I can't. These last few weeks of complete and total silence from him clash with the perpetual thudding in my ears, making me impetuous.

The urge to provoke Agni is overwhelming.

"Oh *no*, is the poor little highborn having a bad day? How very tough it must be to be *you*." The contempt in my voice is palpable. I'm suddenly extremely interested in making him feel every bit as aggravated as he's made me since stepping foot in the north.

Agni frowns, his eyes flitting up and over me with quick disinterest. He then stares above the top of my head, making it perfectly clear that I'm merely a pest he wishes to rid himself of.

I want to be cruel. As cruel as he is.

It's true that the southern captain leaves very few chinks to be found in his armor. However, there is one spot I've noted to be particularly sore with raiders who were most similar to him in the past. I figure now's as good a time as any to test it out.

"What's wrong? Are you missing your mommy and daddy, Agni? Out here brooding about the life you could have had if only they'd kept you in it? How fucking *pathetic*." I spit in disgust.

Those amber eyes darken until they're nothing but ash. Captain Agni straightens before flicking the end of his still-lit paper into the snow blanketed rocks surrounding our narrow trail. I disregard the faintness developing in my legs as he sneers down at me, now fully provoked.

Bullseye.

XXXIII. SWEET TALKING

Agni's fury is a tangible thing, like a familiar scorching rod pressed against my flesh.

"You want a question so bad? *Fine.*" He draws nearer, his features contorting into a sinister warning sign.

"Tell me then," he practically growls. "How does it feel to know your own family disregarded your life so very easily? To know that they didn't find you valuable enough to even consider the loss of your life a *sacrifice*?"

My recoil is instant.

His laugh is sharp and vicious. "Do you wake up every morning wondering whether or not they could *sense* your worthlessness? Or have you come to the highly likely conclusion that you were just some insufferable abomination they simply hoped to rid themselves of as easily as possible?"

Nails dig themselves into my palm as he glares at me without an ounce of pity. "Due to the fact that you were pitched into the sea for fish food, I'd put money on the latter. But that's just me."

"You are such an *ass*," I hiss before shoving him harshly with the intention of returning to my cabin, as I probably should have done in the first place. He catches me by both wrists, where my palms meet his chest in hands that feel like solid iron.

The pounding in my head only gets louder, making it harder for me to control my breathing.

"And you are a *brat*," he snarls, the insult grazing my face from his nearness. "You're such a little tragedy, aren't you? Oh *poor* Boreas, no memory, no family, no home. Just a lowly castaway who's been so sheltered, she has no fucking clue what the world is like outside of her northern haven."

"You know nothing of what my life has been like here." I spit before yanking my hands out of his grasp. His look of utter indifference is so jarring that it incenses me to push him further. I want to delve my way beneath his skin as surely as he's able to peel back mine.

"I don't have a choice in my ignorance, but you do. You and your desperate need for any spec of power or leverage you can gain and then thwart over another living being is *vile*."

Agni doesn't so much as blink at my whetted barbs. The whiplash he's given me these last few months with his drastic mood swings pushes me towards a bottomless spiral. I decide I might as well drag the perpetrator down with me.

"It disgusts me to see how you exploit and then discard anything and everything you don't deem worthy of your highborn sacrifice and gods-given affinity. I'm sure maiming that kelpie of yours meant nothing, not to someone like you—*right*?" My tone is scathing.

His responding chuckle is wry and removed. "It's tamed now, isn't it?"

The apathetic way in which he speaks of such a horrendous act is truly sickening. I feel the skin on my arms tighten, and goosebumps prickle from my wrists to my shoulders, as if my body is trying to erect a barrier between me and the haunting wail of that kelpie reverberating inside my mind.

Agni actually believes his heinous actions are trivial. I have no reasonable notion as to why, but the proof of his blatant disregard feels as sharp as any physical blow. I'm genuinely surprised that I don't stagger back from the impact.

"Those kelpies—they were only *colts*—each of them barely older than foals," I state while angry tremors ripple through my clenched fists. "They had just been separated from their mothers that very morning. For the first time since *birth*."

This parcel of knowledge is one I've been holding onto for a while now. Ever since my debrief after our scoring with Preceptor Beldham. I practically crawled my way up to the nets afterward. I couldn't stomach being around those celebrating the first pillar's completion.

The truth was nearly devouring me whole until Kleio intervened.

Captain Agni brushes past without comment and begins traipsing back in the direction of their docked cardinal ship. The horrible callousness of his attitude bothers me more than it should. It paints me with a shade of anger I've never seen or felt before. For the first time, I get the sense that there might be something worse lurking beyond that wall of unfaltering ice inside.

I stalk after him, one hand hovering over a concealed blade.

"They had no idea what was going on as your *adoring* TideLord Nero hauled them up here to perform." My tone becomes more derisive with every step he takes away from me. "Only that they were desperate to get back to their mothers."

I have no intention of relenting. I'll shout at him all the way to his cardinal's dock if I must.

"You were told to tame it, so then *of course* you had to blind and brand it." I could choke on my own appall. "Heating the bay waters so it had no other possibility of freedom but to attack from outside was obviously your only option. You were practically forced to poison it with your touch and destroy the rest of its life with your insufferable arrogance. It's not as if that creature's life is worth anything to someone like *you*."

Agni pauses his silent retreat in the middle of a patch of evergreens. Their tall, needle-filled branches rise up so far that they appear as if to stroke the midnight sky. I'm quick to take the opportunity and step before him again, quick to get in his face with my rage.

"I want to know *why*. Because it threw you into the docks? Because the kelpie—a wild and free creature by birthright—dared to rebuke your attempt at confining it?"

He turns his back on me once more in insult. And I let out a low laugh in mockery at his pointed slight. It's a shame he can't see just how potent the look of loathing is on my face.

"I should have known—it's beneath you. Less-than. Right? Well then that should absolutely give you the right to punish it however you see fit. You're just so very fucking *important,* aren't you, highborn? So impossibly far above everyone and everything else. So important, in fact, that you were then given a ten. A fucking *ten.* After mutilating a confused and terrified foal."

The months of despising him cling to each word, and I'm rewarded with his sharp recoil.

"Honestly, I can't even begin to imagine how *entertaining* it must be—getting to commit whatever atrocities you want without any sort of consequence. After all, you're just so *bored* here, right? None of it matters. It's all just a game to you—everything is a fucking game to you!"

I'm so furious at Agni's complete lack of emotion that a horrifying prickling sensation begins forming at the base of my eyes. It does not, however, stop my assault. Nor does it slow me in forcing him to drink down the horrors I've kept so tightly bottled.

"They had to kill its mother afterward. Did you know that? The kelpie was sentenced to what will most likely be a very short existence of baiting in The Deep. Its mother was too enraged after seeing her maimed child to be deemed safe enough to remain *alive.*" I'm seething now.

Agni's spine becomes rigid, but I hardly notice. The terrible sadness from that day begins bleeding into the present. A never-ending darkness bears down on my consciousness. It's so familiar that I sometimes think I must have been born with it.

"But that's no issue of yours," I continue on in my rant. "After all, you tamed it. You— "

"I—WAS—BLIND!" Agni snarls, whirling around to face me at last. His voice is like the sharp crack of a switch and its severity splinters the air between us.

Appearing suddenly like some sort of avenging star, the southern captain's gaze brims with a real, vivid burning as he rounds himself on me. I stumble and nearly fall in my fast-moving backward steps. Real fear begins clawing at me from somewhere deep inside my chest.

"I—WASN'T—ABLE—TO—*FUCKING*—SEE!" he bellows.

The look on his face is that of a man on the brink as Agni backs me into one of the thick, moss-covered trunks. "I couldn't even—I couldn't even—*HEAR!*" he shouts the last word, and the space around me heats right through the shield of my affinity.

Agni's eyes blaze furiously while his broad chest heaves from the effort it takes for him to breathe evenly and lower his voice. "I heated the bay because it was a felsic breed of kelpie. They survive in only exceedingly hot waters. I was trying to coax it in not fucking *torment* it!" He pauses to inhale raggedly.

"Then it got spooked and blasted me into that dock. The lightning shot out both of my eardrums, half of my sight, and—and—and I didn't *know.*" Agni's southern accent trills along each word of his lowered voice, thicker than I've ever heard.

His features manage to look somehow both stricken and enraged.

If he notices the chill in the air or white petals dropping from above, he doesn't allude to it. It becomes impossible to swallow, and a sour taste begins working its way up my esophagus.

Yet Agni persists.

"The blood was *everywhere*. I was coated in it—my *senses* were coated in it. I thought maybe I could bridle it again. I didn't know how close it was." He continues fuming. "My arm was snapped in fucking half and—I thought my aim was—I wasn't trying to—I just—" Agni's eyes shudder, and a façade I didn't even realize he was wearing slips.

For a single heartbeat, I catch sight of something unexpectedly broken lurking beyond walls of solid iron. My pulse falters in response, and I physically retreat backwards without thought. Tree bark digs into my spine so hard that I have to bite my tongue to keep from yelping in pain.

Agni swallows tightly, and his next words are so distant that I'm not sure they're truly meant for my ears. "I had it sent to one of my familial estates in Andesite, it will have been accepted on my behalf. It will *not* be forced to bait. I made certain of it. That kelpie will live out the remainder of its long and well cared for life with its sire in the same lands that its mother originated from."

His vision becomes lost while tilting his head up to the stars. The wind's fleeting hands run through his wild, obsidian mane. I'm struck then by how incredibly young he looks, how *anguished*.

For a moment, it feels as though I'm trespassing on something deeply private.

The way his eyes pursue the night sky looks as if he's searching for something. Or rather *someone*. The word longing comes to mind, as impossible as I find it to believe that emotion could belong to someone like him.

The moment is gone just as soon as Agni's unfocused gaze flickers back down to me and his jaw clenches dangerously tight. From the fresh rage now etching into the planes of his face, I know he's remembered just exactly who it is he's talking to.

Agni's sensuous mouth schools itself into an ugly leer while closing the few steps of distance between us. "Alright, *little bastard*. You wanted my attention—you got it. I'm all yours."

The twisted smile he sports is so vitriolic it mangles my insides until I have the urge to vomit right there. Even my affinity is agitated by his imposing form, white flakes now fall thickly, and rime begins crawling every nearby tree. If it wasn't for the equivalent anger radiating off of Agni in the form of brutal heat, the whole area would be blanketed in an inescapable winter.

I'm immensely grateful my voice comes out next as sharp and cold as a splinter of ice instead of quivering with the abject terror pumping in my veins. "I don't want anything to do with you. What I want is to be rid of this trivial od and your excruciating presence as quickly as possible."

So much for Nimra's tactics.

"Excellent." He sneers. "Then let's tick off one of your debts."

A dark shadow passes through his gaze with the curl of his lip, and my breathing turns shallow.

"Since you're so hellbent on casting me into the villain tonight, I think I'd like to return the favor." My teeth bite down into a lip in response to the pure malice lacing his voice. "The stories we've been told about you are honestly a bit *nightmarish*. A little far-fetched if you ask me. I'll admit, I've become rather curious as to whether or not they're true."

Agni lowers his face so it resides only centimeters from my own. It feels as though a gust of air has slipped beneath my skin, and it's nearly impossible to contain my shiver. In a voice as soft as smoke he whispers his request plainly. "Tell me about your first murder, bastard."

The blood drains from my face and pools down inside my boots.

Absolutely not.

My mouth parts in surprise. White tendrils escape from both of my disheveled braids and begin blowing across my face as I stare into Agni's monstrous eyes. His enjoyment is evident.

I regret ever leaving that stupid fucking bay.

"Go on," he orders me. "Describe the first time you took another young raider's life, since you're so very *noble* for a squid. Don't bother sparing me the details—I want every last one. Unless, of course, you would prefer to break our od and sit the remainder of the trials out."

I'm mentally kicking myself for allowing my emotions to run wild and getting into this position in the first place. Agni looms over me like a daunting omen, and I slump further against the evergreen, as if it can somehow shield me from his request. My mouth feels too dry, and my throat tightens uncomfortably.

The southern captain smirks as his hand comes to catch one of the white flyaway strands in my eyeline before tucking it neatly behind an ear. Lightheadedness flourishes inside of me in response to the severity of his capriciousness, and I strain to keep myself upright.

Agni takes my newfound vertigo as the opportunity to lean in closer than before.

His head dips so that mouth hovers again over that place along my throat where my pulse beats most noticeably. Amber eyes glint upwards with amusement. "Scared, are we?"

A nervous fluttering twists around my core in response to the smugness in his gaze meeting mine. I jerk away from his touch, and he stands just as a slip of my power snaps against him with a loud, harsh *slap* right across his face. "Fuck you. Pick a different question."

That was probably not the sort of sweet talk Kleio had in mind.

Agni moves back a step with a startled laugh, one hand holding his newly reddened cheek. For a horrible moment, I fear he'll use his affinity on me in turn and blanch at my own cowardice. His surprise doesn't last long, though. Renewed anger narrows his gaze while rolling his jaw.

Dropping his hand, Agni uses it to catch me by the chin while his free arm presses into the frost-covered trunk just above my head.

"I warned you that I wasn't in the mood tonight," Agni mutters, pulling up on my captured chin and forcing my gaze higher. "*That* is the question I want answered." The threat of immediate incineration is all that stops me from grabbing a weapon. The way the air around us heats in silent warning confirms the prick knows it too.

"You never said I couldn't refuse one—technically," I point out, gritting my teeth against the evergreen bark currently digging into my scalp. It's a bullshit stipulation, but I'll try whatever possible to steer the conversation in a different direction.

"True," Agni says, dragging out the single word while weighing his head to one side. There's a cold calculation in his expression as he stares down at me, considering.

"But you were right," he begins airily after a pause. "What you said about me earlier."

I attempt to frown in question, but it proves difficult with his hand still imprisoning my chin.

"I do enjoy holding this power over you," Agni clarifies, his eyes darkening while his thumb brushes gently over my bottom lip. The trivial motion injects me with a jolt of adrenaline, and I find it almost impossible to keep still beneath him. "I'm not sure I'll ever tire of it."

Keeping my breath from catching takes an alarming amount of self-control.

"You do *technically* have the right to refuse a question. Just as I *technically* have the right to choose another method of repayment." Agni's sizable hand moves almost of its own accord to wrap lightly around my throat. "*If* you were in fact hoping to refuse and still keep the captaincy you swore to your od, that is."

His gaze unfocuses slightly while scanning down my person, and a faint blush stains my cheeks.

I begin internally ripping myself a new one for opening up the clauses to our od.

Stupid.

Fucking.

Moron.

"I do have a few ideas of my own, actually, since we're apparently making changes to the already established agreement. Although I highly doubt you'll like them any better." He smirks.

My eyes narrow on him, not yet sure what he's getting at, but his attention is fixated on my pulse now thudding beneath his palm. Tilting my chin upwards with his thumb, his gaze returns to my questioning face. There's a smugness about his wayward lips that I don't quite understand.

"You see, the only alternative games I can think of playing—the kind that would assuage me in our little deal here—well, they all require *much* less clothing than this," he explains, dropping his hand from my throat in order to tug lightly on a braid. "None at all, actually."

My vision blotches over with spots of red while taking in his meaning.

Agni flashes me a fiendish grin.

"It's your choice, of course, how you wish to keep the od. I should mention, though, the second option doesn't count unless you're both *eager* and *willing.*" His eyes burn brighter with the new stipulation to his game. "So either tell me exactly what I wish to know, or you can follow me back to my quarters right now and see what little sleep you manage to get tonight."

"*Fine.*"

Shock blazes across his face for a split-second before Agni smothers it with cool amusement.

"Which one, exactly?" He asks, leering overtly above me.

Indignation eclipses all my previous caution, and I snatch the front of his crimson uniform. Pulling him closer, ice begins skittering out violently from where my fist clutches the fabric.

I briefly study his eyes as they dance with a goading sort of cockiness.

Then, donning a cloying voice to better imitate that of his admirers, I taunt him in obvious mockery. "Oh yes, *please,* Captain Agni. Bring me to your bed. I want you. I need you. What are you waiting for, *loverboy*? Go ahead and take me—I'm *begging* you."

His gaze darkens at my sarcasm-soaked words, all prior amusement extinguished by my pointed barbs. "*Vos habet nullus notio omnes vias ego vellem efficio vos imploro,*" he mutters softly from the corner of his mouth.

Releasing my icy grip on his uniform, I forcefully shove the smug bastard as hard as I possibly can, despising the ridiculous firmness of his chest. "I'll answer your question, dumbass."

Agni swiftly regains his balance, now a satisfying stretch away from me with a low chuckle. He casually wipes my affinity's remaining powdery dust from the front of his uniform before taking a step in my direction.

He folds his arms and looks down at me expectantly.

XXXIV. FIRST KILL

Blood thunders in my ears and my stomach turns in warning.

But nevertheless, I drag back up the memories I've worked hard to forget. Faces and names I've endeavored to keep buried deep down inside thrash around reluctantly while pulling them to the brutal light of the surface.

I find it marginally easier to control my voice by focusing on the shadow beneath Agni's chin rather than meeting his intent gaze.

"His name was Iver. I was in level two, and he—he was in level four."

Agni tuts once. "I thought that sounded pretty young to become a cold-blooded murderer. I'm impressed. Continue." My lips pull themselves downward in disgust, whether it's towards me or him, I'm not yet sure.

"Iver was talented. *Brek*. He had an affinity for archery like nothing I've ever seen," I admit before stealing a short breath and working to flatten out the debased memory. "Level-two's aren't allowed to leave their cabin's past nightfall, but I used to wander in the dark most evenings."

His brow lifts as if to say, *as you still continue to do.* I roll my eyes at his pointed stare and resume.

"This night in particular, I went to walk my usual path. The one right along the tree-line leading back to the old docks. It's pretty close to here actually, but—anyway, I found I wasn't alone." The sound of my exhale fills the air around us.

My brow creases as the repressed memories begin tangling themselves again.

"It was stupid. I should never have left my bunk, but I didn't want to be there. I just—I just wanted to be *anywhere* else." I don't know why I'm explaining myself other than the fact that Agni requested the details and I would give them to him.

"There was a group of them. Coming back from the boneyard."

The image of that night suddenly resurfaces in painful clarity. I can practically hear their loud shouting and the obnoxious way in which they bragged about recent oblation winnings. Even the midnight breeze can't carry away their lurid scent, it still cloaks them so heavily in my mind.

I had just turned fourteen.

"They were all terribly drunk. This was before liquor was outlawed from the boneyard, obviously." A provision I myself put into place the very evening of my promotion to captaincy.

"I thought I was pretty well hidden within the high grasses and stones. This group of level fours in particular had a certain *reputation,*" I muse. "A true talent for cruelty." My eyes flicker up to Agni's to discover them uncharacteristically hard, his mouth has set in an unreadable line.

My lip curls. "I suppose you might have gotten along with them quite well."

A vein along his temple throbs visibly in response.

"I didn't realize the wind would cause my hair to lift like some damning white flag and give away my hiding spot." Bitterness coats the back of my tongue and I internally spit on the gods for the extreme and unforgivable way in which they branded me. "That was my mistake."

Swallowing the acidity in my throat, I find the words to continue. "They sought me out, knowing just exactly *who* and *what* was hiding from them. They, like you, despised castaways and bastard-borns. I provided them with the unique opportunity of taking out their aggression on both."

Drawing another rallying breath, I wonder idly when my hand grabbed for the small knife now twirling anxiously about my fingers.

"They found me. I tried to run, but they were faster and stronger. They had two more years of experience and training. Not to mention that, being a castaway, I obviously didn't arrive here with any oblations. Assuming the south operates in the same way—well, you know I wouldn't have been allotted weapons without reaching level-six or earning them in a challenge."

I swallow. "That is to say, I had none, and they had many."

I'm not positive at what point Agni took a step back or when I took one forward and our roles reversed. But he wanted to hear the whole story. Every detail.

"They cut my hair off in terrible chunks and told me it was a mercy when I began to cry. Each of them, obviously highborn, explained to me in very putrid words that the color of it was a sign from the gods themselves that they were worth more than me. That they were *above* me by right. They claimed to be taking what was owed to them for allowing my existence here."

Oddly enough, the beating inside my bones is nothing more than a dull thud, lost inside the echoes of time. I barely even notice how black the southern captain's eyes have turned or how his fisted hands have whitened at the knuckles.

"They were quite descriptive with what they intended to do to me that night, how *exactly* they were going to show me my place." I pause with another swallow, an ache has begun forming along my temples and jawline. "So yes, the stories you've heard about me *are* true. When they started to cut away at my uniform with their blades, I let my power slip the leash."

Captain Agni has dimmed into a darkness so absolute that he could be mistaken for the resting place between stars. I can almost forget his presence entirely.

"Iver *was* my first kill, but he was not the only kill I made that night." Admittance to that fact is not a struggle and my lips lift slightly in the corners.

"He had it easy. All it took was one little frigid blast and he toppled right over the bluffs. You know how high the fall is and how sharp the rocks waiting at the bottom are. No amount of archery can save you from that, I'm afraid." I try flattening my lips again, to no avail.

The corner of my mouth hooks ever upwards in recollection.

"Then went Chet. It was winter and as you can probably imagine, it was easy enough to craft an icicle, even having next to no affinity training at that point. Easier still to shove it in his eye socket until it pierced through the back of his skull." The breathy laugh I huff is dark and cold.

"I'd like to claim I saved Byron for last on purpose but it was honestly more so that he got away while I was... *distracted* with Chet." My eyes become unfocused for a moment.

"It didn't take long to find him, the idiot ran back towards the boneyard instead of the north. That was his mistake. His *last* mistake." I chew the inside of my lip while deciding my next words. "I found out about my frostbite ability that night. I found out a lot about myself that night." My lips purse tight in remembrance.

"I couldn't stop once I'd started. My affinity was damn near impossible to tame back then. Besides," I shrug casually. "I was too enraged about the hair of mine he'd taken and tied around his belt as a trophy to even fathom halting."

When I meet Agni's gaze again, I find it filled with flames, but not the ones I'm expecting. They do not narrow in judgment or glint in the promise of damnation. These flames are far more terrifying, dancing and swaying with pure obsidian *rage*.

His mouth moves as if carved from stone when speaking at last. "I heard it was four against one."

It's not technically a question but I shake my head regardless. "I had to leave one of them alive, didn't I? Had to ensure the message was received by anyone else thinking of going after me."

"What was their name? The one left alive." Agni's words are clipped and severe.

My snort is faint. "What's it to you?"

"I'll count it as a question," he offers darkly.

Rolling my eyes to the sky and back at his sudden strangeness, I answer in a tapered breath. "Maybe the worst of them all, funnily enough. He promised to take something *else* from me that night as a trophy. Something much more *intimate* than my hair. His name is Ferris Noll."

Agni nods once and it's almost mechanical in movement.

"Does that satisfy two debts, then?" I ask. "Or do you require even more details to satiate this obsessive need of yours to acerbate me? There are some exceptionally vile things they said to me—really creative, maybe you'd like—"

"*No.*" He spits out the word like it's coated in poison.

Reliving the memory has made it so I'm too remote to enjoy his riled state. I can't even find it in myself to smirk at the way Agni's sickening arrogance has completely abandoned him at last.

"It's safe to say that whatever other terrible rumors you've heard are probably true. I *am* a nightmare. A deviant, bastard-born, castaway nightmare." The pronouncement sounds dead even to my own ears.

A chilling quiet falls between us for an unsettling moment.

Then, Agni lifts the quiet.

He says, *"Oderint dum metuant,"* offering the words to me like a gift.

His eyes remain fixed on my face as they continue dancing in that menacing obsidian. I don't think he even realizes the statement was given in his southern tongue until my head tilts to one side in clear question.

"Let them hate, so long as they fear," he states, explaining their meaning to my undying surprise. "It was my mother's family maxim. Some people in the landmasses use them like a prayer. They say it helps."

It takes genuine effort to repress the shiver that beckons in response and keep my face impassive. The tingling sensation prickling at the base of my scalp stems from more than just my shock at Agni revealing his foreign words' significance for the first time.

Never in my life have more veracious words been spoken.

Never have I felt so completely exposed.

We stand there staring at each other for several more motionless minutes. Assessing one another anew. Reevaluating and remeasuring the enemy as any good raider would.

After a prolonged period of silent calculation, I conclude, "Well, that makes four."

Making to turn back in aim for the northern fortress and my cabin within it, I hesitate. We really aren't so far from where the horror of that night occurred. The knowledge sends a dark wave of unease crashing through me. Dread curdles low in echoed response while I feel their ghosts begin to press about the air, as if summoned by the recount.

That was a long time ago, Boreas.

They're dead now—get a grip.

I lock my jaw, straighten my spine, and resume the course with determination.

A haze of saffron and cedar and something else I don't know the name for trails me every step of the way. For the first time, the scent is not an entirely unwelcome presence. Although I suppose any non-threatening presence would do so near that haunted path on a night as similar as this. How Agni managed to slide himself into that mental category, I haven't the faintest clue.

Just before slipping inside the black stone confinement, I pause to steal a backward glance.

The image of Agni's towering shadow greets me as he watches silently from the other side of the open-air bridge. Releasing a low-lying cloud of smoke in my direction is the only sign of his farewell.

A strange surge of something dangerously thrilling heats my blood in response. I dismiss it briskly, with a sharp jerk of my head.

Giving Agni a flash of my captain-ring finger, I continue on inside, intending to head directly for my bunk. His deep chuckled response to my gesture accompanies me through the entrance.

I'm unnervingly aware of every movement I make under his searing gaze.

For some masochistic reason I don't dare attempt to decipher, I find myself loitering in the hall minutes later, unable to continue on to my cabin. Finally, moving as if no more than a shadow, I creep to one of the many carved-out niches along the hall. My fingers, pale from the lack of sunlight, press against the gritty black wall as I risk another look.

Agni *still* lingers at the opposite end of the bridge.

Observing him while hidden behind the stone recess is a strange sort of relief.

My unfettered eyes are free to study his staggering form and all its dreadful beauty beneath the celestial light. His broad muscular back leans casually against the stone. His upturned chin displays the strength of his jaw, contrasting sharply with the soft outline of his lips as he finishes off the last of his spice.

I've never noticed before how soft his mouth looks. A hand rubs idly against my lower lip.

Moments later, Agni finally turns back around and disappears in the direction of their ship. A fresh wave of that concerning heat begins rolling into me again. It flushes across my chest and drops lower, raising skin as it goes.

Pushing away from the wall, I give myself a thorough shake before scoffing at my capacity for self-destruction. *Depths.* I'm no better than one of his adoring little fan club members that I so enjoy mocking.

Fucking pathetic.

XXXV. Helmsman

The leg I rest beneath our table shakes with unusual impatience.

Preceptor Beldham has turned around no less than four times in the last half hour of today's lecture covering systematic raiding ploys in order to glare at my various forms of fidgeting. I grimace when her piercing blue eyes land on me for what is now the fifth time.

"Captain Boreas, do we need to tie you to your seat this morning or have your leg removed altogether?" Her voice carries out to the back of the room, where the South Regent observes.

Kleio and Herse both flash me quizzical looks, which I ignore. I've been anxious as hell since receiving a message during breakfast carrying Skelm's signet seal. He's requested I meet in his quarters following the conclusion of today's classes. That's *hours* from now.

I hate to admit it but his methods of torture are becoming quite clever.

There are about a million different reasons why our grand preceptor would need to meet with me. They churn my nerves with their passing, each one even more unsavory than the last. The worst of all being Skelm somehow learning of my misstep during Luminalia.

I worry about Kerau exposing me almost as often as I did Captain Agni. He sends me epistles with long written apologies every week. I've yet to respond to a single one. Instead, I shred them immediately after reading before pitching the scraps into the sea.

Seeing as he *is* the captain of a TideLord, Beldham and the others can't very well restrict him from attempting communications with me. Although I'm almost certain she supposes them to be love letters.

Who knew the old bat had a heart?

Pressing my lips into a firm line, I shake my head in silent response to Beldham's chastising. After a considering moment, she drops her petrifying gaze and breaks us off into table discussions regarding successful overwintering ploys. Kleio begins leading our debate, leaving me free to zone out to the sounds of Herse and Greer arguing.

I lean back further in my seat and my ankles come to cross in an attempt to stop their restless movement. I'm trying hard not to brood too deeply over the reason for my summons. Thinking about it won't lessen the punishment.

A fact I know painfully well.

"If she asks to have you tied again, I think I'll volunteer," whispers a dark, sultry voice from just beside my ear.

My pulse stumbles. I hadn't realized how far back I'd positioned myself while mentally spacing. Sliding my gaze to the right, I find Olsson Agni leaning forward in his seat so that our faces are a mere inch apart. A wave of heat floods my system and I quickly work to dispel it before the evidence can manifest on my skin.

"I would prefer to lose the leg," I whisper sharply in return.

His resounding chuckle is semi-frightening, without the typical edge of bitterness that I've come to expect. "*Tu minoris aestimo quam iucundus esset experientia.*" His comment exudes a taunting quality and I'm more curious than usual to unravel its meaning.

Agni's smirk is cocky when he gives me a flash of his brows before turning back to rejoin his crew. I don't even have the chance to respond. Vagar narrows his deep navy eyes in my direction before saying something to his captain in a voice too quick and quiet for me to pick up.

I can't decide if Agni's foreign words sounded more like a threat or a promise. Quite possibly they're both. His little comments, I've come to realize, are each a mind game in and of themselves. They also happen to be the perfect distraction from my anxious brooding.

I'd previously written the southern captain off as an especially irksome, pretentious highborn. One who's used to the taste of power and willing to do whatever necessary to keep it flowing.

His obsession with vexing me in particular I noted as strange but also not so unlike others I've encountered before. I'm well aware others see me as an easy target and there's a distinct message to send by crushing me under their heel.

But lately, I've been reconsidering.

Our interaction that night after the winter storm rattled the very tightly wrapped categorical box I had him packaged in. Arrogant, self-important, spoiled, cocky-little-prick, the labels all read. Now—well—now I wasn't so sure which of them actually fit.

The kelpie and the tragedy of its maiming were one of the large driving nails in Agni's coffin of awfulness. Learning that it was unintended, and what's more, that he felt something very much like remorse over it, has sent me into an existential loop.

If I'm not analyzing Agni properly—if I haven't been this whole time—then I can never hope to form the right strategy in order to bring about his downfall.

And he *must* fall.

Whether I'm willing to audibly admit it or not, Captain Agni and his crew pose the biggest threat to me and mine when it comes to winning The Vault and leaving the north. I won't allow for my own miscalculations about the asshole to be the reason that he wins.

If that is in fact what it comes down to.

The nights I spend twisting and turning in sweat-dampened sheets are now dedicated to deciphering this sudden shift in his character.

Or is it truly another layer?

I struggle to grasp the horrible way in which Agni was so easily able to slide right back into the role of tormentor. He was unexpectedly skilled in countering his own private admission by forcing me to pry out a dark and damaged piece of my soul in return.

I'm not an idiot. I know he's terrible. I know he's cruel and conceited and outright insolent. However, I also now know there is more to it than that.

To *him*.

I've memorized the words he gifted me that night and tucked them away into a dark, shadowed corner of my consciousness. Sometimes I find myself repeating them beneath my breath when ugly images of earlier years break into my thoughts or night terrors drag me from slumber.

Oderint dum metuant.

Let them hate, so long as they fear.

It has indeed become a sort of prayer and repeating them evokes in me an unexplainable calm. I've discovered that they feel more powerful in his rich dialect than in my northern translation. I'm beginning to worry that there is much, maybe *too* much, regarding Agni that I do not know.

Kleio gives me a curious look when I return my attention to their ongoing debate and I throw her a glance that promises an explanation later.

Wrapping up one of the final lessons remaining in our theory of war class, I feel a vexing tug on my braid. I don't bother turning around. I can feel the perpetrator's movements as he stands and passes me, trailing behind the rest of his crew.

Before exiting, Agni pauses to look over his shoulder, finding me brazenly flipping off his backside with both hands and a deep scowl. His response to my obscene gestures is worse than I could have anticipated.

Agni laughs a *real* laugh. Right before his mouth curves itself up into a heart-stoppingly crooked, dangerously-dark grin. An expression I'm positive I've never seen him wear before.

My heart stutters and then pounds furiously against my ribcage, each beat a desperate attempt to remind me to breathe. Heat threatens to give away the brewing storm of new and strange emotions taking root inside of me. My affinity fights against the warmth spreading from the pit of my stomach, unfurling in slow, tingling waves that reach all the way to my fingertips.

I blink and he slips out into the fray beyond.

Kleio's voice echoes back into existence and I have no idea how long she's been talking to me. "Merena, are you alright? We have to get to Darood's class. Anyone late this week is getting waterboarded for level-four demonstrations or something."

"Yeah—that's good. I mean, I'm fine. This whole meeting with Skelm is just messing with my head."

I quickly gather myself and follow her towards the rest of our retreating crew. But my claim is not entirely the truth.

Something is *incredibly* wrong with me.

Every detail of that crooked grin is now seared into my mind.

"What a sick fucking joke."

The evening following Beldham's lecture finds me storming out of our grand preceptor's quarters with an attitude I wouldn't have dared display had I not been so close to freedom.

The thought of kicking down his door *actually* presented itself to me as a legitimate temptation. I swear I saw a flash of outrage in Skelm's eye, as if he could read my momentary consideration.

We're just *so* damn close to ditching this hellish island. The mere thought of not winning The Vault has my insides freezing over in a fit of terrified rage.

"*Well now, Boreas, whose fault is it for choosing a leech as a crew member*?"

Skelm basically spat his list of reasons for his disapproval at me. My teeth grind together in memory as I tear down the stairwell, taking the steps two at a time.

I make it to the main level and stalk the long corridor. The stone's carved recesses reveal the outside world is exploding with delayed symptoms of spring. Icy veins spider the moist walls with sharp crackling sounds in my wake as I veer towards the outdoor lyceums.

In instances like this one, with the internal beating so savage and wild, it's safer for all residents of the Cardinal North if I work off at least a portion of my affinity's violence outdoors. My crew has already started their evening training rounds, I can hear their voices mixing with the ringing of weapons.

The fourth and final trial is not as mysterious as the other three. Each time The Vault rises, every captain *and* their crew are obliged to participate. It's said to be a test of loyalty and leadership. I've had Kleio run training on the side in preparation for the last several months.

It's also no secret that this is when most blood is split. There are no rules once inside those famed kórallian walls. Providing us with the opportunity to settle any and all scores. Rumor was the last time The Vault arose, when TideLord Dolion won, the sea was stained scarlet for a week.

The aura of my rabid power has me chafing at the bit as I storm over the bridge. Its heightened presence is also no doubt why I was able to leave Skelm's quarters in such a fit of rage. There *is* some reasoning behind him forcing kratosbane down my throat before bestowing punishment.

Herse notices my furious approach towards them before the others and whistles at Kleio in warning. My second pauses her instruction with Greer and Davina, allowing Nimra to take over.

Kleio deftly grabs two second-hand broadswords from the pile of various weapons they've dragged out here with Preceptor Oplon's blessing.

My vibrating fingers struggle to unbutton my too-tight jacket until I finally just rip it straight off my body. Readjusting the gold pin and securing back my hair in a huff, I swipe one of the outstretched hilts from my second's hand.

Kleio follows me wordlessly to the chalky, grass-outlined ring we've begun using again for Brek affinity training. Circling each other, I spy the almost invisible lines of concern etched into my second's brow in the fading sunlight. Visible relief flattens those creases after she's studied me enough to find I've come back in one angry piece.

Then Kleio lunges.

Her weapon swings in a broad arc and I grunt while meeting her with my own identical blade, deflecting the attack. The impact of our clash reverberates through my arms but I hold firm and dislodge her. Kleio doesn't give me a moment's rest before pushing forward again with relentless alternating strikes. This is *exactly* what I need and the look in Kleio's eyes tells me that she's very aware.

"So I can assume that went well?" My second is able to tease, now that she's certain I haven't been physically reprimanded.

I dance backwards, parrying each blow as fast as I can. Blood pumps rhythmically in my ears and my mind begins to clear, sharpening for the task at hand.

"Oh yeah, a real tea party in there." I snort.

With a sweeping motion of my palm across the ground, I send a wave of cold towards my second. Ice manifests rapidly, forming a slick surface with the once-dewy grass beneath her feet.

Kleio's affinity springs to life, shimmering around her and neatly dispersing the ice. I've got plenty of energy to spare. I will a bitter chill into my weapon, causing hoarfrost to creep along its blade, then I swing for Kleio again. This time with more precision.

Her power slams up like a wall between us. My strike bounces off the barrier harmlessly but a faint crack forms beneath.

"So what did he have to say?" Kleio presses. Her wall of force burns a brighter shade of violet, pushing me back towards the outer white ring.

"Thirty," I growl with a sharp exhale.

My second drops her shield and pounces for me again. Sidestepping her intention, I pivot and thrust my palm towards the ground. A barrier of frigid spikes emerges between us as I move backwards. Kleio's power reappears before her approaching figure and extends outwards as I regain my footing. She throws me a quizzical look before effectively shattering the brutal icicles separating us.

"Thirty fucking points is all that I earned from the last pillar task," I explain before launching a flurry of strikes, each one aimed to test the limits of her shield.

In the aftermath of Captain Namak's unexpected death, I didn't think much about my current scoring. It seemed too trivial to worry about in the wake of watching all of his crew members and Dhara stumble about like their own hands had been cut off.

It's been more painful than I could have anticipated to observe.

"Well—what were the other scores?" Kleio, ever the optimist, ventures as she blocks my rapid assault with skill. Her affinity's protection wraps tightly around her body to absorb the impact of each blow. Ironically, my second has had more practice than just about anyone else when it comes to resisting me and my affinity's force.

"Fucking better than that. We'll be going into the last pillar ranked *fifth*." The word leaves a sour taste on my tongue and the angry line between my brows deepens.

She retaliates my incessant walloping with a powerful downward swipe, which I barely manage to parry. My weapon arm starts throbbing from the force of her attempt and my teeth press together in determination.

Kleio starts up in her encouragement, "We can work with that. Fifth isn't—"

"Fifth is fucking atrocious," Herse calls, cutting off Kleio's budding words of positivity from the other side of the chalky boundary. "*Damn* Boreas. What were the requirements for scoring this round? See what captain could piss off their grand preceptor the least?"

Despite the anger riddling my veins, Herse's bluntness draws a real laugh from my lips.

"More or less," I shout back. My thoughts shift to Skelm's long list of reasons for docking me points. I avoid the impulse to glance over at where Nimra is currently drilling Davina.

Kleio gives our third a blatant look of chiding, to which Herse rolls her violet eyes. Using the momentary distraction, I charge for my second, swinging my broadsword in a wide arc. Her energy shield fractures slightly under the pressure of my frigid blade and I spot an opening at last.

"She's right, Kleio. It is atrocious. Fifth place is *not* good. I've been ranking in the top three since this whole thing started and now—when we need it most—" I grunt with renewed effort while thrusting my weapon forward, aiming for the identified chink in her armor. "I somehow manage to fuck us all the way down to fifth."

Her affinity shatters with a resounding '*crack*' and Kleio stumbles back, momentarily exposed. I don't hesitate. Unleashing a torrent of icy shards, I send them flying her way. She reacts quicker than I anticipated, raising a smaller, more concentrated shield to deflect each one of the glass-like pieces of frozen evening dew.

"You've gotten better," I praise between panting breaths, throwing a glance of approval at my second.

Kleio grins, a hint of pride in her eyes. "We've been practicing."

Then the concentrated ball of power in her hands explodes outward in a blinding sweep of violet energy. Its detonation forces me to scramble backwards to avoid being slammed across the white ring. I steady myself from the impact of her blast, watching as Kleio also regains her balance.

Questions swim plainly back and forth through those watchful eyes and I shake my head knowingly. "He refused to divulge anything regarding Captain Namak's death. Only the Cardinal East is aware of what occurred and I was very thoroughly informed we are *not* privy to anything more."

Sweat slides down from my hairline to coat my neck and pool at the base of my collarbones. My hands rest on my hips as refreshingly cool evening air works its way in and out of my lungs in a heavy pattern of recovery.

"That was also *after* he deemed it necessary to remind me he would use my skin for a cape if any of us dared to embarrass him before King Nereus and the Driftwood Court."

Greer lets out a low whistle from where she and the others have joined Herse to watch and listen in on our brawl. "Gotta love that man's charm. Always so colorful with his threats."

"An artist, that one," Prisca agrees.

"I think he prefers to be called a poet. You should ask him though, to be sure," Nephthys chimes in.

I might have laughed along with the others if my mood hadn't clouded over so entirely. Nodding to Kleio, we ready ourselves to go again. That blast of energy cost her. I watch the strain of using so much power sliding down the sides of her temples, soaking the front of her undershirt.

My blade glows a pale chilling blue before I blitz my second one last time. She raises up her wall again but it's clearly weakened. My weapon slams down with all the pent-up frustration my meeting with Skelm left writhing inside.

Kleio's affinity shatters beneath me once more but this time she isn't quick enough with her blade to meet mine in deflection. The sword in my grip halts just centimeters from her shoulder. We stand there for a moment, panting and grinning at one another, before slowly dropping our weapons.

As the adrenaline rush from our fight begins to fall, so does my face. I swallow thickly, my head hanging low with the weight of self-condemnation.

"Hey," Kleio says, clapping me on the shoulder. "It's not like fifth place is even going to matter. Don't give me that look—it *won't*."

I know her heartfelt words are just an effort to retrieve me from my brewing disposition. Like she's my own sort of personal life raft. I can almost feel her nearby churning thoughts as she contemplates this new problem.

Kleio's next words are spoken slowly, so there isn't a chance of misunderstanding. "It actually *won't* matter. Because we just so happen to have the best helmsman in all four cardinals."

My head lifts slowly from where it previously studied the snowflake-dusted grass. When meeting my second's gaze, I discover a very familiar mischievous light cavorting about her eyes. Blinking once I tilt my head to study her, I honestly can't tell whether she's joking or not.

"You want to switch?" I ask, my voice unsure.

Kleio nods and her mouth forms a scheming sort of grin. "I think we'd be stupid not to."

For a moment I'm lost again but not to the agitation-fueled storm of guilt. Now I'm enveloped in the newly brightening horizon abundant with opportunity. Mulling over my second's offer, I come to conclude that we actually might just be able to pull it off.

"But—you don't mind? Really?" I press.

She laughs in return. "Mind? Why would I mind? If anyone would refuse to switch, it would be you. Which I wouldn't fault you for, what with the TideLords and King Nereus there watching. But Merena, we could *win*."

Any remaining clouds of my dismay dissipate into the ether and are replaced by fluttering's of hope. I can't believe I hadn't thought of this before.

I grab Kleio's hand, squeezing it gratefully. "You're brilliant, you know that?"

She beams at me in return. Her brown eyes grow warm enough to thaw some of that unyielding ice inside of me. I could almost swear I felt something begin to fracture.

"Alright," I shout with a brisk clap. "Kleio and I have some last-minute changes to go over with you guys." A grin climbs its way up my face as we leave the ring and join the rest of our crew.

We spend the remainder of our time that night re-strategizing. We cover and then re-cover the event timeline of the trial. We analyze for hours all that we know when it comes to finding The Vault and noting the *many* factors that will have to be left up to chance. Finally, we plan out how best to utilize the few remaining days we have to practice our last-minute change.

Not until we finally drag ourselves back to the cabin and I lie down in my bunk for what might be one of the last times do the doubts begin to swell inside.

What if I win and still no TideLord chooses me?

What if my origins are too much to overlook?

How absolutely humiliating that would be. For me *and* my crew. Just the possibility of it makes me want to hunker down and never leave the safety of my sheets again.

If only the evidence of what I am wasn't so incredibly damning. I often wonder just what exactly I must have done to piss off the drowned gods to such a degree. From the white brand around my wrist extending to the identical shade of my affinity mark and then stretching so far as to turn my hair into a glaring symbol.

A part of me thought maybe I would never grow it back out after those assholes chopped it off in a hack job. In the brilliancy of early youth, I thought maybe if I hid it, people might even forget. Maybe, by allowing it to grow so long and obvious, I was inadvertently asking for the treatment I received. Maybe *I* was the one at fault for bringing the attention upon myself.

Maybe I should just make myself as small and invisible as possible, I thought. Maybe then everyone would finally leave me alone. Maybe I could just fade into the background until no one noticed I was there at all.

Then a different part of me raised its head from the deep, dark depths of my blackened soul. It whispered to me tidings of another path.

Maybe, I thought, maybe I should become larger and more terrifying than even those who hunted me in my nightmares. Maybe I should learn to train the beast that prowled beneath my skin and unleash it at my will. Maybe I should take up so much space it would suffocate everyone in the fucking vicinity.

The choice then became crystal clear for my younger self. *Oderint dum metuant.*

Let them hate, so long as they fear.

XXXVI. THE TYTHE

Tantalizingly warm air ruffles past my cheek as I gaze out at the sinking sun. My chin rests on a fist beneath my elbows, currently propped on the stone terrace edge. Scents of brine and salt tease the inside of my nose while I study the arctic waves out beyond. I watch the waters as they heave a ship brandishing the crimson southern flag towards the horizon.

A lip slides between my teeth and I try to steady my untamed nerves. This day has taken a torturously long time to arrive but now that it's here, it seems to have come all too quickly.

Tonight marks our final pillar trial. The one that will decide our fates and potentially take us away from here for good. The anxious beating in my chest at the prospect of what tomorrow morning might bring is so obnoxious that I'm sure everyone on the entire bleeding isle must be able to hear it.

Anxiety peppers my brow and tips my stomach over. The doubts I tossed and turned with from nights prior is suddenly overbearing.

Closing my eyes against the sea air, I force myself to take deep, steady, practiced breaths. I utilize the rhythm that Preceptor Darood has drilled into us for high-stress situations. Inhale a count of four. Pause. Exhale a count of four. Pause. Repeat.

This cycle of breath work keeps me company while I watch the colorful portrait of dusk unfold.

I've always loved this time of day best. When the sun lays down atop the sea and stars begin to wink into existence in the brilliant vividness of half-light. It calls to me, singing some sort of forgotten melody while also unfurling a bit of the tightness inside.

Eventually my unease fades.

After a few peaceful moments, I blow out a long-winded sigh and reluctantly move onto more important thoughts. Tonight's events will begin with the traditional race into The Vaults' famously treacherous kórallian maze. All of my focus needs to be on that. *Must* be on that.

The anticipation of fulfilling Kleio's plan sends a welcome buzz of adrenaline pulsing through my veins. My fingers tap impatiently along the coarse barrier and the bottom hem of my captain's cape lifts idly in the breeze. Both northern crews are set to report down at Giant's Crook right after sunset. The other cardinals have begun departing already.

Our final trial won't begin until midnight.

"Captain?"

Turning away from the waters, I shift to face Kleio hovering in the doorway of our cabin's veranda. The exact same hesitant smile plays on her lips as the day she tracked me down to the wharf and conned me into becoming her ally. My lips flicker upwards at the memory of it. That turned out to be the most important day of my life. Until today, perhaps.

"Raider Hiraeth?" I mimic her formal tone in jest.

"We have something to show you," she says, her eyes dancing with endearing mischief.

The smile I sport stays in place while my brows pull together in question. I give her a bemused tilt of my head in interest. Holding onto her own grin, Kleio motions to what I assume must be the rest of my crew and I watch as the six of them file out into the darkening veranda to form a shadowed line before me.

The wrinkles of confusion beneath my hairline grow as I look them over. Each one is expertly dressed in our newly fashioned uniforms. It's not often the north provides us with new provisions of anything. Just about every scrap of cloth I've ever worn has been third or fourth-hand, at least.

So discovering the carefully wrapped bundle of skillfully crafted regalia left before our cabin's hearth this morning was akin to having gowns made for Luminalia. Better, even.

Having obviously kept our sizes on file from the previous festivities tailoring, each garb was created and labeled individually.

The uniform itself gives the illusion of being a single bodysuit, while in actuality it's two separate pieces. The long-sleeve top is made from surprisingly breathable yet fitted fabric, beginning at the neck and ending at the waist. The bottoms are looser, high-waisted, and made from a similarly lightweight material. They also boast a plethora of pockets, perfect for concealing numerous weapons without weighing you down.

A sturdy onyx belt for sheathing supplies and additional weapons graces each of our hips. Boots the color of midnight cut off just below the knee with outsoles made for any terrain. The waterproofing material of them is rather curious too, like leather but without its typical shine.

My personal favorite part of the suit lies in the details. While we're covered from neck to toe in black, the stitching provides a pop of brilliant azure. That blazing thread work was then taken a step further as each of our affinity markings has been artfully embroidered in the fabric atop the part of our bodies where they reside.

The backside of the shirt currently clinging tightly to my skin displays my affinity proudly in all its wild and unruly patterns. The stitching imitates my marking perfectly as it bursts across my shoulder blades and streams down to the base of my spine without any sort of definitive motif.

Squinting back at Kleio in confusion, she laughs at my obvious puzzlement before stepping into the light of the dying sun. Something glints in her neatly tied braids and shines bright in my questioning eyes.

Understanding takes a moment to dawn, but when it does, my jaw slackens and I blink repeatedly at my second in disbelief. I'm not entirely positive whether I trust my vision, especially after the events following Reed's pyre burning.

But then the rest of my crew steps forward one by one. They join Kleio in the golden evening light and I'm suddenly blinded by them all.

No—it—they *can't* have.

A tythe.

All seven members of my crew, who make up our sacred eight, have streaks of pure glittering *white* woven throughout their hair. A lump threatens to strangle my throat as I scan the group over and over again, in continued disbelief. My mouth opens but no sound comes out. I can't find the words, let alone form them.

What they've done—the statement they're making—*tything* themselves to me. Tything themselves by the very awful token the drowned gods made with my startling shade of hair.

They've taken my deepest, darkest vulnerability and turned it into a show of solidarity. The same way that a TideLord's crew will choose permanent matching ornaments or inkings of great significance on their skin to link themselves by.

What they've done is considered a major declaration among The Order of the Tide Raiders.

A tything is an extremely sacred rite. A way to show that you all belong together as one—*always*. It takes every last shred of my own self-discipline not to sink to my knees and break down in tears. Even so, my chin quivers, and my eyes begin searing with undeserved rapture.

"H-how?" I manage to ask. I'm too stunned to put into words what this means to me, or the gravity of the pronouncement they're poised to make.

Kleio's eyes gleam with the tears I won't afford myself. "I went back to the wharf market the day after we got fabrics for Luminalia," she explains easily, as if it were no more than an errant thought.

My head shakes slowly, a hand coming to cover my mouth as I again examine every one of their beautiful heads. There must be countless strands woven throughout their various tied-back hairstyles.

"But—how did you all—they were worth a fortune!" I sputter in remembrance of how expensive they'd been, fifty-silvers *each*. My widened eyes trace back and forth over the line of women before me again and again.

My brave, rash, idiotic, *perfectly wonderful* crew.

"Well, as you may remember, mommy moneybags over here *did* wash up with a rather ridiculously large oblation." Herse's husky voice is teasing and she gives a pointed cough in direction of my second.

Kleio rolls her eyes. "We pooled together for them but I might have contributed a *little* bit extra."

Herse rubs her thumb against her pointer and index finger while mouthing the words 'money bags' to me in clear emphasis. A bubble of rich laughter escapes me in response. The others break into snickers at Herse's charade while a reddened Kleio waves them off.

"This, however—" My second begins fishing out a small item from her breast pocket. "I *will* take credit for," she boasts, extending the retrieved trinket out for me to see.

I glance down at the small golden band in her hand, then back to Kleio's face in uncertainty.

Laughing gently at my perplexed expression, she explains, "It's a cuff that you put around your hair when it's tied on top of your head. See the holes on the sides? You just slide that hairpin I gave you through them both and it will lock it all in one place."

My gaze returns to the precious golden trinket laying flat in her palm. "No," I say in refusal after a minute, shaking my head repeatedly. "No, it's too much, I can't."

"*Merena.*" Kleio sighs deeply, her eyes looking up at the sky, as if she already knew this would be a battle. "Please, just this once—for me—don't be difficult. We don't have time like we did with the hairpin debacle for me to challenge you to a fight, just for you to win, in order for you to accept the stupid gift."

"Are you saying you *let* me win that fight?" I argue and Kleio's lips press together in a thin line of silence. It only takes a moment to read the seriousness in her gaze before relenting.

"Okay," I surrender, swallowing hard. "Thank *you*." My traitorous voice decides right then is the perfect time to fracture and heat consumes the back of my neck in embarrassment.

Fucking Hiraeth.

I distract myself by removing the gold pin I treasure above all other items from where it's currently hiding my hair back in a tight twist. Long white glittering strands fall before me, identical to those now gleaming on the heads of my crew. I quickly pile them tight atop my head and Kleio demonstrates the accessory use. She places the gold cuff around the base of my hair and slides the pin through the front-facing holes.

"You *do* know what you're doing with all of this, right?" My voice is beseeching while meeting seven pairs of eyes. I need to know regardless of their good intentions that they understand what this will mean.

For good or bad, our futures will be tethered as one. Until the tides take us home.

"The TideLords—hell the Raider *King* and his entire court will be there tonight. I don't— if I can't—" I start stumbling over my own frantic thoughts and have to stop myself. Breathing deeply, I try again. "If I can't get you all where you deserve to go, I don't want the rest of your careers to be tainted by this—by *me*. I couldn't bear it—if I—should things go poorly."

"We know what we're doing," Kleio states, her tone ringing with finality. "We can hand—"

"You can handle yourselves. I know." I finish my second's words and nod at my crew in agreement for once. I will not stop them in this sacred rite. I will allow them to make their own choices, as I should have probably done sooner. "But I need to hear it from each of your lips."

"I understand, Captain," Herse says immediately, her voice low and eyes bright, two streaks of loyalty now frame either side of her face. Greer repeats my third's words and she cracks one of her rare true smiles, strands of white dancing through her single fiery braid. Their claim is followed by Nephthys, then Prisca, Nimra, and finally Davina.

Satisfied, I return my attention to Kleio.

"I have always understood the consequences, Captain," my second states proudly and firmly. "You know I was right, by the way," she adds, her mouth twitching with that once-infuriating amusement. "We *do* make a great team."

Her recounted words from years ago fill me with warmth. The warmth indicative of someone who knows what it is to be loved. Nodding tightly, I accept their decision and the tythe.

"Plus, it's not like we can very well return them," Nephthys comments airily.

Prisca does a terrible job of hiding her laughter. "Yeah, not to mention they're permanent."

My eyebrows shoot upwards and a choking sound parts my mouth. Kleio throws the twins a murderous glare before shrugging it off. "So what? We'll all have white in our hair until *all* of our hair is white. We look badass, it's fine."

Coughing out a laugh, I shake my head and turn to face the stone veranda. I then pretend to gauge how much light we have left before reporting down at the wharf. The hand covering my mouth trembles as I quickly wipe the tears that have begun fleeing freely down my cheeks.

Something internally starts to ache, like a faint splintering sensation coming from just beneath my affinity. Nothing major. Just a small crack, I think. A hairline fracture, maybe.

Ultimately, I decide it's not worth my attention.

I can only pray that the sea breeze dries any remaining evidence of my kvelling.

Unlike my experience with the third trial, we're actually allowed above deck on the Cardinal North's cruiser while it pulls us ever closer to the final pillar.

Also, unlike the third trial, I don't feel nearly as nauseous or half as anxious. Scratch that, unlike the previous *three*. Even knowing the monumental feat we're about to undergo, I have my crew with me. I have Kleio with me.

Their presence enlivens some of the old swagger and confidence that made me such a little conniving shit in years past. Which is good, because that conniving little shit is now integral to winning this thing.

Beldham heads our ship while Skelm is aboard the one escorting Vash and his crew. So far no one has commented on the new tokens my crew members display. Although I'm almost positive that I glimpsed the shadow of a surprised-yet-pleased smile flit across our Regent's face when boarding.

I couldn't say if it was hours or minutes before the ship started to slow but most likely the former. Either way, it's too soon to feel real. Beldham calls us together with the purpose of reviewing the logistics of the pillar in place of Raider Dornon. He is, of course, busy coordinating the event at the viewing colosseum.

The idea of the Raider King watching us—watching *me*—sends the adrenaline already coursing through my system soaring.

Our Regent explains we'll depart from the ship and head for the ocean-bound docks to find our assigned port and speeder. Once cast-off is announced, the cutthroat race into the kórallian maze will begin. From there, we can expect three checkpoints that will lead us down into the heart, where most of the blood is spilt. But more importantly, it's where The Vault lies.

I'm lost in thought, mulling over our planned strategy, when Beldham unties a cloth pouch from her side and pours copper seeds into an outstretched palm. I look at her with a dark scowl.

"Why?"

I don't mean for my tone to hold as much hostility as it does but I'm too distracted by the detestable kernels to correct myself. As far as I'm aware, kratosbane has never been used in this final pillar. Not ever.

Beldham's lips flatten into tight parallel lines. "They were requested by King Nereus. He wishes to ascertain for himself whether those competing this year are truly Brek or Vek. Without the help or reputation of your affinities."

My eyes scour the faces of those seven people I care about most in this world. Each of them has turned varying pale shades of green while eyeing our Regent's hand, and for good reason. While I myself am no stranger to the seed, the same cannot be said for most raiders. Skelm's constant practice of using it on me is not typical in any way. The presence of it during our second trial was only the third time Vash Larceon had ever consumed it.

Those in my crew have taken it once, at most.

My eyes flash back to the contents of Beldham's outstretched palm. "He cannot possibly mean for my entire crew to be without their affinities." I disguise the panic in my voice as disgust.

"Not exactly." Beldham's next words are spoken with careful intent. "There is a choice for each captain." Her piercing blue eyes nail me to the spot. "Either take the kratosbane yourself or distribute it to your crew instead."

I blink away from her intent stare. Then, giving a frown of nonchalance, I pluck one of the metallic kernels easily from her hand. The eruption of aversion is loud and immediate.

"Merena, I swear—"

"Absolutely not you godsdamned—"

"This is not up for debate—"

"Are you fucking insane—"

My crew members' shout at me in a chorus of furious dissent. Ignoring the way every fiber of my being abhors my willingness, I flash them all a quick grin before popping the kratosbane into my mouth. Their angry bellowing becomes unintelligible.

Swallowing the seed so casually feels like a personal treachery. The sharpness of how effectively my affinity is cut off nearly makes me gasp out in pain. I never can get used to that awful sensation.

Artfully concealing any trace of discomfort, I gaze back at Beldham, completely unfazed. She studies me for a moment while Kleio and Herse continue to spew their enragement.

The others have gone eerily silent.

"You will now be entering the final pillar and making your way towards The Vault without access to your power, Captain Boreas. Those checkpoints are designed to *maim*." Beldham's words are sharp and reprimanding but her voice wavers, its tone alluding to one of deep concern.

"Many a skilled raider has been killed before even reaching The Vault's precipice," she states, almost gently.

I nod in understanding, my eyes sliding over to my seething crew. "But they will all have access to their powers. They'll be safe." Or, as safe as I can possibly hope for them to be.

Returning my attention to the stern face of our Regent, I'm surprised to find her eyes are closed. She swallows thickly before opening them and meeting my gaze, her irises brighter than ever before.

Resting the hand not filled with kratosbane on my shoulder, Beldham squeezes it tightly. "You are *unquestionably* Brek, Captain Boreas. Without a doubt, the very best the North Order has ever procured. Flatten them for me, will you?" she asks, calling back to my promise made what now feels like a lifetime ago.

The ghost of a smile haunts my lips.

"I'll see that we do."

XXXVII. CAPTAIN THAROS

Kerau

An eruption of ear-splitting cheers and thunderous applause explodes from the raiders surrounding us.

Their sounds of rowdy excitement are so obnoxious that I'm tempted to put a finger on either side of my head and blast out my own fucking eardrums.

Someone whistles so ridiculously loudly from behind that I actually find myself unsheathing a blade.

The crowd's annoying commotion signals the arrival of yet another cardinal's cruiser. Sure enough, the raucous noise is overcome by the announcer's voice as he introduces the third captain and crew to arrive. Anticipation is so dense in the air that I could probably wield it in place of lightning.

The final pillar will start up here fairly soon.

Shoving the jeweled hilt of my sword angrily back into its holder, I stalk after Lord Raimbaut down the newly cleared pathway, dividing rows of overly excitable raiders.

Keeping my eyes on the bright, multicolored cape before me, I'm sure to maintain the proper distance in the wake of the retreating TideLord. I'm extra careful not to step too far near any of those carrying cups of sloshing drink on either side.

There is nothing Regis Raimbaut hates so much as a stain. I've watched him kill a man, point blank, for the high crime of spilling no more than three red wine droplets along his cuff.

The murderous TideLord in question pauses here and there to chat with those belonging in the upper echelons of the three cardinals and members of the Driftwood Court's lower levels. The ones that are *not* privy to the Raider King's personal viewing platform.

I remain close by, not near enough to be counted in on his discussions but close enough to hear them.

Which is my main objective.

After several agonizingly long conversations regarding things of absolutely no consequence, Lord Raimbaut begins posturing through the massive iron colosseum, aiming for the TideLords box at long last.

One, if not the most tedious thing about working under TideLord Raimbaut, is his overly active mouth and how it loves to gab and gossip. That irritating trait also happens to be *precisely* the reason I agreed to captain under him. That and the fact that he doesn't keep quite as close a watchful eye on his captain's as the other lords have reputations for.

Another necessity.

As anticipated, the open-air box is filled to its barnacle-smattered brim with TideLords, their various crews, and even a few chosen captains, such as myself. All of them mill about talking excitedly over their betting odds for the evening events. Remaining close to the vibrant lord who commands me, I'm better able to catch the main headlines of their conversations.

"*Three hundred on the boy from the west.*"

"*On the boy? I'm putting four hundred on the girl. She's been seated in the top two throughout every task so far.*"

"*I've got two hundred golds saying the northern boy surprises us all. With another two hundred on that girl from the south, just in case.*"

"*I've put down an entire trove guaranteeing the southern boy wins—the elemental. Did you see the size of his affinity markings? That first trial was pure talent, he's got exactly the sort of power and ruthlessness we need more of in The Order.*"

I bite my tongue, withstanding the bitter urge to laugh. *If only they knew.*

"And who will you be wagering your latest spoils on this evening, Blaine? Any captain's manage to catch your eye in particular?" Lord Raimbaut questions Lord Dolion.

There's a hint of amusement in my TideLord's lazy smile. As if he already knows the young Lord's answer but wants all the others to hear it too.

The Lord of Leviathan's matches Regis's languorous smirk with one of his own. His clever eyes of ocean green flicker towards me and where I shadow Raimbaut a few meters back from their group. I find myself subconsciously adjusting my posture beneath his quick study.

TideLord Dolion's notice is all the more unnerving when realizing, not for the first time, how slight our age gap is. I remember him quite clearly from the time we shared together in the north, brief as it was. Though I have to doubt he remembers me. I'd have been nothing more than an insignificant level-one at that point.

Blaine Dolion won The Vault at the end of my first year, making him the last raider among us to do so. To say he was a legend in the eyes of my level is putting it too lightly. He was more akin to a living god, one that we all worshiped from a respected distance.

"What great gambler would ever show you their cards, Regis?" Blaine inquires, his eyes returning to Lord Raimbaut, before taking a swig from the sterling cup in his hand. Those in their mixed group of raiders titter at his cleverness.

"So you *are* intending to take a gamble, then?" Regis pushes mildly.

Lord Dolion smiles faintly and shrugs, nonplussed. His casual demeanor doesn't hide from me the subtle tightening of his grip around the gilded chalice.

Lord Kufko intervenes, having just swaggered in from his group of typical admirers. "Blaine *is* the last raider alive to have made it into The Vault, Regis." His eyes rest coolly over sunset-tinted rims. "I don't think I'd call any wager he makes tonight a gamble, would you?"

"I suppose we'll find out," Lord Raimbaut answers with a practiced chuckle and a breezy smile. The kind that tells everyone else he doesn't really care much about the conversation at hand in particular. It's just idle chatter. Another diverting game. A way to pass the time.

Which is, of course, a lie.

After being given a subtle but firm glance from my TideLord telling me to *get fucking lost*, I make my way down to the furthest edge of the box. Being that I hold the lowest ranking seniority under Regis at present, my crew was put on posting duty tonight. I'm therefore left to endure this whole taxing charade alone.

Standing aloof before the viewing exterior, I note idly that there's nothing beyond this slim silver barrier to stop me or anyone else from falling down a thousand meters into the sea below and certain death just beneath. That also means there's nothing obscuring my view.

My gaze is thrown out like a net and it sweeps avidly over the miles of ocean spanning from the colossal stadium we occupy to the location of the mythic vault itself. Four monstrous pillars made of rough gray seastone rise out of the dark ocean waters and twist up towards the celestial realm above. They reach so high into the night that four stars, the sundown stars, appear as if to sit atop each one.

It's a sight I had hoped for a very long time that I just might get to see. Although I wished fervently to visit them under different circumstances. Tonight

I'm viewing as a spectator only but there is nothing I wouldn't have given to see them as a competitor.

Me and every other raider here.

Second-hand nerves begin manifesting themselves when lowering my gaze to the undertaking that phantoms the base of those otherworldly pillars.

Fifty or so meters tall stands the kórallian labyrinth. The fabled maze glows a pale amethyst and wraps itself protectively around The Vault's location, like a sea serpent encircling its clutch. It's the reason those competing tonight can only hope to reach The Vault's entrance with a slim speeder. The winding passages and many dead ends would tear apart any larger of a ship's hull.

Searching the ocean-bound docks spread horizontally below the hulking coliseum, I loosen a sigh of painful longing. There are eight docks in total, each spaced at a hundred meters apart. My painful longing would be due to the slick top-of-the-line speeders bobbing enticingly at the end of each one.

Letting out a low groan of appreciation, my hands rise up to grip the mollusk-encrusted iron railing in frustration. My fingers twitch with need at the sight of their untouched helms.

As if it's second nature when admiring racing vessels, my thoughts turn to the image of a girl with hair the color of fresh snow. No—a *woman*. A woman with hair the color of fresh snow.

The word jarring seems appropriate when recalling how it felt to see Merena the night of Luminalia. Two years. Two *measly* little years and she had utterly transformed into someone I wasn't quite sure I knew.

Watching her spin in Captain Agni's arms couldn't have stunned me more than if a stray dancing disc had sliced me straight across the throat.

Her and that dress. That *fucking* dress.

The one that has starred in *far* too many of my nightly imaginings. Imaginings that no matter how many women I bed from every port possible *cannot* be satiated. That fact is at least partially to blame for my abnormally dismal mood of late.

Which is idiotic as shit to say the least.

Merena and I aren't strangers, this wasn't some chance meeting. We had history. We'd been intimate on more than one occasion. Yet somehow seeing her that night made it feel like any and all of our previous evenings together were surely just my own wishful fantasies.

It had been genuinely alarming to look at her, let alone *talk* to her. Not that she hadn't been beautiful before. Merena has always been beautiful, damningly so. But now, well, I couldn't really place what had changed exactly. There was this quality about her that was almost ethereal, shimmering just beneath the surface.

Like she was somehow more... *alive.*

More startling even than her striking appearance was the inexplicable restraint she'd cultivated. All that prior wildness had been whittled down in the last few years, etched away bit by bit, sharpening in her a lethal edge of icy control. I struggled in the short moments we had together to coax out traces of the girl I'd once known.

She talked like Merena—*sort of.* I'm not sure I remember her voice ever being so ridiculously alluring. She laughed at our previous misadventures like Merena would have. But then she'd come back with this playful teasing that sent me reeling. I couldn't make sense of it. I've never been closer to publicly bedding a woman in my life.

It was like being trapped inside a paradox. She was her and yet she was *not.* I couldn't even convince myself it was due to the time apart, it was more than that.

I had always been more sure of myself. More mature. More—*intimidating*, I guess. I knew that dynamic between us. I knew *her.*

Until I didn't.

During my last couple of years in the north, she'd *just* started putting her natural talents to good use. Once Merena had found some sort of reason to try, she tore through the ranks.

In my absence, she's clearly earned the respect of those in her level and the ones below. The way those northern raiders looked at her when we passed by was an entire one-eighty from the hostility of before. She didn't even seem to notice.

It was obvious to me how far she's come in reputation, ultimately leading to her captaincy. And I could tell from our too-brief interaction, that Merena holds her position so dear it may as well be the carved out hearts of her own crewmates she's been handed rather than a title. The rank undoubtedly suits her, even if I selfishly missed the hellion of before.

But I hadn't come to Luminalia for Merena.

Not exactly.

Merena sending me that epistle the week beforehand and my appearance that night had truthfully been a factor of convenience. One that turned itself into an opportunity.

My eyes find the dock titled 'ONE' where Captain Agni is helping his crew perform inspections at present. A low growl automatically begins to build at the base of my chest.

Stumbling upon a very unexpectedly grown-up Merena had been one thing but finding her in the arms of Captain Agni was wholly *other*. For a moment I'd forgotten my purpose beyond getting Merena as far away from his extremely possessive hands as swiftly as possible.

Two vitally separate worlds of mine were colliding in such a horribly unanticipated way.

Yet, even though I'd been dreading that night for a myriad of reasons, it was undeniably satisfying to watch as that smug grin of his fell away entirely upon spotting me.

Captain Agni understood exactly why I was there.

I was a messenger. A *reminder*. One from his father to mine, sent through me. A reminder of his orders and of our duty. A reminder to not forget the reason we were in this hellhole in the first place.

I'd been genuinely impressed by his acting skills. He didn't let slip even a hint of familiarity between us. Then again, it's not as if we've ever been friendly before, no matter our familial relations.

The look on his face as he watched me tug Merena off to a private room was probably the highlight of my year. As a boy, I never had anything in my possession so remarkable as to lord over him with. Not even my own fucking power was safe from his greed. So it was incredibly assuaging, not to mention entertaining, to turn those tables for a night.

I don't know why I was even remotely surprised when the spoiled little shit inserted himself. I genuinely don't think he's capable of allowing anyone else a sundamned thing. No matter if that something in particular never truly *belonged* to him in the first place. Outside of the select few males he allows to trail him like hounds, his cruelty towards others knows no bounds.

I couldn't believe he went so far as to tell Merena about the bylaws. Implying that I was trying to get her eliminated from The Vault was a low blow.

Pompous fucking dick.

It was his own malicious form of payback for my appearance, no doubt. Disregarding the fact that I didn't get a say in the matter of our current shit circumstances.

Seducing Merena, or rather being unintentionally seduced by her, had not been the plan when I'd arrived. But once we were alone and talking—I forgot myself. I wanted desperately to know this new Merena as well as I did the old one. So much so that I didn't consider the stakes.

Hers or mine.

I've tried writing to her on countless occasions. Pages on pages of apologies and half-truthful explanations were the best I could do in my current circumstance. Every time the epistle returned to me without a note. Even with the outside contact restrictions, Beldham would have given them to her after seeing my signet.

Depths—I was the captain of a TideLord, I could have dropped by to speak with her in person if I so wished. The thought did cross my mind more than once. Though I also knew dropping in on Merena unannounced while she was so furious with me would likely result in a broken bone or two at best.

After yet another month of silence, I was ready to say screw it and drag my crew from our station near The Deep for a trip up north. I had just sat down to write TideLord Raimbaut some bullshit excuse to visit the old stomping grounds when my epistle returned, *not* empty, for once.

Parchment had been torn, then waded up, before being shoved inside with an aggression that could only come from Merena's hands. After weeks upon weeks of writing an entire tomb's worth of words, I received *two* in response.

'Fuck. off.'

So I had.

An unexpected voice breaks through my brooding with its amusement. "Well, if that isn't a fucking statement, then I don't know what is."

I'm pulled back to an erupting world of cheers and shouts to find the final cruiser has already been docked. The announcer's voice blares loud above our heads as the final captain and crew make their entrance.

Turning to the bemused speaker, I'm somewhat startled to find Lord Dolion's violet-cloaked person standing just a few feet from myself along the railing. His attention remains fixated on the docks below and the emerging raiders. I follow his line of sight to find Merena leading her crew down the floating pathway and towards their docking station.

Disconcerting whispers and low murmurs of dissent begin weaving through the onslaught of noise around us. The reason behind their shaken tone holds little mystery. Not with the stadium orb lights shining so directly onto the northern captain and her crew as they begin to pass the dock labeled 'ONE'.

Each of Merena's seven crewmates has woven streaks of defying white throughout their hair. It is unmistakably the exact same white as their captain's disgraceful castaway markings.

A tythe.

The word is carried out and around us, spilling from every nearby mouth.

In complete disbelief, I lean forward on the railing, blinking hard. I'm not the only one either, countless of those previously milling aimlessly around the box have come to see whether or not the fast-spreading rumors are true. Soon the edge becomes so crowded that I'm forced to stand directly beside TideLord Dolion, though he barely seems to notice.

Within The Order, there is no honor more rare or profound than receiving a tythe.

This is no trivial rite or arbitrary oath, most captains can go their entire careers without hope of ever being gifted one. A tythe is not something that can be asked for from a captain. The honor can only ever be freely given by a unanimous crew. Typically, only once climbing to the rank of TideLord does a raider receive that sort of momentous accolade.

The significance of Merena's crew tything themselves to begin with is unprecedented but the token they've chosen to enact it with is indisputably *dangerous.* My grip tightens on the railing as panic for the girl I used to know racks my system.

What the fuck is she thinking?

Is she insane or just suicidal?

"I'd say she's ballsy. But considering old one-eye's methods, I suppose insanity is also a veritable possibility," Lord Dolion notes dryly, and I realize I've spoken the last of my thoughts aloud.

It feels like someone has me in a headlock, my speech comes out slightly choked. "They can't do that—can they? I mean—she doesn't even have a vessel to swear them on—surely they'll be penalized for this if not eliminated?"

My question is met with Blaine Dolion's humorless laugh. "We're past the point of penalizing, she's already made it to the final pillar." The TideLord shrugs, his eyes still locked on the final captain and crew. "Besides, no Tide Raider, no matter how high ranking, can interfere with the last task. The Vault is beyond even our dear king's authority."

Lord Dolion's words have me glancing around towards the platform rising above the TideLords viewing box, where King Nereus and his court observe. When I don't spot the Raider King immediately among the throng, I turn back to continue watching Merena.

"But—they're glorifying her markings," I counter in a low, urgent voice. "It's a mockery to those sacrificed—it's a mockery of raider tradition—there is no way the court will allow for that to go unpunished."

Agitation grows deeper roots the longer I stare. And I'm not alone in my assumptions. Many of the conversations nearby hum with accusation as more and more raiders realize what sort of tythe-token Captain Boreas's crew so proudly bears.

"Perhaps," Lord Dolion says, his ocean eyes never wavering from Merena's powerful form striding towards their speeder. The hardened face she wears isn't one I recognize at all. It's far too perfect in all its cold unfeelingness.

"But it's also possible they're using them to embrace raider tradition. I'd argue that the core of their intention tonight in tything the crew and captain as one was really to tie themselves further to The Order. What better way to prove that accepting a castaway into our ranks was a worthwhile risk? What better way to show that the gods' choosing was justified?"

His reasoning is loud enough for anyone in the vicinity to hear.

I'm quiet for the next few minutes, lost to thoughts full of sickening worry for Merena and her brash impulsiveness. *That,* at least, is a part of her that has obviously not changed. This stunt of hers also reeks of Raider Hiraeth's involvement.

The two of them should have been separated the night that they were caught running an underground gambling ring. That was during my fifth level, their outrageous wagers were regarding the north's own instructors. The betting pool regarding Preceptor Chie's remaining lifespan having been the most mild of them all.

The only modicum of relief I'm afforded is that Lord Dolion's overheard words seem to have quelled the dissent around us. Cheering resumes again and the turning of my stomach starts to settle. I can only pray his comments have a very distant ripple effect.

For some reason, likely a result of being separated from my crew, I find myself attempting conversation with the TideLord. "You probably didn't know this but we actually overlapped my first year in the north," I comment, shifting slightly to where he stands on my left. "The year you won."

Lord Dolion wears a faint smirk as he turns his famous head of golden curls to face me straight on before stating, "I know." He laughs low in response to my look of surprise. "An elemental doesn't just wash-up to a cardinal without notice. I knew who you were. Just as I'm *sure* you knew of Captain Boreas when she came about. Didn't you?"

He gives me a wink that says he's aware of *exactly* how well I once knew Captain Boreas. A burning sensation heats my chest and I shove back the hair that's cutting through my vision. Pushing away the urge to glower, I give the hero of my youth a noncommittal shrug.

"I suppose."

He smirks again before returning his focus to Merena. "How *did* she manage to come in tonight ranking fifth, I wonder?" Lord Dolion ponders aloud. "I heard her time in the Veil Keeper was remarkable. Pity about the eastern boy though."

"Mm," I grunt by way of agreement. Truthfully, I had only heard of the eastern captain's death upon arrival. Lord Raimbaut mentioned it so casually you would have thought the captain was merely out sick.

"She is rather entertaining, isn't she?" he remarks, leaning ever forward on the slender barrier. When I don't respond, he asks pointedly, "Is that a trait of your all's affinity?"

I turn to him, confusion ripe in my furrowed brow and he glances back at me with amusement lingering in the curve of his mouth.

"The unexpectedness, the—*chaos* that Captain Boreas seems so remarkable at causing," Lord Dolion explains before turning away again. "Is that due to being an elemental? I ask because, from what I've heard, that southern one seems equally as talented in wreaking havoc. I wondered whether that was just a trait within your kind's nature?"

My back stiffens at his words, and my grip on the railing becomes dangerously tight.

Your kind.

As if we're some sort of breed.

"No. I have not found that to be the case," I respond curtly, tamping down on the irritation he's so casually provoked. TideLord Raimbaut would have my fucking head on a shiny, gem-encrusted platter if I embarrassed him tonight.

I don't dare mention the fact that the supposed 'chaos-inducing' Merena he's observed in these trials is nothing compared to the one I knew before.

Lord Dolion makes a low hum of approval. "So it will just take a bit of proper training then."

Sliding my gaze over to the TideLord with more scrutiny, I find I fucking *hate* the way he's watching Merena. His focus follows her cape-clad figure as she moves about their speeder, aiding her crew in their assessment. He studies her movements, his eyes glinting under the star-filled sky with greed, like she's some sort of rare purchase to be made.

A deep scowl twists my features and I struggle to smooth it over. My gaze remains fixed on him until Lord Dolion's lips pull back, revealing perfectly white teeth as he barks out a sharp laugh of surprise. It sends my attention darting back to the floating docks.

What I discover next has me groaning internally and my hands rub down either side of my face in complete exasperation. Lord Dolion's nearby laughter only serves to annoy me more, he evidently understands and enjoys the ploy she's currently unveiling.

Merena has pulled out black fingerless gloves and begun shoving them onto each hand. Her cold demeanor is replaced with a familiar cockiness that whispers tales of her previous deviancy. She once again captures the masses attention when ripping off her captain's cape, exposing the new uniform beneath and her impressive affinity mark embroidered along her back.

My previously inward groan moves outward. I should have known her crew's tythe wouldn't be the only rebellious antic Merena would be involved in tonight. On the other hand, maybe she's not quite as different as I'd feared. Spitting on not one but *two* raider customs in front of the TideLords and Driftwood Court would certainly have tempted a younger Merena.

The announcer's voice blares out obnoxiously again and for the first time I actually pay attention to it. "I don't believe what I think I'm seeing here, Raiders—a strange turn of tides indeed! The first castaway to ever enter the Pillar Trials is making yet another first. Captain Boreas of the Cardinal North appears to be taking over as helmsman for her team!"

"Oh, this is *too* good," Lord Dolion murmurs with a low chuckle.

I fight the snarl forming in my throat in response to his appreciation. A metallic scent tints the air while watching his eyes devour every inch of Merena and her enticingly displayed figure. Their new uniform is expertly form-fitted and without her cape, every tempting feminine curve Merena possesses is made sinfully prominent against the leanness of her toned body.

If my attention wasn't so heavily focused on the TideLord beside me, I would be knee-deep in a world of excruciatingly hard frustration.

As if that dress wasn't fucking bad enough.

Lord Dolion angles his face to me again in request and the hilt of his weapon shines menacingly beneath the starlight. "How *is* Captain Boreas behind the wheel? Tell me."

The demand in his voice frays the remaining edges of my nerves. A very faint crackling noise can be heard whispering about the air. I'm tempted to lie but ultimately know it will do me no good. Unfortunately, the greedy bastard will see for himself here soon enough.

I admit through an almost completely locked jaw, "She is—unexpectedly skilled."

The Lord of Leviathan's handsome expression of smug anticipation bothers me but not near as much as another's. I find Captain Agni immediately upon returning my attention to the docks.

He stares with a predatory stillness, from the captain's position on the bow of his speeder, at Merena slamming down her reflective helmsman visor above a wicked grin I *do* recognize.

The look on his face sends bolts of energy from my fingertips to the railing in my grip.

Several people, including Lord Dolion, curse sharply at the small electric shock that runs through the barrier in my brewing anger but I don't react. My focus remains on Captain Agni's deeply troubling expression.

He's staring at her with the look of a blind man who's just glimpsed the sun.

XXXVIII. MOONLIGHTER 1000

Striding down the ocean-bound docks, we're met with a roar of applause that puts every other one of the earlier trials to absolute shame.

The noisy crowd rattles the driftwood beneath my feet and reverberates around my skull. My demeanor remains remote. My face a mask of unyielding ice. But my insides feel as though I'm about to ride an unbroken kelpie.

As Beldham instructed, we aim for the docks holding eight speeders. One for each captain and their crew. Raider Bedi, having been granted captaincy in the wake of Reed Namak's death, has since stepped up to represent the East.

I begrudgingly locate our speeder resting at the end of the dock site labeled 'FIVE', knowing we'll have to walk past the first four docks in order to get there. I struggle to keep from grumbling out my internal frustration and motion for the rest of my crew to follow in my lead.

I still cannot believe I went from second place to *fifth*. If my affinity wasn't shoved so far down inside, I'm certain there'd be hoarfrost in my wake.

We near the dock labeled 'ONE' and the crowd begins to shift in tone.

I'm well aware of why and there's no stopping it. The orb lights shine down on my crew and their tythe-tokens, illuminating the rite for all to see or rather glare at. Gritting my teeth, I pretend not to hear it. I pretend not to notice the very real discord being murmured along with my name over the towering assembly of raiders high above us.

Approaching the first mooring of the spaced-out docks does not help my temper.

The majority of the all-male southern crew is busy making inspections but each of them slowly drops what they're doing to stare as we pass. It's not only the crowd of raiders above us who have begun to notice the tythe. I can feel their eyes glued to us, studying each colorless strand of shimmering white in open shock.

The only person non-phased by such a sight would, of course, be Olsson *fucking* Agni.

"Oh, *Boreas*?" He whistles, pausing me mid-stride.

Taking a deep breath full of eternal suffering, I throw Kleio a look for her and the others to wait up ahead. She follows my unspoken orders and I stiffly turn my attention to the slim wharf-side.

I find Captain Agni's cocky form jumping down from the side of their speeder with predatory fluidity. His swaggering figure looks lethal as all hell dressed head to toe in crimson threaded black. Locking my jaw against annoyance, I tilt my chin to meet his gaze as he steps before me. The hilts of his twin blades cast him against the night sky into the outline of a daunting omen.

Agni chuckles, no doubt sensing my growing impatience. He holds up one ring-adorned finger in clear reminder before tapping it idly against his lower lip.

"Do be sure to come find me in there, Boreas. I would hate for you to break your od, especially now that it's been ever so *beautifully* tied to your crew," Agni drawls, angling his head of black windswept hair in the direction of The Pillars as his eyes flicker towards my crew waiting ahead.

My mouth purses tightly and he lowers himself slightly downwards, making my body stiffen on instinct. His voice turns to a deep ashen whisper. "*Both* your options are still on the table for my repayment, by the way."

I turn a newly murderous glare on him.

Agni smirks at my obvious irritation with an arrogant shrug. "Just letting you know, in case you were in the mood for something a little more *daring*. Though, now that we're on the topic, I suppose being all the way down in fifth place—" He 'tsks' with a frown in mock disappointment. "That just might make it far too difficult for you to catch up to me in time to get this last little debt of yours cleared."

Blinking slowly, I focus very *very* hard on not removing a knife from my waist and plunging it into his thigh. His amusement towards my internal scuffle is clear in the twitch of his lips. His obvious enjoyment makes it even more difficult to hold back the assault I'm itching to commit.

"I have to warn you, Boreas, I won't be able to slow us down just to wait up for you. However, being the gentleman that I *am*, I'll make sure you have a second chance to keep your captaincy title. For both you and your *lovely* crew's sake."

His tone is so demeaning that it turns my hands into restlessly balled fists.

Agni's eyes rove my homicidal face, shining with smug implication.

"After I win The Vault, you can come help me celebrate *properly* for a night. I'll even go against my no-clothing rule and let you keep that pretty little hairpiece on." His eyes flit to the new golden cuff currently holding my hair up before shooting me a wink. "Then we'll call it square."

"In your *fucking* dreams," I hiss up at him, my lips twisting in disgust.

"Every night," Agni deadpans.

I know what he's doing—getting in my head with his suggestive taunts, riling me up before the final task. He's clearly found a new button of mine to press, one he seems to enjoy even more than all the others. I just wish it wasn't so godsdamn effective.

"You won't have to worry about me catching up—I can promise you that." I sneer, my rising temper making the chafing of my restrained power more intense. "We'll settle this in there as *agreed*," I snarl, ripping myself away from Agni and his bemused expression before he can waste any more of my time.

Swiftly rejoining my crew, we make way for our speeder. Passing by the next few moorings, we're met with stunned silence and expressions ranging from disbelief to pure anger from every captain and their crew.

Behind the south order now ranking first, unsurprisingly comes Brisa seated second. Then, more surprisingly, comes Vash in third. To my shock, he doesn't even lift his head in our direction, nor does Kleio so much as glance the way of their speeder.

My brows furrow as we pass Corvina, who is directly ahead of us in fourth. Captain Leporem's lip curls when spotting the tythe, disdain crinkles her delicate nose in response to the chosen token and I roll my eyes in annoyance.

The announcer's voice booms so loudly that his words override my own godsdamned thoughts as we finally make it to our dock labeled 'FIVE'. I trail after my seven as they head down to our tied-up vessel and begin prepping with inspections. However, all of my previous anger leftover from interacting with Agni dissipates upon confronting our assigned craft.

My whistle is low and appreciative in regards to the speeder we've been given.

It's fucking *nice*.

Nicer than any of the ones I've stolen by far.

The exterior boasts a sleek matte black finish, and the flooring is an equally dark stained wood. Rich seats of supple brown leather illuminate the console, while the stern is situated with a u-shaped bench of pure onyx. My fingers trail along the hull and I begin vibrating with anticipation at getting this thing out on open water, fifth place or not. Soon, my wandering hand discovers the silver lettering gracing the side of the drool-worthy speeder.

'Moonlighter 1000'.

My fingers promptly falter in their exploration.

"Oh sweet depths," I curse aloud. The Moonlighters are a brand new line of raider-crafted speeders we only heard *rumors* about.

How? How are they here? I can only think they must have been donated by a Tide Lord or—

"—of the very fastest in King Nereus's fleet!" The announcers' obnoxious voice echoes back into existence.

My chest constricts and my swallow is tight. *Or* they were donated by the Tide Raider King himself.

Stepping onto the ship, I can *smell* how new it is. I bet this is the first time it's ever seen open water. My hands itch to grab the helm, straddle the console, and see just how many knots this thing can do. But I fight that impulse with an inward groan and instead begin helping the others.

By the time we're done, I'm practically panting in need of getting my hands on that wheel.

"We now ask our captains and crews to begin taking positions. Cast-off will begin in five minutes."

Catching Kleio's eye, I nod at her to take up my place. Then I whip out my leather helmsman gloves from a pocket and begin shoving them onto each hand. I don't think anyone has realized the change in positions yet. Though it's hard to tell with how tumultuous the massive crowd filling the iron colosseum above us seems.

Adrenaline pulses in my veins and a hint of my prior deviancy pulls at the corner of my mouth. With no time to waste, I tear off my captain's cape, exposing my embroidered affinity markings to those watching, and toss it up to Kleio for safekeeping.

Our risky stunt does not go unnoticed for long.

"I don't believe what I'm seeing here, Raiders—a strange turn of tides indeed! The first castaway to ever enter the Pillar Trials is making another first. Captain

Boreas of the North Order has taken place as helmsman for her team, and in fifth place no less!"

Straddling the console, I become too preoccupied with the feel of the expertly crafted wooden wheel and sleek leather-bound throttle to notice the uproar of rowdy raiders. My attention removes itself from ogling the craft at my fingertips to grin up to Kleio standing at the bow.

Traditionally, that is the place I should take. The grand honor that only the captain is supposed to hold. Directing from the front, leading the charge, and all that other bullshit.

But Captain or not, I'm undeniably our best helmsman.

My advanced skills at the helm are a product of my notoriously rebellious youth. In subtle retaliation for my treatment, I spent much of my time stealing speeders and other racing vessels from the wharf for my own personal joyrides. It turns out that a bit of heathenry compulsion might just end up paying off.

I hope it's enough to make Skelm's heart give out.

Doing a quick scan, I realize each and every captain has begun staring at me behind the helm like I've lost my godsdamned mind. From this distance, I can even make out Captain Agni, as he too has turned around to see if the announcer is telling the truth.

Imagining the dumbfounded expression on his arrogant face makes me laugh while donning the last of my accessories. He continues staring from the place at his bow far, *far*, ahead of ours. The thought of kicking that arrogant prick out of his precious first-place position twists my mouth into a wicked grin before I slam down the reflective helmsman visor over my eyes.

"THIRTY SECONDS!"

A savage smile dances on my lips when feeling the ship come alive beneath me. Its buzzing energy is like kindling to my own excitement. Gripping the wheel, I relish the feel of it between my fingers and the console between my thighs. There is no place better in all three realms than behind the wheel of a terrifyingly fast racing vessel. No matter my origins, I *know* that this is exactly where I'm meant to be and precisely what I was born to do.

"TWENTY!"

Not even the announcer's voice counting down our cast-off can delude the elation coursing through my veins. Large drum beats are added to the count and soon the entire stadium is chanting down the time.

My eyes narrow in on the near-invisible crevice in the kórallian maze, located approximately five miles from us across the watery expanse.

I *must* be the first one inside that pocket.

Then I need to lose whoever we run into next.

"TEN."

Taking one last scan around, I make sure my crew is in position. All seven of them hold onto the vessel's iron-bound railing and crouch low to the speeder's floor. Their heads stay tucked in tight as practiced.

"THREE."

My eyes flit towards Corvina in the mooring directly ahead of ours. She's still turned around to face me and has been studying my crew's odd stances with quiet calculation. Understanding dawns in the glower of her face just as I rip back the throttle.

"ONE!"

The moonlighter jolts forward with a daring force and I slingshot us toward the open entrance. The start-up is so volatile it would have sent anyone standing straight off the side of the craft.

We catch up to Captain Leporem's speeder in record time, even with their hundred-meter head start. Her emerald eyes are almost comically wide with angry disbelief at our sudden approach. Their helmsman, Raider Bellum, does a double take at our swift appearance and her nostrils begin flaring with outrage as we come deadhead to them.

Between the crowd's madness at our spectacle of a start and the winds ripping against the side of the speeder, I can't hear too much. But I *am* able to make out the growl of rage that emanates from Corvina when I flash her a grin and punch out in front of her crew with expert ease.

Keeping our speed cranked up dangerously high, the meters are rapidly swallowed beneath the midnight hull of our vessel. The pillars appear closer and Larceon's speeder becomes my next target. I'm confident that with Javin as their helmsman, I can outmaneuver them without too much trouble.

Closing in on the two hundred-meter head start they were given, I enjoy the way in which Vash Larceon turns around to scowl at our rapid gain. I'm not surprised by the blatant look of disdain he gives me up until a year ago it's one I received almost daily from him. But I *am* surprised by the frown he throws Kleio. I'm then fully floored when Kleio returns him one of her own as we inch up through the water.

Looking to Captain Larceon and back to my second through the tint of my visors, I shake my head. I can't afford to pester Kleio right now with questions. Vash calls something over to his seventh, Raider Aio, as she currently mans part of their stern.

The meaning behind his muffled command is revealed in the next moment when a net is hoisted off the side of their vessel and tossed in our direction. I jerk us to the right in order to avoid getting our rudders stuck in the new obstacle. The movement is so harsh that several of my crew members scream in alarm.

"Sorry!" I bark out above the noise.

Vash's moonlighter keeps hold of the netting and drags it so I'm forced to move us further and further outside. I lose meters as quickly as I'd gained them and begin cursing beneath my breath. Racking my brain, I sift through years upon years of secret practice until payoff formulates in the form of a plan.

"Get back down!" I shout loudly. It's the only warning I give before pulling back on the throttle and allowing the other northern craft to move back out ahead of us.

"*Merena*?" Kleio yelps in question.

My teeth lock together as my eyes devour the wake of Larceon's speeder, and I begin steadying our own craft's velocity. My grip tightens so much that my knuckles peeking through the dark glove finger holes are as white as my hair. I exhale slowly, aiming us as close to forty-five degrees as possible.

"Keep low and trim!" I order before taking on their moonlighter's wake with as much precision as physically possible.

A small groan of effort escapes me while I grapple with the wheel against the wake's brutal force. We slice through the chaotic waves and cut to the inside of their speeder with what I can only guess is pure fucking luck. Recovering control of the moonlighter, I smother the throttle.

The feeling of pure ecstasy alights my senses and I crow out loudly as we shoot forward past third place. My victorious shouting is reverberated throughout the night by my crew.

The northern ship's distraction cost us some precious time and even more valuable distance. Fortunately, it seems both Brisa and Olsson are doing a good enough job of slowing the other so that we aren't too terribly far behind either. The typical excited thrumming of my affinity has turned into a sharp clawing sensation due to the suffocation of kratosbane.

The pain helps fuel my competitive nature and reinforces the need to win, the first step to that is gaining entrance to the maze. I glance up to where Kleio remains crouched at the bow, and I see her eyes already on me. Tilting my head down to the throttle, I look back at her in signal. She surveys the rest of the speeder and I wait until she gives me the sharp dip of her chin in silent agreement.

I crack open the throttle.

My laughter is frenzied in response to how efficiently the speeder reacts to my commands. I've decided I *have* to have one of these things. I actually think I'd be willing to trade my weapon arm for it.

Tearing up the midnight tides, our moonlighter begins stalking the two ships currently battling it out for first place. Their silver and crimson flags fly high above the boat's sterns, whipping viciously in the swiftly passing night air.

"Hiraeth—gauge and report," I order Kleio while steadying our speed.

She rises up steadily before pulling out a pair of spyglasses and focusing in on the two crafts. "The West has hooked the South's ship. It looks like they're attempting to cut the grappling."

My smirk meets Kleio's in understanding before I smoothly shift us over and begin claiming the inside line. The look I earn from both the west and south captains upon realizing our impending bearing is an image I would pay an obscene amount of silvers to have painted and hung.

Unfortunately, our unexpected presence fuels the others to make haste in their struggle. No more than a few moments later, Kleio reports back to me with a grimace, "Grappling's cut."

The two speeders ahead of us instantly veer apart from one another.

The crimson-flagged moonlighter immediately drops down in speed, and at first, I don't understand the new ploy. It's not until the slowing south positions themselves closer that I begin piecing together their intentions. Captain Agni strides to the stern of their craft in order to give me a look of pure smugness as they jerk out in front of us and force our speeder to ride inside their intensely volatile wake.

Southern fucking pricks.

Waves begin slamming into us so hard my teeth feel as though they may splinter from clenching so tightly. I try cutting through their backwash this way and that but each time I take a shot at carving up the side, they move right along with me. Agni remains standing at their stern with an insufferable smirk while keeping a precise eye on my efforts in order to restrain us.

"*Such an ass,*" I snarl beneath my breath.

Growling low in frustration, I shout. "Opening her up! Trim the bow—roger?"

I wait to hear my crew members' voices ring back in acknowledgment before sizing up the next trough and immediately strangling the leather pommel. We jolt forward in a burst of savage speed and hit the trough right as another wave roars up before us.

I have no choice but to dive straight through the damn thing.

Salt water rains down all around and my crew scrambles backwards to redistribute weight while I fight for control over the wheel. My filthy swears are swallowed up by the sea spray and thrashing winds until finally, my impulsive efforts pay off. At last, we appear on the other side of the southern speeder.

My shoulders shake with triumphant laughter, while the muscles in my thighs begin to cry out in protest. I won't allow the south the chance to push us again into their wake.

Keeping our speeds dangerously high, I take on the inside line. "Hiraeth—LeRoi—reports?"

"The north is gaining on the west," Herse calls from the stern. "Looks like they're riding the slipstream, Captain."

"DTG is one half mile, South is closing from the starboard!" Kleio shouts over the briny air running its claws through her curly braids. Looking to my right, I find she is correct. Captain Agni and his crew have cut in so close that I can almost see the embers burning in his irises.

I'm extremely pleased to find his hardened expression is one that flickers with contempt-coated outrage. He glances over to where Raider Ophios sits as their helmsman and back. For a moment, it looks like he's *actually* debating taking the wheel from his second for himself.

"Maneuvering!" I shout and my crew hits the deck in preparation.

I flash Agni my captain ring finger, with a grin so cocky it's sure to send him right over the brink and promptly begin wrestling the helm. I push and pull the beautiful wheel until my arms bark out in pain from the effort. Once I'm gritting against the exertion it takes to continue, I chance a glance at starboard and am flooded with relief.

The strategic zig-zagging has paid off.

The southern moonlighter has been effectively shoved further and further away with each of my forceful maneuvers. I spot Agni bellowing at the top of his lungs from the bow of their speeder at his crew, absolutely *furious.* His obvious enragement is satisfying as is, but even better is the dual effect it has of knocking back Brisa and her crew, who were once again on the approach.

Turning back to the widening mouth of the kórallian maze, I grin and yell out, "Heaving to!"

I can only hope all their grips are firm enough when I rear back the throttle and slow us down *just* in time to hit the opening without crashing straight through the ghostly reef.

"*First!* We're first!" Kleio crows loudly between cupped hands.

The others begin howling and cheering over the win now they're actually able to stand. Herse begins shaking me by the shoulders in excitement, while the others all smack my helmsman visor in playful camaraderie.

"Okay, okay—now the *real* trail begins," I tell them coolly, not wanting to get ahead of ourselves.

But my lips have a hard time remaining in a straight line.

XXXIX. TOTAL TRANSPARENCY

"I'm calling it—we're fucking lost," Prisca grumbles from the stern.

"No, we *aren't!*" Nephthys growls sharply, raising the piece of map we were afforded up to the dark sky above us and squinting.

It's the single gift we were given from Beldham before our departure from the north's cruiser. A copy of the only written guide The Cardinal North Order has ever had, containing a vague direction of the kórallian labyrinth and its various checkpoint gates. The walls of said luminous maze rise up around us, standing nearly as tall at the viewing colosseum.

The lack of noise surrounding us now compared to the deafening sounds of before is eerie. It's unsettling to know that whatever happens within these walls, as well as the varying levels between here and The Vault, are our secrets alone. There's no telling how this will change the actions of other crew members and their captains.

A craven part of me yearns for my power's protection.

I remain behind the wheel while Kleio directs from the bow. In such unforgivingly tight quarters as this, I'm still our best bet to win. At least until I'm forced to separate from them whenever we manage to find the first checkpoint.

We've been within the towering borders for ten minutes and I've never seen my crew more on edge. Davina is still recovering from my piloting. Nimra can't manage to stay still for more than five seconds. The twins act as though they might stab one another at any moment. Greer has clammed up entirely. Herse appears to be mentally mapping out murders. Meanwhile Kleio keeps glancing back at me every other minute with the same concern shining in her eyes since I swallowed that kratosbane.

It's enough to send me right over the fucking brink.

"Sooooooo—" I start, having decided someone needs to break the budding tension. It results in catching Kleio's eye and she turns towards me in question. "Are we going to discuss whatever tiff you and Vash Larceon are in?"

That appears to do the trick.

Herse starts grinning immediately from where she stands on the other side of the helm, my words having pulled her out of the moody murder plotting she was previously entrenched in.

"Oh yes, Mrs. Larceon, do tell," she goads, coming nearer to the helm.

Kleio's face turns a brilliant pink while looking between us in annoyance. She opens her mouth to respond but my fourth's voice replaces my second's.

"Oh *shit!*" Greer curses, coming out more like a shriek.

My head whips astern to see the reason for her profanity. Oh *fuck*. Only a few leagues behind us, another moonlighter is coming in hot.

"LeRoi—status report—*now!*" I snap at Herse and begin picking up speed.

My third nods with a spyglass already pressed against her eyes. "Bearing one hundred and eighty degrees, range two hundred meters—gaining."

"Colors?" I question before looking up at Kleio for passageway guidance.

Herse pauses and I risk a glance at her. Her jaw tightens beneath the sharp cut of her white-streaked onyx hair. "Crimson," she finally answers.

I grind my teeth in annoyance. *Of course*.

"Which one?" I grit out while keeping my eyes securely on the deadly maze opening up bit by luminous bit before us.

"The one that tried to kill you," she replies after a beat and my shoulders loosen in relief.

"Alright, then we're going to lose them. Unless you're dead set on murdering Captain Leporem before we've even found the first checkpoint?" I shoot an inquiring look in my third's direction.

"No, it's fine. I can do it later, I guess," Herse grumbles before loosening a wistful sigh.

A low chuckle slips between my lips before I shout "Hold fast!" to my crew over the newly stirring winds. Pulling back harshly on the throttle, I make a sharp stomach-curdling turn into the next passage. Curses and swears ring out from all directions as my crew is swung to one side of the small craft with my efforts.

"I *said* hold fast," I mutter in response to their complaints. Davina, who by far has the least amount of open-water training, looks as though she really might vomit.

"They're still trailing but they lost distance," Greer reports and I bob my chin in understanding.

"Hiraeth—you never answered my question!" I call up chidingly to Kleio while sifting through possible maneuvers. Herse snickers her amusement in my direction and I shoot her a quick conspiratorial grin.

It always helps to have a bit of a distraction to keep me truly focused.

"*Now*? This is hardly the time!" Kleio snaps, her voice rising an octave while turning back in my direction and gesturing to the moonlighter still chasing us from a distance.

Sliding my helmsman visor up to meet her eyes, I shrug with a frown. "I mean, one could say this is the *perfect* time. Once we find the first checkpoint—who *knows* how long I'll survive without my affinity?" I heave out a dramatic sigh, eyeing both my second and third pointedly.

"Alright, we didn't mean what was said on the cruiser. I wasn't trying to claim that you *literally* couldn't survive without your power," Kleio clips in their defense while Herse snorts, her eyes studying the night sky. "We were just angry with you for not even consulting us. It's exhausting to watch you take every *single* blow on our behalf."

My thumbs drum back and forth along the wooden wheel in my grasp as I hum, "Captain's duty is to the crew, no matter the cost. That's the code."

Neither one of them has a retort to that.

"Now circling back to my original question," I say, rotating my index finger for effect. "Care to enlighten us on your relationship struggles? Might be the last chance you get," I taunt my second with another grin.

"Captain, they're gaining!" Greer warns and I slam back down the visor before picking up speed.

I know I'm easily a more skilled helmsman than Raider Bellum. If I can keep up our velocity high enough, then they can chase us round and round this portion of the maze until Nephthys finally figures out how the fuck to navigate.

"Yeah, come on, *Hiraeth*, I thought you were all about 'total transparency' now?" Herse teases Kleio above the sounds of churning water.

A bump of unexpected wake hits us then and everyone bounces nearly a foot in the air before more cursing is thrown about. Kleio's eyes flicker back and forth between Herse and me from where she kneels on one leg at the bow. Those sepia irises hold that rare spark of anger and I fight hard to keep my lips flattened. I'm not very successful.

"You should talk, LeRoi—what was it you were up to in the pool chambers last week, *huh*?" My second asks my third accusingly, her brows lifted in clear taunting question.

This was news to me.

My hands grip the wheel firmer as I glance over at Herse, who is also kneeling, keeping a tight hold of the iron railing. To my utter surprise, my third's face darkens into a deep crimson. The coloring of that abnormal expression reaches all the way to the delicate tip of her sloped nose.

"We already went over this. It was nothing," she growls out.

"Oh nothing?" Kleio's eyes slide to mine with the same goading amusement that has led me into every previous scheme we've ever attempted. "So you were just down in the pool chambers with Vagar Ophios, *alone.* And that was, nothing?"

"The south order second?" I ask, barely stifling my gasp.

My eyes widen behind the tinted visor as I once again glance over at my third. Her violet gaze narrows into a look that says she's contemplating tackling my second right then and there.

"It's not what it sounds like!" Herse snaps sharply before her eyes turn themselves towards me with a beseeching shine. "He stole something of mine and I needed it back."

"Uh—*Captain*?" Greer asks, the tone in her voice the only reason I'm able to pull myself from the sparring match before me.

I huff a deeply agonized sigh at the sight of Captain Leporem pulling up from a nearby passageway and cutting in the space behind us. *Shit*, they must have found a shortcut.

"Mmmm, unfortunately I'm going to have to side with Hiraeth on this one. That doesn't sound very *transparent* to me, LeRoi," I chide Herse, just as a 'thunk' hits the stern.

"How's it going back there?" I shout, risking a glance over a shoulder at my navigator.

Nephthys gives me a wide-eyed look of pure panic and I glimpse the end of an iron arrow lodged into the dark-stained deck. Captain Leporem's petite form, standing atop the front of their speeder with a crossbow in hand, tells me what I need to know.

I turn forward with a long, suffering sigh. "Maneuvering!"

"I'll be transparent when *she* is," Herse snarks towards Kleio but her eyes are glued onto Corvina's smirking form.

Kleio shakes her head in exasperation. "Okay fine. We broke up."

My brows reach for the sky and I look over to see a mirrored expression of surprise on Herse's face. Narrowly sliding into the nearest open passage, my focus is split between the speeding walls of amethyst and the bomb that Kleio just dropped.

"You—*what*?" Greer sputters as she joins the conversation, coming to crouch by Herse.

Kleio gives a curt nod, and a sadness I hadn't previously detected crosses her gaze briefly.

"Ohhh, I am going to *fucking* kill him." My hands tighten on the helm while increasing speed in small increments, and my mouth forms a dark scowl. "You know—the more I think about it—it's honestly better that I don't have access to my affinity. It'll make it that much more satisfying when I gut him with my bare hands."

"Merena, do *not* murder Vash." Kleio gives me a firm look, the whipping winds continue pulling at her uniform braids.

"Come *on*, just a little bit?" I whine in return.

My second shakes her head tersely once more.

"Let Boreas maim the prick a bit, at least!" Herse exclaims, throwing up her hands and Greer nods her head of flaming locks in emphatic agreement.

"*No,*" Kleio reaffirms loudly. "I broke up with Vash. So there is no reason for you to kill or dismember him. There's your fucking transparency—your turn, *Captain*."

My mouth drops wide in indignation as my eyes leave the narrowing, rounded passage to glance up at my second. "What do you mean, *my* turn? I told you guys everything already."

How could they think otherwise? I was almost telling the whole truth.

Kleio shakes her head in disagreement. "No, you told us everything up until that night on the nets. I've heard absolutely nothing else since then."

"What's your point?" I ask, my eyes glued to the course I'm making up as we go. It seems we may have finally lost Captain Leporem.

"There's obviously been some sort of development," my second states matter-of-fact.

With a noncommittal shrug, I frown. "No. Not really."

Kleio and Herse share a laugh that has my frown deepening and the former pushes, "Okay so then what was that little confrontation between you two on the docks? I heard him say something about another option—did our suggestion work?"

My arms strain against their efforts to maintain the wheel as we enter a particularly choppy patch. A memory of Captain Agni's towering form above me, his hand wrapped lightly around my throat as my back digs into tree bark, resurfaces. Heat floods my face without my affinity there to stop it and I am eternally grateful for my helmsman visor.

Swallowing, I strive to keep my tone casual. "Mmmm, no, I wouldn't say that. The jackass just wants to get in my head." An embarrassing flush continues to lap up my neck and over my face and I keep my eyes pointedly on the waters.

"We have new company—Cardinal West starboard!" Herse's barking voice almost makes me flinch. Looking over a shoulder, I find the silver fluttering flag of Captain Bedivere's moonlighter in the broken path mirroring our own.

"Nephthys—UPDATE!" I shout in demand. My hands remain firmly on the wheel while I shoot the twins a quick glance. Prisca blows out a breath and turns her wide eyes toward her twin.

Nephthys looks so stressed out, I think she just might bite someone. "I—the map. It—it doesn't make sense, Captain. I—I'm sorry," she stumbles over her apology, panic tripping her words.

Craning my neck all the way back to the stern, I give Nephthys a swift, disbelieving look.

"ARE YOU A STAR CHARTER OR NOT?" I bellow the words because I'm not able to physically shake her right now. "Fuck the bleeding map and use your gods blessed affinity. FOR CRYING OUT LOUD!"

The twins both blink, stunned for a brief moment.

"Oh *shit,*" Prisca laments, a hand coming to slide down the side of her face aggressively.

"We actually *are* idiots," Nephthys groans loudly while rubbing her temples as she remains kneeling on the stern-sidled bench. "Okay, okay, give me a second."

As a star charter, Nephthys has been blessed with a natural ability for navigating. Unfortunately, with the rise of both landmass and tide raider technology, such a skill as hers is considered Vek and therefore not well trained nor prioritized.

I turn back in time to share a gaping look of complete incredulousness with Kleio. Her cupid's brow twitches with amusement at my display of completely disbelieving fury. As if she can't help it, my second snorts a laugh that cracks my grin, and I shake my head in renewed disbelief.

"Take the next right," Nephthys suddenly snaps in a voice that doesn't belong to this world.

The luminous kórallian passages fly by in the peripherals of my vision and the next opening emerges too fast for Kleio to point out. I grunt from the effort it takes to wrestle the throttle and whip the wheel into submission. The small speeder shrieks in protest as we skirt into the gap and abruptly slow several knots.

"K—keep g—going for the next half-mile, then take the next left exit. That should pull us close to the first gate—I think," Nephthys instructs, excitement returning to her still trembling voice.

I nod tightly in agreement.

Sure enough, half a mile and one steady left-hand turn later, Kleio announces excitedly from the moonlighter's bow, "Checkpoint ahead!"

I squint through the visor at the carved-out mooring located on the far end of the narrow passageway. A dark grin begins climbing its way across my lips with the realization we're the only ones here.

“Prepare to moor!” I call out while skidding up to the lip of the kórall hewn dockside.

Nimra throws Kleio some rope to begin docking and I stand fully from my seat at the helm. My breathing comes out quicker and heavier than I realized while sliding up the visor. Giving them all a swift once-over, I state firmly, “This is where I have to leave you all until Port Capillary.”

It feels like a punch to the gut but this is the way of The Vault. I have two gates to lift before meeting them back at the port. Then we’ll venture onwards to access the heart together and with any luck, I’ll find my way to vault within.

Breathing deeply to steady myself, I rescan their faces. Seven pairs of eyes watch me with varying levels of dread and concern. “You all have your affinities, *please* remember to use them,” I say calmly, my eyes flick over to Nephthys briefly and a flush blooms beneath her copper skin.

“Also, no more bickering from this point on," I demand next while pointing a finger between my second and third in clear emphasis. The former of which gives me a look so completely disbelieving in my own hypocrisy that it coerces a laugh from my lips.

Stepping up to the side of the speeder parallel to the makeshift dock, my pulse begins pounding heavily in my ears. I then remember to remove the helmsman visor and gloves and toss them both into Kleio’s waiting arms. My mouth purses while studying their tythe-tokens once more.

“I request lastly that you all keep each other safe and I do not care what that takes. I do not care about whatever lines you have to cross. I do not care who you have to maim or murder. Your main priority is keeping one another alive until meeting up with me at the port. You do that by whatever means necessary, is that understood?” My tone is cold and unyielding.

Seven voices answer as one, "Yes, Captain.”

I nod and glance again at the dockside. I’m anxious to get going now that we're here.

Not wanting to take up any more precious time, I jump gracefully from the bow down to the fossil-hewn edge and begin scanning my surroundings. A grand cavern crouches before and extends over me. The shrill sound of scraping rock makes me spin around to face my crew.

I discover the ear-splitting noise is due to the pale glowing walls rising up on either side of the moonlighters mooring to lock them in. Then the water beneath our craft begins to descend. Kleio's eyes lock with mine as they start slipping out of view and into the next level of The Vault.

Worry and fear knot up my insides.

"You have to promise us you'll do the same!" Kleio yells over the sound of scraping stones, her voice tinged with barely concealed panic. "You have to swear that you'll do whatever it takes to meet us there. Whatever means necessary!"

My mouth forms a small smile while keeping hold of her gaze as they descend ever lower before I incline my chin sharply in agreement. "I'll do whatever it takes to return to you all. I swear it, by whatever means necessary."

A heartbeat later and they're gone.

Only to be released from the kórallian clutches and into the maze's next level upon my completion of this checkpoint and the lifting of their gate or upon my death. Assuming it's the former, they'll have to reach the second gate by themselves while I work to lift it internally.

XI. THE FOURTH PILLAR

Focusing on non worst-case scenarios, I begin making my way into the mouth of the cave.

My hands flit up to my hair absently and I'm pleasantly surprised to find Kleio's newest gift has worked like a charm. Even with the racing winds and helmsman visor, my hair has been kept neatly away from my face and is still bound tightly in the plait atop my head.

A few silent moments pass before I hit a set of makeshift steps slanting downward. I take them quickly, my feet nimble from years of cliffside galivanting. Sliding out the short sword sheathed at my waist, I meet the bottom of the rocky staircase and am greeted by a wall of stone.

My head swivels 'round to take in the rest of my surroundings, only to find it's nothing but a dead-end outcropping. Brows knitting together, I turn back towards the direction I came from.

My prior calm begins ramping up into irritation.

Pursing my lips, I shift again to face the wall once more, tilting my head to one side in deliberation. I have no idea what compels me to do it, I guess you could call it a sixth sense, all the same my free hand presses itself firmly against the sea stone.

A pulsing beat flutters beneath my touch, and I snatch back my hand in shock.

Blinking several times over in disbelief, I go to test the wall again but a brilliant light steals my attention. Swirling script, like that of the second challenge, etches itself one word at a time into the dead end. My palms begin sweating in earnest and I rub them quickly on my uniform while my heart starts pounding wildly.

The glowing script has fashioned itself into the outline of a tall archway. The words begin and end at the base of the wall so that the whole thing appears to be a door. Craning my neck uncomfortably to one side, I step closer to inspect the very inconveniently shaped words.

Survival requires endurance. Passage requires salt.

My eyes narrow with confusion and I crane my neck again to re-read the short sentence. A frown pulls down on my lips in perplexity. There's no question or riddle hidden within the archway's script, no matter how many times I read it. The unanticipated noise of rock groaning against stone draws me several scuffling steps back from inspection.

I watch with widening eyes as the rough mineral barrier within the archway of glowing script begins descending into the ground below. The opening extends inch by inch, revealing a small circular room framed with plain pale walls and one identical archway directly across my own.

As I step through the newly formed fissure, I discover another figure emerging simultaneously from the opposite opening. My grip tightens around the short sword as the figure steps through its aperture. Dark raven braids appear alongside a keen-edged blade glinting in well manicured hands.

Corvina.

My affinity chained down inside begins slamming itself against the drug in my veins with a vengeance. Worry twists my gut and I begin to doubt a few of my earlier, some might say *brash*, decisions.

Captain Leporem's emerald eyes lock onto mine across the small space. Understanding appears to hit us at the same moment. The luminous script was *not* a riddle this time. Just a statement from The Vault. A demand. This first checkpoint requires salt in order to move forward. Or more specifically, blood.

Incredible.

The one captain whose affinity could make all my training null and void just so happens to be the very first opponent I'm met with. Anger burns bright inside my chest at the injustice of it all. I'm tempted to chuck a dagger in my rage but decide better of it.

Cracking my neck on either side, I swiftly move down into the makeshift arena with a burdened huff. Corvina mirrors my movements, a saccharine smile twisting her features as she comes to take the place across from me. The southern captain puts on a pretty façade but I catch something like unease shining along the edges of those gemstone eyes.

"How perfect. I've been waiting for the right opportunity to repay you," she purrs.

My eyes drop down to that silver capsule covering the finger my frostbite took from Captain Leporem. The sight of it triggers an odd momentary feeling of guilt to flicker beneath my usual aversion. I know I shouldn't feel anything resembling remorse. What Corvina intended to do that day was infinitely worse than the comparatively minor loss of a digit.

I shove aside that very inconveniently noble part of myself and force my lips into a careless smile and flick the blade around my wrist absently. Captain Leporem tracks each of my movements. "Repay me?" I echo in mock confusion. "I think that shiny new *accessory* of yours makes us even."

I smirk, enjoying the annoyance in her gaze at my choice of word. The one the twins use to antagonize Corvina after what she tried to make me do. I figure it's possible that if I get her worked up enough, she'll be too distracted to use that dangerous voice of hers.

Corvina doesn't respond immediately and we begin circling each other in the few meters of space available. Our silent dance doesn't last long. With a flash of her blade in the air near my neck, Corvina's simper transforms into a sneer.

I take advantage of her close proximity when dodging her attack just before connecting my fist with her unsuspecting jaw. Corvina staggers back a step, her emerald eyes turning harder than stone, and swallows what I can only assume is a mouthful of blood.

She lets out a short scoff and we resume circling each other. I watch her warily, preparing to do whatever I must to cut off her affinity should she attempt to use it. No matter how irksome Corvina has been since arriving in the north, I truly do not relish the thought of having to slit her throat.

But I'll do whatever I must.

"You think I care about my fucking *finger*?" The laughter that escapes the beautiful captain is so strange that it almost makes me want to take a step back. I hesitate and she moves.

Corvina's blade goes for my exposed flank and I pivot but she's learned from my very recent example. Her fist slams into my ribs so hard it might as well be the fucking blade. Gasping out for breath, I barely even register her next words.

"My finger is the least of what you've cost me. You don't have the faintest idea of what you've actually done—do you? What your very *existence* has caused?" Corvina's gaze blazes a bright, frightening jade.

My still-recovering body is slightly hunched in pain as her knife comes for my throat. It's clear to me now that she isn't going to stop at just spilling my blood. Corvina wants my life as payment too.

"Of *course* you don't!" She spits in my face just before I block the incoming attack with my forearm.

Satisfaction tilts my lips in response to the ringing sound of her dislodged blade hitting the floor. Not wanting to risk any sort of sly movement from the silver-tongued captain, I tackle Corvina to the ground in the next instant. Tragically, I lose my own fighting weapon in the process.

"By my existence, I assume you mean the drowned god's blessing? Something I didn't get a fucking *choice* in?" I snarl down in question to her struggling form now pinned beneath me.

While forcefully restraining the near-seething captain, I realize with surprise that Corvina looks as disheveled as I've ever seen. Like she's on the verge of some serious unraveling. I try to recount the last time I really took notice of her. Nothing honestly comes to mind since Luminalia.

"Is that why you put ehkinos on those evening stars? To end my existence?" I demand through clenched teeth.

Captain Leporem chokes out a shaky laugh of disbelief. The sound takes effort to escape her throat currently being squeezed between my hands while my knee's pin down her arms. Those emerald eyes meet mine and I discover in them a kind of misery that I didn't believe could exist in someone as beautiful as Corvina. The sight of her anguish feels like a different, very unexpected, kind of blow.

"For the last time I didn't know about the godsdamned ehkinos, you stupid fucking *bitch*!" She hurls back up at me. "You might not believe it, *squid,* but I do have a few shreds of honor left. No matter what your bastard-born ass or anyone *else* believes."

Narrowing my attention upon her hate-filled gaze, I come to the troubling realization that Captain Leporem is definitely telling me the truth. She really, truly, did not intend to poison me that day. Paralyze me for sure, but not murder.

Not *that* day, at least.

Her next words come out with a hysterical quality. "Because of *you,* all of it—all of it—just for nothing." The hold I have on her throat idiotically loosens in my complete and utter confusion.

"*What*?" I ask incredulously.

Corvina's mouth twists angrily before she garners a bit of strength and hurls a massive wad of spit up onto my cheek. More of my hold slips. She takes advantage to free a hand before ripping one of my knives from its perch along the belt at my waist.

I'm forced to roll off the southern captain before she gets the chance to slam that stolen blade into my ribcage. I then scramble back to scoop up my own fallen weapon before wiping off her spit on my cheek with a low sound of disgust.

Corvina, having relocated her previously disarmed knife, stands across from me with both weapons raised. "Everything—*everything* I've done and it—it doesn't matter. He's still—he'll always—and I—I can't—I can't. Gods he's going to *kill* me!" She makes a choking sort of sound that has me going still.

Now would be the perfect time to attack. But for some reason I can't bring myself to take advantage of her crumbling state. Something about the girl seems to be *deeply* coming undone.

"Who or *what* are you going on about, Leporem?" My inquiring voice rings out inside the chamber.

"*Olsson,*" she gasps out his name like a plea and I stumble back a step.

"What in *the depths* are you talking about? He's your—well—and you guys are—well—*yeah*? Surely he wouldn't—you know—would he?" I trip over the words, not believing I even gave them permission to leave my mouth in the first place. Why am I asking questions now?

The fuck is wrong with me?

Corvina's gaze sharpens as she begins recovering herself from whatever sort of mental undoing is clearly ensuing. "Depths you're an idiot—even for a castaway." She snorts angrily. "It's honestly a marvel that you manage to breathe and walk at the same time."

"I don't understand," I say, easily dodging her shoddy foot swipe.

"That's the worst part of it." Her voice is soft and bitter, while rage gleams freely in her gaze.

My brow creases before making contact again with the spine of my blade against her exposed side. She gasps at the impact before letting out a somewhat manic laugh in regards to my outward confusion.

"You truly don't have any idea." Something in her tone makes me pause at the unexpected layer of sadness it possesses. "You can't possibly know why I hate you and yet I hate you all the same. If not infinitely more because of it." Corvina's body begins to tremble, the weapon in her hand shaking with vigor.

I halt my footwork long enough to give her a very queer look. This conversation is so vastly different from any of my interactions I've had thus far with Captain Leporem that I feel as though it's happening to someone else. Maybe it is. Maybe I'm in a dream. Maybe I'll wake up in my bunk to find this day hasn't even begun yet.

"Now I'm as good as dead. And it's all because of *you*!" she snarls in a fit of rage before hurling the knife of mine she's stolen directly for my heart

I very narrowly manage to dodge the incoming weapon. Returning to my feet, I look towards Corvina with bewildered eyes. I've finally fucking had it. "WHAT ARE WE TALKING ABOUT?" I shout in sheer frustration.

She doesn't answer and instead goes for another foot swipe. This one I'm not expecting. I hit the ground *hard* and hiss at the impact reverberating along my bones. Captain Leporem is on top of me with brutal efficiency. Her mouth curls upwards before she lunges low. I'm certain that she's aiming another deathblow for my gut so I move to block her.

I'm not at all expecting her lips to press themselves down upon my own. What. The. *Fuck.*

My eyes fly wide and I emit a startled sound of shock that seems to yank the unraveling captain back into reality. Corvina stares down at me and my completely horrified expression of pure shock. I find her gaze searching my face is brimming with loathing and something a lot like *longing*.

The rest of her person quickly reflects a deep, dark shade of incriminating scarlet. Shoving her off and away from me doesn't take much effort at all.

"Sweet fucking *Soteria*," I stammer to no one in particular while getting to my feet, wiping my mouth with the back of my hand. Well, that settles it then. This is a dream—a hallucination of some sort—*right*? No shot in all the drowned depths is this my current reality.

Corvina wastes no time in jolting up onto her heels and lunging for me again. Deflecting her doesn't take nearly as much skill as it should. Shaking my breathless head at her undone state, I feel no satisfaction in my next maneuver. I drop low while slipping out a second blade and deftly slice through the skin above her unsuspecting ankle.

Her scream of pain rings out into the hollow room like a holy bell. The kneeling tune is swiftly followed by her growl of fresh rage. "I'm going to fucking murder you, *squid*," she promises through a menacing hiss.

I'm already running.

I sprint back towards the opposite opening with Corvina's blood still fresh on my blade. Her struggling footfalls sound from behind and I don't slow a single stride. My hand runs down the crimson weapon before smearing the stolen salt of hers right across the glowing script.

Corvina's injured form manages to drag itself before my archway just as the stone is resealing it's last few exposed inches. Unfortunately, the slim crevice remaining provides just enough space for a dagger to escape it.

The rogue blade shines like a beacon in the night before sinking into the space right above my heart. The last thing I see is the slash of a grim smile and the sparkle of satisfied emerald eyes before the archway closes fully.

My knees hit the ground.

The world has become a spinning blur of light and dark. And it's not because of my injury. The world is really, truly spinning. The patch of fossilized kórall beneath me is the only solid thing as the walls rise up and up and up until finally everything moves sideways.

The unexpectedly harsh pull flings me to the ground. I thankfully have the good sense to fall backwards and avoid pushing the blade in further. The burning pain screaming from inside my chest tells me that this is most definitely *not* a dream nor even a hallucination. Which means Corvina really did kiss me.

Fucking *depths*.

I snort in bewilderment while picturing my crew's faces when recounting this shit.

Once the world mercifully stops moving, I sit up through my agony in order to survey my new surroundings. The only difference I find is that where once was a dead-end wall is now an opening. A brief glance reveals it to be some sort of entrance to a dim looking passageway.

The passageway runs past the room I occupy, like some sort of hall. Or perhaps what I occupy is really more of an alcove. However none of that really matters if I bleed out.

Coming back to my knees, I remove the supplies Davina packed me from my pockets and waist. I don't need to make it pretty. I just need to stabilize the wound before meeting up with my crew again. If I can make it past this next checkpoint, then Vi can get her hands on it, and all will be well.

I just have to get the knife out first.

Easy.

XLI. NO BITE

"Crazy ass southern bitchhhh—" I'm half screaming and half hissing through bared teeth while attempting to pull out the remainder of the blade from its current lodgings.

There's blood, both Corvina's and mine, sliding down over my hands and chest. I'm making so much noise that the hollow passage actually reverberates my painful screams back to me. But I don't care. My breathing has suddenly become terribly heavy and thick.

Someone 'tsks' nearby and I freeze.

"My, what a foul mouth you have, Boreas. I'll have to remember that for later."

My face screws itself into one of angry disbelief. Glancing upward, one bloody hand on the dagger, I lock eyes with the worst person I could possibly be forced to deal with right now.

I try and fail to stifle my groan.

Olsson *godsdamned* Agni stares back at me without a scratch on him. His obsidian hair looks perfectly un-perfect, as though he's just rolled out of someone else's bed. He regards my state through kesar-shaded irises, his gaze flickering to the blade in my chest then back to my face.

Some of that perpetual tan of his appears to pale slightly but his usual condescending smirk still hovers in the corner of his mouth. His suggestive words ring back to me, spiking my temper.

Why? Why is it always him?

I'm surprised I don't shout the thoughts aloud.

"That's just perfect," I mutter with a snort of disbelief.

My grip on the hilt tightens once more and I finally yank free the end of the blade from my skin. I swear low in pain before hurling the dislodged blade directly for Agni's stupidly cocksure face.

His bemused expression flashes to one of blatant surprise before he just *barely* manages to dodge Corvina's incoming dagger. To my supreme satisfaction, he's not left completely unscathed.

"Fucking—*brat!*" he barks out.

A beringed hand cups the new line of crimson-colored torn skin along his throat. I watch as he turns from the room with rage plain in his horribly beautiful features. Agni's angry footsteps sound away, and further down the passage. I let slip a breathless laugh.

Good riddance, asshole.

I know I'll likely pay for that later, and then some.

Now onto the fun part.

Picking up a scrap of medic cloth from the line of supplies before me, I try not to worry about what my crew might be facing on their side of things. A muffled scream slides through clenched teeth as I shove the ethanol-and-salve-coated rag through the cut in my uniform and into the wound.

Davina's healing-soaked cloth begins working almost immediately as I start cleaning out the gash through muffled cries. The agony finally eases down to a much more bearable ache after only a few moments and the lightness in my head mercifully fades. My leech's affinity truly is a blessing.

I should be just fine until meeting with them again, then Vi can heal the wound completely.

"OooOoh, Captain Boreas, whose fault is it for choosing a leech as a crew member?" I mimic Skelm's earlier words under my breath in a whiny impression of his scathing tone. "Whose worthless now you pretentious one-eyed dumbass."

The pain relief from Davina's wound-stoppering salve is so wonderful I find myself laughing while observing the last of the blood now running through the lines on my palms. I watch as droplets of cherry fall down to the dark sand-covered floor for ten hollow beats in recovery.

Coming back to the medicinal supplies, I grab for some adhesive bandaging. Then I make quick work of sliding the black dressing beneath my shirt and unrolling it against my skin. I secure the bandage from under my left arm, across the wound, and up against the other side of my neck.

Once satisfied, I give myself exactly sixty seconds of rest on the cool floor as a reward before hoisting myself up and making better sense of this new location. Much as my crew was, it seems I've been drilled down into the next level within The Vault.

If the reports are to be believed, then this opening will lead to the kórallian tunnels, where I'll find the next gate to lift before meeting my crew at Port Capillary. The similarities between this and our second trial make me wonder if TideLord Dolion had more than a hand in designing it.

Coming to stand before the large hallway opening, I slide a lip between my teeth and quietly contemplate which direction to take. Since the walls spun and the floor moved sideways, there's no real way to know which direction I came from.

In the end, I decided to go in the direction based on my weapon's arm.

It takes no more than two minutes into the dim kórallian passage before regretting that choice.

Captain Agni's distinct silhouette leans casually inside an archway framing the entrance to yet another alcove along the path before me. Burning embers track me as my footsteps slow and I come to a full-blown halt. Years of masking pain come in handy when crossing my arms and glaring at the southern captain without so much as a wince.

"Well, would you look at that, *little bastard*. I waited up for you after all. Even *after* you thought it pertinent to chuck a dagger at my face." Agni's dark voice echoes into the tunnel, while a look of pure irritation alights his sweeping gaze.

Scowling with a huff of equal displeasure, I shift backwards. I'm deliberating on whether or not I should test my luck and try out the opposite direction when the prick sighs in deep annoyance.

"Dead end. Already tried it," he states before pushing himself off from the wall and resuming his stalking down the murky passage in my original direction. Begrudgingly, I follow after while silently removing the short-sword resting against my hip.

Agni eyes me coolly as I come to walk in step beside him.

"Why did you wait for me?" My eyes narrow skeptically in his direction while gripping the leather-wrapped handle tighter.

"Why else?" Agni asks loftily, his eyes darting down to the weapon in my grasp with a pointed smirk before holding up a hand in the air to display his own silver-scarred palm in emphasis

The look on his face is so fucking conceited I'm sorely tempted to backhand him.

"Then get on with it." I'm anxious to be done with this. Hopefully we'll find a fork in the path here soon and be forced to part ways permanently. Assuming one of us doesn't kill the other before then. Which seems rather unlikely.

His mouth twitches in amusement but his gaze remains on the narrow hall ahead. The muscles in my neck tense while holding back my ripening temper, all the control I've worked *so* very hard to master is impossibly lost when he's around.

"Hmmm, but what to ask?" Agni feigns thoughtfulness, tapping that finger idly against his lip again. "I mean, this being your last question and all—well—I need to make it *good*."

Breathing out through my nose, I refuse to meet his goading stare, which only amuses him more. Agni chuckles, the timbre of it is so deep and dark I swear I can feel it running along my bones. "I *could* ask something about your crew. Perhaps what exactly you've planned for their exit strategy after The Vault? That would be all the intel I need for a proper ambush."

Panic grips me in its heathen claws.

"Mmmm, *no*, on second thought, I'd better not. You'll just change it after reaching Port Capillary. Assuming, of course, that you make it there at all," he muses to himself, running an absent hand through his midnight hair.

"Maybe I should make you tell me which one of your crew members is your all's greatest vulnerability? Then, even if you *did* somehow manage to make it into The Vault, we can just play ransom for your prize afterwards."

An image flashes in my mind of kaleidoscope eyes and gentle healing hands.

My insides twist until he finally puts me out of my misery by making it worse. "Although, I suppose that if you were idiotic enough to take the kratosbane for your crew... well then that would now make *you* their greatest vulnerability. Wouldn't it?" he questions darkly.

Fixing my stare at a point in the distance, I do everything in my power to not react.

Unfortunately, that seems to be precisely the reaction Agni is looking for.

The smirk he so prefers turns itself into a cruel grin as my face begins to heat. "Oh, sweet depths, Boreas. Tell me you didn't—not *actually*?" His resounding laughter is caustic. "Just how exactly are you supposing to make it anywhere near The Vault's doors without your affinity?"

I stop walking in order to sneer up at him. "I made it this far, didn't I? As I recall, my speeder was the first one inside the maze. You had—hmm, what *was* it again?" I tap my finger on my lower lip in mimicry of him. "Oh yeah, that's right. You had a four hundred meter head start and I still beat you—*without* my affinity."

Agni has paused as well, his absurdly muscular arms fold themselves over one another while angling his head down to meet my eyes. The mask of disinterest he wears is good, but not good enough to hide the anger shimmering just beneath the surface.

"I suppose they're probably used to you being the source of their deficiency by now anyway," he mutters snidely.

"It's killing you, isn't it?" I ask, pretending not to have heard his latest jibe.

A small smirk hangs in the corner of my mouth and his brows raise in silent question.

"The fact that out there—out in front of the TideLords and the Raider King and the rest of the entire godsdamned Order—you lost to *me*." I laugh, hoping it'll irritate him further.

"The fact that even without the aid of the 'oh so special' elemental abilities—when it comes down to pure talent and skill—you, along with everyone else, now know with *absolute* certainty that I'm better than your fucking best." My expression is smug enough to reel that anger to the surface and I relish the sight of it thrashing so plainly in his eyes.

"Vagar Ophios is not our best helmsman," he growls softly.

"*Oh*? Then who is?" I ask in my best impression of the twin's false innocence, batting eyelashes and all. There is true pleasure to be had in watching Agni's demeanor darken so violently.

His jaw clenches tight before stating, "I am."

Blinking once, I slowly allow my lips to curve upwards on the sides, in the way that I know makes most people want to hit me. "Uh-huh, *sure* you are," I croon, revealing a deeply placating smile before giving him a light tap of my finger on his rock-solid chest.

Before he can retort, I turn back around and continue swaggering along the passage.

His rage is damn near radiating behind me. I tamp down on a grin while fighting to hold back laughter. I think I'm finally beginning to understand the enjoyment behind such mind games.

But of course, he is more practiced at them than I.

Agni's strides catch up to mine far too easily, for my liking. "I've been going about your last question all wrong, Boreas. It can be about anything I wish. No need to limit myself to something so dull as strategy, especially when I'll be winning this thing regardless."

Teeth hold my sharpened tongue in place.

It's *good* to get his attention away from my crew. *Good* to get his mind running in any direction other than around things pertaining to them. I force myself to remember that fact.

"Besides, this was for my own personal *entertainment* in the first place. So I think I really ought to make sure it's something I can savor for years to come," Agni remarks as I pick up my pace and scowl when his stupidly long legs match my gate so arrogantly effortlessly.

"I think I should have you tell me something a little more intimate, Boreas. Something along the lines of—oh, I don't know, how about what thoughts keep you up late at night? Better yet, what thoughts help you to—well, *not* keep you up. You know?"

The overt suggestion in his tone sets my teeth on edge. Kleio and the others will be getting a fucking earful later.

"I'm guessing that 'ole *wonder boy* is still who sets your late-night sails?" Agni asks before flashing me a cruel wink. The withering glare I shoot him only encourages the prick further.

"Thought so." He chuckles. "Do you think it's his *electrifying* sense of duty or that *large* moral compass of his that really gets you going?"

"Is that your question?" I grit out.

"Hardly." Agni scoffs. "Although I am curious as to how poor Tharos will ever get the chance to make you moan like that again after *such* a dishonorable deceit." He tuts distastefully.

Halting mid-step, I turn to look up at Agni with an expression of pure, enraged, disbelief, and he throws me an overt leer in turn. My hand twitches around the pommel in my grasp.

"Oh, was I not supposed to have overheard that part? As you might recall, those tent panels were quite thin, Boreas, and I have to say you really were rather loud. Not that I'm complaining. On the contrary, I enjoyed it *immensely*." The look in his eyes tells me he's thoroughly delighting in every morsel of my humiliation.

Turning back to face the tunnel ahead, I focus on breathing to a count of four. To kill him now would mean breaking our od. It would mean losing my captaincy tied to it. Not to mention basically ruining the lives of everyone I love who just fucking *tythed* themselves to me.

Still, the allure is very much present.

As if sensing my internal dilemma and just unable to help himself, Agni whispers in a wicked voice that is far too near my ear, "Now here's an idea, what if I asked you to tell me *each* of the sounds he gets you to make for him? You'd have to show them to me, wouldn't you? A little vocal demonstration from you, Boreas, is something I would find *very* entertaining indeed."

Scents of cardamom and citrus caress over my shoulders and slip past my cheeks.

"Unless you would rather just choose your *other* very available option," Agni muses to himself in that same richly intimate tone. "In which case I expect I'll just have to learn them all first hand. It's your choice, either way is a win-win for me. I wonder how your dear *Tharos* would enjoy comparing notes with me on how best I find to make you c—"

Blindingly cold fury ensnares my system and I pivot on him. My hand shoves him into a wall and I deeply delight in the sound of his skull smacking hard against stone. Agni glares down at the raised blade's edge, angled squarely beneath his jugular, with a slightly dazed glint to his eyes.

The southern captain's gaze recovers itself into one of deepest loathing when skipping over to where my hand forces him into the fossilized coral. He next turns those coal-black eyes on me. It's honestly deplorable how the weight of his full murderous attention makes a part of me want to balk.

"Is this *truly* your method of getting a woman into your bed, Agni? Drive them to the point of loathing you so fucking much that they're willing to do quite literally *anything* to be rid of you?" My mouth turns down with a look of deep disdain. "Your admirers will be devastated."

"As if I'd ever actually have to try." He snorts, looking away from me in disgust.

My jaw drops at the size of his ego.

"You are completely *delusional* if you actually believe that whatever females are miserable enough to find themselves beneath you aren't either doing so for their own personal gain or fucking *desperate,*" I hiss up at him.

I'm tempted right now to mention my latest little revelation about Corvina. Only a repulsive sense of honor prevents me from being the one to let him in on her newly revealed infatuation.

Agni's hands slide down into the pockets of his pants with a lazy indifference that makes me irate. This ability of his to slip between moods is unforgivably infuriating. He glances upwards for a moment, appearing bored by both my scathing words and the blade close enough to send him back to Nawai with one wrong move.

Od or not, I'm dangerously enticed to do just that.

"I bet you don't even bother *pretending* to try for their sake, do you?" I ask and he meets my gaze again in question.

"Although I'd wager that even if you did, no one in their right mind would ever believe the honeyed words from your lips were born from anything other than your own narcissism." I snort at the absurd idea, which further darkens his gaze.

"It's probably for the best that you don't bother putting in any effort. I'm positive it would only end in your own humiliation." My cutting words are cold as ice.

Agni's lip curls while his eyes dance with obsidian fury. "If you really care to know, those who do come *crawling* to my bed are not under any illusions of the circumstances. I'm there for two things only, pleasure and release. No *feelings* need to be involved from either party."

The way he looks at me makes it evident he finds my ideas of bedding disgraceful.

The laughter I emit is closer to a scoff. "Of course. No banter of any sort allowed either, I'm sure. Not that any of them would want to hear about your whiny little sacrificed life anyway."

My eyes flit up and down his person in a way I know will fan those flames of his.

"Although I *am* curious," I add, my deep tone a mockery of his own just before he hurls me an inquiry specifically designed to slide beneath my skin. "When a woman is in fact desperate enough to look your way, do you just bend them right over without a word? Or do you put them on top and make them do all the *physical* work as well?"

"Care to join me in a demonstration?" Agni's growl is soft and his eyes simmer with all too familiar loathing. I study them, waiting for their waver. His expression remains impressively unreadable but the mind game he's playing at this round is terribly transparent.

"Right," I say slowly, measuring his expression while my chin rises, confidence spurring my demeaning tone. "Because I'm all of a sudden now supposed to actually believe that *you* would ever be caught dead doing anything of the sort with someone like *me*." I'm sure to put enough emphasis to convey both my castaway and bastard status.

Agni is silent for a moment and my self-assurance grows bolder with every passing moment of his reserve. He presses his tongue against the inside of his lower lip, causing his chin to puff out a bit while his gaze searches my face in quiet evaluation.

"Are you actually *willing* to test that theory, Boreas?"

Adrenaline loosens my tongue. "I am, actually."

Agni's brows flash briefly and his look of blatant surprise reinforces my nerve.

"But here's the thing," I say sweetly. "I think you and I both know that, you're *bluffing*."

Irritation sears throughout his gaze and I make no attempt to reign in my rising satisfaction.

"All this bedroom talk of yours is just another one of your very poorly disguised attempts at getting in my head. It's just the latest mind game you've found to play. Another avenue to take beneath my skin. A *ploy* designed to force me into answering your stupid questions and ultimately aggravate me enough to distract me from The Vault entirely."

His face grows more and more unreadable with every word I say.

My smugness is nearly impossible to control while calling him out. "We both know you have no intention of delivering, it's a psychological warfare tactic. There is no real 'second' option. It's a shitty feint, *Captain*. I sincerely hope for the sake of your crew's lives that you're not the one in charge of strategy."

"You're quite certain of this, are you?" Agni's words come out severely clipped.

Watching him is like watching those flames in Skelm's quarters and finding I finally have the courage to spit at them.

"Quite," I agree with a short nod. Then I lean in close enough so that he can clearly hear my next words, dripping with lethally sweet venom. "Because you're nothing but an arrogant, spoiled, unloved, asshole. Who—when it comes right down to it—is all bark and *no bite*."

Captain Agni bends forward against my blade to lower himself closer, not caring one fucking bit as the gilded edge cuts into his skin. My gaze flickers briefly to track the ruby pinpricks drawn in its wake before returning to burning ember-eyes, now less than an inch from my own.

"Then. *Strip*." He sneers.

My focus narrows in on his gaze but otherwise I don't move so much as an increment. My affinity begins stirring restlessly beneath its restraints the longer Agni appears serious. After a moment, his lips pull upwards slowly in smug satisfaction. He leans back against the wall, watching me with cruel amusement at my utter lack of movement.

"Come on, Boreas, we don't have all night."

Vindictive prick.

"You don't actually want to fuck me—you just want to lick your wounded ego," I point out, his unwavering arrogance holding me physically hostage.

"Maybe it's both," Agni argues in a voice like scorched gravel before making a counter maneuver that's too swift to be possible. Quicker than a heartbeat, he leans into my sword, grabs me both wrists, and uses his weight to spin us until the hilt is forced from my grasp.

My mouth parts in angry shock as my blade hits the sandy passageway's floor with a muffled 'thud'. Glancing upwards, I find fresh blood forming a perfect circle around his neck. *His* blood.

Agni's formidable hands find my waist with ease. He pulls me flush against him before turning us over until it's *my* back flat against the wall. I'm reminded again just how much bigger he is, how much larger and stronger every plane that belongs to the body now cages in mine.

A memory flashes of that day in Preceptor Oplon's course. The sensation of his body on top of mine. His weight between my thighs. The flash of his scar as he drives me down into the mat.

My pulse quickens without permission.

I find myself scrambling for a taunt to brandish. "Oh, *of course*. I should have known manipulation would be your kink. Not very original for a highborn, but I guess I'd just assumed your palette was less *debased*."

Agni's hands, still secure on my waist, set me evenly against the wall. My pulse is like a living breathing thing, trying to physically escape my person by any means necessary.

"Manipulation is hardly a fair accusation." His head tilts to study me with raised brows and a deep-set frown. "You *certainly* seemed eager enough a moment ago. As I recall, you yourself just verified your own willingness, did you not?"

My lips flatten at his apt recount, I have no retort to give.

Agni leans down closer, and a hint of citrus begins to tease my senses with the movement. His voice now simmers with unexpected anger when stating, "Maybe I do enjoy a game or two but I am nothing if not a captain of my word. *You* are the one who just put that into question."

My swallow is thick.

"So Boreas, who *is* bluffing here?" Agni asks, his arrogant face turning insufferably smug while looking down at me, waiting expectantly for *my* waver. "Just say the word, admit to your own terribly played posturing scheme and I'll stop."

My jaw clenches while meeting his stare. I absolutely refuse to be the one to lose this match.

He pries a ring-adorned finger inside the neck of my uniform and releases the tight fabric against my skin with a brisk 'snap'. A snarl is barely held behind my clenched teeth at his brazen affront while holding onto his searing gaze.

Agni smirks down at my outrage. "Alright then, let's go, *Captain*—stop dithering."

My eyes remain narrowed on his face, still searching for the hesitation I was *so* certain would be revealed. Instead, Agni's striking features resemble those of an iron veil forged from cruel amusement that then begins lowering itself closer. He pauses when his lips linger beside my ear.

"Boreas," he whispers, soft as ash. "Are you waiting for my help?"

Something unspeakable flutters wildly inside my chest as his thumbs then deftly find the hem of my shirt. The very tips of his fingers begin grazing ever *so* slightly along the skin of my waist and I have to choke down on the sudden urge to gasp.

I know what he's doing—trying to force out my hand.

I'm lightheaded while trying to come up with a strategy.

Any sort of strategy.

"Now that I think about it..." His nose traces the shell of my ear before drifting down to the top of my jawline. The movements send a wave of mortifying tautness throughout my entire being.

"You do seem to require an awful lot of *my* assistance in particular. Don't you?" His taunting words stroke across my throat while his fingers continue trailing softly up my sides. A heat I refuse to acknowledge begins manifesting in my core, intensifying in slow, torturous increments as he lowers his head further with maddening deliberation.

"I wonder why that is," he murmurs, seemingly to himself, before using those sordid lips of his to run up and down my throat before kissing the spot directly beneath my jaw.

It might as well be a knife thrust between my ribs with the way I gasp.

My palms press flat against the stone at my backside in an attempt to rally myself in this newest game between us when a stream of brilliant light flares out behind me. I physically jolt at the unexpected sight of it spilling out and down into the dim tunnel.

Agni's hands drop away from me immediately and he steps back entirely. I notice then that at some point I stopped breathing. Precious air begins to fill my lungs in steady waves of barely concealed respite.

Avoiding the sigh of him altogether, I spin back to face the fossilized wall now rippling with bright, radiant, *white* symbols. Symbols that—that seem to ring a very old and long forgotten bell. The lines that string together my affinity mark begin tingling in response.

I stare at the emblems in quiet perplexity as they continue to unravel themselves further down the kórallian wall.

"Saved by the light, Boreas," Agni says, stealing back my attention with his dark chuckle.

There's a hidden level of humor in the undertow of his words. I'm struck with the most peculiar sense that I should somehow know the additional meaning behind them. Like he's just told me some sort of multilayered punchline but I simply *cannot* remember the joke.

Glancing over a shoulder in question, I find him studying me and the luminous wall intently.

His thoughts are entirely indecipherable.

XLII. LET'S GO BOREAS

The blazing white symbols craft a pattern of tumbling waves that continues down along the tunnel until curving around the next corner. The longer we stand there, the more faded the light becomes, so without another word, Agni and I begin following after the beckoning trail.

My pulse has still not managed to fully steady itself nor has the heat fully left my face. Internally, I'm absolutely furious, both at myself and the pig-headed captain next to me.

Absolute fucking moron.

Just when I thought I was beginning to finally analyze him correctly, he turns around and shows me he can be even more unpredictable than I'd thought. He's downright impossible.

The sound of our boots churning up sand fills the space between us.

I grow more pensive with every step, struggling to bind down the traitorous thoughts regarding what I was about to do. My swallow is tight when reimagining the counterattack I was aiming, the move I was poised to slide into place had the emblems at my backside not appeared.

I refuse to even so much as glance at the prick. I'm glad he doesn't speak. I have no idea what sort of things would leave my mouth if I was forced into a conversation right now.

A pattern of the tides themselves pulls us further and further along for almost twenty more incredibly tense minutes. Until finally the passageway itself halts altogether at a dead end.

"*Seriously*?" I bark in disbelief, breaking the unspoken pact of silence.

Agni remains silent, to a point where I'm forced to turn around in irritation. His eyes don't even flicker towards my questioning scowl, which only riles me up more inside. Instead he remains focused on the dead end wall before us with a contemplative look on his face.

"Touch it," he orders, meeting my eyes at last before nodding to the wall in meaning.

"*You* touch it," I counter immediately, like a petulant child. The edge in my voice is even sharper than usual. Our latest game has rattled me more than I'm prepared to acknowledge.

He snorts before letting out a low sigh, it reminds me of the way Kleio often does when she deems something I do as 'being difficult'. Pressing his palm against the wall, a pale glow emanates from beneath his hand but nothing else happens.

Removing said palm, Agni looks down at me pointedly.

Shaking off the urge to throw another blade his way, I huff out a breath and place my hand upon the stone. It glows like before, except *much* brighter. But nothing else happens.

I'm about to pull away when Agni's hand splays itself right next to mine along the wall. The size comparison between our hands is almost comical to observe. I endeavor not to stare at each of his many golden rings too obviously but I'm not quite sure I succeed.

The pretty ruby one on his pinky catches my eye in particular.

The wall flares brighter than ever before, giving way to a pulsing sensation. Almost like the 'click' of a lock. Just like the one I felt at the checkpoint before.

"That worked," I announce, dropping my hand with confidence.

"How are you—" Agni starts questioning my certainty when the solid wall abruptly begins to crumble. It's not a very wide panel to begin with, so the whole thing collapses in a matter of seconds. His hand just narrowly pries itself backwards before becoming part of the wreckage.

To my undying surprise, Agni starts *laughing,* like he just can't help himself.

Eeking my gaze over to check whether he's having some sort of psychotic break, I'm even more startled to discover that he's laughing at *me*. "*What*?" I ask defensively, and my hands immediately begin patting myself down for anything awry.

He chuckles with a shake of his head. "Nothing." My eyes narrow, I don't believe him for a second.

Agni moves to lean nonchalantly inside the newly made archway before coolly motioning for me to walk through first. When my lips purse in clear annoyance, a smirk again tugs on his features.

The jackass has left me just enough space to enter past him, so long as I press myself up against his person. Breathing out a long-winded huff of irritation, I brush by Agni with the shake of my head, ignoring the unyielding hardness of his chest against mine in passing.

Exiting reveals that we've just discovered a very large, very dark ocean grotto. The warmth of Agni's presence at my backside tells me that he's surveying the new location from only inches away.

I ignore that too.

The cavern is puzzling in its lack of anything besides black solemn waters and I'm not quite certain what exactly it is we've entered. I worry for a moment that maybe this isn't a checkpoint at all, and take a step towards the dark waterline.

Several things seem to trigger at once.

The glass-like onyx surface begins rippling ominously, with some sort of high keening coming from its depths. While a sound, like the whooshing of air, emanates from behind. A backward glance divulges that the crumbled entranceway has reversed into its fully solidified state.

I step past the south captain's annoying statue-like presence to press my palm against the newly erected wall. Nothing. No pulsing sensation. Not even a shimmer of light at my touch.

"We're *stuck,*" I mutter in outward annoyance before cursing beneath my breath.

A low rumbling shudders beneath our feet and abruptly returns my attention to the grotto where new additions have been made. From beneath the ominous surface, two parallel paths of sea stone have emerged. They both extend out to the grotto's midpoint, separated by several meters of dark open water, and end in dual circular platforms.

Glancing at Agni I find his eyes are tracing something on the opposite side of the grotto. I follow his line of sight over to an archway that's been outlined in that same goading white light as before. In the center of the second gate lie two empty sockets, I'd wager they need to be filled in order to open it.

I suppose filled by *what* is truly the question.

Agni and I look back at each other simultaneously. The same idea is reflected in our gazes, as if we had spoken it aloud. An awful lingering heat stirs somewhere down low and I glance away from him with a short nod in silent confirmation.

He takes the left path and I take the right.

Agni's newly reserved state is yet another way to keep me feeling off-footed, I'm sure. It's deeply troubling how easily he manages each one of his many personalities. I get the strangest sense that he's *angry* with me. For what I cannot imagine, but it makes me throw curious sideways glances at his stony face until we both reach the end of our walkways.

Approaching my circular ledge, a table comes into view. Upon it rests a scallop shell larger than my own head. I look over to find a similar table on the opposite platform but only a teeny tiny vial rests on Agni's altar. A smart-ass comment comes to mind and I snort to myself in response.

Peering downwards again, I study the milky liquid filling the ocean basin.

It shines a curious iridescent hue in the dim light and I begin tilting the massive shell over to examine it. A gasp leaves my mouth when two glittering sapphires, one cobalt and the other teal, both roughly the size of my palm, are revealed beneath the liquid's surface. After quickly rescanning the fading archway across the grotto, I conclude that the gemstones must be keys.

"Care to share, Boreas?" Agni drawls, his tone exasperatingly bored.

Ignoring him, I grab for the stones, only to find nothing but liquid. I grab for them again with the same impossible result. I try again and again, becoming more enraged with every attempt.

What the hell?

"There's gemstones at the bottom of this basin and they match up with the sockets on the wall. Pretty positive that they're the keys to open the second gate for us and our crews."

"The issue being?" he inquires airily, his tone grating on my nerves.

"I can't—grasp them. The liquid in here is somehow—impenetrable." Even as I say it, I find myself trying once more to no avail. Agni is silent for a long enough moment before I tilt my head in his direction and find him holding up the impossibly tiny vial in inspection.

"Is the liquid in your bowl a pearl sort of color by chance?" he questions, his voice unusually flat.

"It is," I confirm.

Agni huffs low in obvious annoyance. "Then that would be acheronian poison and one of us is going to have to drink it in order to get to those stones."

My hands remove themselves from the shell basin immediately, just as a sharp 'crack' echoes inside the dimly lit cave.

Turning around, I discover that both stone pathways have broken off from our respective platforms, and I watch in mute horror as they begin descending back beneath the eerie surface to the depths below. Leaving us stranded on our individual dais in the middle of the dark grotto.

"Well, Boreas, it looks like that someone is going to be *you* then," Agni remarks with a slight frown before holding up his tiny vial once again from across the expanse. "This is panacea serum, just a bit more than a dose. I'm going to have to swim it over to you."

"That hardly seems fair," I snap in irritation. "I have to drink a bucket of poison and you have to what—swim half a pool's length?"

The gripe has barely even left my mouth before movement begins churning up the water near Agni's platform. Both our eyes track the billowing liquid in deadly silence as a large obsidian fin with rust-colored spikes, each the size of a rapier, breaks free from the eerie onyx waves.

I don't need to see the rest of the creature to know what lurks below.

A hafgufa.

The thing now beginning to parade in colossal circles around Agni's isolated dais is a monster of old. A massive beast of a fish that's said to swallow ships whole and spit men back out by their bones. Each one of those razor-sharp spikes is imbued with a fatal poison of their very own.

"That ought to even up the participation," he mutters angrily with a snort in my direction, along with a few very choice words, both in his own foreign tongue and mine.

I watch as Agni begins unslinging his twin broad swords before removing his belt in visible annoyance. Something about the movements strikes me as odd. My eyes narrow in on him.

"Why don't you just blast that thing?" I question.

He pauses his weapon removal to lift an aristocratic brow in my direction. "*Blast* it?"

"Yeah. You know—" I push my palm out in a mock imitation of the way I've seen him bring raging spheres of flames to life. "Like that."

His responding snort is derisive.

I grind my teeth in annoyance. "Alright, well, you could at least sear off its fins or heat up the water. I know for a fact that this is not a creature who will enjoy that."

He gives me a queer look before saying slowly, "I'll keep that in mind."

Tilting my head, I study his strange expression further until it dawns on me. " *You* took the kratosbane too!" I gasp, knowing I'm right as soon as I've said it.

Agni's eyes roll skyward and back, his jaw flexing with the movement. His lack of denial is proof enough and he sets about organizing his possessions before tucking the tiny vial into a concealed pocket along his chest.

The knowledge that he took the kratosbane has me somewhat reeling again. Especially after our most recent spar. Yet another piece of his puzzle that just *doesn't* seem to fit.

Once Agni's set on preparing everything he'll need for whatever strategy he's formed, he turns to face me. "It'll be quickest if we go at the same time. That amount of acheronian will probably take you quite a while to get through anyway. It's slow acting but I'll try getting over there as fast as I can."

I scowl at him to cover the nerves beginning to wreak havoc on my insides. "How do I know you'll even give me the antidote? If you manage to make it past that thing, you could just grab the stones and leave me here to rot."

His face appears nonplussed while shrugging. "You don't. You also don't really have a choice."

Always such an arrogant little prince.

"Alright, Boreas—let's go!" he barks out with a determined clap of his hands. Something in his voice reminds me of an instructor. Like an encouraging preceptor urging me onward during a particularly difficult training set.

I nod without argument.

Picking up the basin, I peer down again at the milky liquid, real fear pumping through my veins. Acheronian poison is not your average run-of-the-mill killer. It is both a physical and mental trap. The disarmingly pretty liquid provides a slow, agonizing death while producing both pain and terror for the consumer.

A large splash in the nearby water steadies my resolve.

Fuck it.

I begin downing liquid misery like it's summer wine.

XLIII. SWEETLY

The first few mouthfuls go down too quickly for my body to even react.

Then, on the fourth or fifth swallow, my system seems to register everything at once. The scream I omit is so loud that it startles even myself.

I'm on *fire*.

I'm burning alive from the inside out.

The weight of the heavy bowl in my hands is the only thing reminding me to drink. Meanwhile every ounce of my being is screaming at me to drop it. I've only just begun and I'm already terrified of the pain.

The deviant, reckless, willfulness of my youth steps up to stare down the internal fear. I drink another mouthful, and another, and another.

I drink until I've begun spiraling into an agony that's unlike anything I've ever felt before. Simultaneously, an unbearable yet deeply familiar despair starts pressing in on me from all around. Tears I never allow for slide quickly down my face.

Gritting my teeth, I force myself to keep going.

I discover I'm suddenly twelve again, kneeling in Skelm's office as he brands me for the very first time. It's a small enough line, barely the size of my index finger, but I'd never felt anything like it before in my life. The scream that erupts from me is so strenuous I'm afraid it's going to snap a vocal cord.

But that brand didn't stop me from rolling out of my bunk the next morning and throwing a punch at the first raider stupid enough to look my way.

So I drink again.

I'm thirteen now and Preceptor Ersatz is ironing my hands after I was caught stealing food past curfew. Vash Larceon had been putting sand in all my meals for the last week and I was starving. My cry is high-pitched in anguish, tears flow freely from my impossibly young and haunted eyes.

The next night, I snuck out of my cabin and smashed every single piece of valuable artwork on the entire main level of that dark fortress.

So I drink again.

I'm fourteen with freshly shorn hair, being forced to walk along a path of searing coals for three minutes. One for each highborn life I took. Every time I fall down in pain, my tormentors restart the clock. I feel stone crashing violently into my knees from another world as I endure the unendurable pain.

A week later was the first time I ever stole a speeder and found in it a reason to continue living.

So I drink again.

I drink, and I drink, and I drink until there's nothing left.

I've just been made captain and I kneel once more before that most terrible hearth. Eight large brands, the biggest I've ever been given, are pressed into my back with maddening deliberation.

I grit through each and every one, willfully taking responsibility for and shielding those whom the torture is truly intended. As I will continue to do until my very last breath.

The world tilts backwards.

A clattering sound emanates from somewhere very far away.

I can do nothing but writhe in pain as flames lick over every inch of my person. A fire born of my own deviancy begins destroying me from the inside out.

I endure it.

Year.

After.

Year.

I endure it.

Until I'm freezing cold and don't feel much of anything at all.

"Come on, drink—you have to—*drink,*" someone pleads.

Their deep, commanding voice comes from somewhere far above. It reminds me of an old, familiar beam of halcyon light, penetrating through the frigid surface of my depthless misery. They sound both terrified and inconceivably exhausted.

"You have to drink, *please*—Merena—*drink!*" that halcyon light demands, shouting down at me like the sun to the sea. Something about hearing their low sinful tenor saying my name reminds me exactly how to swallow.

The unmistakable sounds of my crew's laughter begins trickling down my throat. Voices that are the closest thing I have to a home drop one by one down to my core before slowly unraveling inside of me. Relief like I've never felt in my life starts to spread throughout my being.

"There you—go," the very weary sun says, barreling through the last of my bitter cold until the world comes roaring back into existence. "You took it—like a—fucking—*champ.*"

I gasp out in sudden keenness.

It feels like I've been stumbling around inside a midnight fog only to be yanked into a painfully bright high-noon. Sounds and colors are so vivid that my head might just burst from the intensity of it all. I think I groan out in pain.

"It's *s'okay* now—you're okay now—it's over, you're okay," the sun mumbles from nearby, invoking in me the soothing image of dusk. His voice is soft, like the very last rays of light, just before stars begin winking into existence.

That's my favorite time of day, I recall faintly.

The frightening roar of reality finally begins to dull and my senses start returning to their usual state. Blinking hard, I open my eyes at last to the dripstone ceiling above and surge upward onto my forearms in sudden remembrance.

The hafgufa.

The poison.

The gems.

I find Captain Agni lying across from me, soaking wet. His breathing comes in and out in deeply labored heaves. Scanning the waters, I'm startled to find the massive, man-slaughtering monster of old bobbing along the surface with tendrils of crimson pouring out from all sides.

He killed it. *Without* his affinity.

He killed it and then he—

"You gave me the antidote," I rasp out. My throat is unbearably raw and I now remember screaming. Embarrassment colors my cheeks while I roughly wipe away all traces of tears.

He only manages a breathless nod in response.

Agni's obsidian hair plastered about his brow exposes just how startlingly pale he is. Something about the shine in his eyes studying my face strikes me then as *wrong*. I look at him again, with a more shrewd gaze. My assessment halts on the rust-colored spike laying just at the opposite end of his outstretched legs.

It's got *blood* on it.

"Were you cut with that?" I ask, jolting to my knees.

He chuckles softly with another small dip of his chin by way of retort. A deadly blue tint has begun creeping into his lips and something inside of me tilts. I have the sudden urge to vomit.

My face scrunches itself up tight in confusion. He's been poisoned. He had the antidote right there in his hand—and then he just—he just—*gave it to me?* It makes absolutely no sense.

I shake my head in angry frustration. *Why?* Why is he always doing this shit—it never, *ever* makes any sense.

Looking back to Agni, I find him watching me.

An idea comes to mind.

A terrible, horrible, self-destructive kind of idea.

But if he was correct and there really *was* a bit more than one dose of panacea, then—well—*fuck*. I suppose I have to at least try.

Not to mention that if he dies, our od will never be fulfilled, leaving my captaincy title sworn to it completely up to chance. This is what I tell myself when making the decision.

His quickly fading form watches me crawl to him with the ghost of a smirk on his lips and a hint of wickedness in his eyes. The kind that makes me want to punch him somewhere low for what I now have to do.

My face comes to hover a foot above his own, now laying back to study the ceiling. His eyes find mine and I watch as they flicker with an underlying wariness. The raging beat inside of me is just as brutal and savage, as if my affinity were released.

"The—our od isn't finished—so—I can't—I can't let you die." I stumble over the words in a rush to get them out of my mouth before he makes a comment that's certain to make me regret this.

Something bitter flashes through Agni's gaze and strains in his jaw but he doesn't speak.

"The—there's only one way I can think of to get you the antidote." My eyes drift to his lips, now beginning to turn violet, before returning hesitantly to his eyes. "I—you gave me more than one dose and—panacea is quite potent so—I think—well, the—whatever is—I could—you know."

Agni blinks at me, his expression utterly nonplussed, which only makes the thrashing inside that much harder to quell.

Gods, he is insufferable.

I huff a short breath to shake out the last of my nerves, then close my eyes tight and move down to press my lips against his. But an unexpectedly firm hand on my arm halts me no more than an inch from his face.

"No," Agni states.

My eyes open wide to find the very last dregs of that arrogance playing about his features only mere centimeters from my own. The wickedness I glimpsed before in his gaze is now much *much* more than just a hint.

"*What*?" I sputter, bewildered.

He flashes one of his cruelest smiles yet. "Beg me."

I stare at him, mouth open, both shocked and furious. *Surely he cannot be serious?* Unfortunately for me, he can.

Agni's smile grows deeper and his face loses even more of its coloring while taking in my appalled reaction. "Beg me to kiss you, Boreas—or I will die—and I'll take your captaincy right along with me," he promises, his voice coming out uncharacteristically faint.

Outrage flares bright inside and I know he both sees and enjoys it. I study his face for another minute. It only reaffirms to me his sincerity. He would *actually* do it—die and take the od with him—just to spite me. His capacity for getting beneath my skin truly knows no bounds.

"Tik-tok," Agni taunts weakly.

He's becoming colder and colder beneath me with every passing moment. I clench my teeth, hating how even on the brink of death he continues to find ways to best me at every turn. His eyes watch mine intently and they flash fiendishly the instant I find my resolve.

Lowering myself back to his lips, I work hard to shove down the rising heat wave of humiliation. He's saved my life thrice now. I could do this.

I have to.

"Please—*please* kiss me," I whisper.

His answering voice is ashen. "Again."

Growling low in pure frustration, my hand cups his jaw and I press my mouth to his once, twice. "*Please,*" I plead onto his stupidly cold lips. "Please—please *kiss me*," I implore again.

The jackass might as well be carved from marble for all the good it does.

"More," he demands of me.

Sadistic fucking prince.

If it wasn't for my crew, I would slit his throat right now. But I made them a promise and I would not let them down. I'd meant what I said, by whatever means necessary.

So I straddle him, bringing my body down flush against his. My voice takes on an edge of real panic, making the pleas I emit sound truly distraught. "Please kiss me, *Agni,*" I murmur softly against his mouth, desperate as a prayer, my fingers gently tracing the golden lines of his scar.

"I need—I *want* you to kiss me—*please,*" I urge him, my teeth lightly grazing his bottom lip.

"Kiss me—kiss me *please*—I'm begging you, Agni, *kiss me*!" I finally cry out.

He chuckles darkly onto my lips. "Alright, alright, I'll kiss you, Boreas." His voice is rough, almost strained. Alarmingly cold hands find my hips and he turns us over abruptly, dragging me down beneath him. "But only because you begged me *ever* so sweetly."

Before I get the chance to brandish either blade or retort, Agni brings his lips down to mine. I quickly discover his mouth is every bit as soft as it looks, even while ice cold. The familiar scent of spice ushers within me a tide of something truly perilous.

I allow for him to part my lips without hesitation. His tongue finds mine with expert precision and I pray to whichever heathen god blessed me that whatever traces of the antidote left inside my mouth are enough.

Agni's hands find themselves cupping my jaw, around my throat, down my sides, and at my waist, like he can't figure out where he wants to touch me first. Said touches rouse in me a fervor that is alarmingly similar to the tidepool hallucination. Except this time I know it's real.

That awareness only makes my involuntary response to him all the more horrifying.

Sickening desire ambushes me like a well-trained assassin and I begin returning his kisses with mortifying ardor. He tastes even better than I imagined, like cardamom and orange groves and *dusk*. It is truly alarming to realize just how easy falling into addiction would be.

That eagerness, to my eternal chagrin, is *not* lost on him. A soft chuckle slips from Agni, causing my insides to twist with shame. I lash out at his smugness by biting down on his lower lip hard enough to split skin and taste copper.

I'm neither expecting nor prepared for the response it brings.

Agni *groans* into my mouth, deep and raw and carnal. Then his sordid lips set about devouring mine with a kind of hunger I can scarcely even conceive.

Kissing him is entirely different from any of my previous experiences. So different that, in a way, it feels as though I've never really been kissed before. It doesn't erect the expected fluttering's I've received from other boys. Nor can I compare it to the stimulating electricity with Kerau.

This is unmistakably *other*.

It's more similar to the feeling of surfing a great and terrible wave during a summer storm. It provides me the same high as riding a freshly broken kelpie. It fills me with a forbidden pleasure akin only to sneaking out in the dead of night to steal a speeder.

It's like I'm being injected with the exact same stimulant that led me to break The Order's rules time and again. The same dangerous, reckless, heart-racing thrill, I chased after repeatedly just to feel something. *Anything*. Other than my own crushing misery.

"Tell me what you think of me," Agni suddenly demands, low and insistent against my lips. "Tell me what you really—honestly—think of me." His voice is hoarse.

"I find you—*deplorable*," I gasp out truthfully in between breaths as one kiss slides into another and another. He groans low again in response, deepening the angle he has on me. The hand he moves back to grip my throat is noticeably warmer.

"What else?" he bites out.

"I think you're despotic," I admit, my hands threading into his wet, maddening hair with a feeling of dark and secret indulgence.

Agni kisses me harder.

"You're loathsome—and conceited—and terribly insolent," I say, one hand now clinging onto the front of his uniform.

"Yes," he agrees in earnest.

"Downright despicable," I pant.

Agni pulls away slightly, revealing the fire returning to his eyes and the golden hue to his skin. The expression on his face is one of pure ruthlessness as he firmly plants his knees between my thighs, hooks my legs up around his waist, and returns his mouth to mine with a vengeance.

He sets about capturing one of my wrists next, pinning it to the ground above my head. My breathing hitches through the constant collision of our tongues at the unexpected confinement. "*Volo facere inenarrabilia sunt ad vos,*" he murmurs sinfully upon my lips before restraining my other hand so that they're each held prisoner inside one of his iron grasps.

The feeling of combustion becomes concerning.

"Is that all?" Agni taunts.

His vicious scar flashes in the corner of my vision, like real lightning. The image invokes a daunting chill that rises up and over my body like a shroud. "I think you might be a nightmare," I whisper, hardly recognizing my own voice. It's so horribly thick with lust.

Something about that comparison seems to strike a cord for him. Agni shudders above me as if he too can somehow feel the chill of my morbid reverie.

"*More*—tell me more." His debauched command sounds like a devotion. His wicked mouth finds my jaw, then my neck, all the while my hands are locked up tight. I think I could die from this. It feels like some sort of preordained sacrilege.

"You're so—completely—" I can barely think with his lips avidly pursuing my throat. I manage to land on "*excruciating*," in the same instant he finds that spot where my pulse beats most noticeably. The word comes out as a traitorously loud moan of indisputable pleasure.

Every inch of my body feels as if it's just awakened from a thousand-year slumber.

My audible hedonistic enjoyment has the effect of unraveling whatever small increment of restraint he evidently had left. Like the swipe of a match, I feel a spark of undeniable heat physically *jolt* within him.

Agni's mouth returns to mine like he has some sort of score to settle.

Without breaking contact from my lips, he firmly switches over one of my wrists so that both are now held in a single grasp. His newly freed hand begins traversing the sinuous planes of my body in torturous exploration. I can do nothing but writhe beneath him as he ravages my mouth.

"I've never—hated anyone—like I hate you," I confess around his skillful lips.

The sound he makes in response to that admission is dark and depraved.

Agni's hand moves next to my hair and I tense.

Faster than lightning, he pulls out the pin, securing the golden accessory atop my head. My hair tumbles down in damning white waves around me. His lips leave mine and I glance up to find eyes of scorching amber devouring the sight of my newly freed mane.

An old wound twists my gut painfully and causes a pricking behind my eyes, so I look away.

In a blink, he's cupping my jaw and turning my head before bringing his lips flush against my ear. "*Gorgeous,*" he growls murderously low, suddenly furious. " *You're. Fucking. Gorgeous.*" I shiver into the sound of his voice. It's darker and more terrifying than any monster my night terrors could ever hope to concoct.

His nose traces the outline of my ear before his mouth begins pressing searing kisses all the way across my jawline. "So. Gorgeous. It's. *Fucking*. Criminal." Each one evokes from me a horrifying moan and he uses the last one I omit to recapture my lips.

Agni's free hand slips beneath the thin fabric of my uniform and the tight bindings around my chest like a thief in the night.

A calloused palm cups one of my bare ample breasts to find it already taut. Arching reactively into his gentle squeeze, I let out an aching whimper against his mouth while my hips rock upward in response. My core is met with what I can only guess is a godsdamned broadsword at his waist.

No fucking *wonder* he's so insufferably arrogant.

The friction makes us both gasp.

"*Mer—Boreas—fuck.*" Agni chokes on a strangled growl, drawing away from my lips and body once more. I look up through a heady gaze to find him scanning down my person with an almost murderous shine to his blazing eyes. I wriggle against his unyielding hold to no avail.

My heart is slamming so violently inside my ribs that I think it will probably leave bruises of evidence atop my skin. A fracturing sensation cuts down deep along that icy wall beneath my caged affinity, more severe than ever before.

I ignore it.

"What are you *doing*?" I seethe, enraged.

He replies in a voice like smoke, "*Committens hoc to memoria.*" His gaze rakes over me continually while a war I'm not privy to rages in his eyes.

This is a whole new kind of torture. It's quite possibly the very worst form of heat I've ever experienced. I'm torn between demanding to be released immediately and the feeling that if he does not continue touching me, I will in fact die.

Biting down on a lip against my own damnation, I give in and plead.

"*Please* Agni—*more.*"

His kesar-ringed eyes widen before rolling skyward with a painful sounding groan. He draws in a deeply ragged breath and I notice for the first time that there are tremors raging violently through his body.

His hand finds my jaw, a gold-beringed thumb roughly claiming my lower lip. " *Quomodo sunt vos melius etiam quam mea phantasiae?*" he whispers.

With his chest now pressed against mine, I can feel his heartbeat, every bit as violent and savage as my own.

"You'll be *my death*, you know that?" he asks angrily, amber eyes searching mine.

I only manage to nod, too terrified of what might come out of my mouth if I should speak, but not really understanding at all.

His lips take mine, more blistering and volatile than ever before, and I drink with damning eagerness from the delirium of dusk.

This *cannot* happen ever again.

XLIV. RAW

A sound I can only guess would compare to some sort of volcanic eruption shakes the grotto.

It has the effect of ripping the south captain and myself out of the mania of our own creation. Reality comes barreling down on me with the force of a thousand suns.

I bolt upright in alarm, just as Agni rolls off me with effortless fluidity. My breathing is embarrassingly winded while scrambling to my feet. I snatch my fallen hair piece and quickly readjust myself as the ground and ceiling stop their troubling shaking.

Avoiding the sight of Agni's face altogether I stride for the knocked over shell-basin a few feet away and scoop up the two gemstones now free from their poison prison. My gaze then turns to the black waters where I find a new pathway to the opposite shore was erected while we were... *distracted*.

I can feel his eyes tracking me, hot as coals.

Glancing backwards at last, I expect to find Agni's expression smug and insufferable. I instead discover the same emotions of shock and alarm guttering inside his gaze that are filling me near to bursting. His reddened lips are swollen and already slightly bruised, while his midnight hair looks more disheveled than I've ever seen.

The image has a frighteningly intense effect on me.

For a moment we just stare at each other. Our eyes roving over the ravage we've done to one another in a manner of minutes. I feel infinitesimally better to note that his chest also heaves with recovering breaths.

There's a split second in which his eyes flash down to my lips, which feel just as enticingly tender as his own appear, then back to my face fixedly. His posture shifts fractionally in my direction. It looks for a heartbeat like he's about to damn us both and finish what was started.

A shrill shout from somewhere out beyond the dark grotto splinters whatever remaining trance existed between us. We both flinch at the unanticipated noise and hurry for the exit without another word.

I pop the first crystal into its spot on the wall but pause before inserting the second. Turning to look at the south captain, I find his face as remote and emotionless as I've ever seen. It makes an unreasonable part of me instantly angry and my next words come out colder than necessary.

"That concludes our od. We're done now."

Agni blinks down at me, his brows raising ever so slightly. "Obviously."

His condescending drawl has me balling my hands into fists to keep from drawing a weapon. Which, technically, I *could,* and there would be no repercussions for it. The od is done. There's nothing binding us. I could pull a knife on him right now.

I could eliminate our biggest competition before even setting foot in the heart.

"Thinking about slitting my throat now, *little bastard*?" Agni sneers, his tone bitter.

I flinch, glancing down to find a hilt already in my hand with no memory of even grabbing for it. Terrible heat licks up my neck. "It crossed my mind," I answer honestly, meeting his gaze again after sliding the knife back at my waist.

Murderous intensity blazes from the depths of his stare but I refuse to step down, my chin lifts incrementally. Familiar annoyance flickers in his features before he reaches out and roughly swipes the gemstone from my hand. The slight evokes from me an angry snarl of offense.

An overreaction.

Probably.

Agni chuckles, infuriating me even more, and shoves the second crystal into place.

Both stones glow before the arch gives way and swings outwards like a proper door. Agni, being the full-time prick that he is, cuts me off and steps through the exit first. Biting down on the inside of my cheek, I follow after him while a feeling like rage ripples off my bones.

Each of his normally vexing, but overall small jabs, are now a hundred times more provoking. I feel aggravatingly raw. From my still-restrained affinity to my physical being.

The space we emerge into is sheltered by the same fossilized stone as before, but we're no longer secluded by narrow tunnels. Instead, the area is massive, several saltwater rivers weave back and forth throughout. Every one of them leads to a different exit path, a different route to the heart. Caverns open here and there like great big mouths and each waterway is wide enough for a speeder to make it through.

Port Capillary.

A thrill runs through me at the sight of it.

I made it. I *actually* made it to the third checkpoint leading to the last gate before the heart and The Vault just beyond. Which means—my eyes narrow and I scan the mouth-like openings for any sign of my crew. From the corner of my eye, I catch sight of Captain Agni doing the same.

We lifted our side of the gate, so long as our crews found their corresponding entrances they should be here any—as if on cue, the ground begins trembling beneath my feet.

My head turns and I find amber eyes already on me. The sound of rushing water and multiple different octaves of shouting explode into the luminous port, severing our eye contact.

Two moonlighters rush in from parallel cavities, bringing with them a swell of water and loud hostile voices. Excitement and worry fight for dominance as I spot my crew, their tythe-tokens shining like literal beacons in the dim cavern. Excitement takes hold as I count and then recount seven whole and able bodies in total.

Worry steals back purchase as I realize the two speeders are shouting *at* each other. Kleio's affinity can be seen glittering in just the right light as it wraps protectively around our craft. Which is good, because the southern speeder has since pulled seven metal-tipped crossbows on my vessel.

A deep chuckle echoes from a jackass nearby.

The sound floods me with an overwhelming sense of rage. I move for the outskirts of our ledge to get the attention of my crew when a hand of solid iron halts me with a grip around my wrist.

"*What?*" I spit, twisting up to face Agni in a sudden burst of rage. Blood heats my cheeks, and I internally begin strangling the rousing feelings that this very specific touch from him now forever holds over me.

The crook of his mouth pulls upwards in obvious amusement at my venomous demeanor. My hand twitches as I think again about backhanding his overly conceited face.

"Tell your pack of mongrels to drop their weapons," I snap.

Agni frowns, brows-furrowing, shaking his head in mock disappointment. "Now just what sort of parley do you expect to broker here with me using such a viscous attitude as that, Boreas?"

Tearing my wrist from his grasp, I snarl, "*Parley*? This isn't a negotiation you prick. Order them to back off of my crew—*now*."

His eyes blaze, it's clear just how much he abhors my audacity in giving him a direct command. The offense in our gap of societal status is plain in his jaw clenching dangerously tight and my lip curls up high in disgust.

The shouting from beyond heightens further, taking my exceedingly shortened temper with it. Huffing out in frustration, I shove past him forcefully and stalk for the edge of our outcropping. I just barely make it to the lip I'm aiming for when Agni captures another wrist and harshly spins me around to face him. But this time my reflexes are quicker.

My free hand pulls out the blade strapped to my opposite thigh, and with one deft movement, the sharpened tip rests beneath his jaw. Surprise flares bright in his eyes and I laugh, which has the effect of darkening them.

"Let me go and call off your dogs," I hiss, enjoying his irritation at my swift maneuvering immensely. "In exchange, I won't shove this pointy bit of metal through your pretty highborn skull."

He gives me a blink of annoyance before slowly widening his eyes at something high above my head with a low gasp. Like a fucking *idiot* I fall for it and loosen my leverage. He tightens the grip on my wrist, yanking downward before kicking my shin—*hard*.

I bark out a string of outraged curses while he uses the momentary distraction to dislodge the blade from my grip. He grabs my other wrist in his opposite hand. Pulling me closer to his chest, I violently deny the shiver that beckons.

"*Merena*?—MERENA!" Kleio shouts from somewhere behind me, her voice echoed by the others. Their chorus of excited shouts sounds like home.

"Captain—hey! There you—*oh*," Vagar starts calling towards Agni but gets cut off by his own obnoxiously loud barking laugh and promptly switches to their southern tongue. "*Paenitet, sumusne interpellatione aliquid?*"

Their captain before me stills. His eyes leave my face to flit to someone, or rather multiple someone's, behind me. I watch as a cocky smirk eclipses his features, and he flashes his brows in the direction of what I assume to be his approaching crew.

"*Iustus paulum negotium.*" Agni calls back to his second, pulling me close enough that my forearms press parallel to his chest. I begin shoving away from his grip, yet he holds firm, so I seethe up with indignation as close as I can get in his stupid fucking face.

Unfortunately for me, he seems to thoroughly enjoy that.

"*Quid negoti? Genus ubi illa terminus sursum nudus in lecto tuo*?" Vagar shouts, sounding closer now.

Whatever his second in command said was suggestive in some way. The howls of jeering laughter from his crew could tell me that alone but it's also evident in the heat of Agni's eyes and the amusement on his lips as I continue struggling in his grasp.

I am surprised, however, by the sharpness in Agni's retort. "*Nonne iam dixi tibi non loqui de puella?*"

"*Technice vos dixit nobis non loqui puellae directe.*" A new voice chimes in. This one I recognize as belonging to Captain Agni's third-in-command, Adiram Uthra.

Vagar's next comment is clearly taunting. "*Ea satis peritissimus gestatio equitatio lunalevius, ego bet illa posset accipere te ad somnum per noctem enim semel et det manum tuam quietem.*"

"Shut-the-fuck-*up,* Ophios," Agni replies, his tone is low and warning and just a tinge exasperated. It sounds like a phrase he has to use with his second aggravatingly often.

"Captain—give the word—Nimra's positioned." Kleio's voice is closer now from behind and I pause my constant movement. Now it's my turn to smirk as Agni looks briefly confused at my approaching crew before studying my face.

"You would risk being hit if she should miss?" His voice is suddenly caustic. I'm not certain I know where the sharpened edge of anger in his voice is coming from.

My smirk grows. "She won't miss."

Agni's eyes narrow in on my face to study it, trying to judge my certainty. He frowns when it becomes clear I'm not bluffing. "Fine. Ask me *nicely* and I'll call off the boys," he offers in his most patronizing tone.

"Ask you *nicely*?" I bite out.

Agni's smirk returns. "Perhaps *sweetly* would be the proper term."

Before I can riposte, he lowers his head to rest his lips just beside my ear. "After all, we both know you are *ever* so talented at asking me sweetly. Aren't you?" His voice is soft as ash.

Swallowing down the spike in my blood pressure, I pull back slightly to meet his gaze with my own homicidal glare. The look in his eyes meeting mine is one of pure wickedness. I think rage might just be a permanent emotion for me now.

"Agni?" I whisper, leaning in closer.

His kesar-shaded eyes stare back at me with a dizzying array of concealed thoughts. One layer hidden right after another. "Hm?" he asks expectantly, his tone a touch coarse.

"Call off your damn dogs before I put them down myself," I hiss before taking a page out of his book and kicking him square in the shin as hard as I possibly can. *Much* harder than he kicked me.

"Fucking—*brat*!" he barks out in pain.

My crew's eruption of laughter fills the cavern and I yank free my hands easily now that his attention is elsewhere. Scooping up my fallen blade, I make it to the edge where Kleio aims for. Agni's crew lifts their crossbows and my still-snickering second readies her shield.

"*Depone arma nunc!*" Agni snaps, his tone both sharp and peeved and my stomach drops. Kleio's shield has grown stronger in the last year, but I'm not positive whether or not it would be strong enough to take on seven iron bolts at once.

To my relief and stifled surprise, Agni's crew slowly lowers their weapons. The southern moonlighter docks at the opposite bank of the outcropping and their captain goes to rejoin his crew without another word. I despise how riled that simple act of impartiality gets me.

It was just a few kisses for depth's sake.

Get it together, Boreas.

My own craft reaches the ledge before me. Kleio steps up to the bow, her familiar sepia eyes scouring me for all signs of fatal injuries before letting slip a grin. I take her arm in mine and let her pull me into the moonlighter.

My smile is so wide when landing on the deck, I think it just might split my face in two.

"So then—Herse starts yelling at Raider Ophios, saying she's gonna put a muzzle on him and that's when things *really* start to get heated."

Kleio is reporting to me their side of the past few hours that we've been separated while Davina finishes inspecting me.

I'm still snickering from the recount of their escapades when Vi comes to worry over my face and neck. Her hands lightly graze over the blotches on my jaw and throat, the split on my lip, even the marks near my ear. Kaleidoscope eyes blink at me several times over.

"*Merena*," she hisses low.

I give her a look of complete innocence. "*What*?" I ask, matching her tone.

"What the fuck *happened*?" Vi asks, louder than she should.

My scowl is immediate as everyone in the speeder quiets and turns around to see what on Pontus the ever-so-even-tempered Leech Davina is snapping at her captain for. My lips remain tight and I avoid their gazes. This only makes it worse.

Kleio, of course, spots Davina's reason for question with agonizing swiftness. "What—wait—are those—is that from—*Captain Agni*?" Her question comes out in a threatening snarl.

Herse sits up ramrod straight at the helm before risking a look back in my direction. Seven pairs of eyes study me and my most recent injuries with cautious, borderline-murderous interest, and my scowl deepens further. Huffing a sigh, I roll my eyes to the cavernous ceiling and back.

"Technically," I admit, striving to keep my voice even.

"I again ask, *what* happened?" Implores Vi, her hand tensing slightly as it gently tilts my neck.

My arms cross, and I'm suddenly feeling quite raw and defensive. "We were just—um—you know—just *fighting*." Something in my off-key tone and the blushing noncommittal up-quirk of my lips alludes to them that my participation was indeed included very willingly in the event.

Vi relaxes beside me instantly while Kleio lets out an obnoxious guffaw in disbelief.

"What kind of fight, Cap? One for *air*, maybe?" Herse calls over a shoulder in my direction, her brows flashing suggestively.

My face turns a terribly dark scarlet and I sink down low in my spot, giving myself away completely. The entirety of my crew begins gaping at my *extremely* uncharacteristic response and I feel the sudden need to defend myself.

"I was saving his *life*!" I snap.

Kleio busts out laughing from where she sits across from me before taunting, "My my, don't *we* think highly of our skills."

My face reddens even further.

"No it—I had too—see he was poisoned—and we—well—the od wasn't done—so of course it—there wasn't a choice—and—" I start trying to explain but the whole godsdamned speeder hanging on my every stumbling word has me faltering.

"*Annnd*? For transparency's sake, of course." My second grins, mischief practically rolling off of her in waves.

"And—I had the antidote—" a deep flush threatens to swallow me whole "—in my mouth."

All seven of my crewmembers' jaws drop down to the deck of the shiny new moonlighter. Kleio then promptly keens right over and into my lap. I shake my head with a breathy laugh, my eyes rolling upwards at their dramatics.

Absolutely *incorrigible*, the lot of them.

"Hold on, hold on, hold on," Kleio demands, recovering herself back up to face me. "Is *that* what the drama back there was about? Why it looked like Captain-ten-feet-of-pure-fucking-menace was on the verge of kidnapping you?"

"Please," I say, scoffing a laugh. "That was just Agni being an ass for his own entertainment."

Kleio chuckles but then shakes her head of silver-threaded braids. "No, I'm serious, Merena. I thought we were going to be prying you out of his godsdamned hands back there for a second. He looked like he was seriously debating whether or not to just grab you and run."

"It's true," Herse confirms from the helm. "Up until you kicked the shit out of him." She snickers to herself in memory.

"It was *just* a bit of kissing," I state, completely exasperated. Even as something inside of my bones begins to tremble at the mere thought of said kissing.

Kleio, it seems, is exceptionally persistent today. "*Okay*, and then what about right before we left the port for our exit tunnel? He turned back to stare at you like—I don't know." She shakes her head again. "Like he was completely enraged but also—somehow—*amazed*?"

"Oh, that?" I ask, as a deviant smirk begins tugging at my features in memory of said expression.

"Now that was Agni finally realizing I nicked a few of his rings while we were—*fighting,*" I explain with a snort, holding up both the ruby pinky accessory of his I'd admired and, more importantly, his southern captaincy ring before giving them all a conniving flash of my brows.

Kleio glances at the pieces of stolen jewelry and back to my face with something like rapture in her eyes. "Merena, I think you might be a god," she whispers, slack-jawed.

The twins both eye one another silently before promptly sliding to their knees on the ground where I sit and begin bowing over me repeatedly with moronic emphatic worship. Vi actually gets up from healing the blotches along my throat to check on Herse in concern as she's become completely unintelligible while slamming her palms flat against the wheel in amusement.

My fourth begins howling so hard with laughter that she falls off her seat and hits her head near the stern. Nimra struggles through her own tears of mirth in helping Greer back up.

I snort softly at their ridiculous displays while sliding the heavy ruby ornament onto a finger.

The conversation eventually turns back to preparation and navigation through the vein-like rivers as we near the last gate to the heart. I listen to the new adjustments of our entrance and exit strategy while brushing Agni's stolen captain's ring against my lower lip idly.

My thoughts, for one *tiny* moment, become a bit dazed.

Gorgeous, he'd called me.

XLV. SURRENDER & EVOLVE

"Next left," Nephthys directs me.

I ease the speeder into the thinning vein of water, having switched back into acting helmsman after deeming my half hour of recovery much too long a break.

The saltwater rivers leading us down into that heart are a crossword patch of possible waterways and dryland tunnels towards entry. Only my fifth's growing confidence in her star-charting abilities keeps my nerves restrained. I don't think that prior little *distraction* with Captain Agni could have cost us more than twenty minutes but in here, every minute counts.

I can feel it when we're close to the last gate. It's like there's a pulsing sensation in the waters beneath our hull. It reminds me a bit of my affinities' own savage beat.

A lip slides between my teeth in anticipation as we round another fossilized coral bend. The brine-scented tunnel we sail through opens to reveal a very promising archway, just barely wide enough for the moonlighter to make it through. I grit my teeth while keeping us perfectly steady, so as not to damage the hull or get us stuck.

Us losing out on The Vault because we're idiotically jammed in too narrow of a passageway would be *just* my luck. A moment later and the tension in my shoulders eases fractionally in relief as we push out through the other side and into the widening chamber beyond.

That relief is so short-lived, it has to be some sort of godsdamned personal record.

The chamber in question is massive and promising, with an identical archway located at the opposite end. It looks so similar to the other checkpoints that I'm certain it must be the third. Our wonderful problem *now* being the rather large and very powerful whirlpool taking up most of the chamber, effectively cutting us off from the last gate.

The slew of swears I emit beneath my breath at not having my affinity at this very moment in time are damn near lethal. My fucking luck.

Swallowing down my rising temper, I call to Kleio, "Hiraeth—*shield*. I need to keep the speeder stable to attempt making it around the edge."

The churning waters echoing around the room drown out much of my voice and I don't hear Kleio respond. But then a dim violet hue glitters into existence around the bow. My pulse thunders in my ears as I gently press down on the throttle and begin creeping closer to the side of the monstrous whirlpool.

The moonlighter takes to the tug of the vortex far too easily, even *with* Kleio's shield. I curse before reflexively reversing the thrust in an attempt to resituate our angle. That does me no good, we're being pulled in even more now.

"LeRoi—what does backtracking look like?" I yell over my shoulder, fighting back panic.

It might be our only way out of this deathtrap but it's still not an option I'm overly ecstatic to take. Turning back and trying to find another route to the heart would cost us precious time. Time that was made even more precious because of my own stupidly selfish moments of weakness. I hate myself all over again.

The only respite I have is knowing I've got Agni's captaincy ring as well as that ruby one. Without his captain's ring, he can't get into The Vault. Which means that even if he *does* get to the doors first, he'll be forced to wait and fend off anyone else who makes it there before me. Thinking about how much that fact is no doubt pissing him off at this very moment actually makes me laugh during this incredibly perilous time.

"Not an option," Herse answers.

My amusement immediately abandons me. Something terrible wrestles in my gut as I turn around and find the tunnel we just came through has fully sealed itself off. Just like the grotto.

"*Shit*," I breathe.

I can only stall the moonlighter in place for so long. Kleio is already gritting her teeth, trying not to show how much effort it's taking to keep her shield in place. There's no way back, no way out of this but to attempt taking *on* the whirlpool. A fight that I'm almost certain we will not win.

Panic laces through every inch of my being and I begin shoving it back while trying to come up with any sort of maneuver to get us out of this one. If we were out in open waters, then this would be no problem. But locked inside this room, it's basically a death-sentence.

To make matters worse, the pulsing in the water beneath the moonlighter's hull feels as if it's somehow getting more and more powerful. I swear the vortex has started to churn even faster.

The sounds of my crew's panicking voices fight for my attention. Yet some very willful part of my brain is set on sifting through possible avenues out of this. None of which look good for us.

Then—my mind snags itself on a passing thought.

An idea.

A *realization*.

The first gate was like the first trial, 'survival requires endurance', and the second gate was like the second trial, 'alliances and weaknesses.' Then the third gate is—surrender and evolve.

Fuck.

If I'm wrong about this, it'll cost us more than just The Vault. It'll likely be our lives. But the previous checkpoints *all* had the same pulsing sensation as that in the surrounding waters.

There's one way I might be able to know for *almost* certain. "Hiraeth—cut the shield," I demand while sliding the helmsman visor up.

"*What*?" Kleio turns back to look at me like I've gone mad.

"Just for a second—*cut it!*"

She gives me a wary look before dropping the wall of energy around us. I keep a tight hold on the throttle to ensure we remain as stable as possible while steadily leaning my arm over the side of the vessel and into the waters below.

"*Captain*?" Greer's questioning voice is full of concern.

My hand dips gingerly into the frigid churning waters. I can feel that strange, otherworldly beat pressing in around my hand. The same exact rhythm as my own heart. For a moment, my crew members stare at me as if I've just thrown my last remaining scraps of self-preservation into the waters themselves.

I hold my hand down there until—*there it is.*

"What is *that*?" Kleio shrieks.

A rippling white light emerges from the waters around my hand. Exactly like the one along the walls of the Kórallian tunnels. It tumbles out and away as I stand back up to gauge its direction. Sure enough, the playful light chases the swirling vortex round and round before dropping down inside.

"Well shit," I mutter. This settles it, I'm *right.* Which is infinitely worse than having been wrong.

Ignoring my nerves, I turn to face my crew, who are all staring at me with varying shades of shock, worry, and quite possibly awe coloring their features.

I grimace before announcing, “I believe we are going to have to go *inside* the whirlpool.”

Their expressions look as though I’ve just told them I’m secretly in love with Preceptor Bealu and will be running away with him on the morrow.

I flatten my lips and nod tightly to confirm that they all have in fact heard me correctly. Taking a rallying breath, I look back to the monstrous whirlpool churning away at concerning speeds before us.

“That light—” I shout in explanation over the rushing sound of saltwater. "It led Captain Agni and me to the last gate, like some sort of beacon in the dark. If each checkpoint resembles one of the trials, then this would be the third one. Meaning that in order to get past it we have to—”

“*Surrender and evolve,*” Kleio gasps out suddenly, stealing the explanation from my lips.

I turn to my second with a tight-lipped nod of agreement. Her grimace now matches mine, as a sobering understanding has dawned in her eyes. We both frown like veritable mirrors of one another in the direction of the monstrous whirlpool.

"Alright, Cap, let's go then!” Herse shouts, her husky voice is determined and unquestioning.

I turn and rescan my crew as they look at their very possible deaths ahead and back to me with faces full of an unwavering confidence that I don’t really feel I deserve. A deep, dark dread fills me near to bursting when glimpsing their tythe-tokens. I bite the inside of my cheek while thrusting that emotion away and slamming my helmsman visor back down.

“*Alright,*” I shout. “I’m going to do my best to ease us in there and then I’m going to have to cut the throttle and let it take us. Hiraeth—I need you to shield the *second* that I’ve cut it—roger?”

“Roger,” Kleio confirms over the rising noise level. I can tell she’s every bit as aware of the risk we’re taking as I am. Worry is a vise squeezing my heart until it feels like it just might burst.

"Okay—everyone else—keep low and hold on with everything you've got," I demand of them.

I wait to hear their confirmations that they're securely in place before easing off the reverse thrust and angling us slowly into the very edge of the maelstrom. Just as before, the current begins pulling the moonlighter towards it with minimal effort.

I realize now that to have attempted to continue struggling against it around the edge would indeed have secured our death. Once we hit the central eddy, I cut the throttle.

"Throttle back!" I shout at Kleio.

Her shield instantly wraps around the vessel again and it's obvious just how much strain it's causing her to keep this up. She won't be able to use much more of it by the time we hit the heart. My insides roll themselves over at that realization but I fight through.

The whirlpool drags us round and round its perilous edges and we don't put up a fight. My hands cling to the side railing of the helm, and my teeth clench tight against my nerves. The rest of my crew keeps low to the deck, all hands grasping the rail for purchase.

Finally, we make it to the center, where the pulsing is so loud that I think it just might be my own heartbeat currently lodged inside my ears. There's only one thing I can think to do to withstand my welling terror as the maelstrom pulls us firmly into its clutches.

I whisper the gifted words again and again beneath my breath. "*Oderint dum metuant. Oderint dum metuant. Oderint dum metuant.*"

My breathless prayers are echoed by the sounds of my crew's screaming. I feel a tipping sensation beginning towards the bow and volatile saltwater sprays the side of my face.

The world disappears beneath our hull entirely as the monster swallows us whole.

The sensation of our speeder hitting water sends everyone bouncing nearly a foot off the deck. I slam back down against the helm, re-splitting my bottom lip against the wheel.

"Fucking *depths!*" I curse before wiping the blood from my mouth.

The shouts and swears from my crew members are thrown about like debris leftover from a particularly nasty storm. Which, I suppose, is exactly what we are. Blinking hard, I open my eyes, not daring yet to actually believe that we've made it through alive.

My eyes find Kleio's first, then Herse and Greer, Nephthys, Prisca, Nimra, and finally Davina.

All of my seven making up our sacred eight are *alive.* If not a bit frazzled and more than slightly pissed off from the impact of the drop but alive nonetheless.

I quickly scour our new surroundings. We appear to be floating along a dimly lit, green, lazy lagoon.

The passageway is much wider here, making it easier to navigate. It looks promising enough for a slow grin to begin inching across my face. That *was* the last gate. The heart will be just beyond for us to moor at and then go on foot to the tunnels leading to the holy doors of The Vault from there.

I look at Kleio and read my thoughts, clear as day, reflected in her eyes.

We made it.

That grin is promptly stolen after returning my attention to the helm in order to get us up and moving. I quickly come to realize that something is very, very *wrong.*

"This has *got* to be some sort of a godsdamned joke," I mutter angrily as I try the throttle again and again to absolutely no avail. The fall from the last gate must have knocked something loose.

"What's going on?" Kleio asks in alarm from my outward frustration.

"The helm—I can't—something's been jammed," I grumble, trying again to get it to move with no success. I finally slam my fist on the wheel in outright anger.

Breathing to a count of four, I stifle my growing temper before turning towards the stern in order to find idiot number *two*. "Prisca—looks like it's your time to shine. Throttle isn't working," I state flatly to the imp, currently lying lazily across her sister's lap.

She stands with ramrod straight attention and gives me an exaggerated salute. "Aye-aye, Captain!" Prisca quips, her white strands of loyalty shimmering through dual braided buns atop her head.

I roll my eyes in exasperation before slipping off the helm and allowing our resident engineer to take a look at the controls. Prisca's affinity for fixing anything technical or building it from scratch is what some raiders—like the assholes that run the North Order—call *Vek*.

Our speeder continues floating down the lazily winding lagoon as idiot number two narrows in on her gift and gets to work. It's actually quite interesting to watch her take something seriously for once. I stand there in observation while she works in this entrancingly different state until the sound of rushing water and echoing screams tears me from my study while drifting around the next bend.

My head swivels immediately to find the source of the screams but I end up falling short on explanation. I am impressed, however, to find Kleio's shield already locked into place and it somehow appears *way* stronger than before. I look at my second in question regarding her newfound strength and she grins in return.

"I forgot to tell you," Kleio says and my brows raise. "We found out something about Greer's affinity while you were too busy *making-out* with Captain Agni to join us."

My face becomes a crimson scowl of annoyance as my crew members break out into fits of snickering amusement at my second's well-aimed jibe. Kleio's brown eyes dance with goading mischief and I shake my head at her while tamping down on my own grin.

I give her a silent look in clear indication to continue explaining, as I don't currently trust myself to speak. My second laughs again at my deeply reddened face before continuing.

"So you know how our dear Greer's affinity is some sort of energy transfer? One that Bealu and Ersatz couldn't make out any sort of use for with their stunted little brains so they deemed her *Vek* and then tossed her aside?"

I nod tightly with something like violence and a need for revenge simmering behind that restricted wall inside. Looking over to Greer sitting near the stern, I find her face appears a bit flushed and I swear there's a glint of triumph shining in her olive eyes. I whip back around to Kleio with clear interest in what exactly it is they've figured out in my absence.

"Well, if only they had thought to actually *attempt* doing their godsdamned jobs," Kleio says with that rare spark of anger in her eyes that I always enjoy seeing. "They'd have realized that she's basically a fucking jump starter for your affinities. She's got a well of raw energy just waiting to be transferred. Literally one handshake and I'm back to full power—it's insane."

My eyes and mouth are both wide as I face Greer. "Oh *shit!*"

My fourth's face turns as red as her hair as she rolls her eyes while holding back a smile. As if this wasn't a godsdamned game changer for us. Not just for The Vault, but anything that lay in our futures far beyond.

With a continued moronic look of shock, I turn to Kleio. Her grin becomes wholly deviant as we lock eyes and begin wordlessly running through the endless possibilities this new advantage has just unlocked. I glance at Greer in renewed amazement, shaking my head in complete wonder.

"Now *that* is fucking Brek," I state with absolutely no room for challenge in my voice.

My fourth rolls her eyes once more but this time she doesn't hold back on her grin as I beam at her.

Unfortunately, this sweet little moment is quite quickly broken up by the concerning sounds of downward rushing water and another round of bone-chilling screams.

I move instinctively towards the bow and Kleio slides easily out of my way. At last, I step up into my rightful place as captain while we round the next bend and promptly choke on my findings.

Sweet depths.

Down the opening lagoon passage before us, another moonlighter can be spotted.

It lies in complete and total smithereens.

XLVI. BRISA'S TRUTH

"Oh shit," Kleio echoes my earlier sentiment from behind.

I quickly scan the debris to find a silver flag marking it as belonging to the Cardinal West Order.

A teeny, *tiny* bit of tension in my chest eases in response. The source behind those echoing screams is made apparent a moment later as we float closer and I count seven western crew members stuck between half of their speeder's hull and a kórallian ledge.

My eyes narrow in confusion. They all appear to be alive and able to breathe, if not a bit uncomfortable. The reason for their screams must be—I scan them all quickly again—their missing captain. Glancing over at the debris and rushing water falling from their whirlpool opening above, I quickly deduce the cause for such panicked wails and terrified sobs.

Their captain went down with the ship.

Brisa is trapped beneath the wreckage.

I grit my teeth and begin ripping off my captain's cape once more, then quickly removing my helmsman visor and gloves. I'm fiddling with the belt around my waist when Kleio's hand catches my arm and squeezes tight.

"Merena—what are you *doing*?" Her warm brown eyes are filled with alarm.

"Brisa is trapped under the debris—I'm going in to get her," I explain while moving to unburden myself from as much weight as possible.

"Whoa wait *no*—Cap, you can't—you could get sucked under the riptide. The water from above will drag you right under the current," Herse argues, stepping up towards Kleio and me.

"I'm a strong swimmer. I can beat the current. I'll be fine," I reply in dismissal before shaking off Kleio's hold in order to continue on in my hasty preparation.

"Captain, but—the throttle isn't fixed yet." Prisca's voice comes out panicked. "We won't be able to come back for you until it's been repaired. The current will keep pushing us past here—you'll be stuck until we can find you again!" she shrieks.

As the waters pull us closer, I shake my head and start mentally mapping out my best strategy to get the western captain out as fast as possible. "There are tunnel passages all over this place. I'll find one and follow that light towards the heart. You guys float your way there, and we'll meet right back up. No problem."

I step back up towards the bow, the haunting chill of Brisa's crew's horrified wails echoing throughout the expanse. And I then jump in complete surprise at the feeling of Kleio's hand once again pulling me backwards. I turn slightly to look down at her in confusion.

"Merena, you can't! I won't let you risk yourself—think of The Vault. We're *so* close," she pleads.

Turning back around fully, I find my crew's faces are each swimming with so much love, and worry, and fear that I just might fucking drown in it.

Suppressing those overwhelming feelings, I meet each of their beautifully tythed faces before stating very quickly, "You all are clever and brave and—" I give a pointed look at Kleio, still grabbing tightly onto my arm, "persistent as all *hell*. I trust you implicitly. I know now that you will keep each other safe. You have your affinities. You will do whatever needs to be done. I will meet you back at the heart *and—*"

I try for a little brevity to break their rapidly increasing panic and clear the worry from their now alarmingly tearful eyes. "*If* I happen to run a little bit late, just assume I'm busy winning The Vault or I'm *making out* with Captain Agni or whatever else helps you keep calm. Okay?"

I find only the most grievously somber of faces meet my aim for humor. But then six very brave raiders finally nod back at me in grim understanding.

Kleio, however, true to form, *still* does not relent. She squeezes my hand so tightly, I think it might break. Tears of genuine fear for my life fill her eyes and roll down her heart-shaped face as she alone shakes her head in disagreement.

"N—*no* you can't leave us again—we just got you back. We're supposed to be together now until The Vault. That was the deal." Her voice grows higher in pitch with each word. "You *can't*—remember the code? Your duty is to your *crew*—you have to stay here with us," she begs me, completely terrified that not only one captain will be going down with that ship tonight.

We are quite rapidly reaching the exact point I need to dive from in order to reach Brisa.

I'm running out of time.

"*LOOK AT THEM, KLEIO!*" I bellow in order to snap my second out of her spiraling panic.

"Look at them—being *forced* to watch their captain *die*—right in front of their *godsdamned eyes*! My duty as a captain right now is to *Brisa's* crew."

My harshly shouted words have the intended effect. Kleio's eyes at last break away from me to scan the seven western raiders now sobbing in distress. She swallows down her well of worries and at last meets me with a very brave face.

"Okay." Kleio nods, relenting at long last. "You're right. *I just*—I love you so much, Merena, I can't bear the thought of you ever leaving us permanently." Her voice breaks, and more tears slip past her eyes to run down her cheeks.

I smile an extremely rare, soft smile before pressing my forehead down against her own. "You are like the closest thing I have to a heart, Kleio. I'll be back for you, don't worry," I promise her.

Then, before anyone *else* can lose their shit on me tonight, I straighten and turn in order to begin striding down the bow of our moonlighter before promptly diving right off the front.

I plunge down into deceivingly cool waters in a perfect streamline.

The lagoon's frigid temperature is exactly what I need to sharpen my focus and spark up something Brek inside that has nothing to do with my affinity.

The debris is *everywhere*.

Brisa and her crew must have tried to fight the whirlpool with everything they had. I wrestle through layers upon layers of broken bits and pieces of what was once quite a beautiful speeder.

The current isn't as bad as I secretly feared it would be. Which is good as I'm being forced to slip inside the broken shards of the moonlighter in order to get to the captain lodged beneath. A moment later, I finally spot the shine of her silver hair cuffs, like a beacon in the darkened depths. If I wasn't currently holding my breath, I'd sigh out in relief.

I use all my internal strength to make it inside the crevice she's been wedged between to find that Brisa is impossibly *still* struggling to survive.

Brek as fucking hell.

But the western captain's movements are faint.

Her body is just barely resisting death's firm pull, yet those steel-colored eyes go wide when spotting me. Something wary that I don't quite understand flashes in her expression as I make my way near. I don't have long before my own oxygen supply is out, so I quickly assess how exactly she's stuck and find that her captain's cape is making it impossible to dislodge from beneath the hull.

Pulling out one of the only few blades I dared to take in an effort not to weigh me down, I deftly cut off her captain's cape before wrenching her free. Unfortunately for me, this is the exact same instant that Brisa loses her fighting spirit. She immediately becomes a very unhelpful weight that I now get to drag up to the surface.

The gods truly love nothing more than to play with *me* in particular.

Clenching my back molars tightly in aggravation, I once again find that strength inside. The next few moments are filled with me hauling Brisa's body back through the debris with every ounce of water combat training I have.

My muscles and lungs strain in resistance, but somehow they power through.

I gasp out for breath the second we hit the surface to the horrified screams of Brisa's crew.

Their shrieking has turned hysterical now that they're forced to watch me swim her very *limp* body over to the nearest flat surface. Finding that inner strength one more time I tread water and groan out in real pain while pushing a hundred and fifty pounds of dead fucking weight up and onto the kórallian ledge.

When Brisa's body at last makes it onto the side and her weight is removed from me, I gasp out again in relief. But time is ticking. I can feel the countdown inside the beat of my own heart. My hands hit the ledge, and I hoist myself out the waters to kneel before the western captain's sprawled form.

"Hey—*hey*—come on now!" I snap, shaking Brisa by the shoulders.

I try slapping her a few times in order to gauge any sort of reaction, but she remains unmoving.

There is only one more avenue to go.

It's like I can *hear* the gods laughing right now.

"I cannot believe that this is *fucking-happening-again!*" I seethe angrily through my teeth before lowering myself down to Brisa's lips and promptly begin performing mouth-to-mouth.

Four kisses and two rounds of chest compressions later, Brisa's soul returns to her body. It's arrival is made well known by her precipitously vomiting saltwater directly into my mouth.

"Ugh, worst one *by far,*" I mutter in disgust, wiping my face with the sleeve of my uniform after having just spit out the western captain's proof of life onto the kórallian ledge.

Brisa's gasping form darts upwards, and she looks at me with pure fear in her eyes. The echo of her crew's shrill screaming fills the lagoon's tunnel passageway, ringing like a holy bell.

"Dead or alive?" She rasps out, desperately searching my face for something, but I haven't the faintest clue what.

My brows raise high at her expression of terror.

"Um, *alive*?" I answer with a frown, puzzlement narrowing my eyes in response to her tone of voice and choice of words. Brisa begins swallowing down air in great, greedy gulps.

I stand up to wave at her still-trapped crew members. Their caterwauling is giving me a gods awful headache. "You can stop your screaming now—*please*—your captain is just fine!" I shout over towards where they're all in various despondent states of horror and despair.

Pivoting back on my heel towards Captain Bedivere, I motion at her to wrangle in her crew's physically distressing commotion.

Brisa lets out a breathless laugh while her silver eyes shine up at me in complete confoundment, and she sits up fully in order to wave at them. "I'm—I'm really—I'm really *okay*!" their captain calls out in between heaving breaths.

That little act of comfort almost immediately transforms their cries of grief into an even louder commotion. Except this time, their boisterous, headache-inducing noise consists of shouts, cheers, and absolutely *obscene* prayers of thanks.

All thrown in my direction.

I can't help but snort a laugh at their over-the-top display. It reminds me so very much of my own crew. I decide to indulge myself a little by giving them all a grand sweeping bow from across the lagoon. "Thank you, thank you. I will *not* be doing that again."

I sincerely fucking hope.

"I can't believe you—you *saved* me!" Brisa exclaims, still a bit breathless from her return to Pontus.

Shrugging, I respond easily, "I owed you one. Plus, like you said—us bastards have to look out for one another from time to time." Glancing back, I give her a small grin, followed by a wink.

Brisa laughs in surprised remembrance of what she told me privately on the alcove that day that seems so very long ago now. The reason she felt so compelled to warn me about the second pillar trial and the test it would be. Also the reason she made me swear an od.

Because Captain Brisa Bedivere's real name is actually Captain Brisa *Zephyrus*.

Zephyrus being the last name given to those bastards born to the West.

Her father just so happens to be high up enough in The Order rankings *himself* that he was able to pull some strings and get her bastard name erased once she'd made it to captaincy. All to ensure that she was given a truly fair shot during the Pillar Trials.

Something that didn't quite sit right with Brisa after meeting me.

The western captain swallows, still appearing to be in complete shock that she's actually alive, before shaking her head firmly. "That goes beyond owing me one, Boreas. There has *never* been a time in the entire history of The Vault where a captain has saved another one's life."

My grin turns as devious as a drowned god while turning to face her fully. "Would you believe me if I told you you're my second one tonight?"

Brisa's face studies mine, and I'm waiting for her to laugh, but instead her mouth falls completely slack and her eyes again fill with that strange look of terror.

Except now they're ringed with something much more... *devout*. Her mouth closes tight, and she nods once with a solemn sort of seriousness that sends a chill skittering down my bones.

My brows rise high in surprise at the way she's staring at me. But being the little deviant that I *am*, I can't help but want to try to push her just a bit further. So I broadened that drowned-god grin before asking, "And would you still believe me if I told you that you are now the *third* captain I've kissed tonight?"

Her steel-colored eyes widen in shock, and she blinks several times over before finally barking a laugh. "My gods—you know I actually—I actually *would!*" She exclaims in a startling rush of delirium.

I chuckle and decide she's probably a bit too frazzled from her circle around the Netherdepths to properly jest with.

"Is it safe to assume that with your affinity you can get your crew out of their jam? I mean, I would help, but—" I lower my voice with an exaggerated grimace, "I took the kratosbane," and nod in the direction of where seven western raiders remain stuck.

Brisa glances at her crewmates, currently wedged between a hull and hard place, and back to myself standing before her. Her gaze scours my face like she's searching for some kind of answer to an unspoken question.

"What?" I ask before teasing again. "Do you need my *blessing* or something?"

Captain Zephyrus's eyes go wide and round, and I truly begin to wonder about the state of her mental sanity. I watch as she turns to her crew and looks oddly astonished when using her gods-blessed power to remove the chunk of moonlighter pinning them to the ledge.

Once they've all made it safely back to dry land, I rock back on my heels and start focusing on my next task, getting back to my crew. "Alright, then I'm off. Lives to save, captain's to kiss, vault to win," I joke, turning to study the various tunnel openings lining the nearest wall.

"*Wait—*" Brisa cries from behind and I pivot to find her on her knees, looking up beseechingly. "Please, there has to be something I can do to repay you. How can I thank you for this?"

My mouth opens slightly at her unnecessary display of gratitude, and I shake my head in startled confusion. "I don't know, just like—put in a good word with your father for me—or something?"

Brisa nods, a bit too reverently for me to think she's fully recovered from her brain's recent lack of oxygen, but I don't have time to worry about that now. Taking a deep breath, I turn back one more time to face the varying tunnel paths. After a minute of deliberation, I decide to go with the center one.

Once I'm several lengths away from the lazy lagoon's waterway, I place my palm against the wall and watch as that brilliant light once again forms a trail for me to follow. Breathing out a sigh of relief, I begin making my way to the heart and my crew, and with any luck, The Vault.

XLVII. KNIVES' EDGE

I follow that light, which I've begun to find quite trustworthy, and pick my way as quickly as I can through the sandy-floored passageways.

It jumps from tunnel to tunnel, winding me around bend after curving bend. The light seems impatient now. I have to run to catch up with it as it begins disappearing with alarming swiftness.

I don't slow in pace until the shimmer of something gold catches my attention from the very end of the next tunnel. Pausing, my heart skips about five beats.

This cannot be possible.

The light has guided me somehow, impossibly, *around* the heart's mooring and directly to The Vault itself. My returning pulse is a wild thing in my ears. The small flicker of aurelian color at the other end of the long passageway brightens and begins to shine victoriously before me.

I know now for certain that *gold* is my favorite color.

My steps become even quicker and my gaze even sharper as that golden glimmer widens and widens and widens until finally revealing itself to be a monstrously large, resplendently aureate temple. Said temple is elevated on a raised platform, only to be reached by a steep staircase. My jaw drops in wonder as I gaze up at the massive columns shadowing the view of those doors.

I've *found* it.

Before I know it, I'm sprinting up those stairs, taking them two at a time.

My feet are desperate to carry me to the gilded, larger-than-life doors, as fast as they possibly can. There's a hulking roof protruding out from above those dominating columns, which acts as a sort of protective awning. Shadows gather beneath it and grow darker with every stride.

What might just be a hundred footfalls later, I finally reach the very intricately carved archway of promise. The Vault's sacred entrance shines down on me as the veritable vision of our futures. Something even deeper than my caged affinity begins to stir inside.

My mouth parts in wonder while I stand there staring at the answer to each and every one of my childish prayers. It's the golden beacon of my horribly depressing and very tortuous youth. I'd be lying if I said there wasn't a part of me that wants to fall to my knees in reverence.

Honestly, I might have done just that. But the scent of burning spices ensnares my senses.

Movement from the opposite end of the darkened temple catches my eye. I slide my gaze over to find a towering, formidable shadow, leaning arrogantly against one of those colossal pillars.

A shadow with eyes that burn like real fire.

Shit.

A breath catches in my throat as the shadow flicks away it's smoking roll of spice before leaving that darkened corner to become a man.

Captain Agni strides out into the starlight beneath The Vault's shimmering gates, looking sickeningly handsome. A quick scan reveals not a scratch remains on him from our previous encounter. He must have some sort of healer on his crew as well. Yet another piece of his puzzle that I'm not sure I'll ever be able to make any sense of.

His eyes burn brighter than ever. They're almost terrifying in their intensity while scouring my person assessingly. After a moment, the fire in them eases a touch. Yet there's something off about his countenance. He looks tightly wound, anxious, *worried* even.

"Where the *hell* have you been?" Agni snaps angrily.

His captain's ring burns a bright hole in the pocket of my uniform. I fight back my own amusement when remembering just how absolutely enraged he's probably been having to stand here and wait for me to arrive for the gods know how long.

"Wouldn't you like to know, *loverboy*?" I mock to push him further.

He scowls deeply, and I find there's a newly intense deliberation in his gaze as he stares at me in swift evaluation. "Why are you wet? Where have you *actually* been?"

I snort at his outward peevishness before putting a hand on my hip with a casual shrug. "Oh, you know, just off kissing another captain in order to save their life."

His eyes flicker before darkening in typical annoyance. "Very funny."

I smirk before taking a step towards the harrowing male. "I'm not joking."

His shrewd amber eyes study my face and almost abruptly turn outright obsidian when he reads the fact that I am actually telling him the truth.

That's... *interesting*.

"So you just out here brooding again? Or—*oh no*—don't tell me that you're going soft on me now since that kiss, Agni. Have you been here waiting for me? *Pinning* away this entire time."

Agni's lips turn up in a sneer before stating very evenly, "You have something of mine, Boreas. You know that I need it back, and I'd prefer it if I didn't have to force it from you."

I waste no time in drawing the short sword from where it's sidled against my hips along with a few remaining knives. Captain Agni tracks the movement with a mask forged in indifference.

"Something of yours, you say?" I ask, giving him a tight frown of puzzlement and tapping my lower lip in that antagonizing way of his. My brows furrow in innocent confusion before lying straight to his face, "I have no idea what you're talking about."

Agni still doesn't draw a blade. Instead, the southern captain takes a single formidable step in my direction. It has me angling my weapon up higher in anticipation.

His voice drops down to a dark growl when warning me, "Come on, Boreas. Don't make this harder than it needs to be."

"Sorry," I insist with a dubious shrug of my shoulders and shake of my head, not alluding to the nerves swelling up inside. "It honestly just doesn't *ring* any bells." The smirk that then creeps up and across my features is a touch devious and very intentionally provoking.

Captain Agni's expression turns to one entrenched in endless aggravation.

The sound of a blade being released from his person at last rents the night air. My smirk holds firm while he raises one of his dual foreboding broadswords, even as an intense dread begins pooling down low inside at the sight of its fatal edge.

Yet again, I catch sight of that odd newfound deliberation in Agni's gaze.

His amber eyes lock onto mine, and he hesitates for a single second before that daunting, tenebrous weapon of his comes crashing down on me with the force of a falling star. I gasp beneath the harsh impact, and my sword trembles while barely holding off his brazen strike.

Real fear begins pounding heavily inside my veins. Luckily, adrenaline crashes into my system next, steadying my reflexes and sharpening my focus. I dart to the side in an attempted feint maneuver, but Agni anticipates it. He swings the broadsword in a wide arc, and it forces me to dance further away from the golden doors with a string of raider-worthy curses.

"I'll admit your thieving skills are surprisingly quite impressive." The corner of his mouth twitches once in amusement when I meet his stare. "However, I think we're both aware you're not a match for me when it comes to weapon or affinity play."

I give him a look of angry affront and open my mouth to retort when he cuts me off coolly, "That was actually *not* a taunt Boreas. It's a fact. You lack nearly any sort of proper elemental training, and it shows. The way you fight with a weapon versus with your affinity are two completely different styles when they should actually just be one."

Agni frowns, studying me again. "Now give me back my captain's ring so I can leave you here in one piece."

"Your arrogance should really be studied," I retort through gritted teeth just before an opening presents itself. Lunging forward in a burst of speed, my blade grazes his exposed arm. It rips his uniform sleeve and draws a thin line of blood.

I laugh up at him in pointed mockery.

Agni rolls his eyes with the exasperated shake of his messy waves. "That proves nothing."

My amusement is sadly short-lived, as his reaction reveals itself to be terribly swift and brutally effective. It makes me wonder if, just *maybe*, that day in Oplon's class, he was actually going pretty easy on me. The southern captain retaliates with an impossibly powerful blow of his blade against mine. Its impact sends me stumbling several more steps away from the doors of promise.

"*See*," Agni snaps sharply. After a moment, he adds in a more subdued and considering voice, "The best weapon suited to your elemental abilities is also most definitely not a short sword."

A glance at his terribly beautiful face reveals his eyes have narrowed on my person in silent calculation. "Maybe something double-edged though, lightweight, good balance." With another troubling frown, he murmurs, "A xiphos might do."

I'm as bewildered by this interaction as our previous one. What was happening during everyone else's night? They couldn't all possibly be undergoing such disconcerting experiences as I've been.

The gods must really be putting in some overtime here. Or perhaps there is some sort of order-wide psychotic break happening?

Or *maybe*—a strategic part of me wonders—have I somehow managed to unintentionally peel back yet another layer on Captain Agni? Is this strange new behavior just another glimpse behind the iron mask? Another slip-up on his true character?

More importantly—*is this something I can use?*

My jaw sets itself tight before taking advantage of his distracted attention as I aim a quick jab to his exposed flank. The southern captain deflects my attempt with awful proficiency before giving me a truly disappointed look.

"It's like you're *intentionally* going against your own natural rhythm," he berates me.

There's no time for me to retort before Agni begins pressing the advantage. His strikes become relentless. I manage to parry one, then another, but he continues driving me back from the golden doors. It looks so effortless for him—so easy that he doesn't even break a sweat.

This was *without* his affinity.

"Your footwork is decent, at least," Agni notes offhandedly. "But overall, your movements aren't fluid in the slightest. You're much too rigid and tightly constrained for an elemental, especially one with your powers."

"What is going on here?" I snap at last. "I do not recall The Vault requiring a combat lesson before entering."

Agni's thoughts lie hidden behind an iron gate. His eyes meet mine with brows coolly raised. "We've been over this already. I need my captain's ring, which I know that you have. So kindly hand it back over."

I hate how easy it is for him to return to this unfeeling persona. The frightening male before me now does not so much as even *resemble* the one who risked a hafgufa to get me that antidote. The one who so very recently kissed me with such intensity that I thought it really might kill me.

Maybe that kiss actually satiated whatever sort of intimate interest he once had in me. Agni himself made it quite clear that there are never any sort of feelings involved in any of his exploits. He's only in it for two things, nothing more. That realization causes a twisting somewhere between my chest and my stomach.

Fucking pathetic.

I work hard to pulverize the utterly ridiculous feeling before sneering back up at him. "And what if I don't have it *on* me?"

Agni gives me a knowing smirk before divulging, "We already searched your speeder." His chuckle is dark in the face of my immediate doubt. "And your crew was *not* happy about it."

That smirk turns smug as I study his face, searching for the bluff. "See, now, that's when I wondered where it was that you'd run off to. None of your *enchanting* little crew members would say one single fucking peep to me or any of my boys about it. I found their resistance to our interrogation methods quite impressive, actually."

My heart stops beating.

The grip on my sword tightens in panic-fueled indignation, and my knuckles turn about as white as my markings. I struggle to swallow while reading the sincerity on his face. Alarm and worry tie my insides into thickly corded knots.

I'd left them all behind. I left them exposed and vulnerable, and *he* had taken advantage of it.

How could I be so stupid?

"*Depths Boreas*—your crew members have not been harmed in the slightest—they are currently just detained, that's it," Agni discloses with a frustrated roll of his eyes, clearly having picked up on my visible distress. "Suffice to say I'm fairly certain you have it on your person... *somewhere*."

The way those amber eyes scan up and down my body appraisingly, while taking several steps closer, makes a deep flush of betrayal sweep across my skin.

I feint to the left before spinning to the right and aiming for his legs, but Agni sees right through my ruse. His hellish broadsword sweeps low, effortlessly knocking my feet out from under me. I hit the ground *hard*, swearing as the impact knocks the wind from my lungs and the short sword skitters out of reach.

Scrambling back to my feet with one of my only remaining knives in hand proves futile, as the impossibly fast southern captain is already there with his broadsword pointed at my throat.

Agni forces the knife from my hand, and I brace myself for what's about to happen next. But, instead of delivering the final blow I'm fully expecting, Agni presses the flat of his blade against my chest and pins me back flat against the golden wall of the temple.

I meet his stare, only to find that cocky smirk of his ghosting at the corners of his mouth.

My breathing hitches in mutiny as his face lowers down to mine and his lips press themselves against my ear. "As much as I would deeply enjoy it if you gave me the go-ahead to search *every inch* of your person for my ring right now, Boreas—" Agni's ashen words come out torturously intimate. "We regrettably don't have the time nor the privacy for me to properly show you just exactly how *skilled* and *thorough* that I am."

His lips remove themselves from my ear before his darkened, kesar-shaded eyes meet mine with meaning. My heart rate spikes concerningly, and a treasonous blush spills along my neck in response to the too-familiar heat now sifting the embers of his gaze.

"I'll say this one more time. Give me back my ring," he demands firmly.

My chin lifts while keeping hold of his painfully intent stare. "I told you already. I don't know what you're talking about. Doesn't ring a bell."

The annoyance in his face is nearly tangible, and I catch his jaw flexing against it. Agni takes a quick scan of my expression before letting out an irate huff at my continued refusal to concede.

"Your crew is currently unharmed, but that can change *Captain*—if it has to," He states darkly. "Do not force my hand on this one, Boreas. You will not like the cards that I'll have to play."

A snarl of rage escapes me at his very real threat to my crew. Agni holds my now-seething form solidly against the gilded wall. His iron-masked expression remains ruthless and unwavering. He has me on this one, and we both know it.

I give him a look dripping with abhorrence before finally dipping my chin in surrender.

"Front right pocket."

Agni's brutal expression softens, just a touch, in response to my yield. His hand is surprisingly gentle when he reaches into the concealed compartment along the side of my waist before lightly fishing out his captaincy ring.

My eyes avoid him at all costs, and I begin studying the exposed sky above while chewing the inside of my cheek. A faint light can be seen nearing the horizon, transforming the midnight sky into a velvety shade of periwinkle. Dawn won't be too terribly far off now.

"Now, *second* order of business," Agni snaps, returning my eyes to meet his surprisingly very angry face. "Exactly whose life were you just off saving? What cardinal?"

"West," I reply, meeting his gaze, and watch in surprise as his eyes blaze obsidian again.

"*Why?*" he demands.

I frown at his sudden change in mood. "Their speeder was in smithereens after trying to take on a whirlpool in the third checkpoint. The crew was stuck between half of their hull and one of the ledges while Captain Bedivere was trapped beneath the current and debris at the bottom."

His eyes searching my face turn back to amber, and his breathing unexpectedly begins to quicken. "So you're telling me that you went down in there and got her *out*?"

My brows rise at his alarming intensity before I confirm with a tight nod. "I couldn't just stand by and allow a raider crew to be forced to watch their captain die. I do not wish to ever attend another of those terribly somber pyre-burning ceremonies. As I already explained to my second, my duty as a captain in that moment was to Brisa's crew—*that* is the code."

"And then what happened?" Agni pushes, continuing on in the interrogation.

Shaking my head at his strangeness, I explain further, "And then I had to drag her unconscious body over to a ledge and give her mouth-to-mouth. So, as I already said when you first asked, I was *kissing* another *captain* in order to save their *life.* It was a joke," I snap, angry with his ceaseless questions.

Agni begins surveying my face fiercely. His eyes have the same unspoken war raging in them as they did in the grotto, but now it's somehow more intense. The tension in them makes me feel like he's walking on some sort of knife edge, but I have no idea what it is he's wavering between.

It's maddening.

"Well, if you're done interrogating me, then here's your other ring, *prick,*" I mutter angrily before holding up my right hand to reveal my index finger, currently laden with his ruby accessory. My eyes return upwards as they start burning with the very real realization that Captain Agni is going to win The Vault.

"My other one? What do you mean, my other—*oh sweet depths,*" Agni pauses in shock before he begins laughing in genuine surprise. The sound of it is startlingly real and mortifyingly stirring.

"*Deos meos*—you took this one too, and I didn't even realize." He laughs again in freshly renewed amazement, and my pulse stumbles a beat. After a moment, Agni adds softly, "You know, I'd rather you kept that one, actually. I prefer the look of it on your hand much more than mine."

My attention flickers back warily to his alarmingly handsome face now just inches away from my own. His amber eyes currently study the ruby ring on my hand, and I soon discover his mouth is curved into that incredibly rare, heart-stoppingly-crooked, dangerously-dark grin.

My pulse promptly falters before picking up speed in response.

"How are you so good at that?" Agni murmurs in a voice that now feels private, as his gaze flits back to mine in suspicion. That golden scar of his glistens under the waning starlight, and I find there's a divine sort of beauty to it. I have the strangest desire to reach up and trace it.

Swallowing tightly, my eyes don't leave his as I shake my head in silent response. The lingering ghost of that crooked grin on his mouth makes it impossible for me to speak. I watch as his eyes begin to walk that razor edge once more. His breathing quickens while returning to that state of maddening deliberation.

He has his ring, he has my crew as collateral, and he has me physically pinned against the shiny wall of the godsdamned vault with a broadsword at my throat. What on all of Pontus could he be debating at this moment in time?

Unless—is it—*possible*?

"*Non possum credere stupri hoc nunc fieri.*" Agni mutters, his gaze still intense, while his tone has turned angrily disbelieving.

I bite down on my lower lip in complete confusion, and Agni notes the movement. My eyes begin to burn intentionally as I allow just a touch of despair to run along my waterline. Then I watch in satisfaction as Agni finally teeters off the knife edge with the tight clench of his jaw.

"My *death,* I fucking swear it," he growls angrily before his mouth comes crashing down against mine. The feeling of his spice-laden lips injects me with an immediate thrill before his expert tongue makes it past my mouth in order to clash against my own, igniting something dangerously warm inside my core.

It's over much too soon, as Agni then releases me abruptly from both his mouth and blade.

There's a very deep scowl on his face while he next grabs me by the wrist and drags me towards The Vault's intricately carved doors. I blink in astonishment as he then places *my* ring-adorned hand firmly on the holy doors of promise. There's a *pulse* beneath my palm, like the 'click' of a lock.

My mouth parts as The Vault opens in response and I look to Agni in total bewilderment. I cannot believe my last ditch ploy actually worked.

He shakes his head at himself, anger still plain on his face. Yet I catch his lips twitching slightly in amusement towards my startled expression. I open my mouth to say something when the southern captain shocks me yet again by delivering his own strategic blow.

Agni yanks me into his arms with a cocky smirk stating "loophole" in explanation before slipping us *both* through The Vault's opening. The monstrous doors shut behind us with a clang of finality.

And then we're *falling*.

We're falling through what appears to be nothing but waves and starlight.

Agni holds me tightly against his person, and my startled screams of terror are devoured by the firmness of his chest. An otherworldly hum of energy presses in on us from all sides.

Our bodies plunge down through layer after layer of every shade of tide that exists until I can barely even recount my own name. Until I no longer believe my own reality. Until my throat is raw from overuse. Until suddenly there is solid ground beneath me again.

There is no impact.

There is also, mysteriously, no more Agni.

I have to wonder if I might be dead.

XLVIII. DEATH'S KISS

I lie flat on my back on what feels to be the ocean floor.

My breathing comes in and out in extremely shallow waves, while my hands grasp continually at the miniscule granular rocks beneath my fingers. I mentally try to come to terms with what exactly has just occurred. The wall of ice that resides within me is now *completely* fractured.

A large and ancient rhythmic pounding beat sounds from the other side. I'm afraid it's now just a matter of time until whatever terrible thing resides behind that wall comes barreling through.

After several frozen moments, I struggle to my feet from the oceanic flooring to gather my surroundings. I then actually physically stumble backwards and almost fall on my ass at the sight that unravels itself before me in the room I've suddenly materialized in.

That ancient pounding beat intensifies.

I suppose 'room' isn't really the proper term for wherever it is that I am. A pocket realm, like the Veil Keeper, feels more accurate. Someplace in time and space that lies between the borders of our three realms. If that is *truly* the case, then I'd wager to bet that Captain Agni is currently in his own separate 'pocket' of whatever this place is.

I laugh breathlessly in shock as I remember him falling for my ploy. Just the *barest* hint of despair watering my eyes, and he'd relented entirely before handing me over The Vault.

A very terrible part of me wonders what a full-blown tear could do.

I'm equally impressed by his own cunning. I didn't see that little loophole maneuver coming in a million years. As far as I know, there isn't actually a law stating only one raider can enter The Vault. If that is in fact where I am. From what little The Order does know, due to how very few times it's ever resurfaced, The Vault doors will open once in response to one worthy captain's beringed hand before descending back down to the netherdepths.

We are trained as children to be ruthless and cutthroat. We are raised to expect only the very worst from each other, except for those very few that are our chosen crew. There's no way any captain has ever even considered the possibility of going through those doors *with* another.

I force myself to set aside the never-ending questions running up a tally in my mind.

Rows upon rows of monstrously large sea-stone shelves rise up and line out as far as the eye can see. Said shelves appear so colossal that I think they could actually reach all the way up to the celestial realm itself. The staggering height of them is eclipsed only by the amount of them.

No matter how hard I try, I can't find an end in sight. They go on seemingly for all eternity.

"*Agni?*" I find myself whispering moronically out into the mythical abyss. As I already suspected, there is neither sign nor sound of the vexing southern captain anywhere to be found.

Each way I turn, I find only shelves. There's no door or any sort of semblance of an exit. Just as with the Veil Keeper, it seems to me that there isn't really a way back. The issuing of my release will not be up to my own discretion, assuming I am in fact to be released at all.

After several thunderous, stupefied heartbeats, curiosity takes control. I drift over to the nearest monumental structure in order to inspect the objects laden within them. My eyes widen incredulously upon my findings.

These aren't bookshelves at all.

Not a single tome nor scroll to be found in fact. Instead, glass bottles of every shape and size occupy the seastone ledges, each about three meters apart from the next. They're quite similar to epistles in appearance, with two major differences. One being that they're about four to five times the size, and two being that these bottles are already quite full.

Each bottle contains within it a ship.

A ship that resides on *real* churning tides.

I blink several times over in disbelieving incredulity. My hands then come to rub up and down my face in an effort to know whether or not this is really, truly happening.

This settles it then. I'm actually inside *The Vault*.

My breathing turns a tad bit shallow as I begin wandering slowly down the nearest line of shelves. My eyes take their sweet time in devouring each incredible treasure unique to its individual bottle. I just need to decide which one to take as my boon.

Some of the vessels I inspect appear to be trapped inside a storm. Real lightning flashes against gathering thunderclouds within the container's horizon. Tiny invisible winds rage against their different colored sails, making the ship sway this way and that on its dark treacherous waters.

More of those that I study drift on calm and steady seas. Real sunshine refracts through the tempered glass, throwing watery designs onto the ocean floor beneath my feet. These ships rest pleasantly atop their jewel-colored tides. Their variously hued flags billow softly upon what appears to be a faint summer breeze.

I stop my continual perusal entirely in order to closely inspect one bottle that catches my eye in particular. The ship within it bobs menacingly close to the horizon of a dying sunset.

Sails of almost pure obsidian, marked only by branches of *real* golden lightning, wave insolently against the beckoning night. They blend in seamlessly with the ship's matching, cutthroat hull.

The wondrous vessel looks as though it might have been crafted from the darkness between the stars. Something about it tells me that it moves like a daunting omen out on the tides. I continue observing it intently and notice, with no small amount of interest, as a single star falls faintly from the heavens towards the twilight horizon.

'Dusk's Salvation' the ship's name plate reads.

My hand reactively reaches out towards it.

"*Not that one!*" A voice warns me, echoing from somewhere deeper inside The Vault.

I jump nearly a solid meter backwards in surprise at the unexpected outburst. But then my hair comes to stand on end. Not only do I recognize that rich male timbre, but I've heard it quite recently.

The Heimartai.

Hope nearly explodes inside my chest.

If my Heimartai is here, then perhaps that means I'm ready. Perhaps it's *finally* come to tell me of my fate, or at least gift me back my past. One hand grips my single remaining knife as I leave behind the daunting ship and turn to face the direction from which the familiar voice came.

The skin along my arms prickles in the resounding silence, and I walk in a trance-like state further into The Vault. The Heimartai reaches out to me again only a few moments later.

"I ought to have probably had this discussion with you sooner." The familiar timbre reverberates through the hallowed grounds.

Rounding the next hulking line of colossal cases, I catch sight of the creature's faint silvery glow. The thrashing feeling of hope is now almost unbearable to contain. The luminous light proves to be emanating from somewhere much farther into the realm of never-ending shelves.

My pulse and pace both quicken.

I begin sprinting down the monstrous racks of sea-stone ledges. Countless bottles containing countless magnificent ships of every make and color race past in my peripheral. Each one is more tempting than the last, but I'm determined on my course.

This time, I won't let my Heimartai get away. This time I'll *make* it tell me of my past. I'll force my fate from the strange creature with my bare hands and one remaining knife if I have to. I'm close now. The halfway hidden luminance becomes brighter with every single step I take.

"*Did your mother mention what I wanted to talk to you about?*" that rich voice questions. My steps abruptly falter and slow.

Mother?

Is the fate-deliverer playing some sort of game with me now?

The next words it spews are so uncharacteristically warped that I only make out a small portion of the last half. "*—for the good of Pontus. You know we all must make sacrifices.*" Is all I'm able to catch.

Creeping down the last few remaining cases between myself and the warped words, I begin realizing, to no small amount of disappointment, that the silver light doesn't actually belong to my Heimartai at all. It doesn't belong to any Heimartai. That terribly familiar voice instead is revealed to be echoing from the corner of a large fossilized ledge.

Hope dies a very painful death within me.

The silvery light shines even brighter as the voice, the one currently pounding against that icy wall inside of me, begging to be remembered, speaks once more. "

You are like my own heart, you know that Cherrystone? Don't worry, I'll be with you." The deep timbre is incredibly soft, as if speaking to a child.

Something cold grips onto my soul, and I suddenly have the oddest urge to cry. Repressing that frightening reaction takes much more effort than I want to admit.

The mystical radiance begins to fade down into a mere glimmer of starlight, revealing a medium-sized glass bottle as the source responsible. I cautiously drift closer while also trying to remember how to breathe. Re-sheathing my knife, I lean forward and peer curiously inside the strange talking bottle.

A gasp escapes me in response to the sight I'm met with. A ship of complete and utter heart-stopping *perfection* is trapped inside a sea of ice beneath a wintry midnight sky.

The vessel's sleek hull, deck, and masts are all so black that they actually come off with a shimmering opalescent hue. Sharp destructive angles make up the stern and bow, both of which tell me that this ship is without a doubt *faster* than all fucking hell.

I don't think twice before grabbing the bottle. I'm immediately desperate to see each individual inch from every single angle possible. The starlight glittering within it is quite faint. I have to study it quite closely in order to truly get a good look.

My eyes rest almost directly against the glass itself as I watch in open-mouthed wonder while the fantastical ship's previously tied-up sails begin unfurling themselves. My gaping becomes entirely moronic when those sails shake off the ice clinging to them before taking on a unique arch-shape against the arctic chill.

I think my heart has stopped beating.

As if the ship couldn't have been any more suited to me, the colors of those newly revealed sails reflect a gorgeously haunting, luminous shade of iridescent *white*. They glimmer as if shards of the moon itself and dance like ghosts along an ancient midnight gale.

The ship perfectly matches me, my crew, and our unbreakable tythe.

Rubbing the fabric of my uniform over the small golden plate embedded in the glass, I discover two words etched upon it. The two words that declare the name belonging to this absurdly perfect craft.

My thumb no more than begins to brush over the engraved nameplate when an undeniably final, world-shattering *'crack'* comes from within that wall of ice inside.

This time, it is one I *cannot* ignore.

An ocean I never knew I was carrying inside of me swells back up from deep down within. Its volatile tide crashes through that unyielding defense before taking hold and dragging me down to its deep, dark depths.

Time vanishes entirely.

IN A PAST LIFE

"Death's Kiss," I whisper in awe, my thumb brushing against the ship bottle's shiny new nameplate.

My hand clutches a familiar heart-shaped, pendant at my neck. I run the aquamarine stone back and forth along its golden chain idly while inspecting the craft. I'm afraid speaking its name any louder than that will somehow shatter the perfection from within.

Names are *very* powerful things, of course.

Swallowing in amazement, my eyes again scour every inch of the ship with a keen kind of hunger pain I've never before experienced.

"Do you like it?" questions a rich male voice from just a few steps behind. "Your mother came up with the name. She said there was some sort of inside joke to it."

"*It's incredible,*" I proclaim with a reverent sigh before letting go of the heart-shaped pendant and looking over my shoulder towards the owner of said questioning voice and giver of said pendant.

Crushing eyes of sapphire-blue meet mine beneath expertly groomed raven hair held inside a face made specifically to shatter female hearts. The man sits behind a familiar sprawling desk in a grand, darkly-stained, book-filled room that smells of driftwood and mint leaves. He flashes me a striking smile that is both rare and just a touch deviant.

"It's yours," he reveals. That rare smile broadens as both my mouth and eyes pop open wide in amazement.

"*Mine*?" I sputter, not daring to believe him. Father does *ever* so love teasing me.

"Yes, yours," he affirms with a chuckle in response to my overly theatrical surprise before explaining further. "One day, when you're old enough, and more than likely on a birthday or some other such important event, it will be *officially* gifted to you."

I scowl immediately at that idea, to which he laughs. The sound of it is rich and deep, and true, which is a very special thing to earn from my father indeed.

"Until then, I will have it taken where I know it can be kept safe," he states, amusement still twitching on his full winterberry lips. "We'll put it in the family vault."

"But—why can't I have it now?" I whine impetuously, turning around fully to face him with my wide-eyed, childish pleading. "We could keep it down at the docks. I promise that I won't take it anywhere. Maybe I could—I just—I could just *live* in it, maybe?"

Father's arresting face fills right back up with his teasing sense of humor that I alone am privy to. "Oh, now *that* is a grand idea. I can't believe I hadn't thought of it myself. I'll have the nereids move you out of your bedchambers immediately. A ten-year-old living all alone on a ship that they have no idea how to even pilot—it's genius. Your mother will be thrilled with me, I'm sure."

I roll my eyes in annoyance at his jesting while coming to lean myself fully over the side of his grandiose desk. "Fine." I heave out my conceding with an intentionally long and heavily burdensome sigh. "How long do I have to wait then? A year?"

Father bursts out into another round of barking laughter, with a bemused clap of his hands. "Oh *Cherrystone*, have I told you recently that you're my favorite daughter?" His sapphire eyes twinkle as they meet mine.

My lips flatten against the aggravating nickname both Papa and Mama insist on calling me.

I shake my head silently while trying to hold back my giggle at the stupid jest he so often enjoys making. Although secretly, it is my favorite of all the many recurring inside jokes between us.

"I'm your *only* child, Papa!" I exclaim up to his still-grinning face.

"Oh, now *that's* right! How could I forget?" He teases me again.

That striking grin deepens as I *dare* to stick out my tongue at him. So brutal and savage is my formidable father's absolutely terrifying reputation that others often only referred to him around their hushed shadowed circles as 'The Bastard King'. Most, if not all, are far too afraid to even whisper his true name or title. Rightfully so.

Father chuckles at my defiant ways. "To answer your question, my darling, 'Death's Kiss' will be waiting for you after your twentieth birthday."

"*Twentieth*?" I emit a long, suffering groan. "That's like a thousand years from now. I'll never make it that long! I will die from the need to get my hands on that wheel *way* before then!" I claim, pounding my fist in frustration on the table.

Father just shakes his head, once again enjoying my dramatics. "You'll have plenty to occupy your time until then, Cherrystone. Which brings me to the next topic of discussion. Would you mind taking an *actual* seat for me?" He motions with a raise of his raven brows towards my now fully sprawled-out form atop his desk.

I laugh a bit while rolling off Papa's large, important table and into one of the silver, fur-covered armchairs opposite him. Resituating myself inside the large seat, I meet my father's handsome face again and instantly go tense. The male who sits across from me now could be carved from a glacier as he studies me with a slight, yet unnervingly calculating, frown.

Father props an elbow up on the table, his hand coming to rub back and forth over his razor-sharp chin. The way he measures me with his hard 'Bastard King' mask on makes my insides twist a bit in unease. Admittedly, there is currently a decently long running list of things I could in fact be in some well-deserved trouble for at the moment.

Finally, he asks, "Did your mother mention what I wanted to talk to you about?"

I frown while giving the slow shake of my head in confusion. "Mama said that you had something to show me and something to tell me. But she didn't say anything else."

Papa's crystal-like eyes flit up to the ceiling and back with a small snort. "Of course she did," he mutters, shaking his head in humored annoyance with the only woman who's ever managed to slip behind those walls of ice and find out that 'The Bastard King' does in fact have a heart.

His lips purse tightly again before at last taking a deep breath. "Well, I ought to have probably had this discussion with you sooner."

ONE YEAR LATER

"*Cherrystone?* Are you listening to me?"

My head snaps upwards at the sound of a voice as bright and beautiful as a moonlit night.

"What?" I ask, having been lost in some idle thought, once again running that aquamarine pendant back and forth across its golden chain of comfort. The woman behind me laughs, and the sound of it evokes the image of gentle waves lapping against a midnight shore.

A comb made from gem-encrusted abalone runs itself repeatedly through my long, luminous hair. I sit before a shimmering table, gleaming with opulence. There's a veritable treasure trove of glittering powders and liquids, delicate perfume bottles, and polished brushes before me. My hand traces shapeless forms along the treasure trove's surface, pensive.

"I was telling you about *the boy,* Cherrystone."

I scowl deeply in irritation before finally snapping at her. "I do not wish to hear another word about *the boy*, Mama!"

Ever since that day in my father's study, this was all that was ever talked about around me. That was exactly a year ago now. I can practically feel the walls closing in from all around and up and down. My days have numbered themselves all too quickly.

My mother sighs deeply from behind and slows her hand's movements in order to turn me around to face her. Eyes the color of seafoam, held inside an ethereal face designed specifically to rip out male hearts, meet mine. Her perfectly shaped pale pink lips purse softly in the face of my willfulness.

"We've *talked* about this, Cherrystone. You will be meeting him tonight, and it would do you well to make a good first impression. Especially considering the fact that he and the rest of their court will be residing here for the next year. You know how important this alliance is and not just for your father and me. This is for the good of the *realms.*"

My chin remains upwards, unwavering.

Mama snorts an impossibly enchanting laugh at my resolve and shakes her head of luminous white tumbling waves in disbelief at my stubbornness. "You are *so* your father's daughter," she teases with a light tap to my nose, which I swat away angrily.

Her brief amusement quickly gives over to a much more serious sigh. The same one that often comes before a lecture. My bottom lip presses out in preparation while I testily cross my arms.

Mama studies me. Her face is a masterpiece of otherworldly perfection, hinting at her even more powerful origins than my terrifying father.

"You know that his mother and I have been very good friends for a very, *very* long time. I will be sorely disappointed in you if I hear that you've been mean to him tonight."

"Well, I don't care!" I snap loudly. My anger is an impossibly wild thing to tame. "He is both *Celestial* and *Southern*. Everyone knows that they are all cruel and wicked monsters. I've heard the servants whispering about it all. They claim the boy to be a sadistic prince—a thing of nightmares—I've even heard that his eyes burn with real living fire!"

"*Merena!*" Mama hisses low, now truly angry.

Her use of my actual name has me sinking down a bit beneath her scary glower.

"You are both *Nawai* and *Northern*—people claim that to be just as terrifying a thing. '*The little bastard*' I believe is what you're so often called by the other children, is it not?" she asks me quite tersely indeed.

I roll my eyes in order to hide the stinging sensation that her truth provides.

Mama takes another deep breath before continuing. "My point being," she says as her hand places itself gently but firmly over my heart. I meet her seafoam-colored eyes again to find them swimming with so much love I could probably drown in it. "Is that we are *all* filled with many complicated layers. Layers that are just waiting for those who are clever and brave, and in your case very likely *persistent* enough, to peel back."

For once, I don't argue, as my mother unfortunately makes a good point.

I hate it when she does that.

My horribly brash and willful ways, combined with that ancient well of dual-inherited power resting inside, makes most everyone assume that I'm nothing more than a cold-blooded, deviant, *little bastard*. Nothing more than a smaller version of my father. Made all the more horrifying by the inclusion of my mother's bloodline.

I was, in reality, a bit misunderstood.

It also doesn't help that the well of ancient and deadly power inside is not one who likes to be controlled. Not that any of the children here at court were ever brave, clever, or persistent enough to befriend me and find that out.

Mama continues softly, her voice gentle as a prayer, "I also know, from a bit of my own *personal* experience, that sometimes the darker and more frightening the monster, indicates the greater and more priceless the treasure is that they're so fearsomely protecting. If you are brave enough to face the beast and clever enough to slip past its many ploys and defenses, you just might be able to find out what is *so* worth such frightening protection."

She pauses to make sure I'm still paying attention. "You also might just find out what it's like to be held *within* such frightening protection. That is when the real part of the adventure actually begins."

I watch as, for just one *tiny* moment, Mama's eyes become a bit dazed. Her thumb begins to brush idly against her bottom lip, lost in thought.

My gaze searches the ceiling in exasperation at her and her father's impossible-to-live-up-to kind of love. That stupidly dreamy look she has is specifically reserved for when thinking about her and Papa's first kiss. Mama claims it felt as though she'd never been kissed before, like a state of total delirium had overtaken them.

She tells me often that *all* kisses are, in their own right, extremely powerful things.

All of which I personally find to be completely absurd and much too far beneath me.

Mama lets out a small wistful sigh before turning me back around in order to begin weaving a long string of lilac pearls into my hair, like the argument didn't happen at all.

"Now, as I was saying, he likes reading and poetry, so you'll have that in common. His mother says he can never resist a game or a challenge of any sort. Yet *another* thing I'm sure you'll be able to bond over. I'm told he is absolutely enamored with kelpies and spends any free moment he has riding them—can you *imagine*?"

I groan outwardly.

"He is also supposed to be a very good dancer..."

My heartbeat can be heard pulsing in the very air itself as I stand at the top of the moonstone steps that lead down to our outdoor gardens.

A grimace is already plastered on my face while my hands bunch themselves into fists in the crystal-studded black fabrics of my dress. My eyes study the shadow lingering just between our dock's massive ivory columns.

Rich laughter echoes from above, and I spin around to find my father chuckling at my visible crossness. His crushing sapphire eyes glimmer with amusement as I again dare to stick my tongue out at 'The Bastard King' in sheer annoyance.

"Now now, what have we talked about?" Papa chides, but even as he does so, he cracks another encouraging grin at my defiance. A trait that was most definitely earned from him.

"Be nice," I hiss through my teeth.

"Good girl," he says, earning himself one of my most murderous glares. Another of my father's passed-down mannerisms. He tries holding back a laugh and fails.

"Go on now. No more dallying. Halcyon's mother says he's sulking somewhere down by the docks," Papa urges through a chuckle before pushing gently on my upper back towards the moonlit seaside.

"I *know* I *know*. Mama already told me," I huff in reply before taking a step downwards.

Father's hands grab onto my shoulders lightly, and I pause before taking another step further. His voice comes out sounding now like a viscous cold snap from just beside my ear. "If he is *mean* to you, Cherrystone, what do we do?"

A deviant smirk, one inherited from the man above, ghosts my lips. "Kick him where it hurts, as hard as I possibly can," I answer, looking up to flash my father a grin.

Papa nods through his not-so-subtle rolling laughter before shooing me onwards. I do as I'm told and take one step at a time towards what feels like an inescapable fate.

Making it to the dockside, where that shadow becomes a boy, I promptly halt in my tracks. I decide then to take advantage of the unclaimed moment and study my betrothed's appearance before Halcyon has the chance to notice my presence.

My unfettered eyes are free to study him and all his horrible beauty beneath the celestial light.

The hands I fist at my sides have begun to tremble, just a bit, while my stomach twists itself into terribly tight knots. I note that Halcyon is rather tall for a boy who is supposedly only one year older than myself. Mama said he recently turned twelve.

I study him further.

The suit he's dressed in is one of black threaded aurelian. He leans casually against a colossal pillar belonging to our massive dock. The boy's face is turned towards the midnight waters, but the portion of his head that I'm able to view is made up of maddeningly messy obsidian waves.

I notice then that the boy appears to be trembling a bit as well and I begin feeling a little better. He must be nervous too. Then I realize that his shoulders are actually shaking, and I think—I think I even hear the sounds of *crying*. I am admittedly, more than a bit morbidly transfixed.

Boys aren't supposed to cry.

My heart pounds just as wild and savage as ever but my insides actually begin to relax. Maybe this means that Mama was right after all. Halcyon clearly has emotions, which meant that he had to have feelings and some sort of heart. So maybe he wasn't as bad as they all said.

Maybe he's more like me than I thought.

Moving as if no more than a shadow, I come to stand behind him and tap once lightly on his back. The boy physically *jolts* in surprise, almost like the swipe of a match.

He turns around in an angry alarm, and I take several steps backwards as he rounds himself on me like some sort of avenging star. There's a sneer already on his lips, and tears pour startlingly freely down his face. Eyes of scorching amber lock onto mine.

He's terrifying.

My blood turns colder the longer his stare keeps me prisoner. But I am in fact my father's daughter, so I set my jaw and lift my chin, refusing to be the one to look away.

One second. Then two. Three. Four. Five.

The boy is the one to break our staring contest, as he looks me up and down appraisingly in a way that makes me want to punch him somewhere low. My hands tighten into fists at my sides.

It's not until that moment that I remember I've not introduced myself to my own betrothed. The boy probably has no idea who I am or what I'm even doing here, intruding on what is clearly a very private moment. I decide, for once in my life, to give Halcyon the benefit of the doubt.

"Are you *okay*?" I force myself to ask him. An attempt at being nice, as mother and father have insisted.

"*Tu es dulce. Fortasse pater meus dabit te mihi,*" he says, pushing off from the dock's column before taking a harrowing step my way. I immediately move back another few paces at his fast-approaching form. He halts no more than a foot away from where I finally decide to hold my ground.

Halcyon's eyes flash like real fire, exactly like the rumors foretold. He seems somewhat bemused by the fact that I clearly haven't understood whatever it is he's said. I think for a moment that perhaps he can't speak our dialect and find myself saying my thoughts aloud. "You really are a nightmare."

The sleeve of his midnight jacket comes to wipe away some lingering tears. My betrothed's next words unfortunately come out in perfect northern tongue. "And you're *gorgeous*. Who are you?"

Something about the words he says and the intense way he studies my face makes me want to take immediate heed of my father's advice. He takes another harrowing step my way, and I promptly kick him squarely in his exposed shin, as hard as I possibly can.

The boy's ember-like eyes go wide with outrage before he cries out sharply in very real pain.

"You—*brat!*"

I start sprinting back toward the moonstone gardens, my heart beating wild in my ears. Mama was most definitely wrong. This boy is every bit the nightmare that I'd feared. There must be some way out of this.

I have a year to find it.

XLIX. THE SOURCE

I resurface from the ocean within to a trembling that begins in my bones and echoes all the way out into the world of Pontus itself.

Gasping out in sudden keenness for the second time today, I bolt up onto my forearms and swear viscously at the pain that greets me.

My entire body feels as though it's just been flayed alive, while my brain feels like it might have been torn in half. I'm dumbfounded to discover myself laying in front of the now very firmly sealed golden vault doors of victory.

Coming to a sitting position triggers a new kind of pain to flare down my backside. Agony and confusion override most of my senses until I finally register the weight cradled in my arms.

Not daring to believe it, my eyes travel slowly downwards to discover that the bottle containing 'Death's Kiss' truly is secure inside my clutches. A tremor of something ancient and dangerous runs throughout my being at the sight of it.

Holding the beautiful ship closer to my person, I try to remember just exactly *who* and *where,* and *when* I am. Thoughts and images slide painfully back into place, one at a time. My crew, the trials, the captains, the TideLords, the Raider King, our futures—all waiting for me.

The sound of someone *else* gasping out has my head whipping around in alarm. I find Captain Agni panting heavily on his knees a few meters behind me. He looks as if he just finished making the longest and fastest run of his entire life. My eyes narrow in on the bottle nestled inside the crook of his arm before landing back on his face.

Amber eyes lock with mine.

I know immediately from the way his gaze widens slightly in silent question that he *knows*. He-knows-that-I-now-know-that-he-*knows*-me. He knows who I am. He has known *exactly* who I am this entire *fucking* time.

I really will be his death, because now I'm going to kill him.

Agni must see the fury I'm practically vibrating with because he has the good sense to toss his bottle out of reach just as I set down my own before moving in a fit of rage and tackling him right to the ground. He's so incredibly winded that the staggeringly powerful male goes down without a fight. I take great pleasure in hearing his skull hit the floor.

My very last remaining blade is angled against his primary artery in a blink.

Agni's dark brows rise slightly at the weapon while his breathing continues coming in and out in deeply labored waves. I cannot believe him—*just* when I think I'm figuring him out. He's been playing me this whole time, and I didn't even know the *fucking* game to begin with.

"*YOU'VE KNOWN ME ALL THIS TIME?*" I shout, seething with an ancient sort of wrath.

"Yes."

Is all he fucking says.

"So then *you* tell *me* just exactly why I shouldn't shove this blade right through your godsdamned skull, my darling dear *betrothed,*" I hiss through my teeth, absolutely fuming.

"How much—do you know—about our past?" Agni has the audacity to ask in between breaths.

"*Enough!*" I snap, cold and sharp as an arctic blast. "I know that you knew exactly who I was the moment you walked off your godsforsaken southern ship! I know enough to know that you and I have met face-to-face before. Once at least for sure. I remember that night now—the one where I met you down at my family's docks."

Something like bitter understanding dawns in his eyes, and he scoffs an insufferably arrogant laugh that tempts me further to murder the sadistic prince right then and there. Agni utters a breathless string of unintelligible words in his foreign tongue that I can only assume is some sort of lengthy curse.

"Then you barely know anything at all!" he seethes up at me in return. "Because if you had remembered the entirety of how our story goes, then you wouldn't have a blade at my throat—you'd be on your *knees* begging me for my forgiveness. Right-fucking-now!"

His eyes blaze with that same real, living fire. They're just as terrifying as ever with their intensity—possibly even more so. In fact, if I wasn't so livid, I probably would have noted the very real physical changes. Agni has somehow become even more daunting and beautiful than before. He's impossibly taller and broader, and his skin even shimmers with a real golden hue.

Like a beautiful yet absolutely lethal sword forged from some truly divine fire. He's virtually a freshly fallen avenging star.

However, I am much too pissed off right now to bother taking note.

The world around us begins shaking in peril, but I keep the weapon aimed beneath his neck. My teeth clench tight as I study his expression and find it both furious and unwavering. He notices the second that I begin to hesitate in response to the ferocity of his claim and knocks the blade from my hand with *real* lightning-fast reflexes.

Agni then rolls me easily off his person before swiping his bottle angrily from its resting place and roughly yanking me up to my feet. My face is a mask of icy rage as I grab both my fallen weapon and bottle before descending the golden temple steps and beginning to stride angrily towards the tunnel from which I arrived.

There is an iron hold on my wrist in the next instant that has me seeing red. "And just *where* do you think you're going?" Agni demands with barely concealed fury.

My newfound hatred for the southern celestial prick shakes the ground itself as I look back at Agni in outrage. "To find my *crew* and our *speeder,*" I spit, yanking my wrist from his grip. "To get out of this godsforsaken place and away from your infuriating presence as fast as possible so that my crew and I can begin plotting how best to execute you and your crew's murder!"

The jackass rolls his eyes, like I'm being needlessly dramatic. "I already told you—I have your crew detained. They're being held, along with your speeder, by my crew at our mooring. So you'll have to come with me."

The waves of anger emanating from me seem to make the ground around us tremble even harder. Cracks begin riddling the kórallian walls as an otherworldly hum of energy fills the air.

"I told you already they are safe—*my gods,* Boreas." Agni's tone is sharp and peevish. "You have got to be more careful with your emotions right now."

My jaw drops fully, and I look up in complete and utter disbelief at his nerve.

"Oh *what* is it now?" the prick demands, his expression turning to one of irritated confusion in the face of my total affront. "You have very clearly just broken down the wall to your source."

He states it as if I should obviously know what that fuck that is supposed to mean.

I eye him skeptically in silent return.

Agni's eyes close tightly, and his jaw clenches forcefully as a ring-adorned hand swipes down his face in utter aggravation. When he opens his eyes again, I find them coal black. "Are you honestly telling me right now that you don't know a sundamned thing about your own well of power? Do you know *anything* about elementals?"

His anger makes me defensive. I shift the bottle in my arms and snap, "I know about my affinity and I know about elemental powers, you arrogant *prick*. I know that the source of your element is a separate thing from your affinity, and I know that each individual's elemental ability is just slivers that make up that source."

Agni's mouth parts in clear disbelief. His hand goes to roll his jaw before he finally lets out an infuriatingly condescending scoff. "That is just about the stupidest fucking thing I think I've ever heard. *Who* told you that?"

My lip curls up high in response to his brazen haughtiness when answering, "Another elemental, Captain Tharos."

Agni's eyes blaze obsidian for a half-second before that wall of unfeeling iron slams down into place. He lets out a laugh so dry it could start a fire. "Oh-ho-ho, but of course. I should have known that dear ole' *wonder boy* would somehow be involved in this. That now makes perfect sense as to why it's the most asinine explanation of elemental power that there has ever been!"

At my look of simmering loathing, Agni huffs a murderous breath. "Look, we don't have time to go into specifics right now, but you have just tapped into—or more accurately *reconnected with*—a deep well of ancient power that is both incredibly dangerous and completely unstable at the moment. It is directly influenced by your emotions, which are also completely unstable at the moment."

Even deeper cracks form up the luminous kórallian tunnels around us. My mouth opens again to lash out in outrage, but the prick cuts me off. "That was once again *not* a taunt but a fact. Believe me, I know from personal experience the deadly consequences of not getting your emotions in check after that wall inside comes tumbling down."

Something painful flickers in his gaze that tells me he's actually speaking truthfully.

"*Fine,*" I concede, my jaw clenched tight.

We continue walking down the winding vein leading back to the heart, and I try focusing on Preceptor Darood's breathing exercises. Unfortunately, they no longer seem to help me shove down that raging beast. I feel so impossibly raw, truly as if I've been flayed all over my person but even more on the inside. Every question and thought regarding the millions of things I still don't know swell up inside.

I find myself halting to demand from Agni before we take another turn along the passage, "So then what happened? The end of our story—why should I be begging you for your forgiveness? What exactly do you know of me? Who am I? Where did I come from? What happened?"

Agni pauses mid-stride to look down at me with an unreadable expression. I watch as his jaw clenches tight, and he shakes his head at me in silent denial to answer any of my questions.

After *everything*, he has the nerve to refuse me of my own godsdamned past. I'm blindingly furious, and the ground suddenly shifts onto its side.

Agni catches me swiftly in his arms before my face hits the floor. He then sets me back upright firmly and states very evenly, "You need to *attempt* to control your emotions right now, Boreas."

His amber eyes lock on mine intently, and the next words he speaks are very deliberate, like he needs me to pay very close attention to his every word. "It isn't that I don't *want* to tell you the answers to all of your many questions."

I pause and study his face for a moment. "So you're saying that you *can't*?"

A bit of relief eases the burning intensity in his gaze. "Clever girl," Agni says with a small, provoking smirk.

My lips flatten in silent assessment before questioning him shrewdly, "To be clear, are you saying that you *can't,* as in, you are somehow, impossibly, physically, unable to speak to me about my past life? Or are you saying that you *can't,* as in, it would spoil the twisted little games you've been playing with me for your own personal entertainment this *entire* godsdamned year?"

Agni doesn't even have the decency to look ashamed of his prior torment before holding up one finger in silent emphasis that it's the first option. I read the sifting embers in his gaze and, unfortunately, get the sense somewhere deep down in my gut that the improbable claim he is making is actually somehow true.

"Does anyone *else* know me—or who I once was?" I next demand.

Agni's expression flashes for a moment, and I could almost swear there was a glint of sadness in his gaze before shaking his head 'no'. Again, I study him closely and once more feel that same little twinge deep down inside that lets me know it's the truth.

Blowing out a huff of annoyance, I begin marching back down the tunnel. The very air feels like it's pulsing with my anger. I keep trying the breathing method, but every few rounds some random thought will trigger an emotion, and that horribly unruly power within will come swelling back up inside just for me to begin pushing it right back down.

After about five minutes of this internal battle, I lose my hold on the beast, and a great resounding *'crash'* sounds from a tunnel collapsing far too near our passageway for comfort.

Agni halts to give me a look before demanding, "What exactly are you doing right now to control your emotions?"

"Breath-work," I snap.

"And that means what, *exactly*?" he slides the last word through his teeth.

Swallowing my hatred towards the male, I explain, "It's a count of four breathing technique. I breathe in to four, hold for four, exhale to four, hold, repeat. It usually helps me shove down my emotions and restrain my affinity when it becomes too unruly. But it is not currently working as well as it usually does."

Agni blinks once slowly before puffing out his chin with his tongue while his eyes search my face like he's waiting for me to say that I'm joking. When I return him a look of total perplexity, he closes his eyes and lets out a low groan in aggravation. The hand not holding his ship bottle comes to pinch the bridge of his nose, and he looks to the sky while muttering painfully to himself. "*Hoc tam durius futurum esse quam putabam.*"

I watch silently as he eventually swallows thickly and finally returns his eyes to mine.

"So to be *clear*," he says in a mockery of my prior shrewdness. "You are telling me that this *entire* time, you have been bottling up and then shoving down both your emotions and your elemental power as your way of controlling them? And that *no one* has ever taught you *any* differently?"

His tone has me hesitating and my answer comes out more like a question. "Um, *yes*?"

Agni's eyes widen in renewed disbelief, and his hand actually comes to cover his mouth while he shakes his head at me in that newly agitating way. "How are you still *alive*?" He practically explodes, running a hand through his maddening hair.

"*Deos supra et infra.*" Agni chokes. "All this time—I thought you were just being *intentionally* pathetic for the sake of strategy so I played along! You don't even have the godsdamned fundamentals to control what's just been unlocked!" he exclaims, his tone verging on murderous.

"Then what *should* I be doing?" I ask, my voice rising in equal irritation.

"Controlling them, not containing them!" Agni's nearly shouting in frustration.

His eyes blaze so fiercely against the gold of his menacing scar that I actually step backwards in involuntary reaction to their blinding fury. He notices the movement and clamps down tightly on whatever he was about to say next before exhaling deeply.

"Sorry," he huffs angrily, and his irises return to amber. Agni's next words come out softer in tone. "What I am trying to say, is that you should not be actively fighting to restrain the multitude of very valid emotions that you're currently feeling. As an elemental *especially*, you should feel them, and process them, and then *bend* them to your will."

He takes another deep breath. "However, due to the fact that you have had less than zero proper instruction, it will likely take quite a while for you to get to that point."

I look away from him and his aggravating amount of knowledge. Biting down on my lower lip, I begin to worry what this will mean now. I could hardly even control my affinity before.

Agni sighs in outward annoyance before setting down his vault trophy once more and coming to stand before me. I shift the bottle in my arms before glancing up to him with raised brows.

"Give me your hand."

I scowl immediately. "No."

He smirks at my prompt refusal. "I'm just going to show you a trick that will allow you to at least *feel* whatever array of emotions you're currently feeling without bringing the entire maze down around us. Then we can make it back to our crews, get out of here, and you can begin plotting how best to execute my murder."

I snort without thinking, and I'm instantly irritated by my own amusement. Grinding my teeth, I gingerly set down 'Death's kiss' before angrily placing my hand in his. Then I watch through skeptical eyes as Agni gently flips my hand over so that my palm now faces upwards.

"This is the first technique I ever learned," he says, meeting my gaze, and I find his eyes a golden shade I've not yet seen.

It almost looks like sunlight.

"The idea is that each finger is tied to a different array of emotions. The thumb is linked to worry and anxiety, the index finger is your fear, and the middle finger is for bitterness and rage, although—" He stops mid-explanation to let out a dark chuckle. "I think you've already got that one figured out."

I roll my eyes, and he chuckles again.

"The ring finger is tied to despair and depression, and your pinky is for stress or nerves. So when you have an emotion begin to swell up inside, don't repress it.

Instead, just focus on trying to identify what exactly it is. Then take your other hand, use it to wrap around the finger tied to that emotion tightly, and take a very deep breath. It will ease the potency of the feeling, which will then allow it to pass by and roll off of you."

I chew on my lip, thinking through the steps.

"Let's try it out, get the technique down, and then we can get this show on the road. Because I am not risking you getting even one single step closer to my crew in this state. Nor do I think you are willing to risk getting closer to your own."

"How?" I ask, visibly annoyed that I'm forced to accept his help right now.

His upper lip twitches with amusement. "We'll play our favorite game. I'll ask you a couple of questions. You identify how the answer makes you feel, use the method, and then allow the emotion to pass by and roll off."

"Fine. Let's get this over with," I mutter.

He smirks at my obvious vexation. "We'll start with something easy. How do you feel knowing your crew is currently detained—*safely*—by my boys?"

The potent emotions come swelling up inside, and I soon find that my knee-jerk reaction is in fact to beat them right back down. I grind my teeth and deny myself the temptation. Instead, I focus very hard on identifying the monster itself.

It wasn't that I thought that my crew was helpless. They all had each other and their affinities should anything go truly wrong. Plus, they had already done very well on their own. I was very proud of them. So it really came down to them being in a situation where I wasn't there to intervene and didn't know what variables there could possibly be going on.

"Anxiety," I answer with a tight swallow as a shallow tremor runs through the ground.

"Good," Agni replies, nodding for me to try his technique. I wrap my opposite hand around my thumb, tied to the emotion of anxiety, and squeeze tightly while taking a deep breath.

I am a bit amazed at how well the method works. It's like standing up to your waist in the ocean and allowing a wave to pass through you before rolling down to the shoreline. It doesn't mean the situation is gone or the emotion is no longer present. It's just that now it's dispelled to a point where I can think, and see, and act without its interference.

"See, it works."

I look up to find Captain Agni's face is stupidly smug. "And as I've said, they are safe. My boys are under strict orders, and they are just as loyal to me as yours are to you. They're practically hounds. Plus, I'm pretty sure your third has done something to enchant poor Ophios. My second won't let anything happen to them."

I tamp down on my own smirk when thinking about bringing up that tidbit to Kleio in front of Herse.

"Now this next one is going to be a little harder. It's going to be about the *past*," Agni warns me pointedly. "How do you feel when you think of the encounter you remembered between us?"

Resisting the urge to shove down the emotion is admittedly a struggle. His young eyes still burn like an avenging star in my mind as he rounds himself on me. Even now, just the mere memory of their awful intensity makes my pulse quicken a bit.

"Fear," I respond automatically before taking my hand and squeezing the index finger tightly.

I breathe in and out deeply until the emotion has come and gone. When Agni is silent, I look up to meet his stare and find surprise in his eyes, as well as a very deep frown on his face.

"*What?* What did I do wrong?" I demand.

"*Nothing*," he says instantly. "That was perfect. I just—I was not expecting that emotion to be your response. It's a very different reaction than I had assumed it would be. That's my own fault."

"What did you assume it would be?" I ask curiously.

His lips quirk up a bit before he brazenly flashes me his middle finger—bitterness and rage. I let out a laugh of surprised amusement. That laugh, shockingly enough, earns me one of his dangerously crooked smiles. My pulse automatically trips over itself, and I curse myself internally.

"Okay, two more. This one is going to be tough and also about the *past.* But we need to get it out. So just remember, don't fight it. Try to identify it." Agni again warns me before asking, "How do you feel when thinking about whatever *important people* that you might have remembered?"

The question does indeed unlock a bit of a floodgate. I'm no longer standing in the ocean before a wave. I'm caught up in a riptide. My jaw clenches as two inhumanly perfect faces flash in my mind's eye. Faces and their voices that I now cannot believe I ever before forgot.

I don't even know their names beyond Mama and Papa, but I can feel their presence inside me. Which is in and of itself a blessing. It also makes my throat close up and my eyes sear until they begin overflowing with something brutally painful.

"Despair," I choke out and my eyes close tight as tears I never allow for begin to break free.

"*Very* good," Agni says, his voice as soft and gentle as dawn.

When I don't move, he takes my hand and squeezes my ring finger tightly for me. Like he's standing with me in the waters as a tidal wave crashes through. I breathe deeply through my crushing misery. Eventually I'm able to allow it to roll off, and I slump in relief of its passing.

Opening my eyes, I find Agni's countenance solemn and understanding.

"That was really good, Merena. Despair and depression are the very toughest waves to ever withstand. But—" he adds with a quirk of his lips. "I've heard a little rumor going around, made very well known to me by your adoring group of castaway boys, that *you* are the reigning northern surfing *champion*. So I'll be sure to get my autograph before you kill me."

I can't help but laugh in surprise at his very well-played joke. Agni rolls his eyes at my clear astonishment that he has a sense of humor before letting out a breathless laugh himself. He then waits for me to gather my bearings before starting back up.

"Okay, last one." Agni steps closer. "How do you feel about *me* now, with what you *do* know?"

I grit my teeth again while allowing the many different facets of Agni to rise up before me. Now that I knew that tiny sliver of our past, it opened an entire sea of burning questions and warring desires. There were so many layers to him that I haven't yet discovered. So many complicated and completely contrasting pieces to his puzzle that I just wasn't sure how I'd ever figure out.

"Conflicted," I answer honestly.

He takes another step closer with a tight nod in agreement. "That's very perceptive and advanced, *even* for the fundamental stage. It means that there's an array. People are highly complex. Just list as many as you can identify."

Swallowing my spiked pulse at his nearness, I close my eyes and try to focus. "Anger. Annoyance. Irritation. Vexation. *Hatred*." I pause, letting the first wave barrel through with a deep breath, and my voice comes out next, less vehement. "Confused. Unsure. Nervous," I admit, truthfully, taking another deep breath.

Agni's ashen voice sounds from just beside my ear. "And, *physically*?"

I shiver in surprise at his unexpected closeness. He tilts my chin up beneath a finger, and I open my eyes to find him less than an inch from my face.

"Curious," I reply.

Then he does the second thing I never saw coming in a million years.

Agni takes my chin in his hand and gently turns my head in order to softly press a kiss of golden sunlight onto each one of my cheeks. It has the effect of easing the very last ripples from that tidal wave of despair while soothing the awful, lingering rawness, both internally and externally.

Then he drops his hand and steps back away.

I stand there, searching his darkly handsome face intently, as a very loud internal alarm bell begins to ring quite shrilly inside my head. He has just skillfully breached one of the first highly formidable gates that's currently locking up something much more dangerous than my affinity.

I can see it now—the little shine of triumph in his eyes. He knows exactly what he's doing.

Fuck.

"Alright, I think you're okay now. Let's go."

We make it about ten minutes towards his mooring before one more pressing thought shoves itself up to the surface. "Wait," I say, and Agni halts his steps mid-stride to pivot on a heel before looking down at me in question.

"Your name—your *real* name—is Halcyon. Why did you change it to Olsson?" My brows furrow tight in question. Agni gives me a grimace that tells me he can't physically explain why.

I chew on a lip before venturing, "I get the feeling Agni isn't really your family name either?"

He dips his chin to let me know I'm right.

Chewing my lip further, I try to recall why exactly the name 'Agni' feels so correct. I only have those three memories to go off of, but then—something in the energy-laden air whispers to me one single word: *agonizing*.

It's the exact same unexplainable murmur of energy that told me on my Sál Moon to tell The Sons and Daughters my name was Merena when asked. So I instinctively find myself trusting it.

I look back up to gauge his reaction. "Agonizing?"

Surprise flares bright inside his eyes, and he grins with a small nod for me to go on.

"Agonizing—Agni. It was—it was a kind of nickname your parents had for you—wasn't it?"

There aren't exactly memories tied to this knowledge. It's more of a feeling I get from a familiar source that I can't quite place. His dark brows are high now, and his grin is terribly crooked as he nods repeatedly that I am in fact, somehow, correct.

"*Clever girl,*" Agni praises me, more than a touch wickedly. A flush instantly heats my neck and I shake my head in order to dismiss my own body's moronic mutiny.

It's silent for a beat.

I'm not sure why I find myself looking at his face to judge my own memories, but I study those amber eyes while stating, "My parents, they called me Cherry-stone."

His grin softens a bit as he nods once in agreement.

I laugh breathily to myself in remembrance of just how much that nickname used to piss me off. Which is more than likely why my parents would keep calling me it. They both thoroughly enjoyed my dramatics.

Then I try to remember where it came from. Why *did* they call me that very strange name? My brows tug together, and I grow pensive for a moment.

"But I don't know why," I finally admit in defeat while my shoulders slump down a bit.

Agni stares at me in silent calculation before moving his bottle into one arm's crook and starting a new game. He holds up two fingers before me pointedly, and I squint in confusion before taking a guess. "Two words?"

With a small smirk, Agni inclines his chin in response. Then he holds up just one finger, and I start to understand where the game is going.

"First word, cherry?" I venture.

His smirk broadens as I'm playing along. I shake my head at his amusement and press, "Okay, so cherry comes from what?"

Strangely, Agni's eyes grow a bit heated, and I watch in confusion as he slowly lowers his head before running his nose up my neck. My perfidious heart beats wildly, and I stare at him in surprise. He nods repeatedly, motioning with his free hand, as if telling me to think about it.

"My—I—I *smell* like cherries?"

"And you *taste* like them, too," Agni confirms in an exhale, like whatever is holding him back from speaking ceases once I've figured out the answer. The grin he flashes me next is purely sinful.

I flush a damning scarlet in turn before promptly scowling with a roll of my eyes in an effort not to pay any heed to the terribly dangerous warmth sparking inside my core.

But then a very rare, soft-smile lifts the corners of my mouth. Because I now *know* that little portion of the nickname has Mama written all over it. Agni gives me an odd sort of look in response to the sight of that soft smile. Like his heart might have stopped beating.

"Okay, second word—stone?" I question, forcing him back into the game.

That odd look is gone in a blink as his expression quickly becomes a very solemn mask of harsh indifference. He firmly pounds a fist over his heart twice in emphasis.

"Heart of stone?" I guess.

Agni laughs but shakes his head 'no'. His eyes turn upwards to search the sky far above while trying to figure out how to properly explain it. I watch as an idea comes to mind, and amber eyes meet mine again.

"*Brek*," Agni says the word with intent. And suddenly it 'clicks' like the pulse of a lock.

That was right.

I remember it now.

The grin I then reveal is equally rare with the newfound certainty that this portion of the name has Papa written all over it. I was unyielding. I was unbreakable. I was the rock of protection, standing up against the volatile and chaotic storms.

I was stone.

Cherrystone.

L. BEWITCHED

Agni and I journey the rest of the way to the heart in an eerily comfortable silence.

Both of us are pensive and exhausted and spun out on just about every emotion you can possibly think of.

The vault was basically a hafgufa. It had swallowed me whole and then spat me back out by my bones. I'd been put through a whirlpool of so many extreme feelings and realizations that I was most definitely not prepared for. There's a deep sort of fatigue setting in that I'm sure I've never felt before.

I think I could sleep for a week straight.

Dawn is well and truly rising above us as we make it to the last stretch before reaching Captain Agni's mooring. Once again, anxiety and unease swell up inside, but I grip my thumb and breathe deeply through the bitter urge to suppress them.

It was getting easier.

I look up to find Agni giving me a knowing smirk as he turns around and begins walking cockily backwards in the direction of our waiting crews.

"Good girl," he says in response to my use of his method. The praise was a bit offhanded, but once he's said it, something flexes in his jaw, heats in his eyes, and he swallows as that smirk turns sinful. "Oh, I could get *very* used to this little teacher-student dynamic between us."

My hand grips onto my middle finger, and I breathe in and out deeply.

"Impressive," Agni comments, brows high. His expression then turns insufferably arrogant. "I could teach you *lots* of things you know. About your powers, about your element. We could play some games to try and answer your questions about our shared past. I have *lots* of games we could play, in fact. Some of them might *even* allow for clothing." He shoots me a wink while continuing his backwards swaggering.

My hand grips my middle finger even tighter while exhaling the words, "Insufferable asshole."

"Don't you mean—*excruciating*?" Agni taunts with a provoking flash of his brows.

The ground tremors slightly in response, but I otherwise manage to ride the wave of his absolutely agonizing fucking personality. He chuckles darkly while giving me a nod of real approval as we reach the end of the tunnel before spinning back around.

"Now, as I promised—" Agni begins, taking a step out of the tunnel and into the circular mooring dock. "Your lovely little crew is all perfectly safe, and—" he halts abruptly in order to choke on a horrified gasp of profound disbelief.

My heart thunders with reckless abandon as I shove Agni out of my way and step into the heart. I quickly scour the scene to find seven tied-up raiders, each with a locked and loaded crossbow aimed directly over their hearts.

But they are *not* mine.

The grin that forms along my mouth is almost painfully wide while devouring the absolutely delectable scene that's been laid out for me. This is almost as good as winning the fucking vault itself.

Captain Agni's crew of mongrels are tied up securely in a very tight ring. Each one of them is in various states of undress, with hair indecently mussy and their lips undeniably reddened. They also all appear to be seething with rage in response to having their own weapons pointed directly against their own shirtless chests by one of *my* crew members.

My eyes find Kleio's immediately, and for a moment I'm only able to stare, speechless, in complete amazement. Then I lock eyes with the six others of my crew, each one mercifully alive and well, and also in a fair bit of damning disarray.

"WHAT THE *HELL* HAPPENED?" Captain Agni bellows, absolutely furious.

My grin widens further.

"WE WERE BEWITCHED CAPTAIN—THEY *FUCKING* BEWITCHED US!" Vagar Ophios bellows right back, unbelievably outraged.

"Oh, please, you practically crawled on your knees and begged me to touch you," Herse refutes with a snort of cool amusement from where she currently points the end of an iron-tipped arrow right over his heart. My entire crew, myself included, break into fits of pealing laughter.

Raider Ophios flushes crimson before glaring murderously at my third with a face full of ire.

"*Bene. Ophios fuit amissa causa aliquamdiu nunc quae excusatio tua, Uthra?*" Agni fumes in that foreign tongue. His accusing voice is now directed towards his third, Adiram Uthra, whose warm upturned haughty features and jade-colored eyes look towards his captain incredulously.

"*Vide eam!*" He snaps before staring daggers at Kleio, currently holding him hostage. "*Quum femina sicut gloriosus sicut illud, ostendit tibi etiam exigua de studium vos have ut pounce! Mea Deos—non est mea culpa quod illa est unus opus artis!*" Adiram shakes his head of shorn onyx hair in heated exasperation.

I look over to my second with a bit of awe at how uncharacteristically riled Captain Agni's third is. "What did you *do* to him?" I ask, inspired.

Kleio shares with me one of her most mischievous grins. "I *winked.*"

My mouth drops fully open at her unnerving skill before I begin laughing so hard that it sets my entire crew off in another wave of amusement. The southern captain and his mongrels are left more furious than I've ever seen.

Agni begins rubbing his hands up and down the sides of his face with a long outward groan. Vagar responds by stating accusingly, "You claimed there would be no problem without their captain! These are not normal females—these are *sirens,*" he forces the last word through enraged, clenched teeth.

Something about that word triggers me to look closer at my crew. All seven of them were already very pretty girls before, but now that I really take another look... Their natural features appear to have been heightened to become startlingly, hauntingly, *gorgeous*.

It's as if all the things I love about them have been thrust right up to the surface for everyone else to see. There's a kind of ethereal glow about them too. It's subtle, glimmering just beneath their skin, but it's there. The white tythe-tokens shimmering in their hair now provide the illusion of real moonlight shining down on them.

Now the entire Order—no—all of *Pontus* can see just exactly why I picked each and every one of them for my crew. They'll be forced to, whether they like it or not.

It's some sort of added boon from the drowned gods. A second blessing, giving my crew an even deadlier power of protection for those times I can't be with them to stand as the rock between whatever the storm is.

Kleio begins eyeing me strangely and I give her a quizzical look. "You're kind of different now," she says. "You look like you. But you're like... *glowing*. Like it's physically hurting my brain a little bit right now to comprehend how beautiful you are." My second narrows her eyes and cocks her head to one side in confusion.

Brows furrowing, I fish out the tail-end of my long plate still miraculously held in that new golden cuff to find that it is a tad luminous. My hair now very subtly glows in that same shimmering opalescent white as Mama's did in those few unlocked memories I now possess. It's beautiful but also a bit chilling. Like some sort of beacon in the dark.

"You didn't think to tell me that I was now *glowing*?" I turn towards Agni in surprise after having just spent this entire walk back with him.

"*What?*" Agni retorts snappishly, looking back over at me in complete annoyance, still seething from how poorly he's just been bested. "You are always glowing. *Don't* start back up with me right now," he warns before returning his scorching scowl of irritation to his crew members.

"*Quid ego docui tibi de continentia?* One fucking *wink,* and she takes you down?" Agni snorts in visible disbelief before running a hand through his maddening hair. "You're practically hellhounds! But all it takes from these lovely little females is to bat their pretty eyes at you, and you all roll over like lovesick puppies!" he berates before scoffing at his mongrels in disgust.

Such a sore loser.

I begin studying Agni's crew closer and discover whatever sort of second blessing that has clearly been placed on their captain has made its way over to the crew. Each of his mongrels was already stupidly bronze, tall, and quite ruthless to begin with. But now they appeared even bigger and stronger and glowed just a *bit* with that strange golden hue.

They individually appear to be lethal weapons of destruction in their own right. Not quite to the extreme as their insufferable captain, but close. Had I known that *this* was the pack of males my crew was detained with, I would've let Agni have The Vault and come running to find them immediately.

Then I notice, as Vagar is currently shirtless, that a golden branch of lightning has been branded into his skin and flares across the breadth of his chest. I check the other six to find they've all branded that same golden branch of lightning right across their hearts. The same one marring Agni's face.

They were *tythed.*

Tythed by the very thing that secretly haunted their captain so terribly. They must have completed the sacred rite at some point before tonight's events began, like we had done. Their chosen tokens just aren't ones of such outward obvious expression as my crew's. So no one had even known.

I begin biting down on my lip in thought as another alarm bell rings loudly in my head. Another very formidable gate is currently being skillfully breached by the prick. This time, however, it is completely unintentional. Which only makes it all the more horrifying.

Shit.

Agni begins pacing the spot before me quite heatedly. "*What* have I been telling you all repeatedly, this *entire* time, all-godsdamned-year? *Non potes permittere puellam valde splendidam a pari calliditate et calliditate monstri, quod sub superficie iacebat, te avocare*. It will be your all's death, I fucking swear it!"

Agni mutters a few more curses before finally ordering, "Boreas, call off your sirens. *Now*."

Meeting each of my crew member's eyes, an idea comes to mind. One that's sure to push the celestial-southern prick just a touch further tonight. I give them a quick flash of my father's deviant grin before showing my little sirens precisely how to make the final killing blow.

The *kiss of death,* as it were.

Frowning deeply, I turn to face Captain ten-feet-of-pure-fucking-menace with a slow, disappointed shake of my head while 'tsking' three times over. "Now just what sort of parley do you expect to broker here with such a vicious attitude as that?"

Agni's obsidian eyes meet mine, and his nostrils flare with outrage. I derive true pleasure from his anger due to me and my crew beating him and his so very horribly.

"What do you *want?*" he growls in irritation.

My responding smirk is wicked. "Beg me."

Agni's expression turns fully indignant in a blink, and my enjoyment heightens. Near-unintelligible laughter erupts inside the heart from my crew. The south captain's arresting face darkens and I can see it—just how much it's killing him right now to be the one to lose.

Perfect.

"Beg me to call off my sirens, Agni, or I will let them shoot your very handsomely tythed hellhounds—not fatally—but somewhere that *will* hurt," I promise with mock sweetness.

Captain Agni's gaze hardens as he quickly sifts through his tactical options before finally coming to terms with the fact that I do have him beat on this one. He looks towards Vagar and the rest of his hostage crew members, eyes blazing with fury.

"You see?" Agni demands with a brisk 'snap' before pointing in my direction. "*Videstine quam deos-damnatum ieiunium erat enim ea in venire sursum cum quod*? It's fucking intrinsic."

Their captain then carefully studies my unwavering face once more. "*Fine*," he concedes before roughly grabbing my wrist and dragging me back inside the hidden passage. Another wave of my crew's laughter follows us in and pisses him off even more.

Once we're out of view from either of our crews, Agni quickly works through his seething anger and begins analyzing my face. His jaw flexes while quietly calculating something. I'm aware the moment he comes up with an answer to his private query because the beginnings of a cruel smirk flicker into existence in the corners of his stupidly soft lips.

Agni then grabs me by the waist, sets me solidly against the wall, and gets down on one knee.

The action throws me off so much that I find myself immediately trying to press further into the wall that I'm already back flat upon in startled surprise. He proceeds to take my hand with his ruby ring adorning it and brings it swiftly to his lips.

All of my previous nefarious amusement evaporates as I look down in alarm to find his eyes determined and intent. "*Please, Merena,*" Agni whispers my name like a prayer. He then presses his searing mouth firmly against the top of his stolen ring. Irises of pure gold hold me prisoner to the spot.

My gaze narrows at his cruel cunning.

He has found the one and only way that would remove my very terrible enjoyment at watching him beg due to our to-be-inspected-further *betrothed* past.

Sadistic fucking genius.

"Please let my crew go from your unexpectedly deadly sirens," he begs me, brushing his lips reverently back and forth against my hand in a way that causes a tremor to run deep inside my bones. "Or if you won't, then *please* take me as your prisoner too. And I promise I'll worship you, and every inch of your naked body, each night from dusk until dawn, for the rest of eternity."

I frown deeply in response as my chest begins rising and falling with more alarm bells sounding inside my head. He is appallingly skilled at testing my walls. This is not good. Not good at all.

My voice sounds a bit off, even to my own ears, when replying, "Okay, I'll let them go. But I will be *keeping* the ring as my boon."

Golden eyes flare triumphantly, and I know for sure that this one was not unintentional at all. He knows exactly what he's fucking doing and exactly whatever sort of new mind game it is he's playing with me. Meanwhile, I am yet again left in the darkness of the unknown.

Satisfied, Agni gets up from the ground.

I make to leave, but before I can exit, he pushes me gently back against the kórallian wall. Looking up, I find his scarily handsome person far too close for my sanity. Especially with those alarm bells still echoing inside my head.

"*Yes*?" I ask, suddenly wary.

"Second order of parley business," Agni explains with another smirk.

He tilts my chin up with his index finger so that I'm forced to meet his gaze as he speaks in a sultry voice like smoke. "I wanted to make sure that you knew, that the offer I just gave was not a taunt, and will *always* be on the table between us. You just let me know the moment you're feeling daring enough to give it a trial run. Spend one night with me, from dusk 'til dawn. I can assure you that I will not disappoint, and I'm *highly* devout."

Studying his face for the game, I am very much alarmed to find Agni is extremely serious.

He sees my wary study and chuckles softly in response. "Let me know the *instant* you're feeling daring, gorgeous," Agni affirms, before having the outright audacity to use his lightning reflexes and steal a kiss from my unsuspecting lips.

I blink in stunned surprise at the feeling of raw, undiluted *power* that just passed from his mouth to mine. I haven't the faintest fucking clue what on Pontus that just was.

By the time I find my voice, Captain Agni is already swaggering cockily back out to our crews.

LI. THE CHRISTENING

"So do you think we just like, smash it or what?" Nephthys asks.

"*No*—we do not *smash* it!" I gasp, yanking back the bottle from idiot number one's current inspection.

The very beautiful little imp looks over to her equally stunning twin, and I watch them pass unspoken words before Nephthys busts out laughing. "I *told* you she would lose it."

Prisca snorts before resentfully handing over some sort of shared oblation token with a shake of her glimmering head.

Rolling my eyes in irritation, I turn back to face my absolute knockout of a second who is still gazing in wonder at the bottle in my hands. I can't help but smile at her unwavering adoration for the ship. Kleio's been staring at it like this ever since we let the mongrels go and returned to our speeder.

Our crews followed each other's moonlighters, more than a bit resentfully, and made it out of the kórallian maze in record time. By the time we arrived back at the floating docks, dawn had become full-blown morning. The welcome we received was absurdly thunderous and ear-splittingly boisterous.

But mostly it was very, *very* drunk.

So drunk that at first no one even noticed there were actually two vault winners standing before them. Captain Agni had held his bottle up high with an arrogant smirk, and the entire crowd of raiders went inconceivably mad for him. They even began chanting his name. Like he needed any expansion on that massive fucking ego.

I meanwhile was still lost inside my own thoughts from the overwhelming amount of new and confusing information provided while inside The Vault. So much so that Herse actually had to grab my arm with 'Death's Kiss' and raise it up for me in victory.

It effectively snapped me out of my trance, and I returned to a world of complete silence. Silence that erupted into another, much more heavily disoriented, round of cheering.

The TideLords each made their appearances to congratulate us soon after. Truthfully, I was surprised to find that they all strangely seemed much less intimidating to me now.

The way they in turn eyed Agni and myself, plus our crews, was an equally unexpected change. No longer did they gaze down from their viewing platform with little more than a nod or casual smile. They were beginning to measure us much differently now.

There was real fear in their eyes when realizing what the gods had done. There was also a very real and quite ravenous hunger while considering us that hadn't been there before. A *need* among each one of them to be the TideLord that acquires such beautiful weapons for their own personal arsenal.

I could practically taste the highly competitive storm brewing between the seven. The tables have turned. They'll be fighting for us to choose one of them as being worthy of our attention.

To my immense disappointment, I did not get to see the Raider King himself. There has apparently been another alarming development regarding the falling stars on Luminalia that required his immediate attention.

I can't deny I'm beginning to sense that feeling of impending dread that the others have picked up on from that night. It's almost like there's a warning message being whispered in the air. But I just *can't* quite make out the words.

The return ride north was a brand new kind of torture. All seven of my crew members passed out almost immediately upon castoff. I myself was impossibly exhausted and yet couldn't manage to sleep even one single wink the entire time.

This well of foreign yet familiar power humming beneath my skin flat-out refused to allow my body relax enough to slumber. My mind was also too busy running round and round the intense amount of bewildering and conflicting knowledge I'd gained about myself and my past to drift off.

There was a staggering list of questions I'd tallied inside my head from three memories alone. The first of which being my parents. My origins.

As far as I knew, there was no 'Bastard King' in all of Pontus. I'd thought over each landmass, isle, drifter, and all known rulers. Absolutely no one matched that name, reputation, or even came close to my father's physical description. Not to mention the fact that he would without a doubt been mentioned in Preceptor Chie's class as well as Beldham's.

So what did *that* mean?

Then there was thing my mother had said. That I was both *Northern* and *Nawai*. There is no true 'North'. Not anymore, at least. Not for a very, *very* long time. Nothing exists any further beyond our tiny cardinal isle other than hulking glaciers and unpassable seas.

I'm not even sure what to make of the Nawai bit. I know about as much regarding the spirit realm as the next raider. Which is to say, very little. Only the Sons and Daughters with their 'true sight' have access to the mysteries of the netherdepths.

My mother was another question entirely.

I could almost convince myself I'd imagined her up if it weren't for that voice. Mama's voice in those memories was the exact same one I'd heard that day before being struck by evening stars. Then I'd heard it a second time when being forced to beg Captain Leporem and trying to make me kiss her captaincy ring. I had *known* that voice deep down.

And I was always desperate to hear more of it.

The more I thought about my parents in those few precious memories, the more I realized I don't want to know anything more about my past. I'd felt so much love both for and from each of them in those past moments that coming back down to reality was a crushing sort of blow.

They had really, truly, loved me.

Yet here I am, a bastard-born castaway.

I'm left to assume those truths mean there is in fact a reasonable explanation for that ever-present miserable sort of darkness that's always pressing in the back of my mind. I must have done something horrible to lose their love.

If Agni's claims are truthful, and I should be begging for his forgiveness, then that only confirms I don't want to know anything more. Whatever I did must be the reason for the drowned gods marking me so cruelly. Even if my hair had already been white, my brand and affinity mark are just as damning. I don't know why I'm even remotely surprised to realize I must have deserved it after all.

So I'm done searching for my past.

I'll keep my precious memories safe and accept my castaway status as atonement. My focus from here on out belongs solely to my crew and their futures. While I might not be deserving of it, they are each more than worthy of whatever goodness I can bring to this second life for them. I will continue to be their rock between any and all storms.

No matter the cost.

Of course my mind then circled round and round the highly complex puzzle that is Captain Agni. Or rather Halcyon, as I now knew him.

My darling, dear, *betrothed*.

After the night of the winter storm, after learning the truth about the incident with his kelpie, I realized there was more to Agni than what I'd previously written him off as. But I didn't have the faintest clue as to how *much* more there was. Nor did I have any idea the staggering amount of contrasting layers within his possession.

He *is* cocky, and arrogant, and oftentimes intolerably insolent. He can also be cruel and cunning and brutally ruthless. But now I have to grapple with this newest layer. He can be... *empathetic*?

Logically, I suppose him helping me get ahold of my powers was really just as much for his own benefit and the safety of his crew as it was for me and mine. But why be—*sweet*? Gentle, even?

Agni is quite literally an enigma taken form.

We had a past. One that I can confidently conclude ended pretty fucking horribly. Horrible enough for him to believe that on top of everything else I'd been through, I also deserved an entire year of psychological warfare and mental games of torment from him. Which begs the question: how do I even know they've ended?

If I should be down on the ground groveling for his absolution, then I have to think that this whole charade between us isn't over. No, I'd wager that this dance is far from finished.

Perhaps then it's his tactics that have changed.

I know for certain that whatever loathing there is, and evidently historically has been between us, hasn't just disappeared overnight. Strategically thinking, if the tables were turned, I'd be working to adapt my ploys to the enemy and any new external factors presenting themselves.

As any worthy Tide Raider would.

If I were Agni, it would have been in my best interest to play nice. *Especially* when I, the enemy, had just regained access to a highly dangerous and emotionally controlled source of power. It would honestly have been suicidal to be less than cordial. That would explain his little 'golden boy' act.

Though the dusk 'til dawn offer is... troubling.

Agni doesn't make a single move that isn't ultimately to his own benefit. I can't imagine him as the type who would ever actually *want* to be tied down in that sense and most definitely not to me. I think I'm safe to conclude his offer, this 'trial run' as he calls it, is essentially a way to get whatever attraction he feels towards me out of his system.

To eliminate that weakness.

His games with me might just have moved into a much more dangerous territory of emotional destruction. If that's the case, it would only make sense that he'd begin trying to bring my guard down. Using a bit of kindness and some romantic notions as ploys. Once he has me at my most vulnerable, Agni can take advantage and enact whatever it is he clearly believes I've earned myself.

Tactically, it's kind of genius.

The more I wrestled with my inner turmoil regarding Agni, the more I came to realize just how very dangerous he is. Dangerous to *me* in particular. Which, by extension, means he's dangerous to my crew. And I can't allow for that.

If I'm at last understanding him and his true motivations, then the best thing I can do for the sake of my crew is to keep as far away from Agni as possible. While there's a chance, and a growing list of evidence, that I might deserve his retribution, my seven most definitely do not. I can't take any risks when it comes to their well-being.

No matter how addictive a puzzle he may be.

Mercifully, the other cardinals all left directly from The Vault to return back to their own isles far away across the Pontus seas. While the North Order is only a few hours' from the mythic pillars, the other's will have a week at least to journey back home. A few will be stopping at the Driftwood Court in order to properly send off their fallen.

One captain and four raiders did not make it out alive. We were told it's the least amount of deaths there's ever been during The Vault. That fact does not make the loss of Captain Tetsuo's life any more tolerable. The weight of his death very prominently lingered beside me the entire ride back. Even now, I just can't seem to shake it.

Since our very recent return, I've refused to step a foot inside those gates of hell. The last thing I want is for even *one* of those shadows that haunt that dark fortress to return to my crew's eyes. After everything, I just can't bear going back inside.

Not yet, at least.

I'm also fairly certain that I might just murder Skelm, Bealu, and Ersatz with my bare hands if given the chance. I actually found myself debating quite heavily during the last little bit of our journey just exactly how severe the fallout would be. Something about this wave of unlocked power makes me feel every bit as willful and defiant and reckless as the night I washed up here.

Like all those years of punishments and torture I've been through with the intent to break me down have been cleansed away. I'm ready for a fight, itching to cause trouble.

If it wasn't for my crew and their futures tythed to mine, I'd be kicking down Skelm's door right this very minute. To avoid that, I've marched us down to moorings past Giant's Crook and decided to christen our new home. My attention returns to Kleio, currently studying the perfect vessel cradled in my hands, slack-jawed.

"You like it?" I ask with a broadening grin.

Her wide sepia eyes meet mine before whispering reverently, "It's *incredible.*"

My grin broadens further when stating, "It's yours." That grin becomes quite painful as I look around at each of my crew members and proclaim, "It's *all* of yours. It's *ours.*"

All seven of my perfectly wonderful crew members look at me with extremely tight swallows. Very real tears begin lining their eyes, and I catch sight of something a lot like eternal devotion glinting in their gazes. It's a look I most definitely don't feel deserving of.

For brevity's sake, I ask, "Well, let's crack this bad-boy open, shall we?" before pivoting backwards on the tall black tooth-like rock in which I currently stand.

The sea is eerily calm today, with a pleasant warmth in the breeze bringing tidings of summer. A quick scan, however, reveals some ominous-looking clouds gathering far off along the horizon. I don't allow them to deter me from this moment.

Holding the bottle containing our ship up high above my head, I shout the ceremonial words with a commanding air, "I christen thee 'Death's Kiss', belonging now and forever more to the Sacred Eight. Captained by Merena Boreas and her crew of deadly sirens!" Then I hurl my hard-won vault prize into the eerie tides.

It takes no more than a moment before an otherworldly shudder ripples in the waters before us, sending a blast of pure, ancient power *running* throughout the world of Pontus. I shiver in response to the wave of passing energy.

It feels like some sort of harbinger.

The hauntingly beautiful ship, now officially belonging to my crew and I, rises up and out of the arctic waters as the very answer to each one of my childhood prayers.

To my surprise, I find while inspecting the beast in all its terrifying life-size beauty, that there is a previously undiscovered figurehead carved into the front of the ship's lethal bow of obsidian.

It portrays that of a gorgeously sculpted *siren*.

LII. A PROPHECY

Death's Kiss has proven itself to be just as incredible on the inside as it is on the outside. Which really is saying something.

My crew and I take our sweet time carefully walking through to inspect each and every inch of the stunning vessel. We soon discover that nearly every bit of it is even better than the last.

First and foremost, there's a very impressive war room. It holds a long, sleek, black oval table set with leather-bound chairs. Perfect for us to debate around. Maps of every sort plaster the walls, while stone shelves line the entire backside. The shelves themselves are chock-full of scrolls and epistle bottles and numerous other devices I've only ever seen while used in Beldham's lectures.

There's a proper sickbay, stocked with just about every kind of medicinal supply you can think of. Which is very good news for *me*. Strangely though, one of the cabinets contained some extraordinarily rare poisons and antidotes. I even found a rather large jar of kratosbane while poking around. Davina actually blacked out for a minute at the sight of it all. Greer had to jumpstart her back up.

Another trick her affinity is evidently capable of.

We strolled next through the fully-stocked kitchen and up onto the perfectly polished decks. I was then blessed with witnessing and touching the most incredible helm I've ever seen in my entire life. I *also* began to black out a bit and had to take a break before continuing any further.

Kleio and I paused while inspecting the ship masts to exchange twinning delinquent grins. The main mast holds a very large, wide netted, crows-nest atop it. Big enough for eight raiders to sprawl out and look up at the stars, while very likely also getting a little drunk.

Later, we moved back inside the beautiful beast to explore. Down past the shared areas and spaces, we found that each one of us has our very own room and ensuite. This is when the sobbing began, to my wide-eyed alarm.

My seven explained, through their new-found love of tears, that the ship implausibly somehow knew *exactly* who my crew would be. Their bedrooms have been created specifically with them in mind, precisely to their individual taste.

However, that's not exactly the reason behind such startling sobs. Those would be due to small trinkets of happy reminders and cherished things from their previous lives filling each room. It was like a way for them to return to an unreturnable home.

Kleio tells me her bed is the exact same bed she had in the Oyster Court. She claims that it even somehow *smells* the same. My second in command then bawled in it for about an hour after finding a small locket tucked inside her bedside table.

Again, I was alarmed by the unexpected floodgate unlocked. She explained through shuddering breaths that the necklace had belonged to her deceased mother. It was the same one that was lost to the sea after her death when Kleio was quite young.

I laid silently beside her, squeezing her hand tight in mine to help ease the tidal wave of despair. Finally, once everyone is all cried out, we go to find *my* room. To my outright horror.

I make it not more than three steps inside before freezing entirely. "*My fucking gods*—you have got to be joking," I mutter angrily beneath my breath.

Kleio nearly chokes on her surprise after having eagerly followed inside the room right on my heels. Herse strolls in behind her and immediately breaks out into a round of disbelieving laughter.

The rest of my crew similarly follow as they each curiously file on inside to get a glimpse of their stone-cold-bitch, calculating, deviant little nightmare of a captain's new quarters.

The room is, as I have very recently remembered, basically just the grown-up version of my childhood bedchambers from wherever it is that I once upon a time called 'home'. Front and center sprawls a ridiculously large bed that is rather obnoxiously shaped like a *real* open clamshell. It's heaped with plush pillows and wrapped in silken sheets of pale lilac.

The walls reflect a deep velvety shade of periwinkle, the flooring a soft glittering cream, while the ceiling is completely translucent to reveal the sky above. I spot along the left wall a thin pair of stained glass doors that I would guess lead out into a tiny veranda.

In one corner rests a large, also newly-remembered, vanity. It's a veritable treasure trove of glittering powders and liquids, delicate perfume bottles, and polished brushes. The hulking thing is made over the top with its equally large *heart-shaped* mirror.

I hold my deeply blushing head in my hands in complete and total embarrassment as my crew curiously checks out my new digs. Each of them has *very* mischievous grins on their previously tear-stained faces. Once again, I am the rock between all storms. A very-humiliated one at that.

"Merena, this is like a *sexy-princess* bedroom," Kleio claims, breaking the silence at last. Her expression is much too goading while watching my reaction.

"No—*it isn't!*" I snap defensively, to which Kleio snickers.

But after taking another look around, one of my hands cups my parted mouth while coming to terms with a truly horrifying realization. That is exactly what this fucking room looks like. This, of course, only incenses my crew's teasing.

Where are the weapons? The books?

The desk with which to plot our futures and quite possibly Agni's murder?

The very worst part is that I secretly kind of actually really *love* the room. Impractical as it is.

"Oh yeah, 'Cap? What are *these* then?" Herse asks, having found a chest of drawers overflowing with clothes. I look back towards my third, only to find her brazenly holding up an extremely racy set of black lace undergarments that I wouldn't have the faintest idea how to get into.

"*My gods,*" I curse aloud.

A hand comes to pinch the bridge of my nose between my thumb and fore-finger in complete and utter mortification. I doubt my face has been redder in all my life. That causes Kleio to erupt into a fit of laughter that is dutifully followed by the rest.

This is practically mutiny.

"This whole thing is *full* of them!" Herse announces to the room of females now determined to get beneath my skin. Their laughter becomes increasingly higher in direct correlation to the depth of my blush. Incorrigible godsdamned idiots. The whole lot of them.

"Well then, LeRoi, I think you should take some," I retort sharply before glancing at Kleio with a small grin. "I get the feeling Raider Ophios would actually commit treason if it meant he could see you in one. Think it might be worth adding to our list of potential strategies, Hiraeth?"

Herse turns an uncharacteristic shade of pink.

"Oh, without a doubt," Kleio quips, instantly on board with my taunting. "With how eager Vagar was to take you up on your offer to kiss him, I think it might make our top five. If we're ever in need of distracting those morons again, rest assured you will be the first to know."

My third goes back on the offense and looks to me with accusing violet eyes. "*You* were the one making out with their captain during the second checkpoint!"

My face fills with heat once more but there's now a new mixture of terribly confusing feelings tied to that damning kiss. Too much has changed knowing that piece of our past history for me to know what's real between us and what's not. So, for the sake of my crew, I'll have to assume the worst.

"Well, that will not be happening again," I state, my voice a touch cold.

It's evidently cold enough. My second and third look at each other in silent conversation. The others' expressions rapidly turn into ones of uneasy surprise. "What did he *do*?" Kleio demands after a moment, venom thick in her voice.

I swallow while trying to figure out the right words needed to properly walk them through the world-shattering revelations I'd endured while inside The Vault. My past is not something I wish to disclose or explore but if anyone deserves the painful truth, it's my tythed crew.

Taking a deep breath, I start to explain, "When Agni and I went into The Vault, I found out—" But something unexplainable cuts me off.

Time itself seems to stop for a moment.

The world around me begins humming with the very same peculiar other-worldly energy. A sensation of chills overcomes my body. It feels as though I've just put one foot in the past while one remains firmly in the present.

A heinous yet beautiful voice slithers out from everywhere and nowhere to reach my ears.

> *"One soul fated to remember what the world forgot. Only with them may you speak of what was not."*

The blood pumping through my veins begins to slow into a sluggish sort of rhythm. Those words are ones I'm sure I've never heard before and yet all the same ring some sort of long-forgotten bell.

They unmistakably belong to a prophecy.

Or more accurately, they're unmistakably a line from what is likely a much longer prophecy. I have no reasonable notion as to why, but once the thought crosses through my mind, I know it to be true. Just as quickly, the energy is mysteriously *gone*.

Time starts back up.

Once again, I alone appear to have experienced the unexplainable.

I try finishing the sentence I'd begun in explanation only to find that I quite *literally* cannot. The muscles in my jaw refuse to move, my vocal cords are unwilling to work, even my mouth can no longer part. A hand comes to rest against my throat just to verify it's still there.

Kleio's gaze on me becomes concerned.

So Agni really and truly was telling me the truth in that he couldn't physically speak about our past. I'd guess since that little impossibility is true, then this evidently means I'm unable to speak with my crew about those newly revealed memories regarding my previous life.

But *why*?

What kind of fresh hell is this?

Swallowing down the past, I instead state the facts at present. "Captain Agni is more cunning and calculating than I'd previously given him credit for. He's dangerous and I don't trust him."

The room is silent as my crew begins taking in this ominous analysis.

"I knew it," Herse mutters sharply to herself.

I can feel Kleio's cautious eyes on me as I drift over to the wall at the back end of the room. It's hosting a large pair of previously unnoticed mahogany doors. The carving on them is too detailed for me to think they belong to a mere closet. Grabbing onto the ornate handles, I open slowly to reveal the perfect place in which to begin plotting our future course.

My captains office.

A breath catches in my throat while taking in the room. It's three walls of dark-stained wood, all lined with shelves bursting with books. A decently sized rack of standard weapons takes up one corner, and the desk sitting before a wall of floor-to-ceiling windows is sterling, grand, and *familiar*.

It even smells like driftwood and mint leaves.

It's an exact replica of my father's office.

Just *littler*.

LIII. THE TRISKELION SEAL

Seven epistles line themselves up neatly before me.

Each glass bottle sitting atop the replica of my father's grandiose desk bears the broken seal affiliated with a different TideLord. Seven scrolls belonging to those bottles lie scattered about in disarray as I continue making my notes.

I've been offered a captaincy position from every single one. *Even* TideLord Nero.

I could take my pick.

The idea of such freedom is so absolutely ludicrous and entirely overwhelming that I almost wish I didn't have so many options. It would make coming to a decision a hell of a lot easier. Fortunately, I've had a full day and a half's worth of sleep in the comfort of our ship to sharpen my analysis.

I've begun making lists of pros and cons for each and every offer, except Nero's. I took him off the table right away for a few different reasons. The most obvious being that I'm almost certain he is who Captain Agni will choose to take a position under. Ultimately though, when it comes down to it, I won't consider him because I know how he truly feels regarding me and *what* I am.

'The Kraken King' wrote that his offer to *allow* me the opportunity to captain within his ranks was a privilege I should "scarcely be able to dream of due to such highly undesirable origins".

I'd actually scoffed aloud when reading it.

I've narrowed it down to two invitations I find most promising for both myself and my crew. At present, I'm deliberating heavily between Lord Kufko and Lord Dolion. So much so that I've had to start a whole new list of strategic advantages and disadvantages from scratch.

Both offers are nearly identical in what they can provide for our futures and the amount of authority and responsibility I would hold. On the one hand, TideLord Dolion actually has an estate very conveniently located in the Pearl Sea. We'd have the perfect excuse to begin searching for Asha in order to fulfill my second's greatest wish. On the other hand, Dolion's offer also strikes me as just a bit off.

He requested that we set sail tomorrow morning to meet for an in-person meeting at his estate. Then he personally requested that I join him for a private candlelit dinner afterwards.

That isn't exactly the 'off' part.

He actually had the gall to put it in writing that he'd like me to *stay* with him the first night. The last thing I'm interested in is sleeping with whatever TideLord I take a captaincy position under. It's quite literally just a disaster waiting to happen, no matter how handsome or charming he might be.

I wonder if Blaine Dolion is the type of male who'd take that sort of rejection from his inferior and move on. I somehow get the feeling he is *not*.

Which sways me back over to TideLord Kufko.

His offer is just as good and what's better, it's entirely professional. No lines being crossed or beds being offered. Although we would not have the very large added benefit of frequent access and reasonable excuses to visit the Pearl Sea.

I'm rereading each offer for perhaps the tenth time when a knock sounds from the archway to my new captain's quarters. Glancing up, I find Kleio peeking in from the outside corridor with a bit of mischief in her eyes.

"You have visitors, Captain," she announces, before motioning with her head of dual moonlight sparkling braids to someone I can't yet see.

Two familiar little level-ones then appear at her side in the daunting archway of my fearsome father's office. They both hold mixed expressions of fear and awe when peeking hesitantly inside the room. A grin breaks out upon my face almost immediately at the unexpected sight of them and the boys' jaws drop in shock.

Kleio snorts her amusement at their reactions while slipping into the room.

I can't help but laugh before asking, "Well, what are you two little sea devils doing here?"

The pale, red-headed boy remembers himself first. "H–Hi Captain B—Boreas. We're here to deliver a—a message from the G—Grand Preceptor," he stumbles over himself while I rise up from the sterling desk in greeting.

My teeth immediately grind together at the idea of Skelm sending me any sort of message but I knew it was only a matter of time. I cannot avoid reality forever, much as I might wish to.

The green-eyed one with rich ochre skin steps forward without a word and extends out to me a small scroll. I take it gently from his hands and notice plainly the way in which he averts my gaze entirely. When I glance at his partner in crime, I discover the exact same mannerisms.

I also realize they stand stock still, no fidgeting to be seen.

The haunted shadows indicative of a castaway have firmly returned to their eyes.

My blood grows bitterly cold as a newfound hatred for Skelm is born inside. A tremor rumbles from beneath our ship hull and it makes Kleio eye me curiously.

Gripping my middle finger, I work through an extremely potent wave of rage before addressing them once more, "Well, thank you, boys. I really do appreciate your services."

Turning to Kleio, I add pointedly, “Raider Hiraeth, would you round up the others? Let them all know we have two extremely strapping northern raiders aboard in need of payment for their delivery services—if I remember correctly, it was a kiss on each cheek, wasn't it?”

The boys look up in shock, those shadows clearing a bit.

I give them a wink and nod towards a newly grinning Kleio to gather the rest of our crew before turning the small scroll now in my hands. Unraveling it reveals a very brief yet equally demanding message to meet with Grand Preceptor Skelm in his office *immediately*.

It's not as if I can deny his orders but every fiber of my being fervently wants to.

I can't help but feel a deep sense of guilt hit me somewhere low a few minutes later. There is a pang in my chest while watching the impossibly young-looking level-ones who appear to be getting drunk off my crew's beauty as they each give the boys a kiss on the cheek in payment.

I'm supposed to be the rock that stands up against the storms. I remember that now. That meant I was my crew's rock, obviously, but leaving these two and any others like them—knowing exactly what I had to endure here—just somehow feels *wrong*.

I let out a long and burdensome sigh that catches the attention of my second and third. Shaking my head at their identical inquisitive looks, I keep my current calculating thoughts to myself.

I might just have to murder Skelm and the other northern demons after all.

"Is it true you were the first in the maze?"

"It is," I answer the green-eyed boy, whom I now know is named Nuru.

My crew and I are walking back with the level-ones to the dark fortress belonging to the North Order. I find those black spires appear even more foreboding and gloomier than usual with the lack of other cardinals and their raiders to keep things interesting.

"And is it also true that you fought a leviathan with your bare hands?" Demands the red-haired one named Euan from me next.

I hear Kleio's laughter from the end of the pack, where my seven crewmembers trail behind us. They're all under strict instructions to grab their things and say their goodbyes while I'm in my meeting with Skelm. Then we'll meet back up at the ship and make preparations to set sail.

Snorting at the absurd idea voiced by Euan, I shake my head. "No, I'm afraid that one is not true." They both deflate a little and I laugh at their reactions before recounting, "But I *did* see a Hafgufa during the second checkpoint. It was massive, with spikes each the size of a sword."

"Whoa," whispers Nuru in amazement.

"That's epic! Did you fight *it* with your bare hands?" Euan asks me hopefully.

Laughing again at their hopeful faces I admit, "No, I didn't. Captain Agni got the pleasure of fighting the monster while I had the honor of drinking a bucket of acheronian poison."

Their mouths drop open wide in wonder.

"Captain Agni is like the most legendary raider ever!" Euan proclaims before quickly adding, "I mean besides *you,* of course." He throws a sheepish smile my way.

"Oh, is he now?" I ask with a roll of my eyes as we journey ever closer to the skull-like opening.

"Yeah. He's wicked cool but also really scary," Nuru agrees, nodding repeatedly.

Euan says excitedly from where he walks in step right beside me, "He let us try picking up his broadswords and they're way heavier than they look. Nuru almost fell over!"

My brows furrow. "When did he do that?"

"It was a few times actually," Euan reveals while pushing back some loose red locks from his forehead. "Captain Agni and his crew let us practice with them at The Boneyard sometimes."

"Yeah *and* they taught us how to play a bunch of card games!" Nuru chimes back in.

Euan grins wide before adding, "*And* they told us what all the best swear words are. So now we can curse like real Tide Raiders!"

Alarm bells begin ringing and I work hard to shut them off as quickly as possible—I have no idea if this was intentional or not.

I remind myself that Agni is clever and strategic and had an entire year to observe me. He had plenty of time to gather all the intel needed to make me believe whatever version of him he wants me to. This doesn't necessarily mean anything.

The logical thoughts help to push him further back outside my icy boundaries.

A few minutes later, I part ways from both my crew members and the level-ones, now almost level-twos, as they reminded me several times, after kissing them each one last kiss on the cheek. They leave me a touch dazedly and I think I even hear laughter when they round the corner back towards their cabins. A sound that most definitely isn't found in these halls often.

Kleio squeezes my hand tightly with a touch of panic in her eyes but I wave her off, promising for about the fifth time now that it's just a formal congratulations. Nothing to worry about.

I can't tell whether or not she fully buys it.

Climbing the stairs up to the highest black spire, I feel the joy seep right out of me step by step.

By the time I'm standing in front of the Grand Preceptor's archway, I'm having to work through multiple waves of bitterness and rage. That inferno is indeed lit and the windows are in fact closed tight. For a moment, fear strikes me square in the chest.

But I remind myself that I am Brek inside.

I swear I can almost feel my father's presence when striding through that opening.

That impossible notion seems slightly more possible upon entering the room as I meet Skelm's one remaining eye and watch as a flash of true fear shines back at me. The emotion is abruptly swallowed whole in the next blink but I know what I saw. I know for a fact that it was real.

Interesting.

My gaze slides over to two people I'm not expecting to be here witnessing a potential murder this morning. Grand Regent Beldham and Raider Dornon stand before Grand Preceptor Skelm's oaken desk and I get the sense I've interrupted some sort of private discussion between the three of them. The former wears the hint of a prideful smile when looking my way, while the latter holds his typical air of boyish excitement.

All of this promptly disorients me.

"My presence was requested?" I question, hands coming to clasp behind my back.

"It was indeed Captain Boreas and let me say first off that I'm so sorry I didn't get the chance to congratulate you in person," Raider Dornon chirps, stepping my way with his large paw-like hand outstretched.

I lean forward and shake it firmly in surprise.

Dornon's blue eyes shine with enthusiasm. "Truly such a spectacular event from start to finish. To have our first ever castaway participate in the trials and win is nothing short of historical. Not to mention you're a bastard-born in tow! Really quite a phenomenal feat for someone such as yourself, I must say, all things considered."

I know he's being complimentary but the wording makes it difficult to be gracious.

My expression remains carefully concealed behind a plastered smile while nodding in agreement. I catch sight of Skelm's cat-like smirk from the corner of my eye and it riles up something more than my affinity. He's heard the unintentional snub just as well as I.

"Well, do you want the honor of telling her?" Dornon asks, turning to glance at our Grand Preceptor.

My interest peaks while watching Skelm's smug amusement wither away. Dornon takes the momentary silence as his answer and returns his attention to me before handing out a scroll.

Eyeing the odd boyish middle-aged raider once, I pluck the rolled papyrus from his hand before holding in a gasp at the sight of the royal triskelion seal. The three-wave symbol represents the bone and salt crown. My heart starts up with a painfully prominent rhythm in my ears.

Our pillar-trial officiant announces, "You have been called upon to join King Nereus's second fleet." He's practically bouncing from shifting his weight heel to toe in excitement.

My mouth parts and for a moment I stand there stunned.

A captaincy under the Raider King was not something I'd ever dared hope for, no matter how far my career went. To be a captain in his fleet would put me just about one step down in authority from a TideLord within The Order. It would basically make me akin to a TideLord's Admiral.

"Another castaway first. Truly just remarkable," Dornon comments before beginning to search around his person for something. "Ah, here we go. Your new captaincy ring," he says cheerfully while handing over a small velvet box in that same color of sea-glass green.

The only thing not incredible about captaining under the crown; it's not a choice.

When the Raider King calls you into his ranks, it isn't an offer like with the TideLords. It's a command. A small part of me is somewhat resistant to the idea, even though I'd be an idiot not to leap on this opportunity. A willful side I possess just instinctually refuses to bend to anyone.

I swallow down that instinct and instead take the box from his hand with a grateful smile.

Popping it open reveals a decently thick, golden signet ring. The top depicts the three-wave triskelion symbol and inside each wave lies a small gemstone. The left one holds a blue topaz and the right a crimson garnet, while the middle clutches onto a tiny pearl. My rank and initials 'C.M.B.' are engraved right across the top, Captain Merena Boreas.

I slide it onto my right hand's middle finger after moving my northern captaincy ring over to its newly rightful place, adorning my left. It's beautiful and fits like a glove. My heart pounds even harder in the face of such an improbable achievement.

"Congratulations, Captain Boreas." Grand Regent Beldham beams as she too comes to hold out her hand for me to shake. "Without a doubt the very finest the North has ever procured."

I wonder if I imagine the pointed look she slides Raider Dornon's way.

Skelm is the only one who keeps silent. I begin calculating what this little change in rank truly means.

"The details are all there in writing, of course but you and your crew will be expected to set sail by the morning. There will be several meetings to attend and orientations with your fleet before taking on your first assignment," Dornon explains, running a hand through his thinning head of strawberry-blond hair. "Unfortunately, I must get going. Grand Regent, would you mind accompanying me so we might continue our earlier discussion?"

Beldham nods curtly in agreement before briefly squeezing me on the shoulder. "I look forward to seeing you again, Captain Boreas. I'm certain we can expect nothing but great things in your career." Her piercing cornflower eyes are bright with unabashed pride.

I give her a rare smile in turn and watch as they exit, leaving me alone with Skelm.

Twirling the still-sealed scroll between my fingers, I turn to look at the northern Grand Preceptor in a new light. Once more, I feel the intangible presence of my father. It's as if he's standing right behind me. Fear slips through that single beady eye again before a shadow quickly chases it away.

Interesting.

For a moment, it's silent. Skelm dons his perpetual frown and the skin around his golden eye-socket covering tightens as I refuse to look away from him. I refuse to avert my gaze in the proper way that he spent years beating and branding into me.

A smirk tugs onto my lips after another minute of this quiet stare down.

"I guess this now puts my authority above yours in the chain of command within The Order, doesn't it?" I inquire, breaking another of his rules by being the first to speak.

It looks like it physically pains him to incline his head in agreement.

Tapping the scroll against one palm, my mouth purses slightly in thought while I slide on my father's 'Bastard King' mask of glacial indifference before stepping towards his oaken desk. Skelm actually looks briefly inclined to take a step backwards but ultimately stands firm.

Placing both my palms flat on the desk, I give him a good, hard look.

"You should have killed me when you had the chance," I say with a small chuckle, enjoying being the one to delight in *his* fear for once. "I do expect I'll have some reports regarding how this cardinal is run to bring up to the Overseers in the Driftwood Court. I have to wonder how 'within' raider code everything is. Anything you'd like me to be aware of?"

At his lack of sound and movement, I smirk before adding, "Well, I suppose I'll find out."

Pushing off his desk, I turn to leave but stop short at the sight of his blazing inferno.

I realize now how uncomfortable he wanted to make me today before Raider Dornon. The lit hearth, the windows shut, even the short message to meet in his office. He knows all my tricks.

It floods me with my power's need for violence.

The same power he never allowed inside this hellish room while punishing me.

Coward.

Halting mid-stride, I turn to find the crystal bowl brimming with copper seeds along a shelf as the image of two little castaway boys comes to mind. I pull it from its perch in one swift movement and stride for his inferno. Then I fling the contents of the bowl into the raging fires.

Skelm finally finds his voice. "Boreas, I will have you—"

"*Captain* Boreas," I correct him in a voice seeping with every ounce of the defiance he thought he'd stolen from me. I pivot back to face him with a tight-lipped sneer.

My tormentor of eight long years finally blanches before me.

The next words to leave my lips sound like they come from another world. "You can bet that I will be keeping *very* close tabs on the Cardinal North. If I hear one word about another raider being put through your personal punishments, you can rest assured that I will *personally* be dropping by for a check-in. I've got a feeling that your private use of kratosbane is not something that's been approved by the Overseers, is it?"

He looks like he's debating whether or not to speak. I save him the trouble of deciding.

"Do not think for a single moment that I will feel even an *ounce* of pity watching you be fed to the sea." I know he remembers those words because for the very first time, the Grand Preceptor avoids *my* eyes.

"Same goes for Bealu and Ersatz," I warn him before shattering that empty crystal bowl by chucking it harshly into his inferno.

Without another word, I storm out of my own personal room in hell.

I could swear a deep, dark, bone-chilling laugh that could only belong to 'The Bastard King' follows me out in approval.

LIV. CAST OFF

"Captain, do you want to see it?" Kleio asks, appearing once more in the doorway to my office.

"Is it time?"

She nods with a small grin. "The others are already up on deck."

There's clear mischief playing about the lovely features of her heart-shaped face. It confirms that my crew is doing more than just loitering up there.

I follow her through the increasingly familiar corridors and climb up onto the gleaming deck of Death's Kiss to find six of my sirens leaning against the starboard railing. As I suspected, the shine of a bootlegged bottle can be seen glinting off the small sunlight trickling through the overhead clouds as it passes from Nimra's hands over to Greer's.

My fourth takes a drink of the cobalt liquid before Kleio steals it from her grasp in order to shove it into mine. "Drink up, Captain, you're behind," she orders.

I laugh at the grin my second flashes me and obey.

Swallowing down the burning liquid, I join them all along the ship's side to gaze out at the small wintry isle of the Cardinal North. The ocean's steady rocking presence beneath us is soothing.

It's almost not possible to believe all of the horrors and joys I went through occurred in that tiny speck of a place. Eight years, almost everything in my life that I can remember happened there.

It's just as impossible to believe that we're leaving. Scratch that—we've *left*.

None of it truly seems real.

Least of all the triskelion signet ring burdening my hand.

"How long are we to spend at Thalassalis Isle?" Kleio inquires, sidling up beside me and taking back the bottle.

My eyes remain locked on the north, growing smaller and smaller with each passing minute while replying, "Until the full moon ends and then we'll head for the Driftwood Court."

The others standing down the line from us bickering and teasing all go a bit silent. Each one of us is every bit as nervous as we are excited to join the royal ranks of the Bone and Salt Crown.

It's an honor none of us expected to receive and yet a little part of me dislikes not having had the final say in our path forward. All the lists I made and hours deliberating, for nothing.

However, imagining the look on Captain Agni's face when he realizes I outrank him makes all that previous work completely and totally worth it. This opportunity serves many purposes but the most welcome is putting much-needed distance between us. I'll likely only be required to withstand his presence at the occasional assembly meeting, assuming his TideLord brings him along.

The Cardinal North Order becomes a distant spec and the sounds of my crew's arguing and laughter grow louder and slightly unrulier as the horizon swallows that portion of our pasts whole.

The more burning liquor I consume, the more I begin to reflect upon and replay those precious few memories. Those moments that belong only to myself.

I go over them again and *again* until every second of them is burned into my brain and I'm certain I'll never be able to forget them.

I'm lost inside a world of thoughts forced to remain my own when a brilliant agony alights my system. It violently rips me outside of my reverie while running up and down my backside with the exact same searing pain I felt after leaving The Vault.

I find myself moving to my knees as a lethal bout of curses slides past my teeth.

The pain overrides everything else and only Kleio's voice is able to break through.

"*Merena*?" Her pitch in tone is concerningly high.

Stupidly, I scan the seas for signs of danger before turning from where I now kneel in pain before the starboard railing to face my second. Kleio stands where she's been chatting with Herse at the helm while the others have begun playing a card game along the deck.

"What?" I ask, my voice hoarse.

My pulse spikes at the way her mouth is parted in shock.

Herse's eyes are unusually round while informing me bluntly, "Uh, your back is fucking glowing, Cap."

I inhale the calming scents of eucalyptus and clove while lying face down in a place that is both extremely familiar and yet entirely new.

Leech Davina's sickbay.

Her gentle healing hands run up and down my exposed backside in silent contemplation. I can practically feel her thoughts churning nearby and I'm growing increasingly impatient.

"*Well*?" My tone comes out sharper than intended.

"I've never seen anything like it, Merena. I don't know where to even start with this," Davina answers in her own snappish voice.

Both of us are clearly on edge in the face of the unknown.

"No luck yet on any of the tomes we found on board either," Herse chimes in unhelpfully with a small grimace from where she hangs in the narrow doorway of the small infirmary. "But we're still looking. There are plenty of books for us to go through."

"I'm sure we'll find something," Kleio assures me, coming to stand at the end of the cot I'm laying on. I glance up to meet her warm brown eyes and she's quick to blink away the very obvious worry lining them.

Sighing heavily, I tap my fingers along the cushion edge while noting, "Well, at least the glowing has stopped. Plus, it looks cooler now."

It seems my affinity mark has changed.

Or perhaps expanded is the correct wording. It's still that same damning shade of castaway white but no longer does it portray a wild and unruly pattern bursting across my shoulder blades before streaming without motif down the base of my spine. Now it's taken on a sort of shape.

More lines have been added and woven together in order to craft an intricate design made up of beautiful swirling whirls that, when connected, make it look as though a wave is crashing down my backside. It's actually really rather beautiful.

If I wasn't focusing so hard on not freaking out, I'd be pleased.

The problem is, affinity marks don't just *change*. You're gifted your markings when blessed by the drowned gods before your soul returns to Pontus and you inevitably wash up at whatever Cardinal Order the will of the nix leads you to.

We're all more than a little on edge as to what this might mean.

"Oh, it looks badass for sure," Herse agrees while Kleio remains silent.

My second leaves her spot before me on the cot and goes to study the contents of Davina's new work space in quiet concern. She knows the last thing I want is to witness any of their distress on my behalf.

"Does this hurt?" Davina asks, beginning to roll a scented oil across my aching backside.

"No, not really," I answer with a wince as she lightly spreads out the mixture.

Davina laughs with a small shake of her silver-threaded golden mane. "Liar."

It's quiet for a few minutes and Herse returns to relieve Greer from the helm so she can join the rest of my crew currently digging through any and all books lining the shelves of my office. The only noise inside the sick bay comes from the slight creaking of Kleio's weight under the wooden floorboards as she paces around the room anxiously.

Eventually Vi's concoction begins working its magic and the aching in my back slowly lessens little by little. I'm verging on falling asleep as her hands continue dutifully pressing in the soothing oil when my second's voice sounds startlingly nearby.

"Davina, what is *this*?" Kleio questions, her tone strange.

Blinking open my eyes, I glance up to find her holding up a small triangular-shaped glass.

I squint to get a better look inside the tiny vial. It appears to hold a shimmering liquid of gold-flecked green. My brows furrow both in question and annoyance as Davina stops her work to take the oddly shaped glass from Kleio's outstretched hand.

Our resident healer stares at the pretty liquid for a minute before her kaleidoscope eyes dart to Kleio's and a look of surprise alights her features. "Why?" Davina asks, her voice low.

Kleio's cupid's bow presses flat against her full bottom lip before responding slowly, "Because I've seen this container and that liquid before, at the beginning of the year. What is it?"

"Where *exactly* did you see it?" Davina pushes.

I look between my second and eighth in growing confusion as they now sport mirroring murderous expressions. *What in the depths?*

"In Vash's stash of bootlegged liquor," Kleio grinds out. "He had some other weird vials like this one in a bag. I only saw them once. They were all gone by the time we were celebrating the first pillar trial. He told me it was a sleeping drought but that was a lie, wasn't it?"

Davina nods silently and I feel a brewing storm of anger enter the room.

"Okay so what the hell is it then?" I snap, overly irritated to be left out of the loop.

My eighth dips her chin in agreement with my second in regard to whatever unspoken conversation they've been having. I'm slightly alarmed to feel as something like rage begins rippling off our typically agonizingly restrained leech.

Kleio looks down at me before I can voice my budding demand for one of them to answer. I'm even more alarmed to discover a raging fire of anger consuming those sepia-shaded eyes.

"It's Ehkinos."

EPILOGUE

I awake in the middle of the night to discover two epistle bottles atop my desk.

Neither of them am I expecting.

It's been three days since casting off from the Cardinal North. We're due to arrive for my first meeting with the Sons and Daughters at Thalassalis island by mid-morning. The next few days ahead of us I am most definitely *not* looking forward to.

I'm just clinging onto the hope that one of the unnerving cult worshippers will know what's going on with my affinity markings. Here's hoping whatever it is isn't fatal. That would be my luck.

Those thoughts, along with many others, steal me from sleep.

Upon inspection of the epistles, the sea-glass green waxen seal they *both* carry doesn't belong to any of the seven TideLords I'd given my official rejection to, as I'd assumed. Of course, as my rejections were all due to answering my call to captaincy beneath King Nereus, there isn't anything that any of them can say to me other than it's a pity and move on.

Even the TideLords must bow to the wishes of the Bone and Salt Crown.

Upon the bottle in hand, I discover the royal triskelion symbol with the initial's 'C.K.T.' across it.

Frowning in confusion, I open the epistle and remove the first message awaiting me.

It reads:

Merena,

I know you've already made it extremely clear you don't wish to hear from me but I feel I would be entirely remiss not to reach out in congratulations. I'm incredibly sorry I wasn't able to be there to witness your triumphant exit from The Vault.

Lord Raimbaut sent me off as part of King Nereus's entourage at dawn. I did, however, have the great honor of watching you absolutely demolish the other captains in that starting race. A part of me is tempted to take a smidge amount of credit for that zig-zagging maneuver you pulled to throw off those southern assholes there at the end. If I remember correctly, I taught you that strategy the same night we first... you know.

I'm also writing to you with some exciting news and another round of congratulations.

I was notified this very morning that I've called up into service under our Raider King and I'm told that you and I will now be captaining under the same fleet. I know how much this position means to you. I'm so proud of how far you've come. Hopefully, as we'll be seeing one another regularly again, this might give us a chance to get past my prior mistake. Once again, I truly am sorry for that night.

I never meant to put you in that position.

Maybe this is an opportunity for more than just our careers. If you can find it in that little hellion heart of yours, give me another shot. Let me prove to you that I truly am your ally. Whatever that takes.

I'm really looking forward to seeing you again, kid. — *Keran*

This new tidal wave of information has me reeling. Yet the second epistle calls to me before I get the chance to sit and process. Picking up the bottle, I find an identical triskelion signet with the initials 'C.O.A.' stamped across it.

My stomach begins to drop, and I fervently hope that I am wrong about my growing assumptions while quickly opening it up and dumping out the scroll lodged inside.

Unraveling the rolled-up paper shares with me the following message:

Captain Boreas

It's late and I find I can't sleep so I'm writing to you, gorgeous.

Firstly, I'd like to extend my formal congratulations on your new captaincy promotion within our Tide Raider King's ranks. It seems as though we've both been assigned to the second fleet under the Bone & Salt Crown. How… convenient.

Secondly, as we are now to be fellow fleet captains working towards the greater good of The Order, I feel it is my duty to offer to you my personal instruction. You are clearly in desperate need of proper elemental training and could quite honestly use some halfway decent weapon guidance as well. My crew and I unfortunately will not be able to rendezvous with you and yours at the upcoming captaincy meetings and dull orientations that will no doubt follow. See we've already received our first mission from King Nereus and will be tied up until further notice.

Do try not to die in my absence. You have a deeply disturbing knack for finding trouble.

Once I've returned, we can set up a training schedule. Training would, of course, be a no-clothes game. That was a taunt—unless you don't want it to be. Either way, epistle back your answer regarding my very generous offer of some much-needed instruction.

Please feel free to include any filthy words you no doubt have for me in your return letter. I actually highly encourage it—the more explicit and profane your insults, the better. I'd prefer that you were detailed. If you're feeling really daring, you could include a little description for me regarding whatever thoughts are helping you to not stay up tonight. I'll tell you mine if you tell me yours.

Vos habes nulla idea quid genus sordidus res ego volo audire vos dicunt vel modus ego volofacere te gemere. Et sicut ego cogito vos vult mox recordo ego semper id quod volo.

In case you haven't yet noticed, that little kiss you begged me to give you has done something terrible. I'm beginning to suspect that the memory of how you tasted might just drive me insane. It's really quite cruel.

I need more.

I'll dream of you.

Captain Agnis
2nd Fleet, Bone & Salt Crown

Well, this is going to make things significantly more difficult.

Damnit.

My heart rate jumps alarmingly as a complex combination of emotions I'm not prepared to handle begins swelling up inside. It takes me several minutes to work through identifying and dispelling the overwhelming waves just enough to think past them.

Agni is unfairly skilled at this game. Epistilling me like this is virtually cheating.

Sadistic genius.

But he's also underestimating me if he actually thinks I'll buy into his little love letter. He's clearly had far too many females fall before his feet without needing to put in any effort. Too many of those fan club members swooning over a stray compliment or sultry foreign word.

He seriously thinks I'll believe his insinuation that what happened during the second checkpoint has changed his whole perspective on me? One round of albeit scarily addictive kissing, and he's miraculously turned an entire ideological corner? So much so that he's now selflessly going out of his way to *help* me?

Yeah, fucking right.

I could choke on his arrogance.

Maybe I don't recall all the facts of our past but there are things I know about Agni to be true. He doesn't make any moves, good or bad, without his own complex motivations driving them.

Every scheme he has is just as multilayered and puzzling as his character.

As if on instinct, my eyes fall to the silver scar still marring my left palm. The od line between Agni and me. The one that should have disappeared the day after Luminalia. The one that I thought surely after completing the od itself would be gone. Yet here it still remains.

I think I might have underestimated each and every one of our prior interactions.

Agni spent the last year doing whatever he could to get under my skin in absolutely any way possible. He threw me through loop after loop of psychological warfare. But now I'm beginning to see the varying facets in his maneuvers. His offer to train me is also a scheme for him to get close. It's an opportunity for him to find a way to slide past my defenses and get me vulnerable.

There's not a doubt in my mind he'd use it to his advantage. Halcyon is a worthy opponent. I'll give him that.

I focus on the most prominent emotion flaring bright inside, loathing, and use it to quickly epistle him back. The message is short and sweet and if Agni is anything like Kerau, then it'll ensure he leaves me well enough alone.

For a while, at least.

Besides, I'm sure the egotistical prick has more than enough fan mail to keep him busy.

Captain Agni,

Fuck off loverboy.

Captain Boreas,

2nd Fleet, Bone & Salt Crown

DEATH'S KISS

CONTENT WARNINGS

Explicit punishments / torture

Assault & attempted sexual assault (off-page / recounted)

Sexually explicit language

Swearing / foul language

Cruelty towards a creature/ abuse

Death of a creature (off-page)

Themes of grief, despair, depression, anxiety & self-loathing

Child abuse (off-page / recounted)

www.ingramcontent.com/pod-product-compliance
Lightning Source LLC
Chambersburg PA
CBHW020931310726
48980CB00007B/720/J

* 9 7 9 8 9 9 1 9 3 2 9 3 6 *